Praise for George V. Higgins:

"Higgins emerges as a boss of bullet-lettres. He can write dialogue so authentic it spits." —*Life*

"Higgins is very skillful at varying the rhythms of conversations, injecting them with humor and animation and charting the curve from good-natured brutality to vicious brutality." —*New York Magazine*

"Raucous, bawdy yet completely plausible, Higgins' fictional flings are above all, fun." —*ALA Booklist*

"Mr. Higgins is the Balzac of the Boston underworld." —*New Yorker*

Other George V. Higgins novels available from Carroll & Graf:

A City on a Hill
Pennance for Jerry Kennedy

TWO COMPLETE NOVELS BY

GEORGE V. HIGGINS

TWO COMPLETE NOVELS BY

GEORGE V. HIGGINS

COGAN'S TRADE

A CHOICE OF ENEMIES

Carroll & Graf Publishers, Inc.
New York

First Carroll & Graf edition 1989

Published by arrangement with Alfred A. Knopf, Inc

Carroll & Graf Publishers, Inc.
260 Fifth Avenue
New York, NY 10001

ISBN: 0-88184-534-5

Manufactured in the United States of America

COGAN'S TRADE

1

AMATO IN A GRAY SUIT with a muted red stripe, textured pink shirt with his initials on the left French cuff, a maroon and gold tie, sat at the kidney-shaped, walnut veneer desk and stared. "I got to give it to you," he said, "you're a great-looking couple of guys. Come in here about four hours late, you look like shit and you stink. The fuck, you look like you just got out of jail or something."

"His fault," the first one said. "He was late. I stood around there and I waited for him."

Both of them wore black boots with red suede inserts. The first one wore an army-green poncho, a frayed gray sweater and faded blue jeans. He had long hair, dirty-blond, and mutton-chop sideburns. The second one wore an army-green poncho, a gray sweatshirt and dirty white jeans. He had long black hair that reached his shoulders. He had the beginnings of a black beard.

"I hadda get my dogs in," the second one said. "I got fourteen dogs, there. Takes me a while. I can't, I can't just go off some place, leave them dogs out."

"You're all covered with hair, too," Amato said. "You been backing them dogs up to you, I guess."

"Comes from beating off, Squirrel," the second one said. "I come out, I haven't got your advantages, nice business waiting for me, all that good shit. I got to hustle."

" 'Johnny' around here," Amato said, "you can call me 'Johnny' here. Most of the help calls me 'Mister,' but you can call me 'Johnny.' That'll be all right."

"I'll work on that, Squirrel, I really will," the second one said. "You got to make allowances for me, you know? I, like I just got out of fuckin' jail. My head's all fucked up. I got to readjust to society, is what I got to do."

"You couldn't've got somebody else," Amato said to the first one. "This item looks like shit and he don't have no manners. I got to put up with shit like this?"

"I could've," the first one said, "but you asked me, you know, get somebody that was all right. Russell, here, he's maybe kind of a wise ass, but he's all right if you can stand him."

"Sure," Russell said, "and a guy like you, he wants something done, hasn't got the stones, do it himself, I think he oughta try pretty hard, too."

"I really don't like this prick," Amato said to the first one. "He's too fuckin' fresh for my blood. How about going out and getting me a nice tough nigger? I don't think I can stand this cocksucker long enough to tell him what I want."

"Russell, for Christ sake," the first one said, "willya shut the fuck up and stop jerking the guy's chain? He's tryin' to do us a favor."

"I didn't know that," Russell said. "I thought he wanted us to do him a favor. That the straight shit, Squirrel? You tryin', do me a favor?"

"Get the fuck out of here," Amato said.

"Hey," Russell said, "that's no fuckin' way, talk to a guy. The fuck you sell driving lessons to people, you go around talking to a guy like that?"

"This thing I got in mind," Amato said, "the two guys I get to do it're gonna cut up about thirty, I figure. Thirty K. Shitbirds like him, Frankie, shitbirds like him I can buy for eighty cents a dozen, they throw in another free. Get me somebody else, Frankie. I'm not gonna put up with this kinda shit."

"Remember them habes we had?" Frankie said.

"Habes," Amato said, "what habes? We had about nine hundred habes. Every time I turn around that monkey's pulling out something else I got to sign. What habes?"

"They, the ones they bring us down for," Frankie said. "The federal ones."

"On the line-up thing," Amato said, "yeah. The time that big coon come after me."

"Long Tall Sally," Frankie said.

"I dunno what his name was," Amato said. "We didn't have no nice conversation or anything. He was just trying to get my pants off and I was just trying to stop him from getting my pants off, is all. 'Jes hold still there a minute, white boy, I'm gonna shove all my good time right up your sugah ass.' Fuckin' guy. He had white lipstick on."

"The next night he wasn't there," Frankie said.

"The next night I wasn't there," Amato said. "If I had've been that fuckin' nigger wouldn't't've, boy. I got Billy Dunn a wood chisel for that fucker, he was gonna grab him in the yard if I was there. Fuckin' dumb screws, can't always depend on them guys showin' up when you need them like that, guy's liable to learn a new way, he's not careful."

"You were in Norfolk," Frankie said.

"I was in Norfolk," Amato said. "Sit there all day listening to some kid make a fuckin' asshole outa my goddamned lawyer, all I can think about's what Billy's gonna do to that coon, I get back there, and then it turns out, I'm going to Norfolk. Only thing I see that night, there's this nun in a gray thing, there, wants to know, do I wanna learn the fuckin' guitar."

"I know her," Russell said. "She's all over the place. She was up to Concord once. I said to her, I said: 'Sister, I wanted to play the guitar, I would've grabbed a fuckin' guitar.' After that she left me alone. Lot of the guys liked her, though."

"That night the nigger was in the hospital," Frankie said.

"Good," Amato said. "I hope he fuckin' *died.*"

"Nope," Frankie said, "but I seen him. He was missing about three feet of skin off his fuckin' head."

"Hey," Amato said.

"Him," Frankie said, nodding his head toward Russell.

"No shit," Amato said.

"Peeled him like a fuckin' orange," Frankie said.

"More like pulling bark off a fuckin' tree," Russell said. "Guy had skin like nothing I ever seen."

"He came after you?" Amato said.

"Somebody sure did," Russell said, "somebody looked to me like he hadda be the biggest chungo bunny inna world, come after me. I had this blade there, another guy I meet onna way over, he told me, I give him a hundred out of my thing there and he had this blade for me. Said I was probably gonna need it. I bet I wasn't in there ten minutes and that nigger's coming after me. Didn't do it again, though."

"That's how come," Frankie said. "He's a prick but he's got all the moves."

"He clean?" Amato said. "Both you guys clean?"

"*Frankie,*" Russell said, "you been *using* something?"

"Shut the fuck up, all right, Russell?" Frankie said. "Yeah. I haven't had anything but booze since I get out. Not that much booze, either. Mostly beer. I been waiting for payday, I start in on the VO and other stuff."

"You're on pills," Amato said. "You're in, you're on pills. I seen you, don't forget. You were beating the hell out of them yellowjackets."

"John," Frankie said, "the yellowjackets were there. I didn't see nobody serving no beer. I took what there was. I haven't had none of that stuff since I was out."

"How about him?" Amato said.

"*Gee*, Squirrel," Russell said, "*I* wouldn't take nothing. I, ah, I probably had a couple quarts of Ripple and some grass, and I might've had one or two dime bags once or twice, but I just snort them, you know? It's not like I was using something. I go to Cub Scouts, you know? And they pat you down, there, they start teaching you how to tie them knots and everything."

"Smack," Amato said to Frankie. Frankie shrugged. "I ask you to find a guy for me and I got this thing, and all I got to do is do it and we get some very nice money. All I got to do is find two guys that can do a fairly simple thing without fucking it up, and this is the best you can do for me. A fuckin' junkie. And I'm supposed to just let you guys go in there and you're gonna go in and once and for all you're gonna fuck it up, a job that's never gonna come around again in a million years. I don't want to have a whole lot of *fun* with this thing, you know, because I hadda go out and get a guy that looked all right when I got him and then he goes in and he's on the fuckin' nod or something. I want the god-damned money. That's what I need."

"Squirrel," Russell said, "when I was a little kid I used to take off on Cheracol. I didn't have any trouble. When I was working for my Uncle, I used to have to go down in holes for him, you know? The carbon black on my face and go down in them holes with a forty-five in my hand and a knife in my fuckin' teeth and I went

into them tunnels. Every day I went in them tunnels.
If there wasn't anything in the tunnel, that was a good
day. Not so good days, there's probably only a big
fuckin' snake in there or something that wants to eat
you. Kinda bad days, there's some skinny dink in there
with a gun, tryin' to kill you. Bad days was when the
dink did it, or there was a piece of wire in there and
you didn't happen, you weren't paying attention or
something and it's rigged up to something that blows up
pretty quick, or else there's a punji stick in there with a
whole lot of dink shit on it under your hand and you
go into your basic blood poisoning extra quick.

"I didn't have no bad days," Russell said. "I was in
them tunnels almost two years and I didn't have no bad
days. I wasn't buying up Mustangs and teaching little
dumb shits to drive, but I didn't have no bad days,
either.

"The thing of it is, *Squirrel*," Russell said, "when I
was having them days, I didn't know for sure at the
time that I wasn't gonna have a bad one, you know? I
started out, I thought it was all just a matter of balls. I
don't wanna hurt your feelings or anything, but I always
had the balls, you know? And I thought, I felt pretty
good, because I thought that's all it was and I had them
so I was all right. Then I see, I seen them cart out a
couple guys that went in there and put them in the
green bags, you know? And a couple of them, they
didn't have no balls when they come out, on account
they didn't have no luck, they went in that time, and
no cocks either, and that carbon black, don't do a thing
for cuts and stuff. Fuckin' booby traps go right through
it, like it wasn't even there.

"So that gets me to thinking," Russell said. "I'm no
good at thinking. But that gets me to thinking, and I

see, well, I'm in the shit, is what I am, and I can't personally do nothing about it. All I can do is, I can have the balls and the luck, but the only thing I know about is the balls. I just can't have no bad days. Only, I don't know no way to do that. So, I used to come out, and I know, tomorrow I go in again, and the only thing I can think about is, I used up another day. That's all. So I smoke something. And it helped.

"Then I start looking at them other guys," Russell said. "I see them, I was still thinking, and they're all, most of them, at least're smoking. And them guys that're doing the grass, you know? Very heavy on it, and they slow down some. I was, I was keeping track of things. I could see it happening to me, it was happening to them, I got it a little bit and I begin to see, that's what, them other guys, they started on it, it was probably just a little bit for them, too, when they start. You start forgetting things. All you want, you don't care about things, you know? Very funny thing. And then, some of the guys that're older, they drink a lot. And pretty soon they're sick a lot. And that's bad. Their hands shake. They're not paying attention either. And you get in there, there's the wire or the dink or something, well, you're gonna have to have a lot of time to think about it or else you're not gonna have no time at all. You can't let yourself get slow.

"So I try the horse," Russell said. "You got to have something. So I get some of that nice white shit, and what I did was, I used it after, right? *After* I come out again. I haven't got to go back in tonight. First I snort it. Then, a couple times I did it the other way, but mostly I snort it. But I used it. And I liked it.

"Okay," Russell said, "it don't, it makes you feel great, but it don't actually do nothing for you, you know that. When you're in there, doesn't protect you at all. But you been in, and you got out, and you got to go back in again and you don't want to think about that, maybe you're not gonna bring yourself out, you go in again, use up all your luck thinking. So then it's very fuckin' nice. Don't slow you down. Just makes you feel good, and that's what I was after."

"Sure," Amato said, "and that's what you're gonna be after when you're getting ready to go in on this thing I got, and you're gonna get it and you're gonna be flying and you're gonna go in stoned up to your ass and some poor bastard's gonna start hollering or something and he's gonna get shot, and a very good thing that a kid in his fuckin' right mind couldn't fuck up is gonna get fucked up. That's exactly what I'm afraid of."

"He'll be all right, John," Frankie said.

"*Maybe* he'll be all right," Amato said. "Maybe he won't be all right. Maybe *you* won't be. I don't want nobody getting hurt on this. There's nothing, there's no reason why anybody oughta get hurt on this, the guys that go in or the guys that're in there when the guys go in. This's money, just money, nothing else. No fuckin' *shit* and stuff that's gonna get everybody all pissed off and everything. It was something that was gonna be around, it was something like that, all right, I could maybe take a chance. I could take a couple guys that I was afraid'd maybe cock off and wreck it, and take their word for it, they're gonna be all right. So all right, they go in, and they cock off and wreck it, it was a bank or something, it's gonna be there next week for two guys that've got more sense, all right. But this isn't. It's not like that. You fuck it up, it's fuckin' gone, it's gonna disappear. I got to think about this. I got to be sure. I'm gonna talk to some people.

I'm gonna take my time about this thing, as much time I got, anyway."

"John," Frankie said, "I need dough. I was in the can a long time and I haven't found anything. You can't fuck around with me like this."

"My friend," Amato said, "my wife, Connie? Makes great roast pork. She stuffs it, you know? It's really great. The other night she makes roast pork. First time since I been home. I couldn't eat it. I told her, I said: 'Connie, don't make no pork for me, ever again.' But I used to love it, I always said it's the best thing she makes, and she's a good cook. I mean, a really good cook. That's why she's so fuckin' fat all the time, she likes to eat and she likes to cook and she cooks great and she eats it. 'Bacon,' I said, 'ham, I don't care if it does come off a pig. But no kind of pork. You make baked beans, all right? Don't gimme none with the pork on it. The beans I'll eat. Not the pork.' And, well, I went down the clamstand and I ate in my fuckin' car, and I haven't, until a month ago I didn't eat with my family for almost seven years. I still ate down the clamstand. Something got fucked up once, you remember that? I picked a wrong guy for something, everybody's in a hurry, we got to move, we need the dough, this and that, he'll be all right, and I, it, I was worse'n the rest of you. So we take him, and I knew, he's a guy I'm really not sure about. I couldn't tell you what it was, I just knew it, this was a wrong guy. But I take him anyway. And he *was* a wrong guy, and I eat greasy, shitty pork, seems like every day, almost seven years, and my kids're growing up and my business, it's all right, it's not doing as good as it should be, and I'm in the can, and now, I can't get that back, you know? So now, I can't eat my favorite things any more, because they remind me, I'm, from

now on I'm taking my time, and that's all there is to it.
No, I don't care about you, what's bothering you. We
can do something, great, we'll do something. If we can
do it safe and without fucking up something that's really
good and getting ourselves in the shit again. But I ate
the last fuckin' pork I'm ever gonna eat. I had my last
fuck-up. Call me Thursday. Thursday I'll know. I'll let
you know."

2

RUSSELL STOPPED about four feet from Frankie on the second underground platform of the Park Street MBTA station. "All right," he said, "I'm here. We going out there or what?"

Frankie leaned against one of the red and white pillars. "Depends," he said.

"Don't depend on me," Russell said. "I been up since quarter five. I'm *all* beat to shit. And I also, I got a chance to get laid if I don't go out there."

"Don't people get laid at night any more?" Frankie said. "My sister, we're kids, you couldn't keep Sandy inna house at night if she was tied up. Now she's out Tuesday and Wednesday afternoons. I been there five weeks, she's never home them days."

"Must be a fireman," Russell said, "night guy inna fire station. Young guy, too, she's not going out, weekends."

"Or a fuckin' cop," Frankie said. "It'd be the same thing with a cop. I said to her: 'None of my business, Sandy, I just hope you're not rolling around with some fuckin' cop, is all.' She looks at me. 'Why?' she says. 'What've you guys got that cops haven't?' I pity that kid."

"You oughta pity yourself," Russell said.

"I do," Frankie said. "She never had a clean shot, though. She always got around pretty good, I don't mean that. She just never hadda clean shot."

"Nobody ever had a clean shot," Russell said. "What the fuck else is new? I was talking to this girl, she wants me to come over there this after. I said to her, look, I

hadda be some place. What's the matter, tonight? She's
gotta work. She gets off late. I don't care. I been up late
myself before. She's a nurse. She says: 'Look, I'm gonna
wash old men's asses and everything all day. Then I'm
gonna be out on my feet. You think I wanna get laid,
after that? That what you think? I don't.' "

"That oughta be something," Frankie said. "I can just
see what kind of broad she's gonna be, you can screw
off an ad inna paper. Beautiful. Probably got a couple
handfuls of broken glass in there."

"Look," Russell said, "you ought to know. I was
pounding sand up my ass almost four years. I would've
fucked a snake, I could've got somebody, hold it for
me. These broads, okay, you wouldn't want to rape
them if you saw them, you know? But they got the
fuckin' plumbing."

A badly coordinated heavyset man appeared on the
southerly platform across the tracks. He wore white
coveralls and carried a blue plastic pail. He turned his
back and stared at the tile wall. He put the pail down.
He put his hands on his hips. On the wall in red spray
paint were irregular letters eighteen inches tall. They
read: SOUTHIE EATS IT. He stooped and removed a steel
brush and a can of solvent from the pail.

"I wished I could look at things like that," Frankie
said. "I can't seem to get my mind on anything. I
thought, I used to think, boy, if I ever get out of this
fuckin' place, they just better get all the women out of
town that day, you know? But you know what I do? I
sleep all the time. You were to just leave me alone, I
think that's really what I'd do, the way I feel right now
at least. Just sleep and sleep and sleep. That's why, this
thing, I dunno how it is, what he's got in mind. I admit, he's kind of a crazy bastard. But he's at least got

something in mind, you know? I haven't. He come out and the day he come out, he was looking around. And I keep thinking, it's all I do, Jesus, if I could just get some money. I could go out and live like I was a regular human being. But I can't, I haven't come up with anything, no way to get no money. Dean, my brother-in-law, he's not a bad guy, basically, he don't say anything. You know what he does? He reads catalogues. All them catalogues, come inna mail? Son of a bitch, he works, he goes to work at noon, noon till eight-thirty, down the gas station. He comes out, he reads catalogues. Fuckin' electronics catalogues. And she's, he's down there, busting his hump, up to his ass in oil and stuff, she's out fuckin' some guy. So I'm sleeping on his couch and I'm drinking his beer, he don't know me. He's from Malden. Where's he know me from? They got married, I was inna can. But he still, he tells me, 'Look, don't tell Sandy, all right? Because you tell her and she's probably gonna start wondering, how I find this out. But you probably wanna get your ashes hauled, there's this broad I know, she works, her husband thinks she gets off at midnight, I guess. She gets off about ten.' So I say to him, well, I don't tell him, I was inna big hurry for names, Sandy'd be the one I'd ask, he don't need that kind of favor from me. So I just say, I appreciate it. But I haven't got no place to go, where I can take a broad, you know? I haven't got no car. I got less'n thirty bucks. I mean, what am I gonna do?

"So he says," Frankie said, "he says him and Sandy'll go out, I can use their place. Yeah, and probably one of the kids isn't gonna get up inna middle of the night and come out, see how come I'm making so much noise, getting laid onna couch. It's not gonna work, and that's it, it just won't work. I got to get some dough and I can't, this thing John's got, it's the only thing I got in front of me right now. I got to listen to the guy."

"Shit," Russell said, "listen to him. I'm willing to listen to him. He just didn't want to say anything in front of me that I could hear. Fuckin' guy, he don't like me. Okay. But I'm not gonna go around and check myself into something I don't even know what I'm getting into or anything. I did that before. I'm not doing that again. This thing I'm doing, I can do that. It's probably gonna take me longer, get what I need from it, but I can do it. I'm picking my own spots from now on. I don't have to sit around and take no shit from the Squirrel."

"Okay," Frankie said, "that's what I'm saying. You can take it or you can leave it alone, and that's fine. I wished I was you. But me, this's at least ten apiece the guy's talking about. You don't want the ten, all right. But I do. And I haven't got no place else to get it. You have."

"Not that much," Russell said. "I'm not gonna get ten out of this. Five, seven's more like it. No ten. You gimme ten and I'll be gone so fast it was like I never was here. I know exactly what I'm gonna do, I get that kind of dough. But, I don't have to get it from what he's gonna, that he's got in mind to do. It's gonna take me a while longer, but I can get it from what I'm doing anyway, and that, that's on balls, see? Balls. It's something I think up myself, how I'm gonna do this. So, the guy don't like me? All right, I still don't have to kiss his ass, I don't want to. Fuck him. So it's up to you and him. It's up to you guys. You want me, you want me in this, I'll come in. He's the guy with the big ideas. Fine. You want to go and get somebody else, also fine. Don't matter to me."

A blue and white train pulled in from Cambridge.

The doors opened. An elderly drunk stood up unsteadily, ignored the doors open behind him and lurched toward the doors open in front of Russell and Frankie. He
wore black suit pants and a white dress shirt and a
greenish checkered jacket. He had not shaved for several days. There was a large red bruise on his left cheek.
His left ear was bloody. His black shoes were open along
the welting and his bare bunions protruded. He made it
most of the way across the car before the doors shut. He
bent, reaching for the curved edge of the orange seat
with his left hand. It was bloody at the knuckles. He
reeled backward into the seat. The doors shut and the
train departed for Dorchester.

"Must've been a pretty good one," Russell said. "Like
to see the other guy."

"He fell down," Frankie said. "My father used to
come home like that. He was a strange bastard. Payday
was no trouble at all. He'd get his check and work all
day and come home and give the dough to my mother
and they'd go out that night, go shopping. And they'd
come home and watch TV and he'd maybe have two
beers. At the most, two beers. Lots of times you'd come
down in the morning and there'd be the glass on the
table next to his chair, full of flat old beer. I remember,
I tasted it, the first time I tasted it, I thought: how the
hell can anybody drink anything that tastes like this.
And he'd go to work. But then some times, nothing on
the shape-up. Lots of times. And most of them times,
he'd come home and read or something. Never talked
much. But some times, there wasn't anything, see, you
wouldn't know that, he didn't come home, not all the
times but some times. And he always, he knew, he knew
when he was gonna do it. Because when he didn't come
home, when he was late, my mother'd start to get wor-

ried and walk around a lot, and when he wasn't there,
she's saying Hail Marys and everything, when he wasn't
there by seven-thirty she'd go to the cupboard. That's
where they kept the money they didn't use onna shopping. In a peanut-butter jar. And if he wasn't there, the
jar was always empty. Always. And he'd be gone for at
least three days, and when he came home, that's always
the way he looked. He always fell down.

"I remember," Frankie said, "the last time he's up
at the farm. I had to take him up there, and he was,
well, it was mostly my mother. She told me: 'You're
twenty now. You take care of him. I'd do it but I've had
enough. You take him up.' So I took him up to Drop-
kick's. Doctor P. K. Murphy's farm. And I checked him
in and he was as bombed as you can get. So, he just had
new teeth. And he says to me, well, I knew what he
was trying to say to me, he wanted me to take his teeth.
Paid two hundred and sixty dollars for his teeth. Now
what the fuck was I gonna do with the old man's teeth?
I'm probably gonna lose them myself. So I said to the
guy, I said, look, he was probably gonna come out of it,
one way or the other, they better keep his teeth. And
they put them in a box. I saw them do it.

"I go back about a week later," Frankie said. "I mean,
I liked the old bastard. He never hit anybody. Used to
drive him nuts, Sandy's running around the way she
did, he couldn't do nothing about it. But he wasn't a bad
guy. So I went up there, go up there and see him.

"They used to sit around in the back room," Frankie
said. "It looked, they had these tables and a television
and it looked just like a fuckin' bar. I dunno, probably
they wanted it that way. They got a drink at nine
o'clock and one at lunch and one at six, and some of
them, Christ, the whole place, the woods're full of bot-

tles. A guy'd decide, he was gonna check himself in, and he would, and before he did it he'd get a couple friends of his and they'd come down every day and put ten nips in the woods where he said. The guy told me, he said there was one guy, he was stoned all the time and he never went near the woods, and they could tell, they could tell when one of them was stiff, and they started watching him, really careful. And when they, he didn't think they were watching them, see, he come up in his car, and he'd go out in the yard and get under the car with a cup or something, he filled up the radiator with vodka before he checked in. They thought he was drinking antifreeze. They always had guys bringing in enema bags full of the stuff. At night they'd go around and look in the tanks of all the hoppers. Guys always used to stash pints in there.

"So I go up there," Frankie said, "and the old man's got a buddy. One of the guys he used to work with. They're both on paraldehyde. A little glass of water and the guy comes by every so often and he's got an eyedropper, and a pitcher, and he puts some of the paracki in the glass and some water and they sit there and they sip it, and they, the television's going, they're watching quiz shows or something, they dunno what they're watching, they got cigarettes in their hands and those butts'd burn right down between their knuckles and you could smell their skin burning and you'd tell them and honest to God, that was the first they'd know about it. You'd tell them and they'd look and they'd say: 'Oh, yeah.' And take the cigarette out and look at their fingers and then put the fuckin' thing *back*. They couldn't feel nothing.

"The guy's name was Burke," Frankie said. "My old man's friend was Burke. They were both on paracki

and they both smelled like skunks. Just like skunks. That
stuff makes booze smell like perfume. And the old man's
complaining. He's been up there a week and he's feeling
lots better and he wants his teeth. And the guy can't
find his teeth. He goes on and on. Brand-new teeth, guy
can't find his teeth, where the fuck's his teeth, now he
feels good, he wants to eat, where's the teeth. Burke's
asleep in all of this. I think he was asleep. His eyes were
closed. I know he wasn't dead.

"I go see the guy," Frankie said. " 'Look,' I say, 'my
old man wants his teeth. He's in fairly good shape now.
Not gonna bite anybody. Where's his teeth?' And the
guy tells me, same thing the old man tells me. 'I dunno
where his teeth are,' he says. 'I put the damned things
inna box, and the box's still there but the teeth're gone.
Him and Burke, they been talking about his teeth ever
since he come in. I just don't know. I don't find them,
I'll buy him new teeth. I can't understand it.'

"So I go back," Frankie said. "Burke's awake now, at
least his eyes're open, and the old man's all pissed off,
talking the best he can without his teeth, 'Fine fuckin'
place this is, you come in here and they take your teeth,
fuckin' bastards,' it's all ung, ung, ung, he hasn't got no
teeth, and Burke's sitting up straighter and straighter
and finally Burke laughs. And he's got two sets of teeth.
His own, that're his, and my old man's. Looked like a
fuckin' man-eating shark. I thought the old man was
gonna kill him. Gets his teeth back, wipes them on his
sleeve, puts them in his mouth, I think the old bastard
was almost sober. 'See?' he says. 'See, you little shit?
Make something of yourself and stay off the fuckin'
booze. See what happens to you? Get out there and
make some big money and stay the fuck away from
Burke. You cocksucker.' Then he's gonna beat up Burke.

"I tell you," Frankie said, "I think he was right. I always thought he was right."

"You got caught doing it, though," Russell said, "that fat little fuck. And now you're gonna go out and get caught again."

"I didn't meet you at the ball park," Frankie said. "Keep that in mind. You're already pushing your luck again, and you could get grabbed too."

"For what I'm doing?" Russell said.

"Not gonna matter very much," Frankie said. "What've they got over you?"

"Year and a half," Russell said.

"Plus what they give you for doing it," Frankie said. "And all the guys, they'll be shitting all over you, stealing dogs, for Christ sake."

"You know something?" Russell said. "I bet they wouldn't. I bet they wouldn't even violate me for that. I bet they wouldn't. And Jesus, it's gotta be the easiest thing a guy ever did. This morning there, we go out to Sudbury? Those silly shits. They get up and they come downstairs and they let the dog out. They don't know what they're doing. You sit there, I think you could park right in their yard if you wanted. They wouldn't even see you. They let a four-hundred-dollar animal out, right out the door at you, woof, woof, woof, 'Here, boy, here boy,' and you wave a little meat at him. Jumps right in. You tried to go in that house and he was in there, he'd take your fuckin' leg off, probably. But you show him eighty cents' worth of cheap lamb chops and it takes about two minutes and you're on your way. I got this Labrador today, beautiful dog, scoffing down the meat and drooling all over the place before they get the door shut, big tail going whump, whump, whump, happy as a pig in shit because he's eating and he's get-

ting his ears rubbed. That dog loves my ass. You talk
about money? It'll be Saturday before those stupid
bastards even know he's gone, and I'll sell him in Florida
next week for two hundred without even pushing the
guy. Don't take no brains. Just the rocks."

"Two hundred," Frankie said. "John's talking about
ten apiece."

"Yeah," Russell said, "but he didn't say, he didn't
say how we're gonna get it, that he's too chickenshit
scared to do it himself so he wants us to do it and he
just sits back there and takes his piece without doing
nothing. I didn't hear him say nothing about that. He
just decided he wanted to get all pissed off because
somebody might've used something or maybe was doing something or something."

"If he says it's there," Frankie said, "it's there. And
you got to, if the guy's worried about something, well,
he doesn't want to go and fuck it up, is all. You can't
blame a guy for that. He's all right."

"Yeah," Russell said, "yeah. He's so careful, how
much'd you do the last time he got something set up
for you? About sixty-eight months, am I right?"

"Five and a half," Frankie said. "That wasn't his fault.
He did time too, don't forget."

"Forget nothing," Russell said. "He was the guy that
set the thing up, wasn't he? And now he's got another
bright idea. Okay. But me and Kenny, you give me another week with Kenny and we'll have ourselves about
twenty good dogs, and I guarantee you, the coke'll be
there and I'll be where the coke is and I'll have the
money and I am *on* my fuckin' *way*. One month from
today I got a Moto Guzzi and no shit from anybody."

A silver train pulled in from Cambridge. The red
panel on the front read: QUINCY. It blocked the view of

the heavyset man as he finished removing the E in
SOUTHIE and started on the E in EATS.

"So I guess you're not coming, then," Frankie said.

"Look," Russell said, "go and see the guy. See if you
can get him to tell you something about it. I'll be around.
You find out what it is, you're still interested, don't mat-
ter to me. You decide, you want to do it, it's all right,
I'm in. Without knowing. He still wants me out, I'm out.
I'm not gonna waste the whole afternoon on it, though.
That I'm not gonna do."

3

"HE'S GETTING LAID," Frankie said. "He said he hadda choice between coming down here and getting laid, and he decided to get laid."

"Can't blame a guy for that," Amato said. "Somebody put one like that up to me today, I probably wouldn't be here myself. So, I assume you're still in for it, who else're we gonna get? You think of somebody?"

"I didn't," Frankie said. "I don't know, he's still interested. He didn't, the only reason he didn't come down here, he said if you wanted him to come in on it, okay, he'd come in on it. And if you didn't, okay, no hard feelings, he's doing all right."

Amato was silent. Then he said: "Frank, I just don't like the guy, you know? I just don't like him."

"He's all right," Frankie said. "He comes on kind of strong when you first see him, but he's basically all right. And he's very, very stand-up."

"Which, after the Doctor, we could both use," Amato said.

"Yeah," Frankie said. "I wouldn't mind running into that son of a bitch some time again when I felt good."

"I don't think you're gonna," Amato said. "Nobody's seen the Doctor for a while, the way I get it."

"That so?" Frankie said. "I wonder where he could've gone."

"Well," Amato said, "you know, it's hard to say. He was in San Francisco, he was in the service. He was always saying, he'd like to go back there some time. He said it was too cold, it got too cold for him around here."

"That's probably where he went, then," Frankie said.

"Yeah," Amato said. "Of course, this was Dillon, I get this from. He knows a guy."

"Oh," Frankie said.

"Dillon don't look good," Amato said. "He don't look good at all. I was in town the other day and I saw him. He looks white, all white around the gills. I didn't say anything to him, but he don't look good at all."

"Dillon's getting old," Frankie said.

"We all are," Amato said. "Look at me, the way I let that little shitbird of yours get to me the other day? I never would've done that before. I'm yapping at the kids all the time, for Christ sake. For seven years the only time I see the little bastards's once a month or so, and now I'm finally home and I'm giving them hell all the time. I'm always fighting with my wife. I never used to fight with my wife. I used to, she was being a big pain in the ass, I used to kind of roll with the punches, you know? Now I don't. I'm getting old. And I swore, boy, I was in? I swore when I got out I was gonna make every minute count, the rest of my life. You ever get me some place again, I can go to sleep without some asshole shoving his dick through the bars, all right, that's all I ask. And am I doing it? No. Of course I'm not. I'm just as big an asshole now as I was before."

"Russell'd get to anybody," Frankie said. "It's the way he is."

"Yeah," Amato said, "but the way I used to be, I wouldn't've cared if he could piss off everybody inna world, you know? He couldn't piss me off. If he was right for the job, he'd be right for the job. Screw, I'm not gonna marry the guy. All I want, all I would've been thinking about is, is he right for this job, and if I thought he was right, that'd be it."

"Well," Frankie said, "you change your mind or something?"

"I dunno," Amato said. "I been asking around about him. You know, not too many guys and all, I don't want it to seem like maybe I had something in mind. That I don't need. But, well, I'm afraid, I'm afraid he's not the kind of guy we oughta have in on this. You go around this thing inna wrong way, you could get somebody hurt, and I don't want that. There's no reason for that, you know? You hit somebody, you're not gonna get any more money or anything. It's just, it don't make no sense. You got to have guys that can, that're not going to go haywire or something, is all.

"These people," Amato said, "these're not the kind of people, that're around a bank or something, they *expect* maybe some day a guy or somebody's gonna come in there and try to rob them and, it's not their money, people tell them, how they oughta act. They're not that kinda people at all."

"Heroes," Frankie said.

"Heroes," Amato said. "They're a different kind of guys, and they're liable, some of them, you never know when one of them's gonna do it, go right off his ass and start making trouble and then you got to fuckin' shoot somebody, for Christ sake. Some of them, they think they're pretty hot shits. Somebody comes in there that's not absolutely cool, well, that they can see right off doesn't know what he's doing and he's not taking no shit off anybody that wants to fuck around with him, well, then it's gonna be different. *Bad*, different."

"You're not gonna promote that North End thing to me again, are you, John?" Frankie said.

"The barbut?" Amato said. "Nah, this's different. Although I got to say, I still think you could do that thing if you thought about it long enough and you went in there with the right type of guys, knowing what you're doing. A few guys, some day somebody's gonna knock that thing off, and then he's gonna have a whole lot of money. A whole bunch of money."

"I wanna meet that guy, afterward," Frankie said. "I think probably, I'm ever gonna meet him, I better meet him quick, is what I think. Fuckin' thing. You ever look that thing over? There's a guy on the corner in the phone booth. Funny how come the phone company put that thing right there, huh? And then there's always a guy that's sitting up in the window and looking out at the guy in the phone booth. Coldest night in the year, go down there, that guy's in the phone booth. He's not doing nothing. I think maybe that's how he makes his living. I wouldn't want it, maybe, but it's fuckin' steady's what I think. You wouldn't even think anybody'd go out, and there he is, and then there's that alley and I bet there's not more'n fifteen heavies in that room with the pieces all set to go."

"There's still a lot of money in there," Amato said.

" 'So much money they lose it, they lose the dice in it some times,' " Frankie said. " 'You go in and you get it, they're never gonna be able, report it, no government types chasing you around, you just go down past Billy's Fish and up the stairs and you're set for life.' Yeah, and Dillon gets better so fast you wouldn't believe it, I bet, and fifty guys helping him, too. I been hearing about that place since, I think I was about fourteen when I first hear about that place," Frankie said. "The thing of it is, all that time, nobody ever did it. I wonder how come."

"My daughter's fourteen," Amato said.

"Jesus," Frankie said. "It don't seem that long."

"Yup," Amato said. "She's fourteen years old. And the other day, she left her stuff out on the dresser? I see this light blue cardboard thing. I go in and I look. She's onna Pill."

"No shit," Frankie said.

"I couldn't fuckin' believe it," Amato said. "I said to Connie: 'For Christ sake, willya tell me, what's going on here?' So she tells me. 'So what? They're all on it.' I said to her: 'Whaddaya mean, they're all on it? Who're they? What the hell's she doing on it? Tell me that, all right? I don't care about the rest of them.' Oh, so that makes me the automatic bastard. 'You want, you'd probably rather she gets pregnant or something.' I couldn't, I just couldn't believe it, was all. 'Connie,' I said, 'she's *fourteen years old*, for Christ sake. Fourteen. That's kind of early, I think.' "

"I think so too," Frankie said.

"Yeah," Amato said. "So, you know what she says to me? She says: 'How old's Rosalie when you're going with her?' "

"How old was Rosalie?" Frankie said.

"Eighteen," Amato said, "which is a hell of a lot different. Only, of course, I couldn't say that. I always, whenever she asked me, I denied that. And Rosalie wasn't on no Pill then, either. Every month . . . Ah, she was a lousy lay anyway."

"She didn't look it," Frankie said.

"She was, though," Amato said. "Shit, getting into Fort Knox would've been easier. More fun, too. I hadda tell her every time, it's true love, all that shit. I hadda be an asshole, do that. And she, she didn't *do* nothing. It was like fuckin' a stump. I used, she also didn't do nothing *about* doing anything. I used to say to her: 'Rosalie, for Christ sake, will you get something? You don't want to get pregnant, do you?' And then she'd start crying. It's a mortal sin. I don't know. I didn't. I used to think, I was an asshole, I used to think I really had something there. Now, now I dunno why I did it. It wasn't worth anything near like what I hadda put up with to get it."

"She was one good-looking broad, though," Frankie said.

"See the game the other night?" Amato said. "I did. I was home. Connie finally went to bed. Muscles in her jaw got tired. That's what I like about TV, boy. You can turn off the sound. They had this shot of Snead coming up behind this big Swede center's ass. You see that?"

"I was out," Frankie said.

"Well," Amato said, "I seen Rosalie the other night, I seen her down the Artery. Connie had me stop, get some fuckin' bread. That's another thing, I don't know why it is. I don't ask her, do some of my business. Why the fuck've I gotta stop on the way home and do her business? Anyway, I see Rosalie. She's bigger'n that Swede now, I swear to God."

"She was a real good-looking girl," Frankie said.

"Ah," Amato said, "she got married. That's what she wanted. That's the thing she used to worry about, I was humping her. I was worried, why the fuck's she such a lousy lay. She was worried, how the fuck's she marry me, I'm married to Connie? I didn't wanna get married again. I got married once. Once's enough for any guy, isn't crazy. But that's what she wanted. She's pregnant now. About her fourth, I guess. That broad? I bet, she's got legs on her now, I bet she couldn't get my pants on, is how big she is. Everything goes to hell if you wait long enough. Connie says to me: 'You don't like certain things? Okay. You talk to her, Mister Big Deal Father, that's spending six or seven years in prison while she's growing up. You talk to her. You tell her what a bad girl she is.' Of course Connie couldn't've told me, I was in there, what the fuck's going on. How'm I supposed to know it? Shit. There's nothing you can do anyway. It don't matter. It just pisses me off, is all. It pisses me off."

"Look," Frankie said, "I don't mean nothing, all right? I don't care how pissed off you are. You at least got something."

"Still come up dry, huh?" Amato said.

"You know what I did?" Frankie said. "I went down the Probation. Like I actually believe all that shit they're always handing out, there, all that stuff. 'Here's something for you. Place in Holbrook needs assemblers. One thirty a week. Four to midnight. Steady work and it'll keep you out of trouble.'

"Beautiful," Frankie said. "I'm living in Somerville. How the hell'm I supposed to get to Holbrook in the middle of the afternoon? Never mind, for Christ sake, how the fuck I'm supposed to get home inna middle of the night. 'Buy a car. You need a car for your job, we'll help you get your license back.'

"With what?" Frankie said. "I haven't got no money. What am I gonna buy a car with? Why the fuck they think I need a job, I'm living with my sister and everything. So I can keep warm? I haven't got no money, a car. 'Maybe you can get a ride,' they tell me. Right. Hang around the Square every day, I find somebody that just happens to be going down to Holbrook. Just at the right time, too. Assholes.

"'Move down there,' they tell me," Frankie said. "Same thing. I still haven't got no money. I had money, I could move down there, I'd move some place else, I wouldn't be bothering them in the first place. Well, they're sorry. That's all they got right now, that they're pretty sure the guy that does the hiring'll take a guy like me. I should probably go down the welfare and get enough dough, I can move out there. The guy's just sick of talking to me. He wants his fuckin' coffee or something. Okay, that's the end of that. Then I see Russell. He's going right along. He'll probably buy a hotel or something in a couple weeks or so."

"Not on dogs," Amato said.

"He's just doing that," Frankie said. "He's gonna use that to buy something, soon's he gets enough. That's what I'd like to do, I got something in mind like that myself. But first I got to get the money to buy the stuff."

"What is it?" Amato said.

"There's this guy I know," Frankie said. "I see him, he naturally wants to know, how're things going? So we have a couple pops, he's buying, and we talk, and then he says, well, he's gotta go over this place and I can come along if I want, maybe I'll see something.

"So we go down this place," Frankie said, "and it's money. All twenties. Beautiful stuff. I had, I could've bought some of that stuff. I hadda thousand on me, I could've bought twenny thousand dollars of that stuff. And I tell you, it's beautiful. You could move it under a floodlight."

"Better call the guy up," Amato said. "Tell him bye-bye. He's gonna get grabbed. He better pass the first one inna drugstore and get himself a new toothbrush. He's gonna need one."

"John," Frankie said, "wrong. This stuff is really good. The paper's good, the ink's good, the colors're right. I tell you. I really looked at that stuff. The guy that made it oughta go take some of it to the government. It's better'n the real stuff."

"The guy's Chubby Ryan," Amato said.

"I dunno him," Frankie said.

"He's not around," Amato said. "He's in Atlanta. He's doing ten fuckin' years for that beautiful stuff. That funny? You know something? I agree with you. It's beautiful stuff. It's fuckin' near perfect. But Chubby, Chubby knows a lot about printing and all of that, but, see, Chubby hasn't got no fuckin' brains. Just like your friend, there, Doglover. He's all right. He just don't know anything. Guys like him, the guys you're always hanging around with, well, they're the only guys're stupider'n Chubby. Because all that stuff's good for now, except for wiping your ass on it, it's to sell to guys like you, don't know any better, what's gonna start happening to them when they go out and start moving the stuff. That's why the price's so low.

"You know what's the matter with that stuff?" Amato said. "I'll tell you. Chubby took it out to fuckin' Wonderland, is what Chubby did. He hasn't got no brains. He thinks, it's good, he's gonna move it all by himself. He's gonna go out the dog track and move the whole run, he's so proud of that funny. So he did. He moved about ten thousand of it, all by himself, one single fuckin' night. Five hundred of them goddamned beautiful things, and every single one of them's got the same goddamned number on it.

"Now of course," Amato said, "them guys, run dog tracks, they're all stupid, aren't they? Betcher ass. Dumb as shit. Never occurred to them, race track's a good place to pass funny. No, not on your life. So they never train them tellers, look out for anything like bogus. So of course, them tellers never spot anything, the night

Chubby's there, throwing twenties around like he's ape-shit and everything, absolutely not. So they only had about nine hundred security guys and some cops and the Secret Service all over the place when Chubby comes back, the eighth race. And you know what he says? They give him his rights and everything, he don't have to say a fuckin' word, and if he didn't know that already, which he should've, he knows now. And they tell him, he's in the shit for counterfeit. And he looks at them and he says: 'Jesus Christ. I put them in coffee. They don't look new.'

"You know what he did?" Amato said. "They give him his phone call and he calls Mike. And Mike says, Mike tells him, keep his mouth shut. And Mike goes down there, and, Mike knows everybody. So he goes in, and they're all laughing at him, and he knows it, and he asks: 'Why?' And they show him the reports and stuff. And then Mike's gonna go see his client. And he walks inna cell and he looks at him and Chubby says: 'Boy, am I ever glad, see you.' And you know what Mike says? He looks at him, and he says: 'Chubby, this one's for free. Plead it.' And he goes out.

"See," Amato said, "that's your main problem you got today. You got guys that know how to do things but they don't know nothing about having no fuckin' brains, is all. They haven't got no imagination. The only thing they can think of to do is the first thing they can see that looks good to them. Only, five hundred guys already did it before and *everybody* knows what's going on, so you automatically go out there and you do it and they're watching for you and they get you. You got to think of a different angle, something nobody else thought of for a while, or else you got to go down to Holbrook there and you go to fuckin' work. Everything else's a waste of time, and it's dangerous, too, because you're gonna *do* time."

"Okay," Frankie said, "you're the guy with the angle. Tell me what the angle is. Only, don't tell me, it's the barbut, is all. I'm not going down that alley behind Billy's Fish some night and wind up in Everett with a couple in my head. No fuckin' way. I want dough. I'm not getting dead, gettin' it."

"How about," Amato said, "well, look, let's talk about it. Before we decide. You think Doglover there can handle a card game?"

"Well I mean," Frankie said, "shit. Sure, anybody can. They can find one where they can go in and they haven't got to go up against some kind of an arsenal. Those fuckin' things, they just got less money in them'n the barbut's got, is all. Those things're protected. You can't do them unless you're so fuckin' dumb you actually like having everybody going around tryin' to off you."

"There's one you can do," Amato said.

"There's ten I can do, John," Frankie said. "I know of at least ten of them I can do. But then after, somebody, everybody's gonna have at least eight hot ginzos out looking for me."

"Uh uh," Amato said. "Do this one and they'll, they won't even look for you."

"Why not?" Frankie said.

"Because the minute it fuckin' happens," Amato said, "they're gonna know right off, who it is."

"For some reason," Frankie said, "that don't make me feel better, you know, John?"

"Not us," Amato said. "Keep in mind, I know how these guys think. They're not gonna think, they're never even gonna think it might be us or even somebody else.

They're pick one guy, right off, and go find him and whack him out and that'll be it. And you and me and that little prick, if that's the guy we get, we cut up about forty, fifty thousand dollars. No fuckin' sweat."

"I don't know's I go for setting somebody up," Frankie said.

"You're not setting him up," Amato said. "He set himself up. Mark Trattman runs this game. This's the second game Markie's had. The other game got knocked off. Markie did it."

"Ah," Frankie said.

"He did it," Amato said, "and there was all kinds of shit. One of the guys that got robbed was a doctor, and he had a brother was a state cop, and he was mad as hell, he was gonna do this and he was gonna do that and everybody's running around, they hadda give the guy back about, I dunno, three or four thousand, to shut him up, and they go around and see Trattman. And he puts on this great act. And they believe him.

"So everybody pisses blood for a while," Amato said, "the way they always do when the shit hits the fan, and there's about a month or so goes by and everybody, nobody's running any games or anything, and then, I think it was Tommy Balls, somebody says: 'Fuck this,' and he hires about ten guys to stand around and opens up and nothing happens. So they all look at Testa's game, and nothing still happens, and after a while everybody's open again and everybody's happy.

"So one night," Amato said, "the guys're hanging around and they're talking and all, having a few drinks, and finally one of them says how it's funny, they had that thing and everybody got all jumpy and now they're all running again and nobody's tried it again. Probably having more guys around, huh? Well, Markie starts laughing. See, he can't resist it. So he tells them, he did it himself. He got two guys to come in and he did it himself. The guys got five apiece, they're a couple guys carrying hod that he happens to know or something, and he come out of it with close to thirty."

"He's lucky they didn't put him to sleep," Frankie said.

"Well," Amato said, "he is. But you got to understand Mark. All the guys like Markie. He's a genuine hot shit. And look when they find out: when everybody's open again. They'd've found out it was him when the games're all closed and everybody's hearing footsteps and nobody's making any money, then, I think, they would've done it to him. But they didn't. And then, when they did, well, what the fuck, huh? It wasn't none of their money and just as long as it doesn't happen again, because all the customers, you're not gonna get them coming in unless they think it's protected, but the protection's really there, well, shit on it."

"I bet it probably wouldn't happen again that way," Frankie said.

"And that's the angle," Amato said.

"What's it good for?" Frankie said.

"I figure," Amato said, "I was there twice. I been there twice since I got out. I run into Markie one night, I was in town seeing what's going on and looking around and I run into him and we had a couple drinks and he says, he tells me he's got this thing and I should come up. So, twice, both times onna Wednesday. He runs it two nights a week, Wednesdays and Fridays. Now the guys that're there, that come on Wednesday, there's a few that come both nights but it's really a different group the two nights. There was probably, I would say about forty thousand flying around the nights

I was there. There's this one creep that wears fuckin' velvet pants, and he had at least five on him both the nights I was there. So, a little more, a little less. And of course that's just what I saw. Most guys, go to something like that, they'll carry a little more'n what they're gonna let you see, case they get a bad run of cards and they got to ride something out. So you go in there, you're gonna give everybody a nice little massage and everything, you're probably gonna come up with, say, ten more."

"Not bad," Frankie said.

"Now there's guys," Amato said, "I was there, I heard talk, see, Markie just got divorced again and apparently he had a little party, had a couple hookers come in and eat each other and everybody had a great time and some of these guys're pissed off, he didn't invite them. 'Friends only, no customers,' he says. So they get on him, and some of the Friday night guys were there and that's how these guys find out about it. 'They're good customers,' Markie said, 'good customers're the same as good friends, my book.' So I got an idea, there's more dough there onna Friday'n there is onna Wednesday. So the question is, when're we gonna do it? And I think, I still think, a Wednesday. Friday that place's different. During the week it's pretty quiet, but on Fridays and Saturdays they got a lot of people coming and going, getting laid and all, and that's just another fuckin' thing you got to think about, parties going on and everything. And I think, I dunno, I kind of think maybe there's some guys in there, Fridays, don't come Wednesdays, the kind of guys I don't want to get pissed off. I didn't see nobody there Wednesdays, had any muscle. I think it's better."

"How're we cutting this?" Frankie said.

"A third," Amato said. "I get a third."

"That's high, John," Frankie said.

"Not for this," Amato said. "I know where it is and I know what it is. A third's right. You, I don't care what you do. You can get that wild man or somebody, do it for five, get him. Fine with me."

"The guy who goes in with me gets the same's I do," Frankie said.

"Up to you," Amato said.

"You're not going in," Frankie said.

"Uh uh," Amato said. "They'd burn me the minute I came inna door. I'm gonna be a long ways away from that place that night and I'm gonna have a lot of people around me, saw me there. See, that's what, that's why I think of you. All I can really do is show somebody where the thing is. I can't go near it, and I need a guy I can trust, somebody that isn't gonna tell me, they come up with thirty, it's really fifty and they're fucking me and there's no way I can check. I gotta just be the guy that does the brainwork on this. What I need's two guys to do the job the way I tell them."

"All right," Frankie said, "I'm in. Now, what about Russell?"

"What about him?" Amato said.

"I'm still thinking, he's gonna be the other guy," Frankie said. "You get used to that?"

"I don't give a rat's ass," Amato said. "You can go in with Tarzan in his fuckin' spotted jockstrap if you can get him to do it, don't matter to me. I just want, get somebody who's gonna do it right. There's only two things a guy's gotta have, right? He's gotta have balls, which you say the guy's got, and he can't be nobody my padrones know."

"Well, Jesus," Frankie said, "China Tanzi knows me, for Christ sake."

"China don't count," Amato said. "China's in Lewis-burg and he's gonna be in Lewisburg for a long time. Making furniture for the government or something, and theres a lot of guys're not too happy with China anyway right now. They think he probably should've got fifteen or twenty in Atlanta like everybody else that was in that thing, instead of just the five. Shit, he hadda record worse'n anybody else's that was in it, and he gets the five and he's not inna same place and, I mean, that's got to make guys wonder, you know? How come? It was going around for a while, China's not even *in* Lewis-burg. They got him on ice somewhere, they're feeding him steaks and bringing his family around and talking to him. Well, somebody says it's not true. I dunno. But nobody's listening to China much any more. I already thought of that."

"Well," Frankie said, "I'm gonna ask Russell, then. I don't think he knows anybody."

"What'd he go in for?" Amato said.

"It was kind of a wild thing, I guess," Frankie said. "You know how it is, a guy wants to tell you, he tells you. He didn't tell me. But the way I get it, him and another guy, they decided to go after this drugstore, you know? All-night drugstore. Well, it was one of them guys that the boogeys're always after and he hadda gun in there and there was a whole mess of shit. Started shooting and everything, after they got the stuff, and the guy that was with Russell, well, I dunno. They both had the same kind of guns and I think probably what Russell did, he probably swapped guns. See the guy in the drugstore got hit, but he took the guy that was with Russell out on the way. Anyway, Russell goes on trial and it was the dead guy that got all the shit, put Russell up to it and everything. Rus-sell's just a clown that went along with something he

didn't understand and look at his war record and everything. Which I guess was pretty good. So he come out of
it a lot better'n he would've, otherwise."

"You're sure he's not gonna go into this stoned,"
Amato said.

"He's not on anything big," Frankie said. "You heard
the guy. He's a very savvy guy. He knows what he's
doing. He knows what it does. He don't take nothing he
can't handle."

"You wanna be sure," Amato said. "Guys that go
around robbing drugstores, they're not always guys
that're just after money. Some times they're hurting and
they need something and they haven't got no other way,
they can get it. And they need it. A guy like that, he
can't live without it, he doesn't get it, you know?"

"Look," Frankie said, "Russell's a motorcycle nut.
That's all. The first month I knew the guy, all he ever
did was piss and moan, he hadda sell this fuckin' monster bike, he had a Munch, one of them Mammoths? He
hadda sell the bike, pay his fuckin' lawyer. If there's
a bike in this, no, I wouldn't take Russell. He'd go
hairy-assed apeshit the minute he came in. The stuff?
He uses the stuff. That's all. He's not hooked."

"Because one thing," Amato said, "one thing we really
don't need on this is a guy that's going to go in there
and start something off and get some guy. Because then
they'll have to report it and that's when everybody's
inna shit up to his eyeballs. If Markie, Markie did this
before. He was gonna do it again, he'd be just as careful
as the last time, get some guys that'd go about it in the
right way. These guys're his customers. He wants them
robbed, not hit. He wants them back again, they get
time to think about it and forget it happened."

"He'll be all right," Frankie said.

"I hope you're right," Amato said. "Now, the other thing is, this thing's gotta move, all right?"

"All right with me," Frankie said. "I don't do something pretty soon, I'm gonna have to go back and knock onna gate and say: 'Lemme back in. I can't think of nothing and it's starting to get cold.'"

"Because it's just a matter of time," Amato said, "some other fresh bastard's gonna think of it and then it's gone and we haven't got the money."

"No trouble," Frankie said. "I'm starving and he's got to go some place pretty soon with them dogs, and like I say, I don't get my ass in gear pretty soon, I might as well kiss it good-bye. You got the stuff?"

"A car," Amato said. "The kids Connie got, most of them're stupid enough, but there's one of them, probably if he started to get wet and he was outdoors, he'd go inside. I know where there's a nice Chrysler. I think he can get it without hot-wiring his balls. I got two thirty-eights, which oughta be enough. You're gonna have to get your own ski masks or something."

"I'd like a sawed-off for this one," Frankie said. "Something big, scare the shit out of them, you walk in the door."

"You get one," Amato said, "use it. Okay by me. Just don't start taking your fuckin' time about it, is all. We're not the only smart guys in the world."

4

THE 300F DID EIGHTY quietly on Route 128 north.

"She looked really great," Russell said. "I mean, *really*. Beautiful big tits, fucked like it was going out of style. This's really a great car, isn't it? It's like riding in your fuckin' bedroom, but it's still a great car."

"I wished," Frankie said, "one of the things I really wish, I wish you could still get a car like this."

"Keep this one," Russell said.

"Just what I need," Frankie said, "a nice, hot car. No, you can't do it, and there's none of them around that're in decent shape enough to buy. Fuck. Tell me about her some more."

"Wanna blow your mind?" Russell said. "You're not gettin' any still, are you?"

"Tomorrow night I'm getting some," Frankie said. "This goes all right, this's my last night, a priest. Tell me about it. I'll take care my own hog."

"Well, you had the practice," Russell said.

"That's nice talk," Frankie said, "guy like you that was sticking it in Goat-ass's satchel. Very nice talk."

"That's the first rule," Russell said, "a clean old man. I didn't see no broads around, up there."

"Who said Goat-ass was clean?" Frankie said.

"Not me," Russell said. "That's the next rule. If there's no old man around that's clean, take the dirty one."

"I should've had them get you a goat," Frankie said. "I had some clout with the keepers. I should've done that. The rest of us could've watched. You sure you're not fooling around with them dogs, like John said, right?"

"Dogs're liable to bite," Russell said. "I knew a kid, I knew a kid that had a dachshund once . . . never mind that. Lemme give you some advice, Frank: stay away from the dogs. You can get nipped, and what I hear, that hurts. Stick with broads. If you can find one."

"You know?" Frankie said. "I'm not sure I can. Maybe it's the same thing. Maybe they're not making broads any more, either. You can't get a nice hemi, because it's liable to make somebody sick or something, it burns gas, and it's probably, it wouldn't surprise me, there's no more broads, either."

"There's broads," Russell said. "Just like us. There's always broads. Squirrel wants to do something, he knows where he finds us. We go in and we go out and he's having drinks some place, and he gets the same as we do. He knows where we are. The girls? They're the same. They're just as crazy as we are. It's just one crazy bastard taking advantage of another crazy bastard. That's all it is. That broad I was with? She's crazy. She's beautiful but she's crazy. The way she looks, she didn't have nothing to do with that. She don't have nothing to do with the way her head's fucked up, either. But it is. She's fuckin' batty.

"She lives up onna Hill, right?" Russell said. "I go up there, she opens the door, she's naked. Right there. Kind of threw me. She is really a good-looking girl. The stuff I been having, well, it's not like I don't appreciate it, you know? I was in a long time. But this kid, she was something. So I stand there, I'm just looking at her. And she says: 'We're gonna make it, right? You gonna stand there all day?' So I go in and I bang her. Great. And then we're lying there and I'm playing with her and she had some really good grass and it was great. Except she's fuckin' nuts. The girl's completely nuts."

"Gimme the number," Frankie said. "Don't go back

there. I wouldn't want you hanging around with no
nutty women. Just gimme the number. I'll go up there
and I'll read the fuckin' Bible to her or something."

"I didn't say I wasn't going back," Russell said. "I
said she was crazy."

"I don't think you oughta go back," Frankie said.
"You're gonna get in trouble, up and coming fellow
like yourself, hanging around with crazy people. Turn
her over to me. I'll counsel her, is what I'll do. I'll make
her feel better."

"Right," Russell said, "and then she'll do what she
says she's gonna do and you'll get blamed for it and
that'll be the end of you, Cochise. She's gonna kill herself."

"They all say that," Frankie said. "It's the first thing
they think of to say, a lot of them. I dunno why they
do it. They probably, they went to Catholic school or
something. It don't matter. I was going with this girl,
I used to go with? Friend of Sandy's. Had her pants
glued on, for Christ sake. Not a bad-looking kid. She
had kind of buck teeth. Nice ass. She wanted to get
married. I didn't know anything, for Christ sake. I
wanted to get laid. Get married, go to jail, cut your
foot off: I would've done it. I was so fuckin' horny I
would've done anything to get laid. I remember, I
used to go, can you believe this? I used to go fuckin'
parking with this broad. I used to take my old man's
beat-up car and drive and drive and drive, get some
place where she didn't think maybe somebody knew
her father'd see us. Used to go down Chickatawbut, the
reservoir? I was almost twenny years old and this kid
was, what, I dunno, seventeen, probably, and I used
to spend fuckin' *hours* tryin' to get my fuckin' bare hand
on her fuckin' bare *tit*. I think it took me almost a year.

I took her to drive-ins, I took her to dances, I fed her
booze, I breathed in her fuckin' ear, and all I could do,
I could feel her up from the outside. Through the
sweater, through the blouse, if she was really drunk I
could get my hand inside and feel her up through the
bra. For Christ sake. The night, I finally got my hand
inside the bra. *Inside.* I didn't have it unhitched or
nothing, just, I got my hand in there. I came in my
pants."

Russell began to laugh.

"I did," Frankie said. "And I hadda drive home that
way, all stuck together for Christ sake. The guys, I
used to hang around down the Howdy. And I'd hear
the guys, there's all these broads that put out. And I
believed them. And they gimme names. The actual
names. And I didn't do nothing. I used to think, this
was when I was working the oil company, I was gonna
be a repairman, they give you your own little truck and
you make about ten grand a year, now, and you always
got to go out in a fuckin' blizzard about three o'clock
inna morning, oh, it's a great fuckin' life, and I used to
think, well, what I thought was, I got to have a girl
I can respect. I don't want none of them whores. You
imagine that? True love. True fuckin' love. I don't want
no girl that just wants to fuck. I want a girl that just
wants to fuck *me*, and you know what we're gonna do?
We're gonna get married and we're gonna live happily
ever after. That's what we're gonna do."

"With about nine hundred screamin' kids and a
fuckin' house and all that shit," Russell said.

"Right," Frankie said. "So, inna meantime, I dunno,
her father wouldn't let her go out with me more'n twice
a week. Fridays and Saturdays. I could visit her
Wednesdays, but there's always somebody else there

and I hadda be out of there by ten, because she hadda
go to school the next day."

"High school?" Russell said.

"High school," Frankie said. "I'm twenty years old
and here's this broad I'm absolutely out of my mind
over, and she's in high school."

"Some time, I hope," Russell said, "you got over being an asshole."

"I'm not sure," Frankie said. "I remember one night
I get her home, she hadda be home by eleven-thirty,
Friday nights, on Saturdays she can stay out till midnight. I got her home about two in the morning. I
dunno if it was a Friday night or a Saturday night. We
used to go down the Blue Hills Drive In and she'd
French-kiss me and, probably at least one other couple
inna car, and it'd drive me fuckin' nuts. Blue fuckin'
balls. Three times a week. And I get her home and
the old man's up, and he's raring to go. 'Did you do it?'
he screams at me. I played dumb. 'Do what?' You
should've seen his face. It's a wonder he didn't have
some kind of attack or something. She was standing
right there. *'Did you fuck her, you rotten little bastard?'*
I was fuckin' stunned. I got my mouth open, I couldn't
say nothing. I think I came in my pants that night, too,
and I didn't dare look, see if it came through, because
once I did, he'd know, and he's still screaming at me.
'You think I don't know what you're trying to do, you
little prick? You little fucking bastard? You think I
don't *know?'* I thought he was gonna fuckin' kill me.
And she, that little bitch, she was just as rough on him
as she was on me. 'Daddy,' she says, 'your language is
filthy.' And she stomps upstairs and there're the two of
us, looking at each other. He slammed the fuckin' door.

"After that," Frankie said, "after that I can't see her

no more on Wednesdays. Only weekends, and Jesus, every time I go there I expect they're gonna put the old man in the car with us, we go out. So, I start hanging around with the wrong type of guys. And I meet a couple guys, and one of them knows Johnny, and I meet Johnny, and I start doing a few things for John. And you know something? I was still in love with that crazy kid. I probably would've married her. I dunno if her old man would've let me fuck her, I *was* married to her. Maybe Fridays and Saturdays. Long's I got her home by midnight. I didn't know what the hell I was doing. Then I got hooked and they try me, I was in the can the whole time, and they all come to the trial, him too, now and then, and I got the time, there. Sandy and my mother and Janice and everything. Ten years. What's ten years? I didn't know what the fuck was going on. I was, I wasn't even twenty-one years old. Somebody says ten years to me. What's that mean? That judge, you know what he said? 'If you continue in this path, young man, you'll be in serious trouble before you're through.' Then he gives me ten years. Serious trouble. That's probably when they cut your nuts off and make you eat them.

"So they're taking me away, fuckin' old deputy, his uniform's got soup all over it, and they're all crying, my mother's crying, Sandy's crying, Janice's crying, she's havin' fuckin' hysterics. I should've told her, go out and throw the bumper around, always helped me when you wouldn't come across and I sure can't help you now. And the deputy, he wouldn't let them talk to me and I was still punchy, I was on *his* side. I just got ten and I never even got a hand-job off this broad and now I got to go through this? Pissed me off. I said to him: 'Get me out of here.' And she's gonna do this,

she's gonna do that, it was awful. So, I was in about
three months, Sandy comes to see me. Janice's married.
It don't mean anything."

"Broads're different now," Russell said. "You been in
too long. This broad, this broad means it. You can tell.
She's gonna do it, and then the guy that's with her when
she does it, he's gonna have to explain a lot of things,
and that I can't do. You can't do it either. She needs a
good leaving-alone."

"I can make up my own mind," Frankie said.

"She wouldn't give me a chance, for God's sake," Russell said. " 'We gonna do it again?' Absolutely. Just
gimme a minute or so, get it up again. 'I can do that,'
she says, and she blows me. Well, you know, I haven't
been out that long. I'm still pretty eager. And, I knew
what was gonna happen. But I didn't tell her, and she
got herself a pretty good mouthful. Which she kind of
gags on, naturally, and she sits up and wipes her mouth
off and she looks at me and she says: 'Thanks a lot, you
bastard.' I say, I said, 'Look, I didn't know. I mean,
you act like you know what you're doing.' 'Yeah,' she
says. 'Yeah, you probably think I like the taste of
come.'

"So I told her," Russell said, "Goat-ass always did.
Fuckin' guy couldn't get enough of the stuff. Said it kept
him young. 'I never liked it myself,' I tell her, 'but he
did, and I don't know.' So she says: 'You turd. You're
all turds aren't you, you turd. There isn't one of you
that's not a turd.' And there's this big song and dance.
We're lying there and, it's a really nice apartment, got
all these African masks on the wall and everything, and
she's bitching and moaning, the first time wasn't any
good either, it's never any good, she keeps on hoping,
and it turns out, it's not even her place we're in. I

thought it was her place. It belongs to this guy she's going with, the stereo, all the rest of it, it's all his. He's in school. He's gonna get himself some kind of thing and then he's gonna do something and it's all gonna take him about a million years or something and she don't get nothing from him, so she calls up guys, put ads in the *Phoenix*, 'Ex-con, long dong, love and affection.' I mean, she don't say that. But that's what it is. So I say to her: 'Cut the shit, all right? You wanna get laid? I come here, get laid. Never mind all this other shit.' And she's rubbing me up. And she says: 'Well, he thinks he knows everything. And he doesn't think I know anything. So he can treat me any way he wants. But he can't.' And then she says, she says she's gonna kill herself. So I look at her, and this girl really means it. Remember the way Greenan looked there, it was all over the place, they're gonna kill him and he was walking around with a board under his shirt, remember the way he looked?"

"He knew it wasn't gonna do any good," Frankie said.

"And he was right," Russell said. "Can't wear no board in the shower. Well this broad, she looked the same way. I mean it. She did. So, Jesus, that's all I need. I gotta tell some fuckin' cop how come I'm inna guy's place, I don't even know, and this girl kills herself and I don't know nothing about it? For something like that they bring back the chair. So I say, well, it can wait, we make it again, right? And we do. And then, after, I'm *gonzo*. That broad's hoopy. I'd, if I was you I'd stay away from that broad, Frankie."

"I'll think about it," Frankie said.

"Okay," Russell said, "I'll tell her. She's supposed to call me. See, you can't call her there, because the guy's apparently there some times. So she has to call you.

She's supposed to call me tomorrow. She was supposed to call me today, actually, only, I was out. Jesus, you should see the thing I got this morning. I got this big black fucker, German shepherd.

"Guy I know," Russell said, "calls me. Last night. He's looking over this place in Needham. Guy that owns it's supposed to have a pretty good coin collection. Those medals they're selling now? Made of silver and stuff. 'I can get in there like I was getting into bed,' he tells me. 'The both of them work and they haven't got no kids. But they got this goddamned *dog* in there, looks like a fuckin' wolf or something.' So he tells me, I get the dog outa his way, I can have the dog. Plus he'll gimme a fifth, what he gets.

"So I go over there," Russell said. "The house's back from the street and all, lots of trees and stuff. Beautiful. And we go around the back, there's the dog in there, jumping around like he's gonna go out of his mind or something. Barking and everything. 'Okay,' I say, 'let the bastard out.' I'm not going inside and tangle assholes with that monster. 'Let him out?' the guy says. 'You must be crazy or something. He'll kill both of us.' Well anyway, he racks up the window and that fuckin' dog comes out of there like his ass's on fire. I hadda couple wool shirts on my arm and he makes this whip-ass flying jump at me and knocks me on my ass, but I got the arm up and all he's doing, he's chewing the hell out of them shirts. And I'm, he keeps trying to spit them out and I won't let him. And he's growling like a mad bastard. So, I get this stick in his mouth. Now he's not chewing, ack, ack, ack. Then I put six phenobarbs down his throat and I take the stick out and he's got to swallow and I put the stick back in. He almost bit the fuckin' stick in half, for Christ sake, and I had it way the hell back in there, too. Then, I got this rope, and I tie, I hadda slip knot in it. Tie his mouth shut onna stick. Tie his feet, the guy's helping me. I get him inna car. I had Kenny's car. He's a great dog, boy. If I can ever sell him to someboαy, find somebody that wants a dog to kill people with."

"What'd he get in coins and stuff?" Frankie said.

"Nothing," Russell said. "Guy put them inna bank."

"Bull*shit*," Frankie said.

"No bullshit," Russell said, "I know the guy. He came right around. Showed me what he got. Couple cameras, portable color, some silver stuff. He had the paper the guy got, the guy put the stuff in the bank. Guys borrow money some times. It happens."

"That's what I oughta do," Frankie said. "I oughta go down the bank and borrow myself some money. They probably wouldn't mind, last time I did it I was inna can for doing it, I had a gun."

Frankie turned the 300F up the Bedford-Carlisle exit ramp on Route 128. At the island he turned left on Route 12 and crossed 128 on the overpass. Beyond 128, Route 12 was dark.

"Once they see what a nice fellow you are now, and all," Russell said.

"Sure," Frankie said. "I can show them my papers, there. Rehabilitated son of a bitch, is what I am. Well, let's see how this turns out, first."

Frankie took the fifth right beyond the 128 overpass. The Chrysler moved beneath bare, tall oaks. At a slight rise the road bent to the right and a small white sign, in script, said: *INNISHAVEN*. Frankie took the Chrysler right, into the driveway.

"Got a nice golf course here and everything, huh?" Russell said.

"Oh, they got all the nuts," Frankie said. "John was telling me, they got a gym and they got one of them saunas and a massage thing. First you get all hot and then you go and get blown off, I guess."

Frankie drove the Chrysler around the northerly end of the two-story motel into the parking lot at the rear. It was poorly lighted.

"One thing we could do," Russell said. "Instead of going in there and everything, we could just wait out here and grab the guys when they come out."

"Yeah," Frankie said, "and get ourselves a lot of Papermates and Zippos off the losers. Fuck that."

Frankie parked the Chrysler at the front of the driveway, pointing the nose toward the exit. He shut the lights off.

Russell reached into the back seat and came up with a Stop and Shop bag. He took out blue wool ski masks and handed one to Frankie. He pulled the other one over his head. Russell pulled out yellow plastic gardening gloves. He handed a pair to Frankie and put on the other pair.

"Fuckin' things're too thick," Frankie said.

"Look," Russell said, "you take what you can fuckin' get, all right? They got none of that light stuff around. Fat shits're all raking leaves and stuff, this's what they want. Do the best you can. You gonna use the sawed-off or what?"

Russell took a Stevens double-barreled 12-gauge shotgun out of the bag. The barrel had been cut off behind the front end of the stock. The stock was cut off behind the pistol grip. The shotgun was eleven inches long. There were two shells in it. The front of each green shell stuck out a quarter-inch from the sawed-off muzzles.

"Jesus," Frankie said.

"You said you wanted a sawed-off," Russell said. "I told the guy: 'Wants a sawed-off.' He told me, he hadda sawed-off for me like I never saw. This's it."

"Them things," Frankie said. "What is that, double O?"

"Double O when they got made," Russell said. "That's another thing. What they did, they uncrimp the things and pour the buck out and they take them forty-five wad-cutters, you know? Just like the L.A. police. Split them wad-cutters in half, you can get six of them in there. You can clear out a room pretty fast with this thing, I think. You're me?"

"Me," Frankie said. He took the shotgun.

Russell took a Smith and Wesson thirty-eight from the bag and put it in his belt. He zipped his jacket shut over it. He got out of the car.

Frankie got out of the car and stuck the pistol grip of the shotgun into his belt on the left side. The barrels, silver on the edges where they had been cut, fitted in against his body. He zipped his jacket shut over it. He closed the door of the car.

Frankie and Russell walked at a regular pace across the parking lot. They went to the outside stairs that led to the second deck of the Innishaven. The stairs were wood. Frankie and Russell made very little noise.

On the second deck there was light from the rooms, filtering through blue curtains in even-numbered rooms and orange curtains in odd-numbered rooms. In front of each room there were two aluminum-and-redwood chairs, pushed back against the sills of the picture windows.

"Fourth one," Frankie whispered.

The jalousied door of Room 26 was slightly ajar.

Frankie removed the shotgun from under his jacket. He held the pistol grip in his right hand and what remained of the forestock in his left. He carried the gun at waist level.

Russell took the thirty-eight out of his belt. He smoothed the ski mask at his neck.

Russell kicked the door open and went quickly into the room. Frankie came in fast behind Russell. Frankie kicked the door shut and stepped back against it. Russell stopped at the bureau.

There were three round tables, two beds, a bed table, five lamps, a color television set on a chromium pedestal, sixteen chairs and fourteen men in the room. The men sat motionless at the tables, holding playing cards in their hands. There were piles of red, white and blue chips on the tables. There were four men at one table; five men sat at each of the other two tables. Some of the men had tumblers on the tables in front of them.

Frankie nodded toward the washstand and the door, closed, beside it. Russell walked silently toward the washstand.

A thin man in a red Ban-lon sweater, sitting at the center table, took his White Owl from his mouth and put it in the ashtray. He put his cards down, very carefully, face down. He said: "Oh oh."

Frankie shook his head.

The bathroom door opened and Mark Trattman emerged, combing his long gray hair. His head was tilted to the right and he was looking at the aquamarine carpet as he combed. He said: "Okay, you—"

Russell stuck the barrel of the thirty-eight in his face. Trattman looked up, slowly. The muscles in his face relaxed. He looked beyond Russell and the thirty-eight, into the room. He saw Frankie. "Uh huh," Trattman said, "well, I hope you guys know what you're doing. I'll get it."

Russell looked at Frankie. Frankie nodded. Russell lowered the thirty-eight. Trattman walked past Russell to the closet and opened the louvered doors. He took two Samsonite attaché cases from the floor of the closet. He backed out of the closet into the room. He turned and walked toward the bed nearest the washstand. He put the cases on the bed. Russell trained the thirty-eight on him as he moved.

"Can I sit down now?" Trattman said. He looked at Russell. Russell looked at Frankie. Frankie nodded. Russell looked back at Trattman. Russell nodded. Trattman sat down on the second bed. He clasped his hands between his legs.

Russell went to the bed. He shifted the thirty-eight to his left hand. He opened each of the cases with his right hand. Each case was full of currency. Russell closed one case. He left the other case open. He straightened up. He stepped back. He nodded to Frankie.

Frankie stepped forward to the table nearest the door. He stopped at the first man. The man wore a light blue turtleneck. He had gray, close-cropped hair. Frankie held the shotgun close to his face; the re-crimped fronts of the shells were next to his eyes. The man said: "*No.*"

Trattman said: "You guys, don't do that. You guys've *got* all the money."

Frankie said: "What you got in your pockets. Put it onna table."

Trattman said: "Leave the poor bastard alone."

Russell moved forward quickly. Frankie stepped back, away from the man in the turtleneck.

"They'll get you for this," Trattman said.

Russell came up close to Trattman. He touched Trattman on the point of the chin with the thirty-eight. The
other men watched. Frankie watched the other men.
Russell forced Trattman's head back, by applying pressure with the thirty-eight. Trattman's torso bent in a
backward arch as his head went back. He steadied himself by placing his hands flat on the bed. His eyes
bulged. He did not speak. When he was rising off the
bed, Russell took the thirty-eight back suddenly. Trattman relaxed forward. He said: "I don't care, they'll—"
Russell hit Trattman with the barrel of the thirty-eight,
using a chopping motion that caught Trattman at the
base of his neck, at the collar. Trattman groaned but
succeeded in keeping himself upright on the bed.

Frankie stepped forward. He held the shotgun close
to the face of the man in the blue turtleneck. The man
leaned forward in the chair. He took out his wallet. He
removed currency and put it on the table.

While the man in the blue turtleneck worked, Frankie
swung the shotgun to point at the next man. He wore
a pale green polo shirt. The man reached for his wallet.

"Now there's two ways of doing this," Frankie said.
"There's the easy way and there's the hard way. The
easy way's for all you guys to just go ahead and start
doing what these guys're doing. The hard way's to make
us come around and all, which's gonna make me nervous. And, see him?" Frankie gestured toward Russell
with the shotgun. "Me, feeling good, that's a lot like
him, nervous. When I get nervous, well, you oughta
see him, is what I think, but I wouldn't want to. Not
if he had the gun. Which he does. Now what we want,
we want what you got in your wallets and your shoes
and your coats and like that. And them neat little belts
that got the zippers on the inside, them, too, what's in

them. You can either start putting it out now, or you can sit there and act like you haven't got it in your sock or something. Then after everybody's all through putting out what they wanna put out, me and my nervous friend're gonna go around and make sure. And the guys, the guys that didn't remember everything, we're at least gonna knock their teeth out. How's that, huh?"

None of the men said anything.

"Good," Frankie said. "That's the way I feel, too. The less guys that get hurt, the better. So, don't fuck around. Just give it all up and keep quiet and nobody gets hurt. It's only money."

The rest of the men got out their wallets and put money on the tables. Two men removed loafers, with brass hardware on the insteps, and took money out and put it on the tables. One man, in a blue plaid shirt, removed his belt, opened a zipper compartment on the inside and took out four fifty-dollar bills, folded once in half lengthwise. He put them on the table in front of him.

Frankie returned to the door. Russell moved from table to table, collecting the money. He put the money in the open attaché case. He shut the case. Russell put the thirty-eight in his belt. He picked up one case in each hand. Frankie stepped forward two paces. Russell passed behind him and stood near the door.

"I changed my mind," Frankie said. "He's too nervous. He wants to leave. I never fuck with this guy. We're not gonna go over you after all. You been very smart. Stay smart. Nobody's dead. Don't try to follow us."

Russell opened the door and went out. He walked quickly on the deck to the stairs. He set down the bag in his right hand and used the hand to remove the ski mask. He put the mask in his pocket. He picked up the bag. He went down the stairs quietly, with the two cases.

Frankie moved the shotgun back and forth slowly, covering the room. He waited forty seconds or so. None of the men moved. Frankie stood near the door.

Frankie opened the door quickly, backed through it, shut it and dragged one of the chairs in front of it. He waited.

Frankie stepped back from the door. He put the shotgun under his coat. He moved quickly down the deck. He removed his mask as he went. He went down the stairs quickly and across the parking lot. Russell was in the car. Frankie got in on the driver's side and started the engine. The Chrysler, without lights, traveled quickly and quietly down the drive, under the oaks, into the dark.

5

AT FIVE MINUTES PAST TWO in the afternoon the silver Toronado, black vinyl roof, Rhode Island registration 651 RJ, came up Boylston Street and eased into the curb lane in front of a flocked emerald-green-and-white Fleetwood illegally parked in front of the 1776 Pub. The Toronado stopped in front of Brigham's, a car length from the Tremont Street intersection.

Jackie Cogan, in a pilled suede coat, dropped his Salem on the sidewalk, stepped on it, and got into the Toronado. He shut the door. Without looking at the driver he said: "Hang a right and go a couple blocks."

The driver wore a light gray, glen plaid suit. He had very long white hair. He put the Hydramatic in gear. "This isn't near the courthouse, I assume," he said.

"Nah," Cogan said. "Just a big hole. All the construction jocks, that's all there is. There's always three or four of them, sitting in their cars, trying to get warm. Forget it."

The driver turned the Toronado right on Tremont Street. "He was very concerned," he said. "When I told him I called and Dillon said to see you, he was very concerned. How is the fellow?"

"He's not good," Cogan said. "He came in Monday, he was out about three weeks and he came in Monday and he hadda have a guy come in and take over for him. I don't think he was in at all, Tuesday and Wednesday, and then yesterday he called me, the guy he had those days was tied up and could I get somebody. So I did. He's not in today, either. They told, the doctor said if he took things easy, he was inna hospital over two and a half weeks, and then if he took it easy, he oughta be all right this week. So, he's around but he looks shitty, and I saw him, I saw him yesterday. He's still getting it in the arm and he says it makes him nervous, still, not smoking, he'd probably be better off if he was. Says it feels like somebody stuck a knife in his chest."

"He probably won't be able to handle anything for a while, then," the driver said. He stopped at the red light at the Kneeland Street intersection.

"He sure can't right now," Cogan said. "I think, I personally think the guy's in very bad shape. He was, you know, every time I ever saw the guy he was always bitching about how he felt lousy and everything, his stomach was bothering him and if it wasn't that it was something else. But he's really sick now, and you can tell because he don't say anything about it unless you come right out and ask him, and even then he doesn't really want to talk about it. I think he's worried himself."

The light changed and the Toronado crossed the intersection and the driver said: "He told me, when he heard, that if Dillon wasn't available I was to talk to the fellow he sent."

"When you get up the movie place there," Cogan said, "see that? Go down the right there, and there'll be a place you can park."

"Is that you?" the driver said.

"Dillon said where you'd be and for me to go there and wait for you," Cogan said. "I looked around all right, I didn't see nobody else that might've been there to see you. Did you?"

The driver parked the Toronado behind a pink Thunderbird sedan. "Mark Trattman's game got hit a couple nights ago," the driver said.

"I heard that," Cogan said. "Somewhere around fifty-three thousand they got?"

"Well," the driver said, "probably closer to fifty. Two kids."

"Yeah," Cogan said.

"You or Dillon heard anything about two kids?" the driver said.

"You hear lots of things," Cogan said. "I heard they had masks on, for one thing."

"Correct," the driver said.

"So," Cogan said, "maybe they're not kids."

"They had long hair," the driver said. "The people could see it sticking out, from under."

"Look," Cogan said, "my wife's mother's sick and we hadda go over and see her Sunday, so of course we hadda go to church, too, the old bat doesn't get any wrong ideas. And the priest had long hair, for God's sake. And they could've been wearing wigs or something. You can't tell."

"Well," the driver said, "they were dressed like kids. They had dungarees on and they smelled like *animals*, Trattman said."

"Trattman said," Cogan said. "Look, anyway, there's lots of guys that stink."

"Trattman also said," the driver said, "the one that talked had a voice like a kid."

"Trattman said," Cogan said.

"So far's I know," the driver said, "there's nothing wrong with Trattman's hearing, or his nose or anything."

"Nope," Cogan said. "Nothing I ever heard about, anyway."

"But then, of course, when I talked to him . . ."

"You talked to Trattman?" Cogan said.

"No, of course not," the driver said. "Trattman called

Cangelisi, and they got word to him and then I talked to him."

"Oh," Cogan said.

"Is that important?" the driver said.

"Probably not," Cogan said. "I was just wondering, how Trattman decided to call you. I wouldn't've done that."

"Well, I do talk to him," the driver said.

"Yeah," Cogan said, "but I don't, and I didn't know you, I knew there was somebody, of course, but I never heard of you before in my life. Just seemed funny, is all."

"Well, I didn't talk to him," the driver said. "Trattman. But I talked to him last night and I talked to him again this morning."

"So nobody," Cogan said, "nobody's actually talked to Trattman about this."

"Just Cangelisi," the driver said. "Trattman called him from the place and he couldn't get him and he woke his wife up and everything."

"Yeah," Cogan said. "So all we got right now, to go on, is what Trattman told some guy. And that's what I'm supposed to go out and find two kids on, what Trattman told some guy, I never even talked to."

"That's not what he said," the driver said. "He said that I was to call Dillon, and I called Dillon, and then I talked to him and he told me to talk to the fellow that Dillon sent and see what you thought, I assume it's you, anyway, what you thought ought to be done next."

"What happened to Zach?" Cogan said.

"I'm not really sure," the driver said. "They had some kind of a disagreement. I think it was about the way he handled the petition for cert. Zach. He didn't tell me very much about it, but he did say he couldn't represent him any more. I called Zach when he first called me, naturally."

"Zach was with him for a long time," Cogan said. "I talked to Zach a lot."

"Not so long, actually," the driver said. "About five years. No more'n that. When he first started out he had McGonigle."

"Magoo?" Cogan said. "He came up here for a guy and they practically hadda carry him in court in a basket."

"He's had some bad luck," the driver said. "And that was probably before you were born, when he had Mc-Gonigle. Then, Zach told me, well, he didn't have as many problems then. That was really before he really needed a lot of legal work done. But then he had Mindich and then he had the fellow from New York, Mendoza, and then he used Zach. 'It's good trade,' Zach told me. 'For five years it's good business. It'll drive you nuts, but the money's good.' See, according to Zach, he blames you when things don't come out the way he wants them to, and then he gets a new lawyer."

"Zach was the guy I had to talk to," Cogan said. "Nice guy. He helped me set my thing up. Say hello to Zach for me, you happen to see him."

"I will," the driver said. "Now, what do I tell him?"

"Well," Cogan said, "the games're shut down, right?"

"Most of them," the driver said. "Somebody called Testa and he said he'd like to see somebody try to come into his operation. So I guess he's still working. The rest of them're pretty much closed."

"Same thing that happened the last time," Cogan said.

"It's temporary," the driver said. "He told me that. He said as soon as I talked to you, to let the fellows know

what you want. Or Dillon, rather. Originally it was
to've been Dillon."

"I talked to Dillon," Cogan said.

"What does he think?" the driver said.

"Well, the first thing that anybody'd think about in a
thing like this," Cogan said.

"This is the second time," the driver said. "That's
what he said."

"It happened before," Cogan said. "Four years ago,
and now it happened again."

"The last time, I gather," the driver said, "the man
who did it actually was Trattman himself."

"With a couple Indians," Cogan said. "He put on a
big show and all, but it was Trattman. Dillon said he
even used to brag about it some times."

"And nobody found out about it," the driver said.

"Not till after," Cogan said.

"Well," the driver said, "this time they worked him
over a little."

"Once," Cogan said. "They hit him one rap. One. I
think, if I was Trattman and I was doing it again, I'd
probably get at least one rap myself."

"Well," the driver said, "where do we go from here?
What do you think?"

"I don't know enough yet, do much thinking," Cogan
said. "Because, see, I don't necessarily think this, but it
still might've really been two kids this time. Or else it
might've been Trattman. But it could've been some
guys that knew he did it before. So it's one of two things
here. Mark's been spending it a little more lately. He
could've decided, do it again, nobody'd ever think he'd
do it twice. But, you ever been up that place?"

"No," the driver said.

"You know something?" Cogan said. "Nobody's ever

been up that place. Nobody but Trattman. It's, it's just
not the kind of place that guys go. Except, I was checking around, Dillon mentioned this guy he knew, he used
to know, guy was in Walpole and when he come out,
they taught him landscaping, and when he come out
that's what he did, and Dillon said he thought maybe
that guy did some work up there. So I called him.
There's eighty-six rooms in that place. It's way the hell
off in the woods, and there's eighty-six rooms in it, and
except for Markie's game there's not one single thing
going on in that place. In the middle of the week the
guys that're using those rooms're guys that're selling
things, and they work all night. That's all they do. I
talked to Gordon and he said he, when the place first
opened up, he put a couple his girls in there. 'They
went nuts,' he told me. 'All they did all night was sit in
the bar all by themselves and drink. The only guy they
ever saw was the bartender. They're getting fat and
I'm losing dough hand over fist, it was awful.' The place
moves a little on the weekends, but then it's guys that
come in with girls. 'Or fuckin' amateurs,' Gordon said.
'Between the fuckin' amateurs and the fuckin' niggers
you can't do squat anyway these days.' But during the
week? Forget it. Nothing. There isn't even a regular guy
taking action in there, 's how bad it is.

"Now you think about that," Cogan said, "and keep
in mind, I got absolutely no reason, think the guy's
dancing me around. You think about that for a minute.
When'd that game go over? Right around midnight, am
I right?"

"Around eleven-thirty, I guess," the driver said.

"Right," Cogan said. "They go up there and all, most
of the lights're on. 'The place does a good business,'
Gordon tells me, 'it's full almost all the time. It just

don't do no other business.' So these kids, if that's what they are, they go there on the right night and they go to the exact room where it is and they go right in, the door's open, and they take everybody's money. How about that, huh?"

"Trattman admitted that," the driver said. "He said he'd started to get careless. Instead of opening the windows or something they'd taken to leaving the door open a little bit, let the smoke out. He said that."

"Good," Cogan said. "But the guy that's running the games isn't supposed to get careless, you know? He's supposed to think about things like that."

"He was in the toilet when they came in," the driver said.

"I don't care where he was," Cogan said. "He wasn't doing what he was supposed to've been doing, and one way or the other, those two guys knew he wasn't. And they knew he wasn't gonna be, and they knew where to find him."

"Right," the driver said.

"So," Cogan said, "for now it don't matter, Trattman did it or somebody did it to Trattman."

"It doesn't?" the driver said.

"Not to Trattman," Cogan said. "That's where we got to start. We start with Trattman, and we start real good, too."

"Now wait a minute," the driver said.

"I'll wait a week if you want," Cogan said.

"I'll have to talk to him before you go ahead and do, whatever it is you're planning to do," the driver said.

"Talk to him," Cogan said. "I got plenty of things to do. Tell him I said we hadda talk to Trattman and see what he says."

"He wouldn't object to that," the driver said.

"*Really* talk to him," Cogan said. "You can't do anything else, that I can see."

"I can tell you right now," the driver said, "he's not going to okay anything major just on your suspicions. He's very concerned about starting something that'll make things worse than they already are."

"I know that," Cogan said.

"The last time we had somebody handled it was against both our better judgment," the driver said, "and as soon as he got better he went straight to the FBI and started telling lies like you wouldn't believe. It's just a good thing for him that the fellow got cold feet when they brought him in to the grand jury. And it cost us a lot of money to make his feet cold, too, I can assure you. So he's not going to want anybody going overboard on this. Who's going to do it, you?"

"Do what?" Cogan said.

"Talk, have this little talk with Trattman," the driver said.

"Well," Cogan said, "I could. But, I talked to Dillon about this and we think, I better not. Might be better if Markie wasn't too interested in me right now."

"He's going to want to know," the driver said.

"Sure," Cogan said. "Tell him, I talked to Dillon and we think, Steve Caprio and his brother."

"Dillon knows who they are?" the driver said. "He's used them before?"

"Dillon knows who they are," Cogan said. "I know who they are. Barry was on the *Wasp* with me. He's really kind of an asshole, but he was also, the guy that was the champ had to beat Barry, the light-heavy champ, he hadda beat Barry to get there. Steve's all right. They'll do what you tell them."

"I mean it, now," the driver said.

"Oh sure," Cogan said. "I know that. You guys always mean it. You gotta mean it. I understand that. I haven't been around much myself, hardly at all, but I talk to a lot of guys and I know. Now, how're we working this? You calling me?"

"I tell you what," the driver said, "I'll talk to him and then I'll see what he's got to say, and I'll call Dillon."

"Okay," Cogan said. "Then, I assume, you think Dillon's in good enough shape, he can handle."

"No," the driver said. "You said he can't."

"Dillon said Dillon can't handle," Cogan said. "That's why you're talking to me today."

"Correct," the driver said.

"So," Cogan said, "that's what I mean. You want Dillon to handle, call Dillon. Okay by me. You want me to handle . . ."

"I'll call you," the driver said.

"I'll call *you*," Cogan said. "I'm out, I'm out a lot. I'll get in touch with you."

6

STEVE AND BARRY CAPRIO waited together in the door-way of the Hayes Bickford opposite the Lobster Tail on Boylston Street. "I tell you," Barry said, "I wouldn't've recognized the guy."

"Jackie said that," Steve said. "Guy lost some weight and he thinks he's got a wig or something. He's also, he's a pretty sharp dresser now, and he sure didn't used to be."

"Must've come into a little money or something," Barry said.

"Probably not," Steve said, "not what Jackie thinks, anyway. He thinks all of a sudden, guy started spending a couple dollars now and then. 'Probably come outa the divorce better'n he expected,' is what Jackie thinks. He used to be the tightest cocksucker you ever saw."

"Christ sake," Barry said, "he hadda be. The way he used to chase broads alla time? What's he been married, about nine times?"

"Dillon thinks three," Steve said. "Dillon was there. Jesus, Dillon looks like shit."

"Dillon'll be all right," Barry said. "That prick, he's too mean to die. Ever see his eyes?"

"Not particularly," Steve said.

"I never saw eyes on a guy like that," Barry said, "I never saw eyes like that until after I hit them. The first time I saw that guy, I really thought: He's gonna go over. But he doesn't. It's the way he always looks. Those're bad eyes. He's gonna die."

"We're all gonna die," Steve said. "Trattman's gonna die."

"Yeah," Barry said, "but not tonight, right Steve?"

"I haven't got no inside information," Steve said. "I just got a job to do."

"Don't gimme that," Barry said, "I didn't sign up for that. I want you to tell me, Trattman's not gonna go to sleep tonight."

"Not by us," Steve said.

"Okay by me," Barry said.

"He didn't say his prayers or something," Steve said, "I can't help that. But we're not doing it."

"Okay," Barry said. "I just wanna be sure."

"Just what I said," Steve said. "Nothing else."

"Because I always liked Markie," Barry said.

"Everybody did," Steve said. "You, you mostly liked the blonde."

"What blonde?" Barry said.

"Oh come on," Steve said, "the blonde he used to have at the One-Fifteen, remember her?"

"That was the other game," Barry said.

"The game he knocked over himself," Steve said.

"We're lucky, he didn't have us there for that one," Barry said. "I wouldn't've wanted to be there for that."

"Oh for Christ sake," Steve said, "sometimes you're too fuckin' dumb for fuckin' words, you know that, Barry?"

"Why?" Barry said. "The game got knocked over. We was there, we either would've hadda do something about it or else we would've been inna shit, we didn't do something about it."

"Why the fuck you think he didn't have us there?" Steve said.

"That's what I mean," Barry said. "That was nice of the guy. He knows he's gonna do something, he lets us out."

"You dumb fuckin' shit," Steve said. "I gotta have a talk with Ma. I know it now, she was fuckin' the milkman. Maybe the milkman's horse. You gotta be the dumbest fuckin' shit on the face of the fuckin' earth. You embarrass me, you know that? You stupid fuckin' ginzo."

"He did," Barry said.

"You should've worn a helmet, Barry," Steve said. "I mean that. I think you took too many shots inna head. Don't you know why he let us out?"

"He was being a nice guy," Barry said.

"He didn't wanna pay us," Steve said. "If we're there, and we didn't know, he would've had trouble. He didn't want no trouble. He wanted money. He didn't wanna share no dough with us. So he told us not to show up. He's not nice. He's just cheap. Just like everybody else. You dumb shit."

"I still liked the guy," Barry said.

"You liked the blonde," Steve said. "Come on, Barry."

"He was married to that girl," Barry said.

"Jackie don't think so," Steve said. "Dillon, either. She was just something he had around."

"She was a nice girl," Barry said. "I did like her."

"She hadda great big ass," Steve said. "That's all you think about, a great big ass."

"She did," Barry said. "Still, not a bad girl at all. Nice bazooms. She was a good kid to talk to."

"Yeah," Steve said, "right. Talk. Remember that night she come out there inna pink pants?"

"Yeah," Barry said.

"You don't," Steve said. "Still, that was the biggest pink thing I ever saw."

"She was a nice girl," Barry said.

"You wanna be careful," Steve said. "Some night I'll

get drunk and I'll call Ginny up and tell her, you're scoutin' strange tail alla time."

"Steve," Barry said, "you know . . ."

"I know," Steve said.

"Ginny's the best thing, ever happened to me," Barry said. "I know, you're always telling me, I'm a dumb shit. Okay, I'm a dumb shit. But I know some things. The times that girl, I couldn't count them. You can kid around all you want. I don't care if you are my brother. You know what? I get home tonight, don't matter what time I get home tonight, it's probably gonna be late, Ginny'll be waiting up. We'll have a beer and we'll talk. Anybody gives Ginny a hard time, well, I'm maybe a little outa shape. But nobody better call Ginny and get her thinking something like that, or anything, that, especially that's not true."

"Oh for Christ sake," Steve said. "I was just hacking around."

"Not on that," Barry said. "Ginny, Ginny's sacred to me."

"Yeah, yeah," Steve said.

"I mean that," Barry said. "The rest of you guys, all right, you can think anything you want. But not me. Not me and Ginny."

"You mean to tell me," Steve said, "Trattman's pink broad, you didn't fuck her?"

"Nah," Barry said. "I tell you, she was married to Trattman at the time. You don't fuck somebody else's wife. I wouldn't do that."

"Jackie don't think so," Steve said.

"Jackie don't know, is what Jackie does," Barry said. "She told me herself."

"You asked her," Steve said.

"I didn't ask her if she was married," Barry said.

"Barry," Steve said, "I'm ashamed of you. My own brother, and you asked somebody else's girl to fuck."

"I did not," Barry said.

"I'm definitely gonna tell Ginny," Steve said. "You'll be lucky, you don't get a mouthful of plates, you come in after this. You goddamned stud."

"I wasn't married to Ginny then," Barry said.

"Barry," Steve said, "you been married to Ginny since you're twelve, you know that. You just didn't get to church before, is all. Any time Ginny said: 'Jump,' all you ever said was: 'How high?'"

"I did not," Barry said.

"You did," Steve said. "You give up boxing because Ginny didn't want your face wrecked."

"No, I didn't," Barry said. "I give it up because I wasn't no good."

"Who's the light-heavy champ in Sixty-three?" Steve said.

"All right, all right," Barry said. "He wasn't champ for long."

"Who was he?" Steve said. "I forget his name."

"When I fought him he hadda different name," Barry said.

"Yeah," Steve said, "I remember. Tennessee Bobby Walker. Yeah. That's the guy. How long'd you go with him?"

"That was before," Barry said.

"Not much before," Steve said. "Twelve and you TKO-ed him, and then fifteen and he splits you. And, who was that guy on the *Ticonderoga*?"

"You remind me of Jackie," Barry said.

"I remind you of Ginny," Steve said.

"He was always at me, like you are," Barry said. "That night Walker beat me? He was fulla fuckin' shit, and I was hurt. That bastard cut me onna eye and he kept the laces in it all night."

"You did the same thing to him, the time before," Steve said.

"That didn't make it feel better," Barry said. "The only thing that bastard's thinking about's how much money he's out. And I was hurt."

"You should've butted him," Steve said.

"I tried to," Barry said. "Didn't work. He had his head down too low. You know something? That's the thing I liked about Markie. He never saw me fight. All you guys did."

"And we knew you quit because you're chicken," Steve said. "It's all right."

"I wasn't any good," Barry said. "There're guys that're like that, you know."

"I know," Steve said.

"No you don't," Barry said. "You're just like Jackie. I'm not gonna do this. I haven't got nothing against Markie. I dunno why he didn't stay married, the blonde."

"Barry," Steve said, "they weren't married. That was just something that went on a long time. She was letting you down easy. She didn't wanna fuck you and she didn't wanna hurt your feelings."

"No," Barry said, "maybe, okay, but nothing Markie ever had, went on a long time. He'd just as soon get married as fuck around, he don't care. He's not a bad shit."

"No," Steve said, "he's not. He's just an asshole when it comes to the broads."

"I still like him," Barry said.

"So do I," Steve said. "I said that to Jackie. I, I don't want to do this, you know? I really didn't. Markie's not a bad shit. I told him, I said: 'Look, I used to work for the guy now and then. Me and Barry. Jeez, I don't know. He always treated me all right.'"

"Dillon was there too, wasn't he?" Barry said.

"Dillon was there," Steve said. "White's a fuckin' sheet, he don't use no breath to say nothin', it's probably his last. There's dogs, I think, not as sick as Dillon."

"They're both the same," Barry said. "They're both pricks."

"I don't know," Steve said.

"I do," Barry said. "I knew Jackie before I knew Dillon. I didn't work for Dillon, after I worked, after I knew Jackie. Jackie didn't have no work. They're both the same."

"What difference it make?" Steve said.

"You know Dillon," Barry said.

"Yeah," Steve said.

"You know Jackie," Barry said.

"Yeah," Steve said.

"You know the way Dillon looks now," Barry said, "and it's because he's sick."

"He don't look right," Steve said.

"Jackie always looked that way," Barry said. "Always. He's got the same eyes."

"Ahh," Steve said.

"I mean it," Barry said. "I mean it. I did some things for that guy. When the fights're on, and all, you know something? I bet that guy didn't weigh one thirty then, and he wasn't carrying nothing you could see, and you can see things, you know?"

"Yeah," Steve said.

"A little shit," Barry said. "He was always a little shit. And there was a lot of big guys around. And he had dough. And you know something? Nobody ever fucked with him. Nobody. Not officers, nobody. You know why? Because he looked the same way then that Dillon looks now. In the eyes. Like somebody hit him. Only he's not hurt and he's not going down. He's just there. And nobody knew him from the next guy's asshole, then. Now Dillon's sick and he looks the same way. I don't trust that guy."

"He's all right," Steve said.

"He's a mean little prick," Barry said.

"He doesn't act like one," Steve said. "He treated me all right. Any questions I had, he treated me all right."

"What'd you ask him?" Barry said. "What'd he say?"

"I told him," Steve said, "I said: 'Look, I kind of like Markie.' He said: 'I know it. Everybody does. He's a great guy. I told him once: "Markie, you ask girls to fuck, you don't even want to fuck." I said that to him.' And you know what he says? Jackie said: '"I'm staying in shape. Besides, how the fuck do I know, I don't wanna fuck the girl, unless I fuck her? So I ask her, and she says, all right, I fuck her and then I know. After."' I think, myself," Steve said, "I think the guy's afraid, there's some broad some place inna world that's gonna fuck, and he'll die without asking her. That's what Jackie said. 'Guy gets more ass'n a toilet seat.'"

"Well," Barry said, "that's him all right then. He's got one with about a forty-inch setta boobs on her in there. He practically didn't even get his coat off before he spotted her, and he was right next to her before I could even get a dime inna box to call you. He don't waste any time."

"He's been at it a long time," Steve said. "You know that guy, except for when he first gets married, he goes out every fuckin' night? Every night. When he gets married, for a little while he doesn't. Then pretty soon, he does it again. So naturally, the broads he marries, there's always something that tips them off, they're all lizards themselves and he's not home and they start figuring. But you imagine that? The guy's close to fifty, and he's, he's not married, he's never home. Never. You can say what you want about the guy, he is still one strong bastard."

"I hope he's quick, too," Barry said. "This fuckin' dampness."

"He'll be out," Steve said. "All we got to do is be here and wait, just like whoever the broad is. Markie don't waste no time. He knows what he's doing. Half the gash went into that place, looking to get laid, they ended up inna rack with Markie. And he gives them what they're looking for, too. They all, you know something? They don't even know who he is."

"How come?" Barry said.

"Onna one-night stand," Steve said, "he don't give his right name."

"Who's he say he is?" Barry said.

"Well," Steve said, "he knows us, right? And he knows Dillon and he knows a lot of guys. And then there's some guys he doesn't know, some guys that, he just makes up their names. Depends on how he feels. So the thing is, there's probably four, five broads, come in here or some place else one night all pissed off at their husbands, and they think they fucked us."

"That cocksucker," Barry said.

"Hey," Steve said, "you got to give the guy credit."

"Sure," Barry said, "and suppose one of them broads that he fucked and he said he was me, and Ginny finds out, huh? Then I'm deep in the shit and I didn't even do it."

"Hell, Barry," Steve said, "I mean, nobody could recognize you. What's the matter, I thought Ginny trusted you."

"She does," Barry said, "because she knows I don't do that."

"Well," Steve said, "look, he probably didn't say he was you very much anyway. And the girls he meets, they probably don't even hear the name. They're just out to get laid. It's always, he's the head of the fuckin' Mafia. He's got this whole routine he goes through. 'Just in town for a couple days. I'm in and out of town a lot.' He is, too. Except the nights he runs the game, he's here, he's in Danvers, he's in Lawrence, he's all over the place. Then he pulls out this big roll. He's got himself about eighty fifties there, and it's nothing *but* fifties, either. And he's got the rings. And then pretty soon: 'I'm staying with a guy. Can't take no chances onna hotel, you got to sign everything. Can we, can we maybe use your place?' And of course the broad, she hasn't got a place. Well, she's got one, but the old man and the kids're there, and besides, she don't want nobody to know she's from around here. So the next thing you know they're in a hotel and the broad's paying for it. 'He can't take them to his place,' Dillon told me. 'There's no bugs in there, for Christ sake. Bug'd be ashamed to live in that place.' But he's got the Cad and the gold rings and he goes around telling broads all kinds of things and they all believe him and he fucks them all. He's done more for the world'n Christmas, you add it all up."

"Why'd you say that about Danvers?" Barry said.

"Because he goes there," Steve said. "There's this club he goes to some times, up in Danvers. He goes over the Beach, too. The guy gets around."

"Ginny's ma lives in Danvers," Barry said.

"I doubt he fucked Ginny's ma, Barry," Steve said. "You wanna know, though, I'll call her up and ask her for you."

"Some day I'm gonna break your fuckin' long nose for you, Steve," Barry said.

Trattman, wearing a mouse-colored, double-breasted overcoat, emerged from the Lobster Tail with a dark-haired woman in her forties. He raised his right arm, using his left hand to guide her toward the curb. An attendant in a snorkel coat pulled up in a tan Coupe de Ville. Trattman opened the passenger door for the woman as the attendant got out on the driver's side. Trattman closed the passenger door and walked around the front of the car. He handed a folded bill to the attendant. The attendant said: "Thanks," with no sign of recognition. Trattman got into the Cadillac.

Steve and Barry got into Steve's metallic blue LTD hardtop, black vinyl roof, and shut the doors.

The Coupe de Ville headed east on Boylston Street. It crossed the intersections at Hereford, Gloucester, Fairfield and Exeter streets on green lights. Steve kept the LTD three car lengths back, one lane to the right. He went through the Fairfield and Exeter intersections on yellow lights.

"This isn't a bad car either," Barry said.

"You ever decide," Steve said, "stop fuckin' around and *do* something, you can get something for yourself instead of bitching all the time about how everybody else's got something and you don't."

"Fuck you," Barry said. "Last month I hadda lay out close to two hundred and fifty bucks for the fuckin' dentist. Every time I get a couple bucks ahead, something comes along to fuck it up."

The Cadillac stopped for a red light at Dartmouth Street.

"I must be gettin' old," Steve said. "All my friends're having trouble with their teeth. Jackie was telling me, his wife's all hot and bothered, she's gotta have, what're those things, root canals. 'Which is gonna set me back about nine hundred bucks, I suppose, I'm through.' I didn't know stuff like that cost so much."

The light at Dartmouth changed and the Cadillac moved forward. The woman in the Cadillac moved closer to Trattman.

"He's telling her what he's gonna do to her now," Steve said.

"The thing that really did it to me," Barry said, "you know what that son of a bitch whacked me for Maine? Five hundred a day and expenses. I hadda pay him almost thirty-nine hundred dollars. Plus what I hadda give him before, a thousand, take the case in the first place."

The Cadillac had green lights at Clarendon and Berkeley. The Caprio car went through on yellow.

"That's because you're a stupid shit," Steve said. "No asshole inna world would've gone up there the way you did. You, you haven't got no complaint. I think he did all right by you. You had anybody else, you would've gotten hooked again."

The Cadillac stopped for a red light at Arlington Street.

"I'm not putting the hammer on Mike," Barry said. "He's just expensive, is all."

The light changed and Steve followed the Cadillac, turning right on Arlington Street. A man in a light gray Chesterfield, carrying a briefcase, crossed the street in front of the LTD, walking fast and catching up with a tall albino man who wore a lavender cape lined with red satin, and platform shoes. Steve Caprio changed lanes to the right and closed the distance between the LTD and the Cadillac.

"Looks like he's going down the Envoy," Steve said. "Must've got a cheap one this time, gotta pay for it himself. No, I was just saying, ah, it's the same thing. You just fuck around too much. You did something, you could get something. You don't see me or Jackie going up to Maine and being stupid like that, chasing guys around when they're staying with their families and stuff."

"Well," Barry said, "he wasn't gonna pay. He took the dough off of Bloom and then he wasn't gonna pay it back. Bloom hadda get his dough outa the guy. You can't go around letting guys get away with stuff like that."

The Cadillac moved into the left lane at the Statler Hilton and turned left.

"No, he's not going down the Envoy," Steve said. "He's going down the Terrace. She must have some dough after all. Sure, and Bloom gets his dough, and you get, what'd Bloom give you for that shitty thing?"

"Six hundred," Barry said. "I needed the dough. Ginny was starting to get the caps, there, and that was the first time I hadda pay."

"Six hundred," Steve said. "So, you only lost about thirty-two, forty-two hundred on it. Bloom give you what Mike cost you?"

"Nope," Barry said.

The Cadillac went into the Terrace Hotel garage.

"Nope," Steve said. "You ask him for it?"

"Nope," Barry said.

"Sure," Steve said. He parked the LTD half a block

from the garage and turned off the ignition. "So, you almost go to jail again, and you spent on that what I spent on this car. That's what I mean. Sooner or later you're gonna have to start picking your spots, like I do. Otherwise you're gonna spend the rest of your life tryin' to get out of things that you shouldn't've got into in the first place, and you're never gonna have nothin'."

"Look," Barry said, "okay, you got all this talk and shit for me, lemme ask you this: you're doing so good, how come you're still going out and beating guys up, huh?"

"It's not the money," Steve said. "You wanna see how much money I got on me, right this minute?" He moved on the seat, reaching for his wallet.

"No," Barry said.

Steve relaxed. "I got twenty-one hundred bucks on me right this minute," he said. "I don't owe nickel one on this car and I sent Rita's check to her the other day. No, I'm doing a favor for a guy. This thing come up, Jackie's done some things for me when I couldn't do them. . . ."

"Jackie don't beat guys up," Barry said.

"No," Steve said, "but there's things that Jackie does do, you know? There's other things inna world that guys do besides going around and doing things to other guys, Barry. You wouldn't know that because the only thing you ever thought about was how you could grab a fast hundred and never mind what you're doing on the long run. Jackie gimme that thing, when he was getting away from the machines he had in the locations on Route 9, there. He didn't have to do that."

"He couldn't handle it himself, though," Barry said.

"No, he couldn't," Steve said. "But he didn't have to give it to me. He didn't have to say to the guys, 'Now,

I want you to give this thing to Stevie, he's a good guy.'
But he did. So, if Jackie asks me to do him a favor, and
I can get a fast hundred out of it for my dumb brother,
I'm gonna do it."

"I can use the dough," Barry said. He lit a Winchester cigar.

"Why're you smoking those fucking things?" Steve
said.

"Because they're not gonna kill me as fast," Barry
said.

Steve lit an L&M. "Well," he said, "you inhale them,
don't you?"

"Some times I forget and then I do," Barry said. "Not
very often, though. It's like swallowing fuckin' fire
when you do it."

"Sure," Steve said, "and you're not gonna tell me,
there isn't more shit in them're these."

"Shit," Barry said, "I mean, how long've we been
smoking?"

"I started when I was twelve," Steve said.

"Okay," Barry said, "and I was a big asshole then just
like I am now, I did everything you told me to do, so I
was eleven. So, I mean, I been smoking close to thirty
years, it's probably not gonna make much difference
now anyway. Ginny was after me about it, I smoked
them Omegas for a while. I did them, and then there
was that other kind of thing there."

"Between the Acts," Steve said. "I can't figure them
things out, I never could. They smell just like anything
else, when you're the guy that's smoking them. But
when you're the guy that's with the guy that's smoking
them, you'd swear the bastard spent the whole day
burning a cat or something."

"Yeah," Barry said. "So, I didn't have any cigarettes

for over a year now, except when I was up in Maine, there. I had about twenny packs of Luckies in them three days, I can tell you that. But except for that, I been using these things. I don't feel no better, though. I thought I would. Them guys that're tryin' to put you guys out of business all the time, you think you're gonna feel better if you stop. Ginny told me that too. But I don't. I just eat more. Some day they're gonna say you can't sell the fuckin' things any more. That's what's gonna happen."

"Never happen," Steve said. "Look, how many guys are there, you think, can go back and forth like you do? Huh? Maybe two. They're not gonna do that. Shit, they did the same thing with booze. They do it and, well, look, they think they're taxing them now, right? How much taxes you think me and Jackie pay on that stuff, huh? So you think, they can't get the taxes on what they're letting me sell, you think they're gonna, they're gonna be able to stop me from selling them? I pay on about one third of the stuff I sell. Just enough so it's not too fuckin' easy for them, a kid could catch me doing it. And nobody looks at the bottom of them things. So, and they know I'm doing it, and guys're doing it, and they know they can't stop me and they also know, if they didn't let guys sell them at all, they couldn't do it."

"Jesus," Barry said, "it takes this fucker long enough, don't it?"

"Well," Steve said, "you got to allow the guy a certain amount of time, you know. I asked Jackie. I said, 'Great, the guy's gonna get laid and I'm gonna wait around all night for Christ sake.' Jackie says, no, he don't stay out late. He gets what he wants and then he goes home. Never stays out past one."

"I still think it's kind of nice of us," Barry said, "letting the guy get his rocks off like this. Probably how he stays in so good shape."

"He's a fairly smart bastard," Steve said.

"Not tonight he's not gonna be," Barry said.

"Well," Steve said, "I mean, and that's the kind of guy he is too, like about the broads, there. He's not smart enough, he doesn't marry any of them. Some times he's not smart. And the same thing with the games there, see? Most of the time he runs a good game and all, and everybody's happy and that's when he's being smart. He's not making any noise and he's only taking guys that want to get taken and he don't kill it, you know? He don't take them for a lot. And he don't talk about how he's taking them. No, he just sometimes, it seems like every so often he's gotta take everybody for everything, and that's the same thing."

The Coupe de Ville paused at the garage exit and Steve started the LTD. The Cadillac went down a short street and turned west on Kneeland Street. Steve put the LTD in drive and went east on Kneeland Street. In the rearview mirror of the LTD the taillights of the Cadillac receded into Park Square.

"You're sure he's going home," Barry said.

"Yup," Steve said. "He's just too fuckin' cheap, take the Turnpike."

Steve kept the LTD in the middle lane on the Massachusetts Turnpike and did not exceed sixty-five miles per hour. The LTD reached the Allston exit in less than seven minutes. Steve threw change into the tollgate basket and turned right on Cambridge Street. At eleven-fifty he parked the LTD beside a hydrant on Sheridan Street in Brighton and shut the ignition off.

"All right," he said, "it's the third brick one down there on the left."

"The one with the yellow Chev," Barry said.

"The next one," Steve said.

"No driveway," Barry said.

"Right," Steve said. "Cheap bastard parks on the street."

At nine minutes past midnight the Cadillac moved slowly by the LTD. Steve and Barry eased down on the seats.

At twenty minutes past twelve the Cadillac moved slowly past the LTD. Steve said: "If he comes by once more I'm gonna move and give him this place."

At twelve thirty-five, Trattman walked up Sheridan Street, approaching the LTD from the rear, on the same side of the street. When he got to the rear bumper of the LTD, Steve said: "Now."

Barry and Steve got out of the LTD. Barry said: "Right there."

Trattman stopped. He frowned. He said: "You guys, you guys . . ."

Steve pointed a thirty-eight Chiefs Special, two-inch barrel, at Trattman. He said: "Get inna car, Markie."

Trattman said: "You, I haven't got no money on me, you guys. I don't, you guys, I haven't got no money or anything."

Barry said: "Get inna fuckin' *car*, Markie." He walked up to Trattman and took him by the right elbow. Trattman resisted slightly. "The car," Barry said, "you got to get inna fuckin' car, Markie. You're *gonna* get inna car and you *know* you're gonna get inna car, so get inna *car*, for Christ sake."

Trattman walked slowly toward the car. He looked toward Steve. Steve held the revolver steady. Trattman said: "Steve, you guys, I didn't do nothing."

Steve said: "Barry, put him inna back and get in with him."

Barry pushed Trattman slightly. Trattman said: "I mean it. I didn't do anything."

Barry said: "Markie, we're gonna have all kinds of time to talk about things. Just get inna car, all right?"

Trattman bent and entered the car. He got into the back. Steve slid in on the driver's side and shut the door. He turned in the seat and pointed the revolver at Trattman. Barry got in and managed to close the passenger door from the back seat. Steve handed the revolver to Barry. Trattman said: "Why're you guys doing this?"

Steve started the LTD.

"I could, I could do something, you know," Trattman said. "You guys're gonna do something to me, I know some guys and I know the right, I know where to call. You guys oughta think about that."

"You maybe already did something," Barry said. "Maybe that's why you're here, because you did something."

"I didn't do nothing," Trattman said.

"Well," Steve said. "Then, you're all right, Markie."

"You got nothing to worry about," Barry said.

Steve turned the LTD right on Commonwealth Avenue. He turned left off Commonwealth Avenue onto Chestnut Hill Drive. He took the left fork onto St. Thomas More Drive and the right turn onto Beacon Street.

Trattman said: "You guys know me. Why're you guys doing something like this? I thought, you're doing all right, Steve, for Christ sake. Why're you doing this?"

"A guy, some guys asked me to talk to you," Steve said. "I said I'd talk to you. You know, Markie, talk? Didn't you used to have me and Barry around in case you wanted us to talk to somebody?"

"Sure," Trattman said. "That's why I can't understand this, why you guys're doing this to me."

"Because," Steve said, "for the same reason, we used to do things when you wanted us to. Only this time, we're doing it for somebody else."

Steve took the left at Hammond Street and turned right off Hammond into the parking lot behind the Chestnut Hill shopping center on Route 9. He stopped the LTD in the shadows behind R. H. Stearns'.

Steve got out of the car and unlatched the seatback on the driver's side.

Trattman looked at Barry. Barry pointed the revolver at him. "Get outa the car, Markie," he said.

Trattman said: "Please, you guys, lemme talk this over, all right?"

Steve said: "Now, Markie."

Trattman said: "I didn't *do* nothing."

Barry moved the revolver closer to Trattman's face. "*Markie*," he said. "There's things worse'n talking, you know? Right now all we're supposed to do is talk to you, and that's really all we wanna do. You're liable to get everybody all pissed off, you keep acting like this."

Trattman hesitated. Steve reached into the car and grabbed the left shoulder of Trattman's coat. He pulled. Trattman's upper torso shifted in Steve's direction. Steve said: "Markie, you really got to cut this out, all right? You know what can happen to a guy that doesn't wanna do what people tell him. Now don't give us a lot of shit, okay? We're just a couple of guys that've got to talk to you and we're gonna talk to you and you're gonna talk to us, and that's all there is to it. Unless you don't wanna talk or something. Then it's different, you know? You know how things are. Now come outa the fuckin' car before I start to get mad."

Trattman pulled himself forward and got out of the LTD. Barry got out quickly behind him. Barry handed the revolver to Steve.

Trattman stood next to the car, his arms and hands close to his sides. He faced Steve. "I didn't do anything, you guys. I dunno what this's all about, and if I did something then I would, wouldn't I? And I really don't. You guys, you guys've gotta believe me."

"Move around the backa the car, Markie," Steve said.

Trattman raised his hands slightly, palms up.

"*Move*, Markie, you fuckin' little prick," Steve said. "You tryin' to make me shoot you, for Christ sake?"

Trattman moved sideways to the left rear panel of the LTD. He stood with his arms tight against his sides. Steve stood three feet away from him, pointing the revolver. Barry walked around behind Steve and stood at his right.

"Honest to God," Trattman said, "Steve, may my mother get cancer, I had nothing to do with it. Honest to God, Steve. You, can't you tell them that? I know how it looks. I know. But honest to God, Steve, I didn't."

"He didn't do it," Barry said. "That what you were gonna ask him, Steve?"

"Yeah," Steve said.

"That's what we're supposed to talk to you about, Markie," Barry said.

"Yeah," Steve said, "this thing, you didn't have nothing to do with it?"

"Steve," Trattman said.

"What thing was that, Markie?" Steve said.

"Steve," Trattman said. His voice broke. "Steve, did I ever lie to you? I never told you anything, did I?"

"Now?" Barry said.

"Uh huh," Steve said.

Barry took two strides toward Trattman, closing his right hand and swinging the fist back in the motion of a softball pitcher. Trattman jerked his hands up toward his face. Barry swung his fist forward and punched Trattman in the groin as Trattman's torso began to move backward over the trunk of the LTD. When the fist connected, Trattman's torso stopped and began to move forward quickly. His hands dropped from his face. His mouth gaped. His eyes stared. He exhaled and moaned simultaneously. He clapped his hands to his groin. He doubled over.

Barry took a short stride backward. He stepped forward on his left foot and brought his right knee up fast. It caught Trattman on the mouth. There was a cracking sound. Trattman's head snapped up. His body, still in a crouch, sagged off to the left.

Barry grabbed the lapels of Trattman's coat and pulled him up. He leaned Trattman against the car. Trattman kept his head down. He cried. He spit blood and pink material from his mouth. He raised his head. He had closed his eyes. His nose and mouth were pulpy and covered with blood. Some blood and pink material were on his coat.

"What's this thing you didn't have nothing to do with, Markie?" Steve said.

Trattman moved his head once to the left and once to the right. He extended his tongue, then retracted it, tracing the tip of it along his lips. He lowered his head and spat blood and pink material on the pavement of the parking lot.

"He don't answer," Barry said.

"Must be there's nobody home or something," Steve said.

"Maybe I better knock again," Barry said. "Make sure."

"Yeah," Steve said.

"*No*," Trattman said, uttering it in a high voice as "Mo."

"Shut up, you fuck," Barry said. He hit Trattman very hard, twice, in the pit of the stomach. Trattman started to double over with the impact of the first punch. The second brought a rush of air from his mouth. Steve and Barry stepped back two paces, quickly. Trattman fell forward on the pavement and vomited half-digested steak and salad, and blood. He lay on his chest, his head resting on its left side. He breathed noisily.

"Whaddaya think, Steve," Barry said, "you think he's through?"

"Better give him another minute or so," Steve said. "He might have some more in him."

Trattman, his eyes closed, expelled more vomit, blood and pink material from his mouth. It ran down his cheek to the pavement.

"Give him a try now," Steve said.

Barry stepped forward. He picked Trattman up by the collar of his coat, at the nape of the neck. He leaned Trattman against the side of the LTD. Trattman's head lolled off to the left. His eyes remained closed.

"Who're the kids, Markie?" Steve said.

Trattman retched and bled from the mouth and nose. He raised his right hand feebly toward his face. He touched his face lightly with the tips of his fingers. Slowly he shook his head.

"Can't hear you, Markie," Steve said. "Who're the kids, Markie?"

Trattman explored the pulpy flesh around his mouth. He sighed. Tears came from his closed eyes. He shook his head slowly. "I," he said, "they . . . I didn't . . ."

"He still says he don't know nothing," Barry said.

"Yeah," Steve said, "how about that?"

"Think he doesn't?" Barry said.

"Jesus," Steve said, "maybe he doesn't, after all."

"You can't tell about guys, though," Barry said.

"I know it," Steve said. "I heard about a guy once, somebody asked him if he knew a couple guys and he said he didn't. But you know what? He did."

"Better ask him again?" Barry said.

"Yeah," Steve said.

Trattman screamed softly through his bloody lips.

"Pick a place," Steve said, "you don't get all covered with stuff."

Trattman moaned. His head lolled to the right. He got his eyes open as Barry stepped forward again. He saw Barry's right hand, closed in a fist, swing back across Barry's chest until the fist passed over Barry's left shoulder. He closed his eyes quickly and moved, jerkily, to his own left. Barry brought his fist back in a flat arc. The heel of his hand hit Trattman at the right hinge of his jaw. His head snapped fast to the left as the bone broke. His torso stretched upward and to the left, then sagged down. The back of his head hit the edge on the left rear fender of the LTD. When he hit the pavement he was lying on his left side, face up. His eyelids fluttered open, then closed. He gagged softly on something wet in his throat.

Steve walked up to Trattman and bent over him. "Markie," he said softly, "you sure?"

Trattman moaned. His head shifted on the pavement.

"About the kids," Steve said. "It's the kids, Markie, we're supposed to talk to you about. You sure you don't know who those kids are? You really sure?"

Trattman moved his head slightly.

"Because I got to be sure," Steve said. "I really got to be, Markie, that's all there is to it. You make me stay here all night, me and Barry, making sure, I'm not gonna like it. And it's gonna be an awful long night for you, Markie."

Trattman vomited suddenly, a small amount of pink material and blood. Some of it spattered Steve's shoes and the wide cuffs of his pants.

"You bastard," Steve said. He stepped back quickly. He stepped forward quickly and kicked Trattman on the left side of the rib cage, near the belt. Ribs cracked. Holding his foot at an angle, Steve wiped his shoe on the skirt of Trattman's coat. Trattman gasped and moaned and sighed. "You cocksucker," Steve said. He stepped back again.

"Whaddaya think, Steve?" Barry said.

"Get inna car," Steve said. "Strikes me right, I'll back over the prick."

As the LTD began to move, the taillights illuminated Trattman in red. Then he lay in the mist and darkness, breathing loudly and moaning from time to time. Then he passed out.

The LTD left the parking lot at the Hammond Pond Parkway exit.

On Route 9, eastbound, Barry said: "I hurt my fuckin' hand again. I always do."

"Kiss it and make it better," Steve said. "It'll be all right. That fuckin' Cogan, though. I'm gonna make him pay for these clothes that that cocksucker ruined."

"Think we oughta get the car washed?" Barry said.

"I'm gonna," Steve said. "Just be onna safe side. I'm gonna leave you off, and you take the gun, okay? There's a place in Watertown, it's open all night. I'll go there."

"And then," Barry said, "then where're you gonna go?"

"None of your fuckin' business," Steve said. "Why, you wanna come?"

"I'm not gonna be able to sleep," Barry said. "I always have to calm down some."

"Tell Ginny you don't want no beer," Steve said. "Have her give you some warm milk and stuff."

"Fuck you," Barry said. "Whaddaya think, though, about the guy? Think he knows?"

"I don't think," Steve said. "Who the fuck wants to think about him? He's just a shit."

"Well," Barry said, "I mean, I worked him over pretty good."

"Probably," Steve said, "he probably knows."

"He stood up pretty good, then," Barry said. "If he does, I mean."

"He's gotta stand up pretty good," Steve said. "He knows what's gonna happen to him, he doesn't. He knows."

7

FRANKIE PARKED the dark green GTO convertible in front of Amato's Driving School and got out. He wore tan flared corduroy jeans over Dingo boots, a white turtleneck and a doubleknit gray blazer. He locked the car and went inside.

"Well," Amato said, "you still got a good ways to go, but you look a little better, anyway. And the hair's a lot better. You got too much of that spray on it there, though."

"I don't spray it," Frankie said. "I ain't no fuckin' queer. That's gel on it. The guy that cut it gave me the stuff."

"Find another guy, the next time," Amato said. "Also got yourself something to drive around in, I see."

"I was never that hot for trolleys," Frankie said.

"What'd it go for?" Amato said.

"Eighteen hundred," Frankie said. "Plus the fuckin' sales tax, of course. It's in pretty good shape."

"Things're a little better," Amato said.

"Things're a lot better," Frankie said. "I was out last night, me this girl, I had a place to take her and a car to take her to the place in. I got that thing? I had a little beef with the guy down to Probation, there. Can't understand it, I got to have my license back so soon. So I hadda tell my brother-in-law, I went back to get my stuff. 'By the way, anybody asks you, you loaned me the money, all right?' So he looks at it. Dean's all right. 'I'm not asking no questions,' he says, 'nothing like that at all. But I think you're doing better'n me, all of a sudden.' Yeah, it's really great. I was down the Probation and the guy looks at me and he says: 'Nice clothes.' I said: 'Look, the last time I come in, you're giving me the hardeyes, I look like a bum. I figured you're gonna violate me for it, for Christ sake. So now I beat up on my family and get some dough and I finally look like something that didn't come in on a truckload of chickens, and now you're pissed about that.' Yeah, it's great."

"Where're you living?" Amato said.

"Place in Norwood," Frankie said. "Just a studio thing, the furniture was all in it. It's right on Route 1, though. But what the fuck if it's noisy, you know? The noise's all outside."

"The fuck'd you go all the way out there for," Amato said. "I would've thought, guy like you'd stay around Boston some place. I would."

"Well," Frankie said, "it's a little cheaper, you know? And, I know too many guys around right in town. My brother-in-law, for example, I hadda place in Boston, the first thing you know he'd want to be coming over all the time and using the place, and then Sandy'd get all pissed off at me and everything. And, I just thought about it and I figured, it's gonna be more of a hassle living there'n it's gonna be of a hassle to live some place else. The guy down Probation, he got all stirred up about that, too. 'How come you're in Norwood? What're you doing there?' So I told him, guy I know's gonna give me a job there, how's that? Taking care of the building, and I get something off of my rent and everything and I can still get another job and stay out of trouble."

"They check on that," Amato said. "That's one thing they do check on."

"And when they do," Frankie said, "they're gonna call the guy and that's exactly what he's gonna tell them. I'm a maintenance engineer for Hes-Lee Apartments."

"Janitor," Amato said.

"Janitor," Frankie said.

"What's that pay?" Amato said.

"Well," Frankie said, "it pays fifty, sixty a week. Only I don't think I probably oughta try and collect it very often, you know? The guy's, I told him I just got out of the can, and pretty soon I'm in talking to the head honcho, this big enormous Jew. It was his idea."

"He's fuckin' around with his taxes," Amato said.

"Yeah," Frankie said, "or he's got a honey some place or something. I dunno. I don't give a shit."

"So," Amato said, "what *are* you gonna do, then?"

"Well," Frankie said, "that's one of the things I come down, I figured I'd talk to you about, you know? See, I was thinking about some things and I was talking to Russell about some things and he was thinking about some things, but I didn't want to do anything, really, until we see. If things come out all right on that other thing. So, I hear, I hear they did. And I come down."

"Trattman got the shit beaten out of him," Amato said.

"That's what I mean," Frankie said. "So I was wondering, you got anything else in mind?"

"No," Amato said, "I really don't. You know how I know I don't? I stop down the Square in the morning. I go in, get the paper, see a couple the guys, maybe there's something going on. I always did that, before, and the minute I get out, I'm doing it again. I'm like them old guys you see, the first thing they do in the morning's go down and stand up at the bar and have coffee and anisette. Except I don't have no coffee or anything, and instead I get a newspaper. It's just a habit. And, I been doing this for a long time, I always seen the Brink's, every Friday morning. Picking up the dough for the Armstrong factory. Since I was, what, since I was fifteen, probably. I used to do that when I was going to school. I played the dogs something fierce when I was in school."

"Uh uh," Frankie said.

"Well," Amato said, "that's what I mean. How I know, I really haven't got anything. Because when I start thinking about that, I'm not thinking any more. Outside the barbut, no, nothing."

"I still feel the same way about that," Frankie said. "I personally don't think anybody could get past Billy's Fish before you had guys all over you. And that alley, that alley's narrow. I bet it isn't more'n three feet wide."

"You went down there again, huh?" Amato said.

"I was down there the night, the night before last," Frankie said. "I heard about Trattman. So, I wouldn't want to've been Trattman or anything, but I didn't feel *bad* about it, you know? Come out just like you said. I can't just sit around now. I got to get something else lined up. I was thinking, you know? And one of the things, the way guys get back in, they do something, and they plan it right and everything, and they do it and it works. And then they sit around. And then they run outa dough. And then they got to do something else, quick. And they do. And they get caught and they go away again. I don't want to do that. I'm not doing no more time.

"I start thinking," Frankie said. " 'John's right about the other thing, I'm right down here, maybe he's right about this.' So I went over and I looked it over. Of course this wasn't, I think it was Tuesday or something and there wasn't anybody standing around watching everybody, you know? So that'd be different. But, I still don't think it makes much difference, John. I still don't think you can touch that thing."

"You're probably right," Amato said. "That's another habit I got. See, at least I know it. When I can't think of anything I start thinking about that or the Brink's again. I'd like to do that one, you know? It's the kind of thing, it's almost like a sitting duck, except it isn't. Both of them are. Plus which, there's a lot of dough in both of them. And I can always use some of that."

"You haven't been doing good again?" Frankie said.

"Frank," Amato said, "I been getting *murdered*, is what I been doing. I dunno what the fuck it is. I'm not stupid. It seems like, the last good year I had was, you know when that was? I was thinking about it. It was nineteen sixty-two, can you imagine that? I got nothing in sixty-three, nothing. I think I was lucky if I even broke even. And I was getting my *balls* cut off when we did that thing. That's why I went for it, for Christ sake. That's what started making me think about it in the first place."

"That's one of the things I was thinking about," Frankie said, "another one of those."

"Jesus, Frank," Amato said, "I don't know. Those guys, knocked over the South Shore the other day? Buncha fuckers, I dunno who they were. I had about six cops walking up and down out front here, waiting around, see if anybody's gonna come around and see me. They're gonna be thinking about us now, anything like that happens."

"Let 'em think," Frankie said. "I was thinking, the thing that went ragtime the last time, it was Mattie."

"Right," Amato said.

"We had somebody instead of Mattie, that didn't

shit a fuckin' brick when somebody asks him his name or something," Frankie said, "we wouldn't've had no problem at all."

"That's right," Amato said. "Shit, the first time, there, even the Doctor was all right. He must've had the fuckin' rag on or something."

"All right," Frankie said. "And another thing was, we had, I think we probably had too many guys. That's another thing I was thinking about. I think, two guys working oughta be enough. One that's gonna set everything up and then the two guys that never went *near* the place, to actually do it, and then, you keep it down to that many guys, you oughta be able, kind of control the kind of guys you get, you know?"

"We couldn't do it around here," Amato said.

"I wasn't thinking of around here," Frankie said. "What I was thinking, how about down around Taunton some place? How about that?"

"Too hard," Amato said. "I couldn't get down there that often. For Christ sake, I take half a day off or something, go over the Registry and take care a lot of fuckin' horseshit oughta take about ten minutes, I got to talk to a lot of fuckin' stooges that haven't got no manners, it takes me half a day? You know something? I haven't got no real complaint. A guy gets himself elected to something or something, he's got a whole family full of morons, they can't get no work humping the garbage? Beautiful. I'd rather, they're doing something, they're doing nothing and we're all carrying the lazy fuckers onna welfare. But these people, they haven't got no *manners.* I can tell you what they are, you know what they are? They're, they don't give a shit. You can stand there and stand there and stand there, of course you haven't got nothing else to do, and then, they're all sitting around, these young cunts with big tits and everything, and it gets to be four-thirty, they just sit down. They go talk to their boyfriends, about how they're gonna do it inna fuckin' bathtub or something that night, and then it's five o'clock and they hang up, he's running the fuckin' water or something, and they tell you, come back tomorrow. Fuck you, in other words.

"I got the same problem here," Amato said. "Nobody's doing a fuckin' thing. I go down the Registry, I stand around all the time there, I waste the whole fuckin' day, I come back here, you think anybody's doing anything? Wrong. They're all fuckin' around. Talking, bullshittin' and everything. Connie, I give Connie credit. She did the best she could with this thing. I admit it. I come back and it's still running, which I didn't expect. But it's just all right. The kids she got in here, they'll work if you watch them like hawks. But you just let them find out you're not gonna be around for a day or so and watch them goof off. It's something awful.

"Last month?" Amato said. "Last month the bills're almost a week late going out. The checks're two and a half, at least. I had guys calling me up. 'Uh, Mister Amato, about your order?' And then he tells me, three new transmissions he put in, couple tune-ups, I also owe for three tires they hadda have fixed, one of my great customers don't know they got curbs on roads, and the guy's into me for around eight hundred bucks and he wouldn't mind seeing his money.

"So I go out there," Amato said, "the kid's sitting there. She's putting on nail polish, for Christ sake, she's talking to her boyfriend onna phone. I wait. I only pay her, for Christ sake. No reason she oughta stop talking about how they're gonna do it after closing, it's not closing yet and I'm still paying her. No, of course not. She finally gets off. I tell her, Jesus Christ, we can't do business like this. We need a wrecker or something, this guy, he's not gonna send one. '*Mister* Amato,' she says, 'I haven't had *time*. I've been so *busy*.' Jesus. I pay that broad one thirty-five for that."

"That the one with the nice ass?" Frankie said.

"That's the one," Amato said. "Before I get through that silly little bitch's gonna have me in court, and I'm gonna look awful stupid, I'm telling the judge, I got the money, I just couldn't get the girl to hang up long enough to send it out."

"How is she?" Frankie said.

Amato did not reply immediately. Then he said: "Well, okay, yeah. But Jesus Christ, I mean, you still gotta get the work done and everything."

"You don't learn nothing," Frankie said. He was grinning. "I bet when you were a little kid it took them about eight years to get you to stop shitting in your pants."

"I know it," Amato said. "But, I still can't be going down to Taunton or some place every day. I got to keep this thing going even if I can't do anything else, you know?"

"Every day," Frankie said, "that'd be if you're going in when it's open."

"You wanna go in through the roof or something?" Amato said.

"Yeah," Frankie said. "One of them Sunday night jobs. The back wall or something like that. Two guys that knew where everything was, and I figure, somebody went down there once and just made a little map, that'd be enough to go in on. You know what you're gonna have to do when you get in there. All you got to know is where it is."

"You'd have to get a guy, knew bells and stuff," Amato said. "Doglover know anything about bells?"

"I wasn't thinking about Russell," Frankie said. "If I was gonna go in when it's open again, I'd get Russell. But anyway, Russell took off. Him and the guy he's stealing the dogs with. I dunno if he's gonna be back and if he was, he probably wouldn't want to do it. He's gonna deal."

"What's he got?" Amato said.

"I didn't really ask him," Frankie said. "Coke, I think."

"He's gonna make a million bucks off of that," Amato said.

"He might," Frankie said, "and he might just get himself grabbed about six minutes after he starts and then *do* twenty more. That stuff's dangerous. There isn't anything around, you know? Everybody's hunting around and half of them're narcs. I heard a couple guys, they got sixty thousand hits of meth off a terminal down in Pawtucket, and they come back up, these're tough guys, and about ten freaks ripped them off. The cops've got bigger hard-ons for that'n they got for fuckin' coons with fuckin' guns, for Christ sake. Russell's got balls, but he didn't ask me and I don't think this guy he's working the dogs with, I don't think he's in it with him. I don't think anybody's in it with him, which is no way to be if you're gonna do something like that. No, I was thinking, Dean, my brother-in-law. When he was in the service he was Electronics SP, and he still fools around with that stuff all the time."

"Alarms?" Amato said. "I thought the guy works in a gas station."

"He does," Frankie said. "No, but he built one of them quadraphonic things from a kit on the table in the kitchen, and he was telling me, well, when he saw my car? 'Now if I was to get that, if I ever got myself a few extra bucks,' he tells me, he'd build his own color television. It's all the same thing, isn't it? I mean, it's just circuits and stuff, and he knows about that."

"You think he'd go for it?" Amato said.

"I won't know till I ask him," Frankie said. "See, I wanted, talk to you, first, see what you thought about it. I can't lay the place out like you can. I'm all right going in, but I got to have the map in front of me. I don't notice things like you do. So, I wanted, talk to you, first. Before I see him. I think he will, though, yeah."

"He ever do anything before?" Amato said.

"I think he did favors for a couple guys that bought cars," Frankie said. "And he told me, mine needs a tune-up or something, he'll do it for me and the parts aren't gonna cost me anything. He's hurtin' for dough."

"Has it got to be Taunton?" Amato said.

"Shit, no," Frankie said. "I just said that, account of the way everybody's so interested in what we do around here. I haven't got no particular one in mind. What I want, I want the easiest one around to get into, probably one of those new ones that they made outa plastic or something, and that's got some money in it, and maybe some other things around it so you're not bare-ass to the world when you're doing it."

"I took Connie the movies the other night," Amato said. "Some fuckin' thing, and it's over in Brockton there, in this shopping plaza they got. It's, I dunno what the name of it is. One story."

"How about," Frankie said, "take a look at it, and I'll go drive past it too, and then if it looks good we can start thinking about it."

"Yeah," Amato said. "Yeah, I'm beginning to like this, you know? It's funny about a thing, like that last thing, there, you can tell right off, if it feels right."

8

"HE'S AN ASSHOLE," Cogan said. He sat in the silver Toronado. It was parked in the MBTA lot behind Cronin's in Cambridge. "The *way* he's an asshole, he's a gambler. He thinks he's a gambler, at least. What he really is is a jerk. He don't gamble, he *bets* on everything. Jerk of the year."

"I enjoy going to the track now and then myself," the driver said. "I haven't missed an opening at Lincoln in years."

"So do I," Cogan said. "I still do. Even though, every time I go down the track, I lose."

"I don't," the driver said. "Of course I don't bet very much, but I've won three or four hundred dollars in an afternoon, and I very seldom lose more than twenty or thirty dollars. And I have a good time."

"It is a good time," Cogan said. "It doesn't pay as good as writing the stuff down, but it's fun. I go, it's because there's other guys that're going. It's a nice thing to do, get some fresh air and see some people and maybe you even win. You lose? So what.

"Squirrel," Cogan said, "Squirrel don't do that. He never goes down the track, he never goes to any of the games or anything, he just bets on things. And he doesn't bet because he heard about something and he's interested in that and he thinks he's got something. He bets because he's gotta be down on something all the time, it's like he's not gonna be able to live if he's not. He thinks he's gonna win, when he bets, he's always gonna win."

"Some people do win," the driver said.

"I know people that win," Cogan said. "Some of them, get a little something in the horse and they win. Some other guys get something into all the other horses, and they win. And some guys, spent their whole lives doping horses, one or two of them, maybe there's three, I dunno, they win. Except when the other guys're getting to the animals and winning. Then they lose. And they take it in stride. Write it off. Not Squirrel. He loses today, he spent the whole morning onna phone, he's gonna be back onna phone tomorrow, and he's gonna lose again. So pretty soon he's got to go out and get some dough some place, and then something like this happens. You know Mitch?"

"Offhand," the driver said, "no. Never heard of a Mitch."

"Mitch's all right," Cogan said. "He's a guy I know. Now, you take Mitch, he's a real gentleman. I've seen Mitch drop a grand on one race. And Mitch, he's about, oh, I dunno, he's in his fifties. Him and Dillon used to hang around together a lot. When I met Mitch, I was with Dillon. And Mitch, he does all right, but he hasn't got any more dough'n the next guy. He's from New York. So, then he goes and he bets another thousand on the next race. And I've seen him, he'll lose that and he'll maybe even double up on the next one and lose that one, too. Mitch'll drop a lot of dough. But it's something he likes to do. And the day's over, you wanna go out, you couldn't find yourself a nicer guy'n Mitch to go out with. And he runs out of dough, okay, that's it, he goes home. Nobody's got to worry about Mitch. And you won't see him playing again until next year.

"I was down to Florida there, last winter? Going again this year. Hialeah. Mitch's in town, he's staying

over to that place that the two guys had that just got
hooked with Lansky there. I see Mitch at the track. I
ask him, what's good. And he's got a few things, he tells
me: 'You know me, now, Jackie. Wasn't for me, some
guy'd have to invent losers, the tracks'd go out of business.' He knows everybody, the jocks, the hot-walkers,
everybody. They all tell him. 'They all talk to me,' he
says, 'and I listen to them, and I always take their advice and I always go home losers. I'm a lousy horse-
player, is all. You can have what I got if you want it. I
ever get cancer, call me up and I'll give you some of
that, too, and you're such a jerk you'll probably take it.'
I take what he's got. We lose. We go out that night, is
he pissed? Not Mitch. He's just a great guy, is all. 'I
been doing this a long time,' he tells me. 'It's not like
when I went out, I didn't know what's gonna happen to
me.'

"The Squirrel," Cogan said, "he can't do that. He
loses and everything he loses, he can't afford to lose,
and he gets all edgy. He gets nervous. He starts walking around. He's gonna do that, he's gonna do the other
thing. You know what he did? When he was inna can,
he had his wife, she was making his bets for him. I
heard that. And the exhibition games, the Broons? Orr's
got the bad knee, they let Cheevers right out the door,
nobody even tried to stop him, everybody's coasting
anyway, nobody cares about those games, they're all
out of shape and everything, he was betting them. He's
got a good business. I asked Dillon, Dillon thinks the
guy's good for at least twenty, thirty a year on that
business, there's always gonna be kids coming along
that want to drive. And it's not enough for him. He's an
asshole."

"Can't live on thirty thousand," the driver said.

"My friend," Cogan said, "Squirrel couldn't live on ten *million.* If he got it, he'd lose it."

"Well," the driver said, "it's too bad he had to lose at the card game."

"He didn't," Cogan said. "He won there. He was only there twice. He had any sense, he should've kept going back there. He was the only guy in the place that could come close to knowing anything. The guys he was playing against're bigger shits'n he is. He actually won, the two times he was there, about a thousand, eight hundred or so both times. Which of course for the Squirrel's not even carfare.

"A guy I know," Cogan said, "told me, Johnny Amato dropped eight thousand last week alone. Basketball. Kept missing the spread. 'I love the guy,' he tells me. 'He thinks when you lose, it's not because you bet stupid, you probably shouldn't've got down at all. He thinks it's luck. His is just bad. That guy, he couldn't lay off of the sun coming up tomorrow, somebody was to give him a line on it, not happening.' That time he was in the can, you know he just got out the can, practically?"

"What'd he do?" the driver said.

"Robbed a bank," Cogan said. "It was the same thing. He robbed the same bank twice. Actually got away with it once. And then he did it again. He was too far inna shit for the first time to get him out. Hadda go back and do it again, get some more dough to piss away. Got himself this bunch of ham-and-eggers and he sends them down where he does his business and he goes away. He goes down the Bahamas. They got his cars and the guns and everything, and they do it, only, of course, they're as dumb as he is, they miss about sixty and get out with no more'n thirty and he comes home. He got about five, he had so many guys in it with him, they cut it up, and anyway he got in worse shit while he was gone than he was in when he left because he dropped close to seven while he was away. Casinos're not enough for him, he was also calling home and making stupid bets on games any dumb kid'd know enough to give a leaving-alone.

"So he sets it up again," Cogan said, "and those dummies go back in, the people in the bank're starting to think they're gonna be regular customers or something. So they're about three minutes out of the box, you ever hear of the Doctor? Eddie Mattie?"

"Yes," the driver said, "as a matter of fact, I have."

"Okay," Cogan said, "Mattie's one of them. Now there's only one thing wrong with Mattie, which a guy might expect, he's got to have Squirrel think up things for him to do, and that's that he's fuckin'-A-number-one stupid. So he robbed a bank, right? And he's in a school zone or something, is he being very careful and everything? Not him. He's doing close to ninety and they got this lady cop there that's kind of against that, and she waves him down. *And the dumb shit stopped.* She hasn't got no cruiser, she hasn't got no gun, he's got this car if they find it the only thing they're gonna find out's that it got clouted in Plymouth about three days or so before, and he stopped. 'License, registration?' He's practically gargling. So naturally the crossing guard gets herself a run in her stocking or something and about eight real cops and they take him in and there's the gun and the dough in the trunk, and he decides, he's gonna save himself. And he blabs and he blabs and he blabs. And the Squirrel's onna plane, coming home, funny thing, they had the FBI here, waiting for him, he gets off, got a nice warrant and some handcuffs.

So the Squirrel and them did eight or ten. I think they should've done more, myself."

"What'd the Doctor do?" the driver said.

"Three to five," Cogan said. "He was as pissed off as they were. Thought he was gonna get the street, for tipping them in."

"Good deal for the Doctor," the driver said. "He must've gotten out some time ago, then."

"Three or four years ago, I guess," Cogan said.

"He wasn't in on this," the driver said.

"No," Cogan said.

"You're sure of that," the driver said.

"I'm pretty sure, yeah," Cogan said.

"Because he asked me to ask you about that," the driver said.

"You can tell him, I'm very sure," Cogan said.

"Because he never okayed anything on the Doctor," the driver said.

"Is that so?" Cogan said.

"That's so," the driver said. "Told me that himself, when he asked me to ask you."

"Of course some times," Cogan said, "a guy'll get a guy, and the guy'll think, the man wants it. The guy hasn't got no way of checking, you know. You just assume that."

"I understand," the driver said. "This was merely something I wanted to suggest, that he wanted me to suggest. Mattie having worked with people and all. Just a question."

"Of course everybody's got his own way of doing business," Cogan said.

"Of course," the driver said.

"Now, aside from the Squirrel," Cogan said, "we got the two kids. One of them's a guy that Squirrel had on the bank robberies. That one I'm sure of. The other one, I'm picking up some stuff on him, I think, but I'm not sure yet. The guy I'm talking to, he swears it's this particular kid, but I don't know."

"What's the problem?" the driver said.

"The guy's the problem," Cogan said. "The guy I'm talking to. Dillon give me a couple names and I saw them and they're all-right guys but they don't know shit from Shinola about this thing. This guy I got on my own. But I don't know about him. He's close to sixty, at least, and I bet he didn't put in more'n twenty years all told on the street. Every time he did something he got nailed. So he's not very bright to begin with and now he's crazy, and I don't know about the guy, is all. I do know he's queer. He's had everything up his ass. If they're still making Packards he'd have a Packard up his ass. He's soft. You never know whether he's telling you something that happened or he's telling you something he probably dreamed was happening while nine guys're taking turns with him. I don't blame him. He's as soft as a sneaker fulla shit and he can't help it. But you got to think about what he tells you."

"What's he tell you?" the driver said.

"There's this other kid," Cogan said, "this kid he knows, he knows him from the can. He probably used to blow him. He says the kid's a filthy rotten bastard, but the poor guy's scared of shadows and he'd blow dead cats if a tough kid said to, and he wants this guy, get some stuff for him. It's, he says he can get stuff like that, that you mix with the shit you're selling, and the kid asked him. Only the guy says the kid, he wanted the stuff, it's some kind of stuff dentists use, right? Makes your mouth cold."

"Novocaine," the driver said.

"That's what I keep thinking it is," Cogan said. "It's not. He told me what it is, but I can't remember. Anyway, it don't matter, it's like that, and the kid said he's gonna need about two pounds of the stuff. Now he wants four. So the guy tells me. Which means, if the guy's got it right, the kid's coming in with twice as much junk as he was gonna."

"And that means he's got twice as much money to buy dope with," the driver said.

"Right," Cogan said. "And, well, that's really all it means. I got no way of knowing, where the kid gets the dough. I'm trying to find that out. I'm also trying, find the kid. I haven't even got his whole name. This guy, ah, you can't depend on him. Either way. You can't depend on him to give you the straight shit and you can't depend on him to blow smoke up your ass. It's just a fuckin' *thing*, is all, and I dunno what I'm gonna end up doing about it.

"Now this other kid," Cogan said, "him I know. He was on the jobs that the Squirrel and him went in for, and he got out about the same time, and I heard it and I sent down to China and, what about this kid, could it be him? And China said: 'Certainly could be.' So, him I'm sure of. All we got to do now, we got to think about that other kid. He bothers me."

"Should we move now?" the driver said. "Or, do you want to wait."

"I talked to Dillon about that," Cogan said. "Him and me, we both think: now. Games're closed, right?"

"Grant's Tomb," the driver said.

"People're losing money," Cogan said.

"A fair inference," the driver said.

"They don't like losing money," Cogan said.

"Except for Testa," the driver said. "He's still open."

"So what we oughta do," Cogan said, "and me and Dillon both think this, you think about it and it's the only thing to do. We oughta hit Trattman now and get things started so people can get back to doing what they're supposed to be doing."

"Trattman?" the driver said. "What brings Trattman into this? You told me yourself, it's this Amato fellow and his friends."

"It is," Cogan said. "Trattman didn't have anything to do with it. This stuff I'm getting, plus I had Trattman talked to, you're right. I had him asked and I'm sure."

"You ought to be," the driver said. "Your boys went a little bit overboard there. They damn near killed the man."

"When I talked to Steve," Cogan said, "I didn't know that. When I talked to you. All he told me was they worked him over and he said he didn't know anything. That's all I knew."

"I had one hell of a time understanding him," the driver said. "The first time he called, I was out. My secretary talked to him. She didn't get more'n a third of what he said. I had to call him back and I had trouble understanding him. Hell, I had trouble, calling him back. The numbers he left, she couldn't understand what he was saying. I finally figured it out. It had to be Trattman. Cangelisi called me, all upset, and said Trattman called him and he gave me to Trattman, gave him my number. 'Thanks a lot,' I said. 'Look,' he said, 'I didn't sic those monkeys on him. If you didn't, you know who did. You take care of him.' Then when I finally reached him, I understood why the kid had trouble. He's got a broken jaw."

"I heard that," Cogan said.

"He's also got broken ribs and a broken nose and he

got three or four teeth broken and there's something wrong with his septum," the driver said. "And he told me, there was some question about his spleen. He was in the hospital when I talked to him."

"I heard some of that," Cogan said. "He's out now, I understand."

"Must be his spleen's all right then," the driver said. "He's not happy, though."

"Sorry to hear that," Cogan said. "We aim to please."

"He'll be sorry to hear it too," the driver said. "When I tell him. I have to tell him."

"Tell him anything you want," Cogan said. "You're his lawyer and all."

"Trattman blames him," the driver said. "I didn't tell Trattman anything, of course, but you and I both know, you weren't authorized to go that far."

"You know how guys are," Cogan said. "They go out to do something and they get all excited and everything. When I found out, I called Steve. He said Barry, Barry, look, Barry's an ironworker, all right? He's a very tough guy. All of them guys carry, for Christ sake. They're always falling off something or getting into fights and stuff. He's a tough guy. That's why I use him. And Steve said, well, apparently they're about halfway along and things're going all right, and then Barry decided, Barry's very nutty about his wife. You can't talk to the guy about her. I dunno what she is, she's an angel or something. At least he says so. So, things're going along, Steve said, and Barry decides Trattman fucked his wife. She was staying some place with her mother, Barry's up in Maine on some kind of a beef, and I dunno how the hell it got started, Steve don't know either. But Barry gets this idea in his head, Trattman fucked his wife, and that's when the guy got his jaw broken and the ribs. Barry kicked him. 'I oughta bitch too,' Steve said to me, 'I was standing too close to him and the cocksucker threw his cookies on my pants.' I told him, go fuck himself."

"Is that what I'm supposed to tell him?" the driver said. "I was very specific when I talked to you. He told me to be. Shove him around if you want, but don't hurt him too badly. I told you he didn't want him hurt."

"Ah, come on," Cogan said, "of course you did."

"All right," the driver said.

"You guys always do that," Cogan said. "I know that. You guys, you don't know how to break an egg. You want things done all right, you know what you want and the guys to go get it, and you take what you get because that's what you wanted, but you always go out after and you say, you didn't want nobody, do that. Quit shittin' me, all right? They know, they know who Steve is. They know what him and Barry do. Shit, I mean, they're guys that've always been around. When Jimmy the Fox, there, he started to get all jumpy, I had three hundred locations and there wasn't nothing left for nice ghinny boys like him, there, he started making a lot of noise and I heard about it, I turned over forty joints to Steve just like that. They all know who Steve is. They know what he does. He don't know anything. He's just a good guy to have around, and all the guys've used him."

"The thing of it is," the driver said, "he didn't okay it."

"He okayed it," Cogan said. "I told you who I was gonna use. He knows it just as good as I do, Steve's gonna go out and do what he thinks you want him to do. You tell him what you want, he's gonna listen, he's gonna go out and do what he thinks you want. Do matter what you say. And, he okayed it, he had you call Dillon and he had you see me. Now cut the shit. It's not gonna make any difference anyway. We gotta hit Trattman and the man knows it."

"I don't understand that," the driver said. "I thought you believed him."

"My friend," Cogan said, "I do. It don't make a bit of difference. Once before, Trattman did something, right? And he was lying. He was blowing smoke up the man's ass."

"Correct," the driver said.

"This time," Cogan said, "this time Trattman didn't blow no smoke."

"And he got beaten up," the driver said, "very badly beaten up."

"But we're *sure*, this time," Cogan said. "This time, last time we thought we were sure and we weren't. This time we are."

"Correct," the driver said.

"Now," Cogan said, "the guys that go to the games, they're not sure. Well, they *are* sure. They're sure Trattman's got a license, because he can do it and nobody does anything about it. So that's the same thing. So what do you think they're gonna do? You think they're gonna go the games?

"And never even mind them," Cogan said, "what about the guys on the street? Whaddaya think they think, huh?"

"I've got no idea," the driver said.

"They think," Cogan said, "they think: Trattman. He did it before and he did it again. And he lied about it before and nobody did nothing, and now he did it again and all he got was beat up."

"He could've died," the driver said.

"Because he stuck out," Cogan said. "This's his second time, the way they see it, the second time he did it. The first time you do it and if nobody catches up to you, great. The second time you can do it and somebody whales the shit out of you."

"If that's what they think," the driver said.

"Counselor," Cogan said, "take my word for it: that's what they think."

"Ahhh," the driver said. "But still, he really didn't do anything."

"It's his responsibility," Cogan said. "He did it before and he lied before and he fooled everybody, and, I said it to Dillon, I said: 'They should've whacked him out before.' And Dillon agreed with me. Now it happened again. It's his responsibility for what guys think. On the street it's Trattman, nothing but Trattman. Gets fifty, fifty-two thousand, whatever it was, he got about the same, he hadda split something, okay, but he got about the same the last time. And now they break his jaw. He's hurt and he's out what the kids cost him and he's clipped guys that trusted him about eighty thousand, and he's still walking around and everybody knows he did it."

"He didn't do it," the driver said. "Not this time, anyway."

"That's not what everybody knows," Cogan said. "There's lots of guys that'd drink milkshakes for a year, *if they got caught,* for that kind of dough, they had their jaws wired shut. Shit, we're gonna have kids waiting in line, knock them fuckin' games over, they open up again. You got any idea how many wild-ass junkies there are around? If he gets away with this, well, we might as well just forget it, once and for all, and just quit."

"I still don't know," the driver said. "I see what you mean, the public angle, and I don't take issue with what you say about the other people. But I'm not sure how he's going to feel about this, with a man who didn't do what everybody thinks he did, when I suggest that."

"Tell him," Cogan said, "ask him, where the guys come from, in the games. Not from the street. They don't care, Trattman got beat up. They're not gonna come in, is all. Trattman did it before, Trattman did it again. Trattman's through, and he can't do nothing else. Except get laid. He's good at getting laid. Otherwise he can't do nothing for us. We lose nothing there.

"Tell him also," Cogan said, "the guys onna street. They think the same thing, and they're gonna take what they think and nobody else's games're gonna be safe. He's hurt. Big deal. You hit a game and it's big money and the *worst* they do to you, they beat you up. The kids'll start their own union. We're gonna have nothing but guys running around for a while, knocking down doors worse'n cops, and then after a while there's not gonna be no games, no games at all. 'Goin' to a game? Right. Save yourself some time. Go inna room, put your hands up, throw the cash onna bed, you get home early and the wife's glad and you didn't take no chances, getting yourself shot.' Guys're not gonna go for it, and there's no two ways about it.

"Counselor," Cogan said, "go talk to the man. Trattman's gotta be hit, and you put it up to the man, he'll agree with me right off. Give it a try. You don't do it? Forget about the money. He made a mistake."

"A long time ago," the driver said. "He made a mistake a long time ago."

"He made two mistakes," Cogan said. "The second mistake was making the first mistake, like it always is. That's all you get, two mistakes. Tell the man."

"If he agrees with you," the driver said, "assuming that. You can hit Trattman?"

"Yeah," Cogan said.

"How about this Amato fellow?" the driver said. "He seems like the leading candidate to me."

"He's right up there," Cogan said. "Not yet. Wait'll we do Trattman. It'll make him easier, we do that. But sooner or later, yeah."

"Can you handle?" the driver said.

"Right now," Cogan said, "probably not. Not the way things are right now."

"Who?" the driver said. "He knows people, of course, but he always wants to know who was suggested by the fellow I talk to."

"I got a couple things in mind," Cogan said. "That one, I got to think about that one, and I got to make sure. Maybe, maybe we're gonna need Mitch."

"He does this kind of thing?" the driver said.

"Let's think about Trattman for now," Cogan said. "Later on, we can start to think about what guys do. But yeah, Mitch's been at it a long time. One of the best."

9

"It was fuckin' beautiful," Russell said. He sat on the trunk of the GTO and Frankie leaned against a parking meter. The car was parked in front of the Chicken In the Box on Cambridge Street in Boston.

"We leave inna middle of the night, for Christ sake," Russell said. "I said to him: 'For Christ sake, Kenny, we're gonna have to drive inna daytime sooner or later, there's no way we're stoppin' anywhere with what we're gonna have in there. So why the fuck're we leaving when we oughta be in bed?'

" 'Well,' he tells me, 'see, we gotta do it this way. I wanna get the hell at least onna Jersey Pike before it gets light. Too many fuckin' cops around here, heard about fuckin' dogs missing. See a couple guys, carful of dogs, they're maybe gonna get around to stopping us, see what we got to say.' But cops other places, they didn't hear nothing about dogs, nobody told them anything. 'And besides,' he says, 'I did this before. First part of the trip's really something. So, we start inna dark.'

"Then he shows up," Russell said. "See, I couldn't sleep. He told me: 'Get yourself six, seven hours in the afternoon, you can. We got about sixteen hundred miles in front of us. Last time, took me almost three days. So it'd really help, you get some sleep, all them dogs inna car and everything.'

"Okay," Russell said, "I try it. I get up. I eat. I sit around. I let my fuckin' dogs *out*. I let my fuckin' dogs *in*. I feed my fuckin' dogs. That's another thing he tells me. 'When've you been feeding them dogs? At night, probably.' I tell him, yeah, just before I go out, the horsemeat and the fuckin' meal. Keeps them nice and quiet. 'Tomorrow,' he says, 'feed them, lunch instead. Dogs don't know the difference. I want them dogs have a good shit for themselves, before we get them inna car. Also, now, I want you to give them something, all right?'

"I thought he means the phenobarb," Russell said. "Christ, I got myself so much phenobarb I could nod off half the town without doing nothing else. No. Because, see, you dope them just before you load them up, inna car, they all start off with a nice nap. He's got mineral oil. Four fuckin' gallons of mineral oil.

" 'Dump this in their fuckin' food,' he says. 'Give 'em fuckin' all of it. Got any tomato soup? Get about twenny cans tomato soup, mix that up and heat it, right? Just like you're gonna eat it yourself.' I tell him, I can't eat it, it hasn't got rice in it. 'Always tomato rice inna slammer, Kenny,' I say. 'I gotta put rice in it?' He doesn't know anything. The guy's got absolutely no sense of humor and he never did time. He don't know anything."

"He should've," Frankie said.

"There's very few guys," Russell said, "shouldn't've. 'Look,' he says, 'heat it up and dump the oil in. Then pour it in their food and they'll woof it down like champs. Otherwise, they won't. Then, I guarantee it, you make sure them fuckin' dogs can get out, fast, because that stuff's gonna come out of them like they're *waxed*.'

"Them dogs," Russell said, "all I could think of was when guys got dysentery the first time, you know? And they didn't, they never had nothing like you get there, before that, and they didn't know what was gonna happen to them. So them dogs, I put that food down, they practically trample each other, get at it, and I let them out and pretty soon they're all wrinkled up, their faces're all wrinkled and they're squatting and squatting. Christ, you could smell that fuckin' backyard in goddamned Springfield, steam's coming out of the grass like it's on fire or something. My mother comes home, she's about a block away and she starts in on me. 'Where're you getting them dogs from? They'll have the Board of Health down.' I said: 'Yeah, Ma. You know what you did? You hurt my feelings. You shouldn't've come down here, you should've stayed where you are.' My only son, he's in jail, she's got to come down here so she can be around and visit me. Know how many times she visits me? Three times. Three times in almost three years. Brought me a fuckin' cake, once. They wouldn't let her bring it in. 'Shouldn't've put the file in it, Ma,' I said, 'I meant to tell you, Ma, they got the metal detector, there. They can spot the file.' She tells me: 'There was nothing in that cake.' Fine mother she is, I tell her. Shit. I said: 'Ma, you hurt my feelings. Just for that, I'm gonna take my dogs out of here. I'm gonna take 'em out tonight. But just for that, I'm not cleaning up. I was you, taking the garbage out, I think I'd wanna be careful where I was stepping.' She looks at me. 'Figures,' she says, 'fits right in with everything else I got from you. Do me a favor, willya? Don't come back.' I told her: 'I take after my old man. I won't.'

"Now the next thing I got to do," Russell said, "I got to get that phenobarb into them dogs. 'This's kind of tricky,' he tells me. 'You got to take the water away from them by five o'clock, because them dogs, after the oil goes through them they'll drink it all, and then we'll fuckin' *drown* in dogpiss. The trouble is, the last time

I did this we give them the phenobarb about five, before we take the water away from them, and we really gave them a lot, because the time before that we didn't give them enough and they got inna car and they all hadda nice nap and then it's a fuckin' madhouse. So the last time we give them too much and they're all woozy, we get them to the guy, and we didn't get nothing for them, the dogs're sick and all the rest of it. I don't want no more of that shit. I don't want them dogs raising hell all the way down and I don't want them bumping into things, we get down there, either. Give the little ones, half a grain. A grain if they're lively. The big ones a couple grains, and if they're, if there's any of them that're still jumping round, hit 'em again. With the water. Then take the water back. Take some bread and make it in little balls and stick another half a grain in that and give them it around eleven or so, and that oughta do it.'

"I said to him," Russell said, "I said: 'Kenny, I thought I was supposed to sleep all day. How'm I gonna sleep, I'm doing all them things?' And he tells me. 'Take a little dog dope.' So I ask him, he's gettin' dough offa these dogs, how come I got to do all the work? 'Well,' he says, 'I got to do something.'

"He's worse'n fuckin' Squirrel for making out off guys," Russell said. "He shows up, right around midnight, he's got three more dogs. I'm busting my ass all day, getting dogs ready, Kenny's out gettin' more dogs. I said: 'For Christ sake, Kenny, that's'—we already sold some of the dogs to this guy down the North End? Poodles. We had three poodles and he give us a buck and a half apiece on them. Which isn't bad—'that's sixteen dogs we got, mine and yours.' He's got this Caddy limo. Took the back seat out and he had a lot of old blankets all the way back in there, in the trunk. 'Can't put sixteen dogs in there. They'll kill each other.'

"These dogs, he tells me, 'These're little ones.' He's got a couple spaniels and a wire-haired. 'Fit right in, no sweat.' So, we load them up. My dogs're all dopey. He takes the front legs, I take back legs. My mother's looking out of the window. Finally get all them dogs in. Stack them right up. I'm getting in the car, she opens the window. 'That all of them?' Yeah. 'Good. Remember what I said.' Right, and now I understand the old man a lot better, too. She shuts the window, bang."

"You're still better off'n I was," Frankie said. "My mother, she used to come every week. Every single fuckin' week, I'd, I used to sit on Sunday, and the first thing I hadda do was, I hadda go to Mass. Fuckin' guy, every single fuckin' week he talks about Dismas. Oh for Christ sake. Well, no. Some weeks he talks about beating off. Funny, didn't have nothing to say about blow jobs and like that. And then, the good meal, you know? The one that was just as shitty as the rest of them, except it was supposed to be good. Seen a turnip? I see another turnip, I throw the fuckin' thing at somebody. And then my poor old gray-haired mother, her and her fuckin' coat that's all beat to shit, comes in looking like somebody that just got hit on the head. And I got to sit through that. 'I pray for you, Frankie.' 'I made a novena for you, Frankie.' 'I hope you get parole, Frankie.' 'I know in my heart you're a good boy, Frankie.' 'Frankie, you've got to change your ways.' And she's gonna stay, boy, she's not comin' all the way up there, she's gonna leave in five minutes. No, sir. One week she's sick. Sandy comes for a change. 'Anything I can do for you, Frankie?' You bet your ass there is. Chain Ma the bed, for Christ sake. 'She don't mean anything,' Sandy says.

'She feels guilty. She told me, she dunno what she didn't do.' I told her: 'She didn't tell me about assholes like the Doctor, that's what it is,' " Frankie said. " 'Tell her, the next kid, teach him to plan a job right, he doesn't get some fatmouth bastard in there, fuck things up.' She looks at me. 'You want me to tell her, you don't want her coming no more?' Of course I do. So she does, and the next week Ma comes up, you should've seen her. Looked like somebody took her out and kicked the shit out of her. *'Frankie,'* she says, 'Sandy said, you don't want your mother coming up here no more.' And then she starts crying, and there's guys looking at me, and half of them're bulls and they're all gonna tell the parole, 'He's mean to his mother, she comes up to see him and he don't appreciate it.' Oh, Jesus, it was awful. So, what could I do? I told her, come back, Ma, I was just talking. And she did. Novenas, the stations, the rosary, she's going down to Mission Church there and everything for me. Christ. 'I ain't crippled, Ma,' I tell her. 'In your soul you are,' she says. Jesus. I'm lucky I didn't get at her through the screen."

"They don't know," Russell said. "None of them know. They just think, you're in there, you can't get out. That's all they know. They don't know."

"I wished they did," Frankie said. "Putting up with them's something awful. I wished I knew what it was, a guy goes in and they think it isn't bad enough, they got to make it worse. I go in again, boy, I'm making sure nobody knows. I dunno if I can do time again, but I sure can't take the visiting. Shit."

"I'm not going in again," Russell said. "That's what I'm not gonna do."

"You decided, huh?" Frankie said.

"I'm doing everything I can," Russell said.

"And that's what's gonna put you in again," Frankie said.

"Nah," Russell said.

"Sure," Frankie said, "you're going back for stealing dogs."

"Not so far," Russell said, "and never again, either. You know something? The next dog I see, I'm gonna do a wheelie on him, is what I'm gonna do. Dogs, dogs're stupid. You beat the living shit out of a dog, hit him with the pills and he goes to sleep, he wakes up the next day and he's staggering around and all, but he's hungry. All you got to do with a dog, you can do anything you want to a dog, then just wait till he gets hungry and feed him and he thinks you're fuckin' God or something. Except that black fucker."

"Shepherd grab you?" Frankie said.

"That dog," Russell said, "he's the only dog I ever saw, remembers. First time he wakes up, sees me, rrrr, way down in his throat. So, I give him another day. Gets hungry enough, he'll come around. I starved that fucker *four days*. His bones showed, for Christ sake. Know what I get when I go out? Rrrrr. I thought I was gonna have to give him some more of the stick. But he don't come after me, see? Which proves it, that black bastard isn't dumb. He remembers that stick. He's not gonna tackle me. He's just gonna make my life as hard's he possibly can. So, I hadda feed him. I can't sell hairy bones, for Christ sake.

"Now," Russell said, "now he's got me, and he knows it. I try and get him out, he holds back. I practically got to throw him out of the garage. Then he won't, I can't get him in. And he growls at me all the time, still. That bastard, all the way to Florida, we're in this fuckin' rainstorm in Maryland, they had a barge hit the bridge and we either hadda go around or we use the tunnel. Which everybody else is using. So Kenny say, 'We're going around.' I thought I seen rain when I was with my Uncle. Christ. And them dogs're all pissing and farting and shitting and everything in there and we can't leave the windows down, we don't wanna suffocate, and we also don't want to drown. It was awful. I thought dogs was an easy way to make money. It's not dangerous. I was right about that. I was half right. You know what I get for that black fucker, I thought I was probably gonna get twenty million dollars or something? Seventy-five bucks I got for that dog, and I was lucky to get that. The guy we're selling them to, he just buys them, right? He just, he only takes care of them. One of those guys with no meat on him. He doesn't talk. We're there, he's got this kind of beaten-to-shit old farm down outside Cocoa Beach. We're there about half an hour, we're finally breathing again, we been on the road about ten years with them dogs, all of a sudden I notice, his wife does all the talking. 'This one here looks like he's been run over,' she says. She never stops talking and he never starts. 'He sick or something? We don't want no sick dogs here, Mister. I can't let you have more'n twenty dollars for this one.'

"So I say to her," Russell said, "she said she's gonna give me fifty bucks for the black one. 'Look, he's got papers, he's a valuable dog. He's the real thing. He's a great dog. Fifty's not enough.'

"'He hasn't got no papers today, Mister,' she says to me," Russell said. "'He's just another dog now that I got to think about selling to somebody and that means I got to keep him and feed him and look after him the whole time I'm trying to sell him to somebody, and that's going to be a long time. I don't want this dog. I

don't want him at all. You want to take him back with
you? Because that's exactly what you can do, if you
don't like the price. I'll have trouble, selling that dog to
somebody. He looks vicious to me and he'll look vicious
to somebody else.'

"The guy still doesn't say anything," Russell said.
"Now, she's got me, of course. I'm not taking that dog
no place with me ever again. What I want to say to that
dog is 'Good-bye,' and I hope I never see him again. All
the way to Florida that bastard's watching the back of
my neck, he's gonna eat me if he gets half a chance.
She's right. He is vicious. But, he's not being vicious
then. The guy's got him sitting down and the dog's giving him his paw and the guy's rubbing his ears and that
dog is fuckin' grinning at him. He thinks he's home
again with the stupid bastard that bought him to protect the medals. Then the dog, the guy stands up and
the dog stands up too, puts his feet on the guy's shoulders and starts lapping his face. 'Look, Lady,' I say,
'that's a vicious dog? You think somebody's gonna think
that's a vicious dog? Let 'em see him like that.'

" 'Mister,' she says, 'that's the way he is. That's the
way they all are with him. Every dog that comes in
here's like that. That's why he keeps the dogs and I do
the business. Fifty.'

"The guy wakes up or something," Russell said. "He
looks at us. The shepherd's frenching him, for Christ
sake. Guy finally gets the dog's tongue out of his mouth.
'Give him seventy-five, Imelda,' he says.

" 'Seventy-five,' she says," Russell said. " 'Now,' she
says, takes her about three hours to say anything, 'am
I setting the prices here, or are you gonna argue with
me every time he decides he likes another dog? Because
if you are, you can leave right now and take the rest of

those animals with you.' The only thing I wish," Russell said, "I wish that woman could've met my mother. They'd get along fuckin' great."

"You got out of there all right, though," Frankie said.

"Yeah," Russell said. "Went over to Orlando with Kenny, burn the fuckin' car. Kenny fuckin' near killed himself. Went in this orange grove, right? Pulled it offa the road, there's this little dirt road, there. So, Kenny was driving. He gets out, sticks a rag down the gas tank, he hangs it down and soaks it and then he pulls it out and hangs it down onna fender and lights it off. Fuckin' car just blew up. And, he left it in gear, you know? Knocked him right on his ass, it was in reverse. He's a hot shit. Gets up. 'Okay,' he says, 'that's the second job like that I fucked up. I got to do that again, I'm gonna find somebody, knows what he's doing.' Kenny, he didn't have no eyebrows, for Christ sake, hasn't got much hair left, either."

"What was it," Frankie said, "hot?"

"Nah," Russell said, "it was Kenny's car. But what the fuck's a car good for, you had all them dogs in it over two days? Nothin'. It's like riding in a shithouse. So, Kenny had it in his sister's name, she called the cops the day we're supposed to get there, says it got stolen. Then, we got out of there Wednesday. You should've seen those assholes when they search you at the airport, they see me and Kenny. I thought their eyes was gonna come right out of their heads. Four times we got to go through the metal detector. Then there was this guy, I guess he was the newest guy there or something, he had to pat us down. I think they give him the rest of the day off. 'You're gonna let us on the plane, finally,' Kenny said, 'aren't you?' They look at him. 'Mister,' one of them says, 'if you haven't got no weapons on you,

you can ride. You probably oughta ride in the baggage, but never mind that.' Nobody'd sit next to us. We hadda ride way in the back and there was this one stewardess, every time she hadda come near us, she'd look at us like she never saw anything like us before in her life. 'You guys going all the way to Boston?' she says. 'You wouldn't consider, getting off in Washington or some place?' Kenny fell for it. 'This thing gonna land in Washington?' he says. 'I never been to Washington.' See, we didn't stop or anything. 'No,' she says, 'but if you'll get off there, I'll use my influence with the captain and I'm sure he'll agree to it.' The guy on the bus from New York," Russell said, "I come up from there onna bus? I'm not gonna get searched with the weight on me. I thought he was gonna make me ride outside. I fuckin' crashed when I got here, boy. I never been so tired in my life."

"You look all beat to shit," Frankie said.

"Yeah," Russell said, "and the hell of it is, I been up for about a week, you know? And I shouldn't've even slept last night, only I hadda or I would've just fallen down. I got to keep moving till I finish this thing off. I thought I was gonna see the guy with the other stuff this morning, but I couldn't raise him."

"You haven't dumped the stuff?" Frankie said.

"Dump it," Russell said, "Christ, no. I didn't hit it yet. I can't, I probably won't be able to move it till tonight, now, by the time I see him and everything. I know where it is. I can get it, and I haven't got it on me."

"Down the bus station," Frankie said.

"Never mind," Russell said. "I know where it is."

"You're just an asshole," Frankie said. "You know that, you asshole? The kind of chances you're taking, they're gonna forget about putting you away for the stuff when they catch you. They're gonna put you away for being nuts."

"Talk to me about that when I get the dough," Russell said.

"Russ," Frankie said, "this whole town's dry, and it's been dry for three or four weeks. There's more guys running into drugstores now with guns'n you ever saw. They got Goldfinger and that was the end of that. They tossed three guys with shipments this week, for Christ sake. The minute the word gets out, somebody's in with something, everybody goes right out of their minds. There's more heat in this town on that'n there is in the FBI, for Christ sake. Unload, Russ. Let somebody else do a hundred years or so, they catch him with it."

"Not till I hit it," Russell said. "Look, I'm into this, over twelve K, right? I put it to a guy, fast, I don't hit it, what do I get? I'm gonna get, even with things the way they are, no more'n fifteen, sixteen. I take it up a step, I can hit that stuff a whole step with the stuff I'm getting, I can move it to two guys and get twenny-five."

"It's stupid," Frankie said. "It's fuckin' stupid. That's a thousand dollars a year."

"Look," Russell said, "I don't need nothing, make me dumb. You know that, you and Squirrel. Squirrel knows it, at least. Maybe you still think we were smart, doing that. You're just as dumb as I am. You just come around and stroke me some, I'll do any dumb fuckin' thing you can think of. The thing is, though, you and me're different. When this's over, I'm through, doing dumb things for guys. I do dumb things for me, maybe, and then, I get grabbed, okay, at least I was doing them for me. Which means, I get to keep all the fuckin' money. I don't have to give Squirrel nothing for being smart enough to see I'm stupid any more."

"That worked out beautiful," Frankie said.

"Sure," Russell said, "fuckin' cheesecake. Of course there's a contract out on us and all, but it worked beautiful. You and me, we got different ideas of beautiful, too."

"The fuck're you talking about?" Frankie said.

"You," Russell said, "me, and the Squirrel. There's a contract out on us. I hang around here too long, which I'm not gonna do, I'm gonna be as dead as you guys are. I'm gonna go to Montreal. I know a guy that's got something going up there and that's where I'm gonna go. And I'll tell you something: if I didn't, I'd still go."

"For what?" Frankie said.

"Cut the shit, Frank," Russell said, "for the Trattman game. The fuck's the matter with you?"

"What the fuck's the matter with *you?*" Frankie said. "You're the one that's got something the matter with him. Where're you getting this fairy story? You flying or something?"

"Frank," Russell said, "I can add and subtract. There's gotta be a contract. Has to be one."

"Nobody knows we did it," Frankie said.

"I think they do," Russell said.

"They went for it," Frankie said.

"That's good," Russell said. "You go ahead and believe that. It'll make you feel better while the guy's catching up with you. Who's the guy that does the work? Tell him when he sees you, sorry I couldn't wait around. Tell him I went to, tell him I went back inna service, I liked it better when it was a pretty good chance I'd at least get a chance to shoot back if they missed me the first time."

"Russell," Frankie said, "Trattman's practically dead. They beat him shitless. You didn't know that, did you?"

"Shit," Russell said, "of course I knew that. Kenny told me that."

"Kenny," Frankie said, "this's Kenny Gill we're talking about, right?"

"Right," Russell said. "Kenny was telling me, well, he didn't give me the guy's name, but it hadda be Trattman. We're talking, we got all them fuckin' dogs inna car and we got all this time and it's raining and everything, I said to him: 'You know, this really sucks. This is really a shitty way to make a couple dollars. I thought it was gonna be easy, and it fuckin' sucks.'

" 'Well,' he tells me, we get to talking, 'there's not very many things a guy can do.' And he tells me, there's a guy, runs a card game some place, Kenny don't even know who he is."

"Bull*shit*," Frankie said.

"No bullshit," Russell said, "he didn't know the guy's name."

"Kenny Gill works for Dillon," Frankie said.

"So fuckin' what?" Russell said.

"Anything Kenny knows, he got from Dillon," Frankie said. "He's too goddamned stupid to figure out anything for himself. If Kenny knows a guy who runs a card game, Dillon knows, and there was some kind of reason he had for telling Kenny. Nobody ever tells Kenny nothing unless it's something they got to tell him because they want him to do something for them."

"They did," Russell said, "that's what he said. He said there's this guy, he knows these two guys, him and his brother hadda go out and do the number onna guy that runs a card game. Hadda be Trattman. Because the guy knocked over his own game and they hadda teach him something for a change. And them guys, well, Kenny knows them, is all, and they asked him if he wanted to come along, they'd give him some of the money, but he was going with me and the dogs and he couldn't. That's all. 'I give that up,' he was saying. 'It don't pay anything and it's dangerous. I bet them guys didn't get more'n two hundred bucks, and look at the chances they hadda take, huh? The fuck can you do with a hundred bucks. Nothin'.' That's all he said."

"Yeah," Frankie said, "and what'd you say, case Dillon didn't have the whole story before?"

"I didn't say shit," Russell said.

"You horse's cock," Frankie said.

"I didn't say fuckin' shit," Russell said. "The guy told me something. I listened. He never even, I didn't, if I didn't already know something, I wouldn't even've known it was Trattman. You think I was gonna say something, the guy's telling me they just beat up a guy that they know did it before? They just beat him up? Is that all they're gonna do to him? No, I said nothing. Shit, all I could think about was not saying anything, and getting out of here before they find out I'm back."

"You better not've," Frankie said. "John's gonna be mad as hell about this."

"Oh," Russell said, "big fuckin' deal. I got the Squirrel mad. I'll probably have to go to bed without no fuckin' supper. Fuck him."

10

"You think he did," Amato said.

"John," Frankie said, "I *know* he did. Him and Kenny're in that car for three days. Non-fuckin'-stop. He must've spilled his fuckin' guts. I know the guy. I never would've figured him for it, but it's the only thing that could've happened. He was trying to warn me, is all. He finally seen what he did and he was trying to tell me, I'm inna shit. You and me both."

"So's he," Amato said.

"Not in Montreal," Frankie said. "In Montreal he's as clean as he can be."

"There's guys in Montreal, too, you know," Amato said.

"I know it," Frankie said, "and you know it. He apparently doesn't. It don't make no difference. It's what he thinks. He thinks we're inna shit around here, and the thing that proves it is, he thinks he is, and he thinks so from talking too much to a guy that works for Dillon. Kenny must've said something, finally, that tipped him. That's why."

"You brought him in," Amato said. "I asked you all kinds of things about him, you remember. You said he was all right. Remember that?"

"I made a mistake," Frankie said. "How the fuck'd I know this was gonna happen? He was Mister Tight-Asshole before, there was nothing you could've done to the guy, make him say anything. I thought he'd do it and that'd be the end of it. I didn't know he was gonna go to Confession to Kenny Gill."

"You used to hand me a good deal of shit about the Doctor," Amato said. "He was all my fault."

"He was your mistake," Frankie said. "I did a lot of time for your mistake. Now what I want, I don't want to get dead for my mistake. I tell you what, we get this straightened out? You can give me all kinds of shit if you want. I know it. I didn't know he was motor-mouth, but I brought him in and he was. Okay, so what do we do now? I didn't know he was gonna start off and be the big operator. 'I can't waste no time, I just knock over this guy's game for a hundred thou.' I thought he was smart. Now I see, he wasn't, and he's gonna save his ass and then we get the shit. Fuck him."

"You're sure about this Gill kid," Amato said.

"I'm surer about him'n I am about fuckin' God," Frankie said. "Ever go the zoo, see an ape? That's Kenny. Looks like a fuckin' ape, he's all bowlegged and he's got real short legs, too. This huge body, and he walks, he walks like a fuckin' monkey. Hands practically drag onna ground when he walks. You looked at him, you'd think somebody skinned him and put a pair of pants on him and took away his fuckin' club. And, he's stupid. He knows things, he knows how to do things, because somebody told him and he listened and the guy talked real slow, too, nice and loud. Kenny can listen. Otherwise, he's stupid. His idea of talking is, he listens, and somebody asks him something, he goes uh, uh, uh. That's when he feels good. When he don't feel good, he don't say anything. You ask him something, he'll sit there and he'll stare at you, and he thinks about it. He tries to think about it. He's not very good and he's not very fast. You got an hour or so, he'll do his best. That's what he does. Then he might say something. It'll be just the same thing you said to him. He always agrees with you. Kenny knows about, probably, two things. You hit one of them, you can talk. Otherwise, no. And he breathes. He's good at breathing."

"Ah," Amato said, "well, at least he shouldn't be too tough."

"He did work for Dillon," Frankie said.

"Wyatt Earp did things for Dillon," Amato said. "The way I get it, I seen him myself, don't forget, don't matter what anybody did for Dillon. Dillon's gonna die."

"You remember Callahan?" Frankie said.

"No," Amato said.

"Sure," Frankie said, "the lawyer, there. Used to work for the man some times. Car blew up."

"Right," Amato said.

"Kenny Gill did that," Frankie said.

"That happened," Amato said, "we're inna can."

"That's how I found out, it's Kenny," Frankie said. "China told me, he was up onna habe and his wife give him the word. Six sticks on the fire wall."

"That's an awful way to do a guy," Amato said.

"Callahan'd agree with you," Frankie said, "lost most of his stuff in that. Blew his ass off, for one thing. Would've gotten all of him if he had the door all the way closed, he hit the switch. China told me: 'Kenny's nuts. He'd do anything Dillon told him, Dillon said: "Kenny, cut your dick off," Kenny'd cut his dick off, take it right out and start chopping away. There's a lot of guys around that're afraid of Dillon and they don't even know it's Kenny they're really afraid of.'"

"I better have Connie start the car inna morning?" Amato said.

"That's an idea," Frankie said, "and if it don't go off, have her drive over and start mine for me. No, but we got to think of something. I thought, the first thing I thought of, we oughta take Russell out. That's the very first thing I thought of to do. I don't like it, I never did nothing like that, but that son of a bitch, if I'm in the hole, he's the one that got me there, and I could kill him for it, I really could."

"That gonna be such a good idea?" Amato said.

"No," Frankie said. "He already did the damage anyway, and if we put him to sleep it'll just prove it to everybody, that we're the guys that did it. One way or the other, he's gonna go anyway. He's either right, and they're gonna kill us all, or else he's gonna go to Canada or he's gonna get caught with that stuff and go to the jug and he's never gonna come out again. No, right now the main thing we got to worry about is Kenny. I don't think they're gonna send Kenny around to see me. I know him and I wouldn't let him get inside a block of me, I'd take him out. So they got to get somebody else, and that's gonna take them a little time."

"Plus which," Amato said, "I wonder if they'd do it, the way things're going right now. Too much noise."

"They'd do it," Frankie said. "We got to start being very careful and looking around and everything."

"No," Amato said, "nope, I can't figure it. It was Trattman's game got hit. It was Trattman got beat up. Trattman didn't have no other reason, get beat up, and they don't go around beating guys like that up like that for the fun of it. Nope, they're not looking for us. Nobody's even thinking about that thing any more."

"John," Frankie said, "look, I hope you're right. I wanna live a long time. I just got started and I like it."

"I'm right," Amato said.

"You don't mind, though," Frankie said, "I look around a little."

"Frankie," Amato said, "get as nervous as you like. We did it and we're clear. I'm going over to Brockton a couple more times and tend to business. I'll let you know when it's time to stop worrying and go to work again."

IN THE EARLY AFTERNOON, Cogan drank a stein of dark in Jake Wirth's. He sat far back, on the bar side, and watched the bar door. In the dining area, beyond the brass rail, medical technicians and the interns hustling them sat in white jackets and drank steins of dark and gossiped about the New England Medical Center.

Mitch came through the bar door. He scanned the room quickly, found Cogan and started across the wooden floor and the sawdust. He wore a plain Harris Tweed sports coat and gray flannel slacks and a dark blue shirt, open at the throat. His hair was black and short. He had very light skin. At the table he offered his hand and said: "Jack."

They shook hands. Cogan said: "Mitch." They sat down. Cogan signaled one of the waiters; he raised two fingers.

"Uh uh," Mitch said.

"Wagon?" Cogan said.

"Gettin' fat," Mitch said. The waiter approached. "Beefeater martini," Mitch said. "Onna rocks. Olive. Right?" The waiter nodded.

"You had lunch?" Cogan said.

"Onna plane," Mitch said. "I had lunch onna plane. Some lunch."

"Oughta have the goulash," Cogan said. "Basically it's beef stew, but they put tomatoes and stuff in it. It's pretty good."

"They still got that place down the alley, all the bums go and you can get beef stew there?" Mitch said.

"Conway and Downey's," Cogan said, "yeah. Isn't that great beef stew?"

"I used to think so," Mitch said. "Dillon took me in there one time. 'Jesus,' I said, 'you know all the good joints, don't you?' It was one of those lousy days, snowing and everything, Christ, you couldn't get around any place, and we're having all kinds of problems with this guy and Dillon took me in there. He got all pissed off. Any time you want to piss Dillon off, make him think you think he's doing something bush. Sets him right off. That and telling him there's nothing the matter with him. I guess there is, though, huh?"

"This time there is," Cogan said.

"Son of a bitch," Mitch said. "I dunno, I guess, shit, I'm fifty-one years old and I'm getting fat. I don't know, I never had no trouble with my weight. I was about thirty, thirty-five, Jesus, you know something? When I was thirty, for Christ sake, you know who was fuckin' President? Harry fuckin' Truman."

"He's about a hundred years old now," Cogan said.

"For all I know," Mitch said, "he's fuckin' dead. I dunno. I used to, I used to cut down onna potatoes then, that's all I had to do. No more problem. Work out now and then, lay off the potatoes. I could always have a glass of beer when I wanted one."

"Maybe more'n one," Cogan said.

"Well," Mitch said, "once or twice, maybe. But I could do it, then. Now, now I can't do it. Now, I look at a glass of beer, I get fat. Pisses me off. It's that cortisone I was taking, you know? It bloats you. I was, I said to the doctor, I told him, this stuff's gonna get me so fat I'll die of that. And he tells me, no, soon's I stop taking it, I'll go right down again. But I didn't."

"What're you on cortisone for?" Cogan said.

"Colitis," Mitch said. "I was sick last spring, the summer. I really felt shitty. I didn't take that much of it, you know? I wasn't on it for that long. Except, well, I almost got real sick. I was, I hadda see the cock doctor and he gimme penicillin, and I didn't bother to tell him, I'm onna cortisone, and I guess you're not supposed to do that, mix them two things like that. I was really sick for about a week or so. Couldn't get or do anything."

"My wife had to take that stuff," Cogan said, "that cortisone. I think it was that. Maybe it was something else. She didn't gain that much weight, though."

"She got arthritis or something?" Mitch said.

"Poison oak," Cogan said. "She likes to be outdoors all the time she can, she's got this real nice garden. And she was out there and she got this poison oak. So, she didn't think anything about it, probably pulled some roots or something she shouldn't've, and the next thing you know, well, she's covered with that calomine lotion all the time and she's itchy and it just wouldn't go away. So she finally went the doctor, and he tells her, it's in her bloodstream, and that's when she started taking the stuff. It got in her hair, you know? It was all over her scalp and down behind her ears and everything. She gets up before me, she goes to work earlier'n I do, and it used to wake me up, she was in the bathroom, crying, it hurt so bad to comb her hair. So they said, we're never gonna beat it putting things on it, we're gonna have to have you take something. I think it was cortisone. She really went through hell there, for a while."

"She'll probably get it again next year, too, then," Mitch said.

"I know it," Cogan said. "I asked the doctor that, and he said no, that's just if it gets in your blood and you don't take nothing for it to kill it, then it comes back again if you just put stuff on it. But I wouldn't be surprised. Them guys don't always know what they're doing. See, the big problem with her, is, she's got, she's always had this real bad problem with bugs, you know? Bees and hornets and stuff. She's allergic to them."

"Swells all up and everything?" Mitch said. "When I was a kid I used to do that."

"Worse'n that," Cogan said, "she could actually die. She's got, she never leaves the house, she hasn't got a needle with her, adrenalin, I got one in the glove box in the car, I got one in the truck. They told her, you get stung, you get stung above the neck, you got five minutes to get that shot. Twenny minutes below the neck. They told me: 'Hit her the shot. Don't try to get her to the hospital. You won't have time. Her heart'll stop.'"

"Jesus," Mitch said, "that's a tough thing."

"She's a tough girl," Cogan said. "She's lived like that most of her life. 'There're bees in the world,' she says. 'I can't stay inside all my life. What if a bee comes inside?' She told me, she got stung a couple years ago, we're having dinner, this place right on the water and I guess they're hiving underneath it or something and, she don't wear no perfume, of course, and I generally got more brains but somebody gave me some of that Brut and I had it on, and one of the bees comes out and I guess he was probably looking for me. So he lands on her neck and the waiter sees it and, he's gonna be helpful, he tries to brush it away. I didn't see what he was doing, he was already doing it. Well, he missed, and the way he did it, he drove the stinger right in and she *screams*. And she goes for her bag and she starts to turn blue. Well, I had the one I carry, and I practically knock the tables over, getting around to her, and she can't get no breath, you know? So I give her the shot and she's all right. 'Feels just like everybody took all the air out of the world,' she says.

"And every so often," Cogan said, "she puts up with all of this, she knows what can happen to her, we got to go down and see her old lady, and Carol's got two sisters, all right? And they each got about a million kids and Carol's good with them. And her mother hasn't got no sense. She gets this look on her face. She don't have to *say* anything. Just sits there. And she knows what Carol's got, of course, but she looks at her and my wife's tough. 'Ma,' she'll say, '*Aunt* Carol'll have to be the limit, is all. You can't always do the things you'd like to do.'"

"You can't never do the things you'd like to do," Mitch said. "Never. Every time you do, you get inna shit. Look at Dillon."

The waiter, having served the interns and technicians twice, brought the drinks to Cogan and Mitch.

"First of the day," Mitch said. "Except for the ones I had on the plane, anyway." He drank. "Buck and a half for a stinking drink," he said. "They oughta be ashamed of themselves. Fuckin' bandits. No, look at Dillon. There's a guy. I never seen the guy do too much of anything. He'd take a drink, he liked a big meal now and then, I guess he used to get a broad when he needed one. I dunno, I never saw him, but I assume he did."

"He used to go and see his wife some times," Cogan said.

"She was a beauty," Mitch said. He finished the drink. He signaled the waiter. "He told me once, he caught her going through his pockets. I told him: 'I'd kill a broad I caught doing that.' And you know what he told me? 'No,' he says, 'I always like to know, anybody that's around me, how far he's willing to go. Now, about her, I know.' I dunno, I think Dillon's had a pretty lousy time. The only time I ever saw him doing anything, have any fun, was that time he was down in

Florida, there. Too bad for the guy. Did the same thing all his life, I dunno. I wouldn't've done it."

"You still in the union?" Cogan said.

"Nah," Mitch said. "I hadda give that up. There's too many, you know what they're doing now? It's the fuckin' PRs, mostly. You hear about it and everybody thinks: it's the niggers. But it's not. New York, maybe some place else it is. But not New York. New York it's PRs. I dunno what the fuck it is. I been there, I been in New York almost twenty years. The whole time I been there, somebody's been howling for something. It's not the niggers, it's the PRs. Those bastards, they come in onna plane, they own the whole fuckin' town all of a sudden. All of a sudden everybody's got to get down and kiss the goddamned PRs' ass. You get yourself a sandwich and there's a hungry PR around, because, of course, there's *always* gonna be a hungry PR around, they're too fuckin' good-looking to go to work or anything, forget your sandwich. There's gonna be some guy from Washington standing around, giving you the hardeyes. 'Leave him have the sandwich, Jason. He's a spic and he's entitled.' I look around, you look around in New York and all you can see is spics, wall-to-wall spics wiggling their ass. I swear they're all queer. No, I'm selling cars."

"Jesus," Cogan said, "I wouldn't think, it'd pay that good."

"Doesn't," Mitch said, "don't pay for shit. But you're the guy, owns the thing, all right? Now that guy makes out. Guys that've got the same kind of job I have, you really got to hammer ass and get lucky, too, you wanna make a buck. But the guy, he's my wife's uncle, right? I should've married him. Him and me get along fine. So I do all right, and I'm outdoors and you get to go to the meetings and all. It's just for the time being. I go near one of them fuckin' jobs now and everybody's screaming fuckin' bloody murder. I got a record and I got this and I got that, and that asshole in New Jersey, I swear every time the guy picked the phone up he was telling somebody what a hot shit I am, oh, he was a great one. So, you got to wait, it'll die down. It always does. The fuckin' Chinks'll be next. What the fuck, I mean, sooner or later they're probably gonna *have* a fuckin' election and that crazy fuckin' guy that wants to give the world away to somebody, anybody, so long's he's a nigger himself and thinks the niggers oughta own the world, he'll get his ass whipped and then things'll quiet down again. I'll find something."

The waiter brought two more drinks. He was an elderly man, bent in the formal uniform. "Where do you have to go for these?" Mitch said. The waiter straightened up and stared at Mitch. "I said: Where do you have to go for these things?" Mitch said. "I know it's some place outa the building, here, it's obviously gotta be. You maybe even got to walk a couple blocks, take a cab or something. I was just wondering."

"No, sir," the waiter said, "we only have one man on the service and lunch bars today, and he's very busy. Are the drinks all right?"

"Well," Mitch said, "as a matter of fact, no, it's mostly evaporated by the time it gets here."

"Mitch," Cogan said. "Yeah," he said to the waiter, "the drinks are all right."

The waiter went away.

"The next one I'm gonna send in for," Mitch said. "They probably got an order blank in a magazine or something, you can mail it in and then when you get here it only takes them about a week to get you what you want."

"You picked it," Cogan said.

"The only place in fuckin' Boston I know about, I could remember, for Christ sake," Mitch said. "I never come here. You know how many times I come here? I been here, this's the fourth or fifth time I been here in my whole life. I just never come here, is all. Every time I have to go somewhere, it's Detroit, it's Chicago, it's something like that. I was in St. Louis, the last time I hadda go someplace. I just never come here. Guy asked me the other day, I wanna do something. I told him no, I was gonna be out of town. 'Jesus,' he said, 'you going all the way to Brooklyn or something?' "

"You tell him, you're coming up here?" Cogan said.

"For Christ sake, no," Mitch said. "I was just saying, I never come up here much. I suppose, when they needed somebody, they usually must've had somebody else they used to call. Course I haven't been doing much except staying away from a lot of things lately anyway. Or things've been staying away from me, anyway."

"Yeah?" Cogan said.

"Yeah," Mitch said. He finished his drink. He signaled to the waiter and pointed to his glass. The waiter, slowly, began to move toward the service bar. "You don't mind if I drink one of them beers while I'm waiting for that guy to make it in from the airport, do you?" Mitch said. He was reaching for a stein of dark.

"No," Cogan said. "It'll make you fat, though, I thought you said."

Mitch drank some of the beer. "Yeah," he said. "First there was that thing on the phones. Jesus, I could've killed that guy. I mean it. I could've found somebody, gimme the okay, I would've done him for nothing. On the fuckin' cuff. Then, then, well, I hadda leave the hall on account of that. And I wasn't feeling good, you know? So I go the doctor, and he gives me the stuff, and he asks me: have I been under some kind of tension or something. Of course not, just gettin' my name in the paper all the time, more'n Rockefeller, I bet, I used to be a guy that could go in and organize something and keep everything going all right, now all of a sudden I don't do nothing but break people's legs and stuff and throw bombs or something at them. I forget what it was. And I'm getting hell from my wife all the time, naturally. No, there's nothing bothering me. And I take the stuff and I get fat and then I got myself a good dose in Saratoga, I was up there with a couple of the guys, and then they grabbed me down in Maryland on that gun thing."

"What gun thing?" Cogan said.

"I was goin' huntin', for Christ sake," Mitch said. "Me and another guy. You know Topper?"

"No," Cogan said.

Mitch finished the beer. The waiter arrived with the drink. "You didn't bring him a beer, I bet," Mitch said.

"No, sir," the waiter said. "You only wanted the one, I thought."

"You thought wrong," Mitch said. "Bring him a beer, too. I just drank the man's beer on him."

"I don't want any more," Cogan said to the waiter. "It's all right."

The waiter nodded.

Mitch shrugged. "Okay," he said, "don't have no more. Yeah. Topper. Nice guy. Lives out on Long Island. We move out there, guy tells me, I should look him up. 'Getting old,' he says, 'still a nice guy.' So I do. Likes to fish."

"I went fishing once," Cogan said. "Got onna fuckin' boat. All these guys, drinking beer. I look at the guy. 'What is this?' I say. 'I can go the ball game, I want

to watch guys drinking beer.' It was awful. It was rough
and all them guys, drinking beer, they all start throwing
up. Fuck fishing."

"This's surf casting, he does," Mitch said. "You go out
and you stand on the beach and all. It's pretty good."
Mitch drank half of the martini. He belched silently.
"It's just, the only thing wrong with it is, you got to get
up too early. But what the fuck, he wants to go. My
wife starts in on me. 'Jesus Christ,' I tell her, 'leave me
alone, all right?' You ever been shooting geese?"

"No," Cogan said. "That's the trouble, I work. I work
all night and all day and then I go home and I go to
bed. So naturally, I take a few days off, I still live the
same way. My wife, now what my wife's always telling
me, I'm working too hard. And that's true. See, I had this
one operation, and it's all right, but anybody can see
what's happening, it's just a matter of time, the state
starts taking all kinds of action, and it'll still be there,
no question about that, but it's not gonna be as good.
So I started, I started up this thing with the cigarettes,
and I got that thing going pretty good. Six months after
I take it over, it's going like a bat out of hell. So, good,
I hadda get a guy and give him some of it, I still supply
him but he runs the locations I got west of here and I
just take care of the others. So, it's getting better. But
it drives her batty, we go some place and we get there
and then I can't sleep. I'm not used to going to bed so
early, and I stay up and then I sleep late and we can't
do nothing. 'You're exhausted,' she tells me, and I am.
But I tried changing it back and forth and I can't do it.
I been at it too long. I oughta get into something else,
I guess. Better hours."

"You got to change every so often," Mitch said.
"That's one of things, the union thing? It went to hell,

well, I didn't like it. But I was doing it a long time, I was, in a way I was kind of glad too, you know? That's what Topper says. He's seventy, at least, he doesn't do things any more. He was telling me that. 'The trouble with you guys,' he says, 'you spend your whole life, you're doing the same thing and all you're ever doing's getting old. You've got to keep trying new things.' So I listened to him, we're goin' down the Maryland shore, there, a whole bunch of people're just taking over this motel and they're all the right kind of guys, we're gonna hunt geese. So, we go down there, I, there was probably a couple hundred cops around the place? And we've got the shotguns in the trunk. Oh, fuckin' beautiful. 'Where're you going? What're you gonna do? Where're you from?' So we don't say anything, naturally, I mean, they done a lot of things but this isn't fuckin' Russia yet, I think, and everybody's standing around and now they're gonna start searching cars. And I'm gonna ask them, they got any warrants or anything, and I'm really gonna do it. Topper takes hold of me. There's four or five of them standing around, I was really afraid he was going to say something. Just shakes his head. Doesn't even do that, really. Topper's all right. I don't say anything.

"So," Mitch said, "they open up the cars and there's the shotguns, me and Topper's car. It was Topper's wife's car, actually. Two shotguns right there. I just bought the fuckin' shotgun, for Christ sake. I went down the place and I bought the fuckin' shotgun. I hadda have my wife's uncle sign for it, of course, but I actually went out and paid for the thing. Nobody gave it to me or anything. I never even used it once. Guy looks at them. Then he comes over. Treasury. I'm under arrest. Felon in possession. You think, you think I said

a single word to them? No. But what does he say:
'Mister Mitchell,' and then he starts telling me. So, it
probably just happened, they know my record and
everything. I look at Topper. Nope, they arrest him, too.
They know his name. I'm thinking: pretty soon I start
asking around, see how come these guys know when I'm
gonna take a shit and everything.

"'Just for your information,' the guy says to me,"
Mitch said, "'you might be interested to know, we
picked you up at the Throg's Neck Bridge this morning.
You guys've got to learn some day, stop having these
conventions.' So there I am. I'm probably gonna go to
jail for a fuckin' shotgun I bought in a fuckin' store, I
was gonna use to shoot geese with, for Christ sake."

"Jesus," Cogan said.

Mitch finished the martini. He signaled to the waiter,
pointing to Cogan's empty stein first.

"You're hitting that stuff pretty hard, aren't you,
Mitch?" Cogan said.

"I was up all night," Mitch said. "I can never sleep,
I'm going some place the next day onna plane. Them
things make me nervous. Then, I come in like this, I
got to sleep before I'm good for anything that day. I'm
gonna go the hotel, we finish here, get some sleep.
I told the doctor, he was gonna put me back on the
cortisone, it started up again after that thing in Maryland, and I said: 'No.' I don't care what it is, I'll change
my pants three times a day if I have to, I got to get rid
of this weight I got on me. Only I think, well, Topper
feels responsible. And he looks, he's little and he's old
and he didn't take a pinch for about thirty years, I
think. So, they're probably gonna both be his shotguns.
I was just doing an old man a favor, driving him down
there and all."

"Yeah," Cogan said, "but if they don't . . ."

"I do time," Mitch said. "It's very simple. If they're not his guns, I do time. I did it before. If I have to, I can do it again. They're gonna have to practically turn themselves inside out, get me more'n three even with the rap sheet I got, for that. Oh Jesus, do them guys love arresting you. They just love it. They get somebody, they finally get a guy, they know his name, Jesus Christ, you'd think some of them're little kids. Like to bash them right inna mouth, they like it so much. Bastards. But, big fuckin' deal. I do a year. I don't like it, but shit, that's the way it goes."

"Rough onna wife, though," Cogan said. "That's the one thing, you know, Carol can never get it off of her mind, I might get bagged and have to go to jail. Most of the time she don't give me any shit, except about the way I'm out all the time and everything. But every so often, well, they hooked four guys there and they got them in front the grand jury and they asked them, who's the guy they're looking for, you know? Like you say: the guy, they know who he is. And naturally they don't say anything. And then they get this immunity."

"They been doing that down in Brooklyn," Mitch said. "They got everybody in the slammer, and what'd they do? They wouldn't say anything."

"Yeah," Cogan said. "So, the same thing, they go to jail. And if they don't tell them, which they're naturally not gonna do, they're gonna have to stay there. So they're in the can. And my wife was saying, well, I told her, I said, I'm not big enough. And I'm getting out of it anyway, fast as I can. Guys like me, they don't even know I'm around. Those're much bigger guys'n I am. But I can see it. I think, I don't think she could take it, really, something like that happened. Every time they come in and ask for the toll sheets, there, everybody knows, they talk about it the cafeteria. And she gets all worried and everything. 'Just promise me one thing, you'll stay away from phones where they know you.' So, I do. But I'm almost out of that anyway. I don't think she could take it, really, something like that happened."

"None of them can," Mitch said. The waiter delivered the martini and the beer. Mitch drank the beer. He wiped his mouth. He belched, softly. "The last time, the last time she actually took out the papers. And I didn't blame her. She was a lot younger then. But when we're trying that thing, the last day? The jury's gonna get the case that day. I get up and she's already up. I dunno how long that is, but I was up at five or so to take a leak, and she wasn't in bed then. She says: 'Doesn't look good, does it?' Well, what the hell, it didn't. The cop lied on the stand, of course, put me in the place at nine-thirty, it was at least after ten when I got there that night, and the jury believed him, of course. So, I say, no, it didn't. And we go in the bedroom, get dressed. And I'm putting my pants on and I'm watching her, she's getting dressed, I dunno how she does it, the way she drinks and everything, but she always hadda nice body, and I was thinking, you know? Now I'm goin' away again, and she'll start beating the shit out of the sauce and everything, and I *know* she'll play around. Shit, I mean, I don't like the feeling it gives me in the nuts, knowing it, but I wouldn't even ask her, you know? Just because I'm inna can, she's supposed to go without it just like she's inna can with me? So she looks at me. 'This's the third time I've had to do this, Harold,' she says. She never called me Mitch, and she knows I hate that name.

" 'Look,' I tell her," Mitch said, " 'you never know

what'll happen.'" He drank some of the martini.
"'What's gonna happen, you never know.'

"And she says to me," Mitch said, "'Well, you think
you know what's gonna happen, and I think it's gonna
happen, and I don't know if I can take it again.'

"So it happened," Mitch said, "and then the papers
come up and I was gonna sign them, let her have what
she wants if this's what she wants. She went through it
twice. The girl don't owe me nothing. She probably is
sick of it. But then, I asked her to come up and see me,
and I said: 'Margie, look, you know? You want this,
you're really sure, you can have it. But what's it gonna
get you, huh?' She was, she was thirty-nine, forty, then.
'You're still gonna have the kids, you're still gonna have
to know, I get out, I'm not gonna be in here forever and
you're gonna have to see me when I see them. I'm not
gonna stop coming around, seeing them. And, we been
together a long time. Unless, unless you really got somebody else you really got to have, okay?' See, I knew she
was seeing this guy. So, she don't answer me. And I say:
'Look, do this for me. Don't do nothing now. You had,
you know, when I come out last time, we're both a lot
younger then and all, and you hadda decide then.' And
she looks at me: 'And you promised me then,' she says,
'you promised me then, you were all through. And here
I am again, and you'll promise me now, again, and I'll
wait five years and get six more, and then you'll do
something again.'

"'Margie,' I said," Mitch said, "'what can I say to
you? I know. You're right. But all I'm asking, you can
do, wait'll I come out again. Because, I dunno who the
guy is,'" Mitch said, "and I did, of course. I knew about
it two days after she was with him the first time. I don't
blame him, either. 'I oughta at least, you oughta at least

do this for me: I oughta be around the same's he is. Because we always got along all right.' And she starts crying and shaking her head, and I really thought. But she didn't. And it was all right. I think, you know, you know anything about kids? Probably not." Mitch finished the martini.

"You're not having any more of those things," Cogan said. "You'll fall on your ass if you do."

"I can handle it," Mitch said. "I was drinking before you got out of your father's cock. Don't tell me what I do." He signaled the waiter. He pointed twice at Cogan's empty stein. "Nobody knows anything about kids," Mitch said. "But, it's really hard on the kids. I think it was that, probably, what did it to them, the way they hadda be and all. They're no good. Oh, they're good enough. My daughter's all right. But my son, he won't have nothing to do with me. And I think, this's the funny part, all right? I think it probably was that, that she did it for, and it probably would've been better for them if she didn't. I think that's why she drinks so much, now."

"I thought she was all right," Cogan said, "we're down in Florida, there."

"She was," Mitch said. "Look, when I was down there she was all right. When I *went* down there. She really was. I believed it. But see, that was the first time she was all right, and since then, I seen what happened. I talked to some guys, everybody that's got somebody like that, and the first time they shake it, you know, you always think they shook it and that's the end of it. *They* always think that, they think that themselves. But they never do. Nobody like that's ever all right again, ever. I came back, there, I was home about a month and we're going at it left and right, this and that, well, look, I dunno what it is, you know? But I wasn't sorry I hadda come up here, lemme put it that way. She was going at it again. They can't stay away from it when they get like that. The best they can do is, they can stay away from it for a while. I think something finally happens to them. I go away, I go away on this thing again, she'll go down the slide once and for all before they get the gray suit on me. And this time, boy, I find that out, I get the papers again from her, this time I sign them. It's too fuckin' rough for me."

The waiter brought two steins of dark. He set them both in front of Mitch. Cogan said: "Check." The waiter nodded. Mitch drank half of the first stein.

"It's a terrible amount of shit, you got to go through," Cogan said.

"Hey," Mitch said, "look, you know? What can you do? Do the best you can. Think I'm gonna leave the country like some fuckin' draft dodger or something? Fuck that. It don't make no difference anyway. What're we doing?"

"We got this," Cogan said, "we got two guys. There's actually four guys, but one of them's probably not around and I'm not sure, we really want the other one. So, we got two guys, for sure, and one of them knows me, so here you are."

"Well," Mitch said, "am I doing a double or what? These guys hang around or something?"

"Uh uh," Cogan said. "Well, I mean, you wanna take the double, it's all right with me, you think you can handle it. You need that?"

"I could use the dough," Mitch said. "I'm gonna have to try this thing and it's gonna cost me my left ball to do it. You know where the pricks indicted me? Maryland. Not in New York, Maryland. So I got to go down there and everything, and fart around in some motel, and it's gonna mean two lawyers, my guy, that looks like he never got out the garment district in his life, Solly's a great guy, but if a guy ever looked like a sharp New York Jew, it's Solly. And then the other guy, some guy that probably wears overalls or something, so they don't hook me just because I got Solly. Yeah, I need dough."

"Well," Cogan said, "you want the two of them, it's fine with me."

"I oughta take you up on it," Mitch said. "But I think, I'm not supposed to be up here, you know? I'm restricted, New York and Maryland and that stuff, I'm supposed, I'm not supposed, go any place else unless I ask them. Well, I didn't ask. So I probably shouldn't hang around here any longer'n I absolutely have to. And, two's risky, too. No, I better stick with the one."

"Okay," Cogan said. "Now, here's the thing: that's gonna be the guy that knows me. Well, he don't know me, but he's one of the few guys that probably knows who I am, all right? He knows me and he knows Dillon, and if he hears anything, he's gonna figure, he's gonna be waiting for Dillon or me. So, he's the one."

"He got friends?" Mitch said.

"One of the guys that we might do," Cogan said. "He's a kid, he could be around. He's a fairly tough kid, too. The other kid, he's the guy that's apparently not around. So, there might be the one."

"We gonna do anything about him?" Mitch said.

"Right now," Cogan said, "it depends. I honestly don't know. See, the other guy, I got him in mind for tonight. And a lot depends, what happens after that."

"The fuck happened, anyway?" Mitch said.

"One of them fuckin' *things*," Cogan said. "There's

this guy, got a game, all right? And he got some guys, one time, knock it over for him, and then, well, he got away with it. So, and then everybody says: 'Okay.' Then this other guy comes along, and he gets these two kids, and they go in and they knock it over again, right? They think he's gonna get blamed for it again. That's the guy I'm doing. I'm gonna put his light out tonight, I figure, things go all right."

"Dumb shit," Mitch said. He finished the first stein.

"Right," Cogan said. The waiter brought the check. Cogan paid it.

"On your way back," Mitch said, "you think you're gonna be in this neighborhood again this year, you can bring me two more."

"No, you can't," Cogan said to the waiter. He took the second stein. "I'm gonna drink this, even if I don't want it. He's drinking coffee. Bring the man nice black coffee."

"Hey," Mitch said.

"Hey yourself," Cogan said. "I'm gonna have to talk to you. I don't wanna have to go down, see you inna fuckin' tank. Too many guys around down there, listening to other people's business. Coffee for you."

"I won't be able to sleep," Mitch said.

"Watch television," Cogan said.

"I probably won't," Mitch said. "You're gonna line something up for me, instead."

"You gotta have that?" Cogan said.

"Shit," Mitch said. "I'm not working tonight, right?"

"Nope," Cogan said.

"And I'm probably not working tomorrow night, either," Mitch said. "We got to set this thing up, and all. Who's gonna help me?"

"I got a kid," Cogan said. "He's not the sharpest thing

I ever seen, but he'll do what you tell him. You want
him to drive, he'll drive. Anything."

"Is he gonna fuck up?" Mitch said. "Never mind what
somebody tells him, does he fuck up?"

"Look," Cogan said, "this kid'd tear a fuckin' car in
half with his bare hands, you asked him. He's very de-
pendable. But you got to tell him. You tell him, he'll do
it. He'll go through a fuckin' building, he's got to."

"I personally," Mitch said, "I'd rather have a guy
that'd see the building and go around it. I can't afford,
I don't want no guy that's gonna go on no fuckin'
rampage the minute I let him out of my sight. You sure
you can't come in on this?"

"Look," Cogan said, "the guy's name's Johnny Amato.
I know him. I did, he wanted Dillon to do something
for him once, and Dillon couldn't do it. So Dillon told
him, if it was all right, he'd ask me, and the guy said:
'Yeah.' So I did it, and he paid me. He knows me."

"How much does this kid know?" Mitch said.

"Kenny?" Cogan said. "Kenny knows nothing. I didn't
tell him nothing. He don't know you're in town. He
knew it, it wouldn't mean nothing to him."

"I don't want him," Mitch said.

The waiter brought Cogan's change and the coffee.

"I don't want that, either," Mitch said.

The waiter left.

"I didn't say you wanted it," Cogan said.

"I don't want no fuckin' nutcakes, either," Mitch said.

"Well," Cogan said, "look, I mean, you got to tell me
what you want, then, right? Because I don't know."

"Where is this guy?" Mitch said.

"Quincy," Cogan said. "Wollaston, actually."

"I don't know where the fuck that is," Mitch said.

"I can show you," Cogan said.

"But he knows you," Mitch said. "Great. Look, this other guy, the one you're doing?"

"Yeah," Cogan said.

"Do him," Mitch said, "and the way I get it, that's gonna do something to the guy I'm supposed to hit."

"Got to," Cogan said.

"Gonna make him relax, or something," Mitch said.

"I think," Cogan said.

"Okay, then," Mitch said. "So, we got to give him a chance to relax then, haven't we? And you got to get me somebody that can drive a car without running into things, and also you got to get me something. You haven't got anything yet, I assume."

"I was gonna ask you what you wanted," Cogan said.

"Good," Mitch said, "forty-five Military Police. I never use nothing else."

"Okay," Cogan said.

"If you're the guy that's starting it," Mitch said, "it's a great thing. One of them. And a guy that can do things. How long's that gonna take you?"

"Day or so," Cogan said.

"And a car," Mitch said.

"Still a day or so," Cogan said.

"And where he's gonna be," Mitch said.

"Same thing," Cogan said.

"You know something?" Mitch said. "I don't think you can do it that fast."

"I can," Cogan said.

"Well," Mitch said, "then I think you're not gonna and I don't care if you can or not. Now, this's, we're gonna do this, this is Thursday. We're gonna do him Saturday night. That's when we're gonna do it. You guys're all half-assed up here. You don't take the time to think about things. I do."

"Always glad to meet a guy, you can learn something from," Cogan said.

"I been at this a long time," Mitch said. "I messed up some things, but never one of these. Now, that leaves me tonight and tomorrow night. Who's gonna see me tonight?"

"I can't promise nothing special," Cogan said.

"Don't like fuckin', is that it?" Mitch said.

"Never paid for it, anyway," Cogan said.

"Well, company's what I want," Mitch said. "You get me some company for tonight. I'll take it from there. Fourteen-o-nine. I'm in the tower, all right?"

"That," Cogan said, "I'll do the best I can for you. That's something you're gonna have to decide."

12

"HE'S NOT WALKING RIGHT," Gill said. He wore a dark blue tanker jacket and sat opposite Cogan in the Hayes Bickford across the street from the Lobster Tail.

"Of course he's not walking right," Cogan said. "He's hurt. He's all beat to shit."

"It takes him a long time to do something," Gill said. "I seen him, he was getting out of his car. It takes him a long time."

"He's all taped up," Cogan said.

"He's sure slow," Gill said.

"He don't feel good," Cogan said. "You wouldn't feel good, either."

"What're we gonna do, Jack?" Gill said.

"You're gonna drive the car," Cogan said. "Never mind thinking about what I'm gonna do. You just think about what you're gonna do."

"I'm gonna get some money," Gill said.

"Five hundred," Cogan said, "same as always, five hundred. You don't fuck anything up."

"I ever fuck anything up with you?" Kenny said.

"Kenny," Cogan said, "the world's full of guys that never fucked up, and then they did something and they fucked up once and they're doing time. So this's no night to start, not when I'm with you. What'd you get for a car?"

"Olds," Gill said. "Last year's Four-four-two. Nice car."

"Don't get attached to it," Cogan said. "You got everything in it, I gave you?"

"Sure," Gill said.

"The way I gave it to you and all," Cogan said.

"Yeah," Gill said.

"Okay," Cogan said, "all you gotta do is, you got to drive."

"Who is this guy?" Gill said.

"Don't matter," Cogan said.

"No," Gill said, "I mean, really. Who is this guy? This the guy Steve and Barry beat up?"

"Kenny," Cogan said.

"I didn't mean nothing," Gill said. "I was just wondering. I was, there was this guy, really got beat up, he was running a card game. And this guy, he's hurt, I was wondering if it was the same guy."

"Who told you about the guy with the card game, Kenny," Cogan said.

"Jack," Gill said, "like I said, I was just wondering. I didn't mean nothing. What'd he do with the card game?"

"He had a couple guys come in and knock it over," Cogan said.

"Oh," Gill said. "See, well, I couldn't understand it. Steve and Barry."

"You figured I should've asked you," Cogan said.

"I could've used the money, Jack," Gill said.

"You can always use the money," Cogan said. "Thing of it is, and I didn't ask them, incidentally, you got that?"

"Sure," Gill said.

"The thing needed two guys," Cogan said. "That's why you didn't get called."

"I could've got another guy," Gill said. "I could've got the guy I had with me onna dogs."

"Uh huh," Cogan said, "well, okay, Kenny. Next time I need two guys, I'll call you."

"He would've been all right," Kenny said. "He's a good guy. Only, I don't think he's gonna hang around much now."

"Okay, Kenny," Cogan said, "you just keep things in mind, I need two guys some time, I'll maybe call you first and if you can get me a guy, I'll use you. Okay?"

"Okay," Kenny said. "See, I was just thinking, was all, Jack."

"That's your weak spot, Kenny," Cogan said. "Never mind it. Just do like I tell you, everything'll be all right."

"Does he know?" Gill said.

"Nah," Cogan said, "he oughta, but he probably doesn't. I don't think so, no."

Wearing a gray and red tattersall coat, Mark Trattman, his hands in his pockets, emerged from the Lobster Tail alone. The attendant in the snorkel coat started walking down the street.

"Son of a bitch," Cogan said. "Didn't score tonight for a change."

"He was drinking his drink through them little plastic things you're supposed to steer them with," Gill said. "Those little green and white things."

"Yeah," Cogan said. He set his coffee cup down. "Where's the fuckin' car?"

"Around the side," Gill said. "I thought you said—"

"Never mind what you thought I said," Cogan said. "Move your big dumb ass. The guy's going home."

"I don't get it," Gill said.

"Neither's he, tonight," Cogan said. "Never again, either. Come on, for Christ sake, we're gonna get home early for a change."

The yellow 4-4-2 trailed Trattman's tan Coupe de Ville through eight consecutive green lights on Commonwealth Avenue, westbound. Cogan rode in the back, sitting behind the driver's seat. He kept his hands down, out of sight.

"Jesus," Gill said, "he's pretty good at this. He hits them all, just's they turn."

"He knows the speed," Cogan said. "They're set for nineteen or twenty miles an hour, I think it is. Something like that. He does it all the time, for Christ sake. He oughta."

"Jack," Gill said, "what if, what if he hasn't gotta stop?"

"We'll take him home and put him to fuckin' bed then," Cogan said. "Just keep after him, Kenny, and remember what I told you about thinking. Don't worry about nothing. Just you change lanes now and then and everything'll be all right."

On the long hill at the synagogue, the Cadillac swung into the right lane and the brake lights came on as it approached the intersection of Chestnut Hill Avenue. The traffic light was red. A streetcar moved west toward Lake Street beyond the intersection.

"Middle lane, Kenny," Cogan said. "There's three lanes, it goes to three lanes up here. Take the middle." He began to straighten up in the back seat. He leaned over and cranked down the right rear passenger window with his left hand.

The 4-4-2 approached the Cadillac quickly off the left rear.

"Right up even," Cogan said, "nice and smooth."

The traffic light remained red. There were no other cars. The traffic lights on Chestnut Hill Avenue turned yellow.

"Right up next to him," Cogan said. "Then a little bit ahead. Put me right next to him, Kenny. Atta boy."

Gill stopped the 4-4-2 with the open right rear

window even with the driver's window of the Cadillac. Trattman looked lazily at the car. He looked back at the traffic light.

Cogan ran the 30–06 Savage semi-automatic rifle out the rear window of the 4–4–2 and fired five times. The first bullet crazed Trattman's window. Trattman lurched off to the right and was snubbed up abruptly. Cogan said: "Good for you, Markie, always wear your seat belt."

The Cadillac started to creep forward as Cogan finished firing, Trattman bent forward at an angle over the passenger seat. When Gill swung the 4–4–2 left on Chestnut Hill Avenue, the Cadillac was halfway across; it ran up against the curbstone as the lights in the apartments at the intersection started to come on.

13

RUSSELL, CARRYING A BROWN-PAPER BAG, came out of the Arlington Street MBTA station just before six o'clock and turned off Arlington at St. James. At the newsstand on the corner the old man was cutting wire on bundles of the *Globe*. Two men in business suits waited in a light green Ford sedan at the newsstand, the passenger with his head and left hand out of the window, offering change. The driver watched Russell turn right on St. James. Holding the microphone in his right hand, the driver spoke into it: "All units, this is unit three. He finally made it."

Russell crossed the street, pausing for a Greyhound bus to pull into the terminal parking lot, in from Bangor. The driver of the third Yellow Cab in line at the terminal spoke into his microphone: "Unit four to all units. I got him now. He's on the sidewalk. He's about to enter the station."

The light green Ford started moving toward the next intersection. It turned right at Stuart Street and went the wrong way up behind the terminal.

In the station a man in a light blue private security force uniform stood at the top of the stairs, his back to the doors, watching the reflection of the entrance doors in the glass of the windows of the lounge. He wore a hearing aid button in his right ear.

Russell came through the doors, into the terminal.

The man in the light blue suit bent his neck to the left and talked out of the left side of his mouth into the small rectangular bulge in his uniform shirt. "This is unit seven. All units converge."

The two men in business suits left the light green Ford and went to the doors of the terminal on the easterly side. The driver got out of the cab and went to the door on the westerly side. Four men got out of a blue Dodge Polara in front of the terminal. Two moved to the front of the terminal. One went to join the cab driver on the westerly side. One joined the men from the light green Ford on the easterly side. Two baggage handlers, each wearing a hearing aid button, stepped back from the baggage check-in and stood near the doors at the back of the terminal. One of the ticket sellers, in a white shirt, stepped out from behind the counter, moving slowly.

Russell paused to let the ticket seller walk in front of him. The ticket seller roused a drunk, asleep on the bench. He began to usher the drunk toward the easterly doors. After Russell had his back to them, the drunk required less assistance.

Russell went to the baggage lockers on the westerly side of the terminal.

The man in the security force uniform watched from the top of the stairs. He spoke again. "Unit seven to all units. West side, west side."

Russell inserted the key to locker 352 and turned it.

The men from the light green Ford entered the terminal through the easterly doors.

Russell opened the locker and took out a box wrapped in brown paper. He opened the bag and put the box in. Leaving the locker door ajar, he turned toward the front of the terminal. He carried the bag in his left hand.

The driver of the cab entered through the westerly door. The two men in the baggage room went out into the passenger area of the terminal. The men from the Polara came in through the front doors and the man in the security force uniform turned slowly away from the front doors as Russell approached them.

The men from the light green Ford walked up behind Russell, one on each side. When they were half a pace behind him, they took him firmly by the elbows. Russell's body sagged.

The man on Russell's right said: "Bureau Narcotics. You're under arrest." He had a chrome-plated forty-five automatic in his right hand. He stuck the barrel close to Russell's face.

The man on Russell's left had handcuffs in his left hand. He stepped backward without letting go of Russell's arm and swung it behind Russell. He locked one cuff on Russell's left wrist and took the bag from him. He pulled Russell's right arm back and locked the wrist into the cuff. He patted Russell down. He shook his head.

The man with the automatic said: "You're pretty fuckin' obvious, my friend. Matter of fact, you're so fuckin' obvious I was afraid you'd forget where you left the stuff, or lose the key or something. *You've* got a right to remain silent. Anything you say can and *will* be used against you at a trial in a fuckin' court of law. You got a right to an *attorney*, and if you can't *afford* an attorney, us long-suffering good and noble taxpayers'll go out and treat you to the best fuckin' shyster we can find. I think you also got a right to have your head tested, and in your case, I think you oughta, see if there's anything in it at all."

"I wanna make my phone call," Russell said. The agents urged him toward the door.

"They got a real nice phone in the Marshal's office, my friend," the agent said. "It's a great little instrument. You can call any place in the country on it. That's if you know how to dial. If you don't know how to dial, we'll teach you how to do it. If you call long distance, we'll put it on your bill."

"Thanks," Russell said.

"Buddy," the agent said, "don't thank me. I think you're gonna be surprised when you get that bill. You're goin' in for all day on this one, my friend. Unless of course your friend down there in New York figured out how stupid you really are, and sold you quinine or something. All's well that ends well, right, my friend?"

"Shut up," Russell said.

The agents escorted Russell out of the terminal, into the darkness.

"That's not one of your rights, my friend," the agent said. "That's one of my rights. But I got a little deal for you, all right, my friend? Any time you wanna talk, just tell me, and I'll shut up. Just say the word and you have got the fuckin' floor."

"Fuck you," Russell said.

The Polara made a U-turn on St. James and pulled up in front of the terminal.

The agent dug the barrel of the automatic into Russell's rib cage. "That, my friend," he said in a soft voice, "is not the kind of talk I meant. People've been known to fall down a lot getting in and out of cars and so forth when they talk like that. Got it?" Russell said nothing. "And another thing, my friend," the agent said. "Not only are you stupid but you stink. I think you're gonna get twenty years and a bath. I dunno which you need more."

14

"THE STUPID SHIT," Frankie said. He sat in Amato's office. "You know who he picks to call, of course. Me. Only he don't remember I moved, so he calls Sandy, and he got her up and she's all pissed and she calls me and give me a whole ration of shit and then I got to call him and I hadda girl with me. And of course I got to give my name to them, they won't let anybody else talk to him."

"That's good," Amato said.

"Yeah," Frankie said. "Oh, I'm gonna really enjoy this, I can tell. Wants me to come down and see him. 'Yeah,' I said, 'sure, Russell, and I won't have a hundred ballbusters following me around for the rest of my life if I do that, either. No thanks. I didn't have nothing to do with it and I told you what was gonna happen and you wouldn't listen to me.'

" 'Did you tell them?' he says to me," Frankie said. " 'Are you the fuckin' bastard that told them?'

" 'Russell,' I said," Frankie said, " 'nobody hadda tell them. You told them yourself. What am I gonna tell cops anything for? Tell me that, huh? You wanna blame somebody, blame yourself.' That calmed him down some. Well, will I make bail for him? 'Depends,' I said. See, he hasn't got no money left. Spent it on his problem, which I don't think they're probably gonna let him go out and sell, now. 'What's the bail?' Just what you'd expect, his record and a pound of that stuff. One hundred thousand dollars."

"Ten K from you," Amato said.

"Well," Frankie said, "there's guys that'll write one

for five per cent if you wanna handle some things for them now and then, but onna guy like him I doubt you could get it even from one of them. But either way, it's too much, and besides, I tell him, 'Keep in mind, I just got out of the can myself. Where'd I get all that bread?' No, I said I'd call somebody for him, but that's all, he can make his own deal. 'You ask me,' I said, 'I don't even think that's gonna do it for you, though. You raise the hundred, they'll go to double surety or two hundred or something. Those guys aren't gonna let you out. Forget it.'

"So that's what he tells me," Frankie said, "and then he says: 'Frankie, if I don't get out of here, I'm gonna tell them you were in it with me.' "

"Nice guy," Amato said.

"Ah," Frankie said, "he was all pissed off. I don't blame him. And what the fuck's he gonna tell them? I said: 'Russell, get off the pot, all right? You bring me into this, I'll tell them everything you told me about Goat-ass stealing that other stuff, and all the dogs and the insurance thing you had with Kenny onna car and everything. So don't hand me that shit.' He'll be all right. It's just, he's looking at a lot of time. You can't blame him. I asked a guy, he said his guess is, probably eight, ten, something like that. So naturally that means, they probably told him guys've been getting fifteen or so, maybe more.

"Them guys," Frankie said, "I mean, they are *bad*. This kid I talked to, he said they come at you from just about every place at once. 'They tell you,' he said, 'you don't have to say nothing to them. But that sure don't stop them from saying something to you. They toss you in New York,' he said, 'it's gonna take them, always, three or four hours, before you can see a judge, and all the time they're *talking* to you. I think them guys've got cassettes in them. "You're a lost dude this time. You're gonna go in and you're never gonna come out again. You're crazy, that's all. We know you're not in it alone. You better talk about it." ' So, he was probably pissing his pants when he called me. So I told him: 'Russell, I tell you what: I'll get you a lawyer. That's all I can do for you.' "

"The fuck's a lawyer gonna do for him?" Amato said.

"He's gonna do it for me," Frankie said. "He's gonna get Russell off my back. He wanted Mike Zinna."

"I doubt if you can get him Mike," Amato said. "I doubt if Mike'll touch him."

"Oh, for Christ sake," Frankie said. "Of course I can't get him Mike. I can't afford Mike, I couldn't get Mike for myself. And Mike, Mike couldn't do nothing for him. What's he gonna do, the guy's alone and he's got it in his hands? Make it disappear? What Russell really needs is a magician. No, I got him Toby."

"I dunno Toby," Amato said.

"That's because you never had nothing to do with junk," Frankie said. "When they grab you with the junk, you call Toby and you pay him no more'n a grand and he gets you as good a deal as anybody could. The cops all know him. He's cheap and all the good anybody can do for Russell, Toby'll do it, and without going all ape-shit and telling the guy to give them the names of everybody he ever saw.

"Added to which," Frankie said, "there's certain things Toby won't do, and that's good for me. Because Russell's gonna want something else, I figure."

"Somebody hit the guy he thinks put him in," Amato said.

"Right," Frankie said. "So, all right, I'm a bastard,

but there's no way inna world he's gonna be able, get
Toby to tell me that, and I'm not personally gonna go
down and see him."

"Where is he?" Amato said.

"Charles Street," Frankie said.

"You'll get the message, then," Amato said.

"I don't object to hearing it," Frankie said. "You hear
it, you can always say, well, what the fuck, I wouldn't
go around and do something like that on what I heard.
No, if the guy asked me, I'd have to tell him something,
I guess, and I don't wanna do that, you know? I like
Russell. He was all right to me, and I told him, not to
do this. But shit, Goat-ass just did what he wanted, he
went out and stole four pounds of procaine or something like that, and I suppose some fuckin' cop was
bright enough, starts wondering who wants pounds of
that stuff and that was it for Russell. Goat-ass didn't do
anything. And besides, who the fuck am I? I didn't, I
don't know anybody."

"I see where Trattman knows a couple guys or so,
though," Amato said.

"That poor bastard," Frankie said.

"Well," Amato said, "I mean, it wasn't like, you didn't
expect it or something."

"Sure," Frankie said. "But, you know, when it didn't
happen, and Russell was telling me all that stuff there,
then I was scared shitless, it wasn't gonna happen. I
thought it was gonna happen to me. That don't mean,
well, yeah, I'm glad it happened to him. But, I still
wish it didn't even happen to him, you know? Didn't
have to. Like Russell. I knew this was gonna happen
to Russell. I told him. But the fuck, I know the guy.
And I can't do nothing to help him. I don't know anybody."

"He took his chances," Amato said.

"Sure," Frankie said, "and now he's gonna take his time. And you're taking your chances and I'm taking my chances and we're gonna do this thing, sooner or later, and probably they're not gonna get us this time, either. But I was thinking about it, right? Suppose, me and Dean go in the place, all of a sudden we got all kinds of cops around. Who do I call? Who do I call, that's not gonna give me the same kind of shit I give Russell? You know why Russell called me? Because, who else's he got to call? And it's the same thing. If we get grabbed in there, Dean calls Sandy. And what do I do? Have him tell her, get me somebody too? I can't call you, for Christ sake. They'd be waiting for that. I, we haven't got no friends, either. You look at it, you and me and Russell're in exactly the same position, except he's in it now and we're not in it yet."

"Well, Jesus," Amato said, "I mean, this was your idea and everything. It isn't like, I came around and saw you on this one. Shit, you're afraid of it, forget it. Won't piss me off any. I just went down there and did, I did what you wanted. I haven't got no invest-ment in this. I made almost four thousand yesterday alone. I can do without it."

"Won for a change," Frankie said.

"Yeah," Amato said, "I kind of liked it too. Broke even about, the first part of the week. I got fifteen hun-dred or so Thursday after and then last night, another twenty-five onna Knicks. Knicks're gonna take it, this time."

"Yeah," Frankie said. "John, you told me it was gonna snow in the winter, I'd go out and bet against it, you know that?"

"Nice when you win, though," Amato said. "I figure,

after what I been through, I'm gonna be winning pretty good when I start."

"I figure," Frankie said, "I'm never gonna start. I'm gonna stick to things I can figure out."

"Well," Amato said, "what is it, then?"

"How does it look?" Frankie said.

"It looks good to me," Amato said. "It's nice and dark, they backed the block up to where they put the fill and there's a lot of brush and stuff there and signs on the roof that'll cover you when you're up on the roof. It's brick in front, which don't matter, and it's cinderblock in back. The roof's flat. Looks like tar and pebbles, some kind of cheap shit. I'd go in through the roof. There's a grocery store on one side and a place that sells glasses on the other side and I suppose you could go in through there. But I wouldn't. I'd go the roof. The guys in there in the daytimes're those dopes from Northeast Protective that couldn't see a hockey game in Boston Garden. The cops, I didn't do the cops yet. Northeast always works on two, three hour schedules because they don't hire enough guys. But if you don't want to do it, it's okay."

"John," Frankie said, "it's not this job. That's what I'm trying to tell you. It's not this one and it's not gonna be the next one, either, that's giving me the yikes. It's just, ah, shit, I dunno what it is. I don't like having guys after me, you know? I don't care who they're working for, I don't like having guys after me."

15

THE BLACK GIRL, lanky, arched her spine and bent her arms behind her to fasten her bra.

"The first one?" Mitch said. "She wasn't bad. She wasn't good but she wasn't bad, either. She was all right. Seemed like she was in an awful hurry, though."

"Well, after all," Cogan said, "it was probably pretty short notice for her and all."

The black girl adjusted her breasts in the bra cups. Then she walked up behind Cogan's chair on the apricot rug and used the heel of her left hand to touch his right shoulder. "My dress, honey," she said, "you're sittin' on my dress." Cogan moved forward without turning his head. The black girl pulled the white dress out from under him. She put it on over her head, her feet splayed on the rug.

"Shit," Mitch said, "its not that. It's the same thing as it is with everything else. Nobody does anything right any more."

Cogan laughed.

"I mean it," Mitch said. He picked up the glass on the end table next to his chair. "This's empty," he said, looking at it. "Want one?"

"Too early for me," Cogan said.

"Early?" Mitch said. He stood up in his tee shirt and shorts. "After noon."

"Still too early," Cogan said. "You go ahead if you want, though."

"I'm gonna," Mitch said. He went into the bathroom.

The black girl arched her back again to zip the dress.

"Honey," she said, walking around in front of Cogan and stooping, back-to, "could you zip me up?"

"No," Cogan said.

Mitch ran water in the bathroom. "Screwing's no different'n anything else," he said.

"You bastard," she said, straightening up. She turned and looked at Cogan. "I thought you were kidding."

"I never kid," Cogan said. He inclined his head toward the bathroom. "Get your trick to do it."

Mitch came out of the bathroom, the glass full of dark Scotch and water. "Nobody gives a good shit any more," he said. "You ask somebody to do something and you're willing to pay for it, and they say they'll do it and then they about half do it."

The girl backed up to Mitch. "Zip my dress, honey," she said. "Your nice friend there wouldn't do it."

Mitch zipped the dress. "They still want all the money, though, bet your ass on that. No half money, no sir. All the money." He went back to the chair, sipping from the glass. "Half the job. Pisses me off."

The black girl sat down on the bed and put on her red shoes.

"For a guy that's been having himself a regular party for three days or so," Cogan said, "you sure bitch and moan a lot."

"I've been paying for it," Mitch said. "I been paying for it myself. I can bitch about it if I want. You know this broad, this Polly?"

The black girl stood up and straightened her dress. She looked at Mitch. "Honey?"

"Onna bureau," Mitch said. He drank. "Wallet's onna bureau."

The black girl walked across the room, rotating her hips.

"Everybody knows Polly," Cogan said.

"That's what the broad you sent up said," Mitch said. The black girl picked up the wallet.

"There's a hundred and seventy-three bucks in that," Mitch said. "When I get up I wanna find a hundred and forty-eight, got that?"

"*Oh*-kay," the girl said. She removed currency, counted it and put some back in the wallet. She put the wallet down. She picked up the shiny red shoulder bag from the bureau, opened it and put the money in. "No tip, Honey?" she said.

"No tip," Mitch said.

"Because you know, Honey," she said, "I got to give all this to my man. Girl needs something for herself now and then."

"No tip," Mitch said.

"You're the original sport," Cogan said.

"Fuck her," Mitch said. He drank again. "This's afternoon. She's, this one's gravy, right, *Honey?*"

"It's better'n filing," the girl said.

"I wouldn't know about that," Mitch said. "I never did no filing."

The girl walked toward the door. "Well," she said, "it's not *much* better'n filing, some times. But it's, it's *mostly* better. Some times, you know, you get an old guy, and then it's just faster." She opened the door.

"You know, Honey," Mitch said, "some day some old bastard you just milked, he might decide to carve you up some, talking like that. How'd you like that?"

"Jesus," the girl said in the doorway, "I don't *know*. You think I'd *come?*"

"If you could, you might," Mitch said. "Probably not, is what I think."

"Fuck you," the girl said closing the door.

"Which," Mitch said, "is pretty much what I had in mind when I had her come up here. Christ you got some funny gash in Boston. I hadda practically talk her into it. That Polly, there? Same thing. Nothing but french. 'For Christ sake,' I say, 'I wanna get laid. Isn't that what you do?'"

"No, it's not," Cogan said. "Any guy you asked could've told you that. *I* could've told you that."

"You didn't, though," Mitch said.

"Well, you didn't ask me," Cogan said. "Wasn't me that had her come up here. That broad I sent, she was all right, I assume? The guy said she's all right."

"No more'n that," Mitch said. "I couldn't get over it. I said to her: 'Whaddaya mean, french? I happen to like fucking. Who's hiring who, here?' Didn't make no difference at all. You can feel her up, you can finger-fuck her, but you can't fuck her. For Christ sake. A fuckin' blow job."

"It's supposed to be a great blow job," Cogan said.

"When you wanna get laid," Mitch said, "there's no such thing as a great blow job. She's telling me, guys spend two, three hundred a night for what she does. Is that true?"

"I guess it used to be," Cogan said.

"Yeah," Mitch said, "well, you know what I think? I think you're all nuts, letting broads get away with that."

"She's supposed to be afraid of the clap," Cogan said.

"Yeah," Mitch said, "well, okay. That line of work, I don't think you oughta be able to say like that, but I didn't have no luck with her. She, she still didn't fuck anybody that I could tell you about. Her teeth fall out, boy, she's gonna be the hit of the world. But not me. You know something? I'll tell you something." Mitch finished his drink. "I haven't had a real piece of ass since I was in Florida."

"That was one fine-lookin' broad you had down there," Cogan said.

"Sunny," Mitch said. "That was Sunny. I suppose you fucked her too, after I was gone."

"Mitch," Cogan said, "when me and Dillon got there that night, she was with you. When we left, you're still there and, wasn't she still with you? You're there, what was it?"

"Three weeks," Mitch said.

"Three weeks," Cogan said. "And I was there five days, inna middle. How the fuck'm I gonna do that?"

"I dunno," Mitch said. He picked up the glass. "Empty again." He got up. "Sure you won't join me?"

"Not late enough yet, either," Cogan said.

Mitch went into the bathroom. Cogan heard ice go into the glass. He did not hear water running. "Sammy did it," Mitch said from the bathroom.

"The guy from Detroit," Cogan said. "Sharp-looking little ginzo."

"Sammy's Jewish," Mitch said.

"Okay," Cogan said. "I didn't mean anything."

"No trouble," Mitch said. "He looks like a ginzo. I wished he was. But he's Jewish. All the years I known that guy, he still did it. The son of a bitch."

Cogan heard water running in the bathroom. Mitch emerged with a dark Scotch and water. He was wiping his mouth with the back of his left hand. "It's my own stupid fault," he said. "The night before I'm leaving, we're having dinner and he comes over, I introduce them and everything. I don't know why this bothers me, you know that?"

"No," Cogan said.

Mitch sat down. He put the glass on the end table. "I mean, I know. When I'm there, I'm there and she's with me. When I leave, you're there, and she's with you."

"She wasn't with me," Cogan said.

"I didn't mean you," Mitch said. "I mean: any guy. Anybody that's there, she's with him. You leave, she's not with you any more."

"Oh," Cogan said.

"See," Mitch said, "that's what I mean. I know that. I give her, well, last year, I'm down there, I was only there two weeks. No, three weeks. Anyway, that's how many nights?"

"Twenty-one," Cogan said.

"No," Mitch said, "ah, anyway, I had her all signed up. It was fourteen nights. You know what that cost me? Three thousand dollars."

"Now," Cogan said, "that really oughta do it. I wouldn't pay no broad three thousand to do anything. I wouldn't care what she could do. I wouldn't pay it."

"I didn't care," Mitch said. "I was still with the union then, and the guys that had the jobs, they were always very nice to me. You didn't have no wildcats or anything, well, see what I mean? I didn't care. So it's a lot. I'm not in *love* with the girl, right? I only give her for when I'm there."

"She's still a great-looking girl, though," Cogan said.

"She is," Mitch said. "That fuckin' Sammy. The night you saw her, what'd she have on?"

"Tell you the truth," Cogan said, "I didn't notice what she was wearing, so much's what she was wearing it on. Some yellow thing or something. You could see quite a lot."

"There's quite a lot to see," Mitch said. "The night

Sammy comes by, right? She's got this gray thing on. It's like silk, and it's gray, and there isn't any back on it and she's got these mammoth tits, she's really something. I could've beat up five guys with the horn I had on, and I, I had her all them other nights, right? So Sammy comes up and I introduce them, and how long am I there for and how long's he there for, and I'm not really paying attention or anything, we're having some wine and so I asked him to sit down. And pretty soon I got to go to the Men's. So I go, and I'm gone a pretty long time, because I got this huge prong on and I gotta practically stand on my head if I wanna piss in the hopper and not in my own fuckin' mouth, and still, I wanna be careful with it, you know? It was really big. I don't think I could've blinked. I don't think I had no skin left. She's good, Sunny's good about that. Sunny can't get you up, you're probably dead. But this's the last time, and she's not gonna have to. Because I'm all ready to go, I can ever get through dinner. My friend, I don't care what you say, I seen every kind of ass there is, you know that?"

"You've seen it this week," Cogan said. "You been here, what, three days, what I hear you had a look at most of the ass there is in Boston."

"I like it," Mitch said. "That's what it is, I like it. It's like, it's a hobby with me, you know? I never do nothing when I'm home. Nothing. But that's why, I go the races. Once a year, I go to the races, and I get laid. Only this year, probably I'm not goin' the races."

"I couldn't do it," Cogan said. "I'd get all fucked out. You, I think you're probably in good shape. I wouldn't, I couldn't fuck for three days, is all. I couldn't do it."

"I was your age," Mitch said, "I felt exactly the same way."

"Sure," Cogan said. "I got work I got to do."

Mitch drank from the glass. "I used to think the same way," he said. "Then, I dunno *when* it happened, I dunno *why* it happened. I just started doing it. I went down there, the very first time I went down there, I got the suite. I was having a terrible time with Margie, and she finds out about it and she's giving me all kinds of hell about it, you asked her and she'd tell you she drinks because I go down there. Well, it was her or me. But I can tell you, boy, you want ass, get yourself a, there's no ass inna whole wide world like a young Jewish girl that's hookin'."

"I'll keep it in mind," Cogan said.

"That broad," Mitch said, "she was in Oberlin, she was in college, right? And she quit. Whaddaya think of that?" He drank.

"You're gonna be all right," Cogan said, "tomorrow or the next night?"

"I'm all right, right now," Mitch said. "Christ sake. Lemme alone, willya? Well, she quit. And she took up hookin'. Now you get a broad like that, they really go right to work on it, you know? And they get so, they really know their fuckin' business. That broad, Sunny, she's not, she isn't half my wife's age and she knew things which, if Margie knew them she'd go down the station and turn herself in. She really would.

"So, I come back the table," Mitch said. "I finally get rid of that wine without pissing on my own fuckin' chin and they're both there and Sammy's being very polite and all, and finally he leaves and then we finish and I thought to fuckin' God, I can pole-vault up to the room with just what I got of my own, and we go up there and I want to tell you, three thousand bucks, it's not cheap and I don't care whether you got it or not, it's fuckin' expensive, but it's worth it, it was honestly worth it. I give her three for the whole time and that night alone, it was worth it all. Only, I don't tell *her* that, of course."

"Mitch," Cogan said.

"So the next day I get up," Mitch said. "I also get up, but I hadda twelve-thirty plane so it's just a quickie. Just a quickie with Sunny's about nine times better'n a whole fuckin' date with another broad. And then I go down and I get some steam, and I come back up and I got to give her the rest of the money. See, you give them half when you get there and then when you're through, down there, you give them the rest. So I say, I tell her, I really appreciate it, I know what this means, all that time right out in one chunk and all. And she tells me, see, she's out of circulation and everything, she tells me: 'It's all right,' there isn't any problem, and I give her the money and everything, and she's leaving, and, well, she's gonna stay with Sammy the next two weeks and he's hitting her four for it. That cocksucker."

"Look," Cogan said, "this after, I'm supposed to meet a kid, all right? I think I got a guy that can take you around and all."

"I can't go out," Mitch said.

"I didn't mean fuckin' around," Cogan said. "You come up here to do something. For that. I was gonna talk to him and then if I'm satisfied, he can do something without having his brother hold his hand all the time, I was gonna bring him up here and talk about it with you."

"It's all right with me," Mitch said.

"Well," Cogan said, "I'm glad to hear that. Only, it's not all right with me. Because you're not gonna be able, be able to make it tonight, and I don't want this kid thinking about things too long, he's liable to go tell his brother."

"Aw right," Mitch said, "where the fuck is he? Get him up here and we'll set the guy up."

"You," Cogan said, "I'll tell you what you're gonna do, right? You're goin' to bed."

"I'm not tired," Mitch said.

"You sure as hell look tired to me," Cogan said. "You go to fuckin' bed. And, it's two-thirty now, you shit. I'm gonna call you at seven-thirty and I better wake you up, because if I don't, I'm gonna drop a dime on a couple cops I know and they'll take you back where you're supposed to be."

"Yeah," Mitch said.

"No ass," Cogan said, "no more booze, no nothing. You get yourself a shower and go to bed and I'll wake you up and tell you where you gotta be, right?"

"I don't take orders from shits like you," Mitch said.

16

THE DRIVER TURNED OFF the ignition of the silver Toronado and waited for Cogan to cross the trolley tracks behind Cronin's in Cambridge. When Cogan got in, the driver said: "You know, I hate to be a burden to anybody, but life'd be a whole lot easier for me if you could bring yourself to use a telephone now and then to talk about things. They've got pay phones now, anybody can use them. I bet I can even give you two or three numbers in Providence alone that're pay phones, and if you wanted to call me up and talk to me about something, all you'd have to do is call me up and say which one. This running back and forth every time somebody gets a runny nose's raising hell with me. My wife's sick and one of the kids's sick and my practice's going to hell, and that isn't even enough for you, one of the last good Saturdays we're likely to see in a long time I think, and I had to give up nine holes to come up here and talk to you. That's all I seem to do, lately, cancel appointments and drive up here to talk to you."

"You oughta talk to the man, Albert," Cogan said. "Sounds to me like you're the kind of man, deserves a raise. Tell him to get in touch with me. I'll put in a good word for you."

"You're all heart," the driver said. "Okay, I'm here. Let's have the latest bad news. What's messed up now?"

"Well," Cogan said, "we seem to have a little problem."

"We're not supposed to have any more little problems," the driver said, "no little problems at all. I've talked to him and we've done everything you asked. No problems at all, big or little. Tell me one thing you asked for, that we didn't go along with."

"Nothing," Cogan said. "Only, there's a couple things I didn't know."

"Tell me about it," the driver said.

"Mitch," Cogan said. "He can't do it. I had things pretty well lined up for tonight. I know where Amato's gonna be, and I'm pretty sure I can find out before dark where the kid that I'm sure of's going to be. But at least we had Amato lined up. We could do a double, if things went right, or we'd at least get the Squirrel and he's the big one anyway. But Mitch can't do it."

"You asked for him," the driver said. "You and Dillon both asked for him. You said you couldn't do it, and Dillon of course can't. We got you what you asked for."

"What I asked for," Cogan said, "was, I didn't know this, see? I wanted Mitch the way he was a year, a couple years ago. He's fuckin' worthless now."

"What's the matter with him?" the driver said.

"The first thing I heard about," Cogan said, "he's got this beef down in Maryland. He thinks he's gonna do a bit for it and he's scared of the bit because he thinks his wife's gonna dump him if he does. Which, from what he tells me, she is, and even if she wasn't, he hasn't got any idea he's gonna really enjoy doing the bit anyway."

"I don't see what that's got to do with this," the driver said.

"It don't seem to, at first," Cogan said, "except that he's not supposed to go any place but Maryland without getting permission, and naturally he didn't, come up here, so he's afraid to go out and he stays inna room all the time. Because they'll heave him in just for being here.

"Anyway," Cogan said, "he's staying inside and he's fucking everything that jumps."

"He said," the driver said, "when I told him you wanted Mitch, he said it was all right, but it might be the best idea if you could find some way to keep the fellow locked in the bathroom all the time he's here. Well, what is it? Won't he come out?"

"He'll come out if we want him to," Cogan said. "I don't think we do. When he landed here he wanted me to get him a broad, and I thought, what the fuck business is it of mine? I thought he wanted a broad. I called up a guy, guy got him a broad. Beautiful. But what he did was get that broad to give him the names of some other broads, and these aren't hookers in from Lawrence for the night, either. These're girls that see a lot of guys and talk to a lot of guys, and they all know he's in town by now, and that isn't gonna help us. This kid I sent around, I asked for one that's just getting started and doesn't know anybody from a pisshole in the snow. But he also found Polly, he tells me, and there isn't one guy in town doesn't know Polly, and this silly bastard hadda fight with her, for Christ sake. That girl talks to cops."

"Has he lost his mind?" the driver said.

"I think," Cogan said, "I think there's a limited amount of shit a guy can take, and Mitch went over his limit. When I met him he was drinking up a storm, and I said something to him and he told me, it scares the shit out of him when he's got to fly and he can't sleep the night before and he's got to get something in him so he can sleep. So, okay, and I could see there's a lot of things bothering him. Let the guy do what he wants.

"Well," Cogan said, "that was three days ago, and

what he didn't fuck in them three days, he drank. When I left him, he was drunk. Two-thirty in the afternoon, and he was finishing up a fight with another heavy cruiser he got from some place. Really drunk, talking and everything, he can't remember what year things happened, for Christ sake, and I chew him out for it and he's gonna go right out in his skivvies and do the job now. He won't shut up."

"Have you talked to Dillon?" the driver said. "Is Dillon well enough to talk to?"

"Told me he went out for a walk yesterday," Cogan said. "Said he's feeling much stronger, he had a good dinner last night and watched TV. Yeah. Dillon thinks what I think. This guy'll blow the whole thing if we don't do something. He'll get another broad and another jug up there, and if one of the ones he had already didn't get the word onna street, the next one will. We need that guy out of town yesterday, is what we need."

"Well," the driver said, "you invited him up here. Send him back."

"He wouldn't go," Cogan said. "He's hungry for the dough, said he really needs dough. Lost his job or something and everything. He wouldn't go if I told him. I don't think he'd do anything I told him, unless he was so drunk he couldn't think of anything else to do. Which he probably is."

"I can't get in touch with him today," the driver said.

"It's nothing like that," Cogan said. "What I got in mind, I'm gonna get him grabbed."

"Turn him in," the driver said. "Won't he talk?"

"If he thought it was me that did it, he might," Cogan said. "What I was thinking of, this guy I know, he's got this one broad that is tops at setting guys up. She gets in real fights with them, and they give her their fuckin'

teeth to get her out of the room before the cops come. I
was thinking of sending her up there, see, I told him, no
more ass, he's going to work, but he's so drunk he won't
remember whether he had somebody send her up or
not, and he'd take her if he didn't. Now, this hotel, they
don't exactly keep tabs on people, but it's a good place
and they're not gonna want no whore fights going on in
there, and he'll get busted for that and pretty soon
they'll revoke bail on him and back he'll go."

"Kind of rough on him," the driver said.

"Not actually," Cogan said. "Actually, I think it's
the best thing for him. He's gonna kill himself if he
does this much longer. He won't get enough potato
jack in the can to kill him, and if he's not in the can
he'll kill us."

"I suppose he really should talk to Mitch's people,"
the driver said.

"Albert," Cogan said, "how're they gonna know?"

"Ah," Albert said. "I can tell him, I suppose."

"If you want," Cogan said. "Let him make up his own
mind."

"Okay," the driver said, "do it. Now, that leaves us
with Amato."

"I come up with something, I think," Cogan said. "I
think I can set him up myself."

"I thought you couldn't," the driver said. "I thought
he knew you."

"He does," Cogan said. "He also knows the kid, one
of the kids he used on the job. And that kid, I bet, is
gonna know where Amato's gonna be, the next few
nights or so."

"Will he do it?" the driver said.

"I was waiting for you," Cogan said, "I started thinking. Yeah, I think I know a way."

"Will he be all right?" the driver said.

"Oh," Cogan said, "you can't tell."

"Well, it's serious, isn't it?" the driver said. "It's a serious question."

Cogan stared at the driver. "For a while," he said. "Not long, but a while. Talk to the man."

17

FRANKIE SAT at the first bar downstairs in the Carnaby Street, late in the afternoon. He leaned back on the bentwood stool and watched the waitresses chatting, idle until customers came.

Cogan hung the pilled suede coat on a peg and sat down next to Frankie. He ordered a beer.

"Heineken?" the bartender said.

"Yeah," Cogan said.

"Bottle or draft?" the bartender said.

"I don't give a shit," Cogan said. "Draft."

"They always do that," Frankie said.

"It's a pain in the ass," Cogan said. "I wouldn't've come in here, I thought I was gonna have to go through something like that."

The bartender put a frosted mug in front of Cogan.

"I would," Frankie said. "This guy, I dunno how he does it, he's got to have the best-built girls in Boston working for him. I come in here every day."

"I know," Cogan said.

Frankie looked at him. "I never seen you before in here," he said. "I don't know you."

"Didn't say you did," Cogan said. "Very few guys know me. I'm just a guy, is all. I never been in here before in my life."

"How'd you happen to come in today?" Frankie said.

"Looking for you," Cogan said. "I was looking for you and a guy told me, he said you told him you come in here a lot, 'round this time of day, see if you can get up nerve enough, talk to a girl. So I came in. Simple, huh?"

"Who's the guy?" Frankie said.

"Just a guy," Cogan said, "guy, a friend of yours, actually. Knows a little about you, told me where to look you up. Well, he didn't tell me himself. He told a guy, and the guy was up here and he told me. Because I asked the guy, this friend of yours."

"Who's this friend?" Frankie said.

"China," Cogan said.

"Never heard of nobody by that name," Frankie said. He finished his beer and started to straighten up.

Cogan put his right hand on Frankie's right arm. "China'll be surprised to hear that," he said, "very surprised. Here's a guy, concerned about you, your friends're concerned about you, you know that, Frankie? They're worried. Guys like China. China was really, he, well, he insisted I hadda go and talk to you, is what he did. I wasn't sure I oughta bother you, you know? Got yourself a place and everything? 'Sounds like he's doing all right to me,' is what I said. 'No reason I should go around and bother him.' You have got a place, haven't you, Frankie?"

"Yeah," Frankie said.

"Somewhere south of New Hampshire, I bet," Cogan said.

"Right onna peg," Frankie said.

"Norwood, to be exact," Cogan said. "Why'd you do that, alla them trucks?"

"I dunno," Frankie said.

"Now whyn't you relax a little, Frankie, okay?" Cogan said. "You know how it is when a guy, when China wants a guy to do something, you got to do it, is all, China's all down there, locked up and everything, he's gotta depend on his friends, do the right things for guys he's worried about. I'd be embarrassed in front of China, I hadda tell him, he ever found out, a guy he wanted me to talk to, I didn't talk to him. You know how China is."

Frankie leaned back again.

"Have another beer," Cogan said. "Look at the girls. Jesus, I dunno how you can stand the noise out there. Still, I suppose, guys got all kinds of reasons for doing things. Gotta car, too, I understand."

"Yeah," Frankie said.

"Lemme give you some advice, all right?" Cogan said.

Frankie did not answer.

"I had one of them things myself," Cogan said, "they first come out. You got the hood scoops, right?"

Frankie did not answer.

"Ah, come on," Cogan said, "you got the green Geetoh with the scoops. Don't fuck around with me, right?"

Frankie nodded.

"You're gonna have trouble with it," Cogan said, "couple months or so. January, when it gets cold. Fuckin' thing won't run. It'll start but it won't run. You can do anything you want to it, it won't run, and when it's really cold, down around seven, eight below, it won't start.

"Now lemme tell you what you got to do," Cogan said. "You got to pack them scoops. Mine just had the one, the split one in the middle. But, well, you got the two, I bet you're still gonna have the same trouble, the car just won't warm up. You're gonna have to pack them scoops. It's the scoops. Your engine can't get warm in that thing when it's cold unless you run it about ninety miles an hour the minute you get her going, and you do that, you're gonna bend a fuckin' valve, is all. What I used to do, I used to put masking tape right over them scoops. Looks like hell, but it works. Got that? Masking tape."

Frankie nodded.

"You see what I mean," Cogan said.

"Uh," Frankie said, "uh, no. No, I don't."

"Your friends," Cogan said. "Your friends're worried about you. See? I even heard, you're carrying."

"Fuck, no," Frankie said.

"Well," Cogan said, "now, that's good. Because, you wanna be careful about that. You, what, you been out a month?"

"Six weeks," Frankie said.

"Right," Cogan said. "Onna robbery thing, am I right?"

"Yeah," Frankie said.

"Well, there you are," Cogan said, "and that's why it's such a good thing, you're not carrying. You know how those guys are. They're gonna be measuring your dick every time somebody pulls a job looks anything like what you did. You think they don't know you're out?"

"Nope," Frankie said.

"And of course," Cogan said, "they're not gonna get nothing on you, because you're not doing nothing, am I right?"

"Just havin' a beer and watchin' the girls," Frankie said.

"Sure," Cogan said. "Nothing wrong with that..But, they pick you up, even though you didn't pull a job, you're carrying, they're gonna run you again."

"I know that," Frankie said.

"Well," Cogan said, "that's good. That shows, your friends that're worried about you, shows them you must've grown up some since you went in."

Frankie looked at Cogan. "Grown up some?" he said. "A dog'd get born and live and die in the time I was in."

"Well," Cogan said, "yeah, you're right. But, maybe even since you got out. Maybe you grown up some since then."

"Well," Frankie said, "I finally got laid."

"That's good," Cogan said. "How was it?"

"Not so good," Frankie said. "Matter of fact, it was kind of shitty. I naturally got some broad that's been fuckin' since they found out how to do it, and I naturally shot my mouth off all over the place and I got through and she told me I'm a lousy lay. I'm gonna keep at it, though. I figure, can't be too tough to get the hang of it, and there must be some reason, there's so many people running around doing it."

"That's the idea," Cogan said. He made a sucking noise with his tongue and his teeth. "Jesus," he said, "that's too bad. If I'd've only run into you sooner. I should've got on this right away, when I first get the word from China and them. I knew a guy could've helped you along that line. Really knew some great broads. But he's dead."

"Oh yeah?" Frankie said.

"Yeah," Cogan said. "It's too bad. You maybe saw it inna paper. Somebody whacked him out the other night. Markie Trattman. Nice guy. A real nice guy, and what that guy didn't know about getting broads, nobody knew."

"Must've fucked the wrong one, I guess," Frankie said.

"Yeah," Cogan said, "it was either that or something else. He got somebody pissed off, that's for sure. That's the way it is with most of them guys, I think, that get whacked. They get somebody pissed and then something happens. You got to be careful, these days. You do something, looks perfectly all right to you, and the right guy gets pissed off for no reason at all and you're in the shit. Look at China. How long you known China?"

"China?" Frankie said. "Ten years or so, I guess."

"Well," Cogan said, "that's long enough. Now there's a guy, you should've heard what they're saying about China, year or so ago."

"I did," Frankie said.

"Yeah," Cogan said, "and, knowing China, you got to know, it's not true. China'd eat shit before he'd talk to anybody. But the trouble is, some asshole gets it in his head that something's going on or something, and he starts spreading stuff around about China, and of course nobody asks any questions or does anything smart like that. They just talk and talk and talk and pretty soon China's getting all this static, and he wasn't even doing anything.

"Now," Cogan said, "China's a smart bastard. He's down there and he knows he's gotta see somebody and see them quick. So he gets himself a habe or something and they bring him up here and he gets a chance to get the word to a few guys and somebody got in to see him and he told him: 'Look, I'm gonna get a shiv up my ass if somebody doesn't start stopping all this talk and shit, you know? And, I'm not gonna stand still for that. If I gotta protect myself, I'm gonna have to go to somebody and start telling them things, and I don't want to do that, all right?' So the guy comes out and he puts it around and China's all right again with everybody. See, that's what I mean. China's a smart bastard, knows how to protect his ass. Markie, well, he knew a lot about broads, but I guess he didn't know nothing about protecting his ass."

"Kind of hard to cover your ass," Frankie said, "you

don't even know some guy's after you for dipping your wick. Kind of hard."

"Yeah," Cogan said, "but there's other things it could've been, it could've happened. Now Markie, Markie ran a game. And it got knocked over. You know that?"

"I think I heard something about it," Frankie said.

"Yeah," Cogan said. He drank his beer. To the bartender he said: "Lemme have another one." To Frankie he said: "Want another one?"

"I think I'm set," Frankie said.

"Right," Cogan said. He accepted the fresh mug and drank from it. "Good," he said, wiping his mouth. "Nothin' like a cold beer, I always say. Well, now, Trattman always ran that game, right? He had a game running ever since anybody can remember. And he had a game, went over before. He got robbed before. And you know something?" Cogan said. "It was actually Markie, had it knocked over."

"Maybe he did it again," Frankie said.

"There's a lot of silly shits that're running around, saying that," Cogan said. "I actually heard some of that talk myself. And it pissed me off. Because, Markie wasn't no particular friend of mine, you understand, I bet I didn't talk to him more'n once, twice, in my whole life. So, he gets himself in some kind of trouble, it's not up to me, go around and straighten him out. Who am I? Just a guy he knows. Why's he gonna listen to me? But since then, I thought, I should've. I really should've. Because there wasn't nothing to that talk and shit. Markie wouldn't do that again. He was way too smart for that. But see, that's what I mean. He hadda *know*, he hadda know the kind of talk that was going around, and he should've been smart enough, he heard some of it, like China, you know? Do something about it. So some silly shit don't decide he's gonna make himself all kinds of friends, all he's gotta do is whack Trattman out. It's a crazy fuckin' world.

"See, Frankie," Cogan said, turning slightly toward him, "I think that's what China and them think, your friends, that're worried about you. They think, well, they dunno how much you grown up, since you got out, even. They think you need somebody around, knows about things, advise you."

"Yeah," Frankie said.

"Teach you how to cover your ass," Cogan said. "See, like I was saying, it's not what you been doing so much's it is what guys think you been doing, and that's what you got to look out for, and when it happens, well, you got to be prepared to do something."

"Yeah," Frankie said.

"So," Cogan said in a lower voice, "where's he gonna be, tomorrow night?"

"Who?" Frankie said.

"Johnny Amato," Cogan said. "Tomorrow night. Where's he gonna be?"

"I dunno," Frankie said.

"Frank," Cogan said, "you got to keep in mind what I told you. Your friends're worried about you. You wanna finally get laid right, it's your friends, they wanna see you get the chance, you know what I mean? And it's your friends, wanna know where Squirrel's gonna be."

"This's the first time I seen you," Frankie said.

"New friends're best," Cogan said. "Your other one, there, you can't depend on him, you know? Look at what he got you in before. All that time. You could've been out getting a decent piece of ass, 'stead of pounding sand up yours and everything."

"I don't know who the fuck you are," Frankie said.

"Very few guys do," Cogan said. "Oh, China, maybe, and, oh yeah: Dillon. Dillon knows me. You're, you strike me as a pretty intelligent guy. Want me to call Dillon for you, and you can talk to him, see who I am? There's not much to find out, I can tell you that. But you can talk to him. Wanna talk to Dillon?"

"No," Frankie said.

"Well okay," Cogan said. "Where's he gonna be? I know you're gonna know, if you don't know now."

"I haven't got no idea," Frankie said. "I seen John three or four times since I got out. I don't know what he does, nights. Goes home, I guess."

"Okay," Cogan said. He finished his beer. "See you around, Frankie, my friend." He started to get off the stool.

"Wait a minute," Frankie said.

"There's things," Cogan said, "there's things that won't wait. You tell me, you don't know. Okay, I accept that. But I got something to do. I got to find a guy that knows."

"Where John's gonna be tomorrow night," Frankie said.

"And something else now, I guess," Cogan said. "Like where you're gonna be, the day after. You gonna be here again? Gonna come in about three-thirty, drink about four beers, hang around until you eat, leave and go up Pagliacci's like you always do, see what's still breathing enough to fuck, go home around midnight, one o'clock? That what you're gonna be doing day after tomorrow? Or are you gonna be doing something else, so it takes me a couple, three days extra? It's not gonna matter. You could just save me a lot of time, is all."

Frankie said nothing.

Cogan got off the stool. He rested his forearms on the back of it. "Look," he said, "you gotta be realistic, right, kid? You gotta be. I know the guy. I also know what's goin' through your head. He's, you think he's a friend of yours, right? You probably, you probably got something lined up with him right now, am I right?"

Frankie did not answer.

"It don't matter," Cogan said. "I know how you feel. But you think, I bet you figured, that Trattman thing, it was gonna work, right?"

Frankie did not answer.

"Them things," Cogan said, "lemme tell you something, kid: them things, they never work. Guys with bright ideas, you know? Like Squirrel. They all know the end-around, and they're not gonna get something and work it steady and make it work and make it pay. Not them. He's always been like this, always been looking for a hustle, and guys like him, all they ever do is fuck things up. For everybody else."

"Trattman got hit," Frankie said.

"There's all kinds of reasons for things," Cogan said. "Guys get whacked for doing things, guys get whacked for not doing things, it don't matter. The only thing matters is if you're the guy that's gonna get whacked. That's the only fuckin' thing."

Frankie nodded.

"You," Cogan said, "you're one of the few guys that know, right?"

"I dunno," Frankie said.

"Yes you do," Cogan said. "You know very fuckin' well. You, you got a choice. You're gonna be one of the guys that gets whacked out or else you're not. You know that. It's just a matter of time, now, my friend.

Just a matter of time. Him first and then you. That's the way you're going."

Frankie did not answer.

"Except you're in a position," Cogan said, "you're in a position very few of them guys ever get in. You can do something about it. I known very few guys inna position like that."

Frankie did not answer.

"Frank," Cogan said, "I hope you don't think, I'm shittin' you."

"Look," Frankie said, "who the fuck are you? I never saw you before in my life, all of a sudden you're telling me all these things. What the fuck do I know? Maybe you're not even here. I don't know nothing."

"Kid," Cogan said, "I hate to see you go like this. China says you're all right. And you're going for fuckin' nothin'."

"I'm . . ." Frankie said, "Jesus, I dunno."

"Lemme ask you something," Cogan said, "and you think about this, all right? You think, I was to go down Wollaston and see him, there, right now, I was to leave here and drive down there and see him and say: 'Squirrel, it's you or Frankie. Who's it gonna be?' You think he'd even think about it? You think he would?"

"I dunno," Frankie said.

"You asshole," Cogan said. "An asshole like you, it's no wonder you did time. *You fuck kin asshole.* You haven't got no brains at all."

"Look," Frankie said, "look, I . . ."

"I haven't got to look," Cogan said. "Look, I know what's going on. I know what I got to do. I need a right guy."

Frankie's mouth worked. He did not say anything.

"If I get a right guy," Cogan said, "I told them this,

by the way, I said: 'There's two ways this thing can go. The hard way is, I do them both. The other way, I only gotta do one guy.' I took a lot of shit for that. You know how I got them to go along with this? China. China says you're all right. So, I always like China, I can do something for China, I'm gonna. China don't want you hit. Very loud on that point. Says you're a good guy, kind of guy it's good to have around. Okay. But you know where China is. All he can do is come up here and talk. He can't actually do nothing for a guy."

"No," Frankie said.

"I can do something for a guy," Cogan said. "I don't have to, but I can. Now make the pick, kid, and make it right now. I'm gonna do China a favor, I'm not gonna do China a favor. Don't matter to me."

"Lemme think," Frankie said.

"Nope," Cogan said, "no thinking. Go or no go, right now. I got to get going."

Frankie exhaled heavily. "I don't know," he said. "I don't know if I can do this."

"Can you do the other thing?" Cogan said.

Frankie hesitated. "No," he said.

"Well," Cogan said, "that's the selection. So, I guess you know, then."

"What've I gotta do?" Frankie said.

"You gotta find out where he's gonna be," Cogan said.

"I already know that," Frankie said. "We're, he asked me what I was gonna be doing, he's gonna be some place and he wants to call me or something. I know where he's gonna be. He's got a girl. He told me that, before. I told him I was gonna be home, I'd be home."

"You're not gonna be," Cogan said.

"I'm not?" Frankie said.

"No," Cogan said.

"Where . . ." Frankie said.

"You're gonna be with me," Cogan said, "and we're gonna be where he's gonna be."

"Jesus," Frankie said, "I can't do that. He sees me, it's all over. He'll know, something's wrong. I can't do that. I'll tell you, I'll tell you where he's gonna be. I'll do that. But, he's a friend of mine. I can't do that."

"Okay," Cogan said, "okay. That's, you made the other choice then, I guess."

Frankie stared at Cogan. Cogan did not move. Frankie said: "Have I really got to do that?"

Cogan nodded.

"All of it?" Frankie said.

Cogan nodded.

"I got to be there and everything?"

Cogan nodded.

"It's not," Frankie said, "it's not like, there was anything I could do, anybody else inna world couldn't do. It's not that. You, there must be hundreds of guys, you can get. You don't need me."

"Wrong," Cogan said. He put his hand on Frankie's shoulder. "Frank," he said, "it's not like I don't understand what's on your mind, right? But this thing's a problem. And part of it, it's partly your fault. You made a mistake. Now you gotta, you got to do the right thing. You gotta show, you understand, you made a mistake, and you gotta make things right. Otherwise, guys know you made a mistake, right? And that's when they're gonna want somebody to do something, like with Trattman. He never did the right thing."

Frankie nodded.

18

FRANKIE DROVE the Gold Duster quickly through the arch with the orange lanterns into the curving drives of Stuart Manor. The apartment complexes were two-story, the first of vertical redwood planks, the second stucco, half-timbered. The parking areas were filled with Volkswagens, Camaros, Mustangs and Barracudas. There were coach lights with orange bulbs above each door.

"Jee-zuss," Cogan said, "I finally made it. I'm in ghinny heaven."

The small tires on the Duster howled as Frankie took it through the curves to the back of the third complex. "It's a singles place," he said. "You're supposed to live here if you wanna get laid."

"I'd have to get awful horny to drive to New Hampshire to get laid," Cogan said.

"It's not that far," Frankie said. "I thought the same thing, but Johnny got tied up one night and I hadda bring her back up here. It's not that far."

"Seems far to me," Cogan said. "This, this just proves it to me. The guy's a shit."

"He don't have no control, where the girls live," Frankie said. He pulled into an empty space and shut off the engine and the lights.

"He don't have no control," Cogan said. "Period."

"Jackie," Frankie said, "he's really not a bad guy, you know? He's not a bad guy at all."

Cogan slouched down in the seat. The suede coat piled up around him at the neck. He shut his eyes.

"None of 'em are," he said. "They're all nice guys. They just get to thinking, you know?"

"He was always all right to me," Frankie said.

"Sure," Cogan said. "Got you almost six years inna fuckin' slammer."

"That wasn't his fault," Frankie said.

"Kid," Cogan said, "when somebody does something, and somebody, he gets somebody else, and they go to fuckin' jail for it, it's his fault. That's the rule."

"It wasn't his fault," Frankie said.

"Then this isn't your fault," Cogan said. "If that wasn't his fault, this isn't your fault."

"He didn't mean it," Frankie said.

"Hasn't got nothing to do with it," Cogan said, "nothing at all."

A blue Rallye Nova passed behind the Duster.

"That them?" Cogan said.

"Nah," Frankie said. "John, John's got a Riviera."

"I know what he's got," Cogan said. "What I want to know is, that them?"

"Nope," Frankie said. "I'd've said if it was. You got him wrong, you know. That jail thing, he had it worse'n I did, his family and all."

"He's not gonna have to do it again," Cogan said.

"He stood up," Frankie said. "He could've blamed it all on us."

"In a way," Cogan said, "he did."

"He did not," Frankie said. "He never said shit."

"He didn't say shit about you, maybe," Cogan said. "He still called somebody up."

"About what?" Frankie said. "What'd he call up?"

"He knows how you do things," Cogan said. "He knows how you're supposed to, anyway. He knows."

"What's he know?" Frankie said.

"Ever hear of the Doctor?" Cogan said.

"Yeah, yeah," Frankie said. "Dillon says he's dead. I know."

"When're you talking to Dillon?" Cogan said.

"I didn't talk to him," Frankie said. "Johnny told me that, said Dillon said the Doctor's dead."

"He is dead," Cogan said.

"Okay," Frankie said, "you and Johnny and Dillon, the whole bunch of you say the Doctor's dead. Big deal."

"The Squirrel says he's dead," Cogan said.

"Johnny said Dillon told him, the Doctor's dead," Frankie said.

"That shit," Cogan said. "That fuckin' shit."

A brown Maverick Grabber passed behind the Duster.

"Still not them," Frankie said. "Why?"

"Because he knows it himself," Cogan said. "He knows very fuckin' well, the Doctor's dead."

"How's he know?" Frankie said.

"He paid a man," Cogan said, "he paid a man, five thousand dollars, get the Doctor dead."

"Bull*shit*," Frankie said.

"What's his wife's name," Cogan said, "you want me to tell you, tell you what she looks like and everything, used to wear them big gold-hoop earrings? Connie."

"So what?" Frankie said.

"That's the broad that delivered the money," Cogan said. "For the Doctor's ass. Think he'd pay that if he didn't know it was done?"

Frankie did not answer.

"You know why, Frank, he got the Doctor?" Cogan said.

"Yeah," Frankie said, "I know."

"Sure," Cogan said. "Doctor made a mistake, did something he wasn't supposed to. That's why."

"Well," Frankie said, "he did."

"Sure he did," Cogan said. "So'd he."

"It's not the same thing," Frankie said. "It's not the same thing at all."

A maroon Monte Carlo passed behind the Duster.

"Sure it is," Cogan said, "the Doctor got taken out for getting everybody in the shit. And that's what him and you did. You just thought, the only thing that was different, you thought Trattman'd get blamed for it."

A red Capri passed behind the Duster.

"That's what I mean," Cogan said. "You don't get away with things like that. Trattman was the same way. Thought he was gonna get away with it."

"He did," Frankie said. "Once."

"That's what I mean," Cogan said. "You don't get away with nothing once, it happens again."

The bronze Riviera passed behind the Duster.

"That's him," Cogan said.

"I'm not sure," Frankie said.

"Yes you are," Cogan said. "If you're not you got the first all-over hard-on in the world." He opened his eyes and watched the Riviera. It pulled in beyond the back door of the complex.

"How long's he gonna be, kid?" Cogan said.

"I dunno," Frankie said.

"Okay," Cogan said, "I asked you nice. Now, does he fuck her here or does he fuck her some place else?"

"She's got a roommate," Frankie said. "He knows a guy's got a motel in Haverhill."

"Okay," Cogan said, "he's just gonna be friendly, then." He watched as the door of the Riviera opened. He watched the long white leg of the girl. He watched

Amato emerge from the building shadow and walk around the rear of the car. He watched Amato assist the girl from the car and shut the door.

Cogan reached down on the floor of the Duster with both hands and picked up a five-shot Winchester semi-automatic shotgun. He put it across his lap, steadying it with his right hand. With his left hand he took the key out of the Duster's ignition.

"Hey," Frankie said, "I mean, I was gonna start it and everything, we could get a start."

"I know," Cogan said, "but, it's probably gonna get noisy around here, and I known guys, heard a lot of noise, they got too good a start and left somebody standing around with his thumb up his ass."

Cogan watched Amato walk the girl to the door of the apartment complex.

Cogan opened the passenger door of the Duster, exposing the masking tape he had used to seal the interior light switch off, and slipped out of the car. Amato and the girl were thirty-five yards away, embracing at the door. Cogan crouched against the car, his left elbow bracing against the top of the Duster's hood, the stock of the gun tight against his right shoulder.

Amato broke the embrace. The girl opened the door with a key. Amato waited on the step until the door closed behind her. She turned and waved at him, using only the fingers of her right hand. She was smiling. Amato waved back, in the same way. He turned away from the door. The girl vanished up the stairs.

Cogan fired the first deer slug at Amato. It caught him low on the abdomen and hurled him backward against the building. Cogan waited until Amato hit the top of his low arc. Then Cogan fired the second slug. It hit Amato higher, slightly above the belt on the left side, and went through him, taking an angle through his body which sent it through the glass panel of the door at his left. Cogan fired the third shot as Amato hit the wall of the building and started to sag down. It hit him in the middle of the chest, close to the base of his throat, and blew his chest apart. Amato toppled off to his own right in the low shrubbery.

Cogan backed up fast and got into the car. He shoved the shotgun into the back seat and stuck the key into the ignition. "Now gimme that start," he said.

The Duster leaped out of the space, taking the curves of the drive with the small tires screaming.

Three and one-half miles from Stuart Manor, Cogan said: "You're going too fast."

"Jesus," Frankie said, "they're gonna have all kinds of cops up here." He held the Duster steady at seventy on the two-lane road.

"And one of them's gonna catch us," Cogan said. "Slow down."

"I can't," Frankie said.

"Kid," Cogan said, "look, slow down, all right?"

"I can't," Frankie said. "Honest to God, I can't."

"Kid," Cogan said, "my car's in Massachusetts. We got a long way to go. I don't wanna get caught."

"You wanna drive?" Frankie said.

"Yeah," Cogan said.

Frankie pulled the Duster off on the shoulder of Route 64. He opened the driver's side door quickly and got out and trotted around the back of the car. Cogan slid across the seats. Frankie got in on the passenger side.

"Okay," Cogan said, putting the Duster in drive, "now, this means, you're gonna have to dump the gun."

"Okay," Frankie said.

Cogan stopped the Duster on the overpass at the

Shawsheen River in Andover, Massachusetts. Frankie
opened the passenger window and launched the gun
out into the darkness. He started to close the window.

"Wait," Cogan said.

There was a splash.

"Okay," Cogan said. He put the Duster in gear again.
"Grass and stuff don't take care of prints," he said.
"Water does."

Cogan wheeled the Duster into the parking lot at the
Northshore Plaza west of Salem. Behind Jordan Marsh's
there was a blue LTD.

"You know what you got to do, now," Cogan said,
driving toward the LTD.

"Sure," Frankie said. "I go back down to where my
car is and I leave this one and I go home."

"You just leave it," Cogan said.

"Oh Christ," Frankie said, "I wipe it down."

"You're all right and everything," Cogan said.

"*Yeah,*" Frankie said.

"Where's your car again?" Cogan said.

"For Christ sake," Frankie said, "it's down at, it's inna
lot at Auburndale."

"Just making sure," Cogan said. "You couldn't drive
right, there. Some times guys forget."

Cogan pulled the Duster up next to the LTD. The
parking lot was lighted, but empty. Cogan opened the
driver's side door. Frankie started sliding across the
seat. Cogan got out. Frankie slid into the driver's seat.
He put his hands on the wheel. Cogan held the door
handle in his left hand. With his right hand he removed
a Smith and Wesson thirty-eight Police Special, two-
inch barrel, from beneath his coat.

"You're gonna remember, now," Cogan said, holding
the revolver below the level of the window.

"I know, I know," Frankie said, "I dump the fuckin'

car and I get my car and I don't go too fast and I—"

Cogan raised the revolver and shot Frankie in the face, once. Frankie fell off toward the passenger seat. Cogan leaned in the window and put the muzzle of the revolver against Frankie's chest and fired four times, the powder blast burning Frankie's coat. The body shuddered with each shot.

Cogan put the revolver in the pocket of his car coat. He took unlined leather gloves from the other pocket, and a red handkerchief. He began to wipe the Duster down.

IN THE MIDDLE of the afternoon, Cogan parked his flame-painted white El Camino pickup beside the silver Toronado in the lot at the Holiday Inn at South Attleboro, Massachusetts. The sign next to the Toronado said: "Welcome, South Jaycees." Cogan went inside.

In the lounge the driver sat at the bar, dawdling with a large ginger ale. Cogan took the stool next to him.

"You're late," the driver said.

"My mother used to tell me that," Cogan said. " 'You'll be late for your own funeral.' I hope so."

"Had yourself quite a party," the driver said.

"I do the best I can," Cogan said. To the bartender he said: "Beer."

The bartender filled a stein with Michelob.

"Everything's under control now, I take it," the driver said. "At long last."

"You know," Cogan said, "for a guy I'm trying to help out and everything, you're awful hard to get along with. I could've made you drive up to Boston, you know. I hadda go to Framingham, I didn't have to come down here. I'm trying to be nice to you."

"What the hell's wrong in Framingham," the driver said, "sky falling there or something?"

"Nah," Cogan said. "Stevie was outa hundred-millimeters and I had his car anyway and he had my truck, so I went out there and met him and give him some. I like to do a guy a favor now and then."

"Do me a favor," the driver said. "Never do me any favors. I've seen how you work."

"Tell you what," Cogan said, "gimme the money."

The driver handed Cogan a thick white business envelope.

"'Scuse me," Cogan said. He slid off the stool.

"You going to *count* it?" the driver said.

"I gotta take a leak," Cogan said. "Just lemme alone, all right? You make me nervous. I get nervous, I always gotta take a leak. Have some more ginger ale, for Christ sake."

Cogan went to the Men's Room. Cogan returned.

"You feel better?" the driver said.

"No," Cogan said, "there's only fifteen in there."

"Three guys," the driver said. "I'm not sure, I had to ask him whether I should pay you for the kid or not. He said I should."

"He was right, too," Cogan said. "That's five apiece."

"Correct," the driver said. "That's what he told me to pay Mitch."

"Yeah," Cogan said, "but the way I got it, Mitch got inna fight with a whore, the dumb shit, and now they got him in the can. Mitch couldn't do it. I come through for everybody on short notice. From now on, the price's ten."

"Dillon only charges five," the driver said. "He told me that, too."

"Not any more," Cogan said.

"Look," the driver said, "you're filling in for Dillon. You get what Dillon gets. No more. Take it up with Dillon. I can't do anything about it."

"You can't do anything about anything," Cogan said. "None of you guys can. Everything just goes haywire and everything, that's fine, you need somebody, get things straightened out. I'm just telling you, is all, it's gonna cost more, now on."

"Tell Dillon," the driver said. "Take it up with him."

"Dillon's dead," Cogan said. "Dillon died this morning."

The driver was silent for a while. Then he said: "He's going to be sorry to hear that."

"No sorrier'n I am," Cogan said.

The driver sipped his ginger ale. "I assume," he said, "I assume. . . . What killed him?"

"I know the name of it," Cogan said. "I got home this morning, my wife left me a note, they took Dillon the hospital about midnight or so. They told me what it was. That's all I know."

"He died in the hospital, then," the driver said.

"Like I say," Cogan said, "I dunno what it is. All I know's what they told me. 'Myocardial infarct.' You know what that is? I guess it's the same thing, the heart trouble."

"That's what he had," the driver said. "Well, how about that? Dillon's dead. Son of a bitch."

"He wasn't a bad guy, actually," Cogan said.

"No," the driver said, "no, I guess he wasn't. He wasn't a bad guy."

"He always," Cogan said, "he never, well, I knew Dillon a long time, right? It was Dillon, really, got me started, said I oughta get something besides the booking, something that'd be around and like that, you know? He was the guy that really plugged me in. I knew Dillon a long time."

"He knew him a long time too," the driver said. "He had a lot of respect for him."

"Sure," Cogan said, "so'd I. You know why?"

"You were afraid of him?" the driver said.

"Nah," Cogan said. He finished his beer. "Nah, it wasn't that. It was, he knew the way things oughta be done, right?"

"So I'm told," the driver said.

"And when they weren't," Cogan said, "he knew what to do."

"And so do you," the driver said.

"And so do I," Cogan said.

A CHOICE OF ENEMIES

1 On the morning of the first day of Jean Dussault's trial on charges
   of extortion, Joe Gillis used his "State House Viewpoint" column
in the Boston *Commoner* to "put the matter in political perspective." In
the late springtime of years when there was no statewide election in the
offing and no overriding issue up for battle in the General Court on
Beacon Hill, Joe Gillis did a lot of columns that assisted the readers of
the *Commoner* in perceiving connections between politicians on the
Hill and events that did not seem to have much to do with them or their
careers. "Someday," Leo Rosen said when he read what Joe Gillis had
to say about the implications of the trial of Jean Dussault, "old Joe is
gonna reach so far to grab a column out of thin air that he's going to
give himself a retroactive case of spina bifida." And when that day finally came, Leo Rosen did not mind admitting, he was going to take
Joe's State House beat away from him.

"On the face of it," Joe Gillis wrote, "Dussault looks like a man
whose life was spent at most upon the fringes of the Massachusetts political fund-raising world. He has not been an intimate of those who
have been powerful, and he has not been seen that often at the functions that attract them. Indeed, before the Middlesex grand jury handed
up those four indictments that confront him in Superior Court in Cambridge starting today, few seasoned political observers would admit
they even knew him."

Frank Costello, waiting in the Ritz Café for Dory Feldman to arrive
and to apologize for being late for the breakfast meeting he had forced
upon Costello, sat at the table at the window overlooking Newbury
Street squinting at the *Commoner* in the impeccable spring sunshine.
He allowed his upper lip to curl perhaps a millimeter. Because, of
course, Costello thought, with contempt for Joe Gillis in his heart, the
stupid bastards really didn't know him.

"But now," Gillis had written, "as the once powerful labor official puts his reputation and his freedom in the hands of Dory Feldman to defend against the vigorous anticorruption campaign being waged in Middlesex County by the young and energetic Brian Hanrihan, whom many are already mentioning as a prime potential contender for next year's Democratic nomination for attorney general, a noticeable change has taken place. Now there are hurried, secret conferences between top party leaders who will privately concede they are concerned. For they are said to be reminding one another, if Hanrihan's hard-hitting prosecution of the Dussault case brings a conviction, the beleaguered union leader may very well decide to tell the young DA what he knows about the party's fund raising. And that, one longtime observer says, could open a whole can of worms that could lead straight to the ornate paneled doors of the office of the Speaker, Bernard Morgan."

Frank Costello slapped the paper down on the Ritz windowsill and said "Oh, bullshit," softly but audibly to Dory Feldman as the counsel for Dussault showed up at last.

"Hey, look," Feldman said, placing his right hand on Frank Costello's left shoulder, "I realize I'm the one who called this meeting and I really shouldn't show up late for it, but I don't think that the situation calls for genuine profanity."

Frank Costello did not like to be touched and he had trouble collecting his normal composure as he looked up at Feldman with plain irritation. "Oh," he said, "Dory," and he made a perfunctory preliminary attempt to rise. Feldman pressed him down again, quite lightly, and took the chair opposite. He grinned at Costello. Costello said in a low voice: "That fucking Gillis."

Feldman's face lost its expression and he made a small production out of arranging the pink napkin in his lap. He waited while the busboy served him coffee and handed him a menu which he did not take the time to open. When he and Costello were left to themselves, he said: "Yes, Francis, absolutely. Those were my sentiments exactly." He scowled and Costello shook his head just once, keeping the gesture so small that only someone watching for it would have noticed it. "When I went to bed last night I thought I had at least as much as I could handle just defending Jean. I really wasn't in the market to have Bernie's presence and reputation inserted in the starting lineup over there today."

* * *

Leo Rosen, being alone in his studio apartment in Jamaica Plain, did not have to control his reactions to the Gillis column. Gillis had continued: "More and more, the Speaker looks like a very heavy albatross around the necks of party stalwarts already gearing up to battle upstart liberal and reform elements for complete control of party machinery in next year's primary elections. The thinking is that Morgan, for the past several years something of a strong embarrassment to more progressive party elements, may have reached the point where he will have to be eased out of office. Otherwise, one insider noted, the cost of maintaining Morgan in his present place may well drag all of his supporters down with him."

"Uh huh," Rosen muttered, nodding and drinking coffee that had a scum of non-dairy creamer on its surface so that it somewhat resembled a small pot of stagnant toxic waste. "Such as those two tribunes of the public interest, Paul Linder and Andy Boyce, and other ferrets that chat often with Joe Gillis."

The waiter in the Ritz Café delivered plates of scrambled eggs that fluffed up on the china like yellow stratocumulus and poured fresh cups of crystalline black coffee. When he had gone away, Costello leaned toward Feldman and said in a soft voice: "Bernie Morgan isn't dead. No matter what you may have heard or people like Joe Gillis dearly wish." He sat up straight again and regarded Feldman through the thin pillar of steam that ascended from the scrambled eggs. "I was with him just last night, Dory, and he is very much alive."

Feldman took that in and then with delicacy set upon his breakfast. "I'm glad to hear that, Frank," he said. He frowned as he lifted food toward his mouth. "On the assumption, of course, that he wouldn't actually be better off if he were not."

Costello scowled at that, put down his fork, and rested both his elbows on the pink tablecloth. Outside the younger matrons in from Weston, Sudbury, and Carlisle to raid the better shops along Newbury walked quickly past, their acquiring smiles in place and their bright eyes lively in the morning. "I assume," he said, "you mean the Ames Commission."

Leo Rosen for the first time that day inadvertently looked at what he had been drinking of his own free will and set it down away from him on the stained surface of the chromium Formica table in his kitchen-ette. He took the *Commoner* in both his hands and gave his full atten-tion to the revelations of Joe Gillis.

"Otis Ames," Gillis had written, "lurks at the edge of all the thinking done by party leaders on the Hill these days, and it is common knowl-edge that the conscience of the State House, as he has been called, is no admirer of the Speaker's." True enough, Joe, Rosen thought, and on Wednesday you can toss another bombshell by reporting that the sun's been rising in the east and setting in the west for quite a while now, too. "The senior Independent," Gillis had written, "though advanced in years, remains extremely energetic, and can draw upon the wealth of his experience to direct the work of the Commission to Investigate Corruption which Gov. John Tierney rammed through the General Court at the insistence of reformers who believe the time has come to clean up Beacon Hill." Dreamers, Rosen thought, and those who think they can get what they want by hiding behind dreamers.

"Yes," Feldman said with equanimity to Frank Costello in the Ritz Café, "I mean the Ames Commission."

"Ames is senile," Frank Costello said. He ingested a large forkful of eggs.

Feldman steepled his fingers. "Occasionally, yes," he said. "But then again, occasionally he is not. If in one of his lucid periods he gets him-self a reasonably decent staff, and that staff gets itself a witness with his own reason to talk and some stuff to talk about, that addled old man just might do a little damage. After all his years of trying."

Frank Costello chewed and swallowed. He lifted his coffee cup with his right hand and looked at Feldman over it. "I really don't like break-fast conferences," he said companionably. "When I get suckered into one, I like it to get over just as fast as possible. You're telling me that Jean Dussault wants help from Bernie Morgan and he might do some-thing if he doesn't get it?"

Dory Feldman smiled and resumed attending to his breakfast. "Not exactly," he said. "What I am telling you is that this whole shooting match has got me just the slightest bit confused." He dispensed with the smile. "If I should lose this case, Jean Dussault is going to go to jail. Warren Matte's a good judge and he was not born yesterday, but labor racketeering and shakedowns are not the kind of things that you can just brush off. If Dussault gets convicted, Warren Matte's got no choice but to give him some hard time." Feldman paused there and considered whether he might soften his voice even a trifle more. He did so, and under the pretense of shifting his weight so as to toy comfortably with the salt shaker, moved closer to Frank Costello.

"I'll be honest with you, Frank," he said, frowning to show his earnestness, "I don't know if Jean Dussault can do hard time. This is his first trip through the gauntlet. He's middle-aged and he's used to his comfort. If I should ask him now, he'd say he could, of course, and tell me he's a stand-up guy just as he really thinks he is. But there's a difference between boasting and the day when you stand up and hear the judge's announcement that you're going to sleep tonight in Walpole with a bunch of goddamned convicts. That's when a guy like Jean Dussault starts making calculations and wondering why he should be the guy that makes the license plates while all the other fellows that he knows're doing bad things too, get to stay outside and drive around with those plates on their Cadillac Sevilles."

Frank Costello's face showed no change of expression. "Just for the record, Dory," he said, "I have made discreet inquiries of some knowledgeable people."

"As has been," Feldman said with a small grin, "your custom of long standing."

"Absolutely," Frank Costello said, betraying no amusement. "And I am satisfied from those inquiries that your man Dussault couldn't pin a parking ticket on the Speaker or the people that the Speaker has been known to have a drink with now and then. My guys would not know Jean Dussault from Serge Koussevitsky, in other words, and if he's looking to scare people he is looking in the wrong damned place."

Feldman let the small smile reappear. "But even with that inquiry behind you, Francis," he said quietly, "you still came in for breakfast, didn't you?"

Costello arched his eyebrows. "You're an old friend, Dory," he said. "I thought perhaps the strain of private practice had gotten to you finally, and you were going to sound me out about a judgeship." He returned Feldman's smile.

Leo Rosen sat slumped at his kitchen table, the Gillis column lying there in front of him, disgust and bafflement contending for control of his expression. "It has been years," Gillis concluded, "since the last cleanup movement on the Hill foundered on the silence of Rep. William Dealey. Convicted on a host of charges of corruption, Dealey, now in ill health and barely able to perform his chiefly ceremonial duties as State Tributaries and Preserves commissioner, refused to implicate those higher up in the regime of then-Speaker Wilfred Knox. The thinking now is that Knox's son-in-law and hand-picked successor, Bernard Morgan, may not be as lucky. Prosecutor Hanrihan, already mentioned as Ames's choice to ramrod his commission, could see to that. His success in Middlesex during the coming days will be closely watched." I definitely should've been a sportswriter, Rosen thought. At least they know they're not supposed to take it seriously.

"I will ask you for a judgeship, Francis," Feldman said, "shortly after Bernie Morgan wins the Nobel Prize for Peace." His voice was hardening rapidly as he said that. "Listen to me now," he said, "because this could be important. Jean Dussault does not know politicians. But he knows a lot of contractors and other people who know politicians, and I have heard those people who know politicians sometimes give them money when they shouldn't, to get state business that might go to someone else."

"Oh, for heaven's sake, Dory," Costello said. "Are you another one of those folks with the stars in their eyes who thinks Bernie Morgan's gotten rich in office?"

"Hear me out," Feldman said. "I've already told you that I've got some doubts about whether Jean'll stand up and go through if Hanrihan nails him. But if Jean doesn't stand up, those contractors are going to topple left and right, and you and I both know what they'll do when it's their tails in the crack. Bernie Morgan's chances won't be worth a dime."

"The point, Dory," Costello said, affecting weariness. "I do have some commitments in the real world that I've got to keep today."

Feldman's face showed anger fast. His voice became more calm and even softer. "A lot of us don't like the Speaker, Frank," he said. "It's nothing personal, you understand, but there are people who truly believe that something should be done about the mental hospitals this Commonwealth inflicts on those who can't care for themselves. There are really people who think that something should be done to bring about improvements in the education that we give our kids. A surprisingly large number of the voters don't disapprove at all of giving homeless people places where they can get in out of the rain. You'd be amazed, most likely, you and Bernie, if I told you that most of the people getting welfare probably would starve without it, and really can't find jobs that will support them and their families. As odd as the idea may strike you, Frank, the notion does persist that government ought to take some interest in the quality of life in our society."

Frank Costello smiled and said: "Am I to understand that white wine and assorted cheeses are served here with the eggs?"

Feldman glared at him. "Okay, Francis," he said, "laugh it off again, as usual. You married the gorilla when you hitched your hopes to Bernie, and you've done pretty well over the years, so I guess it's only right that you won't tell him when it's time to stop the fucking. But it's not smart, Francis, and that's what startles me when you react like this. Bernie's fat and arrogant, an alcoholic crook. Still dangerous, to be sure, and a long way from surrendering because he has to. But if he doesn't decide that he'll go quietly, Francis, he will be carried out one of these days. And I'm inclined to think that day is close at hand."

Costello did not answer for a while. Then he said: "Are you telling me, Dory, that you're going to throw the Dussault case in order to get Bernie Morgan out of office?"

Feldman stared at him. He made two attempts at a reply before he cleared his throat and finally managed one. "Jesus, Frank," he said, "I'd forgotten how vicious you guys are." Costello gave him no response. "Okay," Feldman said, "but I'm going to finish anyway. Ray Archambault's a good man. He's going to be the Speaker some day anyway. He's clean and smart and everyone can live with him."

"So far," Costello said, "you haven't said much that I disagree with."

Feldman nodded and exhaled to show relief. "Good," he said. "All I'm telling you is that Bernie should get his ass out now and let Ray have the job while it's still worth something and nobody's gone to jail, okay? If Bernie leaves, Otis Ames is finished. No uproar and no scandals, no carnival for Dave Pucci to splash across the front page of the *Commoner*, no heartache and no pain. Doesn't that make sense to you?"

Costello nodded. "Uh huh," he said.

Feldman gazed at him and found the little smile again. "But you're not going to do it," he said.

"That is correct," Costello said. "I have never been disloyal."

2 The witness stood in the middle of the intersection of Charles and Mt. Vernon streets at the foot of Beacon Hill and waved his arms and yelled. It was hot in the late morning sun and the witness had been sweating heavily into his untidy red beard and the green T-shirt with the tear at the love handle just above his belt on his left side. He was about six two, two hundred and twenty pounds. He wore greasy jeans and boots and he stamped his feet while he shouted at Shaughnessey. "You fucking cops," the witness said, "it's you fucking cops, is why things like this happen."

"Look," Shaughnessey said, "whyncha just calm the fuck down and tell me what the hell happened, all right?" He had stained his shirt with sweat and sweat rolled down his temples from beneath the sweatband of the perforated summer uniform hat. He rested his right hand on the hood of the cruiser and then snatched it away from the heat.

"Bullshit," the witness said. "I'm here every goddamned day. Three days a week, I'm here. I see what goes on, this fuckin' street, guys cuttin' in and out, parking all over the goddamned place. And then the meter maids come along and they're handin' out the tickets like fuckin' confetti, and you guys drive by and you never do nothing. I was here last week and I saw a little kid almost get run over, right? And you guys, it wasn't your fault the kid didn't get hit, and I was in *Vietnam.*"

Shaughnessey's cruiser blocked the intersection to traffic proceeding from the Boston Public Gardens toward Cambridge Street on the one-way street. It was stopped in the middle of the four lanes, straddling the broken white lines. There was an orange and white ambulance, marked BOSTON HEALTH & HOSPITALS, parked with lights flashing on Mount Vernon Street, the front of it angled toward the Charles Street Meeting House. Two EMTs in blue uniforms were lifting a body on a gurney into the truck. The head of the victim was uncovered; it lolled restlessly from the side. The victim made unintelligible noises. "You hear me, cop?" the witness yelled.

A fair-sized number of women in their early thirties, some with small children in tow and others with two-wheeled wire shopping carts, had gathered on the brick sidewalks at the Meeting House, across the street at the Charles Street Restaurant, and in Mount Vernon Street itself. Men in work clothes stood among them. They discussed the amount of blood visible on the victim's face. Shaughnessey's partner, Curran, stood near the door of the ambulance, his hat pushed back on his head, his hands on his hips. The conversations of the women and the male pedestrians were drowned out by the horns of the cars jammed up behind the cruiser. Shaughnessey ignored the noise. "I was there myself," Shaughnessey said to the witness. "We oughta get together some time when we both got more time and cut up a few old touches, huh?"

The witness dropped his arms. He stared at Shaughnessey. "The fuck're you talkin' about?" he said.

"Vietnam," Shaughnessey said. "That was the last thing you mentioned, so I thought that was probably what you wanted, talk about. Am I wrong there?"

"You dumb bastard," the witness yelled, "there was . . . , I seen a kid get whacked, *right here.*" He pointed toward the southwesterly corner of the intersection, where a brown and white Boston Cab was parked, unoccupied, next to a hydrant. There was a green Volvo station wagon parked behind it, with an orange Denver boot locked onto the right rear wheel and a cerise traffic warning flyer on the windshield, admonishing the driver not to try to move the car until he had made his peace with the city for unpaid tickets. "See that fuckin' dent onna trunka the cab?" the witness said. He wheeled and pointed toward the ambulance, where the EMTs were pulling the doors shut. "That kid's *head* made that fuckin' dent. See that bike all bent outta shape inna street under the cab? The kid was on that bike and the guy fuckin' knocked him right off of it. On fuckin' purpose. I seen it."

"That what you want to talk about?" Shaughnessey said.

"Yeah," the witness yelled. "That's your goddamned job, isn't it?"

"I'm a public servant," Shaughnessey said.

"Right," the witness said, "and this guy I'm telling you about, he beat the kid up and I seen him do it. You wanna hear about that?"

"Sure," Shaughnessey said, "sounds like it might be interesting."

The witness glared at him. He seized Shaughnessey's right arm at the bicep. His lips curled and exposed his teeth. His whiskers bristled wetly around his snarl. "You listen to me, you fucker," he said. "I'm maybe not one of those rich bastards that you guys're always kissin' ass for, but you're gonna listen to me."

Shaughnessey wrenched his arm away. He bulged the muscles in his neck. "You take your fuckin' hands off me, beaver face," he said. "I'll decide who I listen to, and I also get to decide when I wanna run some asshole into the can for assaultin' an officer."

"I got rights," the witness said.

"You bet your ass you have," Shaughnessey said, "and I got a little card that's got all of them written on it, and about one more move from you and I'm gonna read it to you and then I'm gonna run your sorry ass into jail. You got that?"

The witness stared. He started to say something. "The accident," Shaughnessey said. "Tell me about the accident." The horns blared behind them in the backed-up traffic.

"It was no goddamned accident," the witness said.

"Tell me about it," Shaughnessey said. Curran stood in the intersection as the driver backed the ambulance into Mount Vernon Street, turned back into Charles Street, and headed toward Massachusetts General Hospital, the lights flashing and the siren howling as it wove between the trucks and cars double- and triple-parked north of the intersection.

"Come here," the witness said. He started to take Shaughnessey's arm again. Shaughnessey glared at him. "No," the witness said, "I didn't mean nothin'. Just, come with me. Lemme show you, all right? Down here." He nodded south toward the Beacon Street intersection at the Public Garden.

"Okay," Shaughnessey said. The drivers of the vehicles who had been patient until they heard the siren die away now leaned on their horns. "Hey, Dicko," Shaughnessey said. Curran, in the act of hoisting up his pants, shifted his gaze to Shaughnessey. "Move the car, okay?" He gestured down the street. "Goin' down here with this guy, couple minutes." Curran nodded.

The witness started ahead of Shaughnessey. "Okay," he said, walking between the cruiser and the Boston Cab, "the cab is here, right? And the guy in the car comes up here." He pointed to the left-hand lane of the street. "Right next to the cab. And the light's red and there's a woman goin' across with these two little dogs on leashes, you know? And that's how come I noticed him."

"You like dogs or something?" Shaughnessey said.

"No," the witness said. He turned slightly and looked at the crosswalk. "No, it was because this ginch, she had on these real short white shorts and she didn't have no bra on, neither. Beautiful ass on this dame. I was watchin' her, and this guy comes along and he was watchin' her too. I think this is why he stopped. Light was yellow when he first come to it, and she was onna crosswalk which she shouldn't't've been, but this is the kind of guy, he is something like me, you know? Broads like this can jaywalk in front of him all day long, they got a shape like that and they don't wear much clothes in hot weather. This is not the type of guy that usually gives a pedestrian a break, all right?"

"Just what exactly makes you say this?" Shaughnessey said. "You know this guy?"

"Nope," the witness said, "never seen him before, my life. But I can tell from his car, for one thing, all right? Seville. Caddy Seville. Got the metallic maroon onna bustle and the gold and the pin stripes and the gold vinyl roof and the wire wheels, am I right? This a real flashy car for guys that want a real flashy car but they're not pimps, you know? And this type of guy does not stop his car every time somebody decides they don't care what color the light happens to be, they're gonna cross the street anyway."

"Okay," Shaughnessey said.

"Now," the witness said, walking past the cruiser and pointing to a dark spot on the pavement near the rear bumper of the cab, "this here is the blood from where the kid hits the street."

"I saw that," Shaughnessey said.

"Right," the witness said, "and this car here, this fuckin' Volvo, this was obviously right where it was then because the guy that owns it didn't pay his tickets and get it out of here while all this was going on. Now," the witness said, pointing to two empty spaces at the curb, blocked by a two-and-a-half-ton Ford truck painted white with a bright red Budweiser logo on the front of the box, "this here rig was where it is now, see?"

"Right," Shaughnessey said. "This'd be your rig, right?"

"Well," the witness said, "the company's." He continued toward the rear of the truck, the cars, now moving, passing close to him, the drivers glaring but seeing Shaughnessey and making no protest about people walking in the street. Next to the right rear corner of the truck there was a two-wheeled handcart. "This is where I am standing," the witness said. "I just get the handcart out of the hole inna back there under the box when I see the broad out the corner my eye, so I'm gonna take a look at her, she's crossin' the street. And I'm standin' there, lookin', and the guy inna Caddy comes along and practically runs over me. Don't blow his horn or anything like that. Just if I don't see him, he's gonna run over me. Simple.

"Well," the witness said, "I seen him, and he gets by me and that's when the light's yellow and he sees the cunt start across the street and he stops. Now," the driver said, squinting and pointing north up

Charles Street, "the kid is coming down the middle the goddamned street like he owns it, the wrong way, all right? And he's about thirty, maybe fifty feet the other side the crosswalk when I see him. Puerto Rican, looks like, not very big, about fifteen, maybe. Ridin' a ten-speed. See, that's how I figure he's not old enough, drive, because this ten-speed he's ridin' that he probably stole from somebody, he would've took the guy's car if he could drive. And he's havin' a great time for himself grinnin' and everything, makin' old ladies think he's gonna run into them, and he sees the broad and he speeds up. Get a better look at her. She had really nice tits. Got his shirt off and it's tied around his middle, you know, and he's a nice-lookin' kid, curly black hair, he yells somethin' at her. I couldn't hear that. Don't have to. I know what he prolly had in mind. Same thing's me and the guy inna Cad. Asked her she wanted, sit on his face or somethin'.

"She didn't pay no attention to him," the witness said. "Just kept that motor of hers goin' nice and smooth, everything bouncing just when it should, where it should, and she gets across the street and the kid's already made one guy jam onna brakes comin' down Mount Vernon Street there, because the kid don't give a shit about things like one-way streets and red lights, and he sees the Caddy. He's right inna middle of the intersection and he sees the car, and he heads right fuckin' for it. And he grins. And the guy drivin' leans forward and I see the window go down on his side, because I am lookin' at him from an angle, and the driver sticks his elbow out and the kid's comin' right for him and the kid just dinks the bike a little bit and gets between the Cad and the cab and lays the left handbrake handle right on the Caddy's front fender and starts draggin' it along the paint there, grinnin' like a bastard."

"He did it on purpose," Shaughnessey said.

"Sure," the witness said. "He was having a good old time. You could hear that handle scrapin' the paint—*scriiiitch*—it was *loud.*"

"Driver didn't like this," Shaughnessey said.

"Not at fuckin' *all,*" the witness said. "Hey, you blame him? This's a twenty-thousand-dollar car he's got, this little bastard's wreckin' a three-thousand-dollar paint job? How'd you feel?"

"Mean," Shaughnessey said.

"Sure," the witness said. "So'd I. I don't blame the guy for that. It's what he did. The kid comes crankin' along his fender and he gets the door, the driver stiff-arms him right off of the bike."

"Good for him," Shaughnessey said.

"Yeah," the witness said, "I could understand that, the way he felt. Kid hasn't got no money, pay for the damage. At least clout him inna neck. So far, okay. The kid asked for it.

"Kid falls off the bike," the witness said. "Hits his head onna cab. Bike falls down under the Cad. Kid slides down off the trunk the cab. Lands in the street on his back. Stunned. Driver gets out the Cad just as the kid starts to fall. Hits him right inna balls with the door. Kid's down, like I say, driver's out and he stomps on his belly. Sounded like the ribs broke. Kicks the kid inna head a couple times. Good and hard, too. No love taps. Kicks him inna balls again. Gets back in his car, shuts the door, puts it in gear, light turns green, floors it, runs over the bike and smashes it, and he's gone. That was too much. Hittin' the kid the first time, that I could understand. Beatin' the shit out of him? I dunno. This was a big guy. Little kid, even though he probably did have a knife and stole the bike. But still, this guy must've, he was bigger'n I am."

"How old?" Shaughnessey said.

"Old," the witness said. "Fifty, fifty-five, maybe sixty. White hair. Big bushy headda white hair. More hair'n me. White. Over six feet tall. Fat. But he was in pretty good shape. Fast on his feet, with his hands. This guy did some fighting some time, I think. Not boxing, neither. This was the good old hand-to-hand drill they taught us in Basic. Dirty fighter. Good, though. Very good. He had the whole job done in less'n the time it took the light to change."

"You didn't recognize him?" Shaughnessey said.

The witness frowned. "He looked like somebody that I oughta know," the witness said. "Like, he was somebody that I seen some place, but he wasn't anybody that I knew, you know what I mean? That kind of thing. I didn't know him personally, I know that. I did, I would stay on his good side, after what I seen."

"How about the registration," Shaughnessey said. "Get a look at that?"

"It was numbers," the witness said. "No vanity plate or anything like that. I didn't, I don't remember them."

"Okay," Shaughnessey said. He took out a spiral notepad. "Your name," he said.

"Hey," the witness said, "I didn't do nothing. I told you what happened. Other people, some these other people seen it too, that was just standin' there. You didn't take their names."

"They didn't come forward," Shaughnessey said.

"Jesus," the witnesss said, "you mean that's it? I try, help you guys, it's gonna mean a big pain in the ass for me? That's what I get? Christ, no wonder nobody wants anything to do, the cops."

"You want us to catch the guy, don't you?" Shaughnessey said. "Overreacting like that. Maybe killed the kid for scratching his great big car. Oughta be punished."

"Sure," the witness said. "I want you to catch the guy. You, not me. I'm not a cop. You guys get paid for it. I'm just tryin', help out. I don't need a lot of shit for doin' it."

"You're just drivin' a truck," Shaughnessey said.

"Yeah," the witness said. "And that's what I wanna keep right on doing."

"This truck," Shaughnessey said. He stepped back two paces into the traffic, causing a motorist to swerve a Saab Turbo coupe around him and swear. He read from the side of the truck: "Spring Crest Beverages, Inc., right?"

"Right," the witness said.

"Which is obstructing traffic this very minute on Charles Street and impeding the orderly flow and so forth," Shaughnessey said.

"Hey," the witness said, "that's a loading zone. Liquor store's right there, see?"

"The loading zone's at the curb," Shaughnessey said. "The loading zone is not in the left-hand travel lane. The loading zone's empty and the truck's inna street, and that's against the law."

"Look," the witness said desperately, "I park in those spaces, you know what's gonna happen?"

"Yup," Shaughnessey said.

"Sure," the witness said. "Two cars're gonna double-park me in and keep me there all day and I'm not gonna make my next stop or the one after that and I'll get fired."

"Right," Shaughnessey said, "so as a result, you double-park next to an empty loading zone and fuck everybody else all up so you can stand around looking at broads with no clothes on."

"Are you gonna give me a fuckin' ticket?" the witness said. "For standin' around and wastin' my time when I was tryin', help you and I should've been doing my job and gettin' the hell out of here 'fore you ever knew I was here?"

Shaughnessey snapped the pad shut and put it back in his pocket. "Nope," he said, "not this time. No guarantees tomorrow though, got it?"

"Thanks a lot," the witness said.

"You're welcome," Shaughnessey said. "And here's another piece of free advice, okay? Never grab a cop in the street and yell at him, unless you're a cop too and outrank him. Otherwise, a very bad idea. Liable, get you in trouble."

The witness did not say anything. Shaughnessey went back to the cruiser and got in. He shut the door.

"Get anything?" Curran said.

"Yeah," Shaughnessey said. "Laugh or two. Not much more. How's the kid?"

"Guy did a pretty decent number on him," Curran said. "Possible skull fracture, pelvic fracture, busted wrist, nose. They won't know till they get him at the hospital. Find out what happened, besides he creamed the guy's car and he picked the wrong guy's car to cream?"

"Well," Shaughnessey said, "I think I know who the guy is, if that's what you mean."

"Oh yeah?" Curran said.

"Yeah," Shaughnessey said. "I bet if we were to drive up on the Hill behind the State House and take a look at the Speaker's Caddy, we would see that it's got fresh scratches on the left front fender and a ding in the driver's side door from a bicycle running into it."

"Bernie Morgan got another one, huh?" Curran said.

"Sounds like it," Shaughnessey said. "Clotheslined the kid and then disabled him. Witness said it reminded him of Basic hand-to-hand."

"That's Morgan all right," Curran said. "We goin' up there?"

"Oh, I dunno," Shaughnessey said. "Whaddaya think, huh? Almost noon. I'm gettin' hungry. Awful hot, go runnin' around any more'n we have to, botherin' guys like that."

"You got a point there, my friend," Curran said. "Little air conditioning, little roast beef, cold glass or two. Much better'n tangling assholes with guys like Bernie Morgan that only do what I wanted to do at least ten times a day myself in this town."

"Right," Shaughnessey said, putting the cruiser in gear. "You and every other white man in this world. All Bernie Morgan does is what everyone'd like to do. But he gets away with it."

"That," Curran said, "must be why people love him so."

3 Andy Boyce did not waste time. In the few minutes that he had by himself in the apartment which the legislative leadership maintained in the three-story brownstone on the backside of the Hill, he found half of a Table Talk cherry pie in the refrigerator, along with a pint can of Miller Lite. He took his treasures with him into the living room and made space enough among the greasy pizza boxes and the soiled plastic cups stacked on the coffee table to put the box of pie down while he ate. He was digging at the crust with a white plastic spoon when Frank Costello let himself into the apartment.

"Mister Chairman," Costello said, picking his way through the discarded newspapers and magazines piled haphazardly upon the cheap green carpet, "you would eat shirt cardboards if somebody put jelly on them and packed them in a pie box."

Boyce washed down pie with beer as Costello sat down on the oversized pine chair upholstered in orange and brown plaid and said: "I didn't have my breakfast, Frank, all right? I haul my ass in here on less'n five hours' sleep so I can see you, and it happens I am hungry. So I see what I can find to eat and this was it. Apparently the boys ate all the steak and eggs after I left here around three this morning."

"Uh huh," Frank Costello said. "And what else did the boys do in this luxurious hideaway until the wee small hours of the morning? Did they spend all their time discussing German theologians, or did they actually do something useful for a change?"

Boyce sucked at his teeth. "Frank," he said, "my mentor in the Speaker's office told me long ago that I should treat you with respect, so I do that. I do everything my mentor in the Speaker's office tells me I should do."

Costello nodded. "A sound practice, my boy," he said. "It's being smart like that that's made you chairman of judiciary at your tender age, even though you are too fat for any kid still wet behind the ears and haven't figured out yet this is probably because you eat supermarket pie and beer for breakfast."

"Which is not to say it isn't awful difficult sometimes," Boyce said.

"Bite the bullet," Frank Costello said. "My recollection is that before sundown yesterday Mister Morgan, you, and I had pretty much agreed that we had better find approximately nineteen thousand dollars before this week is out or we are going to have some trouble with some people who've been very patient for a long time, waiting for their money."

"That figure does stick in my mind," Boyce said.

"My recollection further is," Costello said, "that Mister Morgan, you, and I had reminded one another that the Honorable Paul Linder has in the past when he has had too much to drink made mention of an ammunition box that he keeps beneath the floorboards of his bedroom closet."

"You mean the one, I think," Boyce said, "that he says has got over forty grand in it."

"The very one," Costello said. "Forty thousand dollars in gifts made of utter free will to Representative Paul Linder when he was chairman of the Board of County Commissioners."

"I mentioned that steel box to Paul last night," Boyce said. "You understand I couldn't be specific because there were some other guys here that I don't know if I trust with my life like I do my mentor there and you."

"I understand," Costello said. "Your sensitivity's one quality that prompted Mister Morgan and me to entrust you with profound responsibilities while you're still practically a teenager."

"I appreciate that," Boyce said. "I know you're full of shit, of course, but I appreciate it. Anyway, I give Paul the little nudge there like I say, and I can see he gets the idea right away that I am bracing him for a few bucks, although I didn't actually give him any figures."

"And of course the Honorable Linder," Frank Costello said, "immediately understanding that his sterling leader is a little short of cash, at once said that the only question in his mind was how much he should take out of the ammunition box to meet this small emergency."

"Not exactly," Boyce said.

"Goodness," Costello said, "really? A man as eager for political advancement as Paul Linder is? I must say I'm surprised."

"Right," Boyce said drily. "Paul said that he'd really like to help us out and all, but as long's he's got to think about getting reelected every few years here, he's got to hang onto the contributions that his old friends who rent trucks and plows out used to give him now and then when he was making the decisions about which trucks and plows the county rented when it snowed."

"Uh huh," Costello said. "I don't suppose he went so far as to say what position he'd consider sufficiently attractive to make him decide to give up his seat and all of that expensive campaigning that goes with it."

Boyce frowned and smiled at the same time. "Not in so many words, Frank," he said. "All he said was that if he had something like Bill Dealey's got there with the Tributaries and the Game Preserves that's a nice secure lifetime appointment, he would probably be able to see things a little differently."

Costello smiled at Andy Boyce, who smiled back at him. "That little piece of shit," Costello said.

"That's what I thought," Boyce said.

"Poor Billy Dealey's running out like a cheap ballpoint pen, and Linder hasn't got the common decency to wait until the medical examiner says there's no pulse," Costello said.

"Well," Boyce said, "he didn't really *say* that, but I think it's what he meant."

Costello looked at his gold Corum watch. "Where the hell is Bernie?" he said disgustedly. "The bastard's half an hour late and when he gets here we've got this to tell him. Shit. If this doesn't put him through the roof then nothing will."

"The Speaker isn't gonna be here," Boyce said. "Not today."

"Really?" Frank Costello said. "Why? You tell him already what Paul said and he decided to save time and go kill the little prick before lunch?"

"Nope," Boyce said. "I was a little slow in getting off the dime myself this morning, so I called the office before I came over here and said that I was on my way. And Connie there, she told me that the Speaker'd just come in and he was on the phone to his insurance company. Something with his car getting banged up on the way over, I think. She said if I had any sense I would thank God I wasn't going to see him because as many times's she's seen him mad, she never saw him like he is today. She said if he got any worse they were gonna call the zoo and have some guys come over with a tranquilizer gun and a big net."

"Wonderful," Costello said. He pondered. Boyce finished up the beer. "Andy," Costello said, "the more I think about this, the more I think that I'm not going to think of anything that's different from what Bernie, you, and I thought of the other day."

Boyce nodded and looked glum.

"It's not that things've changed since then," Costello said. "I still dislike the idea of going back to this guy in particular and telling him it's time to make another contribution."

"Well, shit," Boyce said, "fuck him if he don't like it. He's got a good contract there nobody had to give him. It's not that we couldn't find another guy that had the right kind of equipment and knew how to build a fuckin' runway, damnit. So what if he don't like the idea so much when it's money coming out of him instead of money coming in? Tough shit for him."

"I know," Costello said, "I know. The trouble is with this guy, he's a rookie at it, you know? Sort of, at least. It's always the same way with these virgins that come in and tell you up and down they know what's going on and they decided it was time they played the same games as the other people who've been at it a lot longer. They tell you that, and then you do it to them, and when they go home they tell you they feel fine, but the next day when you see them they give you the big weepy eye and you know they're mad at you and they're not going to forgive you."

Boyce shrugged. "Frank," he said, "it's not like I have ever said I envied you the things you got to do to keep things running smooth."

"No," Costello said bitterly, "I never did get that impression. But what the hell, huh? It's a dirty job, but somebody's got to do it." He stood up suddenly, a trim, meticulously dressed man in the last stages of his middle years, his suit tailored skillfully and his iron-grey hair barbered expertly, and he looked completely out of place in the clutter of the leadership apartment. "My mother was right when she told me not to go to law school, Andy," he said. "I should've been a brain surgeon like she told me."

Boyce laughed one short bark. "You, ah, want me to tell Bernie what you're doing?"

Costello nodded. "Yeah," he said. "If you can find a half a dozen good strong guys to tie him with some ropes like they use to peg the circus tents down during hurricanes, tell him what you told me about that little turd Paul Linder, and that I'm calling our guy on the island."

"Will do," Boyce said. Then he grinned. "I tell you, Francis," he said, "you're an inspiration to all of us young guys. I hope some day when I'm the Speaker I have got a wise adviser like yourself that I know I can rely on."

Costello smiled at him. "You fresh little bastard, Andy," he said, "that's what I hope, too. It'll serve you both right, no matter who he is."

4 Up island on the Vineyard the mist soaked the clay stripped of its scrub pines and small oaks by Vinnie Mahoney's bulldozers and graders. He stood in the haze and watched. The heavy machinery snarled and roared over the land ahead of him, gnawing at the edges of the receding woods, flattening the tree trunks into the soil and crushing the branches down with them. Mahoney, wearing a tan work shirt and tan twill pants, a hard hat and heavy work boots, stood staring happily at the destruction, his back to the white two-story wooden airport terminal and tower behind him. A single-engine Piper Cherokee wheeled out of the grey sky above the fringe of the woods ahead of him, its gear and flaps down, its wings waggling slightly as the pilot flared it in toward the approach to the runway which Mahoney was lengthening, the laboring noise of its engine increasing as it approached Mahoney and passed low over his head, squealing down on the pavement four hundred yards behind him. He did not shift his gaze from his machines. He smiled. He shifted his feet in the clay and folded his arms.

Off to Mahoney's right and slightly behind him, his machines had cut a temporary road through the woods that bordered the county road connecting Edgartown and Vineyard Haven. It was rutted by the heavy trucks that carted fill away from the airport, and the dirty white pickup truck bounced wildly as it emerged from the woods onto the site of the construction. It came to a stop behind Mahoney, who heard it but did not turn his head. The driver got out and left the door open. He came up beside Mahoney and said: "Shipstead called. Wants you to call him."

"Shipstead," Mahoney said, "that dried-up little cunt-hair. What the fuck does he want?"

"Didn't say," the driver said. "Just that he wants to talk to you."

"Shit," Mahoney said. He kicked at the slimy clay and spattered his caked boots with more of it. "I bet he's got his bowels inna rage about his fuckin' gravel again. Him and his fuckin' gravel. 'Make sure you put down enough gravel. We don't want frost heaves.'"

"What's with him and gravel?" the driver said. "His family inna gravel business or something?"

"Nah," Mahoney said, "they're inna fuckin' bird business. They go out and run around in the woods and chase the fuckin' birds and look at them."

"Birdwatchers?" the driver said. "The fuck birdwatchers care about this? We're not hurtin' no birds. Some nests or something, maybe, few of them trees we knocked down. Ask me, the squirrels was the ones that took the beatin' here. I saw lots of goddamned squirrel nests, we're laying this thing out and staking it. I didn't see that many birds' nests."

"That was before we come in here," Mahoney said. "They did all their goddamned screaming about the birds 'fore I even ever heard of this job. That was over when we got here. They yelled and raised all kinds of hell and they went up to Boston and they screamed and hollered some more, and they lost some more, and the bill went through and the bids invitation went out and here we are. The old ladies with their binoculars and little geeks like Shipstead don't like us any better or nothing, but we're here and they got to put up with us. They just don't like it, is all."

"I thought Shipstead was our lawyer here," the driver said.

"He is," Mahoney said.

"But I thought you said he was with the old ladies," the driver said.

"He is," Mahoney said. "Why the fuck you think he's *our* lawyer? That's what we hire the little cunt-ball for, because he's the lawyer for the old ladies with the goddamned binoculars that're always jumping up and down and screaming about the fuckin' digging that we're doing. His fuckin' *mother's* one of the fuckin' old ladies, for Christ sake. The fuck you think I'd rather do, huh? Fight Shipstead's mother and her pals and Shipstead too, bring in some guy from Boston that goes to Mass every Sunday and he's inna Holy Name Society up in Braintree, so all he's got to do is stand up and they know he's the devil right off down here? Bullshit I will. Gimme some guy like Shipstead, that his own mother's friendly with the birdies, and pay him some money and let him fight with his mother and the old ladies instead of me. You got any idea how many permits we got to have here? Shit. Get him and them and the towns offa my back all at once, let me go dig my hole and make an honest fuckin' day's pay for it, for Christ sake."

"Don't he know, that's what you're hiring him for?" the driver said.

"Sure he does," Mahoney said. "The fuck you think him and his mother dreamed that whole scam up about the fuckin' birds inna first place for? They didn't know us, they didn't know us from the guys that come around and want to sell them magazines. All they know is that this airport's gonna have to get bigger so all their friends that watch the birdies can fly in here from everyplace else with their goddamned binoculars and go runnin' around inna woods with them looking at the birdies. And they like that fine. Fuck the birds, at least some of them, if it means their friends can come in. But that don't mean they object to making an honest dollar off of it themselves onna way through. So they all huddle up and call the play and then they go out and start all kinds of a commotion about the birds, and Shipstead ends up getting the legal business. And everybody's happy, 'cept the birds and the squirrels."

"You gonna call him?" the driver said.

"I suppose I might as well," Mahoney said. "I don't, the bastard'll drive me crazy till I do." He allowed his shoulders to slump. He turned and walked back to the truck.

Mahoney got out of the truck as soon as it reached the sixty-foot tan mobile home in the small clearing off the dirt road to the street. The truck settled on its shock absorbers after the trip and Mahoney slammed the door while he stared at the vehicles parked at the trailer. There were two heavy dump trucks idled there, and another pickup truck. It was parked next to seven Johnny-on-the-Spot portable toilets, six of them roped together in a cluster, the seventh lying on its side on the clay.

"Harry," Mahoney said, as the driver got out of the cab, "where the fuck is Fucillo?"

"Vin," Harry said, "I dunno. He hasn't been here."

"You call the motel?" Mahoney said.

"I called it about nine thirty this morning," Harry said. "His wife called here and said was he around, and I said he wasn't in yet and she said she would call the motel. So I figured, I better call right off and tell Billy she is calling before she calls him up and catches him by surprise. See, I told her I didn't have the number, so she would have to look it up. And I called there and I think I'm gettin' that kid at the desk, what's her name?"

"Judy," Mahoney said with distaste. "Judy. Or Tits. And what'd she say?"

"It wasn't her," Harry said. "It was Mrs. Winton but I thought it was Judy, and she told me it wasn't and said she didn't know where the hell Judy was. And then I asked her for Billy's room, and she tells me he already had two calls, from his wife, and he didn't answer. She must've called there before she called here."

"Son of a bitch," Mahoney said, "he's doin' it again. That son of a bitch. He's not a foreman—he's one big foreskin. All cock, from foot to feathers. It comes to broads, that guy, he is just like a dog and hydrants. He just can't take a look at them and keep on going. Nope, he's gotta get his cock out, every one he sees, and he's got to fall in love with every one he fucks. I wonder where the hell he went this time. This's a small island. He got the other truck?"

"He took it last night," Harry said. "I didn't see it when I got home last night though, and it wasn't there this morning."

"*Shit,*" Mahoney said. "His car's over Woods Hole, am I right?"

"He left it there, last Monday, we come down here," Harry said.

"Okay," Mahoney said, "get back inna truck and go back out to the southwest plat there and get the Flynn kid. He's not doing nothing anyway, most likely, and take him down the Vineyard Haven parking lot and look for the truck. It ain't there, go over Oak Bluffs. Have the Flynn kid get it and bring it back."

"How you know it's gonna be in those places?" Harry said.

"Because that's what Billy does," Mahoney said. "This is the first time, far as I know, he hadda pull his scoot onna ferryboat, but Billy don't let new things stop him. He can't sneak out after dark and drive the girl someplace? Okay, he'll sneak her out at night and take a boat someplace." Mahoney laughed. "Son of a bitch. He wouldn't fuck her at the motel because Mrs. Winton'd catch him. He was with me the day we took those rooms and she was very particular about that. Didn't care about booze in them, but no broads makin' lots of noise. 'Not turnin' this place into no hot pillow joint,' she says. 'This is a respectable place. I got trouble enough with my regular guests bringing people in here, and that's just one-night stands. You guys're gonna be here a year or so, and then you'll leave, and you're not gonna leave me in the lurch runnin' no whorehouse with the selectmen all in a fit all the time.' So Billy took her to the late ferry and they screwed off the island, and my truck's at one of those ferryboat docks. Go and get it."

"What about Billy, his wife calls again?" Harry said. "I cover for him?"

"Shee-it," Mahoney said. "How the fuck're you gonna do that? You can't, is what. She's just as wise to him as I am. Shit, she's known him even longer. She's been wise to him since Kennedy was president.

You're not gonna give that lady no song and dance. Forget it."

"I could say he come in and he's out onna job," Harry said.

"You could also say he went to camp meeting last night and got religion and run off to Africa to save the fuckin' niggers," Mahoney said. "She'd be just as likely to believe you. You tell her some fairy story, she'll get the kids dressed and heave them all inna station wagon and bring everybody down here and come out to the trailer and just sit in it until Billy shows up. You ever spend an afternoon with Theresa and those five kids they've got? I'd rather do a stretch in Walpole, for Christ sake. It'd be quieter. Hah, Terry calls him, and she will, you tell her we ain't seen Billy since yesterday, we tried the motel and he ain't there, and we don't know where the fuck he is. I gave up trying to cover for that guy about twenty years ago. Jesus Christ, it is almost twenty years ago. Son of a bitch. I give the guy credit, he's got the staying power. Wonder how much ass he's had? Prolly doesn't know himself. Son of a bitch."

"Won't she go after him?" Harry said.

"Sure," Mahoney said. "I assume she will, anyway. She'll find him, too. Always has before. She's like Frank fuckin' Buck, bringin' Billy back alive. Cheaper'n us lookin' for him. Oh, and in case she asks, which she will because she always does every time she gets a new guy to talk to in the company, tell her I took Billy off the clock as usual until he gets his ass back here. Because you don't, she'll ask you if you can send his checks to her, and she'll swear up and down when she don't get none because we don't pay Billy for the time he spends out fuckin', she will swear you told her his check'd come as usual. Theresa don't change either, over the years."

"Jesus," Harry said, "he's off screwin' some broad and that's all she cares about's his money?"

"Sure," Mahoney said. "You blame her? Five kids? How the fuck's she gonna feed five kids if she don't get any money? Leave him go stick his dong in every hole that hasn't got a gopher in it, she don't care. Least she's gettin' the night off. She don't want six kids, for Christ sake. All she wants is a roof over the five she's already got, and herself too, and something in the icebox. That's what does it. Theresa gets the word: Billy don't work, Billy don't get no money for Terry and the kids, she saddles up the whole bunch and goes lookin' for him and gets his ass back to work. He can screw all he wants, after the quittin' whistle."

"Jesus," Harry said again.

"Then," Mahoney said, "when you and the Flynn kid get back with the truck—keys'll be under the seat where he always leaves them when he gets a hard-on—when you get back with the pickup, check the Flynn kid out on one of them heavies there and get Gilcreese the fork-lift truck over here and load them fuckin' toilets on it. Have the Flynn kid drive them down the freight ferry dock and they'll put them on the flatbeds they got down there. Okay? Those fuckin' things stink like a bastard. Specially that one that's tipped over, there. Guys're shittin' the woods today, huh?"

Harry shrugged.

Mahoney laughed. "Good," he said. "That's another thing we hadda do for Shipstead and his fuckin' mother. No shittin' inna woods. Bad for the plants or something. I oughta make two or three them old bats go inside one of those portables, some nice hot day, and sit there about five or ten minutes. They wouldn't have to take a shit or anything. Just imagine how they'd like to have to sit in there a couple times a day if they did have to take a shit and they happened to be out onna job when it happened. That'd teach 'em little ladies something. Fuckin' Billy. He was supposed to get them fuckin' sewers outta here the day before yesterday. I hope he gets gangrene from this one."

Mahoney climbed the three wooden steps set against the side of the trailer. He opened the aluminum combination door, the storm-window glass still in place, and then the steel inner door. The interior of the trailer was dim, the light tinted orange by the dirt caked on the windows. The air was heavy and musty. He turned on the overhead fluorescent lamps and blinked as the harsh white light flickered into full strength. There was an air conditioner set into the wall over the small aluminum sink and he turned it on. He washed his hands and dried them on paper towels. He wadded up the paper towels and pitched them, left-handed and awkwardly, toward a tall yellow plastic pail set against the oven of a propane stove. He missed. There were several dirty china coffee mugs on the stove and a teakettle next to them on one of the burners. He shook the kettle and filled it from the faucet at the sink. He put it back on the stove while he rummaged through his clothes for a match. He found one, turned the gas on slightly, ignited the burner, and put the kettle on the flame. He held the match, still burning, with his right hand while he fished a pack of Camels from his shirt pocket and attempted to shake one out quickly. The match burned close to his forefinger and thumb while he fumbled. "Shit," he said, and threw it into the sink. He used both hands to light the cigarette, re-placed the pack in his pocket, and turned to his right where there was a refrigerator. Inside he located a fresh quart of milk behind eight quarts of orange juice.

"Fuck you, Billy," he said, moving the orange juice and taking the milk out, "you and your damned health foods, and then you'd fuck a filter bed, nothing else around." He shut the refrigerator door, opened the carton, tilted it up and drank it in two draughts. He threw the empty container toward the yellow pail and missed. He stood meditatively in place for a moment, taking a deep drag of the cigarette. He belched loudly. He exhaled the smoke and belched again, more softly. He said: "Ahh." He rubbed his belly.

Mahoney walked toward the rear of the trailer. The passageway was narrow, taken up by grey steel file cabinets. There were rolls of blueprints and site plans piled on top of them. At the rear of the trailer there was a large, scarred oak desk, its legs bolted to the floor with heavy angle irons. There were three straight wooden chairs in front of it. The top was littered with square foil ashtrays, a clipboard with a large wad of papers stained by coffee, three empty Coca-Cola cans, about ten stubby pencils, a black telephone, several file folders thick with documents, and three CB hand-held radio transceivers. Behind the desk there was a wooden swivel chair. Mahoney made his way among the chairs and squeezed in behind the desk. He sank onto the swivel chair, picked up the phone, and started dialing. He stubbed out the Camel.

"Lucy," he said, in a slightly truculent tone, "Mahoney. He called me." He paused. "That don't concern me, Lucy. Have him tell the client block his ears or go out and have a cup of coffee or something. I hadda come in off the job for this and I'm gonna go back out the job as soon's I talk to him. Put him on." He paused again. He drummed his fingers on the desk. He cradled the phone between his head and shoulder and lit another Camel. He spat the loose grains of tobacco from his lips.

"Ship," he said, in a more pleasant tone, "the fuck is it this time? Somebody discover a new plant or something that we're plowin' under the last batch inna world? I thought we got all that permit stuff taken care of. Somebody want a new boat?" He waited again. His brow furrowed deeply. "Whaddaya mean, Costello? Yeah, I know Costello's in Boston. What the fuck's he want?" He paused. "You're goddamned right, I'd better come in and see you, Ship. I'm coming in right now." He banged the phone down. He slammed the top of the desk with the flat of his left hand. He stood up and put his hands on his hips. He exhaled smoke furiously. *"Mother*fucker," he said. He sat down again. He dialed a 1 and seven digits. He waited.

"Mister Costello's line," he said. "Mahoney. No first name. He'll know: Mahoney." He paused. "Francis, my boy," he said, "I just had a little chat with our friend Shipstead. That's the guy. Yeah. Thought he had another flap with some asshole about us scaring deers with the machinery or something. Yeah. Turns out, sounds like, it's something else bothers him. Yeah. Said something about, it was off-island. Yeah. Mentioned your name. I don't give a shit what you told him, Francis. I don't give a shit what you told me, either, Francis. Yeah. Well, I am going in now to see him, and I'm gonna find out what you told him, and I better like what I hear, you got that? Because if I don't, I am gonna have to come up there and see you, and you know how much I like gettin' all dressed up and that stuff. Yeah."

Mahoney paused again. He leaned back in his chair and put his feet on the desk. He listened for a long time. He took his feet off the desk and hunched over it, resting his elbows amid the clutter. "Now," he said, "that is very fine, Francis, and it is always a pleasure to talk to you, although I've noticed it can get pretty goddamned expensive every so often. But what I am trying to do here on this island is build a fuckin' runway, see? It's not a whole expressway or a new route to the Cape or anything. Just a plain old ordinary goddamned strip of pavement that planes can land on and take off from. I ain't used to these sophisticated things you're always talking about. I never had this trouble 'fore I got ambitious and I was still building patios, you know? Yeah. So, Francis, this is what it is: I am going in to see Shipstead, and I better like what Mister Shipstead's got to say to me, because if I don't I am going to come up and see you, and we are going to have a nice long chat." He paused again. "About money, Frankie," Mahoney said. "Money and Mister Morgan."

5 Joe Gillis, crowding fifty, listened appreciatively to Paul Linder. They stood on the sidewalk on the easterly side of Bowdoin Street in the sunshine. Gillis leaned against the stone wall of the old Hotel Bellevue, and he chuckled low in his throat. That was how Linder knew that Gillis liked the story.

"Jesus Christ, Joe," Linder said, "I almost shit my pants, you know?

Because I knew what was gonna happen. Everybody who was there knows what is gonna happen, right? Except for somebody that's onna furlough from the Convent of Our Little Sisters of Divine Erections or something. Which Bannerman of course is. So we're all, the rest of us, we're all just standing around there inna woods in Proctor, having a glass of beer and we're sweatin' our balls off and all the Polacks're pitchin' horseshoes and woofin' down the keel-bass-ee there. Hotter'n a fuckin' stove. Not a breatha goddamned air, and all these women with big tits're runnin' around sweating their longjohns soaking wet so they get stuck in the cracks of their asses and if you was ever thinking, even just *thinking*, about fuckin' one of these little blondes with the big tits that those Polacks grow up there inna woods that look like they're gonna make the world forget Hollywood before they're twenty and end up looking just like their big fat momma before they turn nineteen, you would forget about it just looking around. And it's 'Hey Rudy' this and 'How's it going, Stevie?' and all that other shit, and they got a ball game going on.

"Now," Linder said, wetting his lips and looking around anxiously, as though making sure he was not under surveillance, "this ain't nothing for the paper, am I right?" He wore a polyester-knit suit in an odd shade of green. It had a gold thread running through it. He wore a green shirt, the shade of Key lime pie. He wore a green tie with white flowers on it, and a white belt and white shoes. He wore a dark-brown coconut-straw Sam Snead hat with a red, cream, and blue Madras band.

"Not for the paper, Paul," Gillis said, smiling. He chuckled once or twice to show he understood.

"I got your word on this," Linder said.

"Like always," Gillis said. He wore a rumpled brown linen suit. He had a stenographer's spiral-bound notepad jammed into the left-hand pocket of the jacket. He wore a brown fedora and brown shoes. He wore a white shirt which did not have enough tail to cover his paunch and at the same time remain tucked in at his belt—it bulged at the front, and the excess material draped over his buckle. He had grey hair, clipped short. His beard was grizzled and heavy and his skin was transparent; he had shaved before coming to work that morning, but he looked as though he had forgotten to do so. His tie was a brown polkadot which he carried in the pocket of his brown suit and put on when he got to the State House. He had a blue one folded in the pocket of his blue suit in the closet at home, and a red one in the pocket of his blue blazer.

"Okay," Linder said, sighing as though he had obtained a very important agreement. He spread his hands and tried to get Gillis to look him in the eye, but Gillis's gaze kept flashing back and forth from Linder to the side door of the State House across the street. "Are you looking for something?" Linder asked.

"Huh?" Gillis said.

"I said," Linder said, "are you looking for something?"

"Up here?" Gillis said. "Sure. I'm always looking for something when I'm up here. I've been coming up here going on thirty years. Seems like a hundred. I'm always looking for something. I always *see* something, too. Seen millions of things, and I know I haven't seen more'n a tenth of the things there are to see. Some're even worth writing about."

"But, nothing special," Linder said. "You're not *expecting* anything?"

"No," Gillis said. "Just habit."

"Because, see, I was wondering," Linder said.

"Yeah," Gillis said. He chuckled again. "So, tell me what happens in the woods."

"Yeah," Linder said. He hitched up his pants. "Now, see, you got to realize, this is the *western* time they have, after the Cape one they put on down Falmouth, all right?"

"I went, the Cape one, myself," Gillis said.

"Naturally," Linder said. "So'd I. You haven't got some reason, go up in the woods there, you're gonna go the Cape one. You make the appearance, right? People see you, know you're not dead like some of them hoped. You eat the steamers, you crack the lobster, you get your picture taken, you're lucky, Ted Kennedy or somebody else. It happens Kennedy's fuckin' poison in your district, then you go home and you're asshole buddies with the fuckin' *President* or something, right? None of that, the western one. The fuck you wanna go out inna fuckin' woods in Proctor, for Christ sake, tramp around onna goddamned ferns and prolly get bit by a fuckin' snake or something, huh? Knox State Park? Fuck it. You don't. So you stay the fuck home or you take the kids the fuckin' beach or you go the fuckin' ball game or some other fuckin' thing. Watcha buncha fuckin' guys named Butch throwin' horseshoes, they look like they oughta be wearin' fuckin' horseshoes, for Christ sake."

Gillis was laughing. Genuinely laughing.

"I'm fuckin' serious," Linder said, laughing, "I mean it. Those guys out there inna Golden West, Speaker calls it, they look like they oughta be pullin' the fuckin' beer wagon inna fuckin' Budweiser commercials, for Christ sake. These guys're gonna help you? How they gonna help you? You got a big rock or a stump or something maybe, your backyard, the guys the highway department can't get it out with a fuckin' backhoe or something, maybe then they could help you. Come around and you could harness them up and they could just pulla fuckin' thing out without even breakin' a sweat. But otherwise? Forfuckinget it. The only way those guys, they can help you, is if you're running in their districts and they come out onna town with you, go down the tire plant and the brewery and just show up with you and stand there so a buncha guys named Charlie'll know you're all right even though they don't know you, and they will vote for you because otherwise some big bastard named Stanley's gonna come around and pound them onna head so their ears stick out their pants pockets. And I'm not lookin' for no support up there."

"I'll bet Archambault was there," Gillis said.

"Raymond?" Linder said. "Raymond would go to a catfight. He don't care where the fuck it is, Raymond don't. He thinks it might possibly help him, he will go to it. You hear about the time, I heard about the time, this thieving little shit name of Samuelson. You know him?"

"I heard of him," Gillis said. "Isn't he, wasn't he the guy the boys put in up there, run that two-bit rundown trotter track in the woods up near Brattleboro?"

"Sure," Linder said, "same fuckin' guy. About four feet tall if you stretched him, and he just got outta Middlesex onna check thing they caught him at. Then all of a sudden he's the big honcho in this wide spot inna road up in Vermont, Arcadia fuckin' Downs. Harness racing, for Christ sake. They had a fuckin' grandstand there that would've fallen down directly onna fuckin' ground, it wasn't for the fuckin' coata cheap fuckin' paint they put on it. I think they only used about two gallons, see if the nags get enough guys in here, bet onna boat races. 'They don't and we'll burn the fuckin' thing Christmas and get the fuck outta here.' They had mosquitoes up there that're so big the fuckin' Air Force's complaining, they're jamming the fuckin' radars up in Maine there every night they got racing and some fresh white meat comes up from Massachusetts. They had the fighters scrambling every race, eight times a night.

"Somebody," Linder said, "somebody gets ahold of Archambault and they tell him there's all kinds of voters and stuff go this track, and they leave out that most of them're big fat jerks from New York that came up the mountains with their families, two weeks vacation inna fuckin' bushes with nothing to do at night once they bang the wife and get through pickin' off the scabs their poison ivy and peeling their fuckin' sunburns, it's so quiet. So Archambault figures this is where he starts runnin' for fuckin' President or something, he don't give a shit what he's running for, long it's something. And the next thing he finds out, he's agreed to go to fuckin' Vermont. They thought they were gonna have to give him a pill or something, calm him down enough so he could present the trophy the fuckin' horse that wins the feature. Which horse, I think, was too tired after to come up inna winner's circle so they just took him right off to the truck from the dog food factory without waiting in case he fell down and died first, and Raymond hadda make the presentation some little kid that had muscular dystrophy or something and her fuckin' family's from fuckin' *Canada*, for Christ sake. And Samuelson didn't give him any money, either. Samuelson didn't *have* any money.

"Sure, Raymond was out inna woods in Proctor," Linder said. "He'd go the track in Vermont—is he gonna miss the chance, show up with the big glad hand in the woods for a thing that's at least in his own state? Absolutely, Raymond is gonna be there, and a whole lot of guys like him. Keepin' in touch.

"So," Linder said, "there is Raymond running around all over the place so everybody will remember him if the Governor don't live or the Lieutenant Governor don't feel so good or the AG gets himself a sore foot or maybe Bernie Morgan gets the heart attack everybody's been promising for years and they will think of old Raymond when they get old Speaker Morgan in the ground at last, and Bannerman don't know what the hell to make of it. See, he has never been to the western one before."

"Coming from Brookline and all," Gillis said. "How'd Raymond like that, Bannerman there?"

"He didn't," Linder said. "The class act and everything? The liberal conscience of the Democratic Party? Milk for the fuckin' babies and money for their fuckin' mummies. Raymond don't like Bannerman's ideas at all, things he wants. You got to have special education so these forty-year-old niggers can get their high school degrees, because otherwise they won't be able, take the college courses we got for them when we finally catch them mugging old ladies and put them inna can for five or ten years. And you gotta teach the Chink kids in Chink and the

Puerto Rican kids in Spanish. You know why a Puerto Rican don't want a blow job?" Linder said.

"No," Gillis said. He had stopped laughing. He had returned to the appreciative chuckle, the way a cat resumes purring when its food dish is replenished.

"Puerto Rican," Linder said, "don't want *no* kind of job." He paused and Gillis forced a laugh. "So anyway," Linder said, nodding, "Bannerman's been to the Cape one, which he would normally go to anyway, but he has got this wild-ass idea he would like to maybe be governor some day, you guys at the *Commoner* think it would be all right if he was and everything, which you do."

"I don't know what everybody else at the *Commoner* thinks," Gillis said. "I don't consult with them and they don't generally confide in me. Which if they did ask me, it wouldn't change much. I myself personally do not give a shit who is governor."

"Bullshit," Linder said. He grinned uncertainly.

Gillis stopped chuckling. "No bullshit, Paul," he said. "I mean it. Pooch Pucci, maybe. Pooch Pucci may care who is governor. If it's a guy that went to Choate and Harvard with him, he can invite him over to Carlisle in the morning and they can have a Bloody Mary and go put on their red coats. Get on their goddamned horses and go tearing around all over hill and bloody dale chasing a pack of dogs that're chasing a bag of fox piss some kids dragged around in the bushes to keep the hounds busy. If it's a guy that came up off the docks and wants to spend the whole day watching his gumbahs play bocci, Pooch can put on his sneaks and sit with him over anisette and coffee in the morning down in the North End. Pooch maybe cares. He needs something he can do, Sundays.

"I," Gillis said, "I do not. Weekends if I see a pol I did something wrong. On Sunday mornings I go play with my kids. I have dinner with my wife. On Monday mornings I come to work, and on Friday nights I go home. You could put Elizabeth fucking Taylor in the governor's office bollicky-bareass, and it wouldn't make one nickel's worth of difference to me. As long as Bernie Morgan or somebody is Speaker, and John Tierney or somebody is governor, and all the other offices've got some kind of people in them, all they got to be is alive, somebody will be doing something idiotic every single day of every single week, and that gives me my bread and butter. If Jesus Christ Himself was governor, I would still have something to write about. That's all I care."

"Yeah," Linder said, "well, there's a lot of people that read that column of yours there that aren't so sure of that sometimes."

"They're too sensitive," Gillis said. "You know how the boys are. They're always seeing things that aren't there."

"Is Bannerman one of those?" Linder said.

"Hell, Paul," Gillis said, "I'm not even sure that Bannerman's there, and I see *him*. Wasn't for the lead in his shoes, he'd float clear off the ground. Has that guy got any idea of what's really going on in this state, when there's something going on in this state?"

"I don't think so," Linder said. "He sure didn't that day in Proctor anyway. He shows up in his ice-cream suit, you know the one? Looks like he's gonna leave early and go sell Popsicles, the kids at the playground. Just in time to ruin their suppers. Nice white suit. All the guys see him, wearing their bowling shirts and their T-shirts that got various things onna front that say which tavern they're on the softball team, and they're going up to him and looking at him up and down like he was a broad or something, walking around and looking at the back of him. 'Hey, Donnie, ya think, huh? Guy's gonna make his First Communion or something.'

"Bannerman don't register none of this, right? Goes right over his head like it was clouds inna fuckin' sky, where his head is. Tells me he's got to go his sister's wedding down in Newton right after, won't have time to go home and change. Also tells me, it's at the country club they got there, you know? Not at no church or the temple or anything, tells me it's her third marriage but he's still gotta go. The hell's he telling me it's her third for, huh? Business of mine, huh? I don't know what to say. And this is when Morgan shows up.

"Now," Linder said, "you know the entrance, right? The whole drill with the big car like it was the Pope dropping in just by way of no harm, see how the kids in the third grade're doing and are they learning their catechism like Jesus and Sister Mary Helen Douchebag want?"

"I have seen the ritual," Gillis said.

"I think he crabbed that act off of Cardinal Cushing, I swear it," Linder said. "The only thing he could do to make it better, he could come in on a fuckin' white horse, wear a red cape, and wave a fuckin' saber around like he was Caesar or something. George Washington. So he comes in, and he gets out, nice blue jacket, white shirt, no tie, close shave, the whole bit. Must've taken two guys sittin' on his chest for three days, dry him out and clean him up for this thing, I figure, because I seen him drunk myself four nights before at the Claret. He was practically fallin' in the fuckin' soup. Not now, though. Looks like King Kong straight from the barber shop and Brooks Brothers too. And he helps his fuckin' wife out the car. 'Jesus H. Christ,' Bannerman says. 'My fuckin' goddamned word, who the fucking hell is that?' "

"Bannerman?" Gillis said. "Bannerman said that? Bannerman doesn't swear. He wouldn't say *shit*, he hadda mouthful. League of Women Vultures'd be shocked, they knew this."

"I mean it," Linder said. "Don't go sneaking none of this into your goddamned column there now, Gillis."

"Come on, Paul," Gillis said. "Small shit like that? Cut it out. Kind of surprising, though, number of times Bannerman had the knife shoved up his ass and twisted a few times inna State House, never said even *hell* or *damn*. And then Maggie Morgan sets him off?"

"Right," Linder said. He giggled.

"Well, Jesus," Gillis said. "Maggie's harmless enough. Cripes, I've only seen her three, four times, all the years I been here, but she's fairly ordinary. Nice sexy little broad, but ordinary. Small woman? Five feet or so? Sort of dull blond hair, nice build, don't dress to show it off, kind of shy. Looks like a librarian. Librarian in a small town that hasn't got many books. None of them sex books. That the one?"

"The legal Maggie, yeah," Linder said. He was having trouble controlling his laughter. He spluttered. "Thing of it was, Bannerman wasn't prepared for the legal Maggie. 'Who the hell is that?' he says. Guy next to him's one of the Stanleys. Don't know Bannerman. Know him, hell, he'd never even seen anything like Bannerman before that day in his life. Never been out the fuckin' woods since the day he was born, except when he was in the Marines and they sent him Korea or some place. He thought the only kind of people in the world that didn't look like him and Butch and Steve and all the other Stanleys was little yellow bastards that carried rifles and wore padded uniforms and spent all their time trying to shoot you. He looks where Bannerman's looking, at the car. 'Her?' the guy says. 'That's Mrs. Morgan, of course.' 'His *mother*?' Bannerman says. He sounds like he's gonna choke to death. Guy looks at him like he's thinking about maybe he should pound Bannerman onna back, help him clear his throat. I was sort of hoping he would. Guy this size hits Bannerman, even trying to help him, Bannerman's gonna land inna dirt in his nice white suit. 'No,' the guy says. See, he's decided maybe Bannerman's all right, he ain't choking after all. Crazy, maybe. Maybe stupid. But he'll be all right, maybe. Couple kegs of beer'll fix him up. He's gonna be patient with this nut. 'Mrs. Morgan. Maggie Morgan. Speaker's wife. They been married for ages.'

"Now," Linder said, "Bannerman gets all red. He's been parading around up there inna woods, introducing himself and telling everybody he's this great pal, the Speaker's, and it looks like he never met the Speaker's wife, Maggie. Which, of course, he didn't, if it was the legal Maggie you were talking about, because the Mrs. Morgan that the Speaker introduced him to at the Cape thing there was not the legal Maggie Morgan that stays up in the woods and only comes out when the Speaker bangs onna cage and tells her he wants her to come out. The Maggie Morgan that he met down in Falmouth there with all the guys eatin' lobster and clams and lying about their golf scores was the *real* Maggie."

"Maggie Gault," Gillis said.

"Right," Linder said. "Well, if that's her last name, I dunno. The one that says she's Mrs. Morgan and lives in the apartment with him at the Pru over there. That one. The big blonde with the tits like a coupla brass torpedoes out in front of her."

"That's the one," Gillis said.

"Yeah," Linder said. "Well, me and Andy Boyce, the guy from Brighton-Allston?"

"Yeah," Gillis said, chuckling.

"Me and Andy," Linder said, "we're up there sort of showing Bannerman around, you know? Wasn't something we planned or anything. He didn't ask us. Just that we been to the thing before on account of me being with Raymond there a couple times when him and the Speaker was still gettin' along . . ."

"You mean," Gillis said, "before Raymond made it a little too obvious that he was getting a little impatient for the Speaker to retire or die or something. And you and Andy decided you'd maybe get a fresh horse for governor. Like, say, Bannerman?"

"Hey," Linder said, "they still get along all right. There was never any trouble between them two guys, Raymond and the Speaker."

"Uh huh," Gillis said. "Okay, but I still think the Speaker caught on when Raymond kept taking his pulse all the time."

"Nope," Linder said, "they're still good buddies."

"You say so, Paul," Gillis said.

"Yeah," Linder said. "So, anyway, we got to take Bannerman in the bushes, me and Andy, and we tell him: this is the Speaker's legal wife that he's with. And Bannerman's all over us about who is this other broad that he meets onna Cape. I tell you, Joe, it was the funniest god-damned thing I seen in some time. Bannerman has got to be the only guy in the State House that didn't know about the two Maggies. 'Christ,' he says, he's all upset, 'he must be crazy. Bernie must be crazy. Pulling a stunt like that, doesn't even divorce his first wife and marry the second one? Papers ever get ahold of that, it'll be the end of him.' "

"What?" Gillis said.

"That's what he said," Linder said. "He said if you guys ever found out Morgan's got two wives, one that legally is, but really isn't, and the other one that legally isn't but really is, it's gonna sink him."

"Jesus Christ," Gillis said, "he really is about the same weight as a feather duster, isn't he? Does he think people still care about that shit?"

Linder grinned. "Lemme put it this way, Joe," he said, "Mike Bannerman's a hell of a nice guy, and he wouldn't hurt a fly. Hell, he'd be against capital punishment if the guy was convicted of hacking Bannerman's mother to death with a dull hatchet. Sincere as hell. But innocent as hell also. Me and Andy Boyce, we sort of had it with him after that, you know? Jack Tierney never did Brighton-Allston or Third Norfolk any favors, and I could use some help from him in Needham, but Bannerman's not the guy, is what I think."

"Ah," Gillis said. "I assume it's okay, I do a think piece about Mike Bannerman's liberal ideas alienating powerful support among colleagues in the House?"

"Hey, Joe," Linder said, "it's your column. You do what you want. No names, though. You know me, telling funny stories."

"Lemme ask you, Paul," Gillis said. "Just off the top of your head: how's Bernie Morgan feel about Jack Tierney running for reelection, huh?"

"Well," Linder said, "I haven't discussed it with the Speaker directly, right? But I think if Tierney was to show a little more interest in some of the problems that the reps've got, the ones that could help him, I think probably the Speaker'd like to see him renominated."

"The Speaker," Gillis said, "the Speaker is a thoughtful man."

6 First Assistant D.A. Brian Hanrihan, having effortlessly committed to his memory those passages of that morning's "State House Viewpoint" column which he found especially insightful, had spent all

of the first day of the Dussault trial striving to be vigorous and hit hard. He had endeavored simultaneously to keep the entire courtroom under his surveillance so that he might spot and identify those unnamed on-lookers whom Joe Gillis had predicted would be watching closely what he did. He had not picked out any such observers, and he suspected the distraction of the attempt had facilitated Dory Feldman's masterful confusion of his first witness, Henrietta Benedict. The combination of fatigue, frustration, and exasperation had by the afternoon recess left Hanrihan's temper somewhat frayed, and he made a quick decision on the short walk from the prosecutor's table to the entrance of the chambers of Judge Warren Matte: he would assert himself in there as force-fully as possible. Brian Hanrihan at thirty-three had filled out agreeably beneath the cherubic blond curls that framed his face, and he knew that women found his blue eyes and white, even teeth only two of his many appealing features. He believed that he was old enough and certainly in a position lofty enough to entitle him to more deference than Feldman had seen fit to accord him, or Matte had considered appropriate to make Feldman accord him.

"You," Brian Hanrihan declared to Dory Feldman as soon as the bai-liff had retreated from the office and closed the door behind him, "are badgering that witness." As Feldman in the act of fishing a cigarette out of his jacket pocket paused to looked at him with mild amusement, Hanrihan turned to the judge and said: "And you, Your Honor, are not doing much to stop him."

Judge Matte's eyebrows were still going up as he resumed the process of sitting down which he had interrupted at Hanrihan's remark, when Feldman said, almost drawling: "My God, Your Honor, can you beat that? Here the lad presents us with a woman whose resemblance to the late Hermione Gingold unfortunately does not extend to her memory for her lines, tries to lead her through the whole case like she's a spaniel on a leash, and now he has the common gall to scold you for not allow-ing him to do it."

Warren Matte shook his head. He chuckled and took out his pipe. He commenced the ritual of lighting it while Hanrihan stared sternly at him and Feldman subsided into his chair like a large dog lying down. While he played with the tobacco pouch, the tamper, and the match, he cleared his throat and talked. "You know, Brian," he said, "twenty-two years or so ago, when I finally give up the idea I was going to transform the General Court of Wilfred Knox into a place of comfort, hope, and light, and traded my crusader's sword and shield for my black dress, I thought, I actually believed, that I was leaving behind all the circus crap and foolishness that had begun to bore me." He blew out the match with a large puff of heavy, spicy smoke which Hanrihan waved irritably away from his face. "Now here I am," the judge said sadly, "acting as master of ceremonies for another version of Arthur Godfrey's 'Talent Scouts,' except in the one you're putting on I haven't seen a majorette play the accordion or any very fat girls tap-dance to the score from *Annie*. It gets a little wearisome, you know?"

Hanrihan's face became redder. "That woman, Judge," he said, "has spent her entire adult life keeping the books and ledgers of a small trucking company, and that is all she's done. She doesn't answer phones and she does not negotiate with customers. She's got no experience at all in dealing with the public. Naturally when she gets up there on that witness stand, she's going to be completely flustered. Of course she's nervous, with all those people looking at her and that blasted TV camera practically shoved down her throat."

"Rubbish," Feldman said, still in the elaborate drawl he had put on. "That woman's about as stagestruck as Johnny Carson would be. She gave that camera her best side the instant she stood up there, and she hasn't shifted her position once since she went into it. She's a perfect specimen of what I said would be the effect of those cameras on the conduct of important trials. She absolutely loves it."

Hanrihan began to speak and Matte cut him off. "Brian," he said, "the facts here are the facts and there is nothing you can say to change them. Mrs. Benedict is obviously unable or unwilling to offer her testimony without being led. Whether that's because she's not prepared, which would be your fault, or because she's under the impression she's auditioning for M-G-M, which would be her fault, or because Dory here's succeeded in getting her so rattled she no longer knows whether she's on foot or on horseback, it doesn't really matter. What does matter is that it's nearly half past three, and I am going to let the jury go until tomorrow morning. Maybe if she gets a good night's sleep she'll be able to come back in here and stick to what's admissible in this case, which is whether she was carrying non-persons on the company payrolls to cover up kickbacks to Jean Dussault on a sweetheart contract. So," Matte said, "why don't you go out and have a word with her and make that suggestion to her, and then come back in here and we'll see if we can make a few rude guesses about how long this piss-ant case is going to take. Because I'm supposed to sit down on Nantucket, come June first, and I would like to do it."

Hanrihan's neck muscles bulged as did the ones at his jawline. "Your Honor," he said, gripping the arms of his chair, "that's a prejudicial remark and I really must protest it. The Commonwealth has got as much right to a fair trial of this case as Jean Dussault has, and if that's an indication of the attitude you're going to take, I move for a mistrial."

Matte shook his head and looked at'Feldman. Then he let out a deep breath and shifted his eyes to Hanrihan's face. "Brian," he said, "I should not have said that. I admit it. On the other hand, we are in chambers here. The jury isn't present and it isn't on the record. Furthermore, it *is* a piss-ant case, in my opinion, and there's nothing you or I or anybody on this earth can do about that. The best I can do is keep my view of it a secret from the jury. That I will try to do. In exchange I'd like from you your solemn promise that you won't ask me to believe I'm trying Adolf Eichmann here, okay? The Commonwealth will get a fair trial, and that's the best that any judge can do."

"Jean Dussault is a leg-breaker," Hanrihan said angrily.

Matte nodded while Dory Feldman grinned. "For purposes of argument," Matte said, "I'd agree with you even if I didn't know that's probably exactly what he is. But that isn't what you've got him for, labor violence and strikebreaking. You haven't got him for those things because you can't prove that he does those things. So you've got him for what you think you have a shot at proving. Which is, if you manage it, the same sort of cozy arrangement to give people extra tax-free pocket money that's made this the great republic that it is. Illegal, sure, because the people who don't share the pocket money get quite envious of those who do. But still, Brian, a piss-ant case."

"This man," Hanrihan said in a choked voice, "has evidence of wrongdoing that could put an end to the accepted ways of doing business in this Commonwealth," he said. "His conviction—"

Judge Matte put up his hand. "Brian," he said, "please. No speeches. Just go and tell your witness what I said, and we'll wait here for you, and when you've finished with her, come back here and we'll see what we can rough out for the rest of this week, okay?"

Hanrihan looked uncertain.

"Oh, for heaven's sake, Brian," Feldman said, "go ahead, willya? You think Warren's going to bag your case for me while you talk to your woman? Cripes."

"Brian," Matte said. "Take your time. We won't discuss your case, I promise you."

"Well," Hanrihan said, "okay. But I was actually thinking about you guys. It's just I was concerned, you've got reporters here and all, and I know how it might look."

Matte made a small wave. "I'll take my chances," he said. "If the press thinks after all these years that Warren Matte's in the tank, it's too late to worry now about my spotless reputation."

Hanrihan got up and left the office. He did not shut the door all of the way. Matte looked at it, looked at Feldman, and smiled. "Can you beat that?" Feldman, grinning, got up and shut the door. "Jesus Christ," Matte said, "there're days when I really have to wonder."

"He's young," Feldman said.

"I know," Matte said. "He's young and he is gonna save the world, and old Joe Gillis there this morning, everybody's favorite seedy hack, wished him Godspeed in the enterprise. He's probably already drafting his announcement in his mind that he won't seek a third term as attorney general because he's going for the Senate nomination." The judge snickered. "I guess I was the same way myself, pretty much," he said. "We got that big Dump Wilfred movement going in the House, and *Time* latched onto it and did that little piece about the Young Turks in the Massachusetts legislature, and for a couple heady moments I entertained some high ambitions of my own." He laughed again. "Funny thing," he said, "but my constituents in Quincy were nowhere near as impressed by what *Time* said about me as they were by what old Wilfred did to a couple bills that would've meant about four million dollars in state aid for the city. All of a sudden they did not seem quite so proud of me, and when Wilfred set up that transparent deal to get me appointed to the bench, well, I must admit it did have its attractive features."

"Kind of alarming though," Feldman mused, "if Joe Gillis was right about what he said this morning. That kid in charge of a commission with the powers that it seems to have? Do a lot of damage to the notion of due process 'fore he's through."

"Ahh," Matte said derisively, "what the hell are you griping about? A guy in your position stands to make a couple million of his own, the indictments start to come out every day, and the naughty boys start getting worried. You draw Bernie Morgan there, you'd have the case of your career."

"Is that so, now?" Feldman said. "Assuming that a pol can get a fair trial in this Commonwealth, you really think that I'd like Bernie Morgan for a client? Give up my summer's sailing for that pirate?"

"Gracious, Dory," Matte said, "you don't mean that you hate the man so much you wouldn't want to see him get the best lawyer in town. Or that you actually believe somebody else is the best lawyer in the town."

"Absolutely not," Feldman said. "It's much more serious than that. I don't think Bernie Morgan has any money."

The door to Matte's office opened and Hanrihan returned. "Brian," Matte said, his face an illustration of innocence, "Dory and I here were just shooting the shit about one thing and another, and he's just made a startling remark. He doesn't think that Bernie Morgan has a lot of money. You agree with that?"

Hanrihan did not contrive to keep his surprise off his face. "No money?" he said. "Bernie Morgan with no money? Bernie Morgan's got more money than God has, after all he's taken from the till."

"See?" Matte said to Feldman. "You're getting soft in your old age, Dory."

Feldman looked chagrined but somewhat sly. "Son of a gun, Warren," he said. "Well, if you two say so, I guess I must be wrong. But tell me something, huh? If Bernie Morgan's stolen so much money, how come everybody thinks that he's still stealing?"

7 Frank Costello's offices had three arched windows overlooking Joe Twiss Corner and the east end of the State House opposite the intersection of Beacon and Bowdoin streets. It offered him a view of people whose visits to the State House interested him and whose habit of skulking was so pronounced that they indulged it in broad daylight even when their purposes were completely innocent. He left his office only with extreme reluctance, and when he had been kept away from it as he had been that late spring afternoon, he returned to it in an evil mood.

Collecting his phone messages from Yvonne at the reception desk—Costello was the only partner in the firm without a personal secretary, his preference for writing very little down and placing his own phone calls leaving him without the need for one—he provided her with as much explanation of where he had been as he would give to anyone: "I was at the Algonquin Club," he said, "having lunch with some young businessmen who think because they've made some money paving pastures and constructing stores out of cinder block and wallboard they know all there is to know about the world in general and the government in particular."

The businessmen had praised the governor, John Tierney, as honest and sincere. "He is," Costello had agreed. The boldest of the businessmen had stated his opinion that John Tierney was also pretty much a fool. "He is," Costello had agreed, somewhat to their surprise. Therefore, the businessmen had said in confidence to Frank Costello, the next year and a half before election should be spent selecting an attractive candidate and accumulating a large war chest which would enable him to overwhelm the governor in the democratic primary and leave him virtually unbeatable in the general election. Costello, convinced the boldest businessman had been shaving his choice for that assignment ever since he had reached puberty, reacted to the idea with feigned astonishment. "For the love of the dear Lord Jesus," he had said, "why the hell would anybody want to do a damned fool thing like that?"

The self-appointed leader, somewhat puzzled, had explained elaborately and patiently to Frank Costello that this strategy would almost certainly get rid of Tierney. "Of course it would," Costello said, "and that would be a stupid thing to do. Why the hell do you think every man in this state that turned down a Medicare lobotomy and kept his brain instead was backing Tierney with his next-to-last dollar and all the breath that he could muster in the last election, for the love of God? Because he *looks* good, because he *is* good, and most of all because he's probably the biggest asshole that God ever made to look just like a movie hero. I know gentlemen in other states who'd *die* to get a guy like Tierney in as governor. The guy is absolutely *perfect.* There isn't a spot on him, he can rattle off that social justice shit like he was Bing Crosby rolling into 'White Christmas,' and he hasn't got the foggiest idea of how on earth to do it. Christ," Frank Costello said, taking the name of the Lord in vain to show he really meant it, "you get a guy that listens and does what you tell him to, you don't try to get rid of him. You keep him, and you thank the Lord for sending him to you."

Yvonne said she had heard the food was good at the Algonquin Club. "It is," Costello replied absently, shuffling through the messages until he came to Levin Shipstead's. He put that in his shirt pocket and crumpled the rest in his left hand. Then he dropped them in the wastebasket beside Yvonne's neat desk. "It's just too far away from here," he said, " 'way the hell out on Com Ave there. Makes me nervous when I'm not around this neighborhood."

Frank Costello concluded his discussion with Yvonne with that smile and went into his private office. He removed his dark-blue suitcoat and draped it on the Harvard chair between his desk and the door. He went to the desk and sat down. Referring to the message, he dialed the number himself—Costello placed his own calls; switchboard operators often had visitors within earshot, and somehow never understood why they should not repeat aloud the name and number of the person Costello wished to reach.

Costello spoke softly and pleasantly to Lucy when she answered Shipstead's phone in Edgartown, and got some useful information in return. She told him that Vincent Mahoney had been in and had been very angry. She said he had shouted at Mr. Shipstead. She reported that Mahoney had used bad language. She said Mahoney had left appearing to be angrier than he had been when he arrived. Costello said he was puzzled by this. Lucy put him through to Shipstead. Costello made a note to remember Lucy with a poinsettia at Christmas. He sent out nearly one hundred poinsettias each Christmas, and almost as many Easter lilies when they were appropriate. He ran a large account at Boland's Finer Florists in West Roxbury, whose lavish floral offerings were familiar decorations at wakes from Provincetown to Pittsfield; Joseph Boland was Frank Costello's maternal uncle, and the three-figure monthly bills were paid promptly each month from Costello's private petty cash account.

"Lee," he said, when Shipstead came on, "returning your call. You didn't get him calmed down, I take it. What seems to be the trouble?" Shipstead sounded overwrought. "Now, Lee," Costello said, "let's take it easy here. I'm sure we can work this thing out. What set him off?" Shipstead told him. "That surprises me," Costello said. "He knew the amount when he got into this. He knew it was a continuing obligation, if there were complications." Shipstead said that Mahoney appeared to have forgotten what he had known. "Umm," Costello said. "Well, he's coming up here, you say?" Shipstead said Mahoney was indeed planning to go to Boston. "Tonight, eh?" Costello said. "I'll see what I can do. I'm sure we'll be able to work this thing out." He had left his chair and was lifting his coat as he hung up the phone.

Costello emerged from 22 Beacon at his usual moderate pace. He paused on the step and buttoned his jacket. Then he shot his cuffs while he surveyed the Hill. He saw Joe Gillis coming out of the Bowdoin Street door of the State House. He composed his thoughts, waited for a break in traffic, and crossed the street. Frank Costello never varied his regular speed afoot. If his errand was unimportant, the moderate pace made people wonder if it was important. If it was important, his refusal to hurry suggested that it was not. He maneuvered courteously through the small groups of State House employees sneaking out of work early and met Gillis at the southeast corner of the building, next to the granite wall retaining the lawn. He always had time for a word with Gillis.

"Frangie," Gillis said, "you're lookin' fit."

Costello gave Gillis a small smile. "Clean living, Joe," he said. "Whaddaya hear? Anything going on?"

Gillis shrugged. "Shouldn't I be the one asking you that?" he said.

"Go ahead, Joe," Costello said. "Far as I know, there isn't a damned thing going on. Except maybe Brian Hanrihan's ascension into heaven that I read about in your column this morning."

Gillis ignored that. "That means there is and I failed to earn my keep today for Pucci," he said. "You and Morgan aren't gonna spring anything like World War Three between now and the cocktail hour, are you? I was thinking about maybe having a cold glass before I go back to the paper."

"Not a thing, Joe," Costello said. "If Morgan is, he hasn't told me about it. Go ahead."

"Care to join me?" Gillis said. He nodded toward the Golden Dome.

"Ahh, hell," Costello said, "I'd like to, Joe, but I've got a couple clients comin' in this afternoon. Old ladies. Estate plan. You know how it is, smell of booze on your breath and they're gone."

"Those're remarkably long-lived old ladies," Gillis said. "They've been visiting your office pretty regularly ever since I came up here, and that's a long time. As we both know, Francis."

Costello grinned. "The best kind of clients, Joe," he said. "The ones that live a long time and like regular, billable conferences that keep them up to date and reassured."

"Yeah," Gillis said. "I'd really like to see those old ladies some time, Frangie," he said. "Not meet them or anything. Just catch a glimpse of them, you know? Must be hardy old birds, those girls."

Costello grinned again. "I'll try to remember to set it up, Joe," he said. He tapped Gillis on the right forearm, winked, and continued on his way. He entered the State House by the side door.

It was cool in the basement of the building, dim and silent. Costello's leather heels clicked discreetly on the marble floors. He passed the elevators serving the southeast wing and continued on past offices where a few secretaries did crossword puzzles or chatted on the telephone, cradling the handsets between ear and shoulder, buffing nails while they talked. Occasionally a phone rang unattended in some distant office behind a closed door with a frosted glass panel that prevented passersby from seeing whether anyone was doing anything behind it. Costello liked the State House best in the warm weather, when few even pretended to be actually working and no one had the energy to cause trouble.

The operator of the one working self-service elevator at the southwest corner of the State House was sitting on his stool outside the car. He was reading the *Armstrong* carefully and checking off his choices for the day's program at Hollywood Park. He was in his late twenties, the youngest of three strapping sons born to the late Edmund Cahill, Governor's Councillor from Dorchester, and Mary Margaret (O'Toole) Cahill, chief clerk in the Suffolk County Register of Probate. Mary Margaret Cahill was considered the first woman ever to serve on the Council, despite the fact that she had never run for it nor been appointed to fill out a term; as long as Edmund lived, Mary Margaret had her say, and when he died she had been having it so long that no one even thought to commence ignoring her. Her eldest son, Jake, was elected to replace his father. The middle son, Michael, "the one that inherited all of Mary Margaret's brains," was sheriff of Suffolk County and an unannounced candidate for mayor of Boston, who at least once every two weeks issued another statement saying that he was not yet announcing his candidacy for the office of mayor of Boston. The elevator operator was Forgan Cahill. Costello said, "Hullo, Forgie," and went into the elevator.

Forgan did not get up immediately from his stool, and Costello did not push the panel button for the third floor. Forgan had been the victim of a breech birth and his face was distorted on the right side where the forceps had been cruel. Any son of Mary Margaret Cahill's who suffered a breech birth and facial disfigurement, along with being christened Forgan and being called Fahgin', which sounded suspiciously like "fuckin' " when slurred by experienced State House people who did not like any Cahill, had certain privileges. Among them were the $28,500-a-year job operating a self-service elevator, the bookmaking franchise for the southwest end of the State House, which was good for another $700 or $800 a week—considerably more during the World Series, the month before the Super Bowl, the Stanley Cup playoffs, the NBA playoffs, and the week before the Kentucky Derby—and the limitless patience of anyone whose desire for elevator transportation happened to coincide with Forgan's handicapping sessions. Costello stood quietly in the elevator until Forgan finished his immediate calculations, folded the *Armstrong*, stood up, put the *Armstrong* in his right rear pocket, sighed, moved his stool back away from the elevator door, and entered the cab. Forgan punched the panel button which turned on the elevator, glanced back at Costello, nodded as though noticing him for the first time, and said: "Third." Costello nodded. The car doors slid shut.

Forgan operated the elevator with his eyes raised toward heaven, as though ensuring safe progress upwards. He whistled and hummed alternate eight-bar passages from "La Donna è mobile." Between the basement and the first floor he said: "Seen Pavarotti down the Esplanade last week."

"No kidding," Costello said. "Didn't know he was in town."

Forgan laughed quietly. "Most guys didn't," he said. "I run into Linder there the other night, down the Rusty Scupper. You know Paul Linder."

"Yeah," Costello said. "Haven't seen him, a while."

"Stupid shit," Forgan said. "He was pickin' up broads as usual. Tryin' to. Asshole. I know this broad, works for the airlines. Delta? She was tellin' me, he's always down there. Or the Parker House. The Aer Lingus crews, they stay at the Parker House? She was tellin' me."

"Yeah," Costello said. The elevator passed the first floor and continued upward.

"Yeah," Forgan said. "She was tellin' me. The new girls that come on the Boston run, they all get warned 'fore they ever leave Shannon the first time. You go in the Last Hurrah, downstairs the Parker House there? Look out this guy Linder, Paul Linder. Asshole. They all know him. He thinks he wears the green alla time, broads and people'll think he's Irish. Wouldn't matter if they did. Then they'd just think he was an Irish asshole. 'Nother Irish asshole."

The elevator reached the third floor and the door opened automatically. Cahill shut off the power. He turned away from the panel. The call buzzer sounded on the second floor. "I see Linder down the Scupper," Forgan said, "and I say to him: 'You see Pavarotti?' and he looks at me." Forgan laughed. "I knew what he's gonna say, 'fore he says it. 'Didn't know he was in town,' he says. Sure he didn't. Didn't know he was on the earth. Pavarotti? Who the fuck is Pavarotti? I decide, I'm gonna give him the business for a while. Wasn't anythin' else going on.

Have some fun with Linder. 'Sure,' I says to him. 'Governor was there and the Mayor and everything.' He gets all upset. Give him a little more. 'I heard Tip O'Neill was even there.' He thinks it's a time they had for somebody and he wasn't invited. You can see him, he's thinkin' like a bastard: 'Who the fuck's this Pavarotti ginney guy that Cahill's talkin' about?' Only he's afraid, he asks me, that'll mean he don't know who Pavarotti is and maybe he's the fuckin' national chairman the Democratic Party or something. So he don't dare ask me. And I see I got him. 'Yeah,' I says, 'everybody was there. You didn't hear about it or something?' He's got to admit it now. 'No,' he says. 'I must've been down the Cape or something, the family.' Right, the family. Last time Linder seen that wife of his, she caught him comin' out the Lenox with a babe and he hadda tell her it was some lobbyist from the beauticians' convention or something. She was a lobbyist all right. She wasn't hangin' around the lobby the Lenox some night, it was because she was over the Sheraton Boston or down the Park Plaza, drummin' up business. 'Well,' I says, 'I'm surprised you didn't hear about it just the same, even down there. This guy is very big in the Cape and Islands District, is what I hear.' And then I left him. It was beautiful.''

Costello judged that Forgan had finished. He laughed politely and started toward the corridor. Forgan reached around the corner of the elevator door and pulled out another stool, identical to the one he had been using in the basement. He skidded it around and sat on it next to the door as Costello emerged from the car. The call buzzer for the second floor rang again. Forgan pulled out his *Armstrong* and resumed his handicapping. Forgan made trips in the elevator only when a passenger presented himself on the floor where Forgan had stopped with his previous passenger. He did not deadhead up and down all day, picking up people wherever they happened to be, catering to their whims. Forgan believed that most of his passengers hurried needlessly. "They would be in better shape," he said, "if they climbed the stairs more anyway. Especially the lazy bastards that won't even walk down, for Christ sake. No wonder they're always having heart attacks and stuff all the time."

It was quiet on the third floor of the State House. The gallery of the Hall of Flags yielded from the first floor only the occasional murmur of a conversation being conducted in one of the corridors branching off it. Costello's leather heels clicked on the marble. He stopped at the tall paneled double doors of the Speaker's Chambers, knocked once, got no answer, turned the latch and found it locked, rapped once again. He waited. He knocked again. There was no answer. He looked up the corridor and down, and across the gallery to the corridor on the other side. There was no one in sight. He took a key case from his pocket, unsnapped it, selected a key, fitted it to the lock, unlocked the door, and put the key case back in his pocket.

He went into the reception area of the Speaker's Chambers. There were four secretarial desks arranged on the medium blue carpet, the tops of them neat and clean, the stenographer's chairs pushed up flush against them. Costello stared at them, paused, frowned, turned back and locked the doors behind him. He walked past the visitors' chairs along the northerly wall to the doors leading into the Speaker's private offices. He opened the one on the left about two inches.

Along the westerly wall, in front of leather-upholstered chairs and the tall windows draped with light blue velvet, the four women who occupied the desks in the reception area were standing and clapping their hands. Nearest the door was Gineen Foley, who was eighteen and filling her first job out of St. Thomas Aquinas Secretarial School. Gineen had come to work carrying a change of clothes for the softball game that night at Dillman Field in Jamaica Plain, State House Secretaries vs. WHDH All-Stars. She had removed the dirndl skirt and blouse she had worn to work and put on tight white shorts and a red tank top. She was leading the older women in cheers. They were all sweating heavily. It was hot work and they had loosened their blouses and skirts for it. Connie Mulready had found it impossible to perform in the tight slit skirt she had worn, one of several she had bought after divorcing her second husband; she had removed it and was kicking in her pantyhose. Connie did not make it a practice to wear anything under her pantyhose. Her dark pubic hair made a mound under the sheer nylon. Gineen shouted: "Morgan, Morgan, he's our man. If Morgan can't do it, nobody can." She whooped at the end of it.

The Speaker had his buttocks pressed against the front end of his enormous desk. He had removed his jacket and tie and rolled up the sleeves of his shirt. His forearms were heavy. There was an Old Glory tattoo on the right forearm and a naked woman on the left forearm. He was crouching with his hands cupped under the rump of Samuel Kilgore, counsel to the House of Representatives. Kilgore was also tieless and had gotten himself into an approximation of the stance he had used playing center for the St. Sebastian's football team some twenty years before. He grasped a game football given to the Speaker by the New England Patriots. There were two young reps in three-point stances flanking Kilgore; Rep. Andy Boyce of Allston-Brighton was poised in a wide receiver's position off to the easterly end of the line. Costello knew the other one only as Flaherty. The Speaker said: "Aw *right*. Callin' 'n audible at the line. On three. Eighty-eight inna playbook. All-niggers-go-deep play. Hut, one. Hut, two. Hut, three."

Boyce broke from his position as Kilgore snapped the ball. He was still fairly nimble, though running to fat, and he buttonhooked nicely about eight feet from the door where Costello watched. The Speaker straightened up, tried to drop back, slammed against the desk, threw the football desperately, fell backwards onto the surface of the desk, used his butt as a pivot point, flipped his weight upright again, landed back on his feet, and watched with delight as Boyce hauled down the wobbly pass right next to Gineen Foley, who ducked away from the chairs screaming with joy. The Speaker roared and gave the touchdown signal. Connie Mulready screeched in something like an imitation of a whistle, and made the time-out T with her hands. Boyce trotted back toward the desk, shrugging his shoulders in the gait of a player wearing shoulder pads, and the Speaker walked around behind the desk. He reached into the bookcase where the decanters were and took one out. "Now what the hell's this," he said, squinting at it. "Ah, fuck, doesn't matter. 'S not Scotch, then it's bourbon, and if it's not bourbon then it's snot. Fuck it." He lurched a little and poured a large dollop of the liquid into a glass. He tilted his head back and drank it down in one pull. He banged the glass down on the bookcase and said: "Ahhh." The rest of his team crowded around behind the desk and began mixing their drinks. Connie Mulready lifted her skirt off the chair behind her and put it on, taking her time about it but being ignored by the men. Costello pushed the door open and stepped into the room. He applauded slowly, isolating each clap of his hands. "Very edifying, Mister Speaker," he said, "a very uplifting performance, I must say. You should reenact the crucial play for the six o'clock news."

The Speaker, collapsing into his leather chair, had difficulty shifting his vision to the far end of the office. Sweat ran down his reddened face and his eyes were bleary. "*Coss*-tello," he said uncertainly.

"I believe so," Costello said. The other players and the cheerleaders froze in the preparation of their refreshments. "Of course, it needn't've been. It could've been Gillis, for example. Maybe even with a photographer. Not that he'd need one, exactly. What I just saw'd be good enough for a couple nifty columns, without a single picture. He could write about the Speaker's new office-hours fitness campaign. You'd have a prominent part in the story too, Connie: 'Half-naked divorcee joins in romp.' You'd probably get invited to do one of those talk shows or something. Demonstrate your agility."

"The door was locked," the Speaker said sullenly. "Gillis hasn't got no key that door. The outside door. Locked it myself."

"Right," Costello said, "and Gillis doesn't know more'n a dozen Capitol police and a few janitors and a whole bunch of cleaning ladies that've got keys, does he. Nah. Gillis doesn't know anybody in this whole private building here that wouldn't take a twenty from him to show him a regular circus in progress in the Speaker's office. The only thing you were missin' was the wild lions and the tigers and you didn't really need them, all of you clowns runnin' around half-dressed in here."

The Speaker stared at him. "You *want* something, Monsignor? Or're you just over here on a social call, goin' around house to house and visitin' the parishioners when they don't expect you, you can see if they're readin' their Bibles and everything and thinkin' nice thoughts in the afternoon."

This got a dutiful and nervous laugh from Gineen and Connie, but the men began to collect their ties and coats and slide past Costello toward the door. "Shaddup," the Speaker said to the women. "I asked you something, Francis."

"And I'll answer you, something, Bernard," Costello said, "when your harem and your trapeze artists get out of here."

The Speaker stood up again and poured himself another drink. The women filed past Costello and out of the office. Costello walked over to the desk, taking a chair from along the windowed wall and dragging it over with him. "You wanna drink?" the Speaker said. "No," Costello said. "Suit yourself," the Speaker said. He sat down again. He put his glass on the leather-bound blotter. He folded his hands across his lap. He belched. The door shut audibly behind him. "Alone at last, darling," Morgan said. "Tell me that you love me, dear. You ain't knocked up, are ya?"

"Why the fuck don't you shut up, Bernie," Costello said pleasantly. "I've known you for a long time. I know you're kind of an asshole when you're drunk. Most of us are. But you used to get drunk only every now and then. Which meant you only were an asshole every now and then. Now you're an asshole most of the time. Which means you're drunk most of the time. You know what you're gonna do, finally, with this kind of little afternoon free-play period? You're gonna shit in your own bed. Because it's not gonna last, Bernie. The Grayline'll be runnin' bus tours up here. You got away with it today, unless one of Boyce's little chums starts talking some night, or Kilgore gets scared of Tierney and decides he wants to be a judge bad enough to swap your ass for the robe. But you're not gonna get away with it forever. And when it catches up with you, it's gonna ruin you."

"I've been taking afternoons now and then all my life," Morgan said.

"Sure you have," Costello said, "and back when you started, it didn't matter. David Pucci didn't give a shit about the good time Bernie Morgan had with the guys from Katie's Place and the girls from the night shift at the Tampax factory. Fuckin' bartender? Who cared. Besides, you had credits. Soldier boy. Lettin' off some steam. 'He'll settle down, he gets older, gets his wild oats sown.' Trouble is, didn't happen. And you got guys don't like you now. You puttin' your thing in Mulready again?"

"You'd like to know, wouldn't you, Counselor," Morgan said. He licked his chops. "That's the first thing you lighted on, you walked in here: Mulready's bush. I saw you lookin' at it." He laughed.

Costello snorted. "Jesus Christ, Bernie. Lookin' at it? That's like takin' a guy on a ride down the Fenway and catchin' him lookin' at the ball park. It's all around you, for Christ sake. Every time that broad gets divorced she puts the goods out in plain view for the next customer. Cripes."

"Nice piece of ass, Francis," Morgan said. "All broken in. Just like ridin' in the Cadillac. Nice and smooth, no bumps and bounces. Just the thing for a quiet afternoon when you haven't got that much to do except play with yourself." He laughed again.

"Yeah," Costello said, "and I wouldn't even have to worry what'd happen if Maggie found out, would I?"

The Speaker's expression became bleak at once. "You leave my wife out of this," he said.

"Matter of fact," Costello said, "I didn't even have her in it. It was Prudential Maggie I was thinking of. Your wife'd be *easy* to handle, in comparison with that."

Morgan began to rise slowly in his chair, without lifting his buttocks off the cushion. Costello watched with interest. "Very smooth, Bernard," he said approvingly. "Nice execution there. No hesitation, nothing too precipitous that might make it seem like a letdown if you didn't actually follow through, rear up and punch somebody in the mouth, but still that unmistakable menace that'd make a man less well-informed decide that he really might've gone too far this time. What with you dead drunk and all. Unpredictable. Yeah, pretty good. You've still got the moves, Bernie. You could scare the shit out of somebody like Ray Archambault with that, even as many times's he's seen it all these years. Dumb bastard probably thinks he's just been lucky all those times, pulled back just in time before you really got the hair across your ass and got up and beat his fuckin' brains out onna floor of the House. Very impressive."

The Speaker began to laugh. He sank back again. "I'm serious, Bernie," Costello said, smiling slightly. "I am extremely serious. Are you listening carefully to me now, taking in every word I say to you?"

Morgan laughed some more. He nodded. "Good," Costello said, "very good, Bernard. Because you and I have got a little bit of a problem that I think we had better address ourselves to, and it may just take as many as two of your wits to solve it. Have you got them both plugged in?"

"Go ahead, you asshole," Morgan said.

"Vincent Mahoney," Costello said.

The Speaker looked puzzled. "I know this guy?" he said.

"Yes indeed, Mister Speaker," Costello said. "Close pal of yours. As I recall. Least the last time you saw him, when I was in attendance, you assured him that he was that. A close pal of yours. You even called him pal a couple of times. Slapped him on the back and everything."

"The full treatment, huh?" the Speaker mused.

"Absolutely," Costello said, "the full skin, and it wasn't even his mother's wake or anything. You pulled out all the stops. I thought you must've sponsored him at Confirmation or something and raised him as the son you never had."

"Okay," the Speaker said, "you got me. Who the hell is Vincent Mahoney?"

"Vincent C. Mahoney, to be precise about it," Costello said. "Actually, never much of anything until a couple years ago. Small-time construction business. Stuck pretty close to home. Biggest job he had was some shopping plaza they put up in Plymouth or something, and I guess he decided he was in the big league all of a sudden and bought himself a lot of fancy equipment on the cuff. So naturally he was in a tight corner when the bottom fell out of the market and he decided he'd like some state contracts. Just to tide him over. So he didn't lose his bulldozers or something. And that was how you met him. He did the new wing on the technical school lab building and a couple other things."

The Speaker frowned. "He was all right, was he?"

"He was all right, all right," Costello said. "He wasn't all *right*, but he didn't really have anything very big. He was all right. We were satisfied."

"Okay," Morgan said, "got him in mind. Him and a thousand guys like him. What's the problem? He want another job now?"

"Nope," Costello said, "you got him one and he's working on it. The airport expansion down on the Vineyard. Nice little piece of work. Perfect for him."

"So, what's the difficulty?" Morgan said.

"Shipstead," Costello said, "the guy we got down on the island for the thing, his sister's married to that bastard Republican Baxter that's always giving us fits down there, but he's all right, Shipstead is. Shipstead gave him the message that another ten grand was due, and he hit the fuckin' roof."

"Well, Jesus Christ," Morgan said, "why the fuckin' hell he do that? Don't he know, he hasn't got a fuckin' calendar he can look at, he can find out we got a fuckin' election comin' up some year, for Christ sake? The fuck he thinks this is, some kind of goddamned weddin' reception that he goes to and he pays once and that gives him the right, he can dance with the bride every dance if he wants? *Shit*, where'd he get his privileges, for Christ sake? Little bastard."

"Now, calm down," Costello said. "Not gonna do any good, get yourself all in some kind of a state or something. We got to deal with this. The guy is not big time, like I just finished tellin' you. He's been doing really small-time stuff before and this's the first one, I guess, that was going on long enough so he had to make a second payment. He got the idea, he paid it once and that was all of it."

"Well," Morgan said, "he can go and get himself another fuckin' idea, is what he can do. Little son of a bitch. See what I been tellin' you for years, that Wilf Knox always told me before he started hearing dogs barking when he wasn't any fuckin' where near a fuckin' dog, am I right? You should never bring a guy into one of these things in the first place that don't already know what the fuck he's gettin' into before you get him into it. 'There ain't no educatin' these guys, Bernard,' Wilf used to say. He was maybe startin' to travel around some without his fuckin' basket always bein' full, but he was right onna fuckin' money about that, Wilf. These fuckin' cowboys that you just go out and get because they come around and they act like they know what the fuckin' score is. They don't. They never do. It's always a fuckin' mistake."

"Okay," Costello said, "it's a fuckin' mistake and it's a good thing old Wilf isn't here today so he could look at us and say we made assholes of ourselves and we should've listened to him like he always said. Then we'd be seein' Weimaraners just like him."

"Pointers," Morgan said absently. "German shorthairs."

"Pointers," Costello said. "But it's a mistake that is already made, all right? And we have got to deal with the thing where it fuckin' is."

"What do you suggest, wise guy?" Morgan said.

"The first thing is, I'm not suggesting anything, all right?" Costello said. "Mahoney is doing the suggesting at this point. Mahoney is suggesting that we have a meeting tonight and he is coming up here with shit all over his shoes and steam coming out of his ears to see the Speaker and see what is what and how come it is. He is coming up to Boston to visit his money."

"Fuck him," Morgan said. "This little piece of shit thinks I'm at everybody's beck and call that thinks he's got something on his mind like how's he stop being constipated all the time? Tell him to go fuck himself. I got things to do tonight. I got to go to Dealey's time down at Pier Four. You see Mahoney there—whatever this guy says his name is—you tell him how come the sun don't come up in the morning when he wants it just because he did a week's wash and he wants to let it hang out."

"Nice try, Bernie," Costello said. He stood up. He buttoned his suit jacket. "Nice try but no goddamned cigar. You go to Dealey's time. And you happen to see Dealey there and he's not so fuckin' drunk he can stand up for once, you give him all my best. Tell him I hope the guys we've got stand up the way he did for Wilfred."

"Yeah," Morgan said.

"I mean it," Costello said. "You do the best you can to go in there and come out of there so you can still stand up yourself, all right? Because you are gonna have a nice private dinner with me and Mahoney down the Claret, and you are gonna work your fuckin' magic with this guy that thinks he owns a piece of you."

"I'm goin' to Dealey's time," Morgan said. "I'm goin' to Dealey's time, Francis, and then I am going fuckin' home."

"No," Costello said, "you're not. You are going to dinner with me and Mahoney, and you better think of something good between now and the time the waiter comes with the roast beef."

8 Brian Hanrihan found Cpl. James Cremmens in the coffee shop of the Middlesex County Superior Courthouse. Hanrihan got a regular coffee from the sightless man who operated the spigots and paid the pleasant lady who collected the money and made change for the Massachusetts Society for All the Blind. He went over to the white Formica table and took the orange molded plastic chair opposite Cremmens. Cremmens was wearing a blue blazer and a blue shirt and a blue tie. He looked worried.

"I wonder where they get those women," he said to Hanrihan.

Hanrihan stirred his coffee with the small wooden stick provided with the white Styrofoam cup. "Right out of business school, usually," he said. "They get out of high school and they get engaged to somebody and they go to work for a company like Mortimer until they start having babies, and then they go back as soon as they can. Unless they don't have any kids or the guy runs out on them or something so they don't get married after all, and then they don't leave even for a while. There's lots of them."

"Who?" Cremmens said, looking puzzled.

"Mrs. Benedict," Hanrihan said. "Mrs. Benedict that was just on the stand this afternoon and Feldman got her all balled up. I forgot, you weren't there. Where the hell were you anyway? I meant to ask you that. You came in with me when we started, and then I turned around to get something and you weren't there."

"I meant the women that're always at those coffee stands," Cremmens said. "They got them in Suffolk and in Norfolk, down the Quincy District Court, and there's one in the federal building that I see when I hadda be down there for something one day and I wanted a cup of coffee. Except it's just a newsstand, and you can get a Coke or something. They don't have coffee in that one. For coffee you go upstairs the cafeteria, and that, that's not the blind guys. That's like a regular restaurant thing. They always have a woman. There is the blind guy that is supposedly running it but there is always a woman that makes change for him."

"It's in case," Hanrihan said, "somebody wants to try to give him a single and try to get him, make change for a ten or something. You can see how that would happen, the kind of human shit you got floating around in this kind of place all the time."

"Yeah," Cremmens said, "but I wonder who they are."

"Jesus Christ," Hanrihan said, "who gives a shit who they are? They're just women, that's all, women that come in and make sure some thieving bastard doesn't skin the blind guys out of change for a twenty when it's only a single he's giving him. For Christ sake almighty. I asked you something, all right? Where the hell'd you go this after, huh? Where the hell were you?"

"Maria came in," Cremmens said.

"Maria," Hanrihan said. He sat back in the chair and nodded. Cremmens blushed. "Maria comes in the courtroom and I'm all of a sudden standing there with a witness that's practically wetting her pants, and I turn around and my investigator stepped out for a while because Maria came in."

"I had to," Cremmens said. He looked defiant. "You were talking and she hadda tell me something, there was a message, so I got up and I went out to see what it was and when I come back there was nobody around so I went down for a cup of coffee, all right? I didn't know where the hell you went while I was out. How the hell was I supposed to know?"

"What the hell was the message," Hanrihan said, "something that the bunny reported and Maria's got a little problem she thinks maybe you should know about? I pity you, Jimbo, if that happens. Old Sylvia's gonna saddle up a posse and come huntin' your worthless ass, if that happens. She's gonna have you hung fuckin' out to fuckin' *dry.*"

"Cut it out, Brian," Cremmens said. He squirmed in his chair.

"I mean it, Jimbo," Hanrihan said. "I been around longer'n you have and I've seen guys like you that've been married three or four years and they're still not thirty and some hot little number like Maria comes on their screen. Their heads go around just like radar sets and their dicks start going blip, blip, blip in their pants, and they just can't wait to pull those lacey little panties down and stick their pricks in where there's nothing but big trouble waitin' for them. Those eighteen-, nineteen-year-old broads that just got out of school and start going around with their hair down to their ass and wondering what it's like to do it with a married man, they can make an asshole out of a guy in about ten minutes."

"Maria's engaged," Cremmens said.

"Sure she is," Hanrihan said, "and you're married. That's what makes it so exciting, isn't it? She's engaged to the guy that works the late shift over at the *Globe* pressroom and when he's not doing that he's lifting weights and making his body beautiful for hot-pants little Maria, and in the meantime she's cooling off her twat with you, every chance she gets."

"Oh, fuck you," Cremmens said. "You know something, Brian? You think you know pretty near everything."

"Compared to you, most times," Hanrihan said, "I do."

"Yeah," Cremmens said, "bullshit. There's lots of things you don't know shit about."

"Like what?" Hanrihan said. "Name two. Let's hear them." He was grinning.

"This Dussault case, for one thing," Cremmens said.

Hanrihan's grin disappeared. "Like what is it I don't know about the Dussault case? Tell me. What is this thing that I don't know about Dussault? That son of a bitch is going to jail. I know that. What else is there, huh?"

Cremmens shook his head. "I dunno, Brian," he said, "maybe so. But there's a lot of guys that're kind of laughin' at you, sayin' it's not gonna happen like you think it is." He pursed his lips and shook his head again.

"Why not?" Hanrihan said. "Have I got the guy that paid him the money? Uh huh, and his testimony, I have got it cast in concrete. And the guy that the guy got the money from? And the secretary that was in the other office? And Mrs. Benedict? All of them say the same thing. If Dussault can walk this one, him and me and you and the fuckin' judge can go out together in the rain and he's the only one of us that's not gonna get wet, if he can do that. That guy'd need a *miracle* to walk this one."

"You didn't get Mrs. Benedict, though, did you?" Cremmens said. "You had her in there this after, and you knew what she was finally gonna say just like you know what all those other people're gonna say when you get them in here, and she didn't say it, did she?"

"How'd you know?" Hanrihan said. "How'd you know what Mrs. Benedict said? You weren't even there. You were out in the hall makin' goo-goo eyes at Maria and she's battin' the eyes at you and tellin' you what you're gonna get to do to her at night while Bennie's workin' late at the *Globe*. Don't give me *that* shit, James."

"Because it's all over the courthouse," Cremmens said. "It's all over the courthouse every time something happens in that Dussault case that you didn't think was gonna happen. I could be inna closet with the brooms, for Christ sake, and the light out, and something's happened different from what you expected and I would know about it within thirty seconds. Somebody would come by and bang onna door and say: 'Hey, Cremmens, that Hanrihan fella with the big mouth there really know what he's doing in there or what?' You got the idea."

"I know people're jealous of me," Hanrihan said. "I'm used to that. It's just something you have got to live with."

"Oh yeah," Cremmens said. "I forgot, I guess."

"Go ahead, Jimbo," Hanrihan said. "This's something, you wouldn't have any way of knowing about this. Your father, my father was prominent in this area for a long time.

"When I first started out, that was it. 'Only reason Hanrihan makes it's because of his old man.' I heard all that shit a long time ago. The shit about Belmont Hill School and the shit about Harvard College and then some more shit about Yale. I heard it all. It's just something you learn, you got to ignore it. It's envy and there isn't anything in the world you can do about it. I wish there was, but there isn't. It's just something that I've got to deal with, and all my life people're going to be going around and whispering behind my back things that they think might hurt my chances, or how things're not going to work out the way I think they are. But they always have, Jimbo, and that's where they're wrong. They always have, and they will this time, too."

"Right," Cremmens said. "Okay, Brian, whatever you say." He finished his coffee hurriedly and stood up.

"Hey," Hanrihan said, "where the hell're you going?"

"I got an appointment that there's a guy I got to see, Mister Hanrihan sir," Cremmens said. He hitched up his pants. "That was the message that came into the office while you had Mrs. Benedict up there on the stand settling Jean Dussault's hash for him this afternoon, except Dory Feldman wouldn't let you do it, that I had to see this guy. You hear anything that maybe Feldman's got Matte in his pocket, maybe?"

"Oh, come on," Hanrihan said, "Matte's straight. Feldman's been around a long time. He just knows Matte, that's all."

"I hope that's all it is," Cremmens said. "I heard guys, did you leave them two alone in Matte's chambers for a while after they let the jury go home this afternoon?"

"So what?" Hanrihan said. "I had to see Mrs. Benedict, get her calmed down. She has to come back in here tomorrow, for Christ sake. Couldn't just let her go home with her head up her ass, wondering what the hell was going on."

"Well," Cremmens said, "that's what somebody told me, that you left him and Matte alone in chambers and you were out inna god-damned hall, talkin' your witness."

"Oh shit, Jim," Hanrihan said, "they're gonna fix the case in ten minutes while I'm in the hall? I doubt it. I really doubt it. They were gonna do it, they already would've done it long before it got to this stage."

"I hope you're right," Cremmens said. He looked at his watch. "I got to run," he said firmly. "The guy said I should try to be there about five, little before, and the traffic in town and everything, I better leave now."

"Who the hell's in town?" Hanrihan said. "There's nobody in town that's got any possible thing to do with this case, for Christ sake. The hell're you going in there now for?"

"I got to see a man," Cremmens said, "that's got nothing to do with this case, all right? Ten-ten calls me up and leaves an order for me that I should drop my cock and grab my socks and get my ass to Boston to see Otis Ames by five, that is what I do. No questions, Mister Commissioner sir, aye aye and all that shit."

"Otis Ames?" Hanrihan said. "The commission guy?"

Cremmens shrugged. "So I'm told," he said.

"The fuck's he want with you?" Hanrihan said. "He hasn't even got a prosecutor yet. What's he gonna do with an investigator if he hasn't even got a lawyer yet?"

"Beats me," Cremmens said. He shrugged and smiled. He jabbed Hanrihan on the right shoulder. "Maybe wants me, tell him about some lawyers, huh? Recommend somebody?"

Hanrihan frowned. He started to say something and then did not.

Cremmens grinned. "Could be, Brian my boy, could just be, you know. You better be nice to me."

Hanrihan snorted. "Me?" he said. "Nice to you? Why? I wouldn't take that job with a . . . , there's nothing in this world'd make me take that job."

Cremmens put his head back and laughed. "Right," he said, when he had finished. "Absolutely, Brian. I'll tell him that, first thing when I walk in. I'll say: 'Mister Ames, sir, before we get started here and everything, and keeping in mind I haven't got any idea what the hell you want to see me about, I think there's something you oughta know and that is this: Brian Hanrihan, that assistant over in Middlesex that's always gettin' his name in the paper all the time with all those splashy cases? Know the guy? Yeah, Hanrihan. Well, he asked me to tell you, he don't want any part of your operation. He thinks you probably got a breath on you like low tide, and the last thing he ever wants to hear on the radio or something is that you picked him to be your prosecutor and be on television every night. Wouldn't take it for a million dollars and he had to fuck Pussy Galore every afternoon, the cocktail hour, no sir fuckin' ree.' I'll do that, Brian. That's exactly what I'll do. Because I know," he said, jabbing Hanrihan with his forefinger on the shoulder, "I know and you know that there's nothing you'd hate worse'n to see Otis Ames wasting all his valuable time that he could be spending rootin' out corruption in this fair Commonwealth and all that sort of good stuff, thinking maybe that you'd like to help him do it." Cremmens put his head back again and laughed.

Hanrihan looked at him for a long time. "You finished?" he said.

"Yup," Cremmens said.

"I hope the bunny did come back positive, you little fuck," Hanrihan said. "You want to know what I hope, you've just heard it."

9 Following directions he obtained from a lovely, young and supercilious receptionist in the twenty-eighth-floor office of Lines & Ames, James Cremmens marched as the Navy had trained him to march down a long green carpeted corridor, ignoring pictures on both walls of a fleet of merchantmen, clippers, and ships of the line, all of them battling heavy seas under lowering skies. He focused his eyes on Josephine Gately's desk, unoccupied at the end of the hallway. She emerged from Ames's office to his right just as he reached the desk. She closed the door to Ames's office and he halted, coming to parade rest. He decided that he would not salute.

"Mister Cremmens?" she said. She licked her lips. She had been with Mister Ames for a long time and did not believe in going at things hastily.

"Affirmative," Cremmens said.

"*Corporal* Cremmens?" she said.

"Affirmative," he said.

"May I see some identification?" she said.

"Affirmative," he said. He produced a wallet containing his badge and ID card. She barely glanced at it. She glanced back over her shoulder at the door. She moistened her lips again. She squared her shoulders. "I, ah," she said, "I was not aware that Mister Ames had called to ask for you this afternoon," she said.

"Oh," Cremmens said.

"He," she said, looking at the door again, "he must have done it while I was away from my desk," she said.

"Oh," he said.

"Having lunch," she said. "I usually try to place all of his outgoing calls. Personally. They don't go through the switchboard."

"Yes," he said.

"Or something like that," she said. She sat down abruptly. She steepled her fingers and looked at him over the tops of them. "Did he, ah, did he say what he wanted?"

"No," Cremmens said.

"No," she said. She looked down at her desk blotter. She rearranged two pieces of paper that had been neatly arranged before. She stood up abruptly. She smoothed her skirt. She looked at Cremmens and smiled brightly. "Well then," she said, "I guess you'd better just go right in and find *out*, shall we?"

"Yes, ma'am," Cremmens said.

Josephine Gateley opened the door to Ames's office. She peered around it, drew back, and closed it behind her. She shook her head with assurance. "You can't go in," she said.

Cremmens stepped back a pace. "I can't go in?" he said.

"No," she said. "I mean: yes. That's right. You can't go in. Not today."

"What the hell does that mean?" Cremmens said. "I can't go in?"

"Right," she said. She nodded vigorously. "I suggest you go, and come back another time."

"You can't do that," Cremmens said.

"I most certainly can," she said firmly. "I've been doing it for years. I screen everyone who wishes to see Mister Ames. Everyone, Mister Cremmens. That includes you."

"Look," Cremmens said, "I don't know what's going on here, but you can't do this." He patted his left breast with his right forefinger. He winked. "You understand me, Miss Gateley? You can't do it."

"Mrs. Gateley," she said firmly. "Mrs. Donald Gateley."

"No doubt," Cremmens said. "My love to Donald. You still can't do it."

"Do what?" she said, licking her lips again.

"Keep me out of that man's office," Cremmens said. He pointed to it. "That office. The one right there. Behind the damned door."

"I most certainly can," she said. "As I told you, I've been working for Mister Ames for nearly forty years. I've kept many people from seeing him." Her eyes filled with tears. "Many people, Mister Cremmens, many people."

Cremmens sighed. He patted his left breast again. "Mrs. Gateley," he said, "I hate to do this. I really do. Honest. But you're making it awful hard for me to do anything else."

"I am?" she said. One tear ran down her right cheek.

Cremmens nodded. "You certainly are," he said. "Look, we try to do things in a civilized way, if we possibly can, you know?"

"Yes," she said, "I've always heard very good reports about the State Police."

"Thank you," Cremmens said. "We get a matter like this, involves a prominent, respected citizen, member of the community, we try not to create a lot of fuss and unpleasantness about it, you know? Try to keep it out of the newspapers, that sort of thing."

Her left hand went to her throat. "Newspapers," she said. "Are the newspapers going to be involved in this again?"

"Again, ma'am?" Cremmens said politely.

"They were the last time he got involved," she said. "With one of these investigations or whatever you call them. All the time. Years ago. But I remember it. The Dealey matter. Very disruptive."

"Yes, ma'am." Cremmens said. "Well, I wouldn't know about that, really. All I know is, I have these documents, and I really have these documents, and I really have to see him personally. Orders. The contents of that office, well, we have to see them."

"Whatever for?" she said. "They're just the ordinary things that anyone would use to do what he does."

"Please, Mrs. Gateley," Cremmens said, spreading his hands, "I didn't start this. All I know is that it's evidently been alleged, somebody has said, that he may have the tools of the trade in there. And we have to conduct a search of the premises. If they're there, we have to seize them. Simple as that. Now ordinarily, of course, we don't let the subject know that we're coming to search the premises, but in this instance, given Mister Ames's standing in the community, I guess an exception was made. I wouldn't have done it, myself, but somebody evidently thought it should be done. Somebody at ten-ten. Headquarters."

"What on earth are you talking about?" she said.

Cremmens sighed again. He shook his head. He started at her. "Okay, lady," he said, "let's play it the hard way, if that's the way you wanna do it. My orders say: go in there and toss the joint, right?"

"*Toss the joint?*" she said.

"Toss the joint," Cremmens said grimly. "Gambling paraphernalia? Slips? Phones, money, flash paper. Scales, if that's what it is. Procaine, plastic bags. How do I know what he's got in there? Is he dealing drugs, or is he making book, huh? How the hell do I know until I get in there and look around? I don't, is what. So here it is, down and dirty: either you get outta the way and let me go in there, or I'll arrest you for obstructing justice, slap the cuffs on you and take you away. Which way you want it, huh? You tell me." She stared at him, her lower lip trembling, another tear descending over her right cheek. She opened the door and stood aside. Cremmens went in. She closed the door behind him.

The office windows behind the desk looked out over Boston Harbor, toward Logan Airport. A 747 with TWA markings took off from the westbound runway, gaining altitude smoothly, the declining sun orange on its belly as it climbed. Cremmens looked around. The walls were done in blue grasscloth. In the corner to his right there was a large overstuffed chair in oxblood leather with brass nailheads for decoration. There was a fat oxblood leather ottoman in front of it. To the left of the chair there was a mahogany table, roomy enough for five or six heavy books supported upright by brass bookends made of leaping dolphins. At the left shoulder of the chair there was a brass floor lamp with an ivory-colored linen shade. Next to the right arm of the chair there was a small portable bar, the lid open to show a working area with a brass ashtray, fitted with a brass fouled anchor for use as a pipe knocker. Next to it was a rack of heavy pipes, and a brass shell casing filled with pipe cleaners. There was a compact Sony seven-band portable radio and a remote control device for a television set. The television set was on the other side of the room, standing on a rolling cart, turned to face the desk. The screen was showing summations of the day's trading on the New York Stock Exchange. Next to it were three telex machines in sound-deadening cabinets, each printing. There were signs on the first two: DOW JONES and ASSOCIATED PRESS. The third cabinet was blank.

In front of the desk there were four Queen Anne wing chairs, also upholstered in oxblood leather with brass nailheads. The desk was a partners' model, double size. The front half was covered with an oxblood leather-bound blotter on which were piled folders, legal pads, corporate ledgers, stock certificates, and books piled on each other. Cremmens could not see beyond the middle of the desk because of the clutter and because there was a median partition of pigeonhole files, three rows high and tall enough to hide the man behind the desk when he chose to duck down. On the top of the partition there was a brass desk lamp with a green glass shade, and both bulbs were lighted.

Ames had chosen to duck before Cremmens had entered the room. Cremmens cleared his throat, once and then again. Slowly a bald head, almost pointed, with a fringe of white hair cut very short, rose at an angle from the center toward Cremmens's left, so that Ames's left eye, blue, gleaming behind his gold half-frame glasses appeared before the right. The head stopped there in its ascent, the right eye still hidden.

Cremmens halted about fifteen feet from the front of the desk. He stood at parade rest. "Mister Ames," he said. He made his voice as deep as possible.

The head now tilted so that it was level and the right eye appeared. The ascent resumed so that Cremmens could see the broad, long nose and the small white mustache. The head stopped when Ames's chin was still out of Cremmens's sight. There was no expression on the face.

"Ah," Cremmens said, "Corporal Cremmens, sir. You wanted to see me, I believe."

The head made an abrupt gesture off to its right. Cremmens looked puzzled. "Sir?" he said. The gesture was repeated. Cremmens walked toward the desk, slowly at first, then at a normal pace when he was not told to stop. The eyes regarded him intently as he reached the chairs and paused. The gesture was repeated. Cremmens selected the path to his left, went around the chairs, and stopped when he was even with the partition in the center of the desk.

Otis Ames sat in a large tan leather chair, with the brass nailheads at the seams of the covering. His right shoulder was considerably lower than his left, which seemed to have some sort of small hump. Ames was small and he was left-handed. He had evidently been writing with a gold Mont Blanc fountain pen on a pad of white, legal-sized paper when Cremmens came in. His hand was crabbed around against his wrist, as though he had been deformed. He wore a white broadcloth shirt and a black bow tie. He wore red suspenders attached to light brown tweed pants. He glared at Cremmens as though he had caught him doing something that had been expressly forbidden. "Do they teach you to type in the State Police?" he said. His voice was phlegmy.

"Uh, no sir," Cremmens said.

"Well then," Ames said, pursing his lips, "can you type anyway?"

"Some," Cremmens said. "We type our reports."

Ames nodded. "I knew it. Very good idea. You left-handed?"

"No," Cremmens said.

"No," Ames said morosely. "Few are."

"Yes," Cremmens said.

"Nuisance of a thing," Ames said. "All my life. Palmer method to periscopes. Same thing. Right-handed. All of them." He sighed.

"Yessir," Cremmens said.

"Look at this," Ames said, indicating the pad. "See that? One half page." He scratched the pen through it diagonally, once. "Took more out of me than walking a mile." He put the pen down. He clasped his hands over his stomach. He leaned back in his chair. He unclasped his hands and waved with his left toward the Queen Anne chairs. "Pull one of those over. Sit down." He clasped his hands again while Cremmens did as he was told.

"Short notice," Ames said.

"Of what, sir?" Cremmens said. He leaned forward in the chair. Ames looked irritated. "This, man, this. Short notice. Today. Bringing you over like this. Appreciate it."

"No trouble, sir," Cremmens said.

"All my life," Ames said with satisfaction, "done the same thing all my life. Make up your mind and then do it, by God. No use piddling around with things, once you've decided, *hah hah.*" His voice was exuberant at the end of his statement. He stared at Cremmens expectantly. "Am I right?"

"Uh," Cremmens said, "yeah. Yeah, I guess you're right."

"Right," Ames said. He slapped his right palm down on the desk and threw his head back. He said "Hah hah" quite loudly. Once more he stared expectantly at Cremmens. "Right," Cremmens said. "Yes," Ames said with satisfaction. He drummed the fingers of his left hand on the desk top. He watched them for a while. Then he looked at Cremmens again. "You're a police officer," Ames said.

"Yes," Cremmens said.

Ames nodded. "So," he said, "you know what that means."

"Yes sir," Cremmens said.

"Good," Ames said. "Now, you're familiar with the political situation in this Commonwealth, of course."

Cremmens shifted in his chair. "More or less, sir," he said uneasily. "I read the papers and all. Sports, mostly, but I read them."

Ames cleared his throat. "Of course, of course," he said. "Stupid of me. Can't live in this Commonwealth, not know politics. You do live here."

"Yes sir," Cremmens said.

"All your life," Ames said.

"Yes sir," Cremmens said. "Except for when I was in the Navy."

"*Hah hah,*" Ames said abruptly. He leaned forward, clasped his hands on the top of the desk and peered over them as though holding a poker hand and seeking to determine whether Cremmens was bluffing. "I was getting to that. You *left* the Navy."

"Yes sir," Cremmens said.

"Why?" Ames said. "Can you tell me that?"

"My, ah, my hitch was up," Cremmens said. "I signed up and I served the four years, and then when the four years were over, I turned in my stuff and came home. That was the deal."

"You had Q clearance," Ames said accusingly.

"Yes sir," Cremmens said.

"Pentagon," Ames said.

Cremmens puzzled. "Sir?" he said.

"Why'd you leave, then, eh?" Ames said. He studied Cremmens very intently.

"I told you, sir," Cremmens said, "my hitch was up. So I went home. Turned in my gear and went home."

"Just like that," Ames said.

"Just like that," Cremmens said. "It wasn't any, it wasn't like it was any surprise to anybody. I knew it and they knew it. Said good-bye and went on terminal leave and that was it. Poof."

"You were in Naval Intelligence," Ames said.

"Affirmative," Cremmens said.

"Counterintelligence," Ames said.

"Affirmative," Cremmens said.

"Hah hah," Ames said musingly. He nodded several times. "You served four years, Navy counterintelligence, and then your hitch was up and you went home. Just like that."

"Yes sir," Cremmens said. "But see, and I had this job all lined up. I took the exams before I went in the Navy. They told me it'd probably be a few years before they hired me because they weren't hiring then and besides they had this court order that they had to hire so many blacks and women and the PRs there, and I wasn't none of those. So they said to me that they were interested and if I went in the service and got the points for being a veteran and like that, that as soon as they could they would hire me. And I did and just as I was coming out they had this opening that came up and it all went together pretty nice." Cremmens grinned. "I see very few things that go together as nice as that went together, and that was almost five years ago."

Ames nodded. "Jean Dussault," he said.

"Yes sir," Cremmens said.

"You know him," Ames said.

"Uh huh," Cremmens said. "Well, I investigated him, that's what you mean. This case I'm on over to Middlesex with Mister Hanrihan. I don't know him like you say you know somebody. But I know who he is, yeah."

"A very bad man," Ames said. He pursed his lips and shook his head.

Cremmens shrugged his shoulders. "Well," he said, "old Jean there, he's no prince of a fellow like you would say. Like if he was to come around and your father took you aside and said he wanted to, he was thinking of maybe marrying your sister. You wouldn't want him for that, probably, that kind of thing, where he would be around all the time. But if you were to run into him in a bar and you didn't have anything that either one of you had against the other guy, he's not a bad kind of guy from that point of view. I guess."

Ames drew back. He clasped his hands on the arms of his chair. His eyes bulged behind the glasses. "Not a bad kind of guy, Mister Cremmens? Is that what you said?" His voice went up into a croak at the end.

Cremmens cleared his throat. "Well," he said, "I didn't mean, like I said, he's not your regular kind of run-of-the-mill guy that you would just as soon have him around all the time and he would be related to you or something. Because, naturally, he's kind of a hood and everything. But he's not a bad kind of guy otherwise, you understand the type of guy that he is. You see what I mean?"

Ames leaned forward. "Do you mean to tell me," he said, "that this man Dussault? Are you prosecuting him for extortion?"

"Well," Cremmens said, "look, I'm not the one prosecuting him. I mean, I am the cop and I do the investigating that Mister Hanrihan has me to do, that kind of thing. But he is the one that is prosecuting. Mister Hanrihan. He is doing it."

"Hah *hah*," Ames said. He shook his head again. He toyed with the

Mont Blanc pen. "Sad," he said. He did not seem to be talking to Cremmens. Cremmens did not say anything. Ames looked up fiercely. "This Dussault," he said. "Union goon."

"Yes," Cremmens said.

"Did you ever hear, my boy," Ames said, "this Dussault? He killed a man, years ago."

"I heard that," Cremmens said. "Guy named Clancy, down to Braintree there. That he was supposed to have done that. But they didn't, nobody ever proved that he did that. He wasn't ever convicted or anything. He was never even indicted for that thing, that I heard. That's what I heard, anyway."

"That doesn't mean he didn't do it, surely," Ames said. "You don't think that."

"Well, no," Cremmens said, "but, you know, it's kind of pretty close to it, huh? That he didn't do it. Because if he did it there wasn't anybody that they could get that would come in and stand up and say: he did it. Or if there was, that they believed or that they thought that a judge and a jury were gonna believe. You know? That kind of thing. He wasn't ever charged with that."

"Because everybody was afraid of him," Ames said. "That was thirty years or so ago, and people were afraid of him then. Too afraid to step forward and say: 'Jean Dussault killed this man and I saw him do it.' He didn't die of natural causes. You don't think that, do you, Corporal?"

"No," Cremmens said. "It was, I think it was that he was shot two or three times in the head. It was in a bar that he was running and it was after closing or something and he was in there and they saw Dussault go in there that he had to make Clancy unlock the door first, and he went in and there were these shots and then when the cops got there Dussault wasn't there and this guy Clancy was on the floor. Dead.

"But that don't prove he killed him and it was murder," Cremmens said. "Besides, didn't I hear, that there was some kind of talk going around that Clancy'd been fooling around with some broad that Dussault had on the side or something and that was what Dussault went in there to see him about. It didn't have anything to do with no union stuff or anything."

"Does that matter?" Ames said. "Do you really think that that means it doesn't *matter*?"

Cremmens shifted in the chair. He clasped and unclasped his hands. "Well, ah, yeah, it could mean that," he said. "See, if it was some broad they were fighting over, it could've been that maybe this guy Clancy pulled a gun first and then Dussault took it away from him, and while he was taking it away from him there it went off and Clancy got killed. And that would be self-defense. Which it would not be murder, and that would matter. That would matter a lot if it was something like that. And there wasn't anybody else there at the time that could see it and say what it was that happened, so even if it wasn't that, all Dussault would've had to do was get up in court and say it did happen that way and that would be a reasonable doubt. That happens all the time, that a guy gets away with something because either he didn't do it or he did it but there isn't anybody around that can prove he did it like he was supposed to, you know?"

"That gun," Ames said, his face getting red, "that gun that you think they might've been struggling over, that gun went off seven times and there were five of them that went off into Clancy. And you could sit there and tell me this was perhaps an accidental shooting that happened in self-defense?" His voice was much louder and higher at the end of his question.

"I wasn't saying," Cremmens said, writhing in the chair, "I didn't say that. I said it could've been something like that. And that anyway there wasn't anybody that could say that it didn't."

"There was a dishwasher in the kitchen," Ames said.

"I didn't know that," Cremmens said. "How come they didn't ask him what it was that happened? Ask him."

"They did," Ames said. He nodded vigorously. "I asked him. I asked him myself. Because I was a district attorney, an assistant district attorney then and that was my case and I brought him in after the police got through asking him and I asked him myself. Little scared man named Boone. Myself. Asked him." Ames slapped the desk again, hard. "In the kitchen. Came in at six in the afternoon, still in there at two in the morning when the police came and Clancy was on the floor. He actually wet his pants in the office. Didn't hear a thing. Had the water running or something. Nothing. *Wet his pants.* Dussault did that, made Boone do that. Scared the daylights out of him. Murder." Ames nodded, vigorously. "Murder. Jean Dussault murdered Torbert Clancy. Cold blood."

"Oh," Cremmens said.

"But now," Ames said eagerly, leaning forward, "now you've got him, eh?"

"Mister Hanrihan thinks so," Cremmens said.

"Um," Ames said, leaning back again and looking worried. "Hanrihan. Not too confident of his case, is he?"

"Oh," Cremmens said, "confident as hell. Confident as all get-out."

"You're not?" Ames said.

Cremmens shrugged again. "I dunno," he said. "Just, you got to keep in mind, this's my first one like this, you know? I only been investigating like this, for the DAs, for them, like a couple years. And it's been mostly murder and some gamblin' stuff, you know? I haven't done, in this type of case it matters. What you really got to do is you got to get a lotta witnesses that really know what was going on and what it really meant when something happened. Because . . . they got this Feldman guy that is representing Dussault there, and he is pretty smart as it is."

"I know the Jew," Ames said, with some bitterness.

"He, I guess he is Jewish," Cremmens said. "He is one smart son of a bitch, though. He is that. And you got these things in a case like this, that I never had in a case before. And you got people that're doing things, like one guy talks to another guy and the second guy calls somebody up and the guy at the company says something to the other guy at the company, and he tells Mrs. Benedict that when she makes out the payroll for the week for the guys that drive the trucks, all right? She should put down two guys that don't even work there and maybe don't even exist, that you can't find anywhere on the earth, if you know what I mean, because they aren't. And when she brings the checks back the office or wherever it is that they give them out, the guy that hands out the checks is just putting the checks for those two guys that don't exist, he is putting them in his pocket. And then later on he is giving them to somebody that gives them to Dussault or maybe just goes ahead and signs their names to them, the two guys that don't exist. And Dussault is getting the money and just putting that in his pocket. And he keeps it."

"And the company doesn't have any union trouble," Ames said triumphantly. "Which is called racketeering."

"Sure," Cremmens said. "Except maybe the company was a pretty good one anyway, like Mortimer, like it seems to've been they were, and they wouldn't have been having any labor trouble anyway. Because they haven't had any for like twenty years or so before they ever had anything to do with Dussault's union and with Dussault, and the most we can show about it is that they didn't have any for the past two or three years or so. And Dussault was already there for a couple years before that, and we haven't got no evidence that anything was going on then. So what is the beef, huh? You see what I mean, that Feldman or some guy that knows what he is doing can do with this? Because it doesn't look like anything is really going on. At any one time. Mrs. Benedict, she doesn't really know, she can't say for sure that this was what the money was for, so that Dussault wouldn't let his guys have a strike if they wanted. And her boss, he don't know, because he was just taking orders from somebody else that was getting them from somebody else. And all we know, we don't know who is cashing those checks.

"You ever try to prove that there is a guy that don't exist?" Cremmens said. "You got a check that was good when they took it to the bank that somebody cashed for a guy that came into his bar, right? What does he care, the guy don't exist, huh? Long's the check was there and the check was good, and he gave the guy that was spending money in his place, he gave him the money that was the cash for the check and then he took the check to the bank and he got his money back for it all right, you think he's gonna know? Or care? He don't know.

"Nope," Cremmens said, shaking his head, "there is only two guys that really know for sure that there was no regular bet between Dussault and Rickie Mortimer that was running the company for his father on the Patriots game every week, and the Celtics and the Red Sox when the Pats weren't playing, and Rickie never got the odds right, and that is Rickie and the other one is Jean. And Rickie's in the shit himself all over the place because he didn't really own that company even if it did have his name on it. He was just running it, that the other people in the company and the people that bought stock from him in it, that they thought they could trust him and he went and he got himself this bimbo showgirl and sets her up in this condo down to Boca Raton there or some goddamned place and he bought the boat and everything, and I don't know. I just don't know if anybody on that jury there is gonna believe Rickie Mortimer when he gets up there on his hind legs and says Jean Dussault was shaking him down and he was just too scared and innocent but to do anything except sit there and let him do it. And Jean knows, he is the other one that knows, but he ain't likely, he's not gonna get up there and raise his right hand and tell God and all the people that that is what he was doing to Rickie there and giving his own union guys a good screwing at the same time. Nope, I don't think so."

Ames glared at Cremmens. "So *that*, Corporal," he said, hissing, "that is all you think of your case."

"Hey," Cremmens said, holding up his hand, "I already told you, Mister Ames, all right? You can say it is my case and I am prosecuting it and that is all right with me if that is what you want to do. But it's not my case. It's just a case that I got like every other case that I got. The boss of the detectives said to me that if I wanted to get out the uniform and off the Turnpike where maybe some crazy drunk runs over me or some guy that just climbed over the fence at Norfolk and stole a gun that I stop some night for speeding decides he's gonna shoot me in the belly just by way of no harm, the boss said he would put me in and I would go and investigate cases that they gave me to investigate. And that is what I do. Because it is better, safer. Now what I do is, you give me a container and you ask me what is in it, I open it up and I look inside and if it is something that looks like it is ice cream then I taste it and I tell you it is frozen pudding. I don't care, all right, if you got your heart all set on chocolate chip. That don't matter to me in the slightest. There ain't no way in the world that I can get the raisins out of what you give me if there happens to be raisins in it when you give it to me. Or like if you decided you wanted a pizza with anchovies and I went out to see if I could find you one and they didn't happen to have any anchovies lying around that night, so I brought you back one that had pepperonis on it. I'll go pick up your pizza, sir, but I won't make up no anchovies out of the air when they haven't got no anchovies available. Sorry, but that's it. You asked me and I told you. Now if you were to ask Mister Hanrihan, you would get a completely different answer, and maybe you would find that his answer turned out to be right and mine was wrong. Can't do nothing about it."

"Hanrihan," Ames said, "how is he?"

"He was okay this after, when I left him," Cremmens said. "He looked okay to me."

"Is he," Ames said, in a very low voice, "is he, *capable?*"

Cremmens shrugged. "Look, all right? I like Brian. I worked with some guys that I didn't like a whole lot. Guys that thought I was some kind of a bellhop for them. Asking me to pick up their shirts at the laundry and get their kids at school when they're tied up in the grand jury or something and the wife's got their car for the day because there's something wrong with hers. And I don't like that kind of shit. I'm a cop, all right? I'm a professional cop. I had two years college before I went in the service and I can get back to school next fall like I plan, I'll get my degree. Northeastern. I'll get it next spring. I'm taking the summer off. It's taken me this long, who cares if I don't get it next winter, all right? I'm no damned nigger with a driver's license and a state car that you can just go ahead and send me galloping all over the countryside getting the newspapers for you or something. And some guys will try to do that.

"Now," he said, "Hanrihan doesn't. And he is a good guy and everything. He is a pretty good guy and he treats me okay and I treat him okay. So I haven't got anything against him."

"Is he going to get Dussault?" Ames said, still in the low voice.

Cremmens shrugged again. "Says he is," he said. "You go up to him and you ask him if he is going to get Dussault, that is what he will tell you. He thinks he's got Jean's tail nailed to the floor and all he has to do is go over and tramp on it, any time he likes. Like I say, maybe he is right."

"Do you know what that would mean, if he does?" Ames said.

"I can make a pretty fair guess," Cremmens said. "Like you say, Jean's got a reputation and he's had it for a long time. There's lots of people that don't think he's a nice guy, lots of them. He's been okay to me, especially when you think about it that I am the guy that is involved in putting him away. And he's always, he always says hello to Brian, as far as that goes. Who is the guy that *really* wants to put him away."

"Hah hah," Ames said, slamming his left fist down on the blotter, "not while I'm on the earth, he isn't. Not while I'm on the earth. After I'm in it, perhaps, but not while I'm walking on it. Not by a long shot." He grinned.

"Well, ah, no," Cremmens said, smiling, "but see, I didn't know about you and Jean being, going back together such a long way, until I got here today. Anyway, Brian is the guy that is prosecuting him. That's what I mean."

"Yes," Ames said, drawing it out into a hiss. He drooled slightly when he hissed. This seemed to amuse him. He threw back his head again; he laughed without making more than a dry, racking sound like that of a man choking, or in a convulsion. Tears came to his eyes behind his glasses. Cremmens started out of the chair, preparing to help him. Ames waved him off with his left hand. He continued to wheeze. With his right hand he fumbled in his pants for a handkerchief. He found none. The wheezing gradually subsided. His head came back to normal position. He removed his glasses. He gasped three times.

"Well," he said, restoring the glasses and settling back into the chair, "Hanrihan and Dussault. I'll come to the point directly, hah hah. After our little interlude there." He beamed.

"Yes sir," Cremmens said, sitting back in the chair again. "I was afraid you were choking for a minute there, sir."

"No no," Ames said, shaking his head and smiling, "not a chance. The commission. What do you know about the commission?"

"Just that there is one, sir," Cremmens said, "and you're the head of it."

"Yes," Ames said. He nodded several times. "The Ames Commission. A triumph or a joke. All up to me. Ames. That's what the *Commoner* said. You read that?"

"The *Commoner*, sir?" Cremmens said. "Yeah, I read it. I like their sports. That guy they got writing baseball, Kendrigan? I like him. Smart bastard. Tough."

"No no," Ames said impatiently, "what they said about me. Editorial. Column. Gillis. Joseph Gillis. Fraud. Read that?"

"I guess I didn't," Cremmens said.

"Umm," Ames said. "I did." He picked up a newspaper clipping from the desk. "'Whether Governor Tierney's concession to the cleanup movement in government will turn out to be a triumph or just another bad joke will remain far up in the air until Chairman Otis Ames has chosen his staff and given some indication of what he intends to do with the commission. He can assemble a hard-hitting unit that will pursue the trail wherever it leads, and with aggressive use of the unique prosecutorial powers he's been given, carry out his unprecedented mandate until the corrupters are behind bars where they belong. Or he can stage another sham, another travesty of the campaign which this Commonwealth so sorely needs. The choice is that of Otis Ames. A triumph or a joke: it's up to him.'" Ames put the clipping down.

"Yes sir," Cremmens said.

"Nothing but a gauntlet," Ames said, muttering. "Well, if they had any doubt, they won't have it long. Corporal Cremmens, I want Dussault. Get him. Get him convicted and bring him to me. Then we will sweat him until he gives us what we want." His jaw set firmly.

"Sir?" Cremmens said.

"Corporal Cremmens," Ames said sharply, "don't be deliberately dense with me. You know what I mean: nail Dussault and nail him good. Then, when you've got him looking down the barrel of a long, long sentence, bring him to me and I'll make him see the light. Either he talks, and tells the world about the corrupt contractors he's dealt with, or he'll never be at liberty again." Cremmens looked perplexed. "My good man," Ames said, "it's not difficult to understand. Convict Dussault. Confront him with the threat of a heavy sentence, or the choice of testifying before my commission and implicating the crooked contractors. Do you think they'll relish the prospect of jail? I doubt it. We'll give them the same choice we gave Dussault, and they'll crumple, *like Dixie cups.*" He made a fist and slugged the desk with it. "And they, Corporal Cremmens, will in turn give us the men that they've been paying off. Including the kingpin."

"The kingpin," Cremmens said.

Ames nodded vigorously. "Right up the ladder, Corporal. First rung: Dussault. Second and middle rungs: the contractors. Right up to the top. Bernie Morgan and his personal Bismarck."

"Bernie Morgan, sir?" Cremmens said. "The Speaker?"

Ames continued to nod. He grinned and wheezed slightly, but recovered himself. "Morgan, the crook. And his Bismarck."

"I dunno this guy Bismarck," Cremmens said.

"The real brains behind the operation," Ames said. "Francis X. Costello."

Cremmens shifted several times in his chair. "Yeah," he said, "well, uh, okay, you say so. But what do you want me to do?"

"My investigator," Ames said, beaming again. "My first staff investigator."

"Who's the lawyer?" Cremmens said.

"I haven't decided," Ames said. "Hah hah," he said.

"Well," Cremmens said, "I'm not sure of course, but I think Brian's interested."

"Hanrihan," Ames said, nodding again. "I heard that myself. You tell Mister Hanrihan what I want, is that clear? And tell him I intend to get it. Hah *hah.*"

Cremmens stared at him. "That's all, Corporal," Ames said. Cremmens continued to stare. "Do you understand English, Corporal?" Ames said, starting to shout. "That is all. Tell Hanrihan." He was turning in his chair and bending back down over the white legal pad, picking up the Mont Blanc pen. Cremmens got up. Ames peered up at him, grinning. "Tell him," Ames said, "what I said. Remind him of my unprecedented powers. And tell him I'll be here, watching."

Cremmens backed away from the desk. By the time he reached the center of the office, Ames was hidden once again behind the pigeonholed partition. Cremmens could hear the pen scratching. He paused momentarily and cleared his throat. From behind the partition there came an instant response. "That's all, Corporal. Remember, we south-paws must stick together. *Hah hah.*"

10 Around 8:45, the Speaker with his light-blue linen sport coat flapping in the evening breeze and his knitted yellow tie bunched up in an untidy knot at the throat of his shirt stood swaying slightly on the brick pavement at the circle in front of Anthony's Pier Four. He leaned his elbow against one of the black iron dock bollards set in at the curb and stared at the display window where lobsters, swordfish steaks, large king crabs, whole halibuts, and long, fat cod were offered for take-home sale on a bed of crushed ice. His white hair stood up like a rooster's comb in the breeze and even with the support of the bollard which had steadied huge ships against the tides he had trouble keeping his balance. He whistled softly eight or nine bars of "How Are Things in Glocca Morra?", belched, and patted himself on the chest, sighed, belched again, and started the tune once more from the beginning, sometimes whistling it slightly flat and sometimes slightly sharp. A faint smile appeared on his face, disappeared, and reappeared.

At the corner of the building a couple, tanned, in their early thirties, pulled up in a tan Monte Carlo coupe, parked it with the motor running, and got out. The man wore a tan poplin suit and the woman wore a beige jersey dress. The man left the driver's side door open, accepted a ticket from the parking attendant in the orange jumpsuit who came out of his little shack for the mission, and escorted his wife up the pavement toward the entrance. She looked at the Speaker disapprovingly.

"Evenin'," Morgan said, tipping the hat he never wore. "Nice ... *nice* evenin'."

The man took his wife's left elbow and guided her past the Speaker. The man pursed his lips and inspected the Speaker carefully. He did not say anything.

"Match," the Speaker said with some difficulty. The man looked startled and began to fumble in his left-hand jacket pocket. The Speaker made a dismissing gesture with his right hand. "No ... no," he said, shaking his head. "Don't even have a cigar. Not right now. Left it. Inside." He beamed at them. The woman suppressed a laugh and tossed her hair. It was ash blonde and it framed her tanned face perfectly. "Meant," the Speaker said cheerfully, *"match*. You match."

The man looked puzzled. The woman had a musical laugh. It sounded lightly in the gentle air. "Car," the Speaker said, waving vaguely as the attendant drove it around the circle, past the antique locomotive, toward the valet parking area. He grinned. "An' your clothes." The man was still perplexed and his face showed it. "Your suit," the Speaker said, gesturing with his left hand toward the man. "Her dress." He scowled. "Those're your clothes, aren't they?"

The man drew back. The Speaker broke the scowl into another grin. He waved his left hand deprecatingly. He kept his right arm firmly lodged on the bollard. "Sure," he said. "Clothes, anna car, and you both got nice tans, too." He leaned toward them precariously. The man drew back farther. The Speaker leered. "Been out inna sun. I bet," he said. "Down Cape, 'm I right? Little cottage the summer, prolly Chatham? Some place classy like that? Gotta boat?" He lurched abruptly and carefully straightened up again. His tie flapped along with his sport coat. He secured the coat lapel with his right hand, still leaving the elbow resting on the bollard, and stuffed the tie into the jacket, which he failed to button. The tie promptly blew out again. He gazed down at it in frustration, his jowls spreading out over his collar. "Fuck," he said absently. He looked up again. The couple was edging away, the man keeping a close eye on him. "Hey," he said, amiably, "didn't mean *you*. Tie. Hey." The couple was about ten feet away from him, walking toward the entrance to the restaurant. "Didn't answer my, my question." He waved at their backs. "Gotta boat or not, huh?" They opened the doors and stood aside to let another person out. He shook his head and looked back to the display window. "Aw right," he muttered, "then I *did* mean you. Fuck you." He nodded twice and smiled again. He resumed whistling.

Raymond Archambault stepped out of the doorway as the couple went inside. He wore a blue poplin suit and his white shirt was crisp. His tie was a narrow blue with white polka dots, and his hair was grey at his temples. He had made his weekly trip to the hairstylist, and he had touched up his tan with the sunlamp he kept in his office. He looked toward the Speaker, heaped up against the bollard as though he had been a bag of trash discarded by a collector noticing he'd finished his shift. Raymond Archambault studied Morgan for a minute, squared his shoulders, and started toward him.

When Archambault was about five feet away, the Speaker, staring fixedly at the seafood on display and not noticing him, became dissatisfied with his whistling, grimaced, and switched to singing. He sang very softly, and quite slowly, having trouble remembering the words and knitting his brows when he searched for them. He spotted Archambault from the corner of his eye. With difficulty he shifted his position to look at him directly. "Raymond," he said with delight, looking him over, "you're . . . cuttin' a fine figure a man for yourself tonight, Raymond. You piece a *shit."* He threw his head back and laughed, making a sound like barking. He put his head down again. "What's goin' on, huh Raymond? Gotta wake in Lowell tonight? Somethin' like that? Better hurry." The Speaker waggled his finger at Archambault. He tried to look at his watch on his left wrist, could not manage it, and gave it up. He clasped his left wrist in his right hand. "Don't hurry," he said warningly, "missa Sorrowful fuckin' Mysteries, ya know." He released his left hand and waved his forefinger slowly at Archambault. "Naughty," he said. "Naughty. Bereaved family, won't like it. 'Fuckin' Raymond,' they'll say. After you go, they'll say it. 'Fuckin' Raymond. Don't he know he wasn't here, huh? The Agony inna Garden, that stuff? Bastard.' Won't do you no good at all, Raymond, drive alla way up there, missa Sorrowful Mysteries." He grinned.

"Raising our voices in song on a summer's evening, Bernie?" Archambault said. "Airing out the pipes a little?"

The Speaker looked puzzled. "I don't understand," he said with some difficulty.

"I heard you singing when I came out," Archambault said. " 'Glocca Morra,' was it?"

The Speaker smiled. "Oh," he said. He nodded. "Yeah. 'How're Things in Glocca Morra?' Like that. 'S good song. *Brigadoon,* right? Old Gene Kelly there?" He put his head back again and looked toward the stars. He sang in a cracked voice about the little brook.

"Finian's Rainbow, actually," Archambault said.

"Huh?" the Speaker said.

"Finian's Rainbow," Archambault said. " 'How're Things in Glocca Morra?', that's from *Finian's Rainbow."*

The Speaker frowned. "Now, jus' a minute here, Raymond," he said. "I am the Speaker here, right? And you're jus' Ways 'n Means thing there, whatever the fuck it is. Am I right?"

"Right," Archambault said, smiling, "but it's still not *Brigadoon.* You haven't got your gavel here, Bernie. No matter how many times you say it, you can't make *Finian's Rainbow* into *Brigadoon.* Not here. This ain't the House."

The Speaker gazed at him. He had a crafty expression. "You sure of that, Raymond?"

Archambault laughed. "Sure as I am that I'm standing here." He gestured toward the restaurant behind them. "Inside there, maybe you can make Dealey into a statesman and his whiskey disappear, do that without your gavel, but out here, all you got's a buncha dead fish looking at you. Not the House."

"That so?" the Speaker said. He smiled. He pointed toward the window. "You sure that's not the House, Raymond? Looks like the House to me. Looks exactly like what I see, I get up there with alla reps in town looking back at me. Exact same thing. Just as much brains in that window, too, come right down to it."

"That's a bunch of dead fish," Archambault said.

"That's what I said," the Speaker said, "and that buncha dead fishes inna window there looks just like them." He turned his head suddenly to the right, almost losing his balance. "The fuck's that fuckin' kid, my fuckin' car? Must've gone to fuckin' Worcester with it."

"What kid, Bernie?" Archambault said.

"The fuckin' kid in them orange suits that they go and get the car for you," Morgan said. "Him."

"Did you give the kid a ticket, Bernie?" Archambault said. The attendant who had parked the Monte Carlo was entering his shingled hut.

"Course I did," Morgan said. He patted his pockets. "Think I did, anyway." He felt something in his right-hand jacket pocket. He took it out, steadying himself on the bollard with his right hand and reaching across his body with his left hand to get it. He produced an orange ticket. "Well," he said, "looka that, willya? Right here in my pocket, alla time I was blamin' the kid. Huh."

"Gimme that," Archambault said. He held out his hand.

The Speaker pulled the ticket back. "Will not," he said. "What're you gonna do with it, Raymond, huh? Drop it inna harbor, prolly. See, this ticket thing here?" He waved it. "This's my *car.* Can't get my car back, 'thout this. Don't want you, go and throw my car inna water, I can't get it."

Archambault continued to hold out his hand. "I'm not going to throw it in the harbor, Bernie," he said. "It might be better if I did, but I won't. All I'm gonna do is take it over and give it to the kid with my ticket and have him get my car and then get your car, so I can get a good head start on the road ahead of you."

The Speaker shook his head. "Uh uh," he said. "Think you can trick me, Raymond? Think again, pally. I been at this game three hundred years 'fore you were born. I know what you're thinking. Always do. One step . . . hell, *ten* steps ahead of you, alla time." He laughed. "*Briga-doon*," he said.

Archambault dropped his hand. He shrugged. "Okay," he said, "suit yourself. I just thought maybe you'd like me to handle it, before Gillis gets fed up with Dealey and the crowd in there and comes out and sees you like this."

"Gillis," Morgan said with suspicion.

"Yeah," Archambault said, "Joe Gillis. The *Commoner*. You know Joe Gillis. The one with the column? One that drives you nuts so you won't even talk to him? That guy. He'd really like it, see you like this. Him, Ferris from the *Globe* or Collins from the *Herald*. Great stuff."

"I didn't see Gillis here," Morgan said stubbornly.

"Bernie," Archambault said, "the only thing you saw here was that barkeep with the big jug of Wild Turkey and the ice. That's all you saw the whole time you were here."

"I only had one drink," Morgan said defensively.

"Yeah," Archambault said, "well, they must've served it to you in a fuckin' pail, then, because you sure don't look like a man who had just one drink. You didn't have anything to eat or anything."

"Did too," Morgan said. "I had oysters there. Lots of oysters."

"Yeah," Archambault said, "well, you oughta think about layin' off them oysters then, Bernie, because when you eat a lot of them like this they make you act like you're shitfaced."

"Umm," Morgan said.

"Now look," Archambault said, "I got a deal for you, all right?"

"Deal," Morgan said. "Whassa deal?"

"You get your ass inside there in the men's room," Archambault said. "Go in the men's room, it's right inside the door, and throw some cold water on your face and dry it off and take a piss or do anything else you can think of to do. But just stay in there about five minutes, and I'll give the kid your ticket and tell him to get your car first, and then mine, and when you come out you can get right in it and leave. So nobody'll see you, all right? Just get in your car and go straight home."

"My car first," Morgan said.

"Your car first," Archambault said.

"Aw right," Morgan said, handing over the ticket and lifting his weight off the bollard, "but I'm warnin' you, Raymond, it better be here waitin' for me, I come out, and you right here too, or the next thing you know I'll get a cab home and a cab up the office tomorrow and when I get through with you tomorrow night, you won't be Chairman of nothing."

Archambault sighed. "I know, Bernie, I know," he said, "because you got the power."

"I got the power," Morgan said, nodding. "Damned right. Seniority don't matter and party don't matter and who your mother fucked in holy wedlock, that don't matter neither. Not when you're inna goddamned General Court. Because when you're inna General Court, your ass is the grass and Bernie Morgan is the lawn mower. 'Member that, Raymond. Because you got to go back there tomorrow, and I'll be there."

Archambault took the ticket. "I'll remember, Bernie," he said. He turned and watched Morgan weave up the walk to the doors, opening the one on his right with difficulty, slamming into the one on his left and rebounding off it into the entryway. Archambault shook his head. In the cool evening he walked over to the shingled shack where the attendant watched a small black-and-white Panasonic television set. He had found a rock music show and was bup-bupping his mouth and drumming his fingers on his legs as he watched, his body moving back and forth to the beat. " 'Scuse me," Archambault said. The attendant glanced up. "Two cars," Archambault said. He presented the Speaker's ticket. "Get this one first, and when you come back I'll give you mine."

The attendant looked at Archambault with disapproval. "That the guy," he said, "that one that was holding up the pier there?"

"Yeah," Archambault said. The attendant made no move to take the ticket. "Caddy. Seville. Maroon. Gold roof."

"I know which car it is, mister," the attendant said. "I took it from him when he came in here. He was drunk out his mind then."

"Well," Archambault said, "he's drunk out his mind now, too. So get his car and we'll put him back in it and get him the fuck out of here."

The attendant shook his head. "Uh uh," he said. "We got rules around here."

"Really," Archambault said. "Well, that's very nice. We got rules around where that guy and I hang out, too. And one of our rules is that you do what he says. Because otherwise you *die*. So go and get his car for him, because that is what he happens to be saying now."

The attendant leaned toward Archambault. He was very earnest in the flickering light from the television set. "Mister," he said, "I don't know if you understand this kind of thing or not, but there're laws about that kind of thing, you know? Puttin' guys in their cars that we know they're drunk when we do it, and lettin' 'em loose onna road. The owner here, he could get himself sued for that, you know? If a guy like that hurts somebody. So he don't want us to do that. And I don't particularly want to lose my job, all right? Which is what I will end up doing if somebody comes out that door or happens look out one of them windows up there and sees me puttin' a guy in that kinda shape in no automobile, all right? Even if he don't hurt anybody. Won't matter to my ass."

"You through?" Archambault said.

"No," the attendant said, settling back again, "and I don't want to be, either, which is what I just got finished trying to tell you." He folded his arms. "You wanna go back inside there, mister, and find somebody like the owner or somebody else that is running this place for him, and have them come out here and tell me I should put that guy back in his car and let him loose to go outta here and run into the first thing that gets in front of him, you go ahead and do it. Because I don't think you can. And when you do, I'm gonna tell whoever it is that I seen that guy come *in* drunk and I seen him come out even drunker and that's why I didn't go up to him or anything when he didn't come over and give me his ticket, right? Because I figured the longer that guy had to stand there in the air and maybe sober up a little bit the better. Maybe sooner or later one of his friends'd show up. Or else maybe he wouldn't remember until tomorrow morning what he came out here for and he'd just stand here all night and get all wet. But by then at least he'd be sober enough so somebody could give him his car or he could go and find it himself. So, you do that, and we'll see whether I have to go and get his car for him."

"Okay," Archambault said. He reached into his pocket and pulled out a twenty-dollar bill. "See this?"

The attendant looked at it. "Yup," he said. "Take a hell of a lot more'n that, change my mind. I need this job, mister. I make almost three hundred some weeks in this shack and there ain't a lot of it that I can do without. And the way things're going right now, there ain't no place else around that I can find that three hundred no place else. So, you wanna give me six months' pay or something like that, then we can talk. But not for no lousy twenty bucks, am I gonna get my balls in the coffee-grinder, uh uh."

"You talk pretty fast," Archambault said. "You listen even half as fast, you got a bright future in this world. You got any objection, getting his car and givin' it to me?"

The attendant frowned. He looked at Archambault. "Guess not," he said. "You look okay. Provided, you're the one that's gonna drive it out of here. Once it gets onna street, see, I don't give a shit who's drivin' it, long's it's not me that was responsible if it's him that gets behind the wheel. And I'm not one of the ones out onna street at the same time. I don't wanna die."

"Precisely," Archambault said. "Now here is what we do, all right? You take this twenty, and you go get the Seville and bring it up here. Don't waste any time, right? I got him to get back inside for a minute but he's not gonna stay in there forever. Not unless he goes back to the bar, which I doubt he will do. And if he comes out and his car's not here, all hell's gonna break loose. I'll never get him back inside again. And," he said, taking his own ticket out of his breast pocket, "as soon as you drop that car here and I get in it, you get mine, all right?"

"Behind the wheel," the attendant said. "You get in it behind the wheel."

"Right," Archambault said, "you haul ass just as fast as you can down to my car, and bring that down to the street for me, okay? Because I don't feel like walking all the way back up here after we get that Seville out to the street. Mine's the silver Riviera."

"I know which one it is," the attendant said. He stood up, accepting both tickets and the money. "You're really gonna do this, huh?" he said. "You're gonna turn that bastard loose on the streets in that thing when he comes out here? He's gonna kill somebody. Maybe himself. You think you're doing him a favor or something?"

Archambault sighed. "He's gonna come out again any minute, all right?" he said. "I already told you that, once. I haven't got time, argue with you any more like this. Get the car. He'll be all right, I promise you. He's done this hundreds of times, and he always makes it. He's got this weird ability. He can sober himself up, like that." He snapped his fingers. "How, I dunno. Special arrangements with God or something, I guess."

"More like," the attendant said, "more like everybody else onna road when he's out'd better have some kind of arrangements with God, you ask me. So he don't run over them. Because that guy, mister, is drunk and he is dangerous."

"You should see him," Archambault said, "you should see him in action when he's sober, if you think he's dangerous, drunk."

11 Leo Rosen drove the black Kawasaki Spectre motorcycle into the white gravel yard of the two-pump gas station on the back road into Proctor, still crouching low over the handlebars as though taming the hills and curves of the two-lane blacktop through the foothills of the Berkshires. The red night-vision lamps of the speedometer and tachometer shone upward under the smoked-grey Lexan face shield of his black helmet, so that his reddish beard seemed to be smoldering. There were dead bugs spattered out of the warm summer evening on the shield and the top of his helmet, and he flipped it up as soon as he had brought the bike to a stop at the pumps. He shut off the engine, and the crickets could be heard. He straightened up in the dim light of the two seventy-five-watt bulbs, one over each antique pump with its innards exposed below the circular white signs saying JENNEY, and massaged his kidneys with his hands.

The concrete island with the two gas pumps was the only installation in the yard. Ahead of Rosen there was a rump-sprung black pickup truck listing casually to starboard, its back gate hanging down. Next to the road there was an unlighted sign, hard to read in the gloom, on a twenty-foot pole. It said: CITIES SERVICE. On the other side of the pump island there was a low wooden building; two-thirds of it was taken up by two service bays; the remainder was a small office. There was one large window at the front of the office, decorated at the bottom with a window box of pink and white geraniums and petunias that spilled over its edges and trailed almost to the white gravel on the ground. They were illuminated by the light from inside the office. Rosen could see a large rolltop desk covered with papers and a metal gooseneck lamp which shone on the papers and the face of the man seated at the desk. He had his feet up on the surface and his hands clasped behind his head. He wore a Boston Red Sox hat and he was watching something with close attention, out of Rosen's view. There was a flickering light at the edge of the window, mostly blue. The inner, wooden door of the office was open, and the sagging screen door was closed. Rosen could not hear any sound.

He shut off the headlight of the Kawasaki and climbed off, setting the kickstand. It clanked once and clicked once falling into position, momentarily interrupting the conversation of the crickets and the occasional call of a nightbird. He stretched luxuriously. He removed the Bell helmet, using both hands, and rested it on the saddle of the bike. He stretched again and walked a few tentative steps backward and forward, as though making sure he had not lost the hang of it. His feet made the gravel crunch. While he was doing these things, he kept his gaze on the man in the office. The man did not move.

"Shit," Rosen said. He leaned over the bike and removed the key from the ignition, locking it. He walked around the back of the bike and toward the door to the office. He opened the screen door, which creaked, and stepped onto a threshold which bent under his average weight. Directly ahead of him there was an old drum-model Coke machine, about waist-high, with the coin slot in an attachment at the right rear corner. There was a large full-color decal on the front, laid over raised lettering that showed through: Coca-Cola, in script. The picture was of a young girl with curly blond hair and freckles and a baseball hat. She was grinning and holding up a bottle of Coke. The legend under the picture said: THE PAUSE THAT REFRESHES. Rosen said: "Halloo?" He was looking to his left at the man seated at the desk when he said it.

The man did not move. Rosen turned to the left and walked into the main part of the office. His blue and white Nike running shoes had ripple treads for soles, and they made squeegee noises on the faded tan linoleum. There were three chrome-framed chairs padded with maroon vinyl on the left, backs to the window; they were at odd angles, and the stuffing was coming out of the cushions. Directly ahead of Rosen there was a large iron stove with a black flue at the rear. On top of the stove there was a nineteen-inch black and white Dumont television set which covered most of the surface. The Red Sox played silently on the tube, in a snowstorm of interference. An antenna lead had been attached to a pair of separate rabbit ears with black electrical tape—the lead ran off at an angle to a cup hook screwed into the tin patterned ceiling and from there drooped down the side of the window. There were four cardboard tubes about five inches in diameter around the chairs, each of them with a black metal ashtray set into the top for its intended use, and another set into the other end as a base. The man at the desk watched the game. From the rear, Rosen could see that he was not very big and not very tall, and that his hands were permanently stained with grease and oil. There were six cans of Budweiser on the desk, three in the plastic collar, two pushed away from the man, one close to him. There was a black tire iron, the tip polished from sharpening, next to the beer.

"What's the score?" Rosen said.

The man did not turn. "Dunno," he said. "They're playing in Cleveland." The man made *n* sounds into *m* sounds. There was a clicking sound when he spoke.

Rosen said: "Oh." The man remained motionless in the chair. "They," Rosen said, "they don't keep score in Cleveland or something?"

"Far as I know," the man said, "far as I know, they do."

"Oh," Rosen said. "Yeah, I noticed that too sometimes, I'm watching the game. They tell you everything but the damned score, you turn the thing on."

"Not here," the man said. "Sound don't work."

"Oh," Rosen said.

"Yeah," the man said. "Had this set for years. Picture's all right, sound don't work. My father's. He's deaf. Don't matter to him."

"No," Rosen said.

"Grew up this way," the man said. "Used to it now. Ever since I was a kid. Got so's I don't even notice it."

"The score," Rosen said.

"Yeah," the man said. "It's always in the paper, in the morning, how it come out."

One of the Red Sox hit a ground ball through the blizzard on the screen. The shortstop fielded it cleanly and started a six-four-three double play. That evidently ended the inning for Boston. A graphic appeared on the screen, but it was white and illegible in the snow. The man in the chair unclasped his hands and swiveled the chair around, swinging his feet off the desk. He looked at Rosen. "You want something?" he said. He had a deep scar on the right side of his face. It began just below his right eye and made a canyon in his cheek to his top lip, which it left immobile at the corner of his mouth, and continued into his lower lip and chin. He was in his late forties. He had light brown hair which showed under the bill of the Red Sox cap.

"Yeah," Rosen said. "Could I get some gas?"

"Sure," the man said. He wore a green twill shirt with *Roger* in yellow script over the left breast pocket, a pair of green twill pants, and oil-proof dark-brown work shoes laced halfway up. "This's a gas station, isn't it?"

"Yup," Rosen said.

The man stared at Rosen. Rosen wore blue Levi's, a grey cotton work shirt, and a tweed sport jacket under his blue nylon windbreaker. The jacket was longer than the windbreaker, and the skirt of it hung below the waistband of the jacket. There were some dead bugs on the chest of the windbreaker.

"Ain't you awful hot in that outfit, night like this?" the man said.

"No," Rosen said. "There's not much protection from the wind, you get that thing going. Goes right through you without some protection."

"Thought so," the man said. "That's how come they wear them leather coats, am I right?"

"Yup," Rosen said, "that's why they wear them leather coats, all right."

"So," the man said, "how come you don't, don't wear one of them leather coats?"

"I find," Rosen said, finding himself sounding scholarly and feeling foolish, but pressing on with it, "one layer of heavy clothes doesn't work as well for me, I'm not as comfortable in it, as I am with multiple layers. More air gets trapped between them. And then of course, if I get too warm, I can always stop and remove one." He stopped abruptly. There was more that he could say in explanation and the man seemed to be interested, but he was very embarrassed.

The man saw that Rosen had finished, or at least stopped. "You got bugs on you, too," he said.

"From the wind," Rosen said. "Like the car windshields, you know, from fast driving?"

"Yeah," the man said. He nodded several times. He cleared his throat. "Seen a few of those. Son of a *bitch*, get them things off the windshields." He nodded.

"I'd imagine," Rosen said.

"I seen this one guy once," the man said. "He come in here. Been driving real fast. Had one of those foreign jobs there. Ferrari?"

"Uh huh," Rosen said.

"Red," the man said. "Just a *little* son of a whore. Man said it'd go awful fast."

"It would," Rosen said.

"Yeah," the man said. "I figured he was lost, wanted directions. Claimed he wasn't. Lost. Said he got off the Turnpike on purpose. *Liked* the back roads."

"Yeah," Rosen said.

"Yeah," the man said reflectively. "I didn't believe that one. He was lost all right. Had California plates on it."

"Yeah," Rosen said.

"Yeah," the man said. He paused for a few moments and stared at Rosen. "Said he was going to Boston. Claimed he was making this movie there. Didn't believe that neither."

"They do make movies in Boston," Rosen said. "Some movies."

"Little bit of a guy," the man said. "Didn't look like no movie star to me. He wasn't no taller'n I am. He had this rubber thing all across the front of it. Had holes cut in it for the lights. First time I ever saw a car all ready to go fuckin'. He said that was for the bugs."

"You didn't believe that," Rosen said.

"Yeah," the man said, "I did." He made no move to get up.

"Look," Rosen said, "I'm running kind of late. Is there a men's room I can use while you're gassing up my bike?"

"Uh huh," the man said.

Rosen looked around the office. "Could you, ah, could you tell me where it is?"

"Sure," the man said. "Around the back. There's a trailer out there. Wife's in there. She'll be watching television. Don't matter. Just knock once or twice, go right in. Right in front of you."

"There isn't any—" Rosen said, "there isn't any in the station? I kind of hate to just wander in on your wife."

"Stopped up," the man said. "Roots got in the pipe goes down to the septic tank there. Maple roots." He wove his fingers together. "Just like this. Trapped her all up. All the paper and shit didn't get through. Clogged her all up, finally. Have to dig the whole pipe up, find the block. Said the hell with it. Old pipe anyway. Couldn't put it back. Have to relay the whole line. You priced that Orangeburg pipe lately?"

"Can't say's I have," Rosen said.

"Fuckin' dear," the man said. "Too dear for me."

"Yeah," Rosen said.

"Get a backhoe in here and everything? Christ. Fuckin' building's not worth that much. Use the one in the trailer. That works."

"Yeah," Rosen said. "Look, is it okay if I go in the bushes or something?"

The man shrugged. "Okay with me. That's what I do, generally, myself. Don't piss onna wall, though. Wood soaks it up. Sun come out and it stinks." He put his hands on his thighs and seemed to be gathering himself to get up. "You take a piss, I'll put the gas in."

"Fine," Rosen said.

"She take regular?" the man said.

"Yeah," Rosen said.

"I need a key?" the man said.

"No," Rosen said.

The man stood up abruptly. Rosen turned and went back the way he had come. He left the station through the screen doorway and let the door slam behind him. He did not hear the man walking behind him, but he could not defer urination much longer. He let his eyes adapt to the dark. There were some tall trees ahead of him, about twenty feet beyond the last stall of the service bays. He put out his left hand and touched the building lightly with his fingertips. He walked along slowly, feeling the clapboards of the wall and the vertical matched boards of the bay doors, until he reached the end of the building and stopped. The ground was uneven and he went very slowly. Behind him he heard the screen door slam again, and the sound of footsteps on the gravel. It occurred to him that the man might have stopped to pick up a wrench and come out to sneak up behind him and kill him, but he dismissed the idea.

The ground sloped gradually away from the garage. Rosen took a diagonal route away from it, toward the rear. When he reached the back corner he could see the trailer, lighted over the doorway and expanded by a wooden addition. There was a 1956 DeSoto Fireflite Sportsman's Coupe, black and white, parked beside it, the paint on the roof dull in the light. The shades in the trailer were drawn. Rosen unzipped his fly and stood close enough to a clump of bushes to suit him. He relieved himself decorously in the darkness and the leaves, arranged his clothing, and started back toward the front of the station.

The man had removed the cover to the torpedo tank and inserted the nozzle. He was bending over the bike, listening to the gasoline go in. He was holding the pump trigger at minimum flow. He straightened up as Rosen crunched up behind him. He did not take his eyes off the tank.

"This here's a nice motorcycle," he said.

"Thanks," Rosen said.

"I don't like filling these things," the man said. "I seen a guy once, this guy I knew over in Mercer that run a station there, and there was this State Police trooper there that this guy didn't like at all, if you know what I mean."

"Yeah," Rosen said.

"And this trooper," the man said, "he was always making everybody's life hard and giving guys all kind of shit which he could do and get away with on account of how he was this state trooper, see?"

"Yeah," Rosen said.

"And he would just go ahead and do it, you know? Any time he felt like it. And there was this one night when he was riding around all over the place on his big Harley there, and he come in this guy's station all hot and bothered, and this guy takes the pump and this trooper's off getting a Coke or something and the guy puts her on full flow and just sets her on automatic stop, only he jams her so she won't stop, and then he finds something else he can do that he's not near the damned bike. And of course the gas runs all over and down on the engine and everything, and he gets her all cleaned up but he don't touch the coil and the plugs, see? And that trooper starts that thing up and you should've seen that bike go up. I wasn't there, but guys told me, they never saw nothing like that since the Fourth July."

"I imagine," Rosen said.

"So," the man said, "unless I got some reason I want to do something like that, a guy comes in here onna bike, I'm always real careful."

"Glad of it," Rosen said.

"You piss all right?" the man said.

"Yeah," Rosen said. "I never had any trouble yet, anyway. Smooth as silk."

"See," the man said, "ahh, there she is." He shut off the nozzle and lifted it carefully from the tank, avoiding drips. He returned the nozzle to the pump. He wiped his hands on his pants and replaced the cap on the tank. He looked at Rosen. "You went into them bushes," he said.

"Yeah," Rosen said. "I hope that was all right."

"Oh sure," the man said. "Generally go there myself in the daytimes, don't feel like going in the trailer. Nights, though, we sometimes get a skunk in there. Don't smell nothing though, so I'd guess you didn't."

"Just lucky, I guess," Rosen said. "Any particular reason you waited till now to tell me?"

"Didn't think of it before," the man said. "Don't get much night business here. Only reason I'm here, the wife likes them goddamned shows they got on and I want to watch the baseball, so I might as well keep open. Three seventy." He held out his hand.

Rosen pulled a five from his pocket. He handed it to the man, who squinted at it. "You haven't got right change?" the man said.

"Sorry," Rosen said.

"I'll have to go inside," the man said. "I don't carry no change at night."

Rosen started toward the garage, hearing the man's feet crunch behind him. He opened the screen door and held it, but the man crunched on past. "In the trailer," he said. "No money in the station neither, not at night."

"I'll have a Coke," Rosen said.

"Just lift up the cover," the man said. "Coin thing's been busted ever since I can remember. Don't matter anyhow, course, you not having change."

"You can take it out of the five," Rosen said. He let the door slam behind him. He lifted the cover of the Coke machine and took out a king-sized bottle. The opener was still screwed to the side, and he popped the crown off. It fell onto the floor and he left it there. He stepped into the office and stood there, drinking the Coke and watching the Red Sox conclude an inning by forcing a Cleveland base runner at home plate. The electronic blizzard of interference was still severe.

The man walked past the window and entered the building through the screen door. "Coke's twenty-five," he said. "Come to three ninety-five all told, which your change is a buck and a nickel." He handed the money to Rosen.

"Thanks," Rosen said. "Just finish my Coke, and on my way. Saw your car out there, the DeSoto? Nice old car. Oughta fix her up and sell her. People'd pay a lot of money for one of those."

"Can't," the man said. "Can't sell it. That's my dad's car. Always asks me, is his car okay, I go to see him."

"Oh," Rosen said. "That's too bad. He's ill?"

"Twelve years," the man said. "He's not right in the head, mostly. Few strokes. He's in his hospital up there."

"His hospital?" Rosen said.

"That's what I call it," the man said. "He built it."

"Only hospital I ever heard of here," Rosen said, "is the State Hospital. Knox Hospital."

"That's him," the man said. "Wilfred Knox. Wasn't for him, wouldn't've been there."

"He was the state rep they named it for?" Rosen said.

"Speaker, the House," the man said. "Eighteen years."

"Huh," Rosen said. "Good place, is it?"

"I didn't like it, I was in there," the man said. "Dad, it don't matter. He don't know where the fuck he is anyway. He thinks he's still down in Boston, being Speaker. All the people there treat him like he is. That and the dogs in his room."

"Dogs?" Rosen said.

"He had dogs," the man said. "Raised pointers. Pedigreed pointers. He thinks his dogs're there with him. There ain't no dogs. The nurses put a dish of water on the floor every day. When he sleeps, they empty it. Then when he wakes up he pisses and moans that his dogs haven't got any water, and they fill it again. The dogs and his car."

"Well," Rosen said, "how would he know if you sold the car?"

"He would know," the man said sadly. "I never could lie like them nurses can. He would know. I wished I could, sometimes."

"You were a patient at the hospital too?" Rosen said.

The man looked at him sharply. "Yeah, I was. Long time ago, though, and, I didn't see no dogs or anything. I didn't have no strokes. I was just sick."

"Oh," Rosen said.

"It's getting late," the man said. "Where you going?"

"Springfield," Rosen said.

"You better get going," the man said.

"Yeah," Rosen said. He finished the Coke. "Well, thanks for your time and trouble."

"Yeah," the man said. He squinted at Rosen. "Say, you a cop?"

"No," Rosen said.

"Well," the man said, "what're you doing here?"

"Just passing through," Rosen said, setting the Coke bottle on the window sill. "Just passing through."

"I don't believe that," the man said. "I don't believe that, either."

12 Mahoney in a black polyester suit leaned forward in the backseat of the cab and repeated what he had said to the driver. "I didn't ask you that, for Christ sake," he said. "I can see this's the fuckin' Cafe Claret, for Christ sake. They got a goddamned sign right over the door, and the canopy thing here practically out inna goddamned street

that says Cafe Claret on it. I can read, for Christ sake. You think I can't fuckin' *read*?"

The cabdriver twisted around in his seat and looked at Mahoney with mingled boredom and displeasure. He was about twenty-four and he had a brown beard which he had not bothered to trim in some time. His eyes were lidded and there were heavy bags under them. "Hey, man," he said in a slow voice, "you tryin', you wanna make, you after some *trouble*, somethin'? You asked me, get you the Claret, I got you the Claret, aw right? Now you wanna have some discussion or something? Whyncha pay the fuckin' fare, get out the goddamned cab, and just lemme go ahead and go around on my business, aw right? It's only three and a half bucks, right? You can even forget the tip, it's gonna blow your budget. It's all right with me, you wanna feel that way."

"I asked you a fuckin' question," Mahoney said. "I'm gonna get a fuckin' answer if I have to sit here all night."

"Hey, man," the cabbie said, shrugging, " 's all right with me, man. Like, see the meter there? Well, that means we get paid when we're waitin', you know? And like there ain't a hell of a lot of business onna street tonight, like it was raining or a weekend or somethin' and everybody all of a sudden wants to go somewhere all at once, right? So, you wanna sit here, have a nice chat, go ahead, and I'm actually makin' out onna deal. Especially with the engine and the air conditioner not running. 'Cause sooner, later, man, you're gonna have to pay what that meter says and you look at that pisser right now, you're gonna see it's up to three seventy already."

"You son of a bitch," Mahoney said, "you took me all around the fuckin' lot making a buck-fifty into a three-fifty ride, and now you're gonna, you think you're gonna milk it a little more? I'll take your fuckin' head off, kid, and bring it home and feed it to my fuckin' dogs, huh? How'd you like that, punk, bein' breakfast a couple Rhodesian ridgebacks. They'd like it, even if you wouldn't."

The cabbie sighed. He shut the bulletproof partition between the seats, reached over his left shoulder with his right hand and pulled the lever that locked the rear doors with the plungers down on his side of the partition. He turned around again and leaned into the small black grille set into the partition.

"You cocksucker," Mahoney said. He tried the right-hand rear door and could not get it open. He banged on the glass with his fist. The driver grinned. Mahoney hit the partition with his fist. The plastic shivered but it did not give or break.

"This'll stop a thirty-eight, man," the driver said, smiling. "You wanna bang your knuckles and see if you can make them hit like a forty-five, maybe you're gonna get to me. But I doubt it, man, I doubt it." He glanced at the meter and turned back to the grille. "Three ninety, man," he said. "Just lemme know when you get yourself all nice and tired out, finish your exercise in there. Then you look at the meter and put that much money in the little drawer here," he said, patting the pivoting drawer in the partition, "and I'll count it. And if it's enough, I'll let you out and I'll be on my way. And if it isn't, I won't." He grinned.

Mahoney pounded on the partition with both fists. "You mother-fucker," he shouted, "take me the Hack Inspector. You know where the Hack Inspector is, shithead? It's at Police Headquarters."

"Right," the driver said. "And that's on Berkeley Street. And Berkeley Street's one way. And this is Berkeley Street we're on. Up *beyond* Police Headquarters. You want me to take you, Police Headquarters, first you pay me for bringin' you here like you told me to. Then I'll think about goin' all the way around, get to Police Headquarters. Which is behind us. Got that?"

"You fucking bastard," Mahoney screamed, hopping on the seat and beating on the partition.

"My friend," the driver said, "like I say, it's all right with me. You wanna come to the big city, get yourself half in the bag, get in some unsuspecting guy's cab and make a lot of noise and wave your arms around, go ahead. Probably safer'n if you started a whole lot of trouble in some bar somewhere. They would probably pick a couple of guys to come over and quiet you down for disturbin' the other customers. Beat the livin' shit outta you. But this's okay with me, like I said. You wanna rent the arena for your little show, okay by this kid. I don't think it's very good and you're prolly not gonna sell a whole lotta tickets to people, come and watch it, but this's your hall for as long's you wanna rent it. Have a nice time." The cabbie leaned back from the partition, sat back in his seat, folded his arms over his chest, and rested his chin on it. He closed his eyes. Mahoney yelled and pounded the partition. He was heavy enough so his body movements made the cab bounce slightly on its shock absorbers at the curb, and his hollering was softly audible on the sidewalk. It began to get hot inside the cab, and Mahoney sweated.

The doorman at the Claret was Kenny Voss. He had been in the foyer arranging the ignition keys on the board where he put them after parking the customer's cars. He came out onto the sidewalk and saw Mahoney's cab swaying at the curb under the canopy. He ran up to it and peered inside. He rapped on the glass of the right front door. The cabbie looked up and regarded him calmly. Voss made a cranking motion with his right hand. The driver reached across the seat and lowered the window. The noise and thrashing continued in the backseat.

"Hey, my man," the driver said. "How things goin', Kenny babe, huh?"

Voss grinned. "Ransom," he said, "you old dog. I didn't know this was you. What you got in here, one of my customers?"

The cabbie glanced back into the passenger compartment. "I ain't sure," he said. "Usually when it's one of your customers I'm delivering, he don't make as much noise. I dunno what this guy is. Maybe he escaped from the circus or somethin', and they're out lookin' for him right now. Maybe even a ree-ward for him. This could be a valuable animal I got here."

"Well, hey, man," Kenny said, "uh, look, all right? I mean, you can't keep him sittin' here all night and raisin' hell and everything."

"Don't see why not," the driver said. "I ain't got nothin' else to do. And until he pays me, that's exactly what I'm gonna do, too. *Nothin'*, which nothin' includes not doing something else like lettin' him out."

"Look," Kenny said, "let him out, all right? And he'll pay you."

"Sure," the driver said, "sure he will. Prolly give me a ten-buck tip, too. Yeah. I dunno, Kenny. Easter Bunny didn't do so good by me this year, and I ain't seen shit from Santa Claus for so many years I can't even remember. No, thanks, let him out. I get paid, he gets out. That's the deal."

Another cab pulled up abreast of Mahoney's. Francis Costello got out, putting his change in his pocket, and the driver pulled away. Costello looked with interest at Mahoney's cab. Mahoney did not notice Costello. He continued to thrash in the backseat, pounding on the partition and shouting: "Motherfucker cocksucking cuntlapping son of a bitch." He was loud enough to be partly audible outside the cab. Costello looked over the cab at Voss. "The hell's goin' on here, Kenny?" he said. "This guy all right?"

"Seems healthy enough, Mister Costello," Voss said. "Driver says he won't pay, and he won't let him out until he does pay. Guy's pretty mad, I guess."

Costello put his head back and laughed. The driver rolled his window down. "Ah, look, mister, no offense, all right? But see, Kenny's an old friend here, and I got this show I can let him watch, okay, right? I don't know you, see? So I'm gonna have to ask you to make a small offering for admission. We got overhead in show biz too, you know?" He laughed.

Costello looked serious. "I don't know," he said. "I seem to've arrived in the middle, his performance. How long can he keep this up, huh? Don't want to pay you and then I discover he's all through for the night. Suppose he decides to get out the window, huh?"

The driver nodded. He looked serious. "He ain't thought of that, yet. I think he's prolly too fat." He held up his left index finger. "Wait just a minute," he said, "I'll ask him." He turned back to the grille. "Hey, wild man of Borneo," he said, jerking his thumb back toward Costello. "Got a guy here that's willin' to pay a small charge to watch, but he wants to know how long you can keep this up, huh? How long you think you're good for?"

Mahoney stopped in mid-shout. He peered out the window and recognized Costello. "Frankie, for Christ sake," he yelled. "Make this asshole let me the fuck outta here."

Costello stepped back from the cab. "Oh oh," he said.

The driver looked at Costello. "You ah, you wouldn't be acquainted with this citizen by any chance now, would you?"

"It appears I am," Costello said. "As a matter of fact, I was meeting him here."

"Imagine that," the driver said. "What a coincidence, huh? He generally go around makin' this much noise?"

"You fuckin' robber," Mahoney yelled.

"What's his beef?" Costello said to the driver.

"His beef is that I give him the tour," the driver said. "Which, as a matter of fact, I did not. I give somebody the scenic route, man, and I know how to do it. It don't come to no three fifty when I am finished. And I do it to people that wanna go somewhere besides the Claret, all right? Guys gettin' off Pakistani Airlines, guys like them. Not guys like this bozo here that look like they just got through for the day bein' cops onna trolley cars. My guess is this guy ain't taken no cabs in Boston a while. Since about the Vietnam War. You oughta tell him: rates went up."

"How much is it?" Costello said, reaching for his wallet.

"Don't pay the motherfucker, Costello," Mahoney yelled. "Make him let me out and I'll handle it."

Costello stopped in mid-gesture. "You, Vinnie," he said. Mahoney stopped shouting. "You already handled enough of this. You shut your damned trap and let me get you out of it. What're lawyers for, huh?"

"When we got here," the driver said, "it was three fifty. Now," he said looking at the meter, "now with the waiting time it's up to four twenty. Plus the inconvenience, of course. They haven't got no space for that on the meter, but that don't mean there wasn't any."

"Right," Costello said, taking a ten from his wallet, "probably kept you from picking up some Arab that wants to go to Chicago by car, and his limo broke down. This cover it?"

"Yeah," the driver said, taking the bill, "provided I don't have to take any more of his shit, he gets his ass out on the sidewalk."

"No promises," Costello said. "I'll go his bail, but I'm not gonna make myself responsible for his actions when he gets loose."

The driver nodded, his hand poised over the lock release. "Okay," he said, "tell him, though, he better not stand in front of this cab, because I'm gonna leave here like I was launched."

"Right," Costello said. He stood back from the cab. The driver lifted the locks. Mahoney came out of the left-hand passenger door very fast, leaving it open. The driver put the cab in gear and floored it. The passenger door flapped back against its latch from the sudden acceleration, partially shutting. Mahoney waved his right fist and shouted: "You . . ."

"Vinnie," Costello said grabbing him by the arm, "shut up or I'll belt you."

Mahoney wheeled on him. "You son of a bitch," he said, "you getcher hands off me or I'll put you in the hospital."

The cab had reached the intersection of Commonwealth Avenue. Costello released Mahoney. "Quite an entrance, Vincent," he said. "That kid's gonna think you're on furlough from a mental institution. And shouldn't be. And I can't say as I blame him. What the hell were you doing in that cab?"

"Gettin' a ride," Mahoney said, calming down. Costello walked him toward the curb.

"How original," Costello said, nodding. "You were taking a cab in order to get a ride. Where were you getting a ride from, may I ask?"

"Your office," Mahoney said. "I went to your office and you weren't there, so I took a cab here."

"Very sensible," Costello said. "Why didn't you come here in the first place as I told you to do, instead of going to my office?"

"Well," Mahoney said, as they stepped under the canopy, "I was early and I thought I might have a chance to talk to you before we saw Morgan."

"And it didn't occur to you," Costello said pleasantly, ". . . evening, Kenneth . . . that I might not want to have a talk with you at my office?"

"No," Mahoney said, looking puzzled.

"And that that might be the reason why I told you to meet me here?" Costello said.

"No," Mahoney said.

"No," Costello said. "Well, Vinnie, maybe it should have." He shook his head. "Bernie says I didn't bring you up right," he said. "Maybe he's right." He opened the door to the restaurant. It was heavy oak and it opened on maroon velvet carpet and dark paneled walls. The lighting in the foyer was subdued. To the right there was a checkroom, lighted but unattended. It led to the dining room, which was large enough to hold about two hundred customers. There was a table with a large silver bowl of fruit for a centerpiece set against a low planter of boxwood shrubs with very shiny green leaves at the end of the foyer. The dining room was softly lighted, and someone played tunes from *Camelot* on a harp gently in the background.

"Jesus," Mahoney said, "this is nice."

"Right," Costello said, as the maitre d' emerged from the dining room, smiled at Costello, picked up three menus, and approached. "Evening, Mister Costello," he said.

"Ernest," Costello said gravely.

"Your room is ready," the maitre d' said. He pointed toward a corridor off to the left. Costello turned down it. "Thank you, Ernest," he said.

"Hey," Mahoney said, "we're not goin' in there?"

"Right, Vinnie," Costello said, "we're not goin' in there." He took him by the left elbow and steered him down the corridor.

"Look," Mahoney said, "I'm gonna end up payin' for this. I never been in here before. I wanna sit in there."

"All estimable reasons, Vinnie," Costello said, "but I have a better one why we're taking a private room: this is the way I want it. And when you tell me to set up a meeting, I set it up my way."

The fourth door on their left opened into a room about eight feet by twelve, done in the same scheme as the dining room. It had a false window of stained glass, a circular table with six chairs, and a serving sideboard. "I won't be able to hear the music in here," Mahoney said.

"Buy yourself a radio, Vinnie," Costello said. To the maitre d', who was shutting the door, he said: "Thank you, Ernest. When Mister Morgan arrives, please show him right in."

"Where the hell is he?" Mahoney said.

"Suppose we sit down," Costello said, selecting a chair, "and we can have our little chat until he gets here. I don't know where the hell he is. Either on his way here from Dealey's party at Pier Four, if he's been able to tear himself away, or else still at Pier Four, if he hasn't. He's a big boy, Vinnie. He can find his way here all by himself."

A waiter entered and wished them a good evening. "I hope so, Rex," Costello said. "Vodka martini on the rocks with a twist for me. Vinnie?"

"A beer," Mahoney said. "Who's Dealey?"

"Any particular kind of beer, Vinnie?" Costello said.

"Oh," Mahoney said. "Yeah. Gimme a Schaefer."

Costello looked inquiringly at the waiter. The waiter shook his head. "Haven't got Schaefer, Vinnie," Costello said. "Something a little less exotic, maybe?"

"I thought everybody had Schaefer," Mahoney said. "It's what I always drink."

"Bring him a Beck's Light, for heaven's sake, Rex," Costello said. The waiter nodded and left.

"Dealey doesn't concern you," Costello said. "Shipstead concerns you and you're giving Shipstead a whole lot of trouble. What's going on, Vinnie? I thought we understood each other. I thought everything was all settled."

"So did I, goddamnit," Mahoney said. He tugged his collar away from his neck. "I thought this whole deal was all settled and over with a long time ago. That the only thing I hadda do from when I paid you guys the last ten grand was if it was something to do with Shipstead and those fuckin' permits they got more of'n Carter's got little pills."

"You didn't think any such thing," Costello said. "Don't hand me that song and dance. When you originally came to me, I told you what was entailed in these things. We never know in advance what an election'll cost. We need friends we can count on. I made that perfectly clear and you assured me you understood. Now this comes up, and I find you don't understand. Or else you *do* understand but you choose to claim you don't. Which is worse."

"Bullshit," Mahoney said, fairly loudly. The waiter opened the door and delivered their drinks. He set them down on the table and went out again.

Costello leaned forward as the door closed. He began speaking only after it was tightly shut. "Now you listen to me, for openers, Vinnie," he said quietly, pointing at him, "you're not out on the job now, and you're not addressing a bunch of louts that're used to hearing you rant and rave. And you're not talking about somebody moving a goddamned truck from one place to another. Am I right?"

"Yeah," Mahoney, said, "but—"

"Shut up," Costello said, "simple question. Called for affirmative or negative. Answer's affirmative. No explanations needed or desired."

Outside the Cafe Claret on Berkeley Street the Speaker piloted his Seville down the middle of the road. He spotted the space reserved at the curb for patrons arriving in cars and intending to have them parked by Voss. He aimed the Seville toward the space and cut the wheel to the right. He cut it too sharply and creased his right rear fender on the front bumper of a Buick Park Avenue sedan parked behind the space. Voss watched helplessly. Morgan paid no attention to the collision. He pulled forward into the space. He jammed on the brakes, stopped, and wrenched the wheel to the left. He slammed the transmission into reverse. The car jounced from the stop and the shift. Voss started forward toward the car, almost running. Morgan took his foot off the brake, turned his body to look out the back window, spun the wheel to the right and started backing up. With the wheels now cramped hard to the right, and the accelerator depressed, he had enough power to back the Seville onto the curb. He bumped it into the pipe that supported the canopy. He stepped on the brake again. He stared at the pipe, puzzled.

Voss reached the driver's window. He tapped on the glass. Morgan had some difficulty figuring out where the new noise was coming from. He looked out the right side windows, then the windshield, before locating Voss beside his door. He stared at Voss blearily. His lower lip hung slack and his eyes were mournful. He snuffled. His head made small movements, first to the right and then to the left. His lips formed words which he did not fully utter. Voss made a cranking motion with his hand. Morgan threw his head back, nodded enthusiastically, looked down, located the power window switch, and lowered the glass.

"Evening, Mister Speaker," Voss said as the window was opening. "Take care of this for you?"

The Speaker did not say anything. His lips worked and his head lolled. He cleared this throat. He waved his right hand vaguely toward the rear of the car.

"Oh, that," Voss said. "You weren't going fast enough, do any real damage."

"Fass enough," Morgan said. He thought about that. His face brightened. "Oh," he said. He reached for the transmission control. " 'At's easy 'nough," he said amiably. "I can make it go fasser, no trouble."

"No, no," Voss said quickly, opening the driver's door and distracting Morgan. "Look, just leave it alone, all right? The other car's okay. Lemme take care this for you, huh?"

"Kenny?" Morgan said. He frowned. He slobbered slightly. He mopped at his lips with his tongue. He waggled his head. He cleared his throat again. His gaze was fixed on a point just to the left of Voss's waist. He took a package of cigarettes from his shirt pocket. He managed to get one out. He dropped it into his lap. "Shit," he said. He slowly turned his head from looking at Voss's belt and looked down into his own, fumbling at his crotch at the same time.

Voss reached into the car and shut off the engine. He took the keys from the ignition. Two young men with short blond hair and short blond mustaches, wearing tight black jeans with *Gloria Vanderbilt* insignia on the right rear pockets, went by on the sidewalk, their arms around each other's waists. They looked at Morgan and smiled. Voss shook Morgan's left shoulder. "Come on, Mister Morgan," he said, "you got to get outta the car. Dinner'll get all cold."

"Here someplace," Morgan mumbled, still searching for the cigarette.

"Here," Voss said, taking a pack of Merits from his pocket. He shook one out and presented it to Morgan. "Have one of mine, Mister Morgan."

Morgan, still feebly groping at his crotch, slowly moved his head to look at what Voss was offering. "Oh," he said. "There it is." He reached for it. His hand was off the mark by about eight inches.

Voss sighed. He took the cigarette out of the pack and put it in Morgan's grasp. Morgan nodded, several times. He raised the cigarette to his mouth, missing by about two inches to the left. He turned it around so that the filtered end was away from him and put the other end between his lips. He leaned forward. "Light," he said thickly. "You got light, Kenny?"

With his right hand, Voss got a Bic lighter out of his pants pocket. With his left he took out another cigarette from his pack. He pulled it out with his right hand. He reached with his left and took the first Merit out of Morgan's mouth. The unfiltered end was wet. It left bits of tobacco on Morgan's lips. "You had the wrong end there, Mister Morgan," Kenny said. He inserted the new cigarette, filter-end first, into Morgan's mouth. Morgan closed his lips around it like a baby accepting a spoonful of blueberry cobbler. He shut his eyes and a smile creased his face. "Perfect," he said. "Gimme light."

Voss spun the lighter wheel. He held the Bic in his right hand and tapped Morgan on the shoulder with his left. "Right here, Mister Morgan," he said. He held the lighter about two feet away from the car.

Morgan said: "Where?" He opened his eyes.

"Right here, Mister Morgan," Voss said.

"Oh yeah," Morgan said, "there's the fucker." Clamping his right hand on the steering wheel, thrusting his head forward and jutting the cigarette straight from his lips, he tried to lean out far enough to light the Merit. His left hand dangled down onto the rocker panel of the car. He was on the brink of falling into the street. "Not close enough," Morgan said irritably. He moved his head. "Bring it, little closer. How long you think this thing is, huh? Matter with you, Kenny? Can't reach that."

Voss shook his head once. He extended the lighter to the end of the cigarette. Morgan inhaled deeply. Smoke poured out of his nostrils. Feebly he raised his left hand and removed the cigarette from his mouth. "Ahh," he said. He leaned back into the car and settled into the seat again. He considered the cigarette in his left hand. "Tastes funny," he said. He put it to his mouth and took another drag. He expelled the smoke. "Fuckin' bastards," he said. "Look at that, huh Kenny? Thass the reason. Filter on it. They put a fuckin' filter on my Chessfield," He laughed. "Must've done that some time, I wasn't lookin'." He coughed. "Bastards," he said thoughtfully. "Gotta watcha bastard every minute." He put the cigarette back in his mouth and folded his hands across his stomach. He stared out through the windshield and looked pensive. He nodded. He made a motion toward the empty ignition switch.

"Ah, Mister Morgan," Voss said, "you're not joining us for dinner?"

Morgan turned toward Voss. He looked at him suspiciously. "Dinner," he said. "Dinner, huh?"

"Yessir," Voss said. "You drove up here and everything, put the car here for me to park, I assumed you were planning to join us for dinner."

Morgan's expression changed to one of interest. "Oh yeah," he said. "Dinner."

"I mean," Voss said, "it's perfectly all right if you changed your mind or something. Remembered some other appointment."

"No, no," Morgan said, waving his left hand, shaking his head, lifting his left foot out of the car. "No, no other engagement. Dinner."

"Good," Voss said, leaning forward to steady him as he came out of the car. "Because I know Mister Costello and your other guest're already inside."

Morgan stopped halfway out of the car. "Guest," he said to Voss.

"Yessir," Voss said. "Mister Costello and the other gentleman. I don't know his name."

"Son of a bitch," Morgan said with wonder, "guest, huh? Wonder who the fuck it is, huh Kenny?" He grinned.

"Dunno, sir," Voss said. Morgan resumed getting out of the car. "Like I say, sir," Voss said, "I never saw him before. Short man, kind of heavy. Grey hair."

Morgan was all the way out of the car. He gathered himself and stood as straight as possible. "Grey hair," he said, frowning. "Nope. Lots of guys, grey hair."

"He seemed to be upset when he got here," Voss said.

Morgan wavered slightly where he stood, but he kept his balance. "Grey hair'n upset." Morgan said thoughtfully. "Lossa guys, too." He smiled at Voss. "I know lossa guys, grey hair and they're upset."

"I think it was at the cabdriver," Voss said.

"Know lossa cabdrivers, too," Morgan said. The smile widened into a grin. "Gonna have dinner a grey-haired cabbie that's mad at me? Wonder who the fuck that is?"

Voss forced a laugh. "It wasn't the cabdriver that was mad," he said. "It was the grey man that was mad."

"Oh," Morgan said.

"Yeah," Voss said. "*At* the cabdriver."

Morgan winked. "That'd make sense," he said. " 'Cause I don't know any cabbies, I would have dinner with them. Specially they was upset at me."

"Absolutely not," Voss said.

Morgan looked around as though visiting a strange city. "Well," he said, "might's well go in and find out, huh Kenny?"

"Right," Voss said.

"Have some dinner," Morgan said.

"Right," Voss said. "Veal's very good tonight, I understand."

"Always is, Kenny," Morgan said. He patted Voss on the shoulder.

He nodded. "Very good veal, Claret. Always said so. I most likely'll have roast beef, though. Very good roast beef, the Claret. Always said so."

"Right," Voss said.

Morgan lurched away from the car toward the sidewalk. "'Things in Glocca Morra,'" he sang softly. "First, roast beef. *Brigadoon.*" He belched. "Let anybody tell you different." He turned to face Voss, who had gotten into the Seville and was fitting the key into the ignition. "Hey," he said. Voss looked up. "Yeah?" Voss said. "Take good care my car, aw right, Kenny?" Voss nodded. Morgan nodded. He belched silently, and headed unsteadily for the door.

The checkroom was now occupied by the attendant, Dixie Bonds. She was in her early forties and had gained a little too much weight sitting around all day in the Jamaica Pond high-rise condominium that Ernest had bought for them, so she had gone back to work. She had black hair and dark eyes and she puckered when she smiled. Dixie Bonds had cleared over eighteen thousand dollars a year checking coats of customers of the Cafe Claret before Ernest left his wife and started living with her openly. Morgan's face lighted up when he saw her. "Dixie, luvva my fuckin' life," he growled, "the fuck are ya, Dixie?"

"The fuck're you, Bernie?" she said. "Little under the weather tonight, are we?" She laughed.

"You got a nice laugh, Dixie," Morgan said. "I always said that. Woman with a laugh like that, only a broad can laugh like you, make a livin' checkin' coats in weather, people don't even have any coats. Million-dollar laugh, Dixie." He winked at her. "Whaddaya checkin' tonight, Dixie, pants?" He thought that was very funny, and he put his head back and laughed. "Buncha guys sittin' in there, probably, lookin' very respectable, coats'n ties, haven't got no pants on. 'Check your pants with Dixie, you didn't wear no coat. Cheap bastard.'" He laughed some more.

Dixie's smile disappeared as the volume of Morgan's voice increased. She opened the bottom half of the Dutch door to the checkroom and came out into the foyer. She took him by the arm. "Right, Bernie," she said, steering him toward the corridor leading to the private rooms. She opened the first door and ushered him through into Ernest's office. There was a heavy oak desk at the rear of the room, and there was a long red leather couch along the wall to the right, with a coffee table before it. She took Morgan to the couch and sat him down. He collapsed in a heap. He gazed up at her with dim eyes. "Bernie, my love," she said, "I think we have had a little bit too much to drink."

"I dunno about you, Dixie babe," he said thickly, shaking his head, "but I've been in better shape." He snuffled miserably.

"Right," she said. "You meetin' somebody, I assume?"

He nodded. "Coss-tello," he said.

"He's okay," she said. "Anybody else?"

"Yeah," Morgan said. He frowned. "I dunno who it is. Kenny told me, was some guy here."

"Think you better be just a little bit late?" she said.

He nodded.

"Wait here," she said. "I'll order the medicine." He nodded. "I mean it now, Bernie," she said. "No gettin' up and goin' out into the main room." He nodded. "Okay," she said.

Dixie stepped out of the office as a black busboy, about twenty-one, hurried toward the main dining room. He was carrying several napkins and a tablecloth. "Clarence," she said, pulling the office door shut, "put that stuff somewhere and get me a coffeepot two-thirds full of espresso and the rest of the way with half and half. About ten packs of sugar. And a mug."

Clarence stopped in mid-stride. He sneered. "Oh Jesus, Dixie," he said, "is fat lush Morgan in the joint again?"

"The Speaker of the House is in the restaurant," she said, "if that's what you mean."

"Jesus Christ, Dixie," he said, gesturing with the linens, "I got three fat broads from the Hancock that just tipped over their wine, for God's sake. And now I gotta stop and take care of him?"

"You get the coffee," she said, "I'll do the takin' care of. Gimme those." She took the linens. "I'll give'm to somebody else."

"This ain't gonna help him," Clarence said grimly, pulling away. "Just gonna give you a wide-awake drunk, is all."

"That'll be an improvement," she said. "Caffeine and protein and sugar maybe won't make him sober, but they'll help him fake it better."

In the private dining room, Mahoney looked at his watch. "You fuckin' believe this?" he said. "Nine fuckin' thirty. Where the fuck is the fuckin' old bastard, huh? Fucker."

"I think you've got some kind of disease," Costello said thoughtfully.

"The fuck you talkin' about," Mahoney said. "I ain't fuckin' sick."

"There's some kind of a disease people get," Costello said. "Some kind of sickness that makes them swear all the time. They can't help themselves. I think you've got it. It's the only explanation for your vocabulary."

"My what?" Mahoney said.

"Excuse me," Costello said, "I should've thought. You probably can't understand anything else, either. The only fuckin' explanation for your fuckin' vocabulary."

"What fuckin' vocabulary?" Mahoney said.

"Tourette's Syndrome," Costello said. "It's a fuckin' sickness fuckin' makes you fuckin' swear all the fuckin' time."

"Bullshit," Mahoney said. "All I said was where the fuck is he? He's the fuckin' Pope or somethin', comes in any time he wants? I haven't had no fuckin' dinner, you realize that? I get up, I have to get up inna fuckin' morning. I been up since fuckin' five thirty, right? I had my lunch and that is fuckin' it. All I had to fuckin' eat since fuckin' noon. I'm fuckin' hungry. That mean I got somethin' fuckin' wrong with me, for Christ sake?"

Costello sighed. "He'll be here, Vinnie. He said he'd be here and he'll be here. Have another beer."

"Oh sure, have another beer," Mahoney said. "Trying get me fuckin' *drunk*, I won't fuckin' remember what the fuck I came all the fuckin' way up here for?"

Costello sighed again and pushed a small bell button on the wall. "Suit yourself," he said. "I, though, am going to have another drink. I may have ten, as a matter of fact. No use me letting everybody else have a good time for themselves while I just sit around, missing all the fun."

Clarence returned to Ernest's office with the pot of coffee and the mug. Dixie came to the door when he knocked. "You're wasting your time," Clarence said in a low voice. "I don't know why the hell you bother with the old drunk."

She took the pot and the mug. "You probably don't," she whispered back. "But some day when things're slack around here, you ask me or you ask Ernest who got the financing at the last minute when Ernest bought this place and his biggest backer did what backers do best and backed out. And then maybe you'd like to hear how Ernest got his pardon so he could have a liquor license, when everybody said the Council'd never approve it. And the story about the time some guys decided Ernest was gonna pay them five percent off the top of every week or else there was pretty likely gonna be a bad fire here some night after we closed up. You just ask about those things, Clarence," she said, "and you might find out why I bother with Bernie Morgan. Now go mop up after the fat ladies. The linen's on the table with the fruit." She shut the door.

At ten minutes of ten, Bernie Morgan opened the door to the private dining room and closed it behind him. Mahoney glared at him. Costello smiled. Morgan's color was good. His hair was neatly combed. The top button of his shirt was unbuttoned and his tie, neatly knotted, was straight. He did look tired. "Long day, Bernie?" Costello said.

Morgan shook his head. He allowed his shoulders to slump. He suggested a silent belch which he had managed to stifle. "Christ," he said, shaking his head, "a *bitch* of a day." He stuck out his right hand toward Mahoney. "Sorry, kept you waitin'," he said. "I started at it seems like when the sun come up, and I've been going at it hammer, tongs ever since."

"Vinnie understands," Costello said.

"Well," Morgan said, "appreciate that, Vinnie. I hadda go to a time and I just couldn't find a way, get out and come over here." They shook hands. "You must be starving," Morgan said, "know I am."

"Hey," Mahoney said, "look, it can happen, anybody, right?" He looked anxiously at Costello. "Me and Frank, we're just havin' a few drinks, talkin' over a few things. No harm done."

"Good," Morgan said. He took a chair. They all sat down.

Costello poised his hand over the call button. "You want a drink, Bernie?" he said.

Morgan shook his head reluctantly. "Me?" he said. "Uh uh, not just now, thanks." He blinked, rubbed his eyes, shook his head vigorously and coughed. "I'm practically out my feet's it is. What I need's some food. You ever go to those things, Vinnie?" he said. "Political times they have for guys?" He shook his head. "You must. Have to, your line of work."

"Yeah, yeah," Mahoney said eagerly, "I go a few of them. I went to one they had for that guy that's the rep from down there onna Vineyard there. The one that's married Shipstead's sister. I forget his name."

"Wendell," Costello said, as the Speaker frowned, "Wendell Baxter."

"Yeah," Mahoney said, "that's the one. Wendell. Seemed like a pretty nice guy."

"Yeah," Morgan said, "prince of a fellow. 'Less you want him to keep his fuckin' word or somethin'."

"Huh?" Mahoney said.

"Nothin'," the Speaker said morosely. "There're times when I didn't get along so good with Wendy Baxter."

"Oh," Mahoney said. He looked worried. "Jeez, I give him five hundred bucks, too."

Morgan nodded gloomily. "Uh huh," he said. "Fuckin' Baxter. Thinks it's his goddamned island. Gotta have a fuckin' license from Baxter 'fore you can get off the ferry down there. Five hundred bucks. Shit. Baxter never had five hundred bucks in his whole life from somebody. Must've thought he died and went to heaven."

"Still," Costello said, "he does swing a certain amount of weight with the island stuff. Vinnie wouldn't be building that runway down there if it wasn't for Baxter getting out of the way on that."

Morgan glanced at Costello. "Runway?"

"Yeah," Costello said, "the airport runway. Those're important, right?"

"Yeah," Morgan said, "yeah. Sure. Runways're real important. Howsa job comin', Vinnie?" He leaned his forearms on the table and smiled.

Mahoney relaxed. He smiled in return. He toyed with his empty beer glass. "Well," he said, "it's comin' along real good, you know?"

"Great, great," Morgan said. "Glad to hear it." He leaned back in his chair. "Hey, Francis, huh? What the hell, might's well have a drink and order, 'm I right?"

Costello sucked his tongue against his teeth. He nodded. "Oh sure, Bernie, by all means." He pushed the button. "Can't talk business without a drink."

"Right," Morgan said enthusiastically. He nudged Mahoney. "Can't argue that, can you, Vinnie, huh?"

"Absolutely not," Mahoney said, as the waiter entered.

" 'Nother round these gentlemen," Morgan said. "Gimme Wild Turkey onna rocks. Double. Also, we might's well order." The waiter took out his pad. "I want the roast beef," Morgan said, "the prime rib and medium rare. I'll let Francis here order the wine. He knows all about that shit. Vinnie?"

"I, uh, I haven't hadda chance, look at the menu," Mahoney said.

"Shit," Morgan said, "don't needa menu. Have the fuckin' roast beef." He nudged Mahoney again. "It's great here, Vinnie, great roast beef at the Claret. I eat it all the time. 'Less you're one of them fishatarians there."

"Huh?" Mahoney said.

"Fishatarians," Morgan said. "You know, like a vegetarian, them guys that go around and they don't eat nothing but plants? Them guys? All them shitty salads them grey little weeds they got chopped up all over the top of them that taste like you was eating a whole buncha string all cut up? Those're vegetarians. And we got this guy inna House that he's one of them. Crazy little bastard there. Bannerman. Brookline. Only he eats fish. Eats tuna fish. Caught him one day, he's eatin' a tuna fish sandwich there. And I say to him: 'Bannerman, you asshole,' I said, 'I thought you're a vegetarian here and you're eatin' a tuna fish sandwich, huh? What's this, it comes off of the tuna plant or something?' And he says, no, tuna fish and trouts and things like that don't count if you're a vegetarian. It's just the red meat you don't eat. And I says to him that means he must be a fishatarian or something, right? Tunatarian? Sounds like one of them fuckin' crazy, phonusbalonus religions that all them liberals're always belonging to. Tunatarians, huh? Only thing they believe in's the big tuna inna sky. Our tuna which swims in heaven, salad be thy name." He laughed loudly. The waiter joined in giggling. Costello looked disgusted and Mahoney looked frightened. "Thy lettuce come, thy toast be done, on white if we ain't got no rye." Morgan laughed very loudly. Mahoney joined in tentatively.

"I'll have the prime rib as well," Costello said dourly. "Give us a bottle of the Pommard."

"Very good, Mister Costello," the waiter said. He turned toward Mahoney. "The same for you, sir?" he said.

"Sure, sure," Morgan said, "And him, too," he said, indicating Mahoney. "Give him the same. And some potatoes for all of us."

"I'm tryin', take off a little weight," Mahoney said.

Morgan nudged him again. "Plenty time for that, Vinnie, tomorrow. Tonight, my friend, you're at the Cafe Claret, right? No diets here. Make that two bottles Pommard, Richard, or whatever the hell your name is. For thine is the onions, and the may'naise, and the pickles, forevv-ver. Ahhh-men." He laughed very loudly as the waiter left the room and shut the door firmly behind him. Tears sprang to his eyes.

"Jesus Christ," Costello said, "are you out of your mind, Bernie?"

Morgan caught his breath. "Huh?" he said, gasping. "No, I'm not out of my mind." He turned to Mahoney. "Costello here, Vinnie," he said, "confidentially, he thinks he's a doctor, you know? He is always looking at people and telling them he thinks there is something wrong with them. And naturally, him being a doctor and all that shit, he thinks he oughta be the first one to tell them and make the diagnosis, you know what I mean? For example, I don't know how long you guys been here. But I would make you a bet before you get out of here tonight, Francis will tell you there is something wrong with you that you probably never even heard of. This guy knows about diseases them guys inna long white coats over to the Harvard Medical School there didn't even find out about yet. Bet you a hundred bucks. 'Kay?"

"Jeez," Mahoney said, "he already did. Before you even got here, he did that."

Morgan threw his head back and roared with laughter. "See? Didn't I tell you? What's he got wrong with him, Doctor Coss-tello, huh? Something nobody ever heard of, I bet."

"Bernie," Costello said, as the waiter delivered the drinks, "you do tend to wear a man down."

"Yeah," Morgan said with satisfaction, raising his glass. "That's how I do it. Wear the bastards down. That'll do it. Usually right, too. You gotta give me that. Cheers." He drank half of it. He wiped his mouth with the back of his hand. "Ahh," he said. He put his hands on the edge of the table, straightened his arms, arched his back, and exhaled. "Now," he said, "the fuck're we here for, huh? Anybody tell me that? Why we're sittin' around here like the cocks of the walk, 'stead of bein' in the bosoms of our wives and families tonight? Or some other bosoms, maybe huh?"

"I got to go to the bathroom," Mahoney said. He whipped his napkin out of his lap and stood up suddenly. He looked very worried.

Morgan grabbed him by the arm. "Siddown," he said, laughing, "just got here. Don't needa go the bathroom yet. What's the matter, huh? Got nervous kidneys, something? Better ask Francis about that. That what you told Vinnie here that he's got, Francis? Nervous kidneys? Somethin' wrong with his bladder, maybe?" He turned back to Mahoney. "You wanna watch out though," he said, "man your age. Prostate, there. Guy gets into our bracket, our age, you know, figures everything's tickin' along okay, got the wife and the kids're all grown up, huh? And the first thing you know, surer'n fate, hits you right between the eyes. Prostate. Got to go in, have 'em take it out.

"They cut you open with a big knife," he said, making a fast slicing motion with his right hand while Mahoney stood uncomfortably, shifting his weight from side to side, "*whick*, just like that. Just like they're cuttin' open a big fat melon there. And they take it out. And I never heard of one of those goddamned things yet that they didn't go in there for the prostate and they didn't find something else while they was in there. 'Just happened to be in the neighborhood there, Mister Patient, kind of browsing, you know, lookin' around? That bladder there, that didn't look so good neither. So we figured, you know, long's we happened to be in the area and everything, might's well just whomp that out of there, the same time. We got a two-for-one special today, you get the bladder out, no extra charge. And you want a deal onna plastic bags there, which you're gonna need quite a few of, now on? We can give you a hell of a price on ten gross of them things. Too bad you didn't wait till next week, though. We're doin' guts for the same price and throwin' in twenty boxes of the bags and a weekend, Atlantic City. All expenses paid, for two. Take your missus.'" Morgan's face turned serious. "Hey," he said, looking up at Mahoney, "all right? Just kiddin' around. You really got to go the bathroom? 'Cause I was just kiddin' around, you know?"

Mahoney looked very worried now. "I," he said, "I can wait a while, I guess."

Morgan patted him on the arm. "Good," he said, "good. Let's get this business stuff out the way, 'fore dinner. Whyncha siddown there, huh? Always like to get the business done 'fore the food's onna table. 'Don't never talk with your mouth full,' am I right? Know what I mean? What's on your mind, Vincent?"

"I think I will go the bathroom," Mahoney said. He dropped the napkin on the table and bolted from the room.

Morgan waited until the door shut behind Mahoney. Then he laughed, low in his throat. The phlegm rattled. "Jesus Christ," he said, "the fuck these people come from, huh Francis? You tell me that, where they come from? Many years's I've been at it, as many guys I've seen, they never change, do they? Never. Always the same." He shook his head. "Jesus Christ."

Costello did not reply. He toyed with his martini glass. He frowned. "You don't agree with me, Francis?" Morgan said.

Costello pursed his lips. He looked up at Morgan. "You sure you're all right for this, Bernie?"

"All right for what, Francis, huh? The fuck I know?" Morgan said. "I'm here, ain't I? Of course I dunno what the fuck I'm here for, and I don't *want* to be here, but you said I hadda *be* here, and here I am. If it's gonna be somethin' like we all get together and go down the jungle where they're servin' up some boiled missionary from the Maryknoll there so we can tell 'em all we're gonna do for civil rights? Eat with the fuckin' cannibals. No. I'm not all right for that. But if it's something that three white gentlemen can talk about while they have their dinner, sure. Sure, I can do that."

Costello stared at him for a while. "You sure Dixie's coffee's still strong enough to do the job?" Costello said. Morgan blinked. Costello shook his head. "Bernie," he said, "I've known you for a long time."

"I believe that is so, Francis," Morgan said. "You look pretty familiar, at least. Like I seen you someplace before."

"Never mind the bullshit, Bernie," Costello said. "Never mind trying to blow smoke at me like you had some rookie on your hands that you could just intimidate. We go back a long way, my friend, and I know most of your tricks by now. Don't surprise me any more when the little car stops in the circus and the forty clowns pile out of it. I know about the trapdoor in the floor."

"Okay," Morgan said, resting his chin on his hands, "make your speech."

"Once," Costello said, "and once only. When I first ran into you I was a candy-assed kid right out of law school and you were this war hero fresh out of Proctor with the hay stickin' out of your ears. I knew more'n you did about some things then, and you knew more about most things, and besides you had old Wilf to steer you along. We used to tell each other things then, Bernie, and it worked out pretty well."

"This I knew," Morgan said.

Costello leaned back. He toyed with a spoon. "Now," he said slowly, "now I'm not so sure any more. Back in those days . . . well, we haven't got Wilfred any more."

"We still got him," Morgan said, grinning. "You can go up and talk to old Wilf any day you please. Prolly won't make a hell of a lot of sense 'less you want some advice about breedin' dogs. Which I understand he thinks he's still doin'. But if you want to talk to him, he ain't going no place and he's easy to find."

Costello shrugged. "That's what I mean, Bernie," he said, "we may know the ropes now, but we've still got to listen each other, and I'm not sure you pay full attention any more."

"Ahh," Morgan said, dismissing Costello with his hand.

"Okay," Costello said, holding up his hand, "I can go fuck myself. I worry too much and all the rest of that shit. I'll say it once and that'll be the end of it. This guy that you're havin' so much fun with tonight, this hay shaker that you don't believe knows what he's doing, this guy has got your scrotum in one hand and a pair of pliers in the other. He maybe doesn't realize it yet, but that is the combination that he's got. And if he decides to put the balls and the jaws together and squeeze hard enough, he will get your attention, Bernie."

"Bullshit," Morgan said.

"Okay," Costello said, "bullshit it may be, but I'm still gonna finish it. We started off with this guy, he looked like a hundred other two-shovel builders on the make for a contract. The kind that we pick up by the ankles and turn 'em upside down and shake 'em till the loose change falls out their pockets and we scoop it up 'fore it hits the ground. And that's exactly what he was. We read him right. He was dancin' money.

"Now," Costello said, "all of a sudden we find out that this fresh-faced little bastard on the make named Hanrihan's got in front the grand jury one day when the DA wasn't looking and forgot to take his knife away from him before he went out to play a round of golf, and Hanrihan's got Jean Dussault on the hot seat. Right at the same time we're out shaking them again. Not nice, Bernie."

"Jean'll never say Word One," Morgan said. "I known Jean for years. No saint, maybe, but he wouldn't tell you if your coat was on fire."

"Maybe so and maybe no," Costello said. "If he does, he's gonna nail guys he did business with, and there's a lot of them. All two-bit operators like our man Mahoney. All nigger-scared when it comes to guys that come around and start talkin' about puttin' them in jail. And when we checked with Jean it was just like we figured: eight of the guys he's doin' business with happen to be guys we're doing business with, and one of them's Mahoney."

"He's not in the grease yet," Morgan said.

"No," Costello said, "and we better pray he doesn't get into it too, Bernie. Because this guy Mahoney won't stand up. Take it from me. I have looked him over and I know it in my bones. He will fold up like a little boy and spill his guts. And that will be the end of us. I think we better keep him friendly."

"I didn't do anything to make him mad," Morgan said, sounding injured.

"Oh, absolutely not," Costello said. "You might've come in here half in the wrapper. You might have acted like you owned his wife and firstborn son. You might've treated him like you thought he was an asshole. But you didn't do anything that might've made him mad, Bernie. Wouldn't surprise me if he never even went to the bathroom, just got change for a buck and left and put in a call to Ames."

"Hoss shit," Morgan said, but he looked serious.

"Let's hope so," Costello said, as the door opened and Mahoney returned.

"Everything come out all right, Vinnie?" Morgan said jovially.

Mahoney sat down heavily. He folded his hands on the table. He spoke very rapidly but very evenly. "It hasn't yet, Mister Morgan," he said. He looked at Costello. He licked his lips. He looked back at Morgan. He cleared his throat. "Mister Morgan," he said, "I'm not sure you remember me. Which is all right. A lot of people don't remember me. I never did a hell of a lot that'd make 'em remember me. I used to put in swimming pools for rich people, and before that I worked for the guy that put in swimming pools for rich people."

"Nothin' wrong with that, Vinnie," Morgan said heartily.

Mahoney held up his hand. "Just listen to me a minute," he said. "We never had a chance, siddown and talk before. I'm not used to this kind of thing. Never hadda do none of it, I was puttin' in the pools.

"Thing of it is," he said, "aren't that many rich people, I discover. And most of the ones that are, they already got pools. Or if they haven't, even they don't wanna pay what it's gonna cost them to get a first-class job like I do. The only kind I wanna do. They're gonna go with the guy that digs a hole and heaves the concrete on any way it happens to hit and if it don't leak, fine. And if it cracks the next winter they will wish they got me in the first place. But by then it's too late for them and too late for me as well. Because they're not gonna pay me to take the bad job out and start over and prolly find out they shouldn't've dug the hole in that particular spot inna first place, all right?" He nodded. "So," he said, rubbing his hand together, "I decided I was gonna get smart. I'm gonna do construction work, the state. And I bid a few jobs, all right? Nothin' big. Stuff I can handle all right. And I got myself a nice kid that was just startin' his law practice there up in Lexington near where I live, and he makes sure the bids're all in good shape when they go in. But I never get no jobs. I can't figure it out.

"So I sit down with him," Mahoney said, "and we talk about it. We're both new at this racket, dunno the hell's goin' on, and he says to me that he will ask around, some guys he went to law school with, that kind of thing. Maybe know a little more about it. And he does. He talked this kid Brian Hanrihan that went in the DA's office. Family was apparently in politics a long time and he knew a few things my guy didn't. And my guy don't naturally tell him why he wanted to know, but he finds out what you got to do, you want your bid to have a chance.

"Now Mister Morgan," Mahoney said, "I didn't want to do this, you know? The dinners and the cocktail parties there that always cost a hundred bucks or so, okay. I only drink a couple beers anyway, and that's when I really get going and I'm sittin' around watchin' the game or something, not when I'm standin' around in a room with a buncha people I don't even know, got a suit, the tie on and I feel like an asshole, you know? Got so I stop goin', fifty bucks a beer. I just give 'em the dough and I write it off. And here is this Hanrihan guy tellin' my guy I got to do a little bit more. I don't like it.

"I don't like it," Mahoney said, "but you know and I know I did it, and sure enough I get my first job. And I should feel good about that job, am I right? I got the contract that if I don't get it I am gonna have to start thinkin' about layin' guys off. And that is not the kind of thinkin' that I like to do, Mister Morgan, about layin' guys off. I got guys that've been with me over twenny years, guys that've got families and that work hard. And they depend upon me, they're gonna support their families. I don't wanna lay them guys off. And I got a kid finishin' up at Saint John's Prep that is a good kid, he's a good boy, and now he thinks he wants to be a marine geologist there. So he is startin' MIT next year, which God only knows what that's gonna cost me, 'fore I'm through. My two daughters there. One of them went to Regis College and she marries this guy that works in the same office with her. She's in international banking in New York. And the other one gets out of Trinity in Hartford, next year, wants to be a lawyer she says. My wife? Isabel and me, we been married now twenny-eight years and I ain't even looked at another woman. Her idea, her idea raisin' hell is when I tell her some things my guys do, and I tell her about them and she don't believe half of it.

"You see what I mean, Mister Morgan?" Mahoney said. He spread his hands. "I got a good life. I'm a lucky man. I know it. I don't wanna lose it. I am not the type of guy . . . I dunno how to explain this to you, but I am just your ordinary run-of-the-mill guy, you know? Every Sunday I get up. I take a shower and I shave and I go to Mass and Communion. Me and Isabel. My kid that lives at home, he gets up and takes a shower and goes to Mass and Communion with us, right? The girls. I don't think they go any more, but they're not livin' under my roof no more and that is their business if they don't go. Except when they come home and visit or something like that. And then *they* go. You know something, Mister Morgan, how you can eat and everything, you don't have to keep the fast any more before you go to Communion? We still do that. We don't have no breakfast until after we get home from Mass and Communion. Every Sunday.

"This kind of a place," he said, waving his right hand to take in the whole of the restaurant, "this kind of place here? I know it's around. I know that. I'm not stupid. I know there're places where people go and spend a hundred, two hundred bucks on their dinner, don't even think nothin' of it. Just like it was something that they did, and they do it. But I ain't one of those people, Mister Morgan. I know I'm not. Like I was telling Mister Costello, comin' in here. I ain't never been in this place before in my life. I don't belong in no place like this. I know it. I ain't comfortable in here. It ain't a place I would come to, I was on my own."

"You don't like it here, Vinnie?" Morgan said. He spoke very quietly and his voice was menacing.

"Hey," Mahoney said, "I didn't say that, all right? I didn't say nothin' like that."

Costello cleared his throat. "Uhh, Bernie," he said, "Vinnie's all right. He's an all-right guy. Let him finish what he wants to say, huh?" He smiled encouragingly at Mahoney. He looked back at Morgan. "Okay, Bernie?"

Morgan delayed for an instant before he shifted his eyes from Mahoney to Costello. "It was him," he said, jerking his left thumb toward Mahoney, "it was him that asked for this meeting, was my understanding."

"Yeah, yeah," Costello said. "So let him talk, all right?"

Morgan sat back and folded his arms across his chest. He sighed. He scowled. "Go ahead," he said. "I dunno, you apparently got the Indian sign on Coss-tello here, and he's an old friend of mine. He says I gotta listen to you, I'll listen. Talk."

Mahoney spread his hands. "Look," he said, "I didn't mean nothin', all right? And if I give you the impression I did, I'm sorry, all right? I know how come I'm here and you're here and Mister Costello didn't go home his family tonight, if he's got a family. You got a family, Mister Costello?"

"I've got . . ." Costello had to clear his throat again. "Yes. I have a wife. My children are grown."

"Well then," Mahoney said, "I apologize for that also, Mister Cos-

tello. That you're not sittin' at home with your wife right now. Because
that is also my doing and I'm not trying to say it isn't. But see, it's like
with the swimming pools, when I was building them, all right? I was
building you a swimming pool, if you came to me and you asked me
how to build you a pool, and I looked the job over, I would tell you: this
is how much it's gonna cost you, I put in a first-class swimming pool in
your backyard. Or wherever you happened to want it. And you would
most likely show my figures to somebody else that you also had figure
the job. Which if you didn't think of doing that yourself I would've told
you to do, because that is the way I run my business. And he would
probably be lower, a little lower, and you would come back to me and
show me his figures and tell me: See, Mister Mahoney, Grimaldi here
says he can do the job for this, and you want this, and how come it's this
much more, huh? And I would tell you: It's because I can't do no first-
class job for that, Mister Morgan, can't do a first-class job. Now Grimaldi here, or whoever the guy is, maybe his costs're less and he can.
Do it for that and you should think very seriously about givin' him the
job. Which I know for a fact he can't do it for less'n that, a first-class
job, because his costs and mine're all the same and the way he's doin' it
is, he's cuttin' corners onna job. But if you ain't bright enough, figure
that out for yourself, frames and cement's gonna cost him same's it's
gonna cost me, well, maybe you're gonna be satisfied a second-rate job.
Only don't come to me for it and expect me to do it, year or so later it
cracks and you wanna bitch. Go talk to Grimaldi when the water all
runs out into your basement. Not to me.

"Now that is the same thing really that I am doing now," Mahoney
said. "I bid onna thing there, like I did onna first job there with the
school, and say I'm gonna meet all the specs with the gravel anna stuff
like that. Just like I did onna school. And my bid's in line, like it was on
the school. Only this time, you know somethin'?" Mahoney said. "Sure
you do. You always did. The only one didn't know it the first time was
me. You did, but I didn't. I met the specs the first job, but I hadda come
out of the job with almost nothin' I got out of it myself. I took a loss on
that job, matter of fact, and that taught me somethin'. So I put down
the various things I'm gonna use on this job. How much of this and the
best grade of that. And I *know* I'm not gonna put in that much stuff or
stuff that good. I can't. I can't do what I say I'm gonna do and do a
first-class job and make anything for myself. So"—he shrugged—"I
gotta make a choice, I guess. Between a first-class job that I say I'm
gonna do and a third-rate job that I'm actually gonna do if I'm gonna

make some money onna project. Which I got to do, Mister Morgan. I got to make some money for myself. I got to eat too."

"You tellin' me," Morgan said, "this thing's gonna fall apart the day after your trucks leave?"

"Nah," Mahoney said, "nothin' like that. I should go away with this one without anybody ever noticin', matter of fact. Or if they ever do, that we didn't dig as deep and didn't put in as much crushed stone we said we were gonna, which they never look up anyway when something lasts a few years, it falls apart, they never go back and look. Because if this thing ever gets to where it's startin' to wash away, hell, it'll be years. Any place but on that island you might be runnin' a certain amount risk. But they don't get much frost there, account the warm winters, the kind we get up here, and you can get away with things you couldn't in Dedham or something. You'd have frost heaving up to your eyeballs, you did what I'm doing on the island some place in Worcester or something. But there? It'll be good enough.

"Thing of it is, though," Mahoney said, "it won't be as good's I said it was gonna be. But the way things stand, or the way I thought they was standin' anyway, when I hear from Shipstead today and he tells me what I end up havin' to come up here for tonight, I am gettin' worried it isn't even gonna be as good as I was gonna make it. Which would've been good enough. See?" Mahoney tried a small, wistful smile.

"What the fuck do you mean?" Morgan said, in that same low voice, leaning forward onto the table.

Mahoney drew back. He looked at the table. He played with the silverware. He shook his head sorrowfully. He looked pleadingly at Costello, who did not meet his gaze. He looked back at Morgan. "Mister Morgan," he said, "I mean ten thousand more dollars that Shipstead told me this morning I hadda get up from this job and give him. Which I assume means he keeps some of it and sends to Mister Costello, and him and you get some and somebody else prolly gets some. I dunno how it works, once I pay it to Shipstead. That's all I know. And that'll make thirty, Mister Morgan, off a job that's only gonna net me a hundred, hundred and twenty when I started. Before I paid anything."

"That's fuckin' good pay, you ask me," Morgan growled. "Hundred and thirty for, what, four months' work?"

Mahoney sighed. Costello cleared his throat again, but neither of the other two paid any attention. "It's not four months' work, Mister Morgan," Mahoney said. "It's gonna take me over, it's gonna take me almost two years, finish the job. This here is New England, Mister Morgan. We get winter here. It's not as bad's it is some other places, like Vermont, where you start it Memorial Day and pray to God you're finished Labor Day. They got a real short season there. We're not in that bad shape. But I'm gonna end up movin' my equipment back and forth four times, which costs a lot, and tyin' it up a couple years almost, and I have to stay down there and I don't see my family. And hell, I was down to a hundred already when Shipstead called me today and tells me what he told me. Fifty grand a year which I then got to pay taxes on? That ain't much for doin' all that, Mister Morgan. And now you're talkin' about cuttin' it down some more? My bulldozer men and the grader guy, they'll make more'n that with the overtime, tryin' beat the weather, 'n I will, and I'm the one that's takin' all the risks."

"So what do you expect me to do?" Morgan said quietly.

Mahoney sighed again, deeply. "I dunno," he said. He fidgeted. He played with the saltcellar. "Understand, I guess. What I'm goin' through with this. I got, I got the guys from Washington that're always showin' up and counting niggers, see if I hired enough blacks for the job like they say I got to have so many of. You ever try to find a couple black grader operators that'd give up their summer vacations for the same money they can make livin' at home?" He snorted. "Nice try, I end up hirin' guys that're the right color, can't do a fuckin' thing, and I'm just payin' them to stand around. So people can see them. Hell, I caught those guys near anything, any my expensive equipment, I would kill 'em. 'Just go sit inna shade, Rufus, keep your fuckin' hands off my stuff and get your pay the end of the week. Blame the inspectors, you gotta be here at all. I'd like it just as well as you, they'd count you if you stayed in bed all day long, outta everybody's way.'

"I got to hire so many people," Mahoney said, "live on the island. This's summer, right? They're all out cheatin' tourists. Don't get tired'n dirty, doin' that. Construction work? You gotta be shittin' me. They don't want no part of it.

"I got guys that come around and count toilets and guys that make sure nobody took none of the guards off the gears and stuff. Everybody better have their helmets and their goggles on at all times. Jesus," Mahoney said, "I'm not bossin' a job, I'm wet-nursin' it. I feel like I'm runnin' a kindergarten. And every so often some guy comes along and asks me if everything's okay with the unions, and I tell him it is and he tells me Jean Dussault's tied up in Cambridge still and could I spare a little something over the usual, help with his legal expenses.

"You see what I'm tellin' you, Mister Morgan?" he said. "I can't afford no ten grand no more. I shouldn't've done this in the first place, and I did it and I got only myself to blame. I shouldn't've done it. But look at me, willya? I'm sittin' here, beggin' you, for Christ sake let me up."

There were tears in his eyes. He leaned forward. His voice turned gruff. "I was in the Korean War, Mister Morgan," he said. "I didn't win no big medals, anything. But they were still givin' out battlefield commissions then, and I went in a private and come out a first lieutenant. No education or anything. I started off workin' with guys that talked with their fists, I got out, and I made foreman before I was twenny-five. I was runnin' my own company when I was thirty. I met my payrolls and raised my family. I went in bars when my boys got themselves into trouble that they shouldn't've, and I got 'em out. But you know somethin', Mister Morgan? I admit it. I am scared of you."

His voice caught. He started in again. "I know how you say you need all this money, political campaigns, gotta keep the good reps in or they'll make trouble all the time when I bid on a job. Get new guys in there and you won't be able deal with them. Mister Costello told me. Billboards and stuff. I know all them reasons. I heard them. But I'm tapped out, Mister Morgan, and I got to ask you for some consideration now. I *got* to."

Morgan stared at him. The waiter opened the door and brought in the wine. He went to the sideboard and opened the bottles. "Francis?" Morgan said, leaning back.

"Ahh," Costello said, frowning. "Difficult question. Is there some way we could meet these commitments from other sources?"

Morgan glared at Costello. "Okay," he said. "Okay, that's the way it is." He nodded. "Mister Mahoney," he said, leaning forward as the waiter went out and shut the door again, "you make a good argument. You don't prolly know how good. But you know how it is, running an operation. No matter how you plan it, everything always ends up costing a little more than you expected. Are there guys creaming it off the top? Somewhere along the line," he said, shrugging, "probably. Your kind of operation, 'less you follow it like a hawk, your man checks in two loads of gravel, there's one, him and the guy that delivers the gravel do that every day and they split the take the end of the job, both of them show up in new cars when it's over. It's the same thing with us.

"On the other hand," Morgan said, "and you know we're not keepin' any of this, ourselves, I assume."

Mahoney did not look up. He nodded. He played with the salt shaker.

"Course you do," Morgan said. "It's all for campaigning. Guy campaigns for you, you gotta buy him dinner, like that. Costs you money. But on the other hand, I can see the position you're in." Mahoney looked up with hope in his eyes. "Matter of fact," Morgan said, "I'm glad you come up and see me like this, because otherwise I wouldn't know about it. The spot you're in. Am I right?" Mahoney nodded again. The waiter came in with plates of salad and set one to the left of each of them. "Have everybody down there mad at me and I wouldn't even know there was anything wrong," Morgan said, stuffing a wedge of tomato into his mouth and chewing. "Can't have that," he said viciously, picking up the pepper mill and cranking it vigorously over the plate. Then he sprinkled salt heavily. He filled his mouth with lettuce and continued talking as he chewed.

"On the other hand," he said, "I got to think: how can we help this guy? And right now, I'm probably gonna regret this, and I know it's gonna, it's not gonna be just what you wanted to hear, all right?" Mahoney nodded. "But parin' everything down to the bone, I think we can prolly get by with, say, seventy-five." Mahoney looked up with deadened eyes. "Whaddaya say to that?" Morgan said, chewing. There was a small smile at the corner of his mouth.

"Seventy-five," Mahoney said in a whisper. "Seventy-five big ones."

Morgan nodded, smiling. "Okay?"

Mahoney heaved a great sigh. The waiter came in with side dishes of potatoes. "I dunno," Mahoney said. "I don't see how . . . shit. I guess it'll have to be, huh?"

Morgan nodded vigorously. He looked earnest. "That's really," he said, "that's really the best I can do."

The waiter, moving very gingerly, came in with two platters of roast beef. The rib bone stuck over at each end of the platters and the borders of fat dropped over the edges, red juices swimming around the meat. He put the largest before Morgan and the other before Costello. Morgan picked up his knife, transferred his fork to his left hand, and sat admiring the meat. Mahoney stood up.

"Hey," Morgan said, as the waiter came in with Mahoney's serving. "Ain't you gonna eat?"

"Seventy-five," Mahoney said. "I'll get it to you tomorrow."

"No dinner?" Morgan said incredulously. The waiter paused in midstride, staring at Mahoney.

"All of a sudden," Mahoney said in a tired voice, "I'm not hungry any more." He put his napkin on the table and edged past the waiter. "You can take it out of the seventy-five." He went out the door.

The waiter looked inquiringly at Costello. Costello, looking gloomy, shrugged. "Take it back, I guess, Rex," he said. "Man says he doesn't want to eat."

Morgan turned fast in his chair. "Oh no," he said. He pointed to the empty place next to his salad plate. "Put it down right the fuck there, Rex," he said with his mouth full of meat and lettuce, "put it right down there. Mahoney don't wanna eat it, I will." He resumed chewing, noisily. He did not look up.

The waiter glanced inquiringly at Costello. Costello nodded. "As he says, Rex," Costello said, "as he says." The waiter put the roast beef down, his expression showing that it was against his better judgment. "And pour the wine please, too. I'm sure we'll finish both bottles. Right, Bernie?"

Morgan nodded, still chewing and cutting vigorously at the meat. "Absolutely," he said with his mouth full.

"See, Rex?" Costello said. "Always do what Mister Morgan says, and you'll never go far wrong." The waiter poured the wine, set the bottle down, and left the room, closing the door securely behind him. The only sound was Morgan chewing and Morgan drinking. Some of the bloody juice from the meat trickled down from the right corner of Morgan's mouth. He wiped at it hastily and smacked his lips. "Good," he said, picking up the bone to chew. "To prison, maybe," Costello said softly, as Morgan gnawed, "but never far wrong."

13 Driving very slowly and deliberately, Morgan put the Seville neatly into the gated chute that led into the Prudential Center garage. He inserted his parking card in the sensing device that stood on the concrete island defining the left side of the ramp, waited longer than was necessary for the gate to rise before him, and drove with dignity down into the tenants' fenced-off section. He backed the Cadillac into the single space reserved for him—it was an open concrete closet—set the alarm, got out with difficulty in the narrow alcove, and locked it up.

He was still unsteady. When he was out of the cramped parking space he straightened up, touched his right forefinger delicately to the deep scratch running back along the left fender from the grille to the driver's door where the dents were, shook his head, and said aloud in the echoing garage: "Gotta have you fixed, baby." Unsteadily, but with as much dignity as he could muster, he made his way to the elevator to the lobby, called it, walked slowly into the car, and stood with his hands folded over his crotch.

Walter Hackley was on duty, stretching his legs with a little stroll around his territory. Morgan managed to focus him after a short delay, separating the two Walters that he saw and choosing the one on his right. "Good evening, Walter," he said, sounding like Alfred Hitchcock.

"Mister Morgan," Hackley said, gazing at him without any expression. "Howsa wife doing?"

Morgan paused in his unsteady path to the banks of elevators leading to the apartment floors. He made a fluttering motion with his hand. "She isn't," he said, licking his lips, "it's, she's about the same. About the same, really, Walter."

"I saw her the other morning," Hackley said, standing under a hanging fern that loomed over him like a canopy above a throne against the darkness outside the lobby. He took a long time between sentences. "She looked all right. Real nice and healthy. Like anybody that you'd see. I told her so. I said: 'Mrs. Morgan, you look lovely today.' She did, too. I was surprised when I saw her because nobody said she was sick and I see her almost every day when she goes out, so it surprised me. She didn't look sick at all."

"No," Morgan said. He suddenly needed to go to the bathroom, and wondered if he could make it to the twenty-sixth floor before his bladder let go. He cleared his throat and decided that he could. "No," he said, "no. She doesn't. And the way that you or I would look at it, she isn't. It's the doctors. The doctors are the ones who say it. Say she's sick. So," he said, fumbling for words, raising his eyebrows and licking his lips again, "so . . . I guess she must be, eh? Must be. Sick."

"But she looks good, though," Hackley said.

"Yes," Morgan said. "Yes, she does." He gathered himself together and squared his shoulders. He cleared his throat again. He tried a small smile. "Well," he said, "must be getting on. Late." He brought his watch into view but could not choose between the two sets of hands and numbers that he saw. He nodded. "Late."

Hackley looked at his own watch. "Nearly," he said, nodding. "Nearly eleven."

Morgan looked at him, startled, making his own head spin. "Eleven," he said. "Thought it was later. Well, night, Walter."

"Night," Mackley said.

Morgan had the elevator to himself all the way to the twenty-sixth floor. He had also pressed twenty-seven and twenty-eight, stabbing for the button, but that would be something for someone else to worry about. He reached his apartment after slumping twice against the corridor walls, let himself in, and locked the door. He leaned against the jamb and waited for the place to swim into focus.

The lights were dim in the living room. He listened for the television and heard it muttering indistinctly. He cleared his throat. "Home," he said thickly, "home. I'm home, dearest." There was no reply. He waggled his head back and forth, wiped his mouth with the back of his hand, straightened up, and said: "Got to, gotta piss first." He went into the bathroom off the entryway and relieved himself. He came out, fumbling with his pants, and lurched into the living room. She was in there on the couch before the television, covered by the red afghan. She was lying on her side, asleep. He said, uncertainly: "Honey? Honey Maggie, I'm home." She did not reply.

He nodded sagely. He went over to the couch and looked down at her. He brushed her cheek with his left hand. She stirred in her sleep, brushing the chestnut hair away from her right temple. Her face was full and her complexion was still ruddy, partly by nature and partly from the sun at Falmouth. She had not lost any weight, although the doctors had assured her that she would. She told him that she had in fact put on a pound or two, and claimed that she was giving up desserts. She had not done so.

"Sick," he said absently. "Doctors're the ones, say she's sick. Don't look sick to me. Don't feel sick to her. What is *sick*?" He felt himself slobbering. He wiped his mouth again. "Bed," he said. "Gotta go to bed, Honey Maggie." He patted her cheek again, and she brushed at her temple again. He left her sleeping there, the television news at low volume, the dim lamps lighted—the interruption of the sound or a change in the illumination would awaken her. She'd told him she could sleep as well there as she could in bed with him. "Better," she had said. "Johnny Carson doesn't snore when he comes in after I go to sleep." Morgan had replied that he did not snore. "No," she said, "and I haven't got a lump in my left tit. Look, Bernie, it doesn't matter if you snore. Or the lump in my boob. I'm not saying I mind either one that much, or that I'm gonna let anybody do anything about either one of them. Just happens to be something I got to live with, so I will. Nothing serious." She had smiled at him then, and kissed him.

He sat on the edge of their bed, his shirt atòp the pile in the corner he had started with his jacket and his tie, his right stocking in his left hand, his right leg crossed over his left, his body sagging and bulging in the undershirt, his belly lolling over his belt. He sobbed. " 'S got a nice smile," he said. "Honey Maggie's got a nice smile." He finished getting undressed and got into bed in his undershirt and blue boxer shorts. He had the covers halfway up before he started snoring.

He awoke abruptly at twelve thirty, sitting up fast in bed. The apartment was utterly still. In the streets far below, probably on Boylston beneath their bedroom windows, he heard a siren. He listened carefully. There was no sound from the living room. Timidly he felt around in the bed. He touched her right buttock. On the couch or in the bed, she almost always slept on her left side. "Maybe that explains the lump," she said. "I always sleep on that side. Gravity. Like the fat in cream coming to the top of the coffee. Only this's solid and it didn't float. Or I would have it in my right one. So it sank and it's in my left one. I slept on my right, I'd probably have it on my right." He listened very carefully. She was breathing softly and evenly. He relaxed. He took inventory. His head had begun to throb. His stomach felt uneasy. He did not have an immediate urge to go to the bathroom, but he knew there was one in the making not far off. He decided to take care of everything at once. He threw the covers to the foot of the bed and got up. He padded in a crouch around the bed, his head clearer though it did throb, his left hand dragging on the bed. He went into the hall and then into the bathroom before he turned on a light. He urinated. He found his mouth tasted funny. "Oysters," he said. He opened the medicine cabinet and took out a bottle of green mouthwash. He gargled with it and spat it into the sink, noting white threads of mucus in it. "Oysters," he said again. He took out a childproof bottle of Extra-Strength Tylenol. The top was missing because he had thrown it away when he first opened the container. He swallowed three of the capsules. He went back to bed and pulled the covers all the way up to his chin. He patted Maggie on the buttocks. He sighed and went to sleep.

In the morning he would believe that he had started dreaming instantly and had dreamed all night, but he would not mention it outside the apartment.

He was in his late forties. His hair had not yet turned completely white, as it was now. He had lost a lot of weight and had been exercising in the sun. His face was tanned and shining, and his hair was combed back neatly so that it curled around his face as it had when he was a young man. The only difference was the grey.

He stood ramrod straight as he had in the Army when the captain was inspecting his platoon and later his battalion. He wore a priest's black suit, with the Roman collar and the black dickey over the white, short-sleeved shirt. He wore highly polished black shoes, plain toe, and he was in the fourth pew from the front on the left in St. Rose of Lima church in Proctor. He was next to the aisle, his right hand resting on the carved end of the pew in front of him. He looked directly ahead toward the ornate rose marble altar with the tall center spire and the two flanking, shorter spires on each side, the old altar designed for the celebration of the Mass by a priest with his back to the congregation. His mother stood at his left. She was small and frail, in her eighties. She wore a black garbardine dress with a demure white collar, and a black lace mantilla which partially hid her face. She clutched her missal in her hands and kept her head bowed. He smiled happily and looked at the altar. The vigil light in its clear, red vase, on its polished brass pedestal, flickered to show that the Lord was present in the tabernacle. Behind the altar center spire the rose window, showing St. Rose with her arms raised toward a heaven that beamed golden sunlight down on her, was bright in the late morning sun. To the left was the tall window showing St. Christopher carrying the baby Jesus across the torrent. To the right was the tall window showing St. Francis of Asissi feeding the birds of the air. No one stood in the first three rows of the pews of the church, though behind him the church was full. He could hear the other parishioners shuffling and coughing, and he could hear the organ playing very softly: *Mother dear, oh pray for me, whilst far from heaven and thee.* It made him exult and he began to sing softly along with it. *Till in heaven eternally, thy love and peace I share.*

The vestry and sacristy were combined in one room at the left of the altar, the arched door partially concealed by the pulpit which rose four steps above the floor behind the rose marble altar rail. Father Casper and a priest he did not recognize, short and swarthy, emerged from the sacristy now, walked across the altar, genuflected to the tabernacle, and turned to face the congregation. They were both in priests' street clothes. Father Casper smiled warmly, first at Morgan and his mother, then at the entire congregation. The other priest also smiled, somewhat thinly, and Father Casper without saying anything moved to the altar rail. He opened the gates and started down the center aisle, followed by the unfamiliar priest. He stopped at Morgan's pew. He took Morgan's right hand in both of his and shook it, staring deeply into his eyes. "Bernard," he said, "a joyous day." Morgan knew he was sincere, and he bowed his head with happiness. Father Casper released Morgan's hands, reached in and touched Morgan's mother's hands on her missal. Morgan saw that she was crying, the tears coursing down through the ruts of her wrinkled face. "You should be very proud of him," Father Casper said, "as are we all. A son a priest."

Evelyn Morgan smiled at Father Casper through her tears. "I always have been, Father," she said. "Bernard's been a wonderful boy. And, and a wonderful man. Always proud of him."

"And grateful, too," Father Casper said. "You know what the old saying is: to have a son a priest is to go at once to heaven at your death."

"She had her ticket already, Father Casper," Morgan said happily. He put his arm around his mother. He could hear the parishioners stirring and whispering behind them. "She earned her own in this world."

Father Casper continued to smile. "No doubt, no doubt," he said, "but a little insurance never did a man or woman any harm. Shall we go in now for the vestments?"

Morgan edged out into the aisle. "Certainly," he said. "As a matter of fact, I was a little surprised you weren't already in them."

"Oh," Father Casper said, "not today, Bernard. Not for Father Lazzeri and me. Only you in the full regalia. This is your day." He turned toward the priest whom Morgan did not know. "Forgive me, Dominic," he said. "Dominic Lazzeri."

"Ahhh," Morgan said, shaking hands, "and was it your father, perhaps, who played for the Yankees?"

Father Lazzeri laughed. "Afraid not," he said, "no relation, that I know of."

"Just as well, in this part of the world," Morgan said. "My years in politics, I learned: if you're connected to the Yankees, even in the remotest of ways, whether the baseball team or the Protestants, better not mention it. Or else lie about it, if you *have* to mention it."

Father Casper laughed again as they stood in the aisle. "Father Lazzeri's on from the archdiocese of San Francisco," he said. "Observing.

They're thinking of starting a program like yours. The one you took."

Father Lazzeri nodded. "I'd like to talk to you, after the Mass," he said. "Delayed vocations."

"Of course," Morgan said. "Though I must warn you, it'll all be favorable."

"I assumed so," Father Lazzeri said.

"I'm surprised Monsignor Wallace isn't here today, throwing cold water on the proceedings as usual," Morgan said as they stepped onto the altar.

Father Casper grinned, "Easy, Bernard, easy," he said. "He is. He's waiting in the sacristy."

Morgan set his shoulders. "Can't be helped, I suppose," he said. "It is his church and all."

The sacristy was a tall, high-ceilinged room with whitewashed walls and varnished cabinets for the vestments. There were three trays with cut-glass cruets of water and wine set out on the table, together with the vestments that Morgan would now wear on duty for the first time. Monsignor Wallace, thin and small, stood in his surplice and shawl at the window next to the door leading outside, his wizened face scowling, his tiny eyes squinting, his mouth set in disapproval. Father Lazzeri shut the altar door behind them.

"So, Bernard Morgan," Monsignor Wallace said, "you return in triumph to Proctor once again."

"Thank you, Monsignor," Morgan said. "Bless you for your hospitality. That I say my first Mass here, it means a great deal to my mother."

Wallace nodded. "Yes," he said. "First in war, then in politics, now as a servant of the servants of God. I must confess that I had not expected this, though I never doubted you would come to some sort of a dramatic end. You are a man of many surprises, Bernard."

"Thank you, Monsignor," Morgan said, bowing. Father Lazzeri wore a fixed smile.

"Dedicating your life to God at last," Wallace said. "My, my. I thought that sort of conversion had come to an end with Saul of Tarsus. Or at least with Ignatius Loyola."

"I must quarrel with you there, Monsignor," Morgan said.

"Of course," Wallace said without humor, "I never knew a time when you did not quarrel with me. About something."

"I don't feel I've come lately to the service of God, Monsignor," Morgan said. "No one told me that when I was fighting for my country, quite the opposite. And when I was in public service, well, it's not that much different."

"Really," Wallace said.

"Really," Morgan said. "We built hospitals, saw to the housing and the feeding of the poor, attended to the earthly needs of the children of God, that sort of thing. And if we had not built the prisons, there'd be nowhere for the merciful to go and visit those imprisoned in them, would there now?"

"Are you sure, Michael," Wallace said to Casper, "that Bernard took his orders at Pope John Seminary, and not with the Jesuits?"

"Quite certain, Monsignor," Casper said, laughing nervously.

"Yes," Wallace said. "Well, I shan't keep you any longer, Bernard, on this most felicitous day. Just try not to make too many mistakes out there, would you? The parishioners are simple people, but they are used to the Mass as it's usually celebrated and I hope you won't leave them all upset, wondering if they've fulfilled their obligation by coming here today."

"Only if it bothers them, Monsignor," Morgan said, "when I don't take up the second and the third collections from them."

Wallace's face went white, and his lips almost disappeared. He wheeled, opened the exit, and left the sacristy for the yard outside. Casper looked stricken. Morgan said: "Oh my God." Casper said, shaking his head: "It was the woman."

"The *woman?*" Morgan yelled. "The *woman?* That I *loved?* My *wife?* My wife who *died? Honey Maggie?*"

She shook him awake. He could hear her calling afar off and he came up to her voice through a mist, waking to find himself tangled in the covers, shaking and sweating heavily. "What the hell's the matter with you?" she said in her warm, sleep-coated voice.

"I . . . was . . . I was mad," he said thickly.

"For God's sake," she said, "that I knew. But at what?"

He rubbed his eyes. "I dunno," he said.

"You started off snoring," she said. "I got used to that. Then it was some kind of godawful groaning, and I decided that I didn't have any choice but to wake you up. But you stopped. Then all of a sudden you started hollering to beat the band for me, and I decided I'd better come and help, quick. What'd you want me to do, tell Costello off or something?"

"I dunno," he said again.

"Yeah," she said, "well, cripes, the way you were going on about it, you oughta remember. Never heard you this mad before, not even when you were awake."

"Yeah," he said.

"You had a lot to drink last night?" she said.

He rubbed his eyes again and shook his head. "Yeah," he said. "No," he said. "Hell, I dunno. Usual amount."

"Yeah," she said, "well, that's a lot anyway. You better cut down, Bernie, you know it? That stuff's startin' to get to you. You seein' snakes and big fat bugs with teeth? That what you called me for?"

"Uh uh," he said. "This was people, I think. Yeah, just people. None of the kind of snakes that crawl."

"Uh huh," she said. "Well, think about it, okay?"

"Think about it?" he said. "Sure, I'll think about it."

"The booze, I mean," she said. "You better slow it down, lover."

"It was the oysters," he said.

"Oysters," she said.

"Yeah," he said. "I had a lot of oysters over at Pier Four. It was them."

"Jesus Christ," she said, sinking back into the pillow. "Who died?" she said.

"Jesus," Morgan said, "who *did* die? I didn't know anybody died."

"You said somebody died," she said.

"I did not," he said. "Christ sake, I didn't see you since I left this morning. I haven't heard of nobody dying since I left this morning."

"You sure?" she said.

"Positive," he said. "You must've heard somebody else say that. On television, maybe, when you were going to sleep."

She thought about that. "Could be, I suppose," she said at last. She snuggled into the pillows again. "I wished I had your memory," she said, her voice muffled. "Your memory for where you heard things and what things you heard," she said. "It must be great."

"Count your blessings," Morgan said, "that's what I always say."

14 Around 4:00 A.M. the moonlight over the Charles River countryside in Dover began to give way to early sunlight. The frogs and the crickets along the river bank and in the clover of the meadows sloping around the Ames homestead protested comfortably against the

morning; the barn owl which preferred the white pines in the grove behind the house continued to call for companionship.

The house had three sections. The main building was a three-story wooden frame garrison with six bedrooms on the second floor. The ell to the north and the ell to the southwest were one-story additions made during the nineteenth century. The northerly ell contained the kitchen and the living quarters for the cook and the maid. The westerly ell with its long screened porch housed the Ames library, accumulating since the first Ames male settled on the land in 1749, moved from the main house during the nineteenth-century expansion financed by the family's profits from the textile industry and associated shipping interests.

The library had an eighteen-foot ceiling. There were two sets of french doors along each wall. The rest of the wall space, except for that over the fieldstone fireplace at the extreme westerly end and that around the double doors opening onto the main part of the house, was taken up by bookshelves. At the wainscoting level on each of the shelved walls there was a steel track for the wheels of the two movable ladders that enabled the Ameses to reach books desired on shelves near the ceiling.

The diminishing moonlight and the increasing light of dawn came through the french doors and illuminated the gold and rose Kazvin rugs laid side to side on the polished oak floors of the library. The leather of the four couches grouped in facing pairs at the center of the room shone dully, and the cracks of wear in the creases near the tufts were ivory. The library tables, one butted up against the back of each couch, equipped with brass lamps identical to the green-shaded one on Otis Ames's desk in his office, and Queen Anne leather wing chairs glistened in the dull light. There was a tray of glasses and two bottles of Hennessy cognac on the one nearest the desk. The paneled desk between the last pair of couches and the fireplace was covered with books and papers. On the wall above the fireplace there was a glass-fronted shadow box, six feet by four feet, ten inches deep. It contained a Navy ensign, dirty and torn, wih a bedraggled broom, its scraggly bristles aimed upward and its handle festooned with two pieces of line knotted once at each end, lodged diagonally across it. There was a small brass plaque on the bottom of the shadow-box frame. It read: *USS SAND-SHARK 1942–1945. Presented by her Officers and Men to Capt. O. C. Ames. San Diego. 9 August 1946.*

The doors leading to the foyer opened slowly in the dawn and Otis Ames, his white hair sticking up and his balance unsteady, stood naked on the threshold, grasping the curved brass handle of the door on the left with his left hand. He felt his way along it as he made his way into the library, his right arm and hand extended as he proceeded. Groping around the tables and the couches, he kept to the northerly side of the room, careful to walk along the edge of the rug where the fringe under his feet told him where he was. He was small and misshapen in the soft light, his body distended at the belly and almost flat down the back, his buttocks sagging and his knees bowed outward. His chest was somewhat sunken and had only a few wisps of hair. His penis was shrunken and his testicles had ascended to lie close to his abdominal wall. He walked with his feet splayed outward.

When he reached the space between the two couch groupings, he began to sing, at first tentatively and softly, his volume increasing as he gained confidence that he had begun in the right key. By the time he reached the front edge of the desk, he was singing heartily, loudly, and quite well. "Anchors aweigh, my boys, anchors aweigh. Farewell to college days, we sail at break of day, day, day, day." He did not go on to the next lines, but hummed loudly instead. At the desk he came to attention, saluted the ensign and broom, and said forcefully: "Ahoy the *Sandshark*. Permission to come aboard. Never fuck with the dogfish." Sotto voce, he said: "Permission granted." Then he whistled in imitation of a bosun's signal to come aboard. He turned in his place so that he faced the doors he had just entered. He rested his hands on the desk and leaned his buttocks onto it. He surveyed the room. He nodded with satisfaction. "Kistiakowski," he said. He said it again louder, peering angrily toward the doors. "The hell's my exec, goddamnit. *Kistiakowski.*" He paused. He turned slowly to face the desk and bent over it, rummaging through the papers nearest him. "Going on report, Kisty. Warned you about this before."

Dee Scalley appeared in the doorway as her father turned to the desk. She wore a robe of ancient madder, dominated by maroon, with nothing under it. There was a sorrowful expression on her face.

Otis Ames turned again. He raised his eyes so that he stared the length of the room. She stood motionless. He could not identify her. "Kisty?" he said. "You there, Kisty?" He sighed. "Uh," he said. "Uh, Captain retires. Splice the main brace." He coughed silently. He moved toward the brandy tray. He poured a stiff drink and raised it in a toast. "To the *Sandshark*, goddamnit. Best fighting ship in the Navy."

As he raised the glass, Ted Scalley, wearing only a white terry-cloth robe, came to the doorway and stood next to Dee. He had a pitying expression on his face. With his left hand he touched her hair. She looked up at him inquiringly. He nodded toward his right hand, which he held at his side, concealed by the fold of the robe. She took a deep breath. They started into the room, he walking on the right, she on the left of the couch groupings.

Ames, paying no attention to them, put the glass to his lips and downed its contents in one gulp. This brought on violent coughing. He dropped the glass, which bounced once silently on the rug without breaking and rolled under the table. Wracked by the coughing, Ames steadied himself on the table with both hands and lowered his head. He started to walk around it, toward Dee's path of approach. As he did so, Scalley came around behind him. She stepped rapidly into Ames's field of vision. He stopped in his track and stared at her. "Kisty?" he said uncertainly. "That you, you bastard, Kisty?" She held out her arms to him. He attempted to walk toward her, but lost his balance and fell the last step or two into her arms. She moved toward him to prevent him from falling to the floor, taking him by his upper arms. Ames lowered his head as he stumbled. Scalley came up swiftly holding a hypodermic needle in his right hand. He put the point against Ames's right buttock and injected him.

Ames straightened up quickly. *"Hey,"* he said.

"It's okay, Dad," Dee said soothingly.

Ames looked at her stupidly. "You, you're not Kisty," he said.

"No," she said.

He tried to push away from her. "Didn't want you," he said. "I wanted Kisty, goddamnit to hell. You stick me in the ass?"

"Now Dad," she said, "it's all right."

He looked at her stupidly, his head wagging. "You a nurse or something?" he said. "Sure it's all right for you. Wasn't your ass that got stuck. That's why you think it's all right." Irritably, and with a great deal of effort, Ames pulled away from her grasp. She released it gradually, allowing him to struggle but not really seeking to overcome him. He turned his head around and saw Scalley. "Who the fuck are *you?*" he said. He got a crafty expression on his face. "Ah hah," he said triumphantly, pointing his right index finger at Scalley, "you're the one who did it. Stuck something in my ass."

Scalley, the needle again concealed in the fold of his robe, stood quietly while Ames looked around for it. He also spoke soothingly. "Easy does it, Oats," he said. "It'll be all right."

Ames snorted. "Sure, all right. 'Spose you're gonna tell me it's malaria again. Had so many of those goddamned shots myself, it's a wonder there's a mosquito left in the Pacific. Oughta get something, inoculate against *Japs.*" He laughed. *"That* I'd take." His head lolled. With some difficulty, he reached behind him with his right hand and rubbed the place of the injection thoughtfully. His head lolled again and he frowned. Scalley dropped the needle on the table and put out both hands to steady him. Backing up, he guided Ames toward him around the couch until he had him at the center of the cushion. Gently he pushed the old man backward, the edge of the cushion catching him behind the knees and buckling them so that he sat down. His head lolled off to the right. Scalley bent, picked up his feet at the ankles, and hoisted them onto the couch. Ames immediately stretched out as Dee hurried from the room, returning with a pillow and a grey Navy blanket from the hall closet. She handed the pillow to Scalley, who shoved it under Ames's head while she tucked the blanket around her father. Unconscious, he managed nonetheless to snuggle into the warmth of the covering.

Dee put her arm around Scalley's waist. They stood over Ames as parents might over the crib of a newborn infant. "Thanks, husband," she said. She squeezed him.

"Think nothing of it," he said, brushing her hair with his lips. "Just remember this service the next time you hear somebody bitching about doctors not making house calls any more."

"Yeah," she said. "Jeez," she said, shaking her head. "It's really going to start now, isn't it?"

"I suppose it is," Scalley said. "Now that the word's officially out. That he really means it and everything. Can't say we didn't expect it, but still. . . . It's not going to be easy for him, Dee. Man of his age."

"They're going to eat him alive," she said with no spirit in her voice. "They're going to have him for breakfast and have him for lunch, and if there's any left over they'll have that for dinner. If he only hadn't insisted on doing this."

Scalley laughed. "Yes," he said, "just like Alexander insisting upon conquering the known world. Really not the best idea as far as his health was concerned, but sometimes people're determined to do what they shouldn't."

"Okay," Dee said, "let's grant him that. That he has to do it." They turned away from the couch and started toward the doors. "Is there some medical reason why he has to do it in the middle of the night?"

"Dawn, actually," Scalley said.

"Right," she said. "Four bells. The morning watch, is that it? Why can't he take the dogwatch? That'd let us get him bedded down and fit in a decent night's sleep for ourselves. You going back to bed?"

"Well," he said, "I was sort of thinking about grabbing another couple hours before the rooster goes on duty. But I'll have a cup of Ovaltine or something with you if Mrs. Duncan's got a jar of it around. Maybe come up with some breathtakingly simple way to slip him his lithium every day until it's over."

"I don't see how you can drink that stuff," she said. "I think it tastes awful." She made a face.

"It's not freshly ground Chase and Sanborn, if that's what you mean, but there's no caffeine in it, either," he said. "What's he call that stuff you make?"

"Briggs and Stratton," she said, laughing. "I haven't heard him call my coffee that for years. Briggs and Stratton. 'Looks like it came out of the tractor crankcase, Dee,'" she said, imitating Ames's gruffest voice. "'Haven't had coffee this good since I was discharged.' Maybe we could put the lithium in his coffee. Think that'd work?"

"Ought to," Scalley said. "Lithium hasn't got much of a taste anyway, and you could palm off liquid sulfur in that brew if you wanted. Beaker of that stuff and a man'd drink acid without knowing it."

"Suppose Mrs. Duncan gets hold of it," she said.

"Might not do her any harm either," Scalley said. "She's not fully buttoned-up either any more, I notice. Just a little bit off the screen now and then. Wait till it registers on her that he's hired Putter. 'One of the *nay*-gurs, would ya believe, and Mister Ames the foine gentleman that he is, the poor man. We'll have one of them in the White House one iv these days, and mark me words, we don't.'"

"'Just see if you don't go and find that I'm right after all,'" Dee said, continuing in the brogue. "God, if it ever occurs to her why Dad's after Morgan and Costello, it'll break her loyal old Irish heart."

"What do you mean?" Scalley said.

"Because they're Irish," Dee said.

"Oh, I don't think that's the reason," Scalley said. "I'm Irish and he let me in."

"Sure," she said, "and he told you why, too. Too busy watching out the front door lest I bring a Jew in from the law school. Didn't have the time to look for a mick sneaking in the back. Thought you were one of Mrs. Duncan's nephews for the first year or so that you were coming here. By the time he caught on it was too late."

"Well," Scalley said, "he took it with good grace, then. But he's not after Morgan and Costello because they're Irish. Irish politicians, maybe, but not because they're Irish."

"Umm," she said.

"Come to think of it," Scalley said, "I don't think Costello even is Irish."

"Not Irish?" she said, as they left the library. "Francis Costello? Not Irish? Come on, Ted. You'd better get that sleep after all."

"Not that," he said as they passed the Ming vases set on the marble pedestals in the foyer. "I didn't mean *Irish* like that. Blood. The Mafia had a Frank Costello too for a long time, you know. He wasn't even Irish by blood. He was Italian."

"This Frank Costello is Irish," she said, "and this Frank Costello's a politician. Not a gangster, maybe, but as far as Dad's concerned, almost as bad."

"Irish by birth," Scalley said, "but not by the way he lives. And as far as being a politician's concerned, Frank Costello's no more of a politician than he is a broker or a builder or an export-import banker. Politicians happen to be one of the varieties he needs most for what he does, so he uses them a lot, but Frank Costello isn't one of them. He isn't one of anything, except a Frank Costello."

"Forgive my ignorance, O healing master," she said, resting her head against his shoulder as they walked through the foyer into the sitting room where the T'ang horses presided over the table large enough for twelve, "but what the hell is a Frank Costello, as it were. What does it do? Or is that too unspeakably naive of me, to ask that?"

"Not at all, your worship," he said. "A Frank Costello is a sort of latter-day privateer, preying on the sea-lanes of commerce for his own plunder. Generally he's pretty careful to avoid attracting too much attention to himself. Doesn't like it, as a matter of fact. Has a tendency to lie low, like Bre'r Fox. He don't say nuffin'. When he wants something done overseas, he has somebody overseas who will do it. When he wants something done in New York, somebody in Manhattan will respond immediately. He has somebody in Washington, somebody in L.A., and he of course reciprocates and is their somebody in Boston.

"Put it this way," he said, as they went through the butler's pantry and on into the kitchen where the two Garland stoves dominated one wall and the walk-in refrigerator loomed next to the triple stainless steel sinks, "you are a bond lawyer in New York."

"No," she said, "I am not a bond lawyer in New York. I am a fair to middling litigator in Boston."

"For now," he said, "be a bond lawyer in New York."

"Consider it done," she said. "Are you serious about this Ovaltine you mentioned earlier?" The copper pots hung from the racks in the ceiling and the steel kettles stood polished on the shelves.

"It does seem a little silly in these surroundings," he said. "Grind up the coffee. I'll be awake till Wednesday, but probably it's just as well. Grand rounds today. Impress the hell out of the chief when I just let it drop casually that I've been up since four, beavering away at the journals." He sat down at the long wooden table.

"You should be more careful of your choice of words," she said, proceeding to the cabinets.

"Not around Selby," Scalley said. "Selby isn't sure it's dirty unless somebody actually utters the word *fuck* in his hearing. And therefore of course nothing is ever dirty to good old kindly Doctor Selby because he'd go into catatonic seizure if anybody actually uttered the work *fuck* in his hearing, and consequently nobody ever does. Are you still a bond lawyer in New York?"

"Still a bond lawyer in New York," she said, pouring coffee beans into the electric grinder.

"What is that goddamned stuff anyway?" he said. "My mother used to make Chase and Sanborn and it never dissolved the damned spoon the way your coffee does."

"Mocha java," she said. "They used to use it in the leather industry for saddle hides and chaps, but that market sort of died out so they started hustling it for drinking purposes."

"By humans, I assume," he said.

"They're the main ones that took to it so far," she said. She turned on the grinder. Over the noise she said: "You gonna leave me bond-lawyering in New York the rest of the day?"

"No no," he said. "You happen to notice that the market's a little soft in some municipal bonds underwritten by your client bank for the pastoral community of, say, Blackacre, Mass."

"Hey," she said, "you really did pay attention when I was still in law school."

"Absolutely," he said. "Hung on every word. And what you notice about these Blackacre bonds is that Blackacre on close inspection does not appear to have any money."

"Ah," she said.

"Precisely," he said. "This naturally upsets you. Because if Blackacre ain't got no money, and you know about it, pretty soon almost everybody else is going to know Blackacre ain't got no money, and your client's going to have to start discounting those bonds like they were hula hoops or something."

"Which he does not want to do," she said.

"Idea does not appeal to him at all," he said, "and for that reason it does not appeal to you. So, New York bond lawyer, the question for you is what in the hell are you going to do now, wise guy, so your oafish banking client doesn't get fed up with your high fees and start to question usefulness in time of need."

"What I am going to do," she said, "is call up Otis Ames in Boston and say: 'Daddy, quit that damned fool corruption commission thing there and start thinking of a way to pump some money into Blackacre. On the two-step double. You used to be good at this.' "

"Which is why," he said, "it is a good thing that you never went into bond-lawyering in Manhattan. Because Otis Ames isn't any good at that sort of thing any more. He hasn't any clout now, and if he did it'd be the wrong kind anyway. Because his idea of gingering up those Blackacre bonds would be to put together a whole bunch of contingent deals with private businessmen. They would move what they were doing into Blackacre and do it there and juice up the town and its tax revenues. And would probably subscribe to a fair share of those bonds for themselves. And incidentally make lots of money, but that's beside the point. And it's slow, for these days, and it probably wouldn't work anyway. No, nowadays you call Francis Costello, and you say to him: Francis, hightail it over to the State House and collar me a rep or three that can ram through a state guarantee of the Blackacre bonds. And Francis does it, and the state's credit's pledged, and the Blackacre bonds are as solid as a fistful of Hope diamonds."

"And Francis gets a fistful of diamonds for this little service himself," she said. She put the grounds into the filtered coffee maker and poured the water in.

"Uh huh," he said. "And the reps each get at least one little diamond for their trouble, and the taxpayers of Blackacre get their new junior high school or whatever their newest unnecessary passion happens to be, and your underwriting clients in New York sell Blackacre bonds at fat commissions like they were peddling heroin to druggies on annuities. And the Otis Ameses of this world hate you and all your seedy ilk, because that used to be their genteel commerce. But most of all they hate the Frank Costellos who perceived that what could have been done with what your father and his fellow Republicans used to have on Beacon Hill, and now is being done by Frank Costello and his fellow Democrats who took it away from them."

The coffeepot steamed and dribbled black and pungent brew. "When do the three hags appear to stir that vat you're making?" he said.

"Hold your horses," she said, "I haven't put in the eye of a newt or the tail of a fenny snake yet. Don't rush this thing." She jiggled the basket with the grounds in it. She frowned. "Still, though," she said, "there isn't anything that'd knock your eyes out for being illegal in what Costello's doing. Or in what Morgan's doing, for that matter. Maybe some arcane little SEC violation that'd bore everybody to tears for eight years of litigation and wind up in a seventy-page consent decree where everybody admits that nobody did anything wrong and everybody promises not to do it again, but not much more. Dad isn't going to get the lions roaring for their lunch with that, and I don't believe he's far enough gone yet to think he is."

"I don't either," he said. "I think what he's doing is going after them for what they do to keep that stranglehold on the Hill. The one they use to do the kind of thing that's not illegal. Because he thinks there's got to be something rotten in that little tea dance, and he's probably right."

"He probably is," she said. "What do those guys make, twenty grand a year?"

"About that," he said. "It's a part-time job, of course. They try to claim it isn't, but it is."

"I wish I could live as well on eight times that as they seem to be able to do," she said.

"Poor baby," he said, as she poured the coffee into Navy mugs, heavy vessels made of thick white china, adding sugar and cream. "Don't try to peddle that idea at some little function that your father has in this modest establishment."

She set the mugs on the kitchen table. "My family's been acquiring and keeping up this old barn since before King George got grabby and slapped the taxes on the tea," she said. "With what's gone into this place we could live like royalty in Scotland."

"But you choose instead," he said, stirring the coffee, "to do it in Dover."

"And," she said, sitting down, "we earned it, like the ad says on television. The old-fashioned way."

"That's what they think they're doing," he said. He drank coffee. "Jesus," he said, putting the cup down, "if they'd had some of this stuff to pour down the throat of Lazarus, Christ could've saved himself a house call. This'd revive King Tut today, I bet, if you slopped enough of it into him."

"It is rather bracing," she said, smiling.

"You know this colored gentleman your father is going to pick next week," he said. "This Putter guy. He any good?"

She shrugged. "I know him," she said. "I got to know him in those equal opportunity cases. He was good, very good. Not flamboyant. No showboating. Good, competent, well-prepared lawyer who happened to be black. Dad asked me if I knew anybody who could be trusted not to take a dive, and I thought of Lyle."

"And that's all it took?" he said. "He picked him on that?"

"I don't know, really," she said. "He didn't really discuss that with me. Maybe he thinks he's spotted something that nobody else has seen in Putter's public appearances. Maybe they've had some private sessions where Putter came off like Muhammad Ali. I really don't know."

"Because he's black then?" he said. "That seems to be the only thing about him that really makes him stand out."

"That'd explain why he wanted the job," she said. "It wouldn't explain why Dad decided to give it to him. There must be a thousand young lawyers out there that Dad doesn't know from a load of goats, as he'd say, who'd sacrifice their firstborn sons to have gotten that job. But Putter's the one that got it, so he must have shown Dad something that he didn't see in the others. I just don't know what it is."

"Because," he said, "Gillis's column, for example. Monday he had that kid Hanrihan a shoo-in for the job."

"Yeah," she said, "that pompous ass from Middlesex. Joe's usually closer to the mark than that. Hanrihan must've put that bee in his ear. Surprised he swallowed it though."

"He call your father first?" Scalley said.

She looked at him with an expression of mock incredulity. "Doctor," she said, "if you were Joe Gillis and my father was Otis Ames, would you call my father?"

"Only if I meant to dial the time," he said, "and got the wrong number. And if I did, and discovered who I was talking to, that's all I'd ask him for, too—the correct time."

"You'd be lucky if you got that," she said, laughing. "Whenever Dad starts to feel the teensiest bit of uncertainty, that maybe, just maybe, there is such a thing as a reasonably decent Irish Catholic Democrat who frequents Beacon Hill for any reason, he just reminds himself of Joe Gillis. Or else Gillis writes something that infuriates him even more than the stuff that Gillis usually writes, and reminds Dad himself. Joe Gillis is the man God thoughtfully put on earth to enable my father to justify the way he feels about all the rest of them, and I must say God appears to know His business."

He was laughing too. "The funny part of it is," he said, "Joe's really not a bad guy."

"Of course he isn't," she said. "That first time we met him, at the caucus Bruce and Tippy dragged us to?"

"Yeah," he said, laughing harder, "one of those things anyway. Was that the one where we were supposed to demand the pullout from Chile?"

"Something like that," she said. "Joe Gillis liked me fine. He was actually cordial until he remembered that Diana Scalley's name wasn't always Scalley. After that? Well, still cordial, but just the slightest bit distant. No, I don't think he called Dad first. Or second, either, as far as that goes. It's almost summer, remember? Things're slow in this business. You get a story, for God's sake, don't question the damned thing too much. Might collapse and leave you with nothing to write."

"Yeah," he said. "I sure hope to God your Dad locates Kisty before things really heat up."

She patted his hand. "Yes," she said, "good old Kisty. Best exec a man ever had. Too bad he's dead, huh?"

"Yeah," he said, "or that your father's enemies since then haven't always been guys you could tell from the tint of their skin and the slant of their eyes."

She frowned immediately. "Cripes," she said, "I really hope, I hope it's more than that. That old ethnic bullshit."

He patted her hand. "Dee, Dee," he said. "I shouldn't've said that. Of course it is. Honestly. There really isn't any ethical problem I can see in going after Bernie Morgan."

She looked at him anxiously. "How about in what we're doing?" she said.

"Doing?" he said. "Us? You mean: giving up our own house to stay here with him like we were a couple of young teenagers who had to get married and couldn't afford to get their own place? Like: giving up our weekends on the boat so as to make sure he has medical attention standing by at all hours of the day and night? Like: carrying the whole burden of his care so your brother can stay down in Texas there and make a few more millions so that when your father dies, he'll be able to come back here and retire at an early age to become the squire of Dover? Do I think that that's unethical? No, I do not. Do I think it's pleasant? Well, no, as a matter of fact, I don't think that either."

"Not even medically?" she said. "Medicating him like you're doing?"

"So he can function?" Scalley said. "I see nothing wrong with that. Hundreds of people, thousands of people, get through normal everyday affairs with flying colors only because they're medicated. And not just lithium maintenance patients, either. Ulcer patients, hypertensive individuals, all kinds of people with debilitating illnesses. That's what medicine's supposed to do, Dee—make it possible for otherwise sick people to live pretty normal lives."

"I hope so," she said.

"Now Sid Morse," Scalley said. "The other day we had a kid come in. Beating victim. I didn't see the kid, but apparently he got into some dispute with some guy whose car he'd damaged. And the guy had very much the better of the dispute. The kid was conscious but he was pretty badly beaten up. Internal injuries. So here was Sid, this internationally famous urologist, standing there within a foot of the kid when they brought him in, and they asked Sid to have a look at him. See if his kidneys or his bladder had been damaged.

"Well," Scalley said, "the kid apparently wasn't fully able to understand the nature of his situation. He was raving mad. Puerto Rican too, I guess. Cuban. Something along that line. And apparently he doesn't like Jews. So Sid came in to look at him and kid got a look at him, the Jewish afro and the glasses, the nose . . . well, you'd have to agree with me that it isn't really too hard to make a good guess about Sid's ethnic background. And the kid spat at him and called him a motherfucking hebe Jew cocksucker.

"Whereupon," Scalley said, "Sid refused to treat him."

"Well," she said, "I can understand Sid's feelings, for once. I don't think I would've felt much like making somebody who said that to me feel better."

"When you were with the AG's office," he said, "did you sometimes argue cases in behalf of causes you did not agree with?"

"Yes," she said. "Okay. Sid should've treated him."

"And Sid did not," Scalley said. "And as it turned out, by the time they found another doctor free to look at him, the kid's bladder had to come out. So here's this boy perhaps fifteen who'll be peeing into a bag for the rest of his life."

"Was that because Sid didn't treat him?" she said.

"Who knows?" he said. "Maybe the bladder would've had to come out if Sid had seen him right away. Maybe Sid, having skills possibly greater than the gentile who treated him, maybe Sid could have saved it. Doesn't matter. Either way, Sid was wrong.

"That's what I mean," he said, leaning toward her and resting his hand on her arm. "This is a cruel world, Dee," he said. "If we can't help your father, for God's sake, who on earth should we help?"

She looked at him for quite a while. "In case I haven't mentioned it," she said, "I love you very much."

15 In the morning light that came through the two front windows of his fourth-floor office overlooking Tremont Street, Lyle Putter propped his right foot in its black tasseled loafer on the edge of his metal, wood-grained desk, locked his hands behind his head, and looked sardonically at Leo Rosen. He shook his head. "My, my, Mister Rosen," he said, "you look like something that made it over to the Pine Street Inn too late to claim a dinner and a bed last night and had to spend it snoring in the doorway next to the expressway. Is this any way for the power of the press to go about in public in the Athens of America, inviting everyone who sees you to conclude the *Commoner* is out to win our hearts and minds with the outpourings of a bunch of seedy bums?"

Rosen nodded and sat down with a thump. "Go ahead," he said wearily, "ruin what remains of my week. It shouldn't take you long, but what the hell, huh? I start the week with a crazy person and then with two supposedly sane persons who did their best to convince me the first guy that I met was perfectly all right. Today I come into my office, this bright and sunny morning, absolutely bursting with excitement 'cause I decided I'm onto something which will cause the honorable Pooch Pucci to cream his jeans immediately and exempt me from all further assignments until I have completed my blockbuster series on the wretched state of public mental health care in this Commonwealth. And Pooch shat on my head. Ahead of me, I have a whole day of trying to get an interview with our illustrious governor, John Tierney, or at least with somebody on his staff who can maybe give me something I can print about John Tierney's plans for biggety niggers like Lyle Putter, which will at least give me a hundred lines of stuff that I can print to save my miserable ass with Pucci. Now I am come to my very last resort, the eloquent and soft-spoken Lyle Putter, leading moderate voice of civil rights activists between here and Birmingham, and what do I get from him? A dose of shit, of course. My mother was right. I should've played piano in a whorehouse."

"Speaking for us black folks," Putter said, "those two enterprises, civil rights and mental health, they don't seem to go together somehow, do they, Leo?"

"No indeed," Rosen said, sighing. "As a matter of fact, Lyle, I've come to suspect that's what the white folks who elected Governor John Tierney might have been trying to tell you and me and people like us when they did it. That they think you guys are nuts for making lots of noise about how the government still ain't finished yet with doing things for you, and they think guys like me are just as goofy for still pretending that it's news when you guys continue making noise. Which may explain why you're no longer making great strides with the State House, and why when I write about the troubles that you're having making strides, I'm not making headway with the city desk. You dig?"

Putter nodded. "I do indeed," he said. "Andy Warhol's Rule in action. I've been famous for my fifteen minutes, and now my quarter hour is up. What's sadder than the poor player who goes on with the struttin' and the frettin' after the audience has finished paying its attention, huh?" He pondered for a moment. "Kind of humiliating, though," he said, "you ask me. Getting displaced by the dimwits and the maniacs. Some Harvard doctors, maybe, out to save us all from getting cremated in a nuclear holocaust; that would have a certain dignity to it, to be shunted off the stage by people rescuing all of humanity between bites of guacamole and polite sips of spritzers. But nuts and retards? How did they get fashionable again?"

Rosen grimaced. "As it seems to have turned out," he said, "they didn't. I just thought they did. The state's got this medium-sized hospital up in Proctor that the taxpayers decided to finance about twenty, twenty-five years or so ago. They named it after the fellow who was Speaker of the House then, Wilfred Knox. The Knox State Hospital. Which as it turned out was a pretty neat stroke because that is where the Speaker ended up, and where he is today, vague as an angel. Along with lots of other people in regular communication with beings resident on other planets and folks claiming private information to the effect that the world's about to end. There is also a fair-sized population of people who believe they are the targets of KGB assassination plots and stand ready to defend themselves with butter knives and sashweights or any other weapons anybody may be careless enough to leave where they can get their hands on them. Plus some poor souls who came into this world with just about enough intelligence to find primetime television entertaining.

"Now naturally," Rosen said, "where you have got a state facility, you have got state employees, and if there is one thing you can bet the ranch on without worrying one bit, it is that such people will be pissed off about something. And, as Pooch reminded me this morning when I was pitching this great story to him, that something will almost always be that they want more money. Sometimes for themselves, sometimes for the work that they've been hired to do, and every now and then for something that they really need. Only at the instant when they discover that they really need that something, there doesn't happen to be any spare money lying about.

"The Knox State Hospital lash-up," Rosen said, "appears to belong in that last category. The joint's been functioning all these years since Wilfred built it without anybody really paying much attention to it. So since nobody associated with it who's in his right mind has set up a stink, naturally everybody else on Beacon Hill's been quite happy to ignore it. Then about a year ago, something happened and things changed."

"Let me guess," Putter said, "they let an ax murderer out into the general population, and instead of stifling his impulses like all the rest of us who'd like to grab a hatchet and deal sternly with the people who annoy us, he grabbed a hatchet and dealt sternly with some people who annoyed him."

"Nope," Rosen said, "although from my point of view that would have been a better hook to hang a story on. No, what happened was that the old chief of psychiatry decided that he'd had about enough of spending all his days in other people's twilight zones and notified the Commonwealth that he was going to pack it in. Which sufficiently alarmed his deputy, who was even older than the chief, so that he cleaned out his desk as well. Which meant that all of Knox State's medical expertise, between the two of them amounting to about forty-five years, went out the window all at once. And the State Board had to rustle up some more.

"Now," Rosen said, "those jobs don't pay too well by doctor's standards. By the standards of ambitious young newspapermen and most likely by those of promising young black lawyers forgoing what they could make as the token niggers in big white law firms, forty and fifty grand a year seems pretty generous, but to doctors that's not even pocket money. Especially to doctors that've gone on to be shrinks."

"Well, naturally," Lyle Putter said. "In our society, my man, one of the indications that you are not partly nuts is that you're grabbing every dollar that somebody else has not put in his pocket yet. Shrinks have to grub the money, man. Shrinks don't want the people thinking that they're crazy."

"Precisely," Rosen said. "So, what the Commonwealth got when it went out hiring shrinks for Knox was two misfits that had just as much contempt for fifty grand as all their classmates did, but for one reason or another couldn't get their hands on really heavy sugar. One of them's a guy. His name is Ahmed Khan and he's an Indian from India. He's got these big brown soulful eyes which he could use to great advantage if he was a beagle puppy that was looking for an owner and the guy that ran the pet shop would just put him in the window where he could melt the hearts of passersby, and he is rather short. By 'rather short' I mean that he's about five three, and speaking as a man five seven when I stretch, I can tell you confidently that this is not an attribute which helps a man."

"So which is he?" Putter said. "Is he a wimp or does he tend toward the noisy and obnoxious sort, like you have done?"

"A wimp," Rosen said. "My guess is in his heart of hearts he would've liked it a lot better if God had made him a beagle, and he hasn't quite given up hope yet that God may have a change of heart and turn him into one. In the meantime he intends to sit there quietly and stare soulfully at every hardhearted white man he encounters, knowing he is going to get kicked each time and hating them well in advance for kicking him. Which of course every white man that he meets can spot immediately upon meeting him and because he in turn resents that makes damned sure that Ahmed doesn't leave the meeting unkicked and disappointed."

"How is he at the doctoring?" Putter said.

"My guess is," Rosen said, "that he's probably pretty good. Of course you might decide to ask me: how the hell do I know? And I would tell you right off that I don't. But he's still there and he hasn't said he's going to leave after his two-year contract ends next year, and he does have these modest hopes to make the place a little better. So my ignorant impression would be that he's probably competent at least. Maybe a little better than that. He says that a lot's been learned about custodial treatment of the mentally ill and the defective in the past ten years or so, which is a gentle way I guess of making the suggestion that his predecessors were a little bit behind the times, and what he would like to do is make it possible for his sad guests to do something during the day besides sit in the day room and play with bits of yarn. He also says there's some reason to believe that if you can get a fellow who's been violent interested in beating the shit out of a volleyball or going one-on-one with a basketball instead of with somebody else's head you might even have a chance some day of improving him to the point where you don't have to keep him locked up in a cage until the day he dies. Like I say, Lyle, this may be all bullshit and about a foot thick, but if the guy says that a decent gym and a couple athletic fields might turn out to be worth a lot more than they cost, who the hell am I to argue with him? After all, why would he lie? There's nothing in it for him, for Christ sake. He's a fuckin' Indian. He hasn't got six cousins in the contracting business that're gonna go and rape the state for millions putting up a gym and a couple soccer fields. Not here, at least, and I doubt he's got it in mind to put the damned thing in New Delhi."

Putter laughed. "That's the first thing that you think of, isn't it?" he said.

"Well, Jesus Christ," Rosen said, "in this goddamned place it is, of course. The first thing anybody taught me when I got here was that when somebody tells you he's got something that he wants to do that'll wind up making everything between Albany and the ocean into a land of milk and honey, find out if his family's already got the beekeeping franchises locked up. And since I've been here, less'n four short lively years, I haven't seen a damned thing that'd persuade me that I shouldn't think that way."

"Of course not," Putter said. "That's the one part of everything I've tried to do with my people on the board and in the ranks that hasn't worked for shit. I've never been able to persuade them that in a good many cases where we haven't gotten what we wanted, it wasn't because the people that we had to get it from hate niggers. It was because the people that we had to get it from looked at what we wanted and didn't see anything in the request for them, so they torpedoed it. It wasn't racial. It wasn't even personal. It was just good business sense. I'm telling you, my friend, if I could've figured out a way that would've ended unemployment for all the micks in Southie while it was training blacks in Roxbury to qualify for good jobs too, it would've slid through Bernie Morgan's legislature like it'd been on skates." He shook his head and laughed. "Sometimes," he said, "when you want to have some fun, go to one of Tildy Basswick's garden parties up on Beacon Hill and try to get it through his high Episcopal white liberal head that the way to get a redneck to cooperate is to fix it so he makes a profit by cooperating. Tildy is for busing and for housing and for equal opportunity, and his wife Dimpsie is for all those good things plus poetry and drying out at the McLean Hospital, and they must kick in close to twenty grand a year to the Massachusetts Union for Scholarship and Lawful Equality to show they really mean it. They will invite to their tastefully decorated townhouse Virgil Madison in full dashiki, Boston's Most Preposterous Coon and bongo player, bar none, to abuse them and their white-skinned brethren verbally, and they will nod understandingly when I tell them that our chances of cooperation from the office of the governor are slightly worse than those of the North American Man-Boy Love Association, but when I try to tell them that we have got to bite our lower lips if necessary clean through and cut a fucking deal with Bernie Morgan that will get him on our side to fight that asshole Tierney to a standstill, they just tune me out. They don't even hear me, Leo." He paused. "It tends to get discouraging."

"Well," Rosen said, "if you want company in your misery, I think I know where you can find some. Let me know when there's some free time in your busy schedule and I'll arrange for you to meet one Helen Dotten."

"The name is not familiar," Putter said. "Can't be her social conscience has developed far enough to cause her to join MUSCLE and contribute large amounts of money to outdated fashionable causes. Otherwise I would've kissed her ass enthusiastically already many times, and I wouldn't need an introduction."

"Doctor Helen Dotten," Rosen said, "is Khan's assistant. She's the other doctor that they got in the medical bargain basement and she is quite a lady. You know the type, Lyle: early forties, children grown, back to school, gets the degree, comes back into the real world loaded for bear and bent on making up for all that time she lost when she was birthin' babies."

"Ah yes," Lyle Putter said. "Three of those would make a dozen easy. Get them involved in some project and convince them that it's one of the Lord's special programs on this earth and they'll produce more energy for you than you could get out of an atom smasher. As long," he said, "as long as you don't ask them to make coffee, type anything, or run a mimeo machine. Dig a ditch, fix a tractor, put up some scaffolding, or act as drill instructor to recruits in boot camp: those things they will do with fearful dedication. But nothing that sounds like it might be something you would ask a broad to do."

"Right," Rosen said. "Black hair streaked with grey, Morgan Guaranty and Trust Company suits, maybe even leather underwear, but never any bullshit. Helen to the T. It's all she can do to let Khan in his wimpy voice get out a sentence. She sat there in this Polish hard guys' bar in Mercer—the restaurant part's the Blue Eagle Dining Room and they've got the NRA symbol in blue neon in the window; the bar part's the White Eagle and that's in neon in that window—and it was like she was going to wet her pants while he was talking. Which in a way I have to say that I could understand. She was the one that got me all the way out there into the woods, so far north up the Pioneer Valley that it's news when there's a day goes by that they *don't* find bear sign on the back porch. She was the one who'd had at least the brains to get the *Commoner* involved in the thing and see if she could use me to start softening up the governor, or somebody, and here was this guy who happens to be her boss sitting there, hemming this and hawing that, and it was driving her nuts.

"What it was," Rosen said, "on my way up there I had to stop for gas. And also to take a leak, as far as that goes. Not a good idea to ride with a full bladder."

"How about an elastic around it," Putter said. "Would that help?"

"It's not the jiggling I'm worried about," Rosen said. "It's the idea of getting in an accident and having your bladder burst, fill your belly up with all those pissy old bacteria. Bad news. So I stop at this gas station where the last customer that came through was probably John Dillinger fleeing from the law, and there's this guy running it that to my layman's eye looked like he was crazy. I figured I had me one of those New England hillbillies that's about halfway down the stream and still's got only one of his oars actually in the water. Kind that gets spells, you know? Stupid. Slow-witted, and a little strange perhaps. But then we talked a little more and I started to change my mind. He was looking at me like he was seriously considering doing something to me. I told him I had to take a piss and he went into this discourse about not pissing on his garage because the sun shining on it made it stink, and then after I went and pissed into the bushes it occurs to him to tell me there're skunks in there and I was lucky one of them didn't decide to piss right back on me. And I saw this old DeSoto that he had there, and in perfect innocence I said the car was in nice shape, I said that it was probably worth some money, and he didn't like that idea either. Said it was his daddy's car and he would never sell it and he obviously didn't like my small suggestion. He had the knob dialed up to full weird, is what he had.

"So," Rosen said, "we were talking there in the White Eagle about what you can do for crazy people and how they use this Halderol which puts them out of action for a little while but if they've got a lot of customers around the full moon or something like that, they just inject this Prolixin that whomps the nutcakes into never-never land for the better part of three whole weeks or so. And I brought up this guy I met and said, well, given the number of people that we got running loose all over the place like this guy that looked like to me he had a promising career ahead of him in homicidal mania, how the fuck does anybody tell who's crazy and who's not? And where does it say that I get to knock you gaga with a needle because I think you're acting funny, but you don't get to put me into drydock for a month if you think that I'm getting strange.

"Now," Rosen said, "I wasn't trying to start a fight when I said that. It seemed to me like a legitimate question that a layman ought to be concerned about. But Khan there absolutely refused to give me a straight answer. He started gabbing about how *crazy*'s not a word they like to use, and something about how the gradation between someone who's mentally okay and someone who's getting seven channels UHF on his hearing aid is very fine and hard to identify with uniform precision, blah blah blah, and he was acting generally like either I'd insulted him or else he was doing everything he could to insult me by saying in not quite so many words that he thought I was an asshole."

"Well," Putter said, "I don't want to upset you or anything, but I have heard the point of view expressed."

"I'm sure you have," Rosen said immediately. "I would imagine that you or anybody else who spent more than five minutes talking to Joe Gillis would have that diagnosis offered for his own consideration."

"It wasn't Gillis who said it to me," Putter said, "although I must say that your instincts were correct. The person who said it to me brought it up in conversation when we were discussing why it was that every time MUSCLE had something of even arguable newsworthiness to offer, you always seemed to get a beat on everybody else in town. And I thought that seemed pretty easy to explain. I said that Leo Rosen got the beat because of all of the reporters that I'd met from the *Globe,* the *Herald,* and the *Commoner,* he was the most reliable, and that by playing favorites with you I made sure that the story got the kind of attention it deserved not only in the *Commoner* but also on the television news broadcasts. I said in other words that you and I had managed to develop that most agreeable of press and organizational relationships: we used each other shamefully. And I said that I thought this reflected great good judgment on both of our parts."

"Fair enough," Rosen said. "See, I thought that it was probably Gillis because he thinks I'm trying to cut him out of that State House beat he's had ever since the dinosaurs had their last meeting on the Hill, and I don't think Joe misses many opportunities to badmouth me. He's afraid of me. He thinks I want his column."

"And as a matter of fact," Putter said, "he's right."

"Of course he is," Rosen said. "As soon as I can figure out how to finagle my way into some issue that's before the General Court, I'm going to do it, and that'll put me head-to-head with Gillis. When the two of us're covering the same damned story on the Hill, my obvious superiority will be so unmistakable that even an eighteen-karat asshole like Dave Pucci won't be able to ignore it any longer, and that's when I'll bump Gillis and get the political beat. Which if I do it half as well as I am sure I can will make it just a matter of time before I get myself some national attention, and then it's bye-bye Pooch and off to Washington. Why the hell do you think I rode all the way out in the woods last night? So I could have a couple beers with two low-rent doctors who think a couple hours of field hockey every day are gonna be enough to revolutionize the treatment of the mentally ill in these United States? Nah. I went because I figure if they can stir up a little fuss, and I can help them build the fire under the kettle that they're stirring, I'll wind up following them through their dealings with the Speaker and displaying my rare talents where I want them seen."

"Which development, I take it," Putter said, "you no longer see as likely to occur as a result of what you do covering me and the civil rights rodeo."

"Correct," Rosen said. "Two years ago, I did, but now I don't and if you're honest with yourself, neither do you."

"I am," Putter said, "and as you say, I don't."

"The trouble is though," Rosen said, "I appear to have miscalculated somewhat when I thought I saw a route to Washington that wound through Proctor, Mass. At least if Pooch's reaction that I got today is any indication, and since he's the guy that makes all of the decisions that affect me, that is what it certainly is."

"So," Putter said, "that puts you back in here with me, seeing if by any chance there might be one last firecracker left in my organization."

"That's about it, yeah," Rosen said. "Does that offend you?"

"Yes," Putter said. "Not because that's what you're doing here. I don't blame you one minute for that. It's what I'd do myself. But because I'm sorry to say that you're absolutely right. From your point of view, which is quite bad enough, or would be. And also from my point of view, which makes it even worse."

"Ah ha," Rosen said, leaning forward slightly in his chair, "you're quitting, huh?"

Putter stood up and turned his back on Rosen. He looked out the window into Tremont Street. "The Parker House," he said. "If I spend the next forty-two years of my life doing exactly what I'm doing now, I'll be able to walk out of here some night, go across the street, and attend a massive and star-studded celebration in my honor there. Or if their ballroom happens to be booked, at the Park Plaza, the Marriott Long Wharf, or some other hotel with a room big enough to muster three or four divisions in full battle dress. There'll be senators and congressmen and judges, candidates for mayor and maybe President, bishops and rabbis of every blessed creed, brass from all of the armed services, university presidents and captains of industry, and the national anthem will be warbled by whoever's filling in for Ella Fitzgerald when that red-letter day arrives at last."

He turned back to face Rosen again. "That's how it'll be, Leo, if I don't depart from the track that I'm on now, one smooth progress from the dynamic young leader of MUSCLE to conscience of the city with nearly fifty years of doing good to boast of. Doing good, not doing much. All I have to do's behave myself, and all of that will come to me."

He sat down at the desk again and steepled his fingertips. "That, of course," he said, "is if I can somehow manage four more decades of Tomming from the heart. If I can't, well, all I have to do is rip the hanky from my head enough times to scare some governor enough so that he'll decide his life would be more comfy if I were a judge, sending black boys off to jail to do hard labor instead of ragging his ass all the time about making life in his state better for the black folks. And that ain't bad neither, Leo, you know that? It isn't bad at all. I got all that good shit just for the taking. Either way, I got it."

"So," Rosen said, "why not take it?"

"Well," Putter said, "I think that I've decided I don't want it. That's why."

"Interesting," Rosen said. "Can I print this?"

"Let me talk," Putter said. "I'll get to the part that you can print, and tell you when I do."

"Still using me, huh?" Rosen said, grinning.

"Sure," Putter said. "Why stop now? Like you say, Gillis's already putting it out around town that you're an asshole because you submit to our symbiotic little way of doing business. What is there left to lose?"

"So," Rosen said, "it was Gillis who suggested to you that I was an asshole."

"No," Putter said, "it wasn't. It was David Pucci, quoting Gillis to me about you and asking whether I did not have to agree with Gillis."

Rosen did not say anything for a while. Then he cleared his throat and said: "That, ah, that doesn't amuse me quite as much as hearing that Joe Gillis's been complimenting me elsewhere in town."

"No," Putter said, "I'd imagine that it wouldn't."

"Hm," Rosen said, sliding down further in his chair and rubbing his eyebrow with his index finger. He passed his hand over his beard when he had finished that. "I may have to give this some little thought, if Pooch is taking Gillis's evaluations at the same time that I want him to be thinking about making me Gillis's successor. That bastard Joe is smarter than I thought."

"Hard to fight a man like that," Putter said.

"Exactly," Rosen said. "How the hell do I get a grip on him?"

"And that," Putter said, "is the question that I've had to face about my situation also. How the hell do I fight what I've got up against me? It's like fighting with the fogger, that thing they have out in Walpole that they use to calm the bloods when they get rambunctious in Block Ten. Just wheel that pepper-fogger in and blow that cellblock full of tear gas and some other stuff that'll make their eyes smart good and proper and take all the fight out of them. Same sort of thing with me. For enemies I've got a lot of people like the Governor and Bernie Morgan, who refuse to pay me even the small courtesy of worrying about me. The people who finance my organization do not want me cater-wauling up and down the Common and making a goddamned spectacle of myself. As far as they're concerned, those handsome donations that sponsoring members make each year are proof enough that they aren't bigoted. They don't expect me to accomplish anything except show by my visibility that they finance that their hearts are in the best of all the right places. The people who don't like niggers have no reason to fear somebody like me. I'm harmless and they know it.

"Therefore," Putter said, "what I need is the means to do some harm."

"Geez," Rosen said, "I dunno about that, Lyle. What've you got in mind to do? Start taking hostages or something?"

"Actually," Putter said, "what I had in mind is more conventional."

"You're going to run for office," Rosen said.

"Right," Putter said, slapping the desk. "Right on the money, man. Son of a bitch, man, you are *smart*. Would you believe that I already got my slogans?"

"I'd be surprised," Rosen said, "if you told me that you didn't."

"Yes," Putter said. "The first one, this has got my smiling face on it just like I was posing for the cover of the *Rolling Stone*, and underneath it says: 'See? They don't all look like Sonny Liston. Vote for Putter and assuage your liberal guilt, you motherfucking racist honky pig.' And for airplanes over Fenway Park, right about the seventh-inning stretch, I got this banner that says: 'Massachusetts needs a real nigger. Vote for Putter.'" He grinned.

"Lyle," Rosen said, "that's going to wow the black folks?"

"Hell no," Putter said. "For the darkies I got advertising specifically tailored to the wants and needs of their community. I have got: 'Put a watermelon into every pot and some white dude's Coupe de Ville in your garage with all the vehicle ident numbers skillfully erased.' I tell you, Leo, I got campaign stuff that sings." The grin disappeared abruptly. "Shit," he said, "it shouldn't be so goddamned easy to make fun of that idea, should it? I mean, after all, I am halfway intelligent. I've had a more than decent education. I've lived in Boston all my life. I actually have a pretty cordial relationship with the police and no criminal offense record whatsoever. I'm safely but discreetly heterosexual and the only thing that's kept me from being a fine example of a family man already is that I haven't yet decided on the right woman. Or else the right woman hasn't yet decided upon me. And I don't think it's false advertising if I claim I've spent the past six years since law school working for my people and also for the benefit of everyone who lives in Boston, at some financial sacrifice to me."

"It sounds reasonable to me," Rosen said.

"So," Putter said, "with that record, if I were a white boy I would be a natural for public office, right? I get along quite nicely with all the influential people that I've met, and I can say I've done some good and demonstrated that my heart's in the right place. But it happens that my skin is ebony, so instead of being one damned hot prospect for secretary of state in next year's elections, and maybe for the corner office after that, I might entertain a modest hope of sitting on the School Committee or running for the City Council if they put district representation back in. But nothing more than that. This Commonwealth already showed it's tolerant and put Ed Brooke in two offices statewide. Now that's enough of that shit, huh? The rest of you colored gentlemen just sit down now and keep your mouths shut."

"So," Rosen said, "what are you gonna do? Start building up resentment and maybe drinking too much? Or just go around the bend a little ways and start making wilder and wilder statements publicly, until everybody gets fed up with you and stops listening entirely? The alternatives do not sound attractive, Lyle."

Putter stood up again. "Come on," he said, "walk out with me. I've got a brunch at the Copley." He took his suit coat from the closet near the door and shrugged his way into it. "I look at it this way," he said, shooting the cuffs of his red and white striped shirt, "I have spent my life using my natural abilities to imitate the fox."

"The fox," Rosen said.

"Uh huh," Lyle Putter said, nodding. "The fox is very smart and he knows many things. The trouble is that unless the fox goes up against somebody he can outsmart, he goes hungry. And that's what's been happening to me. The people I am up against are also foxes, and know just as many things as I do. So I have come up empty.

"Now," Putter said, "the skunk is an entirely different matter. The skunk is fairly stupid, and he knows only one thing. But that one thing he knows is more important than all the things the foxes know, all put together. And that is why the foxes generally avoid the skunk, and when they find they can't avoid him, act very carefully so as not to get him pissed off. Literally.

"My discontents," Lyle Putter said, opening the door with the frosted glass pane in it that read *MUSCLE, Inc. Lyle Putter, General Counsel* and ushering Rosen out into the corridor ahead of him, "my discontents and the idle hours that I have spent in contemplation of them have left me with enough time to follow pretty closely the actions of the General Court in its past and illustrious legislative session."

"Cripes," Rosen said, going into the corridor and waiting for Putter to lock the door behind him, "you really must've been bored."

"Not totally," Putter said. "There are nuggets in that sludge that Bernie Morgan and his henchmen turn into our statutes. One thing that they did, for instance, was put John Tierney on a small hot spot by appearing to have granted him his wishes for a crime commission."

"Oh," Rosen said as they walked down the corridor, Rosen's rubber soles squeegeeing on the marble, "big fuckin' deal that is. From everything I hear, that legislation's got as many holes in it as your better class of sieves. And just to make things even worse, this guy that Tierney picked to run it still thinks Cal Coolidge should be drafted for another term and hasn't heard about Japan surrendering. So even assuming that old Ames there manages to come out of his fog long enough to nail somebody like the Speaker to the mast, what good's it gonna do? The legislation setting up his unit is defective, and Morgan's boy'll blow it right out of the water."

"So what?" Putter said. "Nobody except lawyers knows the difference between indictments and convictions. Or gives a shit, at least. If Ames gets Morgan named by the grand jury for stealing anything, even a box of giant paper clips or something, that'll do the job and finish him. So what if Morgan gets the charges blown out before he comes to trial? As far as the voting public either knows or cares, everybody's known for years that Bernie Morgan was a crook and stealing millions, and Otis Ames has gone and made the race results official. Morgan doesn't have to do time or anything, you know. All anybody has to do to him is nail him in the papers and that's the end of him."

Rosen stopped walking for a minute. He was frowning when he replied to Putter. "Uh, Lyle," he said, "I have to say I've got some trouble with that. What you're saying."

"Trouble?" Putter said. The grin was back again. "You mean to say, Leo, it bothers you to think somebody might consider taking Morgan out on some trivial indictment that won't stand up in court?"

"Not that somebody might," Rosen said, "not that at all. That you might? Yeah, that bothers me."

"No shit," Putter said. "You're serious?"

"Uh huh," Rosen said, "I guess I am."

"Son of a bitch," Putter said. He took Rosen by the left elbow and slowly they resumed walking toward the elevator banks. "Now," Putter said, "let me be sure we have this right, that we're both talking about the same thing. We agree that Bernie Morgan is in the forefront of every backward movement in this Commonwealth."

"Yup," Rosen said.

"And we agree," Lyle Putter said, "that Bernie Morgan is corrupt in every way that God has made it possible for one mere human being holding office as the Speaker of the House of Representatives of the Commonwealth of Massachusetts."

"Well," Rosen said, "one slight reservation here before I can endorse that. We can agree that Bernie Morgan has the reputation of being the biggest crook his generation has produced. And that in the normal course of human business, you do not get that sort of reputation unless you have worked reasonably hard to get it."

"In other words," Lyle Putter said, "we can concur that he's a crook. Furthermore, a pretty big crook. But we're not able to say at this point what precisely is the total dollar value of the money that he's stolen."

"Or made it possible for his friends to steal," Rosen said. "Yes. We can agree on those points. It's probably not very much. Those guys come cheap."

"And that," Putter said as they turned the corner to reach the elevator bank, "by making corruption the hallmark of his administration, he's completely dissipated the resources of the Commonwealth that might have been applied to improving the lives of its citizens." He punched the button to summon one of the six elevator cars that traveled in the wrought-iron-framed shafts.

"That's a pretty flossy way of putting it," Rosen said, "but yeah, that's been the general consquence of his way of doing things."

"Well," Putter said, rocking back on his heels and grasping his right wrist in his left hand, "I think he's considerably overdue to get what's coming to him."

"I agree," Rosen said.

"And I think the Ames Commission, however imperfect it may be, is the only instrument we seem to have available for giving it to him," Putter said. "Therefore I am willing to use it."

"Especially since," Rosen said, as the middle elevator in the triple bank before them arrived at the fourth floor, "you think that if you associate yourself with that commission, people like me may point out regularly that Lyle Putter is the chief engine of the Ames Commission, Ames being pretty groggy as a result of his advancing years. And you'll end up a household name in Massachusetts, a knight in shining armor, and probably a shoo-in for some high office state or national when Bernie Morgan's all hung out in the wind."

"Let's put it this way," Putter said, sliding open the iron grillework doors and holding them for Rosen, "that does enter into it, sure." He entered the car behind Rosen and let the doors slide shut. The car started its descent. "Does that make a difference? Should it?"

"Yes," Rosen said. "It makes a difference because if the law set up some half-assed organization to go and grab a two-bit vicious landlord out of Allston, and a lawyer like you by looking at it could see any charges coming out of it wouldn't be worth the powder to blow them to hell, so that the landlord when he'd been grabbed would walk right out the courthouse door again without one word of his downfall appearing in Pooch Pucci's paper, you wouldn't touch it with gloves on. Would you, now?"

"Nope," Putter said.

"So," Rosen said, "the fact that Morgan is corrupt is bad, and we agree on that. And you are good and we agree on that. And the commission sucks and we don't have any argument there. But you tell me you're in a position where you can tie up with the commission and that will give you a fine opportunity which you propose to take. And I say that's pretty goddamned cynical, Lyle, and I'm surprised at you. I'd even go so far as to say that I think what you're telling me means Morgan really has corrupted the whole Commonwealth, if somebody like you is willing to do what you say you're going to do in order to destroy him."

The elevator reached the bottom floor and Putter hauled the doors open. He was smiling now. "Jesus Christ," he said, "you've still got some Long Island liberal Jew in you, Leo, I do believe."

"I suppose I have," Rosen said. "I don't see anything wrong with that. What am I supposed to do, be just as cynical and stupid as Joe Gillis covering politics in this place, so I get so I think what those fat bastards do is funny? Is that what you'd like to see me do? I don't believe I can do it, Lyle. I don't believe I want to do it, if I can." At the inner doors leading to the vestibule on Tremont Street, Rosen stood aside to let Lyle Putter pass. "Just out of curiosity," he said, "how'd you happen to get involved in this whole scam anyway? If you don't mind me asking."

"I don't mind you asking," Putter said, going through and opening the outer door onto the street, "as long as you understand we haven't reached the part yet where I've said that you can print any of this."

"Fuck," Rosen said. "Okay, so how'd you get it?"

"Ames's daughter, " Putter said. "She's a partner at Bolter, Ryan and Decicco. Dee Scalley's her married name. Would've been a federal judge by now if Jimmy Carter'd been reelected. That equal opportunity lawsuit we brought against the Fibre Density Tech people? She was the supervising partner on the case. It ended pretty much to everybody's satisfaction, no real blood shed on either side, and she mentioned to me that her old man was looking for a general counsel. Somebody that didn't have connections to the group that Morgan's built around himself, which I by God can prove I haven't or the black folk would be doing a lot better than they are. And she asked me if I would be interested. Which I said I would be and I talked to him, and this is where we reach the part that you can print, Leo, he's going to tell the world that I'm his lawyer next week. So this week, if you like, you can say that I'm depressed about the snail's pace of civil rights programs in Massachusetts and I'm giving serious consideration to leaving MUSCLE soon to look for more rewarding responsibilities elsewhere."

"Uh huh," Rosen said, "and then I just might segue into informed speculation that you might be heading for the Ames Commission."

"If you like," Putter said.

"Which," Rosen said, "since you've already got the job, will make it look to Pooch as though my contacts on the Hill, at least as far as the commission is concerned, are considerably better than any that Joe Gillis has come up with."

"He hasn't even heard a name yet, has he?" Putter said.

"Yeah," Rosen said, "some guy named Hanrihan. He surfaced in 'State House Viewpoint,' beginning of the week. So Joe Gillis is going to end up looking like an asshole on this one, at least."

"I imagine," Putter said as they stepped out onto the sidewalk, "you'll be able to endure that small embarrassment of Joe's." There was very little traffic on Tremont. Three cabdrivers leaned on their cars and talked outside the Parker House; business travelers eating early lunches of fruit salad decorated with alfalfa sprouts sat at window tables reading *Time* and *Newsweek*. Putter continued to stare at Rosen. "Couldn't you?" he said.

Rosen scowled. "Yeah," he said. "Yeah, I guess I'm whore enough for that." He sighed. "I'd better be," he said. "That is, if I intend to keep on making a living in this racket."

Putter clapped him on the shoulder and grinned at him. "Atta boy," he said. "I knew that I could count on you to see the light."

Rosen looked sharply at him. He was already edging toward the heavy iron fence enclosing the Old Granary Burial Ground where his Kawasaki stood chained on the sidewalk. "That doesn't mean I like it, though." He unlocked the bike, stowed the chain in one of the panniers, struggled into his helmet, wheeled the bike over the sidewalk into the street, flipped the starter, and glanced back toward Putter as the bike rumbled among the buildings. "Offer you a ride over to the Copley?" he said.

Putter shook his head. "Somehow I don't think so, Leo," he said. "I think I've started growing up at last, and I don't want to take risks needlessly."

Rosen nodded once. He got onto the bike and roared off down the street, drawing the face shield of his helmet down. Putter watched him go, still smiling. Then he walked across the street, first checking to make sure there was no traffic coming, and addressed one of the cabbies. "The Copley, please," he said, getting into the last cab in the line. The driver of it glanced at him, nodded, and separated himself from the other two. "What I said about not taking niggers," he said, "all right? It don't apply to Oreos."

16 Bernie Morgan struggled to escape from the tangle of the bedclothes he had made during the night. It took him quite a while, and he broke free only by getting his torso out and sitting up, so that he could light a cigarette and think about how best to get at his legs and feet. The first drag of the Chesterfield made him cough hoarsely and deeply, and he had to be careful how he held the cigarette near the blanket as he doubled over with the spasms. He was straightening up, his face red and his eyes rimmed with tears, when Maggie in her quilted light-green housecoat swept into the bedroom and switched on the portable television set on the bureau in front of him. He shook his head fiercely, telling her that he did not want it turned on, and she overruled him.

"Now now, Sunshine," she said, "the whole world's up and cheerful and you've got to catch up fast. No feeling sorry for yourself with that blockbuster hangover I'm sure you've got. You brought it on yourself, you jerk, and we don't allow complaining here about pains we brought on our own selves."

He attempted to speak, coughed four more times, and took another drag.

"Good," she said, "very sensible. Coughing up your guts from last night's booze and butts, best thing in the world for them's another dose of Chesties. That's my Bernie-boy, always knows what's best for him."

"Cut it out," he rasped, as the picture appeared on the television. He stared at it. "The fuck is that?"

" 'Nancy's House,' " she said triumphantly. "I just knew you'd want to watch it, since you told me what you've got on for today." He looked at her without comprehending. "Doctor Helen Dotten," Maggie said. "She's going to be on 'Nancy's House' this morning, telling all about the drooling idiots in the state hospital system and how she's got a personal appointment with the Speaker of the House today to get his backing for the bill to buy them all mink jockstraps. Or whatever the hell it is she's got in mind. You'd know that better'n I would."

He waved feebly at the screen. "Turna fuckin' thing off," he said. "I don't wanna listen her."

"Well," Maggie said, "that's just too bad, because you're *gonna* listen to her. She's coming to your office. You let her pester you into an appointment and now you're going to have to hear what she's got to say. And you might as well get a preview right in your own bedroom so's you'll know what to expect."

He coughed again mildly. He put the cigarette in the ashtray on the night table next to the bed and threw the covers off. "Oh ho," Maggie said, "getting ambitious, huh? Gonna make the big push and get out of bed at nine fifteen? Should I alert the paramedics, have them standing by?"

Morgan stood on his feet, swaying slightly, and plucked at the elastic waistband of his blue nylon shorts. He belched. "You're gonna fart next, I suppose," she said. "I like it a lot better when I go on those raids with you and get to share the booze and beef when it's on the way in, 'stead of sitting here at home and all I get's the gas it makes when it starts on the way out."

He belched again. He stared blearily at Nancy Caughey, who was holding up a can of dog food and explaining why it was much better than dry dog food that came in paper bags. "Silly bitch," he said. "No wonder her fuckin' husband turned queer. Jesus, look at her long enough, the fuck'd want to try another broad?"

Maggie looked at the screen and looked back at Morgan. "I dunno, Bernie," she said, "if Nancy could see you while you're lookin' at her, she might have some questions to ask about my sanity, too."

He coughed again and started toward the bathroom. "Never mind," he said. "Just get me some juice, all right? And turn that fuckin' thing off. I got to watch that fuckin' Dotten broad, I'll watch her in the living room."

Maggie stood up as he passed. "Yes sir," she said, "one fresh-squeezed Smirnoff, colored red, coming right up." He grunted.

Morgan appeared in the living room in his red silk bathrobe with the white silk piping and the Harvard University crest emblazoned on the breast. He wore Japanese rice-paper slippers and he had combed his hair. He sat down in his Barca-Lounger and tilted back to raise the foot-rest. He took his Bloody Mary from the end table next to him and sipped at it. "Ahh," he said. He lit another cigarette from the pack in his bathrobe pocket. Nancy on the big screen in the living room stood in a kitchen layout with a small woman who wore a cardigan and held up a black cast-iron skillet with a yellow substance in it. "What the fuck is that shit?" Morgan said.

Maggie lounged on the daybed and sipped at her own Bloody Mary. "Creole omelette," she said. "It's got green peppers and shrimp and to-matoes in it. Sounded pretty good when she was making it."

"Looks like shit now," Morgan said. Nancy told the viewing audience that the omelette went especially well with stewed tomatoes spooned on top, and crispy thin fried potatoes on the side. The screen showed a picture of an omelette cut and served as she described it, with a sprig of parsley. "Looks like the fuckin' cat came in and threw up on the dish," Morgan said, "all that red shit runnin' out of it. Oughta get a bandage for it, 'fore it bleeds to death."

"Oughta get a bandage for your eyes," Maggie said, " 'fore *you* bleed to death. What the hell was it kept you out gettin' shitfaced again last night, for Christ sake? Some other short-hitter find an extra fifty in the gutter and invite you out to see if you could drink it all?"

"They had another time for Dealey," Morgan said. "I hadda go to it."

"Good Christ," Maggie said, "what's this, about the tenth one? Guy's had more parties'n they've got country music awards on the television there. Every time you turn around, seems like, they got another time for Dealey. You guys're gonna drown him in booze before the stuff he drank already gets a chance to kill him."

"He's got a lot of friends," Morgan said. "This one was the Worcester

County guys. Look, he's gonna be dead a long time. That family his, they're gonna need every penny he can scrape together for them. No use waitin' till he's dead, try to raise it. He's dead, no way he can hurt then with somebody, callin' somebody up, you don't help out his family. Now, at least he's still around. He can go these things and look around, and if a guy ain't there or he didn't do the right thing with a check or something, Billy can still pick up a phone and call me, one the other guys, and let us know somebody didn't give a shit about him when they knew he was in line at the check-out stand. He ain't too sick for that."

"Jesus Christ," Maggie said, "that what he's doin'? That's pretty good. I always thought Billy Dealey was kind of an asshole, and now here he is, he thought up a way, he can go around hauntin' people before he's even dead. That's pretty smart. No use takin' no chances, you might lose track where some guy is after you're dead and you can't locate him to haunt him. He don't show up and pay his dues at Anthony's before you die, you kiss-of-death his ass before you go away yourself. He's not such an asshole after all."

Nancy introduced a young quartet dressed in lederhosen and Bavarian peasant skirts. They wore green loden hats with feathers stuck in the bands. Four men with tubas stood smiling behind them. "Now what the fuck's she gonna do?" Morgan said. "I thought the Dotten broad was gonna be on with some handpicked maniacs for us to see. Some guy come in in his johnny and eat some of the rug, maybe. Wilf put on a dog show, maybe, for us. The fuck's she got here? This some of them that think they're reelectin' Hitler or something?"

"They didn't get to the part about the hospitals yet," Maggie said. "They always do it this way on the show. They start off with Nancy singing a song. Today it was 'Snowbird.' She's actually not bad, you know?"

"I don't look at her that regular," Morgan said. "I'm usually down at the chickenhouse in the morning this time, robbing the eggs off of the hens so I can hurry back up here and watch the dumpy broad tell me how to mix 'em all up with the shrimps and tomatoes there and make everybody sick just lookin' at them. No wonder the hens don't like me even before they catch me choppin' off their boyfriends' heads for Sunday dinner."

"Then after that," Maggie said, "she has the news summary that Gerry usually gives, only he's on vacation this week. So they had some other guy whose name I didn't happen to catch. That's for the people that're too lazy to get up and watch the news when they're supposed to on 'Good Morning, America' or anything. Only of course you're even too lazy to get up on time for the summary Nancy gives you."

"Told you," Morgan said, "I'm still down the henhouse." The Bavarian band omm-pah-pahed and the young quartet sang "Edelweiss" and did a polka step. "Look at that, willya," Morgan said. "Now you could show me that, and if I didn't know I was watchin' it on this show, I would swear this is something somebody took pictures of the last Holy Name Society thing they had Saint Stanislaus's parish. Jesus Christ. This is fuckin' awful. Who watches this shit?"

"Hey," Maggie said, "watch your lip. I watch this shit, for one person. I watch it and I learn all kinds of things I didn't know before."

"Yeah," Morgan said. "Like how to take perfectly good scrambled eggs and ruin them by puttin' a lot of shit in them so they look like they got shot when you stick a fork in them."

"Not all the time," she said. "They have some good recipes on there some times. They had a good way of makin' roast chicken the other day. Stuffed it with chestnuts, which I never heard of before."

"Neither did I," Morgan said. "The hell they think they had there, a squirrel or something?"

"And then also," she said, "they have things about your health. Once a week they have this doctor come on and he tells you about new advances in medicine and things like that. Very interesting."

"I bet," Morgan said. "Tell a bunch of dumb broads what they oughta do about their periods so they don't drive everybody nuts when they get the rag on every month."

"A couple weeks ago," Maggie said, "they did have something like that. Premenstrual depression. It was very informative. I wished I'd known some of those things before I turned forty-five. All those cramps and stuff I went through. I could've taken something for that, if I'd've known about it."

"Couple good stiff shots of rye," Morgan said. "That's what my mother always took. Worked all right for her, far as I could see."

"Sure," Maggie said, "couple stiff shots of rye. That's what your mother took for everything. Cripes, your mother, that one time I met her in the office she'd been takin' a couple shots for it bein' a rainy day for Christ sake, I think it must've been. Wasn't any other reason I could see. She was drunker'n a goat. Probably didn't even know when she was havin' her period."

"Could be," Morgan said. "She thought as long's she went to church every morning, everything else she did was on the cuff. She was a good old broad, though. Never saw her messin' up her head, lot of shit like this."

"That's just because they didn't have any of it then," Maggie said. "She didn't miss it because she didn't know what she was missing."

"Yeah," Morgan said, finishing the Bloody Mary, "like this Nazi orchestra they got here."

"They'll have something worthwhile in a minute," Maggie said. "Just wait and see. This is the entertainment part."

"Yeah," Morgan said. "Tell you what, all right? Get me some more juice while they finish entertaining me, okay?"

She took his glass, got up, and started toward the kitchen. "Speaking of Dealey," she said, "and what's happening to him, you maybe oughta give that a little thought yourself."

"What?" he said. Nancy was thanking the Bavarian group. She turned to the camera and told her viewers she'd be right back "after these important messages." "Right," Morgan said, "toilet paper and floor wax I'll bet."

"What?" Maggie said from the kitchen.

"Nothin'," he said, "I was talking to the TV."

"Yeah," she said, "well, that's what I mean. The kind of thing I mean. I think you're startin' to lose your buttons a little bit."

"What the hell do you mean?" he said. "See, I was right. Toilet paper. Look at the fuckin' broad, rubbin' it on the kid's face. Now she's rubbin' it on her face. That is not how you test if the toilet paper's any good, lady. What you wipe it on, it's the other end you wipe it on. And what you wanna know about it is whether the damned stuff lets go when you're using it and leaves you sittin' there a whole handful of shit in your hand. Not how it feels on your fuckin' nose or something. Jesus. Good goddamned thing they haven't got you sellin' Trojans. Pull one of them things over your head, you'd suffocate to death."

"What in hell are you talkin' about?" Maggie said, returning with the second Bloody Mary. She handed it to him.

"Trojans," he said. "Dumb broad's sellin' toilet paper, wipin' it on her face. That ain't what you wipe toilet paper on. That's all."

"Oh," Maggie said, sipping from her second drink.

"Now," Morgan said, as an ad for underarm deodorant came on, "watch what they do with this stuff, right? They're gonna deodorize their goddamned wrists. You got sweaty wrists, this is definitely the stuff for you."

"Yeah," Maggie said. She sat down and leaned forward. "Bernie," she said, "will you listen to me for a minute for a change?"

He shifted his gaze from the television set to look at her. "I was listening," he said.

"You were not listening," she said. "Now, just listen, all right? I'm worried about you, you understand that? You're wreckin' your health. You get what I'm saying?"

"I should drop a few pounds," he said.

"You should *drop* a few pounds? Bernie, for the luvva Mike, you are at least seventy, maybe eighty pounds overweight."

He shifted uncomfortably in the chair. He frowned. He drank from the Bloody Mary. "Nah," he said, "not that much. Thirty, forty, maybe. Not that much."

"Bernie," she said, "you have got tits. You have got bigger boobs than mine, all right? And I am not a flattie. I am a thirty-six C, for Christ sake, and your tits're bigger'n mine are. It's not supposed to be this way, Bernie, that the guy's got bigger knockers'n the woman has. If you wore a bra and your belly wasn't so big they can sort of rest on it like you had them on a shelf or something, you would stick out more'n I do with your big jugs."

"Hey," he said.

"Hey nothin'," she said. "And your ass, Bernie. You got a satchel ass. It looks like you got a week's supply of clothes you're carryin' with you when you stand up, you got such a big ass. It looks like Rhode Island when you stand up from the back, Bernie. Like the bottom of your spine was Attleboro and the top of the crack in your ass was Pawtucket, for Christ sake. And it goes all the way down to Westerly, too, before it looks like your legs finally begin at the back. It's your thighs. You look like your legs don't begin until you get to your knees. That's why your ankles're so swollen all the time when you take your socks off and it looks like you was unwrapping sausages. It's because you're carrying way too much weight."

"I'll go on a diet," he said. "Hey, look at Nancy. The hell's this guy she's got on now?"

Maggie glanced at the screen and immediately turned back to him. "This is some guy named Macaroni or something like that," she said. "He wrote a book about solar energy."

"Well," Morgan said, "the fuck's the Dotten broad? I thought it was her you got me up to see and now I'm sitting here taking all this shit about I'm too fat."

"This's the way they always do it," Maggie said. "They have some writer that comes on every day and he talks about his book and they hold it up so everybody can run out and buy it."

"The fuck you gonna read it?" Morgan said. "Spend all your time watchin' guys play the tuba, when you gonna have time read the guy's book?"

"Bernie," she said, "I don't give a shit when you read books. You're wreckin' your health, and I'm gonna talk about that until the Dotten broad comes on and you may just as well get used to the idea."

"I said I would go on a diet," he said. "Jesus, I think you're doing the impossible. You're actually makin' me look forward, hearin' what the Dotten broad's got to say."

"It's more than just losing weight," she said. "It's the stuff you eat, too, that you got to change. In addition to not so much of it."

"I eat good food," Morgan said. "I don't eat no shit like that bloody omelette that dumpy broad was making when I sit down here."

"You eat food that's full of cholesterol," she said. "All that meat and stuff. You're going to have a heart attack if you don't watch out."

"There is nothing wrong with roast beef," he said. "And furthermore, you give me all this great stuff about my health, who are you that won't do what the doctor's telling you that *you* should do there, huh? Wanna tell me that? What is this? You go to the doctor and first he tells you that you got to have an operation or you will die, and you say: 'Fuck you, I will not do that,' and then you turn around and he tells you all these things that I should do because I am too fat but I feel fine, and all of that part of it is gospel? I don't get it."

"This is not coming from my doctor," she said. "Him we will leave out of this. This is stuff that everybody knows, that is all over the place and all you got to do is pay attention. Like for example, where you insist on drinking all the time to keep Dealey company on his way out the gate, you want to be careful you don't go all the way with him, right? For this you need zinc. You should be getting zinc in your diet."

"For what?" he said.

"For your stomach," she said. "You should be getting some zinc every day and you don't in your diet. On account of all the drinking that you do that flushes the zinc out your system every day."

"I don't need any goddamned zinc in my stomach," he said. "For Christ sake, Maggie, you want me to galvanize my fuckin' stomach? I don't carry the booze around in it like it was a fuckin' pail or something, you know. It goes through, 'way I understand it, and that's it. Zinc." He snorted.

"And you also," she said, "you don't get any potassium, which you also need. You never eat any bananas. I bet the whole time we have been together, all these years, I have never once seen you eat a banana."

"Maggie," he said, "I eat what I eat when I eat it because I am hungry and that is what I happen to be hungry for. I am not interested in becoming a flashlight battery or anything, all right? All I want is to have my dinner. And I will tell you a little secret, all right? I am going to keep on doing that. I am not gonna go in the Claret some night and sit down and Ernie or Dixie comes up to me and I order a fuckin' kid's chemistry set, medium rare. Ain't gonna happen. So stop battin' your gums over it."

"Then," she said triumphantly, "you have got to stop drinking then."

"You just lost me there," he said.

"Like with Dealey and them," she said. "Drinking. Getting yourself smashed every night. What that does is it just washes all the good stuff out of your system, in case you should be getting any of it purely by accident of course, and that is why you are getting daffy sometimes."

"I am not getting daffy," he said, "and I am not gonna stop drinking with Dealey until they put his name up on one of them little black signs with the white letters on it that says *Friends To See* at the top of it and your name goes under that and then they have the little white arrow that points to which room he's in. And you sign the book there on the stand before you go in and tell everybody who's in there that you're sorry that the guy's pump stopped. I know Billy Dealey a long time and I know a lot of guys with Billy Dealey that happen to know that I know Billy Dealey a long time. And what he done for me and Wilfred. And I am not gonna make myself look like some kind of asshole that all of a sudden forgot what Billy Dealey did for a whole bunch of us when he could've just stood up and spilled his guts and got every one of us in a whole mess of shit. Uh uh, I'm way too old to start acting like that, I'm gonna call in sick all of a sudden now when Billy Dealey's lookin' for a little moral support, his old pals he went to the can for."

"Bullshit," Maggie said. She sat up straight and folded her arms. "I was workin' there at the time all that shit was happening, remember. I was right there in Wilfred's office and I knew exactly what was goin' on. And Billy Dealey wasn't no big hero when that happened and that stuff about the Turnpike started. You can maybe sell somebody else the idea that he was Gene Autry or something and he saved everybody from going to prison there, but I know it ain't so and so do you, and I ain't buyin' it."

"Well," Morgan said, "then you are wrong, is all. Because he did. If Billy Dealey, all he had to do was say that Wilfred and them was behind what he was doing with those contractors, Maggie, and it would've been 'Good Night, Ladies' and 'We'll see all you guys in the shop where they make license plates before too long.' That first crime commission there, Maggie, you maybe forgot but there's a whole bunch of us that didn't, all right? Those guys were serious, Maggie. Ames and all them other bastards. They had the wind up them and they were gonna hang every one of us if they could just fit the goddamned ropes around our necks there. And it was Billy Dealey that stood up and took the blame for everybody."

"He didn't have no choice," she said. "He was in that scam up to his balls."

"And he got caught at it," Morgan said. "He happened to be the one guy that they nailed about fifteen minutes after they came out of the box. And he had two choices. He could trade everybody else and if he would've, they wouldn't even've charged him with anything. Never mind send him to prison and also take away his ticket, practice law, for life. Which the bastards did. They would've made him into the fuckin' Prince Galahad of the fuckin' Commonwealth, for Christ sake. Sterling silver goddamned squealer and given him a job for life."

"He couldn't've stayed here," she said. "Somebody would've run over him or something if he'd done that."

"Christ sake, Maggie," Morgan said, "stay here? If he would've done what they wanted, he could've done anything he wanted, anywhere in the world. You know what those families got, the businesses they got? You like Chinese food? They got a branch office of the family bank in Hong Kong that they can send you to. They make the fuckin' Mafia look sick, them Wasps. Ride around in a fuckin' ricksha all day and eat rice till your fuckin' eyes slant. Don't wanna leave the country, good old U.S. of A.? Fine. Texas suit ya? We got Texas. Go down to Houston there and dig oil wells or something. They got stuff in the Caribbean and they got stuff in South America and if you like cathedrals or you always wanted to live in Rome and eat spaghetti with the fuckin' Pope, they can also find something for you there. They had a price on Wilfred's head then, Maggie, and also one on mine, which was lower but still would've been just about anything Billy Dealey could've dreamed up that he wanted for giving them my scalp. All he hadda do was swallow and say he would testify about what I had done with them guys that had a lot of trucks and plows and stuff and wanted some of that money. And understood they could have it if they shared some of it. And he could've been their lawyer in fucking Buckingham Palace if he wanted for the rest of his life. And he knew it, too. And he still didn't take it. He come to me one day in Wilfred's office when old Wilf was really startin' to get the shingles flyin' off his roof there, and he told me. You know that. Wilf didn't go nuts because he got old there, for Christ sake. He got old because he was goin' to the fuckin' can until Billy took the fall, and he knew it. And after that was when he went nuts. Fuckin' Ames and his fuckin' asswipe Yankees. They drove old Wilf nuts and they would've probably driven me nuts too, if Billy hadn't stood up and stopped them.

"No, Maggie," Morgan said, "Dealey is a go-through guy. And now it is the time to stand up for Billy Dealey, and I am gonna do it and so is everybody else that oughta do it, and if I catch any guys that should but don't, I will remember them and take care of that after Billy's out of the way."

Nancy came back on after a commercial for real estate brokers who wear gold blazers and buy any houses they can't sell within a set period of time.

"Now," Nancy said, smiling brightly as the camera dollied back from a conversational grouping where she sat with a grey-haired woman in a tailored blue suit and a white silk blouse, and a small brown man who wore a brown tweed sport coat and a brick-colored knitted tie, "after all that excitement it's time for us to consider the problems of those less fortunate than ourselves. I think we often tend to put the sick and the ailing out of our minds and just go about our work each day, taking care of our families and doing our own little jobs, and never even think about people who can't take care of themselves. Don't you agree?"

"No," Morgan said. "Half the people I meet every day are assholes who can't take care of themselves and spend all their time as a result going around and fucking everybody else up."

"Shut up, Bernie," Maggie said. "I want to hear this."

"She's the one asked the question," Morgan said. "I was just an-swering her."

"With us today," Nancy said, as the camera closed in on the woman, "are Doctor Helen Dotten, M.D. Doctor Dotten is the deputy chief of psychiatry at the Knox State Hospital in Proctor, Massachusetts. Am I right there, Doctor?"

"Who's the little brown motherfucker?" Morgan said. "I never saw him before."

"Shh," Maggie said.

"That's essentially correct, Nancy," Doctor Dotten said, shifting in her easy chair and tugging at the hem of her skirt. She smiled nervously and touched the hair at the back of her right ear. She pursed her lips. She folded her hands at her waist. "Basically what I am is Doctor Khan's assistant at the Knox Hospital, and at several other Massachusetts State Hospital facilities as well."

"Right," Nancy said, smiling dazzlingly as the camera switched to the small brown man, "and this is Doctor Ahmed Khan, M.D., is that right, Doctor?"

Morgan leaned forward and stared at the screen. "He's a fuckin' Indian, for Christ sake," he said. "He's one of those shifty little bastards from India that's always coming over here and going the Harvard Medical School and always yappin' and hollerin' about we got to send every fuckin' dime we got to India because all his people're starvin' to death and they barely got energy enough left to spend all their time fuckin' their brains out. And makin' more little brown babies that can starve to death unless we all take off all our clothes and sell our cars so we can feed them."

"Shut up, Bernie," Maggie said.

"That's right, Nancy," Dr. Khan said, writhing in his chair but keeping his face impassive.

"Are you a Pakistani, Doctor?" Nancy said. "From Pakistan, I mean?"

"The fuck difference does it make, for Christ sake," Morgan said. "Goddamned little groundhogs wiggle their way into this country, they're like eels. They're all gonna get to be hotshot doctors and go back to India or wherever the fuck they come from and make all the sick people better with all the medicine they learned here. Yes, sir. And then you turn your back on them a minute and they've graduated and they've got all the fifty-thousand-dollar-a-year jobs we set up in our hospitals for *our* doctors to take. And then they start bitchin' about that, how we're discriminatin' against the little bastards that didn't go home like they said they were gonna, because we're only payin' them enough for one Mercedes and their wife's got to drive a Thunderbird or some cheap American car like that."

"Indian," Dr. Khan said. "I am from India, Nancy." He managed a very formal smile.

"India," Nancy exclaimed. "And I know our viewers will be interested in this, you went to medical school in this country, Doctor Khan?"

"Course he did," Morgan said. "Get over here and suck off the Americans all the way through school, us payin' the way, and then when he gets out he knows where to go to land a nice soft state job and get his first fuckin' Mercedes. New ruby for the wife's forehead, probably, too. The fuck's he want now, a yacht?"

"Yes, Nancy," Dr. Khan said, "I went to university at Cambridge and then medical school at Boston University."

"Oh, pisser," Morgan said. "Cocksucker hasn't been back that sewer he came from since he got out, and he isn't goin' back either. He ain't a fool, Nancy. He's fuckin' little grabber that likes what we got one shit-load of a lot better'n he likes what he left back home. He ain't god-damned fool enough to go back and leave all this. Bitch about it, sure, but try and get him leave any of it."

"Oh," Nancy said, "so you got your bachelor's degree at Harvard and then your medical degree at BU."

Dr. Khan looked diffident but determined. "Ah, actually, no, Nancy," he said. "I matriculated at Cambridge University. In England. I took my baccalaureate there, and then I came to this country. To study medicine."

"Sure," Morgan said, "that's why he's bitchin' now. Probably had a fuckin' Rolls-Royce when he was over there. 'S why he's mad now. Mercedes's a comedown for the little fucker."

"Oh," Nancy squealed, clapping delightedly, "Cambridge, *England.*"

"Yes," Dr. Khan said. He smiled agreeably.

Nancy reached forward across Dr. Dotten who leaned back slightly to let her by, and touched Dr. Khan on the left arm. "Because you see, Dr. Khan," she said, "with our viewing area, which includes Cambridge, *Massachusetts,* of course, I just assumed that when you said *Cambridge,* you meant *Harvard.*"

"Yes," Dr. Khan said, smiling less comfortably.

"Well," Nancy said, sitting back and smoothing her skirt, smiling into the camera, "now that we have our little geography lesson for the day all straightened out, for all of our viewers, not only the ones in Cambridge, Massachusetts, but also for those in Providence; Burlington; Keene, New Hampshire; Portland; and of course all our dear friends in the Maritime Provinces who tune us in every day and are so faithful about telling us how much they enjoy the show, we'll want to hear of course what Doctor Dotten has to tell us about these poor unfortunate people." Nancy held up her right index finger. "But, before we get to what Doctor Dotten has to tell us, and I believe you have some tapes with you that actually show the conditions you're going to be describing, is that right, Doctor Dotten?"

"Yes," Doctor Dotten said grimly.

"We'll hear these important messages," Nancy said. The camera dollied back and Nancy could be seen chatting animatedly with Dr. Khan as a commercial for a toilet bowl cleaner replaced them on the screen.

Morgan looked at Maggie and laughed. "I got to hand it you, Maggie," he said, "this is really gonna help me when I talk to this broad today."

"Cut it out, Bernie," Maggie said irritably.

"I mean it," Morgan said, chortling, "this broad's tippin' her hand left and right to me, being on this television show here with good old Nancy like this. So far I found out that her sidekick there was on the British tit before he got on the American tit, and that they got some home movies of the poor slobbering bastards they're supposed to be taking care of. Which they are gonna show me as soon's they make sure there ain't no shit stains in my toilet. I mean, this is real progress, Maggie. This is the kind of stuff that sort of takes your breath away, am I right? Makes you understand how many things there are that you don't know shit about."

The toilet bowl cleaner ad ended and one for paper towels came on. "Maybe," Morgan said, "maybe they'll have some pictures of Wilfred pattin' his dogs, you think, Maggie? It's been years since you've seen old Wilf. That oughta give the old heartstrings a tug, they show Wilf sittin' there with his thumb up his ass and some goofy look on his face. Really make the day, huh, and these two assholes lettin' old Nancy there use them to entertain the herrin' chokers up in Nova Scotia with their home movies of the poor ninnies in the home they're gettin' paid for takin' care of, 'stead of runnin' down to Boston and bein' on television, huh?"

Maggie sniffed. "I liked Wilf," she said.

"Well, I know that," Morgan said. "That's what surprises me, you know? That this kinda shit don't make you mad, these two shapers usin' him and all the other nutcakes to get more dough out of everybody else for themselves. I would think if you knew somebody that was in the booby hatch and he wasn't gettin' taken care of, it'd make you mad the people that's supposed to be lookin' after him was going around and showing off on TV instead."

She did not say anything. He took another pull of his Bloody Mary. "You know what's gonna happen next, this fuckin' circus you got me watching here? Lemme tell you, because I can tell you without even seein' it. Nancy's gonna come back. She's gonna find out whether Doctor Dotten's hobby's fixing flowers or growin' rutabagas. She's gonna let Doctor Dotten finally say something. Doctor Dotten's gonna say they got a lot of people in the home that haven't got all their marbles and they need taking care of. Doctor Dotten's gonna say we got to spend more money taking care of them because none of the people we got taking care of them seem to be getting quite as rich as they'd like to get from doing it. You got that? It's the same thing every time. Fuckin' Bannerman's got hundreds of these bastards he can call out like the militia any time he wants and have a parade around the State House. It's always the same thing: There's some people that's bad off, which the state has got to take care of, and the state *is* taking care of them, only it's not good enough care because the people that the state hires to give it aren't gettin' rich themselves doing it. So therefore we have got to give them some more money. Fucking process liberals. You find something that's wrong, don't matter what the fuck it is, and then you get a whole buncha assholes to holler about it until we appropriate some money, make it right. And then it's all over. Because after that the fuckin' thing we're fixing never gets fixed whatsoever. It just gets worse. The only thing we can ever do about it, once we start doing something about it, is give more money to the people that talked us into doing something about it in the first place. When according to them it was nowhere near as bad's it is now that we're doing something about it."

The commercials ended and Nancy came back on. "Now," she said, "we're really pressed for time here so I want to get right to Doctor Dotten and what she has to say." Nancy turned to Dr. Dotten. "May I call you Helen?"

"Please do," Dr. Dotten said stiffly.

Nancy put her right hand on Dr. Dotten's left arm. "Helen," she said, looking very earnest, "I think you told our people that you started in on your medical career relatively late in life, is that correct?"

"Yes," Dr. Dotten said, looking irritated. "I went back to school after my children were grown."

"And," Nancy said, glancing at Dr. Dotten and then at the camera, "with so many women today doing just that, I know our viewers would be interested. Had you finished college before your children, before your children were born?"

"No," Dr. Dotten said, sighing and allowing her shoulders to slump. "No, I had two years of college at Syracuse before I was married."

"And then you interrupted your college education to have . . . how many children, Helen?" Nancy said.

"I interrupted college to have one child, Nancy," Dr. Dotten said, straightening her shoulders. She held up one finger. "One child. I had my children one at a time. Not as efficient as in litters, but that's the way I chose to do it. I stopped college to have the first one. I got knocked up."

"Oh," Nancy said brightly, "and then how many . . . what?"

"I got knocked up," Dr. Dotten said pleasantly. "Impregnated."

"What?" Morgan said, slamming the footrest of the Barca-Lounger down on the floor and springing forward in the chair.

"Oh," Nancy said, putting her right hand to her throat.

"Yes," Dr. Dotten said. "In those days, this was back in the middle fifties, Nancy, as I'm sure many of your viewers out in the woods will remember very well, and when college and pregnancy outside of wedlock coincided, college got the quick shuffle and the girl got married. That was what I did. I finished my sophomore year and was married and had the baby. Lovely baby, I must say."

"Yes," Nancy said uncertainly.

"I had two more after that," Dr. Dotten said. "Became pregnant with them in the same fashion that I'd gotten pregnant with the first one. I'm sure several of your viewers are themselves familiar with the procedure. But then, of course, I was married. So it was less, well, shall we say *hectic*. I had the little gold band, you see, so that made it all right."

"Yes," Nancy said, glancing desperately from side to side. She cleared her throat. "And then," she said, "after your children were grown, you went back to college, finished college, and then medical school, is that right?"

"Not exactly," Dr. Dotten said. "What happened was that I lost the little gold ring. Well, not the ring exactly. The man that went with it. He took off with a younger woman from the Midwest regional office, and there was no way I could compete with her. My kids were away at school by then, had very little time for me, and my husband desperately didn't want a ruckus over the divorce. He was willing to be very generous to avoid one. So I thought it over, decided I'd rather have some money and do as I pleased with the rest of my life instead of spending it hitting the bottle, took the money as the saying goes, and ran. Went to Flower Medical School, and ended up in Knox State Hospital. Where to my astonishment I discovered there actually were people who were more miserable than I thought I was. These people really do live in the pits, Nancy. For them, plain misery would be an improvement."

"Oh," Nancy said weakly.

"That man over there," Dr. Dotten said, pointing to the left of the camera which was trained on her, "is waving at you. He's been waving at you for quite a long time now."

"Yes," Nancy said. She focused to the left of the camera. She arranged herself in the chair. She nodded, twice, firmly. "Well," she said, "I'm sure all of you out there agree that this has been a fascinating visit with Doctors uh, Ahmed *Khan* and Doctor Helen Dotten. Don't go 'way now, 'cause we'll be right back to tell you about tomorrow's exciting show."

Morgan slammed his right fist down on the arm of the chair and guffawed. He doubled over in the chair and laughed. Tears came to his eyes and he choked. After a while he recovered. He looked over at the couch where Maggie sat with no expression on her face. "That," Morgan said, "that was great. That is the funniest thing I've ever seen on television." She did not say anything. "Uh, Maggie," he said, "didn't you think it was funny?"

She seemed to come to. She looked at him inquiringly.

"Funny," he said, "didn't you think that was funny?"

"No," she said. She shook her head. "No, I didn't."

"Good Christ, woman," Morgan said, "when she said she got knocked up? Did you see the look on old Nancy's face? She looked like her vibrator'd just shorted out." He chuckled again. "Christ," he said, shaking his head, "now I really am looking forward to meeting this broad. She's a hot shit."

"She could've been talking about me," Maggie said.

"You?" Morgan said. He slumped back in his chair. "How the hell was she talking about you? Her boyfriend knocked her up in college. They got married. Had kids. He found a young pussy and took off. What's that the same thing as you?"

Maggie looked at him sadly. "It's true," she said. "That could've been Maggie Knox up there instead of that woman doctor, whatever her name was, only talking about her husband running off with me instead of some number in the Midwest regional office. I did the same thing."

"One of us," Morgan said, "one of us is clean out of his mind, and I don't think it's me."

"She couldn't compete with me," Maggie said. "When you got down here. I was younger than she was and more sophisticated. You were here all the time. It was easy. I was right in the same office and I just took Maggie Knox's man. Took him away from her."

"She didn't put up much of a fight, I recall," Morgan said.

"She didn't even know she was in a fight," Maggie said. "Not until it was over, anyway. Wouldn't've mattered. She couldn't've done anything."

"Jesus Christ," Morgan said. He lit another cigarette.

"You know what I think?" Maggie said. She was frowning.

"No, as a matter of fact," Morgan said, "I don't. And I'm not sure I want to."

"Look," she said, leaning forward and gesturing with her hands, "we got to face facts. One of us is gonna die before the other one does."

"Good Christ," he said, "is this where you were going with the bananas and stuff before that broad got knocked up on television there? No wonder I couldn't follow it."

"If I was to bet," she said, "I would bet it would be you. On account of what you do to yourself. And you won't stop. I know that. You say you'll go on a diet and you'll cut down on the booze, but you won't. You mean to, but then somebody gets to buying rounds and you say: 'What the hell.' And the next thing I know you're coming home late again, drunk again."

"I said," he said, "I said I'll . . ."

"I know what you said," she said, "you've said it before. It doesn't mean anything. It's just the way you are, and sooner or later it'll kill you.

"I'm no teetotaler," she said. "I don't claim that. But I'm not as rough on the stuff as you are. So instead what've I got? Cancer in my tit."

"You don't know it's that," he said.

"Oh yes I do," she said. "The only reason I can say I don't know it's that for sure is because I won't let them cut me open to find out. And the reason I won't let them find out whether it's malignant or benign is because I know it's malignant."

"Bullshit," he said.

"No," she said calmly. "I could tell you that a woman knows what is going on in her own body like a man doesn't, because we get reminded every month for so many years. We think about it more and we pay more attention. But you'd just laugh at that. What I can tell you is that cancer killed my mother when she was just a little older'n I am, and my aunt about the same age, and my sister in San Diego's got one of these things, and two cousins of mine died from it. If they knew what killed my grandmother, my mother's mother, in the Azores, they would probably know it was this too. But they don't.

"All the ones that die in this country," Maggie said, "had the surgery. United States of America. Best doctors in the world. Cut off this and then go back later and cut off something else, and go in a year from now and cut out all the stuff inside. And then the radiation and the chemotherapy and all your hair falls out. You look like somebody that they found walking around in one of those German concentration camps. And I don't want to do that. The pain there isn't much that anybody can do anything about, except one person which is you and one thing. And when the pain gets real bad I will do that thing."

"Maggie, for Christ sake," he said. "Don't talk like that."

She shrugged. "It don't matter," she said. "I never need to mention it again. If you go first, you won't know, I will do it. And if you're still around, well, you will know. But you can't stop me. I won't be a burden to you or to anybody else, including me. I am not going to suffer the way I've seen other people suffer, and that is the end of it."

"Cripes," he said, sagging in the chair.

"There's nothing to be upset about," she said. "Nothing that should get you talking to Walter Hackley about me or anything like that, when you come home stinking drunk and he starts pumping you for every piece of information you've got in you. That's just the way it is. And that's what I have to think about and you do too."

"I didn't say nothing to Hackley," he said.

"Well," she said, "somebody did. Because he knows about it. He asked me how I felt a few weeks back, and he asks me now every time he sees me. And until he started asking me how I was feeling all the time, which he never did before, there was only two people in this building who knew there was anything wrong with me. And I know I wasn't the one who told him, so it had to've been you. Nothing you can do about it now. Just don't tell him nothing else we talk about if you can help it, okay? Guy's nosey."

Morgan did not say anything. "The only thing I hope is," she said, "if my number comes up first, I hope nothing happens to you, and I've been thinking about that. You know what scares the shit out of me? That I'll be gone and you'll wind up with that cunt Mulready, just because she's handy."

"Maggie, for Christ sake," Morgan said. "Mulready? You got to be shittin' me."

She looked at him with a smirk on her face. "Bernie, Bernie," she said, "give me some credit, all right? Connie's like a switchboard in the State House. There's not a rep or senator, or any other guy, that hasn't had his plug in her at one time or another. Nobody who wanted to, anyway. Everybody knows that."

"I never fucked Mulready," he said, acting hurt.

She laughed. "Right," she said, "and Ted Williams never played left field for the Boston Red Sox. Don't get too upset, Bernie, huh? It's okay. The women used to laugh about it in the coffee room. Sooner or later, every one of us had to come in and make the announcement. Her man got off the reservation and Mulready was waitin' for him in the bushes, all set to hump as soon as he came by. She's like a thing where they dip sheep. It's like every cock in the State House has to get marinated in Mulready before it's ready to do anything with. Nobody minded. She never could get a man to keep, except for those two jerks she married, and she likes gettin' laid. She's not, it's not like she gets possessive of anybody or anything. It's like she's convinced that somewhere in the world there is a perfect cock, and if she keeps looking for it long enough, she'll find it. She probably will, too, she don't get Dutch elm disease or something first."

He did not say anything.

"Still," Maggie said, "Connie's gettin' along in years now, and she might be looking to the future. Get one cock for keeps while there's still one available for her. And yours'd do as far as she's concerned. Got some power, little money? Not bad. She would set her hooks for you the minute I was out of the picture. And that, that I wouldn't want to see while I'm up there with Billy Dealey lookin' down on our old pals and how they're making out without us. Or maybe if Dealey's gonna be there, looking *up* at old pals and makin' sure there's places saved for them at the roast the devil runs.

"So," she said, "I've been thinking about that, and what I decided was that if I die first, you should go back to Maggie Knox."

"You have got to be shittin' me," Morgan said.

"Nope," Maggie said, "not in the slightest."

"She would fuckin' kill me," Morgan said. "She would wait until I was asleep some night and then she would cut my cock off and watch me bleed to death."

"Hah," Maggie said, "that tells me how much you know about Maggie Knox. She might stick an icepick in your ear, you got her mad enough, but she would never do a thing to harm your pecker. She's too much like me to do a thing like that. Revenge, murder's one thing. That I could understand, and so could she. But that? Spoilin' your own fun is just plain stupid. Guy's liable to live, and there's nothing left to play with.

"Nope," she said, "that's why I'm advising you, Bernard. You don't know nothing about women. So just listen to me, and if it comes to that, go back to Maggie Knox and tell her you've seen the error of your ways and you want to come back home. She'd take you in a minute. Brag all over the place how you come crawling back, most likely, but she'd still take care of you." Maggie stood up, stepped to his chair, and kissed him on the top of his head. "Just like I do, Bernie babe," she said, "you want another juice to get that motor going?"

He seemed to come out of a reverie. "Yeah," he said, "yeah. Jesus Christ, the things a man hears when he thinks that he's heard everything. If I didn't have to go into the office today, I'd stay here and really learn some stuff."

17 The garage at the right of the main entrance to Massachusetts General Hospital was built in layers of concrete connected by broad ramps, wide enough to allow angle parking on both sides and two narrow lanes of slow and carefully driven traffic in the middle. The first floor, which was flat, was set aside for medical staff, as was most of the first ramp, ascending to the second floor.

Herbert McCluskey, the chief of security for MGH, oversaw his outdoor territories from the front seat of a Chevrolet Citation sedan painted white and made to resemble as much as possible a Boston Police Department cruiser. McCluskey did not share the view of publicly employed police officers who disliked the adoption of compact cars for cruising use; he did not travel long distances around the grounds of MGH and he did not regret the loss of comfort, but he was mildly grateful for the comparative ease of piloting the smaller car up and down the ramps.

"Now," McCluskey said to Shaughnessey and Curran, illustrating with his hands as they stood between his sedan and their BPD cruiser on Blossom Street in the warm June morning sunshine, "I am about to enter the garage for my first tour of the day. Make sure my watchful lads did not leave any derelicts dead in the stalls or overlook the bodies of any tasty young lab techs who as usual last night completely disregarded our advice and walked in here around two in the morning all alone and got raped before they maybe got murdered. This is not my favorite part of the day's work, but I like to keep an eye on things, you know what I mean. More than once I arrive and find a young and promising doctor and a young and promising nurse all snuggled up in a sleeping bag in the back of a Datsun Two-eighty-Z, naked as a couple snakes under that broad expanse of glass in the rear window. And I then have to tell them this don't give a comforting impression of our crack medical facilities to the families of sick persons who arrive to see how their loved ones are doing under our attentive care, and also it would be a good idea to ditch the empty wine bottles that they got in there as well. Some place out of sight would be good for that. If the high moral tone means I got to worm that Chevy between the lanes of parked cars that got abandoned more than they got parked, so be it.

"As you know," McCluskey said, hitching up his pants and accepting the light of his Tiparillo from Curran's Bic, "as you know, we have been having a little additional spice around these precincts recently, which is why I asked for you two guys to be here."

"All the sheet said that we got," Shaughnessey said, "was unusual degrees of vandalism."

"True enough," McCluskey said, "as far as it goes. Which is not far enough. As usual. When this whole thing first started, what I thought we had was some disgruntled orderly or something that took a dislike to some arrogant son of a bitch with a medical degree that ordered him around too much. Told him to lick the bedpans clean or something. And he didn't like it, so he stuck a metal nail file in his pocket one night when he was leaving and did a little number on the medic's Coupe de Ville. It had *Kike Suck* scratched in the hood, and while the doctor always seemed pleasant enough to me, he is a Jew and I figured somebody had it in for him. If you are a Jew and you do something mean to somebody, he will, he is liable to call you a kike. Just like if I do something nasty, he will call me a honky mick pig. Jews should know this, and expect it, I think. Too bad, but you got to be polite to your servants now that they got evil dispositions and nail files, if you want to have nice things of your own.

"The next day," McCluskey said, "we get another complaint. The message this time was *Kike Fuck*, which was slightly different although the sentiment was about the same, and it was etched in the trunk instead of the hood, but the Sedan de Ville belonged to a woman named Edelstein who's in research. Still a Jew, okay, but pretty hard to understand how this woman who does research all the time with people that she's known about twenty years and always got along with all right, how she got somebody pissed off enough to mark up her car. No patient died that she could be blamed for. Began to worry me a little. Maybe we got some little Nazi in here I don't know about. I don't like nuts like that. Never know where the little fucker's gonna strike next.

"Day after that," McCluskey said, "two *Kike Sucks* and one *Kike Eat Shit*. Our lad is branching out some. Don't want to get bored, I suppose. Three more Cadillacs, so that hasn't changed, and the sentiment is still basically the same even with the variation in the choice of words. But one of these Cadillacs belongs to Doctor Selby. Doctor Selby has many faults, gentlemen. For one thing he is a prick. But being Jewish is definitely not among those faults. Doctor Selby is about as Jewish as Myles Standish was, and he comes from a better family, too, hear him tell it. And the white Coupe de Ville is the property of Julia Boylan, whose son Matthew is the Catholic chaplain to the sick and dying at Mass General. I never heard no reports about her being Jewish neither. A little casual about what kind of physician rank the mothers of Catholic chaplains're entitled to when they come on their maternal calls, perhaps, but old Julia has a fine eye for fast horseflesh and a perfect willingness to share a hot tip with a broken-down security guard if she meets him now and then, so we don't say anything about it.

"That was the day before yesterday," McCluskey said, "and that got me a little more concerned. Not because my friend Julia got customized but because I am now getting convinced that indeed we got a little Hitler on the loose and I don't know who the fuck he is. Obviously it's a kid that doesn't know the actual names of the people he's getting at. This is somebody who thinks that everybody who parks a Cadillac at MGH is a doctor, and is Jewish, and beyond that he don't much give a shit. So I sit there at my desk and my lads go about their daily rounds escorting the volunteer Jesus freaks and the winos and the bag ladies from out of the operating rooms of the Massachusetts General Hospital that they find their way into where they do not belong and have not been invited, and I decide that this little business in the parking garage has gone on long enough. What I am going to do is catch the little bastard and have a talk with him, you know what I mean, considering he is probably a juvenile and I know what is going to happen to him if I turn him over to the custody of the Boston Police and our one-hundred-percent virgin-wool juvenile court system."

"Nothing," Shaughnessey said.

McCluskey nodded. "Exactly what I figure," he said, "nothin'. I figure what I will do is this, okay? Some time during the day or the night he has got to be in there. He ain't mailin' those greetings to all the Caddy owners. He is delivering them personally. And all of the Caddy owners who are coming in to my office and giving me what-for on account of his activities are doing so around the middle of the morning. Don't get any people screaming at me after lunch. Not about this little gambit, I mean. Got people yelling at me after lunch about other things, of course, never a shortage of people yelling at me, but not about this. The people getting scratched are people that come in before breakfast for one reason the other, like Father Boylan's mother comin' in to receive at his celebration of the Holy Sacrifice and put in a good word with Jesus for the favorite in the fourth at Suffolk, and then leaving after breakfast, for example. Therefore, the little bastard is coming in here about when the chickens get up and he is leaving before it's time for morning coffee. Maybe he's doing this at all the hospitals, and we happen to be his first stop of the day. Like the canteen truck.

"Now," McCluskey said, "it is not for nothing that I spent twenty years on the force in Cambridge learning modern police techniques, am I right? The way you catch your criminal is to outwit the bastard. I figure he has got to go in that goddamned garage to do his dirty work, and the reason nobody ever catches him is that he knows how to get in and get out without anybody spotting him. There is the main entrance in for cars and motorcycles and so forth, which we got covered now. There is the exit out for cars and stuff, around the corner there, which I got two men in a car on. There is the door down at the corner on the Cambridge Street driveway that I got a man standing at, and there is the door on the corner opposite that I got two men at. So I figure what I will do is this, all right? I will get one of the guys from around the corner at the exit there and I will put him here. And I will ask you guys if you will be good enough to go down about halfway on the main driveway and sit there so as to be prepared in case he comes out over the side of the stalls there and starts hoofing it down the street. And sort of watch for him in case he gets away onto city land and I can't chase him no further. And I will go inside and see if he is in there this morning and I can flush the little fucker out of there."

"In your car," Curran said.

"In my cruiser car," McCluskey said. "I said I think this little bastard's got a nail file, but the thought has crossed my mind that he may be using something a little more dangerous, or have such a something on his person if he isn't using it for this artwork he's been doing."

"Very sensible," Curran said.

"I also," McCluskey said, "I also do not particularly desire to take out my service pistol and shoot the little bastard for decorating on the cars. I would like to, don't get me wrong, but somehow I don't think that I'd better. That don't mean I want to discourage you gentlemen from shooting him, of course, if the opportunity should present itself, or that if he decides to get really hard to handle with me, I would not use reasonable force to subdue him."

"Herb," Shaughnessey said, "if you find you have to use reasonable force, uh, use quite a lot of it, okay? I mean, if this fellow should come at you now with a knife or something, am I right? You got what I see as a pretty heavy responsibility here, the lives and safety all these medical people and helpless patients and that sort of thing, and you would want to be sure that you didn't take any chances on him getting away and hurting some poor defenseless citizen."

McCluskey licked his lips and smiled. "Well," he said, "yeah. Of course."

"Otherwise," Curran said, "it sounds pretty reasonable to us. Any time you're ready."

McCluskey lifted his walkie-talkie off the front seat of his cruiser and spoke into it, directing all units to take up positions. Each reported in. Shaughnessey and Curran got into their cruiser and turned down into the driveway leading up to the main entrance of the hospital, their car pointing toward Cambridge Street. McCluskey got into his car and entered the garage.

Shaughnessey parked the cruiser at the curb in the sunlight and put the transmission in park. The radio grumbled along and the early haze of the day made the sunlight shimmer. The morning rush-hour traffic moved bumper to bumper up Cambridge Street. Shaughnessey slumped in the seat, imitating Curran. "Gonna be another fuckin' scorcher," Shaughnessey said.

Curran yawned. "Yeah," he said. He snorted. "Broads'll be out shaggin' their tits all over the river bank today, boy. Oughta plan to hit there about twelve twenty, snap the siren on, and watch 'em sit up and take notice."

"Well, Jesus Christ, I mean," Shaughnessey said, "we got to, haven't we? Part of our regular patrol duties. Got that moped rapist still on the loose and everything, got to protect the flower Boston's womanhood from him, at least. And besides, they'd be terrible disappointed, we didn't show up and startle 'em like always. Probably complain to the mayor or something." He made his voice falsetto. " 'What happened to those nice young police officers that're supposed to startle us everyday just before twelve thirty so we forget we unhitched our bras and sit up with our tits inna breeze, huh? Another budget cutback? We didn't get to air 'em out today.' "

Curran laughed and yawned again. He regarded the garage reflectively. "Gee, Danny," he said, "I dunno about you, but if I was a doc at the General, I'd feel a lot safer carvin' up some opera singer inside that hospital today, knowin' Herbie was on the job in the garage, protectin' my Cadillac from vandals. Wouldn't you?"

Shaughnessey snorted. "Right," he said, "even to the point of using deadly force. Only if necessary, of course. Here you got hundreds of thievin' boogies strappin' on their felony shoes right now in Rox-ber-ree, woofin' down the Twinkies for a long productive day of rippin' gold chains off of well-dressed ladies shoppin' Downtown Crossin', rapin' coeds in the bushes near the jogging paths around Jamaica Pond, stickin' shivs in bread-truck drivers droppin' off bread in Lower Mills, drivin' all the commuters nuts with their ghetto blasters on the Forest Hills trolley, and McCluskey's got a fuckin' posse bigger'n the one that Hoover had for Dillinger chasing one damned kid that don't like Jews or Cadillacs or doctors at the MGH. I tell you, boy, it makes a man feel warm inside, seein' how we allocate our scarce resources of trained law enforcement man-hours."

"I was thinkin'," Curran said, "I was thinking maybe what I ought to do is unclamp the Remington there off the dash and have that old twelve-bore at the ready when this new model Jesse James comes out here tryin' to make good his escape, huh? Whaddaya think, Dan, cut the bastard down with about a pound and a half of double-O buck right at the knees as the felon flees from judgment?"

"I dunno," Shaughnessey said, "McCluskey might be afraid you'd spatter one them Cads in the garage there. Ricochets, you know? That buckshot really bounces on the concrete and everything. Might even bank one off of a pedestrian's belt buckle there and crease a Rolls-Royce in that bin. Then there'd be hell to pay in several languages."

"You got a point," Curran said. "I didn't think of that. Jesus Christ, huh? Ain't that old Herb a darlin' though? I bet old Joe Kennedy didn't have to dodge as many cops as this when he was runnin' in a whole boatload of Cutty Sark during Prohibition. One fuckin' kid."

"That guy down at the corner there," Shaughnessey said, nodding toward the security guard who stood with his arms folded near the green metal door, "I'm getting a little worried about him. Don't know if he's up to this, you know?"

Curran considered him. "He's not what you'd call real active," he said.

"No," Shaughnessey said, "he isn't. He showed a little sign of life there a minute ago when the brunette crossed over the traffic island to the inbound side there and he had a good view of her ass, but otherwise I wonder if he's in the best of health."

"Well," Curran said, "he'd have to be, wouldn't he? MGH cop? Can't be sick—they'd slap a new kidney in you 'fore you could say 'Blue Cross.' Have you back out on the street in time for the big evening rush hour when the panhandlers start bothering all the women volunteers going home."

"I suppose," Shaughnessey said. He was about to say something more when a siren bleated in the garage.

"Aha," Curran said, "looks like we got something." He sat up straight in the seat. Shaughnessey put the car in gear and backed up so that its rear bumper was even with the curb of the exit. Both of them turned to look at the garage. The siren continued. "I do believe he's coming down," Curran said. "Really gets the old adrenaline pumpin', huh, Dan? Just like days in the Mounties, floggin' them huskies across the snowfields, runnin' them thievin' Eskimos to Nome."

They could see the green roof lights flashing now as the cruiser descended the ramps of the garage. "Poor bastard, Herb," Shaughnessey said, "won't let him have the blue lights like the real police officers do. Wonder if he's got his own tank and helicopter yet."

"*Holy shit,*" Curran said, "if this ain't the fastest outpatient I ever saw comin' out, he'll do until the bastard comes along."

Hector Julio Delgado, his teeth bared and his shoulders bent over the handlebars of a silver Fuji ten-speed bike, his legs pumping hard and the tail of his shirt, tied around his bare waist, flapping behind him, shot out of the exit ramp at approximately twenty miles per hour. He took the turn behind the BPD cruiser with his body at an angle of about thirty-five degrees to the pavement, straightened up as he sped past Shaughnessey's side of the car, turned fast through the pedestrian cut in the traffic island in the center of the driveway, rode the wrong way toward Cambridge Street, saw the security officer at the corner of the building, and turned again up Cambridge, riding fast against the traffic for an instant and then cutting across to the lane headed toward Government Center. He forced the white-maned driver of a maroon and gold Cadillac Seville to jam on the brakes as he made the maneuver, pulled over, stopped short, put his feet down on the ground and slumped on his bike, looking at the Seville. He watched it move back into line, the driver shaking his fist and swearing at him. Hector Julio Delgado grinned at the driver. After a while he shifted the bike into low gear and started slowly up the hill, staying about three car lengths behind the Cadillac, stopping at the curb out of the line of rearview mirror vision when the driver did, and taking the same turns up toward the State House in the pleasant morning sunshine.

Herbert McCluskey pulled his cruiser out of the garage and parked it in front of Shaughnessey. He got out of his car with his shoulders slumped, stared at the street where his officer was standing, inspecting his nails, shook his fist, and shouted: "Randall, you sorry bastard. Get your ass up here." The officer looked up, startled, pointed at his own chest, nodded, and started up the sidewalk. McCluskey came up to the cruiser, his face red and his hands clawing at his pants. "Well," he said, "at least I'm making progress, right? Now I've seen the little bastard."

"Yeah," Shaughnessey said, "but you haven't seen much of him and you didn't see him very long. 'Less when you saw him he didn't have on a head of steam like he had when he dropped by to see us. He was *gone*."

McCluskey nodded. "I know," he said. "Don't suppose there was much point in you chasing him, huh?"

"Chasing him?" Curran said, his voice ascending in volume as he spoke. "Where the hell were we gonna chase the bastard? Out into that traffic, for Christ sake? Who the fuck is he, the Lindbergh kidnapper?"

"Yeah," McCluskey said. "Look," he said, "I'm not saying . . . I just wish we could've collared him, is all. He got another car today. Saw him doing it. El Dorado this time. I think it's one of the guys in cardiology this time, and if it's the one I think it is, there's gonna be hell to pay. Guy's wife's a lawyer, too. Probably sue me."

"Well, shit," Shaughnessey said, "it's good for them lawyers now and then, get a little personal taste of crime. Make 'em think twice 'fore they make a whole buncha new rules, we got to take the little bastards out to dinner and a ball game 'fore they let us arrest them."

"Yeah," McCluskey said disconsolately.

"Hey look," Shaughnessey said, "at least you know what the little bastard looks like now. Fifteen, about, right, Dicko?"

" 'Bout that," Curran said.

"Yeah," Shaughnessey said to McCluskey. "We didn't get what you'd call a good long look at him, but the light was good and I could recognize him. Latino. Fifteen or so. Maybe a hundred and forty pounds or so, no more'n that. Black hair, no scars visible, blue jeans, grey silk shirt tied at the waist."

"And a *very* good bicycle rider," Curran said.

"Yeah," Shaughnessey said, "very good bicycle rider. Last seen going for a ride with the Speaker of the House of Representatives."

"Huh?" McCluskey said.

"Morgan," Curran said, leaning across the seat. "Bernie Morgan." He sat back up again. "You thought it was his car too, huh, Dan?"

"Yeah," Shaughnessey said. "Looked like that barge of his anyway." To McCluskey he said: "Morgan was drivin' to work. Kid slipped into the traffic and followed him."

"Huh," McCluskey said, "better watch out. Kid'll have him Jewed by midnight."

"Yeah," Shaughnessey said, putting the car in drive. "Well look, huh? We'll be running along. Whyncha see anybody in the hospital knows anything about that kid, huh? Might get a line on him. Find him, can't be much tougher'n catchin' him."

"Worth a try," McCluskey said, "worth a try, I suppose. Give Doctor Scalley something to think about besides my job, when he finds out about his El Dorado."

18 Meredith Hawkes was used to dealing calmly with agitated reporters who arrived excited to see David Pucci. She did it by delaying and distracting them. She caused the delays with her earphones, which her nephew had converted from their designed use with a Sony Walkman to fit the editor's dictation recorder; when she had them on, she could not hear what anybody in the outside world came in

and said to her, and she made it a practice not to remove them until she had finished the paragraph that she had started or the visitor had visibly calmed down. The distraction she accomplished by choosing jersey and silk clothing which clung to her figure; this morning she was wearing a rose-colored dress with a deep neckline and a gold chain that dipped into her cleavage where a little lace showed. She made Joe Gillis wait for several moments, shifting his weight from foot to foot and snuffling, while she typed up Pucci's humorous remarks to be delivered ad lib to the semiannual meeting of the New England Society of Newspaper Editors on Nantucket Island. When she was satisfied that she had kept him waiting long enough, she took the earphones off and tossed her hair.

Joe Gillis spoke while looking at his watch. "I had an appointment," he said. "An appointment to see Mister Pucci at ten. You made it for me yesterday."

"I know," she said, "and I'm sure he'll apologize to you himself. It was just that by the time he found out he'd be delayed and called in, it was too late for me to get in touch with you."

"Oh," Gillis said. "Do you know what it was?"

"Yes," she said. "Squash."

"Squash," he said.

"Yes," she said. "Mister Pucci called me from the Harvard Club and told me his squash tournament game had been rescheduled for one hour later and he'd be in after that. And to please get in touch with you and postpone your meeting. He will be here, I assure you."

"Yes," Gillis said.

"You and Mister Rosen, both," she said. "I missed him too, as it turned out, but he called in from wherever he was, so he got the message."

"Rosen," Gillis said.

"Yes," she said. "Leo Rosen."

"I asked Mister Pucci for an appointment yesterday afternoon," Gillis said. "When I heard from the desk that my column interpreting the Putter appointment wasn't wanted, I called here and I talked to you and I asked you if I could speak to Mister Pucci and you said that I could."

"I remember that," she said.

"So do I," he said. He nodded vigorously. "Vividly. I spoke to Mister Pucci and he said that he would see me here at ten. And now here it is nearly ten forty-five and he isn't here yet."

"That's correct," she said. "As I told you, Mister Pucci's squash game was pushed up and he was delayed. He called and asked me to call you and I called your home but you'd already left. I think it was your wife I spoke to."

"My wife's name is Claire," he said firmly.

"Yes," she said, "your wife. Claire."

"Well," Gillis said, "I had. I had my grey slacks at home but I had to stop at the cleaners." She looked puzzled. "To drop off my suit and to pick up my jacket," he said, fluffing the lapels. "I spilled something on it at one of the functions I attended for the paper."

"Yes," she said.

"That was why I left early," he said. "Wasn't home when you called."

"Well, Mister Gillis," she said, "there's no real harm done. He will be here. All you have to do is wait a few minutes more, and he'll be here."

"But Rosen," he said.

"Leo Rosen," she said with a hint of impatience.

"I know who he is," Gillis said. "What I want to know is why he's coming in here for this meeting with Mister Pucci when I was the one who requested the meeting with Mister Pucci in the first place."

"I don't understand," she said. "Mister Pucci told me to call Mister Rosen and tell him to come in after Mister Pucci talked to you yesterday."

"But," Gillis said desperately, "it was my meeting. I was the one who asked for it."

"I know that," she said.

"Well then," he said, "why does Mister Rosen have to come in for it?"

"Because Mister Pucci asked him," she said. "Or rather I did, on Mister Pucci's orders."

Gillis's shoulders sagged. "Miss Hawkes," he said, "I've been working here, for the *Commoner*, for a little over thirty years. I started here as a copyboy. I worked for Mister Pucci's uncle."

"I know that," she said. She smiled again. "Sometimes like this I bet it seems like you've spent the whole thirty years just waiting for one or the other of them to get his appointment book straight."

Gillis waved his hand. He turned to the window again. He unbuttoned his blazer and put his hands on his hips. He chewed his lower lip. Through the cut in the curbs that led into the entrance roadway he saw Leo Rosen come into the driveway on his black Kawasaki. "And there he is now," he said.

"Well," she said, "you can straighten it all out with him then. He should be up here in just a few minutes." She inserted a fresh piece of stationery in the typewriter and lifted her earphones preparatory to putting them back on.

"Miss Hawkes," he said, turning to her again, "this is Rosen that's coming. Not Mister Pucci."

"But I told you Mister Rosen was coming," she said.

Gillis's face was getting red. "Miss Hawkes," he said severely, "my column was bumped again today."

"Yes," she said.

"This was the third Wednesday in a row," he said.

"Yes," she said.

"Perhaps you're not aware of the significance of that," Gillis said.

She shrugged. "Far as I'm concerned," she said, "means Mister Pucci and the others decided they needed the space more for something else."

Gillis looked stricken. "Miss Hawkes," he said, "when I was breaking in to this business, which was not all that long ago, a column was something that you earned. I earned my regular column. My two during the week and my Sunday piece. Nobody gave it to me."

"Yes," she said patiently.

"A column is a particular voice that you develop over the years," Gillis said. "It becomes a part of your identity. In addition to the regular contributions of hard news, the facts, the column is your opinion of the meaning of the facts. Analysis."

"Yes," she said.

"Having it means that you are an expert on your particular beat," he said.

"Yes," she said.

"That confers a certain status upon you as a reporter on that beat," Gillis said. "In addition to reporting what is happening, you are also a critic of what is happening. Your ability to get at the facts is enhanced by the power that you have to put them in their proper perspective for the readers. Your sources are more cooperative, careful to see that you are kept fully informed."

"Yes," she said.

"When the column is bumped once," Gillis said, "that is one thing. Understandable. And of course when you go on vacation and another writer fills in. That, too, also understandable. But when, as has happened to me, the column is bumped three times when you are here, the only possible inference that the reader can draw is that you no longer enjoy the full confidence of your editors, as a critic. That you are being downgraded. You see?"

"Yes," she said.

"Well," Gillis said. "That is what I wanted to talk to Mister Pucci about. My column has been given over three Wednesdays in a row to Mister Rosen. I think I am entitled to an explanation. Don't you?"

"Seems pretty obvious to me," she said. "They thought what Rosen wrote was more important than what you wrote, so that was what they printed."

Gillis went pale. His mouth worked and nothing came out. He fluttered his hands.

"Are you all right?" she said.

He swallowed twice and nodded.

"Can I get you something?" she said. "Glass of water or something?"

He shook his head negatively.

Rosen came through the city room and into the reception area. His beard was unkempt and his necktie was loose at his collar. He wore an unzipped, blue nylon windbreaker, clean chino pants, and desert boots. He tapped on the glass of the partition as he came in. "Hey, Merry," he said cheerfully, "Joe. Hotter'n a bastard out there."

Gillis stared at him. Hawkes came out of her seat and started toward Gillis. Gillis's eyes bulged. He teetered. "Jesus Christ," Rosen said, "the hell's the matter with you, Joe?" He stepped forward toward Gillis, who raised a hand feebly to keep him back. Hawkes came at him from the side, took him by the left arm, and steered him backward to the Naugahyde chair behind him. He sat down heavily, making his fluttering movements with his hands. She bent and loosened his tie. "Merry, for God's sake," Rosen said, "he having a heart attack or something?"

"I don't know," she said, "get Mrs. Bowles down from the infirmary, pronto. Extension's on the Rolodex."

Gillis fainted, slumping in the chair.

Gillis came to with Mrs. Bowles standing over him, armed with smelling salts. Flanking her were Rosen, Hawkes, and Pucci. The glass partitions were crowded with onlookers who had left their desks in the city room to watch. Gillis shook his head. "Shit," he said weakly.

Hawkes, Rosen, and Pucci asked in chorus: "Are you all right, Joe?" Mrs. Bowles thrust the smelling salts at him and he pushed them away. She grasped his left wrist and began to time his pulse. "Any pain in the left arm, Mister Gillis?" she said, staring at her watch. "No," he said.

"Any constriction in the chest?" she said. "Uh uh," he said. "Nausea?" she said. "No, no," he said, shaking his head impatiently. "Don't shake your head," she said. She put his wrist down. "Your pulse is a little rapid," she said, "nothing serious. Look up." He looked up at her. "Yes," he said. "What day is it?" she said. "Wednesday, goddamnit," he said, "the day my column's supposed to be in, and it isn't."

Pucci laughed heartily at that, and slapped Rosen on the shoulder. "He's okay, Mrs. Bowles. He's concerned about his column, he'll be all right."

"He said that's what he wanted to see you about, Mister Pucci," Hawkes said.

"No reason why he can't," Pucci said. "You feel up to it right now, Joe? Or do you want to put it off, take the rest of the day off and come in tomorrow, talk about it?"

Gillis shook his head. He swallowed. "May I have some water, please?" he said. Hawkes handed Bowles a paper cup of water. Gillis drained it.

"You're starting to get your color back now," Mrs. Bowles said. She addressed Pucci. "I think he'll be all right now, Mister Pucci," she said. "This hot weather. Salt deficiencies sometimes. Fairly common. You do any physical work outdoors today, Mister Gillis?"

He nodded. "Changed the oil in my car, 'fore I came in," he said. Mrs. Bowles nodded sagely. "That's probably it," she said. "Take it a little easy until you get straight on your pins, all right? I'll send a Coke down to you. Get that blood sugar back up." The onlookers began to drift away from the glass. "You'll be all right," she said again.

Somewhat elaborately, Pucci stood aside to let Gillis pass into his office first, followed by Rosen. Pucci, his face flushed and the ends of his hair still damp, went in last, removing his tan poplin jacket, which he hung carefully on the coat tree just inside the door. Rosen and Gillis sat down at the editorial conference table. Pucci, fussily taking a pen and notepaper from his desk, took his usual chair at the head of it.

"Well," Pucci said, inclining his head toward Gillis, "in a dual sense of the phrase, Joe, you're the cause of all this excitement today, the one who asked for the meeting as well as the conductor of the preliminary exercises, as it were." He grinned. "So, if you feel up to it, why don't you begin."

Gillis looked at Rosen with distaste, then at Pucci. He nodded and cleared his throat. "Yes," he said, "I think I can manage. Now," he said, leaning back in his chair and unbuttoning his blazer, frowning, resting his left forearm on the table, drumming with his fingertips, "as you know, Dave, I've been here a long time. Am I right?"

Pucci beamed and nodded several times. "Well yes, Joe," he said, "yes indeed. One of our oldest employees. In terms of service, I mean."

"And that," Gillis said, "well, unless I'm very much mistaken, that gives me a certain amount of seniority around here."

"Yes," Pucci said enthusiastically. "Yes," he said, "close to thirty years, if I'm not mistaken. I won my squash match, by the way." He beamed again.

"Congratulations," Gillis said perfunctorily. "Yeah," Rosen said.

"Puts me in the quarter-finals," Pucci said. "First time in about six years. They say you lose the old snap on it, when you get older, but damned if I don't seem to be getting mine back." He winked. "Better tell the girls to watch out, huh?" He laughed.

"Yeah," Gillis said. "Congratulations," Rosen said.

"Well," Pucci said, "what were we talking about here? Some seniority claim, was it? Let's see if we can't get that out of the way first."

Gillis steepled his fingers. He peered at them. "Dave," he said, "I've always felt that the best way to go about things around here has been absolutely straightforward about what's on your mind, am I right?"

"Absolutely," Pucci said. "If we have one firm company policy here, that's always been the keystone of it. And as far as your seniority's concerned, Joe, some matter of vacation time preference or something like that, well, all we have to do is consult the starting date when you and the other fellow, whoever it may be, Joe, regardless of who it happens to be, and we'll soon have it ironed right out to everybody's satisfaction. No reason for any doubt on an issue like that, and we don't want any."

"Well actually, Dave," Gillis said, "it's not as simple as that. A vacation preference, I mean. It's the column."

"The column," Pucci said. He frowned. "You know anything about this, Leo?"

Rosen stared at him. "Uh uh," he said.

"Gee," Pucci said, "I, uh, I haven't heard anything about the column."

"Well," Gillis said, "you wouldn't actually have to hear anything, Dave. What it is is, the column's been bumped the past three weeks. I assume you made that decision. Were aware that it was made, anyway. Approved it."

Pucci gazed at him. "Well, Jesus Joe, I mean, you really shook me.

Wasn't there a 'State House Viewpoint' in today?" He grinned. "I know *I* thought there was, and I certainly should've missed it if there wasn't. And anyway, Joe, I thought this was a matter of seniority you wanted to discuss here."

"There was a column," Rosen said laconically.

Pucci leaned back. "Well," he said, "I'm glad to hear that. I thought something must be strange, there was no column and I didn't even notice it. Now, of course, different thing, there was one but it didn't happen, stick in my mind. I always say that column's one of our most important contributions to the local coverage. Kind of embarrassing, it wasn't there and I didn't even notice it got left out. 'Course, in case of a major story or something, hurricane, assassination, that sort of thing, well, that'd be different. But barring fire, flood, or act of God, well, 'State House Viewpoint' is always right there. Has been for years. People're used to it. Expect it."

"And I'm the guy that writes it," Gillis said.

"Not today's, you didn't," Rosen said. "I did."

"No," Gillis said, "not quite right there, Leo. I did write today's SHV and I did put it into the computer. Just like I did last week for Wednesday and the week before that, too. Trouble is, what I wrote didn't get printed. Instead it was something that you wrote, under my logo, SHV."

"With my byline," Rosen said. "Which was where it should've been, because I was the guy that wrote the words that were in the column."

"And that," Gillis said, "which I found out yesterday was going to happen today, was why I asked to talk with you, Dave. Not with him," Gillis said, indicating Rosen, "but with you."

"Hey," Rosen said, rising from his seat, "I didn't ask to come here. I had some stuff I wanted to do this morning at the State House. I'll be glad to leave."

"It's okay with me," Gillis said. "Wasn't me that asked you."

"Hey," Pucci said, holding up his hands as a crossing guard might, "hey, hey, *hey*. What's going on here, guys, huh? I thought we were all in the same line of work here, trying to put out the best possible newspaper we can, right, guys? What's all this stuff about leaving and not wanting to come in here in the first place?"

"I didn't ask him," Gillis said.

"And I didn't ask to come," Rosen said.

Pucci sighed. "Guys, huh? Gimme a break here. I asked you to come, Leo, after Joe asked to see me. I didn't know what Joe wanted. I did know I had something that I've been meaning to bat the breeze about with both you guys, and since Joe, here, was coming in, I thought this'd be as good a time as any, do it. Have we got the seniority thing out of the way, first? Because if we have, then we can get to what I wanted to discuss."

"No," Gillis said, "we haven't. We haven't even touched on it."

"Well, damnit, Joe," Pucci said, smiling and spreading his hands, "you've got to, somebody's got to bring one up before we can do that. Have you got a seniority matter?"

"Yes, goddamnit," Gillis said, " 'State House Viewpoint.' With Rosen's column in it instead of what I wrote. That is the seniority issue."

"Cripes, Joe," Pucci said benevolently, "that's not a seniority issue. Not a seniority issue at all."

Gillis's mouth dropped open. "I don't," he said, "I don't understand. It's not a seniority issue?"

Pucci chuckled. "Well of course not, Joe. Never has been. 'State House Viewpoint' isn't something that you occupy because of seniority. It's the space where the paper's always run a column of State House analysis on whatever seems to be the most pressing political issues of the day. The best-written piece on the most important issues. Not a seniority thing at all." He snorted. "You didn't think that was another damned obligation we just heaped on you when you'd been here a certain length of time, did you? Hell no, Joe. You didn't get any extra money for doing that, did you? Along with the news stories you cover? Course not. And you didn't ask for any extra money, either. Which was nice of you, of course, but I just assumed you had the same understanding of the thing we did. It was part of the State House coverage and whoever happened to do it best for a given day, that's who we ran."

"I don't believe this," Gillis said.

"Believe it?" Pucci said. "Why wouldn't you believe it?"

"I've been writing SHV for almost eighteen years," Gillis said. "When Paul Roan retired back years ago there, I took over for Paul on Sundays and Dave Samuels did the two during the week. He didn't want the Sunday one, and your uncle said I could sort of feel my way into it with the Sundays and then when Dave retired or didn't want to do it anymore, I'd take over the two weekly ones as well. And that's what happened. Dave retired and I took over the whole three of them. Almost eighteen years ago, I started doing that."

"Well darn it, Joe," Pucci said, "my uncle, my God, he's been retired since LBJ was president, for God's sake. You never got any indication from me, did you, that you actually *owned* the State House column?"

"Sure I did," Gillis said. "You let me keep it. You never said anything to me about somebody else doing it. When I went on vacation or something, I was always the one who made arrangements for somebody else to fill in for me. And it always said down the bottom that so-and-so was doing it while I was on vacation. I never had any reason to ask you."

"Well, Joe," Pucci said, "I guess I'm glad this's finally come to light now, this misunderstanding we've apparently had for so many years here. Let's get it cleared up before it goes any further. 'State House Viewpoint' is where we print the most trenchant analysis of political matters that we happen to have on hand for that day. You've been doing it for eighteen years? Wonderful. That means you were earning your keep, Joe, and that's an enviable record you've compiled. Eighteen years virtually without a break.

"But now," Pucci said, "this Ames thing here appears to be heating up, and you know you went with that Hanrihan kid, you had him doped for general counsel back the end of May, I think it was. And then it turns out to be this Putter fellow that Leo here happens to have an in with that nobody on our competition can match. *You* told me *that.*

"Well Joe," Pucci said gravely, "it just seems to make sense to me. You know what I mean, when you've got the issue and you've got a guy who's uniquely qualified to present it, Leo knowing Putter as he does, gee, I think you've just got to run with it. If you're going to put out the best damned newspaper every day you think you can. I think it just makes sense, Joe."

Gillis looked at him. He opened his mouth, closed it, blinked, looked at Rosen, wet his lips, looked back at Pucci, and opened his mouth again. "I . . ." he said.

"Look," Rosen said in a flat voice, "I think what Joe's concerned about here, and I am too, Dave, is just exactly what the hell is going on with 'State House Viewpoint.' "

"Well," Pucci said jovially, "now that, at least, from my point of view, you understand, I don't have any trouble answering that at all." He beamed at each of them.

"Yeah?" Rosen said.

"Well," Pucci said, "I mean, I think I've already answered that. Is what I mean to say. Made my thinking just about as clear as I possibly can on that point. Just what I said."

"You mean," Gillis said, "about the column being the best piece of political analysis that you happen to have on hand at press time."

"Yeah," Pucci said, "sure. What else, huh guys? What else would you expect to get printed? Always go with your best stuff. I mean, after all, that's elementary good journalism, isn't it?"

"Dave," Rosen said, "I don't want to sound dense or anything, but at least for me this isn't answering the question that Joe raised and that I guess I also have, to a certain extent."

"Well, *damnit*, Leo," Pucci said, "hey, let's get it answered, okay? Because I've got Jack Tierney coming by here around noon for a luncheon here with some people, one of those damned nuisance things that you have to do, Governor asks for a working lunch and what're you gonna do, huh? Turn the guy down? I mean after all, we may not agree with everything the guy does, but we still ought to have the latchkey out for him. Good opportunity, too, I think, find out what direction the guy's thinking's taking. Trends, you know, am I right?"

"What the hell's the Governor doing coming here?" Rosen said.

"He's having luncheon," Pucci said mildly. "Nothing wrong with that, is there? Little tomato soup and some veal in the publisher's dining room? These sessions, you can get some important exchanges in the course of them. I think they're valuable. I know, there's a certain amount of dissent on that point around the city room, but I've talked it over with people, and that's where I come down on it. I think they're valuable."

"I've been trying to sit down with the Governor for over, it must be over two months now," Gillis said. "I bet since the baseball season started I've had at least fifteen matters that I wanted to talk to him about, one on one, and get the trends of his thinking. He won't see me. The closest I can get to him is one of his jerk-off press conferences."

"Well," Pucci said, "that's the point, isn't it, Joe? He wants the chance to talk off the record, sound things out and find out what the thinking on them is around the community. Before he commits himself publicly to you and the guys from the *Globe* and the *Herald* and all the television cameras. I think that's a prudent way of looking at things. Sit down and talk with some of the people in banking, real estate, the universities, communications, get a feeling for how things look in the high-tech areas and that kind of thing. Man has to keep a certain perspective on things, no matter who he is."

"Okay," Rosen said, "why wasn't Joe invited to this lunch? I assume you weren't invited, Joe."

"No," Gillis said, "no, I wasn't invited. I didn't even know about it. Matter of fact, one of the things I originally planned to do this morning up at the State House was take another shot at getting his appointments guy to block out an hour or two of time with him for me, so I could throw some stuff at him and see if we could get something a little harder than this fluff he's been dishing out as a steady diet lately. Not that I expected to get very far with it, dealing with that operation. It's like slugging pillows. After a while your arms get tired, and the pillows're just as good as new. The guy just won't see me."

"Well?" Rosen said.

"Cripes, Leo," Pucci said, "I can't do anything about that, if the Governor won't see Joe. I mean, that's his prerogative, it seems to me, whether he wants to block out an hour here for Joe and another hour there for this guy and then one for that guy. I mean, you can see the position it'd put him in. He couldn't do that just for us and not for the *Herald* and the *Globe.* They'd be raising hell over there. Plus the television. Man's got to keep his time free, get his work done."

"No, Dave," Rosen said, "not that. Not why he won't see Joe. Why didn't you invite Joe to this luncheon? And me, too, for that matter, since we're both apparently writing the 'State House Viewpoint' column now?"

"Wait a minute," Gillis said, "I didn't hear anybody saying that. That you and I were both writing the column."

"Well goddamnit, Joe," Rosen said, "as a practical matter, that's where we're going, isn't it? The first one I did, I didn't know I was doing it. Ames made the announcement about Putter, and I'll be candid with you, I pretty much knew it was coming, on account of being close to Putter, so I had the profile and the prediction stuff all done and ready to go on-line. Not for the column, though. I didn't have any idea they'd run it as a column. And the second one, which was really a followup, I basically did that for the Sunday before, and then when it didn't run I just assumed I'd recycle it for a progress report type of thing down the line. But they printed it in the column the next Wednesday. Today's was the first one that I actually wrote, as a column, for the column. But after three in a row like this, I think we have to say that I'm writing for Wednesday, and you're writing for Mondays and doing the Sunday one. I mean, I don't see what other interpretation we can place on what's happened, do you, Joe?"

"Well," Gillis said, "there's certainly no arguing with you, Leo, and you understand I don't have any hard feelings toward you on this matter, I hope."

Rosen made a dismissing wave. "Sure, sure, Joe," he said. "There's nothing personal here."

"Good," Gillis said, "good. Long's that's out of the way. But what I do have to say is this: Sure, you've been writing the Wednesday column, for the past three weeks, and I've been cut down to two, the Monday and the Sunday. But I wasn't aware of any decision being made that that was the way that things were going to be from here on out, and quite frankly, Leo, I don't know how willing I would've been to agree to it, if I'd been asked, you know?"

"Well," Rosen said, "I can understand that naturally, Joe, but the fact of the matter is, and as I said I had no part in things turning out so they are the way they are, but the fact of the matter is that they have turned out so that I'm doing Wednesdays and you're doing Mondays and Sundays."

"Correct, as of this week, at least," Gillis said. "Next week we may open up the paper, both of us, and see where they've got Carnes from Sports doing 'State House Viewpoint.' "

"Yeah," Rosen said, grinning, "or what's-his-name from Arts, the guy that does all the rock groups."

"Okay then," Pucci said, putting his palms on the table, "so are we all in agreement then?"

"I dunno," Rosen said. "What were we arguing about?"

"Doesn't look to me like there's much chance of us agreeing, Dave," Gillis said. "We can't even seem to agree on what it is we don't agree about, to start with."

Pucci laughed and shook his head ruefully. "Well look," he said, glancing at his watch, "I do have that luncheon set up, so let me get to what I wanted to talk to the two of you about, okay?"

"Might as well," Rosen said. Gillis nodded.

"Now," Pucci said, spreading his hands, "what we seem to have on our hands here is a situation where what Leo knows a lot about, which is this colored kid here, Putter, and what you know a lot about, Joe, which is Ames and Morgan and all those guys he's got around him, is we have the situations coalescing, if you get what I mean." He locked his fingers together. "And the way I see it, the best approach we can have is this sort of ad hoc thing that's sort of sprung up these past three weeks or so, if that's what it is, and I think so far it's worked pretty well. So we'll just continue with it and see how it works out on a long-term basis. Whaddaya say, huh? Joe? Leo?" He looked back and forth anxiously and brightly between them. "Good," he said, without giving them a chance to answer.

"Now," he said, "this means, what we are going to want from you, Leo, is that you're going to have to get up to speed fast on this Morgan fellow here, am I right, Joe? Because there's a lot of history here that Joe knows all about and we're certainly not going to lose the benefit of that. Don't want to. So, Leo, I'll want you to get on that motorcycle there of yours and just go bombing the hell around all over the place, and I'll want you to have the benefit of Joe's advice on just where the places are that you'll want to touch bases on. Am I right about this, Joe?"

"I guess so," Gillis said. "I suppose you could begin to make some sense out of Bernie Morgan without ever having been out to Proctor there, but I don't really know how the hell you'd go about it. The guy's a regular capsule of the place he comes from. The people."

"Any special place I should go?" Rosen said. "Particular people I should talk to?"

Gillis shrugged. "I don't envy you," he said. "It's a long ride out there, and there isn't much to look at once you get there, but I think you oughta go to Knacky's."

"Knacky's," Pucci said. "Wasn't he a prizefighter back in the forties, out of Springfield? Seems as though I recall hearing him mentioned. Knacky Driscoll. Something like that."

"That was Knocko," Gillis said. "Knocko Fogarty. Middleweight. Ranking contender out of Holyoke in the late fifties. Got his bell rung once too often. Never heard much about him after that. Naw, this is Knacky. Knacky Kasko. Only thing I think he ever did was run this joint. It's in Mercer."

"I thought Morgan was from Proctor," Rosen said.

"Right," Pucci said, "right. Proctor. So'd I. Isn't that right, Joe?"

"That's where he's from," Gillis said, "but that's about all Proctor is now: where Morgan comes from. Used to be a joint there where all the boys hung out. He was the bouncer there and then he ran the joint. Right after the war. It's in the clips. I did a long takeout on him and the joint, I forget the name of it, when Wilfred Knox went daffy and they hadda lock him up, and Bernie took over. Katie's Place, that was the name of it. Burned down, good many years ago.

"Anyway, Leo," he said, "like I say, it's a long ride which I don't envy you none, and it's a pretty tough bar, unless it's changed a lot since the last time I was in it. So watch your ass in there, and I mean that. But that's where Bernie's boys moved to when Katie's Place burned down. They must be gettin' old now, though. Maybe they've calmed down some, like the rest of us have. And, what the hell can I tell you? Ask some questions. Talk to some people. See what they got to say. You're a reporter. You don't need me tellin' you how to cover a story."

"Thanks," Rosen said.

"Okay," Pucci said, exhaling loudly and standing up, "aw *right.*" He slapped his right fist into his left palm. "Now this," he said, "this's what I like to see, huh? This is the way a bunch of guys get together, run a newspaper."

Gillis and Rosen stood up slowly. They started to leave. "You guys," Pucci said as they reached the door to the reception area, "you two guys haven't got anything else on your minds that we can work out today, have you? Because I have got that luncheon I told you about." He was picking up his phone as he spoke.

"Nope," Rosen said.

"Nothing springs to mind," Gillis said sourly.

Gillis and Rosen went out into the reception area and looked out the windows just as the Governor's long dark-blue Cadillac limousine, flanked by two state troopers on motorcycles, turned in the roadway, followed by two unmarked white sedans. They stood and watched the motorcade glide down to the entrance. Hawkes, having glanced up and smiled, resumed typing.

"The Governor," Gillis said. "Take a good look, Leo. He's right there. Governor of the Commonwealth of Massachusetts."

"Right," Rosen said. "His Excellency. Pretty soon he's gonna be right in the same building with me. Eating lunch."

"How about that, huh?" Gillis said. "Hard to imagine, isn't it, the governor eating soup and veal just like you or I would. And right in the same building."

"Yeah," Rosen said breathily. "I'm definitely gonna have to write to my mother and tell her about this one. She'll never believe it. Her own son, just a humble newspaperman, in the same actual building with the incumbent governor of Massachusetts. I might actually get to *see* him." He gulped, twice.

"I dunno, Leo," Gillis said, "you're younger'n I am. I'd want more, 'fore I'd be impressed. I'd want, oh, nothing outrageous, you know, but I think before I'd be impressed I would want to touch the hem of his garment or something. I wouldn't ask too much. Nothing ambitious like maybe have a *conversation* with him. Just touch the hem of his garment."

"That'd be enough," Rosen said. "I'm not sure I could stand it, though. There'd be a definite possibility I would come in my pants."

"The thrill of it all, you mean," Gillis said.

"Yeah," Rosen said. "You know what I'm gonna be when I grow up, Joe? I just this minute decided. I'm gonna be an editor, and then I'll be able to do interesting things all day, like play squash and eat lunch with motherfuckers. Won't that be great?"

"Great, Leo," Gillis said, "great. Say, uh, Leo?"

"Yeah?" Rosen said.

"Did you, uh," Gillis said, "you got any fuckin' idea at all what was goin' on in there just now?"

"Sure," Rosen said. "Dave Pucci just proved that Mother Nature endowed him with two cunts. No pricks; just two big twats." Gillis laughed. "It's true, Joe," Rosen said, "unless I missed something, Dave Pucci has just gotten finished fucking two guys at once, and that has to take dual matching twats."

"Right," Gillis said, "and he isn't even breathing hard."

19 In the residual mist of early morning hubcap-deep around the mobile home and the DeSoto behind the gas station on the Mercer Road, Roger Knox had started the car and backed it up to the garage. He had driven it into the service bay nearest the office, positioned it over the grease pit, shut it off, and gone to work on it. He did this once a month in warm weather, when he kept the old Ford pickup truck with the plow attached and rusted fast in the second service bay, switching the vehicles in their parking places when the snow arrived. Taking care of the old black and white Firedome Sportsman occupied one day of each of Roger Knox's months, and they were the twelve days that he enjoyed most in the year. He hummed "The Caissons Go Rolling Along" while he did it, entertaining himself the whole day through.

He had the Champion spark plugs out, seven of them on the oil-soaked workbench, one of them in the red vise where he was cleaning the electrode with emery paper before checking the gap and replacing it in the cylinder, when Candida brought his lunch out to him. She took the tray into the office and set it, napkin-covered, on the desk. She sat down very carefully on one of the torn maroon vinyl chairs, so as to avoid catching the light fabric of her sky-blue stretch pants on one of the protruding spring ends. She set a bottle of pearlescent-plum nail polish on the ashtray standing next to the chair, opened it, and let the dauber rest in the bottle. She took a pack of Virginia Slims from the tray and lighted one with a cardboard match. With the cigarette in her mouth, squinting her left eye against the smoke curling up over her cheekbone, she began to paint her nails. She crossed her legs and swung her right foot in its white sandal back and forth in time to Roger's rendition of the field artillery's song. She could hear the sound of the emery paper on the electrode.

Candida finished two nails on her right hand before she took the cigarette from her mouth and stopped to admire her work. She blew smoke on her polish and said: "Roger, honey, you comin' for your lunch?"

The humming and the sanding sound stopped in the service bay. She heard him inhale deeply. "Roger," she said, "you hear me?" She held up the two painted nails and inspected them in the light. "Yo," he said. "Your lunch is out here," she said. "I got your lunch ready and I brought it up here for you." "Uhh," he said. She heard the sanding sound resume. "Roger?" she said.

"Well," he said, "I guess I heard you. I'm just tryin', get this here plug taken down here so she looks right to me."

"I declare, Roger," she said, starting on another nail, the cigarette back in her mouth and bobbing as she spoke, "I don't see how there can be anything on any of them plugs. Car hasn't hardly been driven at all since the last time you took it up the hospital and then on down Knacky's, and that's all it's been driven. I didn't drive it any."

"Well," he said, the sanding continuing, "somethin' happened to it. There's some of that varnish buildin' up on the plugs every time I tune her now, seems like. I think it's something they're putting in the gas there. Or leaving out, more likely, anything that was costing them some money. It's probably that. Besides, I drove her in to Springfield that time there when I had to get that goddamned Bendix drive for Peterson's piece of shit there that he calls a Chevrolet. There was that, and that time we went over to Chicopee from Knacky's and seen the State Roll-Offs there."

"Well," she said, holding the third nail up and turning it in the light from the large window, "I didn't go either one of those trips." She took the cigarette out, tapped it, and replaced it in her mouth. "Roger," she said, "you gonna eat your lunch or what? It's gettin' cold sittin' here."

"I don't care," he said, taking the first plug out of the vise, setting it on the workbench, and installing another one. "I don't mind cold food. I had enough cold food, the army and when I was in the hospital there, I thought that's the way it's supposed to come. Cold. Don't bother me none."

"Well," she said, "it does me. I made that food up hot and I don't like to sit here and just see it gettin' all cold like that."

The vise squeaked as he cranked it tight against the flange of the spark plug. "Well, shit," he said, "don't do it then. You can get up and go sit in the house or you can get up and eat it yourself, 'fore it gets cold. Won't matter to me."

"Roger," she said, "if I had've wanted any lunch, I would've *made* lunch. For myself. I didn't make no lunch because I didn't want no lunch. Besides," she said, "I got to lose some weight anyhow. I'm gettin' too fat."

"I didn't notice," he said, sanding the new plug. "I didn't notice you seemed to be puttin' on any extra weight."

"You never notice anything anyway, about me," she said. "You didn't even notice I wasn't on those trips you were talking about there."

"What trips?" he said.

"Roger," she said, starting on a fourth nail, "the one to Springfield you were talkin' about and the one to Chicopee there. I didn't go on either one of those trips."

"Well, goddamnit," Roger said, "I didn't say you did go on those trips. I just said I went on them trips and that was probably why, with the new gas they're puttin' out, the plugs're getting this varnish on them all the time. The car went on those trips. That's all I was sayin'."

"But I didn't," she said, "and that's what I was sayin'."

"Well then," he said, "the chances are your plugs're probably all right. I'll have to take a look at them some time, you want. I'm workin' on the car's right now, though. You'll have to wait, I finish this job, 'fore I can get to you." He giggled once.

"Roger," she said, "that ain't funny."

"Okay," he said, "it ain't funny."

"Well," she said, "it isn't. I don't think it's funny, me sittin' here watching your lunch that I made get all cold and you makin' fun of me like that, won't even come out here and eat it, I go all the trouble of makin' it for you and bring it all the way up here like this."

"Oh Jesus Christ," he said, "all right." She heard him slap the emery paper down on the workbench.

"Roger," she said, "you comin' in here now?"

"For Christ sake, woman," he said, "God almighty, yes, I am comin' in there and eat my goddamned lunch."

"When you do," she said, "I would like a Coke. From the machine there. I am dyin' for a Coke all this time, and you just stand there workin' on your old car all the time."

"Well, goddamnit, Candida," he said, "if you wanted a Coke all this time you been sittin' there naggin' at me to come and eat my lunch, why the fuck didn't you just get up off your ass that you say's gettin' too fat anyway, and get yourself a goddamned Coca-Cola? You know where the goddamned machine is after all these years. It don't run around much, I noticed."

"Yes I do," she said, inspecting the fourth nail, "and I also know for a certain fact that it's been broken all these years and the thing don't work, so you got to lift up the cover there and fish out the Coke from that cold dirty water with your bare hands there. And I am doing my nails anyway."

She heard Roger opening the Coke machine. "I don't see what the hell you're complaining about that," he said, shutting the lid and opening the bottle, the cap clinking into the receptacle. "It wouldn't make no goddamned sense if you was to have to go and take a quarter out the register every time you wanted to get a Coke for yourself, so that then when the man come I would have to open up the coin box there and get out our money that we just took from our own cash register there when we wanted a Coke. I ain't gonna go all the trouble and expense of havin' something fixed that's just gonna result in me makin' more things to do for myself." He came into the office, carrying the Coke. "What in hell you doin' your nails for?"

She looked up at him through the cigarette smoke. "I am doin' my nails, Roger Knox," she said, "so my nails will look pretty in case somebody ever decides that they would like to take a look at my nails. Which I know isn't likely to be you because you never notice anythin' I do to make myself look neat or nice around here anyway."

He handed her the Coke. "Well goddamnit," he said, "then I got the same question which I had before. How come you're doin' your nails? That color looks like you got them jammed. Bruised them, it makes them look like."

She accepted the Coke with her left hand, holding the dauber out away from the polish bottle, and drank from the Coke bottle carefully.

She set it down on the floor beside her chair. "That," she said, "that tastes good."

"Well?" he said. "How come you're doin' that there?"

"Because," she said, "maybe somebody else might see me and decide they would like to look at my nails and see if they liked how they looked." She inspected the fourth nail, was satisfied, and started on the fifth one.

"Well," he said, moving toward the desk, "who the hell is that gonna be, huh? You gonna come out and sit here and change places with me and wait on who comes in for a tank of gas or they want their oil checked or something? You're gonna wreck them pretty nails pretty fast if you start doing that type of thing. What the hell is this?" he said, lifting the napkin.

"It's chorizo," she said, "which you like and you know it." She pronounced it shur-*rees*. "Fried chorizo. And scrambled eggs which if you tell me they're all cold now, I wouldn't doubt it after the way you let them sit there all this time. And some fried potatoes which are by now all greasy. And that's all."

"There's some green stuff on top of the eggs," he said. "You gonna tell me stuff started growin' on them while you're sittin' there tryin' get me to get your Coke for you?"

"That's chopped parsley," she said. "I put it on top there because I thought it would make them look pretty."

"Huh," he said. He sat down. There were two one pint cans of Budweiser on the tray and he popped one open. He drank deeply from it. "Ahh," he said. He looked at the tray again. "I don't see no toast here," he said.

"Yeah," she said.

"Well," he said, "I don't. How come?"

"Well," she said, "I didn't make you no toast. So as a result I didn't put no toast on there and that's probably how come you don't see none."

"Shit," he said, "I got a good mind, you know I don't like to eat my chorizo without no toast. It's too hot for me without no toast to kind of give my mouth a rest when I'm eatin' it."

"Well," she said, examining the fifth nail, approving of it, and starting on the thumb of her left hand. She uncrossed her legs and put her right leg up on the chair so that she could sit on it. She had to stretch her upper body in her yellow tank top to reach the dauber into the nail polish bottle on the ashtray beside her. Her breasts strained against the fabric. Roger stared at them. "Well," he said. "Well," she said, "I got to say that I don't see how that particular chorizo you got there could possibly be too hot for anybody to eat, the way you left it sittin' there about three hours 'fore you decided to come out here and eat it after I went to all the trouble cookin' it up for you and fetching it up here like I did. Your mouth shouldn't need no rest from that chorizo."

"Goddamnit," he said, "it's not the kind of hot that it gets from bein' cooked that I need the toast for. You eat chorizo. You know there's hot stuff that's in it before you cook it. Spices. That's what I need the toast for."

She started on the sixth nail. "You are shit out of luck then, Roger, I guess," she said kittenishly, "because I didn't make you no toast today. Eat them potatoes and eggs with it like you would've eaten the toast if I had decided I would make you some today. Or you can always drink some of the beer if you feel your mouth gettin' hot. You like beer all right, Roger."

"Yeah," he said morosely. He started eating the chorizo. "I'm gonna say something to that guy from the company the next time I see him."

"Who," she said.

"From the company," he said. "The guy that comes here from the company. I'm gonna ask him what is it that is makin' all this varnish all of a sudden? I ain't doin' anything different than I ever did, and I'm gettin' all this varnish makin' up and I want to know what is doin' it."

"I didn't know you was thinking of painting anything," she said, holding up the left thumbnail.

"I ain't," he said.

"Well, varnishing then," she said. She approved the thumbnail and began on the index finger.

"I ain't thinking about varnishing nothing either, goddamnit," he said. "Jesus, this chorizo's greasy. I ain't had anything that was this bad to eat since they gave us that baloney when I was up in the hospital like they give us in the service."

"I didn't think of that," she said. "I should get some of that since you say it tastes the same. I bet it's considerably cheaper'n chorizo, too, and if you can't tell the difference then what is the difference, huh?"

"You start giving me baloney," he said, "and I will personally beat the shit out of you." She laughed. "I mean it," he said, "you just go ahead and you laugh at me if you want, Candida, but I mean it and you just go ahead and try me out if you don't believe me, there. I ain't gonna ever eat no baloney in my life as long as I live again." He ate more chorizo. "Fuckin' stuff," he said.

"You ain't gonna beat nobody up, Roger Knox," she said pleasantly.

"That's what you think," he said.

"That's what I think," she said. "When you gonna have time? You're gonna be painting something that you haven't even decided what it is. Or if you did you won't tell me. So when're you gonna have time, beat anybody up? You ain't."

"I'm not gonna paint anything," he said. "Where'd you get all this idea about painting things?"

"Well," she said, "you said you were gonna talk to some guy about getting some varnish. Ain't you gonna paint something with it, after you get it?"

"I got the goddamned varnish," he said. "Don't you ever listen one goddamned word I say? It's on the sparking plugs. The ones in the engine. It's this stuff that makes up on the plugs and it's got to be from the gasoline that he is selling me. Because I ain't changed nothing about the way I do things with the car, so it's got to be that."

"You don't do nothing with the car, Roger," she said. She finished the index finger and began on the middle finger of her left hand. "Much of anything, anyway."

"I use it for what I want," he said. "I use it for that."

"And that ain't much," she said. "It's like you was rooted here or something. Shit."

"Huh?" he said.

"Oh," she said, dabbing at the middle fingernail, "I just smudged it. Shit. Now I'll have to let it dry and then take it off with the remover and do it all over again. And I hate that remover. It stinks so. Gives me a headache."

"I thought you quit using it," he said. "Because of that. I ain't smelled that stuff around for years."

"Because I did," she said. "But that was because I quit doing my nails. You do your nails, you got to use the remover because you got to get the old stuff off before you put any new stuff on. Or like this, when you smudge it while you're putting the new stuff on. Like I always do."

"Then why're you doing it?" he said. "If you don't like the smell or something. There ain't no need of it."

"I dunno," she said, dabbing at it. "There," she said, "maybe I fixed it." She went on to the left ring finger. "You wanna go out some place, it's nicer if you did your nails. That's all."

"Oh," he said. "Where you goin'?"

"Huh?" she said.

"I said where you goin', goddamnit," he said. "Where're you goin'?"

"Oh," she said, "I dunno. I was thinking I might go with Maggie tonight."

He put his fork down. He chewed for a moment, frowning. He picked up his fork again, pointed it toward the plate, stopped it in midair, looked at her again, stopped chewing, resumed chewing, looked down and then up again. "Where's Maggie goin'?" he said.

"Don't talk when your mouth is full of stuff," Candida said absently squinting at the ring finger. "It looks like you had a whole mess of garbage in your face there that some pigs didn't get around to eating."

"I ain't so goddamned sure I don't," he said, "this shit you're feeding me that I haven't even got no toast to eat with it. I asked you a question."

"I heard you," she said. She started on the left pinky finger. She interrupted and reached down to the floor, picking up the Coke, taking a drink, and replacing it on the floor. She went back to painting the nail.

"Well," he said, stabbing the fork at the meat on the plate so that the tines made a clank on the plate, "answer me then. Where the fuck is Maggie going all of a sudden that you decide you're going with her?"

"I think she said," Candida said, looking critically at the pinky, "I think she said something about going down to Worcester there."

"Worcester," he said, shoving the meat into his mouth and chewing. "Worcester, huh?"

"I think so," she said complacently. "Some place around there."

"What place around there?" he said. "The fuck is there around Worcester?"

"Well," Candida said, putting the dauber back in the bottle and spreading her fingers, "there ain't a hell of a lot actually, Roger. Not when you come right down to it. That I recall, at least. Not . . . a . . . hell . . . of a lot. I dunno, it's been so long since I been there though. Maybe they put up a tall building or something. Be fun to go and see anyway. Trees and stuff're nice, and I like the view down there in the meadow and everything, but it would be kind of nice to see a couple of buildings some time that was more than two floors, you know? And traffic lights and street lights. Stuff like that. Guys walking around with suits on and driving something besides pickup trucks full of shit and hay and dirt and stuff. I could go for that."

He glanced at the edge of the desk where the tire iron lay. He looked at it for a few moments. He looked back at Candida. He licked his lips. "I wanna know," he said, "what it is Maggie's doing down in Worcester that you're tellin' me you're gonna go down there and do it with her all of a sudden, is what I want to know."

She looked at him demurely. "I don't know what Maggie's doin' down in Worcester, Roger," she said. "I ain't got the foggiest idea what Maggie's gonna do in Worcester. She just told me she was thinkin' about goin' down to Worcester and did I think I would like to come along with her, and I said I kind of thought I would. For a change. I'm gettin' sick of it, you and me kitin' off to New York all the time and goin' to shows, dancin' and eatin' out and listenin' to music, you know? It gets so I just get sick all that excitement. I thought it'd be nice tonight for a change, while you're sittin' out here by yourself and watchin' the ball game on television, I might like to go down Worcester with Maggie and see what is goin' on there, for a change."

"You and her're always talkin'," he said.

"Yeah," she said, "we talk." She rested her hands on his legs. She looked down on them. "I should get some of them cotton balls for when I do this," she said, "keep them apart when they dry. Maggie uses them between her toes. I guess you don't need them for your fingers, though. Easy to keep them apart." She spread the fingers of her left hand, then her right. "All you got to do," she mused, smiling, "is just *spread* 'em when you want to, and they go right apart, nice as you please. Stay apart, too."

"What?" he said.

"Your fingers," she said. "You can spread your fingers apart." She held up her hands. "See? So your nails don't touch and smear while they're gettin' dry. Can't spread your toes like that. Maggie uses cotton balls, keep them apart." She slipped her right leg out from under her and placed her foot flat on the floor next to the left one. "I wonder if I should do my toenails. Probably not. Haven't got no cotton balls, spread them apart."

"What do you two talk about?" he said.

"Well," she said, "whatever we want to. Girl talk, you know? What we seen on the television. What this one is doing and that one is doing, that we heard somebody was doing. Gossip. Maggie gets that. I don't get out enough, get around, hear what is going on. But Maggie does. What we are thinking about doing. Stuff like that."

"Well then, goddamnit," he said, "that's what I asked you. What is Maggie doing that she is thinking about going down to Worcester tonight, huh?"

"I ain't sure," Candida said. She smiled. "I don't know as she said, exactly. She said something about them having a sale, down at the Caldor store, I think it was."

"Maggie's going to Worcester to buy something?" he said.

"Yeah," Candida said, "it's possible, you know, that somebody would want to go to Worcester and buy something. People do that sometimes."

"There ain't nothing that they got for sale in Worcester that you can't go in the store right down the street in Mercer and buy the same exact thing," Roger said. "That is a lot of bullshit, that Maggie is goin' down to Worcester and she is going to buy something. Bullshit. I don't believe that. That she told you she was going to do that."

"Well, Jesus Christ, Roger," Candida said, "now you can't just go and say that. You don't know. Maybe they got a kind down in Worcester that they don't happen to have in the stores in Mercer, huh? You ever think of that? Like maybe she wants a refrigerator and all they got in Mercer is a GE and she wants one of them Westinghouses there, one of those things that has the freezer side by side with the other part. Or in a different color, maybe. Gold."

"There ain't no goddamned need of anybody havin' no damned gold refrigerator," he said.

"There is if somebody wants one," she said.

"No," he said. "White. Refrigerator should be white."

She shrugged. "Well," she said, "I can't help that. She's your sister, after all. I just talk to her while she's here waitin' for you to work on her car or something. I'm just bein' polite when I sit and talk with her. Maybe you better tell her about not needin' no gold refrigerator."

"Talk," he said, "and drink. The two of you was half stiff when I finished workin' on her car last time."

"And then there's sales," she said.

"Sales?" he said.

"Yeah," she said, "sales. You know, Roger, when they sometimes decide they're gonna sell something to you cheaper than they was first asking for it? So much off the regular price? So you can buy it and save yourself some money? They do that in Worcester sometimes, I hear."

"You ain't gonna save yourself no money," he said, "driving all the way to Worcester to buy something you can buy in Mercer. That's all there is to it. You got to figure, what, you figure it is free for you to run the car all that way? Springfield'd be closer. Don't have to go to Worcester."

"Do if Worcester's where you decided you want to go," Candida said. "And that's where Maggie decided she was gonna go, I guess, and I decided I would be going with her."

"Yeah," he said. "Well, and I was planning, I get finished with the car, I was gonna take a run up and, I was gonna take Rocky and go up and see Dad."

"Go ahead," she said.

"Yeah," he said, "but I was goin' this after."

"Go ahead," she said.

"Well," he said, "there wouldn't be nobody here, watch the station, you're goin' off to Worcester with Maggie, buy this big gold refrigerator that they got on sale down there, she says."

"So what?" she said. "Close the place up. Won't do no harm."

"Customers," he said.

"Shit," she said, "customers. How many, two? At the most. Nobody ever comes by here in the afternoon anyway, except some asshole, get free air for his tires and maybe pay you twenny-five cents, one bottle Coke. What you gonna lose on that sale, huh? Two cents?"

"Well," he said, "I wouldn't lose nothin', you was here to watch the place like usual when I go up to see Dad."

"Well," she said, "that's true. But I think, I just happen to think my trip to Worcester's more important than that two cents you didn't make off somebody stoppin' by for free air and a Coke. So they'll have to go thirsty if they come in here before you get back from the hospital. They can get Coke someplace else, though. They should be all right."

"I was thinking of going down to Knacky's after," he said.

"Well, Roger," she said, "that is all right. There ain't many people that show up here after five or so anyways. And you generally get back from Knacky's around nine or so, no drunker'n you usually are when you just been sittin' here drinkin' beer all night and watchin' television, so that won't do no harm."

He stared at her for a few moments and worked his mouth. "Candida," he said, "I don't want . . . . You remember what happened, that cop down there."

"Yeah," she said, holding up her fingers and spreading them again. "I remember. I dunno, maybe that middle one, maybe it still is so you can see where I smeared it some."

"Yeah," he said, "well."

"Well what?" she said, putting her hands down.

"I don't want nothin' like that, have to do nothin' like that again," he said.

"You didn't have to do nothin' like that before," she said. "There wasn't no need of you actin' like that, that time. That cop wasn't doin' nothin' with me, was he?"

"No," he said.

"And he didn't say he was doin' nothin' with me," she said. "He wasn't sayin' nothing like that."

"No," he said.

"And that cop," she said, "from what you did to him that you didn't have no damned reason to do, from what you did to him he sure ain't gonna be doin' nothin' with me now, me or anybody else. Right?"

"Well," he said, "there could be somebody else."

"Roger," she said, "I don't see what it is that is makin' you talk like this. I didn't have nothin' to do with that cop."

"No," he said, "it was Maggie he was talkin' about. That was gettin' everybody else talkin' about Maggie."

"Right," she said.

"And Bernie," he said, "Bernie wasn't gonna do nothin' about it, the things that cop was sayin', and neither was Dad. Because they weren't here, and they didn't give a shit. They was down in Boston and they didn't give a good *shit*, neither one of them. They were down in Boston there, both of them, and nobody was laughin' at them when they went in to Katie's for a glass of beer there or something. Everybody was all impressed with Dad and Bernie. I was just up here and it was me that hadda take it all."

"Well," she said, "I told you at the time, and you didn't listen to me and you didn't listen to Maggie, that you should talk to her and see what she had to say about it."

"Well, goddamnit," he said, "I did that. I talked to Maggie."

"Yeah," Candida said, "and then you went and did what you did to him anyway. You didn't pay absolutely no attention what Maggie said."

"I didn't believe her," he said.

"Well," she said, "I don't see what I can do about that."

"Well, goddamnit," he said, "I can tell you what you can do about it, and that is you don't go off down to Worcester with Maggie. That is what you do about it, goddamnit, Candida."

"I don't see what me goin' down to Worcester with Maggie for a sale they got at the Caldor there, what that's got to do with something that happened with a cop all that time ago and probably didn't even happen then. It was probably just something he was saying."

"It was something he was saying," Roger said, "that people didn't have no trouble believing it. People didn't have no trouble at all, believing what he was saying about Maggie Morgan, what he was doin' with Maggie Morgan that was the rep's wife and the Speaker's daughter and my sister. They didn't have no trouble at all believing that, that Maggie was just goin' out and whorin' around all over the place out around here while Dad and Bernie was off down in Boston doin' things. And here I was, still up here, and what, I was the only one left around here that could do anything about it. Was *gonna* do anything about it. That was all. And so I did something about it. But that don't mean I want to have something like that happen again."

"Well," she said, "I don't think nothing like that's liable to happen again, unless people start sayin' Maggie went down to Worcester there and bought a refrigerator and you think Bernie oughta get upset about them saying that and come home and do something about it."

"And I don't want you," he said, "I don't want you goin' around with my sister neither."

She laughed. "Why, Roger?" she said. "You 'fraid I'm gonna do something with Maggie like that cop said he was doing?"

He did not say anything for a while. Then he said: "You know what I'm 'fraid of, Candida." He did not say anything more.

20 "You never saw Bernie in Katie's Place," Costello said to Archambault in the dining room on the second floor of the Algonquin Club. The elderly waiters in black trousers and short white jackets moved quietly about the room, serving platters of oysters on the half shell and vodka martinis straight up with twists of lemon, the humidity condensing on the outside of the glasses.

"Uh uh," Archambault said, toying with a Manhattan on the rocks. "He told me it'd burned down."

"It did," Costello said. "Early sixties, I think it was. It was about a year or two after Kennedy got shot. Jack Kennedy, I mean. It was just the building that burned though."

"No people hurt?" Archambault said.

"Oh," Costello said. "No, no, I didn't mean that. People. Far as I know, there weren't. Don't believe there was anybody in there. In the glory days it was a rooming house on the top two floors, used to take in traveling salesmen and the newest teacher in the grammar school. Until she found a man and got herself married and settled down. Whereupon of course she promptly got herself pregnant, had to finish out the year and quit, and they'd get a new teacher and start the whole process all over again. Otherwise it was mostly transients."

"Transients," he said. "There's a vanishing breed. I wonder if there is such a thing as a traveling salesman anymore. This side of Caribou, anyway."

"Must be," Archambault said. "We get a twisted view of things, being in the city all the time the way we are. I know I feel it, when I stay home a few days. And I'm less'n an hour from the State House, you come right down to it."

"Yeah," Costello said, "but that's what I mean. It's the roads. When Bernie and I were freshmen here, crowding thirty years ago, it would've been unthinkable for him to commute. For me it was a different matter. Millis? No sweat. But for Bernie, Route Nine to Route Twenty and then off even deeper into the woods once he got to Mercer, it was out of the question. The people in his district didn't even think about it, the idea that their rep could possibly commute to the State House. Still don't, far as that goes. Bernie hasn't lived in Proctor since the day he was elected, although when you come right down to it now, there's no real reason why he couldn't. The Turnpike and all. He could be home in an hour and a half easy."

"Well," Archambault said, the corners of his mouth twisting slightly, his eyes fixed on his glass, "maybe your average Joe could do it in less than an hour and a half. Bernie, Bernie might be lucky if he made it at all."

Costello looked at him quickly. Archambault raised his eyes and met Costello's gaze. Costello nodded. "Yeah," he said, "yeah. You're right. I don't like it, but you are."

"It's really gotten to the point, Frank," Archambault said, "the point where . . . look, nobody wants to be the first guy to come out and say it, am I right?"

"You're right," Costello said. He drained his martini and signaled to the waiter. "You want another?" he said, gesturing toward Archambault's glass. "Might's well," Archambault said. "This kind of talk makes a man thirsty." Costello indicated to the waiter that they wanted another round. "It's a problem," he said to Archambault.

"It sure is," Archambault said. "All of us . . . well, mostly all of us, we feel a certain amount of obligation to Bernie, you know? He was there when we got here. In place. Sort of a given, the kind you'd get in a mathematics problem. 'The sun is here and the earth revolves around it. The moon is here and it revolves around the earth. One plus one is two and two plus two is four.' That kind of thing."

"Was Wilfred gone when you got here?" Costello said.

"No," Archambault said, draining his glass and setting it down. "Technically he was still the Speaker, but in actual operating fact, he wasn't. He'd already slipped pretty badly when I came in. Nineteen sixty-eight. The year Bobby'd been shot. Wilfred had the title; Bernie had the power." He shrugged. "Seemed to work all right. Wilf still looked pretty good, even if he was six bricks shy a full load. Couldn't tell it to look at him."

"True," Costello said. "Are you saying Bernie is a different case?"

Archambault considered. He raised the glass again, empty except for the maraschino cherry, and squinted at it in the light. "You know," he said, "you look at the way that stuff congeals on the glass, the only way you can get it all out is to emulsify it, use hot soapy water on it, and you've got to think: this stuff can't possibly be good for us. Looks like oil spill in there. Like an oil slick down near the docks where the tankers come up." He put the glass down. He leaned forward and folded his hands on the white tablecloth. He stared at Costello from behind his horn-rimmed glasses. "Sorry," he said, "once a high-school science teacher, always a high-school science teacher, I guess. You were saying?"

The waiter arrived with the fresh round, served it, and departed. Costello allowed himself a small smile. "Ray," he said, "I asked you to come here, right?"

"Certainly did," Archambault said, smiling. "Henry the Eighth invited Catherine of Aragon to visit England for a spell, too."

Costello grinned. "True," he said, "but I'm not proposing marriage. All I had on my mind was a free and candid exchange of views."

"Yes indeed," Archambault said, raising his glass. "Well, here's to intestinal pollution. Cheers." He drank.

"Am I going to get it?" Costello said. He raised his glass. "Confusion to our enemies," he said. He drank.

"Within the limits of prudence," Archambault said. "One is cautious in the presence of the king's henchman."

"Ouch," Costello said. "Henchman. That has a nasty ring to it."

"It may be a trifle strong," Archambault said, "but as others see you, Frank, it's not far off the mark."

"All right," Costello said, "accepting it for the moment. Would you concede I have a reputation for keeping my word?"

"Absolutely," Archambault said. "You didn't get where you are by letting your gums flap."

"Okay," Costello said. "That understanding then, seal of the confessional."

"Seal of the confessional," Archambault said.

"Now," Costello said, "let's talk about Bernie."

Archambault frowned. He toyed with his glass again. He looked up. "Frank," he said, "the guy is a friend of yours."

"Close friend," Costello said. "Has been for years."

"Nobody wants to hurt him," Archambault said. "Partly because, well, for some people it's the only reason: he's still dangerous. He can hurt you back if you hurt him, and nobody wants to take the chance on getting hurt by Bernie Morgan. Much safer to wait it out, let somebody else bell the cat and take the damage that comes from doing it. Time'll take care of him if none of us does."

"I know," Costello said.

"And nobody wants to hurt you, either," Archambault said. Costello looked at him with disbelief. "I'm not shittin' you, Frank," he said. "I'm not trying to tell Frank Costello that his pals in the legislature worry every day about whether he slept well the night before and enjoyed his modest dinner." Costello laughed. "It ain't because we love you that we love ya, Frank," Archambault said. "It's because we're fuckin' scared of you as well, you get my meaning." Costello nodded. "And that," Archambault said, "is because you've still got some control of Bernie, and when he's in control at all, he's still a force we've got to reckon with."

"I know," Costello said.

"The question is," Archambault said, "the question that's on our minds is how much control even you've still got of Bernie, keeping in mind that nobody else, including Bernie, seems to have any."

"Well," Costello said, "Boston Maggie's still got him pretty well in hand. And Proctor Maggie can jigger him around a little if she has to."

Archambault waved that away. "Boston Maggie's a formidable lady," he said. "They dragged me down to Battleship Cove in Fall River for a Veterans' Day thing about two years ago, and they got me up to the *Massachusetts* and I immediately thought of Boston Maggie. If I ever saw a frigate in a battle dress, she's it. But she hasn't messed with one of us in years. She just takes care of Bernie.

"Proctor Maggie's harmless unless you want the same job in the welfare office that she's got earmarked for some cousin with leukemia," Archambault said, "in which case she's a Tartar, so that takes her out of the picture. And that leaves Frank Costello standing by his lonesome, the only remaining member of the Praetorian Guard. One of us might be able to piss on Bernie's boots and convince him it was rain, but only for a little while, until he could locate you and ask you what it was that made his cuffs all wet. Then the game'd be over, and whoever started it would be the loser.

"The thing of it is," Archambault said, "the more people start to wonder whether even you've got any control left over Bernie, the more likely it is that pretty soon even you won't have any. You can have a guy beheaded now if he gets out of line with Bernie, and you find out about it. Just like you could ten years ago. But there's only so many times you can chop people's heads off, Frank, before you and Bernie're left standing there all by yourselves. You'll win for a while, but there'll be a whole new trible come in to replace the guys you've knocked off, and you'll never get the new guys into line. You haven't got enough of Bernie left to work with."

"This I know," Costello said, "this I know."

"Which leaves me with a question," Archambault said. "What're you gonna do about it? You've got some time left before the floor collapses under Bernie and he drops through out of sight like a stone. Not much time maybe, but some. You can wait it out and retire with him and Wilfred's old organization."

"I'm too young to retire," Costello said. "I've got at least fifteen years of useful life left on the Hill. I'd go nuts, put out to pasture at my age."

"Then you've got two choices," Archambault said. "You can start to ease Bernie out now and get somebody else in before he falls apart entirely, or you can wait for him to shatter into little pieces and hope to God someone succeeds him who'll be moderately friendly toward you."

"Take my chances, in other words," Costello said.

"Pretty much," Archambault said, "yeah."

Costello picked up the pencil the waiter had left next to the pad.

"You want to order?" he said. He sighed, and turned the pencil end for end.

"Might as well," Archambault said. "Did he mention a steak sandwich?"

"If he didn't," Costello said, "he should've, because they always have it." He wrote down two steak sandwich orders and shoved the pencil aside. The waiter came at once, glanced at the pad, and said: "How would you like your steak cooked, Mister Costello?"

"Medium rare for me," Costello said. "Also," Archambault said. The waiter nodded and left. "I never gamble," Costello said.

"No," Archambault said.

"It's not that I have any principles against it," Costello said. "I don't care if other people want to gamble. I just never did."

"No," Archambault said.

"Not on football games," Costello said, "not on elections, cards, the weather, or the Red Sox. When I play cards, it isn't gambling. It's not the kind of thing that interests me."

"No," Archambault said.

Costello snorted. "It's the one thing," he said, "the one thing about me that Bernie, as long as we've known each other, that Bernie's never quite been able to understand."

"I didn't realize he was a gambler *too*," Archambault said.

Costello looked at Archambault appraisingly. "You mean, in addition to his other manly virtues?" he said.

Archambault shrugged. "I didn't," he said, "but I'll let it stand. He is a man of appetites."

"Perfect," Costello said, nodding, "absolutely perfect. A man of appetites. Yes indeed. Appetites and no checks on them. I must remember that."

"Be my guest," Archambault said.

"He's always been that way," Costello said, "at least since I've known him, and he was too young then to have gone through too many changes. At first I thought . . . well, at first I didn't think much of anything. When I first got to the Hill I was one of two hundred and forty prospective governors of the Commonwealth. Thought I was, at least. Didn't stop to consider that getting elected rep's one of the surest poisons for gubernatorial ambitions ever devised by the hand of man. What was I, twenty-seven? Brash. Fresh out of Millis. You ever been to Millis, Ray?"

"I grew up in Avon," he said. "Do I need to've?"

"Probably not," Costello said. The sunlight played on the leaves of the trees on the Commonwealth Avenue promenade outside the club, and the only sounds in the dining room were murmured conversations and clinking tableware. He toyed with the salt shaker. "The only thing about Millis that was different," he said, "made it unusual, unlike any other small New England mill town sliding into evil times, was . . . well, this is what I assumed anyway, was that it happened to've been chosen by God as the place for me to be born and grow up. Nothing else."

"Same with Avon," Archambault said. "I still live there now, keep the home fires burning like you're supposed to, and all the people I grew up with that're still there and go nowhere else, ever, they always tell me that it's special. And it isn't."

"And you always tell them that it is," Costello said.

"No question about it," Archambault said. "The sunfish in the pond are fatter, the snow in the winter is deeper, and the kids in the schools are brighter than anywhere else on the earth. I do plan to keep on getting reelected, you know. I may be something of an idealist now and then, but I do plan to keep my seat."

"That's the way to go about it," Costello said. "All that stuff I read in the papers all the time, that stuff that people're screaming about left and right, no matter whether it's the bottle bill or the hazardous waste disposal ban, war, peace, or anything in between, I don't believe for one minute that that stuff actually matters a pile of shit until you get to the point where you're running statewide. It just doesn't, that's all."

"Well," Archambault said, "with reservations. Some of those crackpot things we can get ourselves involved in, practicing foreign policy and that kind of thing, it looks pretty silly, but I wouldn't care to be Andy Boyce shaking hands with the home folks in Brighton-Allston and explaining to the good Irish ladies why I voted to condemn the IRA, for example. Those things can be time bombs."

"Granted," Costello said, "but still, generally true. When the people elect a rep, those that've got the slightest idea of who the hell they're voting for when they vote for a representative in the General Court, they vote for the guy they still see down at the bowling alley Thursday nights. 'You know, Steve Beasely's kid, the one that bowled a six-ninety-nine for the fire department inna roll-off last year.' Beasely's kid may also be the guy that voted to amend the excise tax because he sees a lot of people around that're way too fat and he's for anything that'll encourage exercise, even if it is a tax, but if he bowls every week for the fire department and got four strikes back-to-back-to-back-to-back one time, and 'Remember the time, the Thanksgiving Day game, he ran back that kickoff a hundred and three yards from his own end zone and beat Cumberland?' he will get reelected. Politics until you get statewide, it's just not on a high intellectual level."

"Which of course is how Bernie and I and the rest of us manage to keep a foothold in it," Archambault said.

"Sure is," Costello said. "Up in Proctor there, where they have the annual cookout for the western part of the state?"

The waiter arrived with the steak sandwiches and placed one before each of them. He brought A.1. sauce and put it on the table. "Anything else, Mister Costello?" he said. "Please," Costello said. "A bottle of the cabernet. Okay with you, Ray?" Archambault, meat already in his mouth, nodded. He chewed, swallowed, and said: "I was there. Back in the early part of May. Knox State Park."

"Knox State Park," Costello said. "You call it that and you will never win a vote shaking hands beneath those oak trees out in Proctor, Massachusetts."

"How come?" Archambault said. " 'S what it is, way I get it. Bernie had the damned thing named after Wilfred. Retirement tribute. We all voted on it, governor signed it, everything. Knox State Park. They got a nice little sign there, says it. Plain's anything."

"Yeah," Costello said, "but as far as the people're concerned, that's *all* Bernie put there. And that's all Bernie claims he put there. God grew the trees. God made the ground too rocky to tempt anyone to farm it. God put in the brook and God gets the credit for the Odd Fellows' Grove."

"Odd Fellows," Archambault said.

"Yeah," Costello said. "The Proctor Odd Fellows. Remember that organization that used to have the three chain links and some motto on them—Liberty, Equality, Fraternity, something like that?"

"Yeah," Archambault said, "the Odd Fellows I remember. I.O.O.F. Competition for the Masons and the Knights of Columbus."

"Right," Costello said. "Well, it was their grove. They had it before the state came in and took it over and named it after Wilfred."

"Over twenty years ago," Archambault said, dabbing at his mouth and taking another bite.

"Over twenty years ago," Costello said. "But not as far as the people in Bernie's district're concerned, twenty years or two years. Until everybody dies off who always referred to that clump of trees as the Odd Fellows' Grove, it will be the Odd Fellows' Grove, and that's all there is to it. Doesn't matter if Bernie puts up fifty signs saying something else, it'll still be the Odd Fellows'. You call it Knox and they will know right off you are a foreigner."

Archambault grunted. "Same in Avon," he said, "same in any town. They name the football field after some hero and the junior high after Kennedy and the goddamned traffic island in the middle of the main street after Herbert Hoover's horse, and nobody ever calls it by that name again. Waste of time."

"It is and it isn't, I suppose," Costello said, cutting his steak. "Anyway," he said, "that's what I'm getting at. When I first ran into Bernie, that kind of stuff, only about Millis and not Proctor, that was all I knew. About politics. I knew a lot of other stuff, but that was out of books. It was also pretty much all he knew. Oh, he had the advantage of Wilfred to bring him along, he had that. When Bernie first came to the Hill, he didn't exist without Wilfred. Wilfred was the old fox from the woods. Bernie was just the new kid he was training."

"His son-in-law," Archambault said.

"Right," Costello said. "Big, rough-hewn, gawky kid. Lot of swagger with his war medals, scared of nothing that stood in shoe leather, drink anything that wouldn't drink him, rather fight than fuck, and rather fuck'n do anything else. Straight out of the goddamned bushes."

"Hasn't changed much in what, thirty-odd years?" Archambault said, grinning.

"Ah," Costello said, "but he should have. You for example, you look pretty good." The waiter brought the wine. He uncorked it and served it.

"Thanks," Archambault said, looking mildly surprised. "I try to get a certain amount of exercise, watch what I eat."

"Not that," Costello said, "although that shows as well. Your clothes, I mean. Nice grey suit, well cut, fits you without being showy. Tie, pocket handkerchief. You're one of the few reps I see that never seems to be in need of a shine. And you never look as though you've just had a haircut or else've gone without one for about three months."

"No," Archambault said. He stretched in the chair. He grinned. "My wife tells me I'm as vain as a woman," he said. "She's probably right. But I'm not comfortable, going around and looking like a slob. When I was at Suffolk Law nights, we had Dory Feldman for trial practice, and he told us something that confirmed just what I'd always thought all along. 'When you go into court,' he said, 'forget all that baloney about dressing poor so the jury'll think your client really needs the money because he had to hire such a seedy-lookin' lawyer. Holes in your shoes and your pants all rumpled. You're supposed to be a professional advocate, whether you're representing a beggar or a rich man who's going to be a pauper, once he's paid your fee. Look like one. Look like a man who knows what he's doing, confident of himself because he's confident of his case.' So I do."

"Where you get your clothes?" Costello said.

Archambault shrugged. "You want the truth," he said, "I'll tell you what I don't tell other people. I know a guy up in Lawrence that's the manager in the factory where they make the Dorset line they sell in Louis and Press and those places. Straight Ivy. Natural shoulder. Stuff goes about close to four fifty a three-piece winter suit now, I guess. It's nice stuff. And my mother and father planned well. They made me a perfect forty long. It's like the suit they put on the rack was custom-tailored for me. There is no reason in the world for me to buy a made-to-measure suit. So I have them hem the pants and put my initials in the lining, and my friend sells 'em to me off the line for around two hundred bucks. Same with sport coats, slacks, everything. But ordinarily, somebody asks me where I get my clothes, I tell 'em I shop Louis."

"You tell 'em that in Avon?" Costello said.

"Yup," Archambault said.

"Must be there's no men's store in Avon," Costello said. "There was, you'd never get away with that. Shopping in Boston. Lose the next election for that kind of social climbing."

"You think so?" Archambault said. "I sort of don't. There isn't a men's store, as a matter of fact. People are shopping the malls all the time now, but I don't think that'd make any difference. They've known me too long where I come from. It's like . . . it's almost like they take a certain amount of vicarious satisfaction, you know? I realize that sounds snotty, and I don't mean it that way. Because there can be times when it's kind of a pain in the ass for me, you know? Sunday night, football games're over, I got to hit a wake there really isn't any reason I should hit, barely knew the guy, but I'm the rep and somewhere back when the dinosaurs were walking around Massachusetts it got written down that reps go to wakes. So I am going to have to haul ass and go.

"But," Archambault said, "I also know this: unlike Joe the Twitch that runs the gas station, it is not going to be enough, if I just throw on a sport coat and a tie and show up at the funeral home. Uh uh. I've got to shower, I've got to blow-dry my hair, I've got to shave neat and put on the aftershave lotion, and I've got to wear a tie and coat that's different from what I wore to Mass that morning. Because if the people who saw me at Mass in the morning in my tweed sport coat don't see me at the wake tonight in my blue blazer, they are going to say to themselves: 'Ray didn't put himself out much for this one, did he now?' And it will be just exactly like I never went at all, never mind what tie I happened to have on. It's like Bernie says, Frank: 'It's a funny fuckin' business sometimes.' "

Costello chuckled. "That was Wilfred's too," he said.

"Doesn't matter whose it was," Archambault said, "still true. The clothes're part of what my voters elect. It's like they've had a chance to study me, watch me come out of UMass with the chinos and the corduroy jackets and the desert boots, the long-hair bit gettin' the master's at Bridgewater, the time I spent teaching the sophomores about first class levers and the juniors about periodic tables of the atoms, the first campaign when McElroy dropped dead halfway through it and it was too late for anybody else to file against me and the rules say that when you think one candidate's too young but the other guy is dead, you got to elect the one that's breathing—they went through all that with me, you know? I get in there with all my crackpot ideas because McElroy's dead and I'm not, and Joe Gillis does a story about me and the other young hotshots that're going to put an end to bossism, and . . . ,"

". . . and ruined Warren Matte for all time," Costello said, "to the point where he wasn't good for anything but a judgeship."

". . . and ruined Warren Matte and some others," Archambault said, nodding, "and when the dust cleared and the smoke blew away, I was still standing there. A little barbered, a little better dressed, a little smoother on the stump, a little more polite to my elders, and as it happened with no opposition in the primary.

"That was the key to it, Frank," he said, putting his fork down on his plate and wiping his mouth with his napkin, "that was the absolute key to it. I can't claim it was my idea, and I didn't even realize at the time how important it'd be. Because being young and cocky, I naturally figured I could go out and whip anybody after putting in a full term on the Hill. I probably would've gotten my ass handed to me, some good hardworking, tough-talking woman or a retired banker with lots of time on their hands'd taken it into their heads to run against me. But everybody was doing something else at the time, I guess, and nobody ran against me. I had a free ride, and that was the key to it. Because once I'd had two terms, it really was my seat to have as long's I showed I still wanted it enough to go to wakes and act polite around the senior citizens. The first two years I was being allowed to keep the seat warm and prove I didn't deserve to have it, or wasn't as good as somebody else that decided he ought to have it. After that, since then, it's been mine to lose. Which I do not intend to do."

"Going to run statewide?" Costello said with innocence.

Archambault grinned. "Ten years ago, Frank," he said, "ten years ago, you asked me that and I would've done the neatest little pirouette around that question that you ever saw. Job didn't pay much then, and I was ambitious. But now? My next birthday I'll be forty-one. My oldest is fifteen and my youngest is eleven. There's one in between and four years between them, and it doesn't take too many brains for me to figure out that I'm going to need some heavy college bread before too long. A lot of it.

"Now," he said, "the salary's going up. I'll be grossing fifty grand from this job next year when that little piece of legislation goes through after the primaries. There are many gentlemen my age who would like very much to be making fifty grand from anything, up to and including stuff that could get them put in prison, but everything I do's absolutely legal and pretty good fun, too, and it brings me fifty grand. And it is mine. All I got to do is keep it.

"Then," he said, "we have the small but flourishing law practice, as we like to call it. Nothing too flamboyant, none of the whoop-dee-do with the TV cameras and the big flashy cars. Just a nice steady law practice, me and three other guys who know our responsibilities and pull in about forty apiece a year after the rent and the secretaries.

"If I run for governor," Archambault said, "several things will happen. Only one of them is even the slightest bit appealing to me. First, I lose my seat and my leadership position, so bye-bye fifty grand. That is for openers. Then I spend close to a million bucks, at least, trying to get my name recognized by the most influential faculty members at Bumfuck U., so they will plan me a media strategy and talk me up as the light of the world in the papers and when they get on TV themselves— some of this million I raise from other people giving it to me out of the goodness of their hearts and because they want me to do naughty things for them when I am governor, and some of it comes out of my own jam pot, now and in the future. I start retreating from my nifty little law practice, of course, because I won't have time for it when I run and I can't keep it when I win, *if* I win. Which means kissing good-bye to another forty grand plus whatever the practice'll be worth some years from now when I try to get back into it. And then finally I either win and become governor for four years, which gets me in return for giving up ninety grand just about the same money I gave up leaving the legislature alone, never mind the income from the law practice. Minus the debts I've run up going after the job. Or else I don't win the election. In which case I don't even get the state troopers driving me around for the next four years. All I get is the debts and no damned way to pay them off. Except, of course, grovel around and kiss ass to get money again.

"That, Frank," Archambault said, picking up his wine glass and turning it in the light, "that does not strike me as the sort of program which a thoughtful man would follow." He drank from the glass. He set it down. "Ahh," he said, "fine stuff. Very little of that served in the teacher's lunchroom at Avon High School noontimes. Unless they're smuggling in a jar in a paper bag to take the chill off or something these days. And that, Frank, is the kind of reasoning that makes me say today: No, no statewide office, thank you just the same. Now: why do you ask?"

Costello drank wine. He savored it on his tongue. "They do do a good job with that house wine here," he said. "I have to give them that. It's not too dear and it tastes very good."

"Frank," Archambault said.

"Right," Costello said, "why do I ask? Well, why do I? What do you think?"

Archambault grinned. "You drive a hard bargain, Frank," he said. "You buy the lunch but I have to do all the work."

Costello smiled. He lifted the glass again. "It is a very nice wine," he said.

Archambault's grin went away. "The way you taste it," he said.

"I enjoy the taste," Costello said.

"You didn't learn that from Bernie," Archambault said.

Costello sighed. "No," he said, "no, I didn't."

"Because Bernie," Archambault said, "no matter what it is, Bernie puts it down his throat like he's afraid it'll evaporate if he keeps it in the glass too long."

Costello sighed again. "Katie's Place," he said.

"I don't follow," Archambault said.

Costello put the glass down. He laid his knife and fork on the edge of his plate. Half of the sandwich remained on it undisturbed. He frowned. "He never really left it," he said. "Not even during the time he was in the service, I think, although of course I never knew him until after he'd come back and been elected.

"When I first got to know Bernie," Costello said, "if you want the truth I thought he was an asshole. I was single then, Ray. My time in the evening was my own. I thought I was a pretty sophisticated article. I had a college education, and I hadn't gotten it in the company of that collection of noisy buffoons who'd taken the trolley to Boston College together, graduated together, and taken the trolley back down Commonwealth Avenue, it seemed like, to take their appointed places in the General Court. I'd been to Middlebury; I didn't think a pair of skis was shorthand for two Polish voters in Chicopee. My family wasn't wealthy, not by the standards of the great world outside, but by those of Millis we were well-to-do. You went to Suffolk nights while you were in the legislature? Well, I went to Columbia, days, and that was all I did. Did that make me better than it made you? No. Did I think it made me a better man than you? Yes. I was quite sure of it, as a matter of fact. And you can imagine, Ray, if I thought I was a better man than the graduate of Suffolk, how far superior I must've felt toward Bernie Morgan.

"That big rude piece of shit," Costello said, shaking his head. "Bernie Morgan'd never been *any*where. Of course I was leaving out his little tour of Europe at the expense and behest of Uncle Sam, all that brawling around that I'd managed to avoid by contriving to be born just a hair too late—that hadn't added to his luster at all. Not for me. He was just an ignorant lout fresh from some hillbilly preserve out in western Massachusetts. If he hadn't interested me, I would've sneered at him.

"I was slumming then, you see, Ray," he said. "Of a Tuesday evening I might stay in town and go to Symphony, or stay in town and go out raising hell with Bernie Morgan. If I went to one place I heard Charles Munch play Mussorgsky, and if I went to the other I heard Frankie Laine's record of 'Mule Train' played over and over again to the accompaniment of much loud laughter and lots of stories about broads and sports and men who'd just emerged from prison. The Munch was more elevating but the Morgan more exciting. As you said, a man of appetites.

"I'd never had those appetites," Costello said. "I hadn't had them until then, at least that I was aware, and I haven't had them since. It was a very curious experience for me, visiting whorehouses, sitting in on bustout poker games, competing to see who could drink the most cheap whiskey, singing raunchy songs in bars till three A.M. It fascinated me. I don't mean that I didn't take part. More that I only seemed to. I was there and I drank just as much as anyone else, but every minute while I was doing it, I was preparing for the headache and the next day's awful stomach. I never really got any enjoyment out of it. And what I said about gambling? I never did really gamble. I played a lot of poker with Bernie and the men he knew, and I won a lot of money at it too. A lot for those days, at least. Five, six hundred dollars a crack. But it certainly wasn't gambling, because those men got drunk when they drank, and it didn't exactly improve their concentration. All I had to do was wait until the booze walloped them, and then move in and take their money from them. It was easy. Not very fair, to be sure, but five or six hundred dollars a week extra comes in handy, no matter how well-to-do your family is.

"I only spent four terms in the legislature," Costello said. "When I left, Wilfred'd started patting dogs that weren't there, and Bernie'd eased him out and into the home. By then I'd been there long enough to see it mattered less and less to anybody, including the people of Millis, how I cast my single vote on any issue, or what I had to say in debate on any legislation to my fellow lawmakers. What mattered was the packaging of all the votes, and the preparation of the legislation that those votes affected, and the presentation of those packages to the public and the people who would be affected by them when they became law."

"Fixing, in other words," Archambault said.

Costello pondered. "Lobbying," he said, "expediting, accommodating, adjusting: I've heard it called by lots of names. The names that sound evil are the ones used by the people at least temporarily unable to do it to their own benefit and to prevent other people from doing it for themselves. The nice ones are the names used by the people who temporarily enjoy the power to get things done the way they want them done."

"Whatever you want to call it," Archambault said, "you've gotten rich at it."

"Richer," Costello said. "I never said I started off in a log cabin, and I never had any desire to wind up in one. When I went to work, I did it with the expectation that I'd get money for it, and that is what I've gotten.

"Bernie," he said, "Bernie never took quite the same approach. It's not that he's ever disdained the money. Far from it. Proctor Maggie lives in a fine fieldstone house with a sauna bath and a screened-in porch overlooking a big meadow that'll never be built on unless she goes into the contracting business and starts putting up houses herself.

Bernie paid for that land and that house. Boston Maggie and Bernie live in a lovely apartment and when Bernie takes everybody's life in his hands when he gets behind the wheel, it's the wheel of a Cadillac. They've got a lovely summer home in Onset, though God knows why they'd want to put it there or why the hell they'd want to build a house that looks like the nineteenth hole at a Mafia country club, but they appear to be happy in it. They take winter vacations at places in Florida that probably inspired the architecture of their summer place, now that I think of it, and Bernie spends a lot of money on his clothes even if he does buy stuff that makes him look like an out-of-work faro dealer. He's taken the money, and he's enjoyed the money, and God knows he's spent the money, but that was never really what interested him about the game.

"What interested Bernie," Costello said, "what interests him now, is not the outcome but the game itself. The first year I was in, the first year of my first term, I think it was his second or his third term, he talked me into going home with him for something or other. I don't know what the hell the official excuse was—I took it as an invitation to go drinking and wenching out in the woods, and being curious, I accepted. That was just what it proved to be, too. Well, not the wenching so much. We concentrated on the drinking.

"That area," Costello said, "it's pretty sleepy now, I guess. Years since I've really spent any time up there. Bernie keeps his fences mended, not that he has to do a great deal to accomplish that, even to this day, as much as it's changed. But it was boom town then. The Fisk Tire plant in Chicopee was running full-bore and if there wasn't as much Korean War munitions money floating around as World War Two'd put in circulation with the Rolls-Royce engines and the guns being built in Springfield, it was close enough. The textile mills hadn't packed up and vacated the plants along the Connecticut then and headed south for scab labor—everybody was riding high. Especially in Proctor, where the once and future Speakers both came from.

"Bernie took me to Katie's," Costello said. "Keep in mind that I had credentials as a member in good standing of the Hard-drinking Big-talking Chowder and Marching Society, and I came sponsored by the Mikado of the organization. If I'd been Casper Milquetoast, escorted in by Bernie, I would've been treated like Bluebeard and greeted like Long John Silver, but I wasn't without my own abilities either. I fitted right in.

"It was basically a saloon in a big grey three-story house that'd probably started out as a stagecoach inn for Post Road travelers turning north and heading for eastern Vermont. That's a guess. It was pretty rundown even then. But the porch, veranda, really, ran around three sides of the building and it was all gussied up with afterthought-ginger-bread. So that building'd been there a long time before automobiles. There was an old red barn out back that looked like it'd had about six drinks too many itself and was sort of slouching off to one side in the weeds, trying to decide whether to fall the hell over or stand there another night and day and think about it some more. There were a couple of busted old wagons outside the barn, and parked behind them there were three or four old LaSalles or something that'd probably be worth a lot of money today if somebody'd only had the foresight back in the crash of Nineteen-twenty-nine to shore up the barn and run them inside and put them up on blocks.

"There was a big dusty yard out in the front," Costello said. "This place was right in the center of town, although I'm inclined to think that the place was there first and they more or less located the town to suit the convenience of the inn. All the sidewalks and the side streets radiated out from it and all the cars came into it and parked in the yard, every which way. It looked like the staging area for a gypsy caravan the night I was there, people yelling at each other, swearing and cussing to beat the band, backing into each other, having fistfights and rolling around in the dust, two or three couples passionately embracing in cars, oblivious to all the commotion around them."

"It sounds like a circus," Archambault said, laughing. "Or a fire in a Mexican whorehouse."

"It looked like one too," Costello said. "Looked like I'd always imagined some down-at-the-heels Mexican border town'd look on Sunday afternoon after a bullfight, Tijuana, maybe, all the inhabitants drunk as rats and raising hell without regard to age, race, sex, religion, or country of national origin. The only thing missing was a man selling balloons and pennants.

"Bernie," he said, "Bernie wasn't fat then like he is now. He wasn't goat-shouldered, either. Looked like a lumberjack and walked right into that maelstrom like he was Paul Bunyan himself come to bring order out of the chaos. After that night I never wondered again how he kept his head in all that uproar around prorogation when they keep pushing the hands of the clock back from midnight so they can holler and yell some more in the well of the House. Made the House look tame, out there in Proctor, and Bernie was king of the hill. Made his way through it shaking hands and slapping people on the back like Patton greeting the troops after victory.

"Inside," Costello said, "it was just like outside, only it stunk worse because there wasn't any fresh air and people were smoking and spilling beer and most of them apparently hadn't washed since they got through doing hard physical work. It seems like it must've been summer, we were there, but it wouldn't've mattered anyway. With all the people inside it would've been an inferno with the furnace off and the windows wide open in January. Wall-to-wall humanity, roaring like lions and having the time of their lives."

"The Fourth of July, maybe?" Archambault said.

"Couldn't've been," Costello said. "I was still in office when I went up there with him. Fourth of July, I would've been home in Millis looking solemn. My constituents were pretty tolerant of their dashing young bachelor rep, but there were some minimum standards that I had to meet. Besides, Fourth of July and national celebrations of that order, I think they probably had a human sacrifice or something in Katie's Place and I didn't see one of those. But they would have had to do something like that, set it apart from the regular Saturday night free-for-all and the reenactment of the battle of Lake Champlain they went through every time the softball team won a game.

"The owner was there that night," Costello said. "Maury St. Catherine, known to one and all as Katie. One of those short cigars shaped like a plum tomato in his mouth, end of it all wet and chewed, fat face, and a body like a bowling ball. Round, short-legged, filthy mouth, Grabbed Bernie the minute he came in, pulls him aside and me with him. Couldn't understand a word the man said. Made us stand near the jukebox. I thought my fillings'd get taken out by the noise. Katie gets up on the bar with the help of several friends, bartender hands him a beer stein, Katie turns around and flings it at the lamp hanging over the door. Makes this tremendous crash. Perfect bull's-eye. Glass falling down all over the place, had to've been cutting people, light bulb filaments flaming away, and here's this goddamned crazy saloonkeeper wrecking his own joint and making everybody quiet down: 'Goddamned fuckin' animals,' he yells, 'shut the fuck up a minute, this Morgan can deal with this prob-*lem.*' I never did find out what the prob-*lem* was supposed to be. The busted light maybe.

"There was a cheer," Costello said. "The sort of cheer there must've been in the Colosseum when the Christians were all huddled in the center of the ring and the lions came out of their pens. Bernie climbs up on the bar, which puts him so close to the ceiling he has to duck, and I don't see how he's gonna deal with any prob-*lem* in that uncomfortable position. He grins and he waves and that place went absolutely wild. Jesus Christ, it was frightening. That crowd went nuts. They would've stormed out the door and torn a bishop limb from limb, if Bernie'd told them to.

"He puts up his hand," Costello said demonstrating. "Instant and total silence. 'Ya got any beefs,' he said, 'I'll be here all night. Come up and tell me about 'em.' There was another cheer. He stayed the rest of the night too. About ten people did come up to him. I saw him with my own eyes give away about fifteen hundred bucks of his own goddamned money, cleaned out his pockets. And then borrowed about seven, eight hundred more from Katie before he left. Which I happen to know he paid back because he gave me the money in Boston the next week and I wrote Katie a check. Bernie didn't keep a checking account in those days, either. Then after he invites all the down-and-outers to come up and tell him their tales of woe about their poor starving families that wouldn't've been starving if they didn't spend so much on beer in Katie's Place waitin' for Bernie to come and give them money, he says Wilfred's sick but sends his best, which draws another cheer, and finishes by announcing that the next round's on him. Which that also was, as a matter of fact. Then he got down with the crowd ready to crown him king of Proctor and surrounding towns, and another cheer goes up, and instantly they were right back to raising hell and doing exactly what they'd been doing before.

"Some time around sunrise," Costello said, "long after closing time anyway, Katie poured the last of the revelers into the yard and finally barred the door. We sat there drinking coffee and Katie made some scrambled eggs, and Bernie put the linings of his pockets back in. And then at long last we got up and went to the house that Bernie and Proctor Maggie had before they built the one she lives in now. And before Bernie discovered Boston Maggie, at least on a permanent basis."

"He was still fully married to Proctor Maggie then?" Archambault said.

"Well," Costello said, "to the extent that he took some precautions against loathsome diseases, and that he always went back to her after he'd been out on one of his adventures, he was. And also to the extent that then at least she didn't generally put the make on anybody he brought home, at least that I was aware of. She didn't on me."

"She did on me," Archambault said.

"So I heard," Costello said. "At the Odd Fellows' Grove?"

"Uh huh," Archambault said.

Costello sighed. "Yeah," he said, "well, I can't say I'm surprised. Recent years, she's started doing that when she's with him. Baiting him, I guess. Just reminding him, he put her aside but she's not out the picture yet."

"Why me, though?" Archambault said.

Costello shrugged again. "You were handy," he said. "If you hadn't've been there and somebody else had been, it would've been somebody else. If nobody else'd been, it wouldn't've been anybody."

"Was Bernie pissed off about it?" Archambault said. "Because it wasn't my fault. He saw it, he should know that."

"As a matter of fact," Costello said, "way I got it, he didn't see it. She told him about it, brought it to his attention in the car, when he was driving her home after the time. Said you put a move on her, and she had to fight you off."

"Oh, for Christ sake," Archambault said, "I really resent that. I've had people say all kinds of things about me, some calling me stupid and some others puttin' it around I'm stealing everything that's not locked up, and I can more or less shrug that off. But I don't fuck around and if I did I wouldn't be so goddamned stupid as to try it with the Speaker's goddamned wife, for Christ sake, no matter how horny I happened to be. Besides which, she's about fifteen, twenty years older'n I am anyway, isn't she? I'd go for something younger if I was going to take a chance on Katie stickin' a hatchet in my ear some fine night while I'm sleeping. What the hell did she want to go and do that for?"

"Bernie says," Costello said, "Bernie says she thinks she's Marlene Dietrich now. Greta Garbo or something. All the young studs nuts for her body. Her skill in the sack. Don't worry about it, Bernie didn't take it seriously. Just laughed it off. Told it to me as a joke, matter of fact. 'Old broads,' he says, 'they get simple too. Kind of nice, us old guys gettin' silly, they have to go through it too.' "

"Shit," Archambault said. The waiter came and glanced inquiringly at Costello, who nodded. The waiter began to take the plates away.

"It's really nothing to worry about," Costello said. "She can't do anything to you. Bernie's the only one who'd matter, and he knows she's the one that did it. Or tried to do it. Still jealous, I guess, she is, after all these years that he's been with someone else, and all those someone elses he was with before he settled down with Boston Maggie."

"Yeah," Archambault said bitterly, "kind of sweet, huh? True love lingers on, through all the adulterous liaisons."

"You may not be far wrong," Costello said, "leaving your sarcasm out of it. Those two, they live in a far different world than you assume. Or I would like." The waiter brought coffee cups and served them. "Dessert, gentlemen?" he said. They both shook their heads. "That morning," he said, "Bernie is broke and we go back to his house. It was just about rooster time. I assumed we'd be going to bed. It wasn't the first time I'd stayed out all night with him, but always before when the dawn's early light arrived, we toddled off to beddy-bye. Not Bernie. He threw his coat on the couch in the house, rolled up his sleeves and went out to the garage. And pretty soon there he was, out by the fence in his suit pants and the shirt he'd worn the day before in the House, whitewashing the fence.

"By then," Costello said, stirring cream and sugar into his coffee, "Proctor Maggie was showing signs of life. She came into the living room where I was trying not to fall asleep and at the same time sleeping off a drunk while I was still somewhat awake, and I called this marvel to her attention. She was not in the slightest surprised.

" 'Does it every time he comes home,' she said. 'Stays out all night raising hell, then comes home and starts whitewashing the fence. That fence doesn't need whitewashing. It's perfectly fine as it is. But he always gets his butt down there unless it's pouring rain, and does those sections right next the road. Must be two, three inches of whitewash on that stretch of fence by now.'

"I asked her why," Costello said. "Was this man I thought I knew, was he completely nuts?

" 'Nuts like a fox,' she said. 'All over the Pioneer Valley this mornin' the hellions're sleepin' it off, but not without first telling all kinds of wild stories about how Bernie Morgan was back down at Katie's last night, drinking my father's favorite joint dry until sunup. So the older people'll be out today with their milk for the market truck and their errands to do in town and the things they've got on their mind that ought to be done different there down in Boston if only their rep didn't stay out all night raisin' hell every time he comes back to his district. And every single one of those old busybodies'll make it his business to drive past this house on his way in or out of town, even if it means he has to make up an errand in town that he doesn't really need to do and drive ten or twelve miles out of his way, using time he can't spare and gas he can't afford, to take a look at that hell raiser Morgan's house. And there he'll be, out in the front, working away harder than any of them, always ready to stop for a minute and hear a man's views on what oughta be done down in Boston there. Or take out a pencil and a piece of notepaper and jot something down he wants to remember to bring up on Beacon Hill when he gets back. Job for somebody, maybe. Tell what it is that needs to be done up in Granby. I tell you, Frank, it works like a charm. He's got the drinkers from last night and he'll have the deacons by noon, and there's not a hell of a lot of ground left to cover, 'tween the two of those extremes.'

" 'But he hasn't had any sleep,' I told her.

" 'I know it,' she said. 'You know it. The hell raisers know it and the right-thinking citizens know it and so does everybody else that might have some wild idea of running against him. Bernie Morgan never needs sleep. There's some people that think he's an angel and some people that more than suspect he's probably the devil, and it doesn't matter much which side you come down on. Because either way, would *you* want to run against that guy? Whatever he is? Whatever he is, he's more'n you are.'

" 'He surely is,' I said, 'I got to get some sleep.' And Bernie's out there in the sunrise, painting away at the fence, and she sort of smiled at me and told me about his commanding officer. Met him at a reunion of his outfit, she said. 'He told me Bernie was bulletproof,' she said. 'He said he didn't believe it, the things that Bernie kept doing in combat, things that were clearly impossible for any man to do, that would obviously get you killed. And he just did them. And this captain told me when Bernie got hit, the day he got hit he didn't know whether Bernie was the most surprised guy in the outfit or not, because the rest of the guys'd been seeing him do these things that were sure to get him killed for years, seemed like, without even getting touched. They'd started to believe it too.' She told me, kind of dreamy, you know: 'I dunno what the hell it is I married,' she said. 'The only thing I'm sure of is that I got the only one. There can't possibly be another Bernie Morgan.'

"So," Costello said, "weird as it sounds, I think it's very possible she still loves the guy. Still trying to make him just the littlest bit jealous."

"Huh," Archambault said.

"The trouble is," Costello said slowly, "what Bernie keeps forgetting and she apparently hasn't noticed yet is that it was a pretty long time ago when he was doing those things. Could do those things. If he was bulletproof for a while in the war, he used it up. And if he was bulletproof in the things he did around here and the things he's still doing around here, he isn't protected anymore. And that," Costello said, "that is the trouble. Heroism. Personal stuff. To Bernie, that is politics. What he did in Katie's Place, handing all the money out, beggaring himself, where everybody could see him. Distributing the jobs down by the fence, where nobody that was trying to get one for himself or his idiot kid'd ever have to admit there never would've been a job if they hadn't gone to Bernie for it. None of this crap with imagemakers and television strategies and and all that shit with polling.

"Demographics?" Costello smirked. "For Bernie, demographics is the guys that stay up late and drink—them you meet in Katie's. And the guys that stick to the straight and narrow, come by early in the morning, them you get down by the fence. Social programs? Hand out the fifties in Katie's. Government retirement and disability plans? Hey, Dealey was always a good guy, you have a couple, three, hundred-dollar-a-headers for him, that should keep the family goin' until he kicks off and we think of something else. Personal, Ray, personal. That's what he's doing to this day. The same thing he was doing then in Katie's Place. Only Katie's Place ain't there no more, and Bernie Morgan's not a hero any more."

"Look," Archambault said, leaning forward, "I know you're close to the guy, Frank, I know this. I know you've been with him a long time and this's more'n your run-of-the-mill problem that you've just got to do something about, okay?"

Costello nodded. He looked down at his coffee cup and stirred.

"Bernie Morgan," Archambault said, "I saw Bernie at that time they had, the first time that they had for Dealey down at Pier Four. Back in May?"

Costello nodded again. He did not look up.

"He was drunk," Archambault said, in a very low voice. "It was about eight, nine o'clock in the evening, and he was stopping people coming in the restaurant to eat. He wasn't a little happy, Frank, maybe a little noisy, uh uh. He was absolutely shitfaced. He had me confused with one of the reps from Lowell, or maybe Methuen. I had to bribe the attendant to get his car for him. The kid said he wasn't fit to drive. I had to drive Bernie's car out onto the street before he could get behind the wheel." Archambault leaned back in his chair. "And you know just as well as I do, Frank, that I shouldn't've let him drive."

"I know," Costello said.

"He's a drunk, Frank," Archambault said. "It wasn't the first time he's been out accosting people on the street. It wasn't the first time he's been visibly plastered in public. It wasn't the first time he got behind the wheel of that landcruiser and started weaving all over town, trusting to dumb luck and God he doesn't run over some old lady that can't get out the way of him fast enough."

Costello nodded again. "I know," he said miserably.

"And if that doesn't put him behind bars," Archambault said, "and what a picnic the *Commoner*'ll have with that one, huh? Bernie Morgan in the slammer? Not to mention the *Globe* and the *Herald* and some of the fresh bastards they've got. Make us all look like assholes. This big crusade we got, pass the bill to lock up guys that drive drunk, and the first drunk that gets locked up is the Speaker of the House of Representatives. But even if that doesn't happen, Frank, there's still something else, and that worries me more."

"Yeah," Costello said, "I know that one too."

"Okay," Archambault said, leaning forward again, "you called this meeting. What does he do about the Ames Commission?"

"I don't know," Costello said. He looked up. "I can't get him to face that thing. I talk to him about it, about anything, and he just sloughs it off. Something he'll worry about some other time, when he gets around to it. Probably go away anyway."

"Frank," Archambault said, "it won't go away. It's not going to go away. Ames is senile. We all know that. But he has got that goddamned law that I told Bernie we never ought to let come to a vote and he laughed at me, and he has also got a giant hair across his ass for Bernie Morgan. Which now that he has hired himself this nifty nigger prosecutor he is probably gonna find a way to scratch."

"Well," Costello said, "they haven't got anything yet. That I know about at least."

"They will," Archambault said. "You mark my words, they will. Don't underestimate this black kid, Frank. I hear he's mean and I hear he's a very ambitious young boogie, out to make a name for himself. He can manipulate Ames if he wants, so long's he gets Morgan. And Ames, I don't care what anybody says about his statutory powers being constitutional or not, he'll exercise those powers and he'll nail Bernie. It won't do the slightest bit of good down the line if Bernie gets himself released from the penitentiary on the grounds that Ames shouldn't've had the powers to put him in there in the first place. He'll be ruined, and that's all Ames wants. Ames gets Bernie and he'll die happy. It's all there is left in the world for Ames: Bernie Morgan's scalp. Bernie says that bill was booby-trapped? He's right, and he's the booby they're going to put into that trap. You, Frank, you have got to cut Bernie adrift. Period."

Costello, looking down, spoke indistinctly.

"What?" Archambault said, "I couldn't hear you."

Costello spoke again. "I said," he said, looking up, "I said: I know." There were tears in his eyes.

21 On Billy Fucillo's second day back on the job at the Vineyard Airport, the Flynn kid decided on his own to be helpful and move a front-end loader out of the way of a grader. He put it into a deep muddy ditch at a precarious angle. Billy Fucillo, with Vinnie Mahoney his only protection from a world that otherwise confronted him with his angry wife, Theresa, and the pending statutory rape charge that had made Theresa angry, was on his very best behavior and determined to do nothing that would get Mahoney mad. He had gone up to the office trailer and interrupted Mahoney at his lunch to ask him if he wished to supervise correction of the problem. Vinnie said Fucillo was damned right he did, and went down to the ditch to stand in mud up to his ankles and stare at the front-end loader.

"I would have to say that you are right, Billy," he said. "From what I can see, you are right. There is a problem." The Flynn kid stood next to Mahoney and looked worried. "I would have to say that the only way a man could get on that thing and drive it out without being fairly sure that the thing was gonna tip over on him would be if he had a personal guarantee from God. That is what I would say, yes sir. I don't know why that fuckin' thing didn't tip over already, when it went in there in the first place." Mahoney turned to the Flynn kid. "You got any idea why that thing ain't tipped over already?" he said.

The Flynn kid looked very worried and scuffled his feet. "No, sir," he said. He looked down at the ground.

"Well, Jesus Christ," Mahoney said, "now that kind of surprises me. Here you are, you got this, what've you got, about half a college education so far?"

"Yes sir," the kid said miserably.

"Sure," Mahoney said, "that's what I thought. John Flynn never steered me wrong yet. Tells me his kid's finished two years, Georgetown University, of course it's true. How'd you do it?"

"Well," the kid said uncertainly, "I saw Eddie Wright was gettin' ready to start up the grader there, and the loader was in his way, so I figured I'd move it for him. I watched people driving it all summer so far. Didn't look too hard. So, and then it got away from me, I guess is probably the best explanation for it. And there it is."

"No, no," Mahoney said. "I *know* how you got it so it's liable fall over on the first poor son of a bitch gets up on it and tries to drive it out of there. That I know. That's easy. You did that by trying to do something that I recall telling you right at the beginning not to do, which was: 'Don't operate nothing till you been checked out on it and then don't operate nothing without somebody that saw you checked out on it and knows what you can do with it, without somebody like that telling you to operate it.' So you decide today you're gonna be a wise-ass and operate something that you ain't been checked out on, without anybody that seen you being checked out on it telling you to do it, and you got it pretty near ass over teakettle in the ditch as a result. That ain't hard to figure out. Man don't need two years of college, dope that one out in a second. You got in this shit by not doing something you were told to do, and by doing something you weren't told to do and that you knew damned right well you shouldn't be doing.

"What I want to know," Mahoney said, "is how somebody dumb enough to get in that much shit has made it through two years of college at Georgetown University without cuttin' himself to death on something like a coathanger or something, he's so damned dumb he's willing get up on a piece equipment that beats the shit out of a hundred thousand dollars and damned near wreck it and kill himself when he don't know shit about running it. That's what I want to know. And you're gonna be a doctor, your dad tells me? Jesus Christ, I know one thing: I ain't gettin' sick, no matter what anybody says.

"Billy," he said, "all right. You're right. I don't want nobody getting up on that thing and I end up paying workmen's comp to him the rest my time on earth. Take my pickup over and tell Eddie Wright back the Cat over here and hitch her up and haul her out by the ass. Okay? And then bring my truck back the office."

"Okay," Fucillo said. He went over to the truck and started it up.

"And you," Mahoney said to the Flynn kid, "you come over here with me and we're gonna find a nice dry seat in the sun and I'm gonna try to tell you again the difference between something you been trained how to operate and something you stay away from like it was a fuckin' sausage maker and your cock was the next piece of meat might go into it."

Harry bounced up to the ditch in the other pickup truck. "Vinnie," he said. "Back the office. Couple guys there from the commission. Wanta see you."

"Jesus Christ," Mahoney said, "the commission. Which commission, Harry?"

"I dunno," Harry said. "They didn't say. Just said they were from the commission and they wanted to see you. Don't think they said, anyway. I got them some coffee."

"Harry," Mahoney said, "there's about, you got any idea how many fuckin' goddamned commissions there are? There's thousands of the goddamned things. I'm gonna start servin' coffee, all the fuckin' commissioners come here, I'm gonna have to take out an option to buy fuckin' Brazil."

"I don't see what the fuck difference it makes, Vinnie," Harry said, "you standin' here and yelling at me how many commissions there is. There's two guys from one of them commissions up the office right now, and they said they wanted, see you. Don't matter shit and goddamn which fuckin' commission it is, does it? You're still gonna have to see them."

"Bullshit," Mahoney said. He kicked at a clump of drying mud. "Goddamned commissions. You know what it is, don't you? I know what it is. They're countin', they're down here countin' niggers again."

"They was just down here a couple weeks ago, doin' that," Harry said.

"Don't matter," Mahoney said. "That's what they're doin'. They love to do that, count niggers. They must think there's only a certain number of darkies and we all got together in the business and just go shiftin' 'em around from job to job. Soon's they're counted here, ship 'em over to the next place. Keep 'em one step ahead the commissioners, comin' 'round to count them. Hope to God none of them damned commissioners get to recognizing any of them, realize all they're doin's countin' the same niggers all the time. 'Hey Clem, all right? You had the commissioners this week? You did? Good. We ain't, and I got a feelin' they're comin' over. Send the niggers over my place tonight. I'll ship 'em on over to Jake soon's the commissioners count 'em here.' " Mahoney chuckled.

"Well, Vinnie," Harry said, "that's what it is, I think we got a certain amount of trouble starin' at us."

"Why is that?" Mahoney said. "Didn't our fuckin' niggers show up here today? First this kid here starts puttin' the equipment inna ditch and now you're gonna tell me we ain't got a full supply of niggers, keep all the commissioners happy? Jesus Christ, Harry. Tell you what, kid— get in the truck with Harry and go out to town there and round me up ten, a dozen good-sized niggers, okay? Bring 'em out here right off and put 'em lying down and sleepin' in the bushes. Get hold some beer and wine bottles, too, scatter 'em around, so they'll look just like the ones we usually got here. Don't want the commissioners catchin' on, we're switchin' niggers on 'em."

"Yeah," Harry said, "and that is what I mean. One of these here commissioners *is* one."

"Is one what?" Mahoney said. The Flynn kid started laughing softly. "You shut up," Mahoney said furiously to the kid. "Is one what, I asked you," he said. "A nigger? You tellin' me they got niggers countin' niggers now?"

"I didn't," Harry said. "What I told you was that there was some commissioners here. I don't know what they're doin' except they want to talk to you about doin' it. You're the one that started talkin' about countin' niggers. Not me."

"Shit," Mahoney said.

"Okay," Harry said, "shit. But you still got to talk to them. Get in my truck here and come on."

"I can bring your truck back up for you when Mister Fucillo gets back here with it," the Flynn kid said.

"No," Mahoney said, getting into Harry's truck, "you done enough driving for one day. Fucked up enough, my vehicles. Stay here and do what Billy tells you." He got into Harry's truck and slammed the door.

"Now look at this, willya?" Mahoney said, as Harry jounced the truck over the mauled earth, heading back to the trailer. "You see why it is a man can't get anything done any more, and those bastards're always coming down here from the authority and asking how come the job ain't going along? The first thing that happens, the minute you take your eye off of anything, some punk kid that don't know his ass from third base gets it into his head he's gonna do something he ain't got no fuckin' idea whatsoever in the whole wide world how to do, and he gets everything all screwed up. Which means me, and Billy, and Eddie

Wright, and the big Caterpillar there've been wasted for about an hour each. Three man-hours and one hour the 'dozer time.

"And I no sooner get that shit straightened out," Mahoney said, "and you show up. And now I got to go back the office and stand around with my dick hanging out of my pants goin' back and forth with a couple of guys that don't know shit about the job, talkin' about somethin' that hasn't got shit to do with the job, until they get tired of it and decide they give me enough shit for one day, they can go back their fuckin' offices and write their fuckin' reports say I'm three-point-one niggers shy a full load of what the state would like to see for a reasonable number of niggers on this job. Which also, of course, hasn't got one goddamned thing to do with the actual job or whether it is getting done, not one fuckin' thing at all. And then the head nigger in charge up there in Boston will read their reports and he will decide, *he's* got to come down here and jerk my chain around for half a day or so, telling me I got to dream up some kind of magic so all of a sudden I will have black guys and Puerto Rican guys and all them other minority groups practically falling all over each other, they're so crazy to work for me on this job. And that'll be another jerk-off wasted day.

"You know why it is the government's always screaming and yelling that we don't give the government a full day's work, a full day's pay, on a government job like this?" Mahoney snorted. "It's because the government won't leave us alone long enough, get any work done. We got to spend all our time entertaining the fuckin' government instead, shootin' the shit with a buncha fuckers that don't give a shit about no airport and whether any planes can land at it. All they want to do is make sure we hired every fuckin' Micmac Indian between here and Halifax, every black guy couldn't get a job playin' basketball professional, and all the people that live here on the Vineyard and can tell a cow apart from a fuckin' lobster so naturally they should do great workin' construction, am I right? And that is what we are doing. We are fucking around all day, is what we are doing, and the runway is just something that we got here to do in case there ain't nobody from the state happens to come by and tie us up all day, we shouldn't be sittin' around playin' cards or something."

"Look," Harry said, "I can't do nothing about it."

"Of course you can't," Mahoney said. "Quite naturally you can't. I didn't say you could. How the fuck could you do anything about it? You're still workin' for a living. Still out actually doing things all day

that will make something. You ain't got a job workin' for the government, so you can go to work Monday and spend the whole day thinkin'
how you can go drive somebody nuts on the Vineyard at least one day
this week and get the hell out the office and go have some fresh swordfish on the taxpayers. What the fuck is that?" Mahoney said, pointing
toward a blue Jeep Cherokee four-door parked at the office trailer.

"That?" Harry said. "The Jeep?"

"Yeah, the Jeep," Mahoney said. "You think I was asking you what
one of the trees is, maybe?"

"That's their car," Harry said. "The one that the commissioners
come in."

"Fuck it is," Mahoney said. "That's a State Police car there."

"That ain't no State Police car," Harry said. "That's a Jeep."

"I know it's a fuckin' Jeep," Mahoney said. "I also know it's a State
Police, it's a Jeep that the state cop that's here has got for when he
wants to go chasing out over the beaches and snagging kids rowin' in
with those big bales of marijuana they're always gettin' in here. That's a
State Police Jeep."

"Well," Harry said, slowing the truck to a stop at the trailer, "so
what? It's still the car that the commissioners come in."

"So this," Mahoney said, squaring his shoulders and unlatching the
door to the truck. "Those commissioners are tied up with the cops.
Which is not the same thing as I was talking about, I think." He got out
of the truck and climbed the wooden steps into the trailer.

Lyle Putter in a tan poplin suit and Jimmy Cremmens in his blazer
and grey slacks were standing in the kitchen area of the trailer, drinking
coffee from plastic cups. Mahoney shut the door behind him and looked
at them in the cramped area. "Vinnie Mahoney," he said. "My guy here
says you want to see me."

Putter and Cremmens introduced themselves. "We're, ah," Cremmens said, "we're from the Ames Commission."

Mahoney moistened his lips and frowned. "The Ames Commission,"
he said. "Ah, look," he said, gesturing toward the office area in the rear
of the trailer, "we, ah, we could go in here and sit down and have a little more room, huh?" He did not wait for their answer. He led the way
between the file cabinets into the cluttered working space. He sat down
at the wooden desk. He lighted a cigarette and dropped the spent
match into one of the foil ashtrays. Putter and Cremmens sat down in
the two wooden chairs. "I don't," he said, "you guys got any identification or something?"

"I haven't," Putter said. "I'm the general counsel." Cremmens took his credentials case from his inside jacket pocket. He shoved it across the desk to Mahoney.

"State Police?" Mahoney said.

"Yes sir," Cremmens said. "I'm assigned to the Ames Commission. Work with Mister Putter here."

"Oh," Mahoney said. "I don't think . . . I never had no dealings with this Ames Commission before, I don't think," he said. "This something, my lawyer should've told me about?"

"Mister Costello?" Putter said mildly.

Mahoney shrugged. "Him," he said, "or Ship. Mister Shipstead. The lawyer down in the town there. He's the one we use on this job mostly. This something I should've heard about from him?"

"Him," Putter said, the corners of his mouth twitching slightly, "or Mister Costello. Francis Costello. You do know Francis Costello? Attorney Francis Costello?"

"Sure," Mahoney said, shifting in his chair, "I, ah, I know Costello."

"Get legal advice from him, do you?" Putter said.

"Well, uh, yeah," Mahoney said. "Yeah, I get legal advice from him. If it's something, I think there's something I oughta get some legal advice from somebody about, I might decide that I would ask Mr. Costello about it. Or if I was down here like I have been mostly since the winter was over, Mister Shipstead, him being right here, you know, and generally he is more familiar with the various things that're connected with this job, you know? It would all depend. I also got another lawyer at home, one that I use for the company. My wife calls him quite a lot for things that don't have anything special to do with any particular job I might be away on, you know?"

"I see," Putter said. "But you do know Mister Costello."

"Yeah," Mahoney said. "Uh, look, all right? Can I ask what this's all about? I mean, I got a buncha guys out there I like to keep pretty close tabs, what's goin' on. I just had a kid put a piece of machinery in a ditch, you know? I like to keep an eye on things at all times."

Cremmens cleared his throat. He looked at Putter. Putter nodded. "Mister Mahoney," he said, "are you acquainted with a Jean Dussault?"

"Dussault," Mahoney said, "Dussasult." His brows furrowed. "Jesus," he said, "I might be. I wouldn't want to come right out and tell you, I wasn't. But my God, you meet so many guys, this business, you know? What's he do, I might've run into him someplace."

"You're not sure?" Putter said.

"Well," Mahoney said, "I'm not sure I did and I'm not sure I didn't, you know? I, like I say, you meet a lot of guys, doing what I do, and one of them does one thing and another one does another thing and they don't, they don't all of them always stick in your mind, you know?"

"Sure," Putter said, comfortingly.

"Yeah," Mahoney said. He moistened his lips again.

"For example," Putter said, "somebody like Bernard F. Morgan."

"Morgan," Mahoney said.

"Yeah," Putter said easily. "Morgan. The Speaker of the House? Big guy? White hair? Early sixties? Kind of loud, dresses . . . he dresses so that if you saw him once you would remember him. Drives a Cadillac."

"Cadillac," Mahoney said.

Cremmens nodded. "Cadillac Seville," he said. "Maroon body, gold top. Pretty impressive car."

"I never seen his car," Mahoney said. "I don't think I ever seen his car. I did, I didn't know it was *his* car, you know what I mean? I might've seen his car some time but I didn't know it was his when I saw it. Didn't mean anything to me, is what I mean."

"You have seen him, though," Putter said. "You'd recognize . . . if you were to see Bernie Morgan, if he were to walk in that door we just came in right now, you would recognize him."

"Recognize him," Mahoney said.

"Yeah," Putter said. "You would know who he was."

"Well," Mahoney said, "yeah. Yeah, I would know who he was."

"Say hello to him and so forth," Putter said.

"Yeah," Mahoney said, "I would say hello to him. I would say hello to President Reagan if he was to come through the door, you know? And I knew it was him."

"And you would know it was President Reagan, of course," Putter said, with a smile.

"Yeah," Mahoney said, "I think I would. I never met him or anything, and I been a Democrat all my life, but I think I would recognize him. From television and everything."

"Ever seen Mister Morgan on television?" Putter said.

"I might've," Mahoney said. "It's possible. I dunno. I don't necessarily keep track everything I see on television. I probably did."

"But at any rate," Putter said, "if Mister Morgan were to walk in here now, and you recognized him and said hello to him, it wouldn't be, you wouldn't be recognizing him from having seen him on television."

"No," Mahoney said.

"You would be recognizing him from having seen him, because you had seen him in person," Putter said.

"Yeah," Mahoney said.

"Where did you see Mister Morgan last, Mister Mahoney?" Putter said.

"Hey," Mahoney said, "you wanna tell me what this is all about? Is this something, I oughta call my lawyer about and have him here while we're talking?"

"Whom would you like to have here, Mister Mahoney, if we were to tell you that it very well might be that sort of thing?" Putter said. "Mister Shipstead, who's familiar with this job, as you tell us, or Mister Costello, whom you also know to be a lawyer? Or perhaps the lawyer at home that your wife uses to ask about things having to do with the operation of the company generally?"

"Well," Mahoney said, "I don't know. I guess that is one of the things I would probably want to ask my lawyer about. Which lawyer I should be talking to about whatever it is that you want to talk to me about."

"I see," Putter said. "But it might be that you would want to discuss the matter with Mister Costello."

"Could be," Mahoney said. "Could be, yeah. I wouldn't want to rule it out. Not until I knew what it was I was talking to somebody about."

"You have, then," Putter said, "gotten legal advice from Mister Costello."

Mahoney thought about that. He nodded. "Yeah," he said, "yeah, I have. I have gotten legal advice from Mister Costello."

"Along with other kinds of advice?" Putter said.

"Well," Mahoney said, "I suppose so. I mean, I'm not a lawyer, you know? So, it would probably, I would probably have to ask a lawyer whether this particular advice that I got from Mister Costello was legal, or was it some other kind."

"Such as, for example," Putter said, "*il*legal?"

"Now just a goddamned minute here," Mahoney said, straightening up in his chair, "I think we oughta maybe get six, a half dozen things straight right now, Mister Putter, okay?"

"That's our purpose, Mister Mahoney," Putter said smoothly, nodding toward Cremmens. "Mine, and Corporal Cremmens here. That's all we're here for, to get a few things straight. And we hoped we could do that, just coming down here and talking to you on an informal basis."

"Good," Mahoney said. "The first things is, I didn't invite you in here. You come in here and you was waitin' for me in here when I got back. Nobody that I heard so far said anything that'd make me believe I had to talk to you. I'm doing this on account, I'm trying to be cooperative, you know? And now you decide you're gonna sit there and ask me if I'm doing something illegal? Lemme ask you something, Mister Putter, since we come around to asking questions here. Just who the fuck you think you are, huh?"

Putter's jaw clenched. He started to get out of his chair. "Okay, Mister Mahoney," he said, "I guess that takes care of our visit here. You'll be hearing from us, I can assure you."

"Fine by me," Mahoney said, clasping his hands over his belt buckle.

"And when you do, Mister Mahoney," Putter said, shaking his index finger at Mahoney, "you won't find us half as friendly as we were when we arrived this time."

"I can stand that," Mahoney said. "Next time I'll know you're coming."

Putter shook his head. "I wish I could understand it, Jim," he said to Cremmens, "you try to give a guy a break, and he starts swearing at you."

"I got a deal for you, Mister Putter," Mahoney said. "Next time you come, you can swear at me, and I get to accuse you of committin' crimes. Then we'll be even. See how you like it, guy comes bustin' in your office and starts making accusations."

"I didn't make any accusations, Mister Mahoney," Putter said.

"The shit you didn't," Mahoney said. "If you wasn't inferrin' something when you asked me that business about doing something illegal, I don't know what the hell it was."

"I wasn't implying anything," Putter said.

"That wasn't how it sounded to me," Mahoney said.

"Then you misunderstood me," Putter said, sitting down again.

"I thought you was leaving," Mahoney said.

Putter sighed. "Look," he said, spreading his hands, "you've got to give me a little consideration too, Mister Mahoney. I know it upsets people when I come in and say I'm from the Ames Commission."

"Don't upset me none," Mahoney said. "I don't even know the fuck this Ames Commission is. You could come in and tell me you just got here from the moon, far as I'm concerned. I never heard of Ames. All upsets me is you coming in here and all of a sudden you're asking me if I'm a crook. That's what I don't like."

Putter exhaled. "And," he said, "I know it upsets some people still further when I show up and they see that I'm a black."

"You got it wrong there, too, Mister Putter," Mahoney said. "It don't upset me you're a black at all. I can see it upsets *you*, but there ain't nothing in this world I can do about that."

Putter made a wry face. He shook his head. He looked at Cremmens. "Is there any point you can see, Jim, continuing this?"

Cremmens shifted in his chair. "Yeah," he said. "Yeah, I think there might be, Lyle. Like we said, we do need Mister Mahoney's help, we can possibly get it."

"True," Putter said. He nodded.

"Like you said coming down here today, Lyle," Cremmens said earnestly, "we can do it without him, sure, but it'd be a hell of a lot easier with him."

"Yes," Putter said. He nodded again. He was silent for a few moments. He spoke to Cremmens again, as though Mahoney had not been there. "Look, Jim, all right? I seem to've gotten us off on the wrong foot here. Why don't you see if you can put this thing in perspective for Mister Mahoney, huh? And I'll just sit here and listen."

"You want me to, Lyle," Cremmens said, "and he's willing to take some more time, hear me out."

"Oh, no problem there," Mahoney said. "I shot the whole day anyway. Might's well piss away a little more of it, find out what the hell's going on here anyway. 'Sides me being accused of doing something I don't know diddly-shit about."

"Mister Mahoney," Cremmens said earnestly, "lemme start at the beginning, okay?"

"Shoot," Mahoney said.

"Be patient with me," Cremmens said, "and I think you'll be able to see where we're coming from. What it is we're hoping to get from you in the way of cooperation. Then, you see what's going on, you decide you want to talk it over with your lawyer, any lawyer you like, well, we'll just stop, go away, and you can do that, okay? And no hard feelings."

"Okay," Mahoney said.

"Okay," Cremmens said, taking a deep breath. "Now, bear with me, okay? While back, this Jean Dussault that Mister Putter mentioned, he was convicted a few days ago in Cambridge of labor racketeering. What he was doing was setting up what we call sweetheart contracts. Know what those are?"

Mahoney shrugged. "I know what they are," he said. "I heard of them. I ain't never had one."

"Okay," Cremmens said, glancing at Putter and then back to Mahoney. "Now, I don't mean nothing by this, okay? But that's not what Mister Dussault told us."

"Told you," Mahoney said.

"Yes sir," Cremmens said. "Dussault's turned into a witness for the Commonwealth."

"I thought you said he got convicted," Mahoney said.

"I did," Cremmens said. "But he's awaiting sentencing, and he expects to get at least three years that he will have to do if he loses his appeal. So he's decided he'll cooperate with the Commonwealth before he even gets sentenced, and then maybe he will get his sentence suspended so he won't have to go to jail after all. What he's doing, Mister Mahoney, he's cutting his losses."

"*Vinnie,*" Mahoney said.

"*Vinnie?*" Cremmens said.

"Call me by my first name," Mahoney said. "I'm more used to it. All this respect, this Mister shit, I ain't used to it." He grinned.

"Okay, Vinnie," Cremmens said, sticking out his hand, "*Jim.*"

"Jim," Mahoney said, shaking it.

"Well," Putter said, "might's well join in. *Lyle,*" he said, sticking out his hand.

"Same to you, Lyle," Mahoney said, taking it, "Vinnie. Sorry I popped off there."

"Forget it," Putter said. "I wasn't blameless myself."

"Because, see," Mahoney said, "I always tried to run a clean operation. I just sort of see red, you know, somebody says maybe I didn't."

"I understand," Putter said. "I chose my words poorly."

"Okay," Cremmens said, grinning. "Now, if . . ."

"But I still don't think I ever heard, this Dussault guy," Mahoney said.

Cremmens held up his hand. "Bear with me, like I said," he said. "Basically," he said, "what he's telling us, and keep in mind we're just at the initial stages now, checking out what he says, documents, that kind of thing—we're not sure ourselves yet that he's telling the truth, and that's what we're trying, that's one of the things we want to find out, all right?"

Mahoney nodded.

"These guys will add a little something now and then," Putter said, "soup up their stories some, they figure it'll help them."

"Well," Mahoney said, "he said anything about having any sweetheart contracts with my outfit, that's what he's doing all right. Because I never paid off a union guy in my life. I heard of cases where it was done, but I never done it. I've never had to do it, either. Always had very good relations with the unions. Never had no trouble at all. Everybody else in the world's on strike, Mahoney Construction's just workin' right along as usual. Any time there's been a strike, I just get the guys in and I tell them, all right? 'Whatever the settlement turns out to be, favor of you, favor of me, that's what we're working under, as of today, this minute.' And that's what we always did. Retroactive. Never had a strike in over twenty years. Proud of that. Not one lost day, strike. Anybody tells you different, that Vinnie Mahoney slipped him a little something under the table to bag the unions, well, he is lying, is all. Lying. I never did it."

Cremmens frowned. "Right, Vinnie," he said, "and this is where it gets complicated, a little bit. Dussault doesn't say he got something from you, all right? He says he got it from somebody else, to keep the boys working for you when other companies were having trouble."

"I don't see who he could've," Mahoney said, frowning back. "My wife does all the payrolls and stuff. I do the land stuff. Not the actual checks, I mean, but I decide who's gettin' paid. Same with equipment and so forth. I don't see, I don't think she ever gave nobody no money, and I know I didn't."

"Dussault claims," Cremmens said, "he says you've got a guy working for you, for your company, name of Billy Fucillo."

"Sure," Mahoney said. "He's out onna job right now. Billy Fucillo. Been with me ever since I started. Good guy. A little hard to keep track of, sometimes, but a good guy, basically. Good worker. Foreman."

"Dussault says he knows Billy Fucillo," Cremmens said.

Mahoney shrugged. "Maybe he does," he said. "Billy gets around some when he ain't workin'. I don't know who he knows. He could know this Dussault fellow. Could be."

"Dussault says he got his payoffs from the Mahoney Construction Company from Billy Fucillo," Putter said.

"He says Fucillo was paying him off?" Mahoney said.

Putter nodded. "That's what he says."

"So I wouldn't have labor troubles?" Mahoney said.

"That's what he says," Putter said.

Mahoney looked worried. "I'm havin' trouble believing this," he said. "I dunno, I can see I got to talk to Billy about this. Have a talk with him. Find out just what the fuck is going on here."

"Vinnie," Putter said, "just off the top of your head, all right? Does Fucillo have access to company funds?"

"You mean, like money?" Mahoney said.

"Right," Putter said.

"No," Mahoney said, shaking his head. "No, he don't have no access."

"Does he get money from you?" Cremmens said.

"He gets paid for what he works," Mahoney said. "I got to pay the guy."

"Would that include," Cremmens said, "a thousand dollars a month for incidentals?"

"You mean," Mahoney said, "like, a grand a month, that I didn't owe Billy for what he did himself on the job?"

"Yes," Cremmens said.

"No," Mahoney said. "Absolutely not."

"So," Putter said, "if Dussault said he got a thousand dollars a month from Mahoney Construction, from Billy Fucillo, as part of a sweetheart contract to keep the boys in line, your best answer would be that he couldn't have, because Fucillo didn't have access to a thousand dollars a month in addition to his salary?"

"Sure," Mahoney said. "I might forget I treated to coffee one day, but a grand a month going out, I think I would remember."

"And," Cremmens said, "going back now to that job you had last year, when your company put up the new laboratory wing, offices and a couple classrooms, at the State Technical School in Taunton. Remember that?"

"Sure," Mahoney said, moving uneasily in his chair.

"Did Billy Fucillo have access to any company money then, except what he earned for himself?" Putter said.

"Well, geez," Mahoney said, wriggling, "uh, that's, that's over a year ago, we started that job, right? I dunno what he had. I suppose . . . I'd have to check some records and stuff."

"He could've?" Putter said.

"Well," Mahoney said, "you know how it is. We had a lot of guys there then, and some of them lived quite a distance away and they wanted to cash their checks, and the banks where they lived, they didn't know us, you know? Supermarkets and that stuff. Wouldn't cash our checks for them when they got home and their wife goes out with it and tries to get the butcher, give her some meat and cash the check. So I think . . . Billy might've, we could've set something up so those guys, to help them out, you know? Give them their checks on the job and then Billy would have the cash there to cash them for them before they went home."

"Uh huh," Putter said.

"And," Cremmens said, taking some folded notes from his jacket pocket, "would those checks, would those've been drawn on the New Bristol Trust and Fidelity Bank," he said, "account number oh-one, seven-two-four, oh-oh-five, three? Mahoney Construction Company? Vincent C. Mahoney and William A. Fucillo, authorized signatures?"

Mahoney exhaled. "Uh," he said. "Yeah," he said, "yeah. They could've been drawn, they could've been drawn on that account."

"And," Cremmens said, "if those checks drawn on that account, the bank's microfilmed records, indicated that the sums averaged precisely one thousand dollars a month while you were on that job, that Fucillo drew? Would that sound about right?"

"Ah," Mahoney said, "well, ah, I suppose, yeah, it could be. I suppose. See, like I said, that account, we had those guys that lived a good distance away, you know? Cashing their checks for them."

"How many guys, Vinnie?" Putter said. "Would you know, offhand?"

Mahoney exhaled again. "Ah," he said, "geez, no, I wouldn't, I, ah, I really wouldn't, you know? It wasn't something, you know, I didn't pay much attention to it. It was just something that we did, help those guys out."

"Three or four?" Putter said.

"Well," Mahoney said, "like I said, I'd have to, I'd have to check and all, but I suppose, yeah, three, four. Probably about that."

"What's the average wage in your business, Mister Mahoney?" Putter said.

"Vinnie," Mahoney said.

"Sorry," Putter said. "What's the average wage, Vinnie?"

"Well, ah," Mahoney said, moistening his lips, "it, ah, it varies, you know? It varies."

"Sure," Putter said. "This varying wage, though, huh? Would you say that last year you had as many as four employees in the construction business, the whole time you were building that lab wing in Taunton, that were averaging sixty-two dollars and fifty cents a week?"

"Huh?" Mahoney said.

"A little over a buck fifty an hour?" Putter said.

"Uh," Mahoney said, "ah, no. No, I wouldn't."

"Right," Putter said smoothly. "Which would be what four employees' cashing checks each month for a total of one thousand dollars would represent, right? About two hundred and fifty bucks a month each? Sixty-two fifty a week? Buck and a half an hour?"

Mahoney licked his lips. "Ah, I guess that'd be," he said. "Yeah. That'd be about it. No, no, I don't think we had none of them."

"Can you think of anything else," Cremmens said, "that would account for Fucillo's withdrawals of a thousand dollars a month from that account, Vinnie?"

"Jesus," Mahoney said, sweat appearing around his nose, "I, ah, I really can't. I think I better get ahold those records there, and also Billy. Ask him where the hell that dough was going. That's quite a lot of dough, I don't know where it went."

"That's what we thought," Putter said. "And, up until the end of last week—well, I'll be candid with you, Vinnie, okay?"

"Sure," Mahoney said.

"Well, you'll be able to understand it, I'm sure," Putter said, "we were really, we had a strong desire to talk to Billy Fucillo. You'll understand that, I'm sure."

"Uh," Mahoney said. "Yeah. Yeah. Right."

"Because you certainly wouldn't be the first guy," Putter said warmly, "that had one of his employees playing fast and loose with the company cash, acting under the misguided belief that he was doing something his employer would want him to do, when what he was in fact was breaking the law, a fairly serious criminal offense, a felony, and his employer would've been horrified if he'd known what was going on."

"No," Mahoney said.

"Right," Cremmens said. "Dussault mentioned several companies like yours, Vinnie, as a matter of fact. And you know what? Three of them so far, in three of them it turns out the owner had no idea at all what some employee was doing, behind his back. And those employees, of course, they're in pretty serious trouble now. So serious, in fact, that one or two of them've suggested that they'd be willing to testify against their bosses. Say their bosses actually did know what was going on. Which of course means ... well, you can imagine what it means. Puts the bosses in a position where they're going to be the ones facing criminal charges, having to prove they didn't know what their employees were up to. Pretty tough row to hoe."

"Yeah," Mahoney said, looking morose.

"The trouble is, in this case," Putter said, "and this is what we found out just last week before we had a chance, come down and see you, this one's a little different. Because it's not just a matter of us going up to Fucillo there, with your permission, of course, and asking him, well, why was he doing this."

"It isn't?" Mahoney said.

"Nope," Putter said. "Because the thing of it is, you see, Vinnie, we're in kind of an awkward situation there with Billy Fucillo that we didn't find ourselves in with the other foremen we've talked to, including those who've now gotten back to us and say they've decided they want to blame these schemes on their employers, right?"

"No," Mahoney said.

"Where Fucillo's concerned," Putter said, "we can't just go up and talk to him. Because he's already under criminal charges. Fairly serious ones, too."

"He is?" Mahoney said.

"Yeah," Cremmens said. "Just a matter of course, normal procedure, we ran his name through NCIC—National Crime Information Center, computer—and he came up, there's a rape charge pending against him. We sort of figured you'd know about that. Where it's supposed to've happened here. Started here, at least. He was missing a while, wasn't he? Nobody knew where he took the girl?"

"Well," Mahoney said, "*yeah.* About three weeks. But that thing, I thought, he told me he thought that thing was gonna probably blow over. I guess the local cops were gonna talk to the girl's mother or something, and she, I guess the kid's the town pump, you know what I mean? And he thought it was gonna blow over. Last I heard, anyway. He didn't seem like he was too worried about it."

"Well," Cremmens said, "it's not that simple. See, this isn't just a rape case, where it's pretty much up to the victim whether the charges're gonna be dropped. This's a statutory rape case. Girl was underaged."

"Well," Mahoney said, "I mean, she can still go in and say she don't wanna testify against him, can't she? I mean, she don't have to, she decides she doesn't wanna get all the embarrassment and everything."

"Not that simple, Vinnie," Putter said. "There's a public policy involved here. The attorney general, the Commonwealth, the Commonwealth and society in general have got an interest in older guys not latching on to the young girls. The ones that're underaged. So even though the girl and her family might say: 'Well, we're going to drop it,' that might not be the end of it. The AG might say: 'Yeah, that's okay for you. But we want to teach these guys that haven't been teenagers for a long time, they've got to make damned sure they're dealing with adults here when they start hitting on some kid.' See? Because otherwise it'd be too easy, guy picks up a young kid and then the possible embarrassment she'd suffer winds up letting him off the hook, scot-free."

"Yeah," Mahoney said.

"I mean, after all," Putter said, "I know your three girls're grown up now, and you never had to face anything like this. Your family was lucky, kids went to good schools, doing well in their careers now."

"How'd you know that?" Mahoney said.

"Well," Putter said, "that's not important. It's fairly easy to find out, you know. We've got access to all kinds of information, and naturally we make use of it. To know who we're dealing with. But that doesn't matter. All I'm saying about Fucillo is that the AG might not drop the charges even though the girl might say she did want to. Make her testify and put Fucillo in jail, as an example to anybody else who might be thinking about robbing the cradle."

"Jail?" Mahoney said.

"Sure, jail," Putter said.

"Jesus," Mahoney said. "Terry'd kill him."

"That'd be his wife?" Cremmens said.

"Yeah," Mahoney said absently.

"Not to mention," Putter said, "the embarrassment to his kids."

"Whew," Mahoney said.

"Now," Putter said, "up to now, at least, the AG isn't involved in Fucillo's case."

"No," Mahoney said. "I didn't hear that he was."

"It's the DA," Putter said. "Normal thing where one of these things is involved. DAs handle it."

"Yeah," Mahoney said.

"And," Putter said, "we don't know, we haven't heard that the DA is interested in making an example of Fucillo. Or that the AG has any interest in doing it."

"Well, then," Mahoney said, "I don't see . . ."

"Point is," Putter said, "the AG's got the power to take over the case, if he wants, take it right away from the DA and say: 'I'm gonna make an example out of Fucillo. Throw him in the can.' Then it wouldn't matter what the DA thought, either. Fucillo'd go to jail. If he was convicted, of course. Which from what I know of the case, he's almost certain to be, if it's tried. Pretty cut and dried."

"Yeah," Mahoney said.

"This is one," Putter said, "that'd take a good prosecutor about twenty minutes to prove. There's no defense. Jury'd find him guilty without leaving the courtroom."

"Yeah," Mahoney said.

"And then," Putter said, "if the guy ever had any curiosity about how it might be to make it with a boy, he'd be well on his way to finding out."

Mahoney looked up fast.

"Homosexual rape," Putter said. "It's a virtual certainty for a man going into prison anyway, but when he's going in for statutory rape, he can bank on it. It's too bad, but there's no way to prevent it in our prison system."

"His first night in the general population," Cremmens said, "after he gets out of the New Man Section, *whammo*, right up the ass." He made an uppercut with his right fist. "Couple weeks in there, he's completely eligible for active membership, the FFA."

"FFA," Mahoney said.

"Fist Fuckers of America," Cremmens said.

"Jesus," Mahoney said.

"Right up the old ass," Cremmens said again.

"Yeah," Putter said. "But, as we say, we're not especially eager, when a man's up against this sort of prospect, to just bust in and talk to him, you know? Without him having any chance to think things over and talk to his lawyer. Because if the guy's got information that we think the Ames Commission needs, well, he should have it in mind if he's in a position like your Mister Fucillo is that the Ames Commission has the powers of the attorney general. All of 'em."

"All of 'em," Mahoney said.

"Right," Putter said. "If the AG can take over a case like Mister Fucillo's, we can. And we can do exactly the same thing to him that the AG could do. No matter what the girl wants. No matter what he wants. Which, and I'm being candid with you now, Vinnie, is exactly what I'm very much afraid Mister Fucillo should expect, if he decided to lie to us about this money that Mister Dussault claims he got from the Mahoney Construction Company."

"I see," Mahoney said.

"Now," Putter said, "since we're in this kind of awkward position where Mister Fucillo's concerned, we thought, well, it might be better for everybody concerned if we *didn't* talk to him."

"You don't want to talk to Billy?" Mahoney said.

"Not at this time," Putter said. "What we'd like to have him do is sort of search his memory and give some thought to whether what Mister Dussault tells us has got any truth to it. And if he remembers that it has, or even thinks it might, get in touch with his attorney and then have him call us and make an appointment to come in and talk to us about it. And then, of course, to the grand jury."

"Grand jury," Mahoney said.

"Yeah, Vinnie," Cremmens said, "we empaneled a special grand jury just last week for stuff the commission turns up."

"Now what we hoped was this, Vinnie," Putter said. "What we hoped was that you would tell him pretty much what we've told you, okay?"

"Uh," Mahoney said. "Yeah, yeah, I see."

"And maybe, while you're at it," Cremmens said, "a couple other things."

"Like," Mahoney said, "like, uh, what?"

"Well," Putter said, "the way we get it, on this rape case, Fucillo was off with the girl about three weeks, more or less."

"Yeah," Mahoney said. "Last month there, and this."

"Yes," Putter said. "Now, one of our powers, and this's how that New Bristol account came to our attention, is that we can subpoena from banks. And we put a subpoena on the Haven Trust here in Vineyard Haven. I think the company's got an account there. Similar to the one you had on the Taunton job."

"Right," Mahoney said, licking his lips again.

"And we find on that account," Putter said, "we've got the copies of the checks and the statements, the deposit slips and the checks that went into it, all the traffic, the activity in the account, that one of those regular withdrawals was made while Fucillo was off with the girl, and you seem to've signed for it."

"Uh," Mahoney said, "I don't recall . . ."

"Yeah," Putter said. "Probably doesn't mean anything. And there's another item that we were hoping somebody could explain to us, as well."

"There was?" Mahoney said.

"Yeah," Putter said. "An item, withdrawal, of seventy-five hundred bucks. Also over your signature. While Fucillo was on the loose. You got any idea what that might've had to do with, Vinnie? Cashing some more checks for your laborers, while he was off with his cutie?"

"I, ah, I dunno," Mahoney said. "Not offhand."

"Yeah," Putter said, standing up suddenly, and glancing at his watch. Cremmens stood up as well. "Well," Putter said, "look, okay? We've got a plane to catch. Back to the mainland. New Bedford. And we've got to cut this short. But, look Vinnie, okay? See if you can talk to Fucillo about this, explain it all to him and why we didn't come to him directly, on account of him being a defendant in a criminal case that we could end up prosecuting, and see what the hell the two of you can work out, huh?"

Putter and Cremmens, smiling, stuck out their hands.

Mahoney stood up very slowly, wiping the palms of his hands on his pants. "Yeah," he said, mumbling. He cleared his throat. "Yeah," he said, extending his hand mechanically, "I'll, uh, I'll certainly see what I can do."

They left him standing there, shoulders sagging, behind the desk. They went out through the kitchen, down the wooden steps, across the mud, and got into the Cherokee, Cremmens driving. He stuck the key in the ignition, backed the Jeep around, and headed out to the road. Putter slumped in the passenger seat.

"Well," Cremmens said, "whaddaya think?"

"What do I think?" Putter said, grinning. "Let me ask you something first, Jimmy, okay? Does it bother you that I'm black?"

"Nah," Cremmens said. He grinned.

"Me neither," Putter said with satisfaction, "not when I got one of you honkies hung up on a hook like we just had him."

"So," Cremmens said, "whaddaya think?"

"Easy," Putter said. "One word. *Bingo.*"

22 "It's sad, really," Helen Dotten said to the Speaker, settling herself in the blue leather chair opposite his broad desk. "This isn't medical talk now, because there isn't really anything that we can do about the sadness of dealing with them. Wouldn't matter if we had all the oil in Alaska to sell to pay for their care. They're lost and con-

fused and the worst of them are living inside their own heads with monsters and dragons and the good Lord only knows what kinds of demons. I know it sounds cruel, but nothing we can do and nothing we can persuade you or anyone else to do, nothing will change those facts. And maybe that's the saddest thing of all."

"So," Morgan said mildly, "why bother? I mean, this isn't a slap in your face, Doctor. I don't mean it that way at all. But what difference will it make, anything we do? Will the patients know, will they notice any improvement?"

"Perhaps," she said, "but it's more likely they won't. Their families will. And we of course will. The staff. In a way it's tougher facing them than it is facing the patients every day. The patients can be sort of amusing, and I don't mean that unkindly. They don't realize what they do, the things they say, they don't mean them to be funny and they'd be very hurt if they thought that you were laughing at them and not with them, but they do have that insulation. They're never really entirely sure what's going on, no. It's just static to them, what goes on in the real world. The relevant broadcasts are the ones they have inside their heads."

"Because," Morgan said, "the reason I ask, my brother-in-law was in there for a while. I'm not sure you know that."

"Oh yes," she said. Her lips crinkled slightly. "Yes, I know that. Roger Knox. He still visits his father fairly regularly. Not frequently, but regularly. Once a month. Your . . ."

"My father-in-law," Morgan said, with a small smile. "Yeah, I'm aware of the legal relationship. I'm not sure he is, any longer, but I am."

"You don't come to see him, though," she said. "The staff . . . look, I'm going to be candid with you. Is that all right?"

"Like you were with Nancy on the television show this morning?" Morgan said, grinning.

She smiled, but she also reddened. "She got on my nerves," Dotten said. "I'm afraid I have a low threshold of tolerance for giddy people like that. It's bad enough when you spend every working hour dealing with people who don't understand the simplest things because they genuinely can't. They'd like to, but it's beyond them. And then you come up against somebody like her, somebody who enjoys a position of considerable influence, somebody who could really grasp a problem and present it to people who have their own problems and really aren't much interested in hearing all about somebody else's problems, but will listen if you give them half a chance, present it correctly. And then she turns out to be such a . . . fool.

"We had high hopes for that show, Doctor Khan and I," she said. "We had to get up very early this morning to drive down to Boston in time to sit around for almost an hour and a half drinking coffee and eating doughnuts because that was when they told us that we had to be there, before we actually got on. The lady with the eggs and the singers and the dancers were much more important to them than we were, we and what we had to say. They took us around the set like dogs being shown a strange kennel, letting us sniff the furniture and get used to the surroundings. I suppose that was so we wouldn't cry or bark when we were actually led out in front of the cameras. Then they shooed us back out into the hall to sit and drink coffee for an hour. All I could think of was that this is the way we treat our patients sometimes. Like nitwits. But our patients *are* nitwits, or at least they're supposed to be. And we can't do much else. Incapable of caring for themselves. I thought we arrived there with the assumption that we could care for ourselves and had something important to say. And instead she wants a geography lesson from Doctor Khan and then she treats me like some clone of Germaine Greer. It was frustrating."

"Speaking of which," Morgan said, "where is the little brown mascot you had with you this morning? He wander off or something on the way here?"

Dotten looked at him sharply. "Doctor Khan," she said, "Doctor Khan and I had an appointment with the Governor. The Governor started it late. Apparently he was off pressing the flesh at some luncheon and that was more important than seeing us, keeping an appointment that he'd made a long time ago. So Doctor Khan and I agreed that he would keep the appointment with the Governor, and I'd keep the appointment with you."

"Well," Morgan said, "look at it this way. If you don't get anything accomplished, talking to me, at least you won't walk out of here all covered with bullshit. Which is the problem that your sidekick's likely to have."

She nodded. "I know," she said. "I suppose I'm getting myself and my patients in trouble today instead of helping them, but it wasn't by chance that I left Doctor Khan to see Governor Tierney and came here myself to see you. I've met the Governor before. I haven't met you. I figured no matter if you did live up to your reputation as a stinker, I'd

still be ahead of the game. I feel like I've been subjected to general an-
esthesia when I come out of a discussion with the Governor. He makes
Nancy seem absolutely brilliant by comparison."

"So," Morgan said, smiling, "I'm the big bad wolf at Knox State Hospital, huh? That because I don't come around to see old Wilfred, or is it
something that makes even less sense?"

"It's partly your father-in-law," she said. "He's something of a favorite with the staff, you know."

"He oughta be," Morgan said. "For that matter, so should I. The two
of us, we built that place. Wasn't for him first, and then me, they
wouldn't have those jobs today. They tell me they can't make enough
on them to buy houses for themselves in Florida, and I guess that's kind
of too bad. But I'm not telling you anything you don't know, Doctor, I
tell you half those birds couldn't catch their own worms if they hadda.
That hospital there, it may be old and gettin' a little bit run-down, but
most of us are and it's still a pretty good tit for them as wants a job for
themselves and something to eat."

"Did you expect lifelong gratitude?" she said.

Morgan laughed. "Sister," he said, "if I expected gratitude for anything I did in this job, I should call you up and tell you, heave whoever's
in the room next to Wilfred's right out on his ass, because I'm cleaning
out my desk and coming up and checking in tonight. No," he said, "no.
I didn't expect gratitude. Way I look at things, I'm lucky, I get through
a day and nobody actually took out a gun or something and tried to go
and shoot me.

"Besides," he said, "and I wouldn't say this out in public where anybody'd hear me and start trying to make something out of it, but where
the hell would I come off anyway, looking for gratitude? It ain't my
money that I'm spending, whether it's enough or not. Don't matter at
all to me. That's tax money. There's a certain number times we can
spend it: one. We spend it on Knox State and Bridgewater, and Tindall
and Melanson, and all those other places that we got for people that
keep getting into trouble or setting their clothes on fire or something.
It's not my money. It's just money that we're not going to have available to spend when somebody like you comes in here screaming from
the Department of Corrections or Natural Resources, they want more
cells for prisoners or more wetlands for ducks or some other goddamned
thing.

"Makes me laugh," Morgan said. "I hear other guys doing it when
they're running for stuff. I hear myself doing it, I decide it's time I went

back home and put in a few days showing the flag and making sure that everyone remembers that it's good old Bernie Morgan that makes the water come out the faucet every time you turn the handle, and you'd better vote for me again. It's all bullshit. The other guys, maybe not all of them know it's bullshit, and they're the ones we like best of all, because we can make them vote for things we want voted for or else they won't get the stuff that they think's gonna make them look like Jesus with the home folks, and that's really what's important to them. They think they're missionaries, some damned thing."

"Mister Knox," she said tentatively, "on those rare occasions when he talks, he sometimes says things that suggest that attitude."

Morgan snorted. "Sure he does," he said, "we all do. Only he's saying those things now where other people, like you, can actually hear him, when he's not running for anything. Which proves he's soft and oughta be right where he is. You start thinking like that, in this job, you're doing the Lord's work, it's time to quit. In here, when you're actually in office, in this office that you're in right now at least and I'm in every day, *forget* it. That's bullshit. If we do a certain amount of juggling and back-and-forth and trick little dodges we can work with year-end budget deficits and stuff like that that nobody outside here ever bothers, try to understand, which is a damned good thing for us, we can make it look like we are spending more cash than we're taking in. We're magicians, every one of us, and all the people like you that wanted money and we got it for them, cripes, you fall all over us. Next time you have a banquet at your joint, by God, you're gonna remember us, because you figure if you don't you won't get another dime next year, and you are absolutely right. And you're gonna make us honored guests and present us with a plaque if we really did every last thing that you wanted and a few more things besides, or with a scroll if we come up a little short but you still got hopes for us."

"Or a Revere bowl," she said.

"Ahh," he said, "unusual. That's only if you heard it pretty good that we happen to be the guy that's getting the payoff new administrator's job and we're probably gonna be your actual bosses of the joint when the current legislative session's over, so you'd better get us greased up pretty good so we don't come in and start making everybody spend all forty hours of work a week, actually at work. Or going over the expense accounts or something. I always figure, somebody gets up on his hind legs and hands me a Revere bowl, I always figure I better get my ass right back in here early the next morning and see if Ray Archambault or somebody like him's sitting at this desk and making some appointments. You're a politician, boy, you spot a Revere bowl and you better figure somebody's got you a free ticket to a political cremation and you're gonna be the guest of honor. When that fire goes out and all that's left is ashes, they'll be *you* and you're what's going in that pot they're giving you."

"Remind me," she said, "when you give us all we need this year at Knox, not to give you a Revere bowl at the banquet in March."

"That question, Doctor," he said, "that question isn't likely to come up, I'm sorry to say, and I wouldn't want you to go getting all your hopes up here too fast."

"Oh, come on, Mister Morgan," she said, "have a heart. I'm having a very discouraging day, down here in the big city. Can't you give me one piece of good news I can take back with me and use to get me through the long, hot summer?"

He smiled and stood up. "Come here," he said. He stepped from behind the desk to the carved door on his right. She sat on the chair, poised to get up but still undecided. "Aw," he said, beckoning, "come on. It's not the shithouse or something I'm gonna show you, though there are some people that'd like to tell you different. Come here." He opened the door. She got up and walked over to it. He stood aside to let her look through.

The door opened into the well of the House, onto the raised platform leading to the Speaker's desk and lectern. The chamber was empty except for two white-shirted doorkeepers dozing at their desks at the doors to the corridor outside. The blue leather chairs had been dusted and the representatives' desks, arranged in semicircles around the Speaker's platform and the clerk's desk below it, were neat and orderly. The sacred stuffed cod hung over the doorway.

"Looks pretty dignified, right?" he said.

"It does," she nodded. She spoke in a hushed voice.

He laughed. "It isn't," he said. "You should see it when we're pushing to adjourn and the boys come back from various places with a bit more in their buckets than they were built to carry. Gets kind of noisy in here then. People start exchanging compliments and other remarks. Every so often some guy will really get ticked off and start a little dustup. But it's a nice room just the same. You can hear everybody pretty good, especially when you don't want to, but if you got that big wooden hammer that they let me use, and the block to bash it on there, you can generally make it so the only voice they hear is yours. Old Wilfred there, when he got the wind up him, he looked like a blacksmith with that gavel up there, whaling it down on the desk like he was driving railroad spikes. Had a voice on him like a bull, and when he got mad, he'd just roar. You probably heard stories about me, yelling at people."

"Well," she said.

He laughed again. "Don't lie," he said, "and don't bother, try to water them down. They're true. I practically give myself a hernia up there at least three, four times a year. We have got about a half-dozen guys in here that we cannot get rid of them. The people in their districts just keep sending them back and sending them back, no matter how bad we screw the poor bastards where they live that really need things that we really oughta give to them. We have sent guys out, finally, guys to run against them, tell them clowns right out to their faces, this is the voters now I'm talking about, tell them: 'Look, okay? Bernie Morgan and the guys, they hate old Malcolm's guts.' Or whatever the guy's name is that we happen to hate his guts so much we're not doing nothing for his district. 'And what you got to do, ladies and gentlemen, if you got any hopes of ever getting grass seed even planted in the divider strips along the state roads here, let alone getting it cut, you have got to put old Malcolm out to graze. Because Bernie and them, they're never gonna give old Malcolm nothing.'

"I practically sent letters to those districts, myself," Morgan said. "We got one guy down on Martha's Vineyard there, name of Baxter, Wendell Baxter, that's done everything he can since the day that he walked in here, crab my act and complicate my life. And I've done everything but take an ad out in the paper down there tellin' them that they'd better get rid of Baxter pretty soon because my patience's wearin' thin and pretty soon I'm gonna call out the Ancient and Honorable Artillery and set them up with a navy from the Department of Natural Resources and have them go over there by sea and shell Oak Bluffs some day and blow those campground Protestants they got living there right into the loving arms of Jesus. And do they listen to me? Nope. Next year, every two years, Baxter goes out of here and back down home to Edgartown and tells them like he did two years ago before that which made them think if they didn't have old Baxter up here making everybody's life miserable for them, they would have the Russians quartering soldiers down at the Yacht Club or some other goddamned thing. And every two years, regular as clockwork, the new General Court has its opening session and there stands good old Wendy Baxter, lookin' like he's constipated, waiting to be sworn in."

She laughed. "Now Baxter," Morgan said, "old Baxter is the kind of guy I mean. Baxter's got to be about five years older now'n God is, and the only reason that I guess he ain't with God now is that God don't want no part of him, God being, as you know, a good Democrat, and the Devil won't take him on account he doesn't want to have old Baxter yelling at him all the time down in the fiery furnace that he's got to send more of Hell's revenue back to Vineyard Haven and West Tisbury. Baxter's been here, he was here when Wilfred became Speaker, and he was here, he'd been here, for a good many years when I first come in on my own. The guy comes with the building, and he used to get old Wilf so riled I thought he'd blow up and explode. I tell you, Doctor Dotten, there ain't no doubt whatsoever in my mind today that if old Wilfred's living where he really ought to be today, and he is, in the home, well, by God, Wendy Baxter's one strong reason why he's in there. I saw Wilfred personally break two gavels in one day trying to shut Baxter up, and I broke one of them myself on that old bastard.

"Now, sister," Morgan said, "you take Baxter and you multiply him by one hundred and fifty-odd, and that is what I got out in front of me every day the House's in session and they all happen to be here. Used to be worse—two hundred forty of us back when Wilf was running things. Plus me, and there's plenty of the Baxters that're mortally convinced and you will never get them to believe otherwise, that I am just like Baxter too, only about ten times worse and a hundred times more dangerous because I got the gavel. And when you get all done imagining that, that is the august and dignified body that you are asking me to get you money from. See? It ain't magic that you want, Doctor, it is sheer firepower." He turned toward her and waved toward his office. "Now," he said, taking her by the left elbow, "let's you and me leave this place where it's the lions and the Christians every time they sound the gong, and go in here where it is nice and quiet, sometimes even downright sensible, and the real work gets done sometimes, when it gets done at all."

He returned to his chair behind the desk, waited for her to resume her seat, sat down, and folded his hands across his belly. He rocked back and forth in his chair a couple of times, and sucked his teeth.

"I have read what you want," he said.

"It's a very modest and reasonable request," she said.

He nodded. "I agree with you," he said. "It's a very modest and reasonable request, and you ain't got a tinker's damned chance in hell of getting it."

Her face got red. "Well, Mister Morgan," she said, "I must say, everything they told me about your charm and graciousness was true." She started to get up. "Thanks for your time," she said.

"Easy does it," he said. "I didn't say I thought it was a bad thing you want to do up there, the facilities you want to add. I didn't say I thought three hundred, four hundred grand, was too much. Didn't say anything like that. All I said was that you ain't gonna get it. You wanna hear why, and how maybe you might stand a decent chance of getting it? Or you want to stomp out of here instead and hustle back to Proctor and tell everybody they were right and Bernie Morgan really is a bastard as they can tell from the fact he never comes to see old Wilfred there that's sick and misses him?" He shrugged. "Me, I personally don't give a shit which you do. You can't hurt me with my people, and I haven't got yours behind me anyway, no matter if I turn into Jesus tomorrow and announce that every one of them is saved. They'll still vote against me anyway. You get it and they'll say it was in spite of me. You don't get it and they'll say that was because of me. So, it's up to you."

She sat down again. "I'll be frank with you," she said, "I . . ."

"Lady," Morgan said, "I know that you'll be frank with me, so stop telling me you're gonna be, all right? I knew you were gonna be frank with me before you ever walked into this office. You're the lady that told Nancy on the television that you got knocked up. I've had lots of people come in here all smiling like a bunch of assholes that they are, and they think they're so damned smart they're gonna bullshit Bernie Morgan to his knees. And you know what they did? They left here with their pants all wrinkled and their poor souls troubled, too. You don't shit the shitter, ma'am, but I didn't figure that you'd even try. So it don't impress me that you didn't. Stop bragging about it."

"Okay," she said, "what's the story on my three hundred and seventy-one thousand dollars?"

"Simple," he said, "you didn't ask for enough."

"My turn," she said. "You have got to be shitting me. You tell me I'm not getting it and then you're telling me that it's because I didn't ask for enough of it?"

"Yup," he said. He tapped the file folder on the desk. "You want to build a field house and a pool Olympic size, put in some whirlpool stuff and in a couple years add on a basketball court and a place for badminton indoors."

"Correct," she said. "A large part of the problem that we have, especially as we get more and more younger patients in the hospital population, is keeping them occupied. Their physical energy has to be dissipated, Mister Morgan. The reason, a good part of the reason the night staff especially has trouble with them is because they simply do not get enough exercise during the day to sleep during the night. These people are not physically ill. Many of them are or could be in pretty good physical condition. They need to work off all that excess energy during the day. And this is also activity for which they don't need to learn verbal skills first. They don't need normal intelligence, or intelligence functioning in a normal way, to swim or maybe bat a volleyball around. The only thing that puzzles me is why this sort of facility wasn't installed in the first place, when the hospital was built."

"Simple," Morgan said, "Wilfred didn't think of it, and neither did I. So it didn't get put in there."

"Well," she said, "forgive me, but that looks pretty stupid, from where I sit. All you really succeeded in putting up was a warehouse for the ill, a place to keep them from the time they either get sick, or if they were born retarded, get too big to manage at home. Until they co-. operate and die. Which isn't much of a facility."

"Absolution granted," he said, making the sign of the cross in the air, "no Our Fathers and no Hail Marys, either. Because we really didn't give a shit about building a facility, see? And this is where you look pretty stupid, if you don't mind me being frank for a change. Not that it matters, because I'm gonna be anyway.

"You see, sister," he said, hunching forward at the desk, "what you—"

"Excuse me," she said, "I'm not a nun."

"And I'm not your brother, either," Morgan said. "I'm calling you *sister* and any other reasonably respectable name I happen to because that's what I happen to call you when I open my mouth. And it's my office, sister, so that's the kind of the sort of thing you have to get used to, when you come into it."

"I don't like it," she said.

He shrugged. "Another on a long list of things that I don't give a shit about," he said. "Now, you wanna hear how you can get your stuff you want for the idiots and those folks? Or you wanna lecture me about women's lib and that crap? Your choice, but I got to warn you I have got a habit of walking out of those sessions when I run into them somewhere else, and shutting them down when I hear them starting here."

"You're a very rude man," she said.

"Lady," he said, "I hope you didn't think I was really gonna turn out to be just a lovable old fella you could jolly up and then go back and tell your pals that I was just a perfect lamb, because I'm not. There's a reason why I've got the reputation that I've got—I deserve it. Now, I deal with crazy people in this place all day, just like you do in your place all day. So I got hopes that maybe you and me can talk some sense. You gonna listen to me or not?"

"Very well," she said. "I still don't like it, though."

"Understood," he said. "Now, what you've got to do is get your facility, that you want, by showing people like me how giving it to you will give us something we want. And that's the way you sell it. You want a pool? Fine. That is so many construction jobs and so much cement and stuff right now, and a filter system and that stuff, and then later on some lifeguards and some people to take care of it."

"How many?" she said.

"I don't know," he said. "I should know, though. You should've told me, as the rep for the district that the hospital's in, because I'm the first guy that you've got to get promoting this thing: how many jobs. Right off the bat. You should've sent me this here bill and said: 'Mister Morgan, you old bastard, you give us this and you'll have twenty construction jobs, for a year or two, and then about eight, ten permanent jobs that anybody's idiot cousin can do that's just a little too smart to get into the hospital as a patient.' And I would start translating that into votes in a district which like every other district's got no, zero, none construction business to speak of, and little lights start flashing in my head and they're all green and they mean go."

"I see," she said. "The patients don't matter. It's just the goodies for you."

"Not yet, you don't," he said. "The patients're gonna matter, matter like a bastard, when I announce this thing. Absolutely. But the people I want to impress with this haven't got shit's worth of interest in them unless they got members of their family in there."

"Which you, of course," she said, "have."

"But Doctor Dotten," Morgan said, "I already vote for me, you twerp, and no matter how repulsive I may find me, I am loyal, see? So I will probably always vote for me, no matter how mean that I may think I've been to all the goofy people I got locked up in my district. Okay? You sure you haven't been in that laughing house of mine too long? It hasn't started to affect you, or something? I'm beginning to wonder: is being dumb contagious?"

"Okay," she said, "okay. Sorry I mentioned it."

"The people I want to impress," Morgan said, "are the unions and the suppliers and those guys, right now. And then the people that'll get permanent jobs when the damned thing's built. And I've already got some of them impressed. But I'd like more. How can I get 'em?"

"I don't know," she said.

"By making it bigger, Goldilocks," Morgan said. "Add on a baseball diamond, some tennis courts, maybe a rink, huh? Everything that you can think of. And instead of just making it a hospital thing, put it on the grounds, sure, but make it a state recreational facility. Now you're showing me how to make more jobs, sell more cement, probably some chain-link fence, and at the same time set up a nice little recreational facility for the people in my district. I never was that strong with tennis players, right? More and more of them around now. Maybe this is my way to do it."

"Do you seriously think, Mister Morgan," she said, "that the people of the community would associate with the patients in such a facility?"

"You mean, with the halfway houses and all the uproar they start up every time we think about opening one and the word gets out?" he said. "No. Do I think they'd be willing to share those facilities, so the folks from the funny farm could have the indoor pool and the stuff they can use without getting loose or hurting themselves three or four days a week, and the regular people have to themselves the rest of the week? Sure. No question about it. We've got that now, on a limited basis, the hospital grounds. They're always having busloads of people go up to those grounds and run around in the woods all day."

"I know," Dotten said. "When I first went to work there, there was a whole big group of little people. Midgets, dwarfs? Some sort of organization of them. They came out to pick wild flowers in the meadow and have a picnic. You should've seen the patients when they saw the little people scampering through the flowers. It was really funny, although of course we couldn't laugh. There were the dwarfs and midgets, who I guess hadn't realized they were on a state hospital grounds, and there were the people in the hospital whose view of reality is pretty distorted in most cases anyway, and they couldn't decide what in the world to make of each other."

"Well," Morgan said, "that's the way you do it. It shouldn't be too hard, put a new proposal through. Send it in, we'll ram it through committee and see what chance we've got."

"Really," she said. "And that's all there is to it."

"No," he said. "Financing. You don't want it by straight budget appropriation. That's more taxes. Bond issue. Tax-free bonds for the bankers to sell, makes them happy, tax-free interest for the rich people, which makes them happy, and consequently makes it easier for me to sell. Because, after all, you are spending money, no matter how you got it, and that always makes those fellas nervous. Got to put something in there so they come around to where they see the wisdom of your plan."

"It's all self-interest," she said, somewhat resentfully.

He grinned at her. "Well," he said, "it ain't beanbag, pal. But you know, it's not exactly quite as grubby as you think it is." He got up suddenly, jamming his hands into his back pockets and arching his back so his belly protruded still further. "Ahhh," he said, "all these years' sittin'. Gets you right inna small the back. It's not the knife which you've been half-expecting somebody to plant in you every day you come in here—it's the sacroiliac instead. Shit." He walked slowly toward the tall windows looking out over Beacon Hill toward the river. There was a high summer afternoon haze over it. "Nice night for the ball game," he mused. "I should get tickets." He turned to face her. He shook his head.

"I know what I'm doing," he said, as though apologizing for something. "I know what I'm doing here. In case you were wondering."

"I'm sure you do," she said. "It's just that it seems so sort of, well, ordinary, you know?"

"Oh," he said, "not what, the mechanical things I told you to do. Sure, I know them. By this time I oughta know them, how if you wanna get something through here, you oughta go about it. But not that. I mean, what this place is, you know?

"I first come here," he said, looking out the windows again, "I didn't have no real set ideas, what this place was. I didn't think about it like it was a hockshop, like most people these days do, now. And I didn't think it was something like it was when John Hancock and those fellas got all pissed off at old King George there and told him where he could go and stick his tea. I didn't really know what I was getting into." He faced her again. "You see?"

She shrugged. "I guess so," she said.

He smiled. "Probably not," he said. "It don't matter. You see or you don't see, I still didn't. I do, now. I come down here, you know why I come down here? Because I really didn't have anything else to do. What was I doing, huh? I was basically a bartender. And a bouncer. A sort of supergrade bartender and bouncer, sure. Old Maury called me *manager*. But I wasn't no manager at Katie's Place. It didn't need no manager. All it was was a gin mill. Bunch of guys who all of a sudden got back from a war and didn't have their asses totally shot off, everybody's treating them like heroes and they're making better money than they ever made before, those guys were thirsty. Gonna catch up on all the good times that they missed while they was fighting Germans if they went to Africa or Europe, or Japs if they got sent the other way. Katie's was just the place, it just happened to be the place they started getting together. And I happened to be one of them.

"We get these double-domes coming in here now all over the place," he said, "and they got the notebooks and the graduate assistants and the fuckin' tape recorders, and they want to start out in the morning with you when you get up out of bed and they're not gonna let you out their sight until you go to bed that night. If it makes a noise they're gonna tape it, and if they can't tape they are gonna write it down. And if you tell them you don't want to see them taking notes, you can depend on it that you'll be able, watch them memorizing it. And all the time it looks like they are doing everything they can to keep from getting sick at their stomachs, from watching what you're doing and the way that you are doing it. That's what it does to them: it makes them sick at their stomachs. You can see it happening, right in front of your own baby blues."

The Speaker shook his head and smiled. "And we know why it is," he said, "what it is that makes them act like that and makes them look the way they do. These professors from the universities, the young reporters that ain't been around us and our jobs and seen the way we do them long enough to understand things? They come in here, all they know about the State House is John Kennedy came up here right before he became president, and he made this real crowd-pleaser of a speech so there wasn't one dry eye in the whole House when he got through. About how everybody that's in politics, especially in Massachusetts, is some kind of angel of the Lord, or ought to be, at least. And they've all seen the movies of him doing that, slinging all that bullshit and looking like he should've been a knight done up in silver armor, and they come up here looking for him. Who never gave a shit about state government. And what do they see when they come into this place? Guys who do give a shit about the Commonwealth. Me, and a lot of other ordinary guys that eat too much and drink too much and never had all the advantages when we were growing up so heavy hitters in the Mafia would want to share their girl friends with us and Marilyn Monroe would sing us 'Happy Birthday.' But naturally, of course, they don't think about that cheap sex stuff and JFK, when they come up here looking for him and they find us. They just look at us and you can see them thinking what a bunch of low-down dirty animals we are."

Helen Dotten made her voice soft and spoke very tentatively. "I don't mean any insult," she said, "but don't you maybe give them just a little reason to think that?"

"Uh huh," he said, and nodded vigorously, "you bet we do. Sometimes, there are times when we even make a special effort to make sure they get disgusted even more than they already are. Because, see, even if we are a bunch of rats and weasels in this building, even if we are just dirt, there isn't anything that says we have to like it when some hightoned bastard drops around and spits on us. And we *don't* like it, either."

He paused and reflected for a moment. "Those people that come in here and get sick at the sight of us," he said, "we know why that is. They've all got theories. They went to Boston Latin School or one of them prep places and they read Plato's *Republic* or some other goddamned thing, and they think that's the way the government is run. They think Plato knew the score, and when all the presidents and senators and guys like Alexander Hamilton made speeches, it was all for real." He took a deep breath and turned that thought over in his mind. "Yeah," he said, nodding again, "that's what's the trouble with them. They take us aside and they tell us what those guys said, and this is different. They heard all of that stuff in classes and they think it's all for real." He turned and faced her. He chuckled. "When the fact of the matter is, Doctor, we almost never hear from Alexander Hamilton in here. John Hancock, I guess he must be devoting all his time to the insurance business these days. Somebody told me old Sam Adams is dead. As long as I've been in this place, and it is quite a while, I haven't heard a single word from Plato about this year's budget deficit for human services. It's almost like he isn't interested.

"Well, this ain't no class we're running here," the Speaker said, "although sometimes by mistake it's got some class. It ain't no seminar in government that we thought up and we're all actors in it like them assholes out at Sturbridge Village that go around all day in scratchy clothes pretending to shoe horses and build wagons they can pull, like nobody ever thought of automobiles. We didn't come in here to pose— we came in here to make deals. You know what I bet? I bet old Sam Adams there when he was raising hell about the king, I bet he had a little dodge going on in there one way or other, if the Revolution didn't work out he was gonna be a tax collector or some idiotic cousin of his was right in line to get some nifty job.

"Well," Morgan said, "when I come in here, see, I wasn't carrying any heavy theory shit around with me. I just, old Wilfred said that he could cut me up some of his real estate that he was representing, and I was marrying his daughter and his son did not look like he was gonna turn out very promising, so Wilfred said to me, well, would I run? And that is why I ran. I couldn't lose, I knew that. Wilfred had Proctor sewed up like it was the best quilt that his dear grandma ever made. He could've gotten Joseph Stalin in here if old Joe'd looked to him like he might need a steady job and that he'd play the game to get one. That's the only reason that I did it. Wilfred wanted me to do it, and it looked about ten times better'n the next thing that I had available. Which was wait for Maury to get knocked off by any one of about ten hundred things he had that one of them was gonna kill him sooner, later, and then inherit his barroom and make my living doing that. Which I didn't want to do. It's kind of fun grabbing guys by the collar and the pants and giving them the bum's rush when you're twenty-five or so and big and you know more about trench fighting than they happen to remember at the time you're doing it, because they're drunk. But that didn't look like no career that I would like a lot when I was fat and fifty like I am now. And besides, I like to take a drink myself from time to time, and that happens to be one thing that you cannot do when you're the guy that's selling them."

"I've heard that," she said, with some dryness.

"I'm sure you have, my dear," he said. "I'm sure you've also heard that now that Jesse James is dead and gone to his reward, I am the biggest robber still alive in this republic we got here, from sea to shining sea. Which that at least I know cannot be true, because if it was I would have a lot of money, and I am sorry to assure you that I don't. Them two things you can believe or not and it's your completely personal choice. Myself, I do not give a personal shit, and you don't even have to tell me what you have decided, when and if you do decide to make a choice. That, as we say, is irrelevant.

"So I come in here, just like Wilfred wanted, and that was one of two big things that Wilfred wanted me to do that worked out pretty good. The other one was marry his daughter, who is Maggie, and that did not work out so good."

"Should I ask why?" she said. "I hesitate, because you'll most likely tell me that it's none of my business. And be right, too."

"It doesn't matter," Morgan said. "Doesn't really matter much, one way or the other. It's nowhere near as interesting as people like to make it. Very simple, really. Maggie is a small-time girl, small time and small town. She liked it where she was in Proctor, and she liked me where I was, in Proctor. And she looked at Wilfred and she looked at me and she thought what I was gonna do was be a younger version of her father. Be a rep and live in Proctor. She didn't come right out and ask me if that was what I planned to do, but if she had I would've said it was, because if I expected anything that would've been what I expected. There wasn't any reason then for Wilfred Knox to live in Boston all the time, when Margaret was growing up and he first run for rep. I guess he did it some then, when he didn't have to, but that was for some reason other than because he hadda, and I never asked him what it was. Booze or broads or maybe both, most likely. That's generally the reason now when guys that aren't in leadership and don't have to be in Boston all the time decide all of a sudden that they have to be in Boston all the time and immediately they have got themselves a small pad here and you can't pick a gin mill for yourself no matter where you happen to be at the shag end of nowhere without running into one of them, either with his arm around some bimbo, murmuring sweet nothings in her shell-pink ears, or flat on his ass on the barroom floor, drunk as a fuckin' owl. I tell you, sister, it's a scandal, the things that're always goin' on. It'd bring a blush to any maiden's cheek." He put his head back and he laughed. "This is all brand-new, of course," he said. "You understand that."

She laughed. "Of course," she said. "There was no sin when our grandparents ran the world."

"Absolutely not," he said. He wiped his eyes. "Anyway," he said, "I dunno what Wilfred was doing down here when he wasn't legislating, because he never told me and I never got around to asking him. I did get to know his wife, my charming mother-in-law, good enough so that whatever he was doing I could certainly understand what it was that probably made him do it. But I never asked him and I never caught him at it, so I don't know what it was."

"Because you were up to something yourself?" she said.

"Actually, no," he said. "I moved down here full time almost from the first day I was sworn in. Not right from the first day, you understand, but not long afterwards, either. Because this outfit was changing fast after the war. And it really was a full-time job. The Turnpike wasn't there, then. It wasn't what it was when we lads went off to defend the Stars and Stripes in foreign lands against the yellow peril and the mean old Huns. When they left it was sort of a Republican·men's club that come to order every now and then to look around and see if anything'd been missed the last time they went out stealing everything, and if there had been they made plans to take it, took it, divvied it up, and then went home again. Until one of them noticed something else that nobody thought of taking the last time, and then they'd all come back in here again and take that. There wasn't any perspiration and that sort of thing involved. They owned it and they ran it and it was theirs. Just like the big law firms and the companies and the banks and all those other things they owned that really were what interested them and what they spent most of their time running. For them this was a hobby.

"Now," Morgan said, "after the war, the Irish started flooding the joint, and things began to change on all them birds. Guys like, you heard of Otis Ames?"

She looked doubtful. "Isn't he, doesn't he have something to do with some commission or something?"

Morgan nodded. "Right. The Governor's Commission to Investigate Corruption in State Government. Which is actually the Governor's Hunting License to Old Otis Ames to Bag Bernard Morgan and Get Him Out the Way. Otis Ames is out to cut my scalp, my dear. And he's got a license from the Governor to do it."

"Why?" she said.

"The Governor finds me inconvenient," Morgan said. "He's a religious lad, I hear, or so he claims when he's making one of his fine speeches at a Holy Name Society or some other lash-up, and I don't doubt he prays each night and has probably made at least a couple dozen novenas and weekend retreats to have some angel strike me dead by morning. But it hasn't happened yet. I dunno whether God likes me, or He don't like me especially but by accident I seem to be doing something He approves of. Maybe He's just got too many other things to think about right now. But He ain't done it yet. And so every morning John J. Tierney wakes up between his satin sheets and opens up the paper and starts with the obituaries to see if I am dead yet. And every morning so far he has not found my name. He's been disappointed. So he decided to take matters into his own hands. And somebody in his office with some brains, who I have not picked out yet but I know there must be one in there, someplace, give him a little nudge and told him Otis Ames hates Bernie Morgan worse'n Ames hates every other Irishman. Which is quite a lot. So what the Governor should do is fit Ames out like he was some heavy cruiser that the Navy's building down Fore River and send him out to blow me out of here and into Walpole where they teach you how to make the sturdy wooden furniture for use in our state office buildings. And this will mean that John J. Tierney will be able to put his own pet guy in this office, he thinks, and tell him that he'd better do just what John J. Tierney tells him to, or he will find he isn't getting his cereal in the morning or his fairy story and his milk and cookies when he goes to bed at night. And then everyone in Massachusetts will be living in the promised land. So that's what Tierney's doing and that's what Ames is doing."

"Can he do it?" she said. "Ames, I mean. Can he get rid of you?"

"Gettin' nervous, sister?" Morgan said. "Here I give you all these surefire tips for getting what you want from me, and now you're wondering if maybe it's worth all the effort? You're gonna get it all done and come back down here with your eyes bright and your tail all bushy, find some slick new article behind the desk who never heard of you and doesn't know what kind of no-shit broad you are?"

She laughed. "Yes," she said, "yes. The seminar's kind of fun and all, even if it isn't exactly what I expected, but there is that nagging fear, you know. Should I run back to Proctor and sit up all night to get the new proposal done?"

"Well," he said, "if you haven't got much of anything to do that is better, it's okay with me. But you probably don't have to. I figure that I've got . . . Look, all right? I don't know if Ames is gonna force me out. Or if he gets me out, if he can put me in the slammer. I know that's what he wants to do, but I don't know yet if he can do it."

"Why?" she said. "Why's he so all fired up against you?"

Morgan returned to his chair and collapsed into it. He exhaled noisily. "Short answer?" he said. "Short answer is: he thinks I'm Irish."

"You aren't?" she said.

"Aha," he said, "you thought so, too."

"I assumed so," she said. "You, after all, everything you represent, at least as far as I know . . ."

"I know, I know," he said. "Friend of mine that happens, he's a Yankee, so Ames'll talk to him and let him hear what he has got to say, Ames has got a minor package on one night. Sherry, I assume, or some cheap brand of Scotch—those Yankees don't generally get caught knocking back a few beers, and unless someone else's buying it they don't drink nothing dear, but there's some of them that drink to excess now and then too. They keep it quiet better, though. Anyway, Ames is snarling and everything about that mick Morgan, which is me, and my friend tells Ames that Morgan isn't Irish. Which as a matter of fact I'm not."

"What are you?" she said.

"Easier to tell you what I'm not," he said. "I'm Not Polish and I'm Not Canuck. And I'm from Proctor so that means I should be Irish, but I'm Not Irish either. I'm Scotch and English, mostly, on my father's side, and about a quarter Irish and God nows what else on my mother's. Mongrel. But just about the time I showed up in politics, Tobin here and J. Howard McGrath and Farley, Jim Farley, and Frank Murphy and all of them fine broths of lads in Washington was into politics and elbowing folks aside to make room for all the other Irishmen that wanted to get in. And that was going on here. And I look Irish, and I drink like people more or less expect an Irishman to drink, and I found I got along all right with all the micks who thought I was one anyway, so, noticing no reason to correct them, I took me place in line and waited for me proper turn. And here I am. Which is what Ames said when my friend let the cat out of the bag that night and told him I'm not Irish. 'Well,' says Ames, with a sneer, 'he runs with them by his own choice then, and as far as I'm concerned that makes him worse.'

"See, Doctor," Morgan said, "and there's nothing in this stuff that would require the kind of psychiatric information you've got to explain, the Irish come in to politics to the point they are today, without having any other interests to keep them busy. They had nothing else to do, like Otis Ames and all his clan that had their law firms and their money to look after and didn't want to spend their days and nights on Beacon Hill, hatching plots and dreaming up new ways to spend the people's money. Ames and his friends had neater ways of getting their hands on people's money. They didn't need new laws and new facilities like state hospitals and swimming pools and dingy stuff like that. But the new guys did. We had to think up ways for the government to run things, because we'd gotten to the point where Wilfred Knox, who was nothing better'n a swamp Yankee and consequently very little better'n an Irishman as far's those boys from Marblehead and Dover were concerned, had the controls to it. He didn't have the wheel to all the Yankee businesses, and neither him nor anybody else like him was ever going to get those businesses, so what we hadda do was do the best we could with what we had. And that is what we did. And what we're doing still. And that's why Ames hates us, and me especially because I'm the head villain in charge. Or was, at least, when his kind finally gave up and packed their tents and stole away like Rudolph Valentino."

"But," she said, "isn't Tierney Irish?"

"Nah," Morgan said. "He's a Hoper. He wants to be a Protestant, and from what I hear the micks hold the opinion that the Protestants are welcome to him. He sucks the Yankee ass every damned chance that he gets. Ames probably thinks the kid's a joke, as in fact I do myself, but the kid'll do what Ames wants him to do. Besides, Otis Ames is getting old. He can't, he hasn't got a lot of years left to be choosy. There's a distinct possibility I'll outlive the old bastard and he'll die out the last in the line of Morgan haters, knowing that there's nobody alive to take his place. All those old wars are over now, except for Ames and me. It's kind of funny, really—I'm not rightly in it, and thanks to Ames it turns out I'm the biggest heavy. And time is on my side." He laughed. "You know," he said, "if the guy didn't hate me so much he's determined to destroy me, I could feel sorry for a man like that. The Last of the fuckin' Mohicans, he is. Must be kind of sad, close to eighty like he's got to be, and here's the guy that represents every last thing in the world you hate, running the show and younger'n you are, so it looks like pretty soon you'll die, die knowing that he'll drink a lot of Hampden beer that night and then go out and piss the whole of it on the fresh dirt of your grave. Must be tough."

"But he does hate you," she said. "Why? Is it personal? Too, I mean. Seems like it'd almost have to be. In addition to the political thing. All these years, I mean, to have kept it up so long."

"Yeah," he said. He sighed. "It's both. Political, sure, but politics is personal the way we play it north of Washington, at least. Anything that's political around here, sooner or later it's personal. Usually, sooner.

"He was in the General Court before the war," Morgan said. "Had the family's seat from Dover. It was theirs, the way they looked at it. Just like Wilfred's and mine were ours. Still is, as far as that goes. 'Cept Wilfred's don't exist any more. That was one of the eighty that went when they cut the House. Noble sacrifice on my part. You think I want some fresh bastard taking Wilfred's place and looking to sit in it and give me trouble? Bullshit, I do." He got up and went to the windows again.

"Otis was young and so he went to war, of course," Morgan said, looking out the window toward the river again. "Jesus," he said, "it's pretty on this hill when the weather's nice, you don't let yourself start thinking about all the vicious little fights there's been on it. But then, of course, no fights, no fun.

"Anyway," he said, turning to face her, "Otis went to war. And since he was Harvard and an Ames and all those other fine things, he went to war with a commission. He was an officer when he started out. I hadda get mine the hard way, by not getting myself shot when everybody else in my platoon didn't have the good judgment to avoid it."

She laughed. "Actually," he said, "I shouldn't be talking like that. He was a brave man, from everything I heard, and I can assure you that I would've heard about if he'd clucked even once, or showed any sign of knowing anything about being scared. Because that kind of news travels fast. He went in the subs, which is shit-ass duty, officer or not, danger-ous as hell then and damned little fun too, when he could've probably gotten himself a nice quiet desk to command, the contacts that he had. Went to the Pacific. Out there a long time, too. I mean it, Doctor Dot-ten, even if it does near break my hard old heart to say it: Otis Ames came back from World War Two with a record any fellow could've been proud of, and if he was, he had a right to be.

"Thing of it was, I guess," Morgan said, "I guess he thought he was the only one that did. That because he had the Silver Star, well, with his name and everything, the old Speaker getting ready to step down and all, the job was sort of his to take by right. Like some kind of an inheri-tance, you know? They said at the time that he was planning to be gov-ernor and he didn't exactly rule out going down to Washington some day, either. Jesus," he said, laughing and shaking his head, "can you imagine how it must've pissed off Otis Ames when the punk Irish kid that had some money and got his PT boat sunk right out from under him was the one that ended up down there instead of him? Must've rotted his ass for him.

"So," Morgan said, "he comes back and the time comes and Wilfred is Ames's opposition. This was my first term. Nineteen fifty-two, right after the census that they had the redistricting after, that Wilfred'd used to make my district for me. Wet behind the ears. Didn't know shit. And Wilfred didn't know much more. All he knew was that the swampers and the micks didn't want Ames in as Speaker, and they couldn't, they didn't apparently want to run a mick against him right off. So: Wilfred. He looked harmless enough, keep the seat warm for a few years until some hotshot came along that they could all agree to give it to, nice homespun, no-enemies type of fellow, and they put him up.

"Now at first that was okay with Wilfred," Morgan said. "But then he sort of got used the idea, decided that he really wanted it. Guess he didn't like some of Ames's airs and graces or something. And it starts to turn into a real dogfight. And Wilfred's running as this farmer type of guy, he don't want the reps that don't know him thinking he's a boss type, which was what he was deciding he was gonna be, once he got himself sneaked in here with the hay sticking out his ears, so he uses me to do the dirty work for him instead.

"I didn't give a shit," Morgan said. "Come down here in the first place more out of curiosity'n anything else. What'd I have to lose, huh? I didn't, I wasn't looking for anything really, so everything I had already was pure gravy, and I start to do a little work behind the scenes for Wilfred. Which wasn't getting either one of us too far, you want the truth. I was too new.

"Then they have this bigtime dinner for all of Massachusetts' heroes," Morgan said, "and being one of them, the way the Army told it anyway, I got invited, just like Otis Ames did. Because he had that Silver Star. And I had one so I went too. I went with Henry Toporowski, this Polish guy I knew from Chicopee that had one of his own, and I knew him from home so we went together.

"Now," he said, "lemme tell you something about Polacks. You have probably heard some jokes about dumb Polacks, which I guess're funny unless it happens you're a Polack and you're smart. Because that's what Henry was: smart. He was one smart Polack, and if it hadn't been for this cerebral hemorrhage that Henry didn't plan on back about twelve years ago, he would've been a very rich Polack as well. Henry knew a lot of things about buying real estate, and Henry moved out west to Los Angeles back a year or so after he got out the service and started buying it as fast as he could swing the deals. Henry'd been in the Navy, and his home port was San Diego, and he had a pretty good idea of what the Southern California land was going to be worth some day. Except he died first. Well, not first. But before he got the corner on all the money in the world, which I guess was what he had in mind.

"Anyway," Morgan said, "I am standing there with Henry, at this banquet, and in comes Otis Ames, who is acting like he won the war in the Pacific all by himself. Which like I say, although he was a brave man and I take nothing off of that on him, Henry had some part in doing too. And Henry didn't like the way he saw Ames acting. So he says to me: 'You know that bastard?' And I tell him that I do. And Henry says to me: 'If that bastard ever starts giving you the old song and dance about how he put the Japs back in their cellars with that goddamned submarine of his that ducked out of sight every time anything with guns come hull down the horizon and it didn't have our flag, you just ask him what it was that happened to my old pal Eddie Kistiakowski that come from old Chicago there.' So naturally I was interested, not knowing what was gonna happen a few years later when Ames and Wilfred're fighting for the same job, and I asked him a few questions. And he tells me that this guy Kistiakowski from Chicago that he knows because every Polish hero knows every other Polish hero, I guess, Kistiakowski got drowned one day when he was in the conning tower and Ames sees a Jap battlewagon coming and he took his sub down so damned fast that old Kisty took a swim. And it was a pretty long swim, too, which he couldn't make too good because his hand got caught in the hatch when they shut it and Ames had his chief or somebody hack it off so they could bolt it down to dive where the cruiser or whatever it was couldn't reach them. And Henry tells me that the other Polacks on the Ames sub figured Kisty didn't have to swim too far anyway, because with all the blood coming from that stump he must've had where his hand used to be, one of the sharks that used to hang around to see if there'd be something left to eat when guys got through shooting at each other probably had him for a lunch or something like that."

"Ooh," she said.

"*Ooh* is right," Morgan said. "Well, I didn't think a hell of a lot about it at the time, like I say, and then some time goes by like the song says and I'm in the legislature and here's this same goddamned war hero running against my pal Wilfred Knox, whose daughter I am gonna marry. So there is one day when Ames has got some one of his cheerleaders up there bellowing in the chamber there and the guy is going on to beat the band about how Otis is the biggest hero anybody's seen since General MacArthur or some other guy that never had much interest in being around where there was bullets in the air, and it was scoring points. You could see that. This wasn't like it was when Vietnam was on and guys didn't even wanna mention that. No sir, this was when a war record was strong medicine. And the reporters're there, lapping it up like it was Jack Daniel's whiskey and it was free, all that they could drink, and I can see this isn't doing Wilfred one damned bit of good. So I stood up and put the question that if the Honorable Mister Ames was such a brave and dauntless captain like this gentleman's assuring us, and would like us to consider his war record when we come to cast our votes, which of course he did want because Wilfred was too old to fight and didn't have the record except for some reserve shit when the war was on, well maybe then he'd like to tell us how it was that Eddie Kistiakowski didn't get to come inside that afternoon when the submarine *Sandshark* made a crash dive to avoid engaging the enemy off the entrance to the straits of some damned thing or other in the Philippines. See, I knew the name, the place that day. And I go on to say that the only information I have got is that this poor bastard was trying get back inside when Captain Ames give out the order to leave him drown and shut the fuckin' hatch and whomped the guy's hand off to save his own precious hide."

"Wow," she said.

"Not even that," Morgan said. "Dead, perfect silence. And Ames after what it seemed like about half an hour gets up on his hind legs, the tears're streaming down his face, and says he didn't have no choice, and this and that, it was either he was gonna sacrifice this Polack from Chicago or else this Jap cruiser was gonna sink the whole damned boat and everybody that was in it, and they practically had to carry him away when he was through. Which is exactly what he was. Through. And from that day to this, he has hated me with a passion that makes what Captain Ahab and the whale had going look something like a wedding breakfast."

She looked at him and stroked her chin with her forefinger. "Well," she said, "I can't say it's hard for me to see why."

He shrugged. "Me either," he said. "Oh, I tried to patch it up with him a few times later. Turns out from what I heard from other guys that knew about it, later, they said, what Ames did, and what he said he did it for, it was right. He didn't drown the Polack, it was curtains for the whole boat. But by then it was too late. Wilfred was the Speaker and Ames, he was out of politics. Except as far as I'm concerned. If that guy lives to be a hundred, he will still be after me. Just like he is today."

"And will he get you?" she said.

Morgan shrugged again. "If he doesn't," he said, "sooner or later, somebody else will. I've got a lot of enemies out there now, beyond the walls of this office. Some of them have desks in the chamber. Some of them are writing for the newspapers. Some of them don't even know me from a hole in the ground, but they've been brought up so they hate my guts, and so of course, they do."

"Is the stuff there?" she said.

"You mean: if they want to get the goods on me," Morgan said, "are the goods there for them to get?" He shrugged again. "Thirty years in politics? Making deals? You tell me. If one of my enemies doesn't get a clean shot at my ass, maybe somebody I don't even know's an enemy, somebody I don't even know at all, somebody like that will. It's just a matter of time. If I sit in this office long enough, for God's sake, one of the people that I used to call a friend will probably end up doing it. Just to get the job, you understand, and no hard feelings, Bernie. This is a nice job, Doctor Dotten. It's a job that lets you operate statewide, without ever running outside your little district. The pay ain't bad now, either. You have to run in here, of course, but this ain't like the Congress where the Speaker gets elected but the committee chairmen all get their chairs by seniority. Here, I decide. If I don't like you, doesn't matter if you've been sitting on Judiciary since the glacier melted. If there's some rookie I like better, he gets the job and you get the back of my hand. Ray Archambault, you know him?"

"I've heard of him," she said.

"Talented guy," Morgan said. "Wants this job and wants it bad. Got a nice safe district down in Avon there. Takes good care of it. Be a good Speaker. I'd vote for him myself, didn't mean I couldn't be it any more. He's the chairman, Ways and Means. Know why? Because that's where I put him. Is that the second-highest office, next to mine? Not supposed to be, but is it? Yup. Ways and Means is that. I made it that way. Should Ray have it? Maybe not. Too much power, give a guy that wants my job. Ray may start to fester before I decide the time has come to go. He does, and I'll destroy him. Simple as that.

"Now," Morgan said, "Ray's a friend of mine. If this's how I treat my friends . . . huh?"

"It must be tough to be your enemy," she said.

"Right," he said, "so, one of my friends could do it to me. Guy like Ray."

"So," she said, "how do you protect yourself?"

"By knowing when it's time to go," he said, "like Wilfred didn't. They had to cart him out of here. Much as he liked me, much as he never let my little problems there with his daughter change the way he felt about me, he wouldn't leave go of this office and let me have this job, not until he couldn't hang on any more. Just couldn't do it. When they carried Wilf out, that's when I got the chair. And he didn't like it, even then. He stood right on this carpet there and took one last look around him and then he looked at me, and shook his head, and cried, and then he left. 'I never thought you'd be the one,' he said. Off to the booby hatch. Still think I'm mean because I don't go up and see him? Show up and just remind him what he was and what he ain't no more, and who it was he blames for doing it to him? Still think I'm a bastard 'cause I don't do that?"

"Are you sure," she said, "are you sure that he'd remember?"

"If he didn't know me," Morgan said, "no, then he would not remember. But then there'd be no point, me going. But if it was one of those bad days, from my point of view, like it was the last time, I wheeled him down to the solarium in his chair with the white blanket on his legs and he's picking at the edge of it the way old people do when they're thinking about how pretty soon they're gonna have the final fittings for their shrouds, goofy as a goddamned angel he was, humming and drooling along down to the sunroom with his faithful son-in-law pushing him along, and then when we got in there all of a sudden the light hit me or something, and he recognized me. And he remembered. And it was awful. You could see him recollecting, see it go right across his face, the way he felt the day he left this office and went off to rot, the way he put it, in the booby hatch. See it, see it, see it. He let out this godawful yell, couldn't understand it, fortunately, unless of course you knew what he was trying to say, like I did, and the tears come pouring out his eyes. I hadda get the nurse to take him back and give him some drugs, I guess, to calm him down before he had some kind of an attack that would've killed him."

Morgan turned and faced out the window once again. "No," he said, "no, I don't think I'll go back to see him right away again. I didn't enjoy that last visit a whole lot." He cleared his throat. "For now I think I'll leave that little chore to Roger. He ain't got one hell of a lot on his mind, what I hear. Do him good to have that duty on his mind, polish up the old DeSoto once a month, drive it up and park it right in front the rhododendron bushes that me and Wilfred had them plant out front the entrance, make the place look pretty, wheel Wilfred down the sunroom, have the dog along, let fat old Rocky put his big old faithful head on Wilf's lap and get it patted, Wilfred look out of the window, see his car in front his shrubbery, and that'll probably be the best thing I can do for both of them. Better'n having Roger out with absolutely nothing on his mind, maybe spots a motorcycle and goes off his trolley again, I think."

"Motorcycle?" she said.

"Yeah," he said, facing her again and starting back toward the desk. He spoke absently. "You seen Roger?"

"Yes," she said. "I've seen him the few times I mentioned, when he comes to visit his father."

"Yeah," he said, rearranging some items on the blotter, "he's got a scar on his face. Motorcycle."

"It's a big scar," she said.

"Yeah," he said. "He tells people sometimes that he got it in the war. That's his war wound to compare with mine. How he got it, they had him in the signal corps when he got drafted. Korea. Never got there, though. To Korea, I mean. He was on training maneuvers one night out some place in the bushes, on his motorcycle, hit a patch of sand or something, whacked his head on a tree. Always wondered if that's what it was, made him funny. That's Roger's war wound. Hates motorcycles though, that lad, now. Knows 'em and hates 'em. To this day I think he burned that cop chiefly because he rode a motorcycle. Huh."

She did not say anything, but looked at him as though expecting him to say something more. He toyed with a pencil on the desk, turning it so that it pointed toward her, then away again. "Probably doesn't matter, though."

"No," she said.

He looked at her and seemed to be collecting himself. He cleared his throat again. "He seems all right these days, I guess," he said. "Roger."

"So far as I know," she said.

"You've, ah, you've seen him?" Morgan said. "When, when he visits Wilfred there?"

"Yes," she said. "Generally. It's just about like you said. He parks the car in front and we let him bring the dog in even though we don't allow dogs in the hospital. Because it's Mister Knox and all. And Roger and the dog go to his room and wheel him down to the sunroom, or out of doors this time of year. If it doesn't happen to be raining. They travel very slowly. The dog's lame. I think it's getting blind, too."

"Probably is," Morgan said, nodding. "Old dogs don't learn new tricks, they say, and everything I've seen says that it's true. Just get lame, have trouble seeing." He chuckled, once. "Then they get put to sleep. Be more humane for us as well, I sometimes think."

She did not say anything. He pushed the pencil against the edge of the blotter and put his hands in his pants pockets. He cleared his throat again. "Well," he said, "anyway. If that answers your question. About them getting me, I mean. If they don't I'll either stay on here too long, or else some fine day I'll wake up and I'll say: 'Enough of this shit, Morgan. Time to pack it in.' And somebody like you will be astonished to discover, some weeks later, that their bill for a new basketball gymnasium or something now includes an exhibition hall, convention center, and a museum of the age of transportation or some such thing, together with provision for construction of three high-rise hotels with a total of three thousand rooms and twelve world-class gourmet restaurants. All to be supervised by a state authority headed up by a director who gets to hold the job for life and gets paid two hundred K a year for watching out for everything. And it'll go through the legislature like a greased pig, ushered smartly along by Ray Archambault or somebody just like him, and the next thing you know, the bulldozers will be pulling up and here will be the new director unanimously chosen by vote of all his pals, which are mine, and he is me, and Ray Archambault is the new Speaker of the Massachusetts General Court, already making plans to run for governor. Which naturally is the way I would prefer to see it end, and the way I think it probably will. But guarantee it? That I cannot do."

"There are no guarantees then, Mister Speaker," she said, rising up to leave, "no guarantees at all?"

He smiled at her. "No guarantees, Doctor Dotten, ma'am," he said. "No guarantees at all. Just living by the word of God, and keeping your left hand high." He smiled.

"I thank you for your time, sir," she said, extending her hand. "It's been a real education."

"You're more'n welcome, ma'am," he said, accepting it. "God willing, some day I may even have some more."

23 Brian Hanrihan shortly before five thirty in the afternoon sat by himself in the dim coffee shop in the basement of the courthouse, his tie pulled down from his collar and his expression glum. The woman and the blind man had pulled down the metal curtain that closed the area behind the counter from the public space, but left the access door open on Hanrihan's assurance he would close and lock it

when he left. He had a cup of coffee he had salvaged from the pot on the hot plate and a small plastic stirrer he employed to disturb the surface of the liquid now and then. A folded and stained copy of the *Commoner*, bedraggled after several readings, lay on the table next to him.

Jimmy Cremmens, hurrying, came to the door of the shop, saw Hanrihan in occupation, halted in confusion, then decided it would look worse if he obeyed his impulse to depart and walked in slowly to join him. He did not immediately meet Hanrihan's challenging gaze, but glanced desperately at the curtain at the bar, then licked his lips, before he gave in to the total awkwardness he felt and spoke to Hanrihan. "No, ah," he said, gesturing at the serving area with his left thumb, "chance of a Coke or something, huh?"

Hanrihan regarded him with what he hoped was an expression of fatigue and mild contempt. "Well," he said, "that depends. A crackerjack detective like the guy that Ames has got out shaking all the bushes for the bad guys between New York State and the ocean, this fellow Cremmens from the State Police that this Rosen guy says in the *Commoner* could probably find Amelia Earhart if they let him sniff her socks, he would most likely go around the side there and let himself in behind the counter and just help himself. And leave the money on the register, of course, because a guy like this here Cremmens certainly would never cheat a blind man that depends on what he makes from Coca-Cola there for his paycheck."

Cremmens looked at Hanrihan helplessly and very clumsily did as had been recommended, bumping into the doorjamb as he entered the serving area, dropping something metal when he was out of Hanrihan's vision. Hanrihan increased the volume of his voice so that Cremmens would be able to hear him over the racket he was making. "I got to say, Jim boy," he said, "that was some piece that Rosen had about you and your legal companion there, the *Commoner* this morning." He paused to let Cremmens reply, but heard only more muffled clattering. He smiled to himself and went on. "That fuckin' Putter there," he said, "I got to say he does sound like one goddamned tiger when it comes to hunting down the wrongdoers." He stopped again, and once again he got no answer. He heard the door of the refrigerator shutting. "Apparently this Putter guy," he said, "once he got that job with Ames, he knew just what to do. Quick as a flash he was on the phone to Dory Feldman, telling the Head Jew of the law profession there how it damned near broke his poor black heart that Jean Dussault'd been convicted by that ruthless bastard Hanrihan, even though old Dory and the judge did everything they could to save Jean from the slammer. And the next thing anybody knew, Jean was over there in Putter's office, the very same night after the jury'd come back here and said it was Hanrihan that they believed, him and his witnesses, just crying his eyes out and pouring his heart out to Corporal Cremmens of the State Police."

Cremmens, a plastic cup of coffee in his right hand and a plastic cup mounded with vanilla ice cream in his right, emerged from the serving area, straightened his shoulders, and marched to Hanrihan's table. He put the two containers down, jerked one of the chairs out, sat down on it, and faced Hanrihan across the food. "Brian," he said firmly, "I know you're pissed off at the world, and I know that I'm most likely the guy you've got at the very top of your shit list. It isn't fair, Brian, and you know it isn't fair, but if that's the way you want to feel about it, go ahead. There ain't a fuckin' thing in this world I can do about it."

Hanrihan worked his mouth into a contemptuous expression. "By Jesus, Jim," he said, "I got to hand it to you. You're just as quick as Rosen says you are. I couldn't fool you for a minute, could I? Son of a bitch."

Cremmens dug into the ice cream greedily. "You got to excuse me," he said, "while I eat this shit before it melts. That bastard Putter's had me on the steady lope all day today, and all day yesterday, and I'm not really sure when I had my last meal. So you'll just have to go ahead and rank me out while I am eating."

Hanrihan nodded as Cremmens stuffed a spoonful of ice cream into his mouth. "I can do that," he said. "Certainly wouldn't want the newest version of the Lone Ranger out trying to end evil in the Commonwealth and getting fainting spells while he was doing it."

Cremmens swallowed as he nodded. "That's okay, Brian," he said, "but I want you to understand, I didn't have a thing to do with what the paper said this morning. Not one fuckin' thing."

"Oh," Hanrihan said, making a small wave, "perish the very goddamned thought. It never crossed my mind, that you and Putter might be playing footsie with reporters and that might explain why the pair of you got such a writeup this morning. For a minute, I thought it was an obituary and both of you outstanding public servants'd dropped dead. Goodness, no. Jesus, I would never think anything like that."

Cremmens, having unloaded a second gob of ice cream into his mouth, shook his head, waved the spoon, and lisped through what he was eating. "I didn't thay nothing 'bout Putter," he said. "Lyle and Rothen are palth." He swallowed. "But as far as I'm concerned, Brian," he said, "none of that shit came from me." He looked at Hanrihan earnestly. "Why the hell would I want to do it, for Chrissakes? Publicity don't do me no good. The people at ten-ten don't feature the guys on the street getting ink, for God's sake. Does a soldier like me mostly harm when his name's in the paper."

"It does," Hanrihan said, "if he's planning to stay in the State Police, after he gets through the job that he's on. But if he's planning, for instance, to resign from the SP and open an agency for private detective work, commercial security, that kind of shit, it could do him a shitload of good to be known as Sam Spade in the papers."

Cremmens, conveying another huge gob of ice cream precariously on the white plastic spoon, looked at Hanrihan with an incredulous grin on his face. "For the love of Mike, Brian," he said, "have you blown your porch light out or something?" He put the ice cream in his mouth.

Hanrihan said: "I don't think so, Jim boy. What else would I think, for Christ sake? You work on the Dussault case with me and you spend the whole time that you're on it telling me we'll never hook him. Then when I get him on trial, you're already halfway out the door."

"There wasn't much left for me to do, Brian," Cremmens said, interrupting. "I did what I had to do, the investigation. Trying the case? That was your job. And ten-ten knew that, that my job was done, which was why they yanked me out of here and assigned me to Ames. That wasn't my doing." He took a deep swig of coffee. "Brian," he said, "you oughta know I would've rather stayed here. Maria ain't down at the commission, you know. She's still over here. Don't you think that I'd rather be here, where she is, with nothing to do all day long except get into trouble with her? Like you were always accusing me, back when I was over here?"

"Ah yes," Hanrihan said, still annoyed but off-balanced by what Cremmens said, "the delicious Maria. How are things with you and the lady these days, now that your name's in the bright lights and all?"

Cremmens nodded. He drank some more coffee. "Not so good, since you ask," he said. "She liked it lots better when I was around all day long and she had a real married man to show off. Now, with the way Putter's running my ass, I'm on the road more'n I would be if I was back in the bluebird, out chasing the drunks all night long on the Turnpike." He shrugged. "I can't say you didn't warn me, I guess, but it does kind of get me pissed off."

"Lyle Putter a bad overseer," Hanrihan said. "That how the former slaves act when they get in the driver's seat, Jim?"

Cremmens snickered. "That could be it, I suppose," he said. "But shit, the guy's flogging the duck day and night. The day before yesterday, there, we got three guys that we've got to talk to out between Worcester and Fitchburg. And we do that and that keeps us out on the road until around nine o'clock at night, which does tend to cut into the time for the loving.

"Then," he said, "today was New Bedford, Fall River, and a little plane ride around lunchtime, just in case I might be getting bored."

"The hell're you flying to?" Hanrihan said. "Dussault have accounts in New York that you're chasing?"

Cremmens snorted. "Not that I know of," he said. "But if he did, I will be down there before the month's out, and no doubt about it. I'm telling you, Brian, if that guy knew Churchill, I'll be in England before Labor Day."

"Cripes," Hanrihan said, "what's the big production for? How much stuff you guys need, hook a few bastards and scare the shit out of them, so that they'll harpoon the Speaker?"

Cremmens looked sardonically at him and explored his teeth with his tongue. "More than we've got, that's for sure," he said. "A helluva lot more'n we've got, Brian. Because," he said smiling and tapping the paper, "we haven't got *nothing* so far, and it doesn't matter a *shit* what you read in the paper that's different."

Hanrihan's face displayed a deep frown. "For Christ sake, Jim," he said, "what the hell're you telling me, huh? I give Putter this guy on a regular platter, I know he can make guys that can make the Speaker, he's practically pissing his pants he's so eager to talk, and now he can't make a case? This spearchucker there that's in charge, he incompetent? Or is Ames so soft in the squash that he's fucking it up?"

Cremmens shrugged again. He leaned back in the chair. "You tell me," he said. "My own guess is that these guys that Putter's gone after're much cuter'n anybody Putter's gone after before. They're tricky, and they know how to stall. They don't have to pretend that they like him, like all of the people he's dealt with before. They dance him around and they tug on his rope, and he doesn't know what to do about it. This guy that we flew to the Vineyard to see? Fella named Mahoney. Strange as it seems, this guy looks like the best chance we've got. And that's only because he's more scared and more stupid, or maybe just not as used to the game as the others. But we've got his balls in the juicer, and if he doesn't think of somebody to call between now and the end of the week, we'll give 'em a squeeze and just maybe he'll

talk. And you know something, Brian? He'd better. Because," Cremmens said, sucking his teeth, "he's the one guy that we've got. The only
one that we've got. And it don't look like there's a platoon of others out
there that we're gonna find."

Cremmens stood up suddenly. He slapped his hand on the table. "I
gotta go," he said, "I got to pick up some of my stuff that I need from
my office upstairs, and I'm already late for Maria. Which is gonna get
me in even more shit with my wife that I haven't seen since last Thursday, and I think she may be starting to suspect something." He inhaled
deeply. "Ah well," he said, "so it goes. That's the way it was in those
days, movin' west." He slapped the table again. "Probably see you tomorrow," he said, "you're still around at this ungodly hour when I
come back for my stuff."

Hanrihan seemed lost in thought. "Yeah," he said absently, waving
his hand, "yeah. See you around. And good luck."

Around 6:20, when he was certain that he was alone in his office,
Hanrihan made a call. He ignored the phone book resting on the top of
the small television set on his desk and dialed Directory Assistance. He
asked for the number of Attorney Francis Costello on Beacon Street in
Boston. He dialed that number. The lady at the switchboard asked if
she might say who was calling. "No," Hanrihan said pleasantly, "I'd
prefer not to say." She thanked him politely enough and put him on
hold. A man's voice replaced hers. "Without asking who I'm talking
to," Hanrihan said, "my name is Brian Hanrihan, and I'm about to become a former Assistant District Attorney of Middlesex County. I'd like
to come in and talk to someone about a contractor named Mahoney. He
has a job on Martha's Vineyard, I understand." The male voice said that
it was possible that there would be someone in the office who might be
interested, and asked where Hanrihan could be reached later that evening. Hanrihan gave his home telephone number.

24 In the early evening, the man on the stool next to Rosen in
Knacky's Bar in Mercer wore a Caterpillar Diesel hat and a
dirty tan tanker jacket with the sleeves pushed up on his bare forearms.

His hands were grimy and he had an aluminum splint on his right index finger. It stuck out when he picked up the schooner of Miller Lite. "The gas station guy," he said, "yeah. That'd be Roger Knox." He stared into the mirror behind the bar. He lifted the schooner and drank deeply. He set it down again. He wiped his mouth with the back of his hand. "Roger's an odd duck," he said. He thought about that. He nodded. "Roger's always been an odd duck."

"Is there something, uh, there something wrong with him?" Rosen said. He lifted his schooner of Bud and drank deeply. He wiped his beard with the back of his hand and flicked foam off his mustache. The man in the tanker jacket shifted his attention from the mirror to look at Rosen. He moved his mouth as though he had been chewing. "I didn't mean anything, or anything," Rosen said.

"You're not from around here," the man said.

"No," Rosen said. "I was. I was passing through here a while ago and I needed some gas and I stopped at his station. I guess it's his anyway. Cities Service, I think it said?"

"Jenney," the man said. "Citgo now, but it used to be Jenney. On the Mercer Road."

"Yeah," Rosen said.

The man lifted the schooner and drained it. He wiped his mouth again. He nodded. He belched silently. He put the schooner on the bar. The old Miller sign flashed endless changing colors at him. "Arthur," he said, "more beer." He returned his gaze to Rosen. "Because if you was from around here," the man said, "you wouldn't need to ask. Roger? Yeah, I guess there is something wrong with Roger." He shook his head. Arthur in a white shirt and white apron folded in half and tied at the waist arrived with another schooner of beer. He set it down, lifted the empty, and looked inquiringly at Rosen. "You want another beer?" the man said.

"Oh," Rosen said. He lifted his schooner. "Yeah," he said. "Bud."

Arthur nodded. He did not move. Rosen lifted his schooner and drained it. Arthur picked it up as soon as Rosen set it down on the counter. "I know," he said.

"Arthur never forgets what a guy orders the first round," the man said as Arthur went back to the taps.

"Oh," Rosen said.

"Prides himself on it," the man said. "I was in here one night, must've been ten or twelve years ago. Guy comes in, sits down. 'Beer,' he said. Arthur don't say anything. Goes to the cooler. Takes out a Bally

Ale. Opens it, gets out a glass, puts it in front of the guy. Guy pours it and drinks it. 'Arthur,' I says, 'I finally caught you. You must be slippin', not listenin', what the customer says any more.' Arthur looks at me. 'Think so?' he says. 'Yeah,' I says, 'guy asked for a beer. You give him an ale.' Arthur looks at the guy. 'Hey,' he says, 'guy here,' meaning me, 'thinks I give you the wrong drink, you ask for beer and I give you ale.' Guy looks up at me. 'It's the same stuff, jerk, beer and ale. I like Bally ale better for beer'n I do Bally beer. Okay with you?' Sure, it was okay with me. Not gettin', a fight with a guy because he wants to think beer and ale's the same thing. Ale makes you smell like skunk piss, of course, but he likes that flavor, let him go at it's what I say. 'He was in here before the war,' Arthur says. 'Gives me this big argument, ale'n beer's the same thing. I give a shit? Not me. Ale's beer, far as I'm concerned, he wants to pay for it.' Then Arthur looks at him. 'Come to think of it,' he says, 'I haven't seen you. Where you been?' Guy looks at him. 'Nam,' he says. 'I got drafted. Got my old route back again when I come back. Gimme 'nother one.'

"See what I mean," the man said. "Arthur, all the time that guy's away, must've been years, he remembers this guy that had one ale with him and said it was beer. You come back in here twenny years from now, sit down, ask for a beer, Arthur's still here, you'll get Bud. Guarantee it."

"Huh," Rosen said. Arthur brought the fresh schooner and set it down in front of him. Rosen pushed a dollar across the wet bar at him. Arthur took it and rang up sixty cents. He put the change on the counter next to the first batch of change. "So," Rosen said, "what is it that's wrong with Roger?"

"Good question," the man said. "Arthur," he called down the bar, "you got any idea what's wrong with Roger? Roger Knox?"

"Hey," Rosen said, "I was just asking, you know?" The man waved at him. "Don't matter," the man said.

Arthur pondered. "Nope," he said. "I thought I did, for a while. Thought it was his wife there. Then I thought maybe I was wrong, it was his father. Then I started thinking I was wrong and I was right in the first place, and it was his wife. I dunno."

"Roger," the man said, "see, Roger's old man was the Speaker. The House of Representatives?"

"No kidding," Rosen said.

"Yup," the man said. He nodded again. He drank some beer.

"Speaker. Had the job for years. He was a big man around here. You been onna Turnpike?"

"Sure," Rosen said.

"Right," the man said. "You ever count the exits and the on-ramps?"

"Can't say's I did," Rosen said.

"Try it some time," the man said. "They first put that road in, the truckers, they all noticed it. Had guys comin' through, they couldn't figure it out. 'Son of a bitch,' they would say. 'There's about fourteen, fifteen exits on that whole goddamned road between Albany and One-twenty-eight outside Boston, for Christ sake, and seven of 'em're between here and the next pisshole town. The fuck's goin' on here? Some huge army thing around here or something?"

"There's Westover," Rosen said. "Chicopee."

"Oh sure," the man said, "and there's the armory in Springfield. Used to be anyway. Went out of business. Government closed it. Buy all our rifles from Japan now or something, I guess. And there's Monsanto there in Ludlow, except Monsanto wasn't *in* Ludlow until that road come through and all them exits all of a sudden opened up. Lots of companies did that. And all of them companies that did that all of a sudden started hiring people and paying taxes in towns that just happened to be in Wilfred Knox's district, am I right? Plus which, old Wilf had about two hundred jobs, seemed like, that he could get for people on the toll road." The man shook his head. "Old Wilf was a cute bastard," he said. " 'Fore he lost his marbles there, old Wilf was about as cute's they come. That son of a bitch, he looked like this big stupid farmer and he almost never had anything to say that you could pin him down on later that he said it to you, you know? But he was sure smart. He was the smartest bastard in this part of the world until he went off the beam there. And then he got as soft's a sneaker fulla shit, and they finally hadda put him inna home. The Knox Hospital. Which course was another thing he made the state put up when he was Speaker. See what I mean about smart? He got soft there, no question about that, but he had sense enough, he made the state put up a place where he could go and live out his years when he got dippy and he couldn't do anything any more."

"Shrewd," Rosen said.

"Sure," the man said. He drained the second schooner. "Arthur," he said. He kept his gaze on Rosen. "And when it finally did happen, he couldn't get his pants on from the right end any more, he had everything all set so his son-in-law moved right in, his old job, which is where he is now. Bernie Morgan. And if you think Wilfred was shrewd, which he was, well there ain't no flies on Bernie, either. Bernie Morgan took damned good care of things. Himself especially."

"Whaddaya mean?" Rosen said. Arthur appeared with two more schooners and placed one before each of them. Rosen took out another dollar and paid him even though his second schooner was still nearly full.

"Bernie ain't's smart as Wilfred was, when Wilfred was smart," Arthur said, taking the money.

"Well, shit, Arthur," the man said, "course he ain't. Road's all built, for Christ sake. Businesses're all here, right? He ain't got so much to be smart *about*, for Christ sake. The fuck you want him to do? Throw Monsanto the fuck out and get somebody else new, come in there? That wouldn't accomplish nothin'."

Arthur rang up the sale. "Didn't say it would," he said. "Just said: Bernie's not's smart as Wilfred was. I ain't takin' nothin' away from Bernie." He turned away from the cash register and put the change down. He spread his hands on the bar. "Thing proves it, far's I'm concerned, is I don't think Wilfred ever swiped much of anything just for himself. Least, nobody ever *said* Wilfred was swipin' nothin' for himself, and if that don't prove he was smart, I dunno what would. Because Wilfred done pretty well for himself down in Boston there while he was busy doin' so much that was good for everybody else. He done it quiet, you know? Nobody noticed. They see that there road goin' through and all that business comin' in with the jobs and all, and there's old Wilfred, out takin' all the credit which he probably deserved, but he's gettin' richer himself the whole time too. And nobody ever noticed nothin'. Didn't say nothin' about it if they did, at least."

"They were afraid of him, is why," the man said.

Arthur shook his head. "Well, shit, Norris," he said, "goddamnit, you're not gonna sit there and try to tell me, nobody's afraid of old Bernie now, are you? 'Cause I ain't gonna let you infer I'm that stupid that I was to believe that, if you said it."

"I didn't say that," Norris said.

"No," Arthur said with satisfaction. "No, you didn't say that. Because if you was to tell me that nobody's afraid of Bernie Morgan I would just tell you to go on ahead and finish your beer and leave. I know a guy that's afraid of Morgan and he's sittin' on your stool and wearin' your hat and drinkin' your beer right this very minute. Ain't that right,

—

Norris? You're afraid of Bernie, and there ain't no use pretendin' anything else. Not with anybody like me, that knows you, least." He picked up a cloth and started wiping the bar.

"You had some trouble with Morgan?" Rosen said.

The man looked flustered. "Goddamnit, Arthur," he said, finishing his beer and shoving the empty schooner toward Arthur, "will you get me some more beer and go ahead and do your business without stoppin' in the middle of it, tell everybody else's private business this guy, huh? People oughta decide that for themselves."

Arthur took the glass and moved off toward the taps. "I didn't tell him none your private business, Norris," he said. "You're the one that's havin' this conversation with him. All I said was Wilfred was smarter'n Bernie and you said people were scared of Wilfred and I said people're scared of Bernie, too. And that includes you. That's all I said. And I still say Wilfred was smarter, when he was smart."

"They still had Katie's Place then," Norris said. "That was where all Wilfred's friends went. They didn't come here then any more'n they go in there now. You know what it is about you, Arthur? It's you, is what. Most people that decide they want a glass of beer, they don't ever say to themselves: 'Well, I think I'll just go on down to Knacky's now and have myself a glass of beer.' Like they used to, 'fore Katie's burned down. They don't mind Knacky, Arthur. It's you that they don't like."

"Bullshit," Arthur said. He come back with the beer. He studied Rosen. "You come in here for a glass of beer, didn't you?"

"Yeah," Rosen said.

"Right," Arthur said, "and you don't know me, right?"

"That's what I said, Arthur," Norris said. "That's exactly what I just get through sayin'. This guy don't know you and that's why he come in here. I bet he don't even know who Bernie Morgan is."

"Well," Arthur said, "all right we'll just ask him. He's sittin' right here, ain't he? Whaddaya say, mister, huh? You ain't afraid of Morgan, are you?"

"No," Rosen said. "I don't even know the son of a bitch."

"See?" Arthur said. "Only," he said to Rosen, "I wouldn't say that, not in here, I was you."

"Right," Norris said. "Minute you say it, some son of a bitch'll get up and beat the shit out of you."

"This's where Morgan's friends hang out?" Rosen said.

Both Arthur and Norris frowned. "I don't know as I would say that," Norris said. "Would you say that, Arthur?"

Arthur leaned his forearms on the bar. "Look," he said to Rosen, "the guys that're friendly with Morgan, they come here now just like the guys that were thick with Wilfred Knox used to go to Katie's Place when Maury St. Catherine was still alive. Morgan was the bartender there, which was how he met a lot of the people that helped him get where he is today, and those're the people, the ones that're still in with Morgan, that drink in here. In Knacky's."

"What happened to Katie's?" Rosen said.

"That wasn't here," Arthur said. "Katie's was in Proctor. See, this's Mercer. Katie's burned down. What was it, Norris, twelve, thirteen years?"

"Not that long," Norris said. "It was after, it was after Roger had all his trouble there. And that was what? It was after Wilfred, it was after they put Wilfred in the home there. Which would've been about eight, nine years. Call it ten years. No more'n that."

"Okay," Arthur said. "Ten years ago, call it, but Katie's'd gone to hell long before that. Started downhill right about the time Wilfred got that new district made up that he was giving to Bernie. And Bernie run for that and he won, which didn't surprise nobody that had a half a brain on his neck, and then he quit spendin' enough time in Katie's. And Katie by then was pretty old. He was too old for years to run that place, which was how come all of a sudden Bernie just about took it over and he run it. Katie didn't have no kids, except for the one daughter."

"Right," Norris said. "Candida. Except she was his niece, wasn't she? I didn't think Katie had no kids of his own."

"No," Arthur said, "she was his daughter. Him and Candy's mother got divorced when she was a kid and her aunt raised her. Or his wife ran off or something. Either way. Katie's sister there. The one that had the goiter. Used to be a bitch, talk to her, that goddamned big thing wobblin' around her chin, keep your mind on what she was sayin'."

"Okay," Norris said, "I always thought she was his niece and that was why she was always hangin' around over there."

"Don't matter, she was his niece or his daughter or just some stray he happened to pick up that followed him home," Arthur said. "That wasn't why she was always hangin' around Katie's. Uh uh."

"Candida," Norris said to Rosen, "Candy was hot to trot."

"She was always in Katie's Place," Arthur said, grinning, "because she got it in her head there was a good number, stiff pricks in there, and for a long time there that was all Candy had on her mind, was a good stiff prick."

"She was a hot little number all right," Norris said.

"You betcher," Arthur said, nodding his head and licking his lips. "You got no idea," he said to Rosen, "you got no idea how it was, right after the war. You just got no idea whatsoever what it was like around here when all the soldier boys come home from the war. I don't care how much that Japanese pussy they had or all them French girls and the German broads, they was just about crazy for some good old American vay-gina, is what they were. And there was plenty of it around for them, too, am I right, Norris?"

"God damned right, Arthur," Norris said, also grinning and licking his chops. "There was about six of them that were always ready for it, seemed like. Get off the late shift over to the tire plant in Chicopee there and all you hadda do was find some bar and sit yourself down next to any broad that didn't have a guy sittin' next to her, and it was all you could do, finish one beer 'fore she had your cock out and practically givin' you a blow job right there inna bar. God damn, it was good. And you happened to be on the early shift so you're getting off work in the afternoon, same thing. Didn't matter what time of day it was. Hear all this talk about the kids now with their livin' together and everything, they don't know shit what it was like then."

"And Candida and her cousin there, Evelyn Seeger," Arthur said. "They were cousins, weren't they? I always thought them two was related."

"I don't know if they were related," Norris said, "but they sure were friendly. My God. Didn't matter which one of them you got, you were gonna get your pipes clean that night. Old Evelyn there, remember that night when they had the party for Jaworski that was in Japan there and he got home after everybody else'd been back for almost a year? Him?"

"Good guy, Teddy," Arthur said. "Knocked up some broad in Chicopee and hadda get married all of a sudden. Never amounted to a god-damned thing after he did."

"Old Evelyn, for Christ sake," Norris said, "she went to that party and there must've been about thirty guys there, it was in the Odd Fellows' Grove there, in the summertime, and goddamn if Evelyn didn't take on the whole bunch of them. Stood right up and said anybody that wanted her, could have her. And just about all of us did, too, I think. You did, didn't you, Arthur? I know I did."

"Oh sure," Arthur said. "Good Christ, sure I did. I didn't have no brains then. Would've stuck it in a goddamned lady skunk, I could've figured out some way to get the tail up without gettin' sprayed."

Both men laughed loudly. Rosen forced himself to join them. He drained his schooner to shorten the obligation. He put it down. "More beer, you get a chance, Arthur," he said. Arthur stopped laughing and looked at him suspiciously. "I don't know your name," he said.

"Oh, for Christ sake, Arthur," Norris said, "he just heard me callin' you Arthur is all. He don't mean nothin'."

Arthur looked at Rosen with narrowed eyes. Rosen said: "Hey, sorry." He offered his hand. "Leo," he said. "Leo Rosen."

Arthur took his hand and shook it slowly. He studied Rosen. "Rosen," he said. "You got that beard there too. I see. You Jewish?"

Rosen sighed. "Ahh, for Christ sake," he said, "everybody always says that. I wish to God that immigration guy that wrote down my great-grandfather when he come in this country for the first time'd put down Rose, like he was told. I'm English. I mean, originally. Family's been here over a hundred years. American now, I should think."

Arthur released his hand. He smiled. "Could be worse," he said. "Guy might've put down an Irish name. 'S what happened to Morgan's family."

"Morgan's not Irish?" Rosen said.

"Nah," Arthur said. "He's Scotch. German, something like that. He grew up in Proctor. If you're not Polish in Proctor then everybody assumes you're Irish. He ain't Irish. He was Catholic though. Maybe his mother was Catholic. Morgan's mother Catholic, Norris?"

"Yeah," Norris said. "Her brother there was a priest. Inna missions. Her maiden name was Carr."

"Was not," Arthur said immediately. "Maiden name was Kenney."

"Arthur, for Christ sake," Norris said, "her maiden name wasn't Kenney, goddamnit. Her maiden name was Carr. Her father was the guy, his name was Fred and he run the sheet-metal shop over to Willimansett there, next the Piels brewery before it closed down. And they were all Catholic. The whole Carr family was Catholics."

"You don't know that," Arthur said. "I distinctly recollect, her father was Charlie Kenney that had the place in Chicopee there that they used to have the ice cream stand out in front in the summer. My father used to take me there when I was a kid."

"You're fulla shit, Arthur," Norris said. "For Christ sake, I think you're the one that's gettin' goofy now. They're gonna have you in the next room to Knox's up the hospital 'fore too long, you keep on like this inna way you're goin'."

"Don't gimme that, Norris," Arthur said, "I used to go there with my father. You don't even remember Kenney's ice cream stand? You're the one that's gettin' old. Losin' your memory. That happens, Norris."

"I remember Kenney's ice cream stand all right," Norris said. "I'm just saying Kenney wasn't Morgan's mother's maiden name. She was a Carr from the family that the guy did the sheet-metal work."

"Anyway," Arthur said to Rosen, "Morgan's mother was a Catholic, all right?"

"Right," Rosen said.

"Leo, right?" Arthur said.

"Right," Rosen said, grinning.

"You want another beer, Leo?" Norris said.

"I'm all set, thanks," Rosen said, finishing the partial schooner and lifting the third one, full.

"Well," Norris said, showing his empty toward Arthur, "I'm set for another one."

"No, you're not," Arthur said, shoving it back. "I'm talkin' right now. When I get finished you can have another beer."

"Hey," Norris said, "this was conversation I was having with Leo, here. He's the one, he asked me about Roger."

"Yeah," Arthur said, "well then, since he's your guest I assume you won't mind waitin' until he's ready another beer. What was it you wanted to know about Roger?"

"I wasn't, really," Rosen said. "I was just sort of thinking out loud, that I was wondering if the guy that ran the gas station out on the Mercer Road there, he was all right in the head, you know? I was there one night and I needed some gas and it seemed like he was sort of funny, you know?"

"Well," Arthur said, "you ever been married?"

"No," Rosen said.

Arthur grinned at Norris. Norris said: "Nope, you couldn't've been. Well, lemme tell you. If there is something wrong with Roger sometimes, that is what it is, if you asked me."

"I didn't even see his wife," Rosen said. "It was . . . he was talking funny, for one thing, made me think that. Wonder."

"That's his teeth," Norris said. "His teeth don't fit right. Roger used to get in lots of fights when he was younger, and finally he didn't have no teeth at all his own left, so he . . . I guess he must've ordered some new ones or something from the Sears catalog and didn't get the right size. It's hard to understand him."

"Huh," Arthur said, "it's also his head. Anybody ever tried, stop

Roger Knox from fightin', he wouldn't be in the box he's in now, the poor piece of shit. You know what he did once? He got himself a pretty good load on and, this was when he was working at Siebert's Socony station, after old Wilfred took that piece of land on the Mercer Road and bought him and Candida the trailer and set 'em up behind that station that nobody'd used since old man Whitman woke up one morning and he was dead. You know something, Norris?" Arthur said. "That Roger, there never was a fuckin' thing that Roger could do right and get it right and then just leave it alone the first time he done it now, was there?"

"Never," Norris said, nodding. "Roger had his head up his ass since the day he was born, you ask me. You could tell from the way Wilfred treated him. Wilfred never had no hope that kid'd ever amount to anythin'. I don't even think, you know something? I don't even think Wilfred was even at all that much surprised when Roger got it in his head that Candida was gonna be his one true love there and he was gonna marry her. The town pump. Hell, the county pump. You know what else I think?"

"No," Rosen said.

"I think," Norris said, "that I'm not gonna chat with you no more pretty soon, you don't drink that fuckin' beer you had sittin' in front of you about three days now, like you're waitin' for it, turn to gold or something. Because until you drink your beer, this asshole Arthur here isn't gonna give me no more beer and all this talkin' to you's making me dry, is what it is doing."

"Oh," Rosen said. He picked up the schooner and chugalugged it. He put it down. He wiped his mouth. " 'Nother beer, Arthur?"

Arthur straightened up. He looked at Norris. "He's gonna want one too now, you know," he said to Rosen.

"Fuck," Norris said, "yes, I do. Any reason I shouldn't?"

"None I can think of," Rosen said. "Give him a beer, okay?"

"You sure?" Arthur said. "You had a promise from him there, that he'd shut up if he couldn't have any more beer. All you had to do was nurse that one like he generally does when he's looking for a sponsor, we would've had a nice quiet conversation." He set the beers down on the bar.

"I'm not sponsoring him," Rosen said, taking a five-dollar bill from his pocket. "I didn't say anything about that."

"Certainly did," Arthur said. "Told you I wouldn't give him no more beer unless you ordered some. You just ordered some. There it is. That'll be one twenty."

Norris laughed. Rosen shrugged. "One twenty," he said. "Could've been worse, I suppose. You guys could be running a card game."

"So," Norris said, drinking, "Roger decided Candida was his true love and he was gonna marry her."

"Besides," Arthur said, "he thought she was knocked up, way I recall it."

"There was talk," Norris said, "but there's always talk. Christ sake, she was pregnant then, she must be still pregnant now, because she ain't had the baby yet and it must be close to twenny-five years now, they been married. Set a goddamned record for pregnancies, that one would, if she was."

"Didn't I hear she had the baby," Arthur said, "and it was born dead or something?"

"Nah," Norris said, "that was Morgan's wife, I think. Maggie Morgan. And there was another one, that was glad to see Johnny come marchin' home."

"She was promiscuous too, huh?" Rosen said.

"She fucked around some, that's what you mean," Arthur said. "Not's much as Candy and them though, would you say, Norris?"

"Nah," Norris said, "nowhere near as much. Maggie there, she was a little more choosy, you know what I mean. She was after Morgan from the giddyap. She might've let some the boys have a little taste of tail, but it was always Morgan she wanted. Set her cap for him right off. Which, come to think of it," he said, "that may've been Wilfred's doing too, that put that idea in her head. He never made no bones about it that Roger wasn't gonna be the one that came after him in the political line of work, at least. And Bernie, he didn't have no money or anything, and damned little schooling, but that son of a bitch, huh? He was a natural-born politician."

"He sure was," Arthur said. "Here he was, he was nothin' but a bro-ken-down hardware peddler's kid, that had three other boys beside Bernie that he couldn't feed and keep dressed right either, and all his damned mother ever did was go to church there. I think when they built the new Rose of Lima there she was in the plans. They thought she hadda be part of the building, she spent so much time in church. And what the hell you gonna think's gonna happen, a kid like that? His brothers, I don't even know what happened to them. I know the second-oldest got himself killed in Italy or something during the war, and I think Gabriel there, the youngest, I think he went out west or something. He was some kind of a teacher or something. And I heard Ronald went in the priesthood, but I'm not sure. So what's the kid got going for him, huh? He could play football, and that was all. He was a good football player. His first couple years high school, he was startin' talk that he was gonna get a scholarship to Holy Cross or something, but then he lies about his age and gets in the service and everybody figures, well, that'll be the end of him. And he got wounded . . ."

"He was wounded bad," Norris said. "He got hit at Anzio, I think it was. They didn't even think he was gonna live there, for a while, and then that he'd be in a wheelchair all his life, prolly wouldn't be able to walk or anything. And then he comes home here, and sure he's a hero, but we hadda fuckin' shitload of heroes back in nineteen forty-five, for Christ sake. Every time you turned around, for Christ sake, there was some kind of hero that was tryin' take your job or sayin' you should work for him instead of him having to take orders from you. So that wasn't gonna do him much good, and he couldn't play football no more. And what happens? Maury St. Catherine hires him, work nights tending bar and being a bouncer, and pretty soon it was Bernie Morgan that was running Katie's Place and even Katie didn't make no secret of it. Hell, Katie acted like he was proud of it. Treated that kid like he was a son. Took him everyplace."

"Yeah," Arthur said. "You wouldn't think this maybe, Leo, that a guy like Katie'd mean much inna world, guy that's running a bar in Proctor, but Katie had one hell of a lot of connections. That bastard'd been everywhere. I don't know all of what he did, and there was probably a lot of it that wasn't strictly legal. But like when somebody like Maurice Tobin or Paul Dever was running for governor, they would always make it a point to come through Proctor and stop in at Katie's Place and say hello all the boys. And if they couldn't actually come there, they would make sure Katie was with them when they got to Springfield or Holyoke, wherever they happened to be. He always went the Democratic National Convention, there. Always."

"Of course he did," Norris said, "he was a fuckin' delegate, for Christ sake. The hell else you'd expect him to do? Stay home, wait for somebody to call him up and tell him how it came out?"

"Yeah," Arthur said, "but I was just saying and all, that Katie, all he was was a saloonkeeper, but he was also, he knew a lot of very powerful guys. See, and when Bernie comes along there after the war and Katie just took him under his wing, you know? Sort of adopted him. And then, he was always very thick with Wilfred there, Katie was, he seen to it that Wilfred appreciated what a nice kid this Morgan kid was gettin' to be. And that was just about what Wilfred wanted."

"Right," Norris said. "That's what I said. Wilfred never had no hopes for Roger, even if he was his own kid and everything. Roger never did have a full duffel he was traveling with. You could see that. I dunno if it was when Roger decides that Candy was gonna be the Virgin Mary that Wilfred finally threw in the sponge on him or whether it was just something that he always knew from the day that Roger was born and he first seen him, but he had two kids, which was Maggie and Roger, and Maggie being a broad which they did not fool around in politics in those days, and Roger always being kind of a crazy asshole, Wilfred took on Bernie. And like I say, Bernie is smart. He takes a look at Maggie Knox and maybe she was fuckin' around a little, but so was a lot of girls then and their fathers didn't have no political connections. So Wilfred marries her off to Bernie and that just set the whole damned thing in cement. And old Roger there, pretty soon he gets himself in the shit like everybody always figured he was gonna, sooner or later, surer'n fate, and that was it."

"What'd he do, exactly?" Rosen said, drinking his beer.

"Oh, shit," Arthur said, "he done a lot of things. Mostly what he did was get in fights. And mostly what he did was lose the fights at first, because Roger as you probably noticed isn't very big. So he got in the habit carryin' a piece of pipe around with him and he would whack the guy with that. Which got him in a certain amount of cop trouble. Fistfight's one thing, lots of guys get in them. But a thing with a pipe like that, he got a lot of grief for it. He was in court a lot.

"So," Arthur said, "there was this state trooper that used to patrol around here out of the Monson barracks there, motorcycle. And he thought he was pretty hot shit and he liked to bust Roger's balls for him. And he was around here long enough, he heard some stories about Candida which of course was all true. And when he wanted to yank Roger's chain for him, he would say something about Candy bringing home any money these days when he happened to be down here there some afternoon and see her gettin' off the bus after she'd been shopping in Springfield or something. Real wise-ass bastard. I don't blame Roger, gettin' mad at him. So one night, Roger was working down Siebert's at the time, one night this cop comes in to get some gas and he goes to take a leak. And Roger does something to his bike so it exploded. Cop got hurt pretty bad. Fried his balls and his prick for him, I understand."

"Roger Knox did that himself?" Rosen said.

"Yeah," Norris said. "He did that. It was a pretty long time ago there, though. He used to keep his own place on the Mercer Road open days because there was still a certain amount of trucks using that road then, and at night he would go down Siebert's and be the night mechanic. Pick up some extra cash. Roger always was more'n an ordinary mechanic. He was good. And he was down there one night and he set the cop's motorcycle so it would blow up when he started it."

"Because he told me about that," Rosen said. "Only he said it was somebody else that did it. And it was an accident."

"He said that when they took him into court," Arthur said. "His lawyer did, anyway. Said he was out of his head and didn't know what he was doing. That thing there, split personality. So they locked him up in the hospital that his father built. He was in there about three, four years. And then while he was in there, Wilfred and Bernie both got ahold Candida and they told her she wasn't to take no chances getting Roger, doing something that would get Roger upset again when he come out. That would make him think she was peddling her ass again. Because if she did, and he did something as a result which she already knew he was capable of doing, they would put her out inna goddamned rain for the rest her goddamned life. Or she could just live with Roger, and not do anything, but that was all the choice she had. Because otherwise they were gonna make sure Roger never got out. And I guess she took it. She's been there ever since anyway, with him. Never see her go anywhere, she don't go with Roger. And that ain't often, because Roger don't like to go much of anywhere. 'Cept in here for a few beers, he gets restless or something. Then home again."

"Well," Norris said, "she went someplace today." He lifted the stein to his mouth and drank deeply. He set it down. "Without Roger," he said.

"Well, goddamnit," Arthur said, "now how in hell would you know something like that?"

"Because I seen her," Norris said. He belched slightly. "This goddamned finger I got here," he said to Rosen, brandishing the splint, "I broke this on the job, see?"

"That's just a load of shit, you know," Arthur said to Rosen. "That's just the kind of shit old Norris here thinks up when he gone and did something to himself by accident and then the next thing that he thinks of is the same thing that he thinks of the minute that he comes in here and sees somebody that he didn't see in here before. Which is how he can fix it so he will make some money off of it. Tell some story out of it and he will get some money. So he broke his goddamned finger there, probably when he was trying, get his prick out of some place which he shouldn't have put it in the first place, and he sits himself right down before he even goes down the hospital there and dreams up this whole big song and dance how he broke it workin' down the fire station."

"Well, Arthur, you asshole," Norris said, "I did break it down the fire station like I said, and you know that." He nodded three times. He spoke to Rosen. "They had me, the chief told me there was something wasn't workin' right the pumper hose reel there, where she takes it up, they got this winch it run off. And by Jesus I am here to tell you he was right. I don't know what somebody did to that thing, but I start her up there and she don't go at all, and then I start reachin' around so I can see what's wrong in there, and that son of a whore, she just fired up like a bastard there and caught my finger there and jammed it."

"I ain't even," Norris said, "I'm not supposed to be working with this. But this is the day all the guys at the station go down to Boston, the annual ball game, so out of the goodness my heart, I am working." He nodded again and looked sorrowful.

"Bullshit," Arthur said.

"Well," Norris said, draining the beer, "you wouldn't think that if you ever had to do some work sometime instead of standing there and making jokes about people that spent the whole day fightin' grass fires down Robinson's goddamned ravine out there on the Mercer Road when you're supposed to be down at the doctor's office having him look at your broken finger. The bastard Robinson. Every year he burns it over, like he ain't supposed to, and every year that lyin' bastard says the kids must've set it. Kids'd never get down in there—nobody could."

"So that's where everybody is tonight?" Rosen said. "At the ball game?"

"Well," Arthur said, "everybody except me, because I get paid for being here, and him, because he'd come in here anyway just like he is, even though he's on the clock, the station, and claims that he is working, and you, and pretty soon old Roger Knox."

"What the hell do you mean, Roger Knox, Arthur?" Norris said. "You don't know old Roger's coming in here. Now you just quit makin' up all that shit and go get me and Leo here some more beer."

"I guess I do know it though," Arthur said. "I can stand right here lookin' out the goddamned window and see old Roger park that black

—

and white DeSoto car of his right next to Leo's motorcycle there across the street and walk all around it like he was trying to remember if that was the one that trooper rode, and I never seen old Roger yet drive down here in that car without stopping in here for some beer before he got back in that car and drove her home again. I can see pretty good when I want, you know, Norris. Just because some of us's eyes going bad, it don't mean that mine are."

Norris grunted. "Well all right then goddammit, Arthur," he said, shoving his mug toward him, "then this'll be my last beer for tonight here and I'll just get on back down the fire station once I finished it."

"Not till Leo orders," Arthur said, "unless you think you're gonna pay for one your own without reciprocating Leo for all the beer he bought for you."

"Goddamnit, Arthur," Norris said, "I'll buy a beer for Leo. I can do that all right. Leo," he said, "you're gonna be my guest for this one."

"Hey," Rosen said, grinning, "that's not necessary, Norris." He pointed toward the change on the counter. "I only bought one round there. I still got money working. And it don't make no difference to me anyway. I'm on expenses."

"Well, Leo," Arthur said, "now, you never should've told him that. That was one goddamned thing you never should've mentioned to old Norris here. Just about the worst thing in the world you ever could've picked to say. He's liable now, he's gonna stick by you until you finally look up some morning and it begins to bother you, is he like some dog that picked you up and decided he was gonna follow you back home and live with you for life."

Norris beamed at Leo. "Expenses, huh?" he said. "That mean you got some guy that pays you back what you spend in here drinkin' beer with me?"

"Sure," Rosen said.

"Well, I'll be goddamned," Norris said. "How about that, Arthur?"

"Uh huh," Arthur said to Rosen, "now you made it even worse, which I would not have believed that you could do, if you had told me that was what you had in mind before you went and did it. What's he's gonna want now, you know, he's gonna keep you sittin' there until he finds out whether there is some way he can get this guy you're workin' for, hire him direct to sit here and drink beer with himself all the goddamned night. Old Norris'd give a man a full day's work·for a day's worth of full pay on that job, *every* day. Wouldn't you, Norris, huh?"

"Yeah, Arthur," Norris said, "you heard what the man said there.

Never mind all that usual bullshit you're always handing out. Just get your big fat ass moving there and fill our mugs up there, and take it out of Leo's money there. Leo's gonna get it back."

"Yeah," Arthur said, taking the steins and heading for the taps. "One thing I'd like to know though, Leo, all right?"

"Sure," Rosen said.

"Well," Arthur said, drawing the beers, "what I'd like to know is why the hell this boss of yours'd want you to sit here and drink up all the beer you can with Norris, huh? Because, way I understand it, most bosses that they pay expenses their employees, right, they expect get something for it. And the only thing your boss's got a goddamned chance of getting from you doing this with Norris is maybe he's gonna hear about you met the biggest bullshit artist in the whole goddamned Pioneer Valley, and sat on a stool here talking to him while every goddamned thing 'tween here and Worcester burned right to the ground because he was the whole goddamned fire department for the town the night you drank with him."

Norris nudged Rosen. "Pay no attention to him, Leo," he said. "You can probably see what Arthur's problem is." He winked. "A very jealous man, old Arthur is, you know? He's got this bad habit of his he's got, he never did really lick it. And what it is, it's that he's jealous. So don't pay no attention to him."

Arthur finished drawing the beers and started back. "And then when you get through telling me that," he said, "you can try explain to me how in God's name you can stand it, any job that means you got to sit and listen Norris half the night while he gets himself two-thirds the way inside the bag."

"Well," Rosen said, lifting the fresh mug, "the first is easy. My boss pays me to go where he says and do what he wants me to do when I get there. Which I have already done for today. But the agreement we got with the company, the guys like me that work for it, if we're a certain distance from the office when it's quittin' time, they have to buy us dinner and a few drinks. Well, not the few drinks, but they also have to pay us gas money, and since I don't want no dinner and I ride that motorcycle which does not use much gas, I can have all the beer I want. And since even when I'm not having any dinner, when I'm entitled to have dinner, and I'm having beer instead, and because I don't like to drink alone, I'm buying beer for Norris here, and my boss is paying for it." He touched the mug to his lips, pulled it back, elevated it slightly, said: "Cheers," and drank.

"Well," Arthur said, "then that explains it then. But I'll be god-damned if I think it makes a lot of sense. I think what we need's another party to decide that, whether it makes any goddamned sense at all." He raised his voice as Roger Knox in his green uniform and Red Sox cap entered Knacky's tavern. "Roger," he said, "you old bastard, you come over here and see if you can decide something for us."

Roger Knox paused on the threshold of the barroom. "Well, Arthur, goddamnit," he said, "I don't know's I want to do that. I come in here and I had two fights so far today and I'll be goddamned if I think I want another one. I ain't won one fight yet, you know."

"Well, Roger," Arthur said, "this ain't no fight you're gettin' into here. Who the hell've you been fightin' with anyway?" While he talked he walked down to the taps and drew a Bud. He put it on the bar in front of the taps. Roger walked slowly over to it, licking his lips. He lifted it and drank. He put it down. He rested both his hands on the counter and stared at the mug of beer. He licked his lips again. He picked up the mug and drank again, emptying it. He shoved it back to Arthur. He nodded. He pointed toward the mug. Arthur filled it. "You hear me, Roger?" Arthur said. "Who the hell've you been fightin' with?"

Roger took the refilled mug, raised it to his mouth, and drank a third of it. He set it down. He rested his hands on the counter and belched softly. He turned his head toward where Norris and Rosen sat. "Norris," he said.

"Roger," Norris said, raising his mug. He drank.

Roger raised his mug again and drank. He set it down. He hunched slightly over the bar and peered past Norris. He jerked his head toward Leo. "That your motorcycle parked outside there 'cross the street?"

Rosen turned on the stool, looked out the window, nodded, turned back, leaned past Norris, and said: "Yup."

"Yeah," Roger said. "Seen you before, I think." He turned to Arthur. "Where the hell is everybody, Arthur?"

"Well, Roger," Norris said, "they all went to the ball game. This's ball game night."

"Oh yeah," Roger said. "I forgot. They came home." He drank beer. "Huh," he said. "They were in Toronto last night, I thought."

"Right," Arthur said. "So, who you been fightin' with, Roger?"

Roger rested his hands on the bar again and tried twice without success to force a belch. He shook his head. "Well," he said, pressing his chin back against his neck, "the first fight that I had today was with my wife." He tried to belch again and managed it. "Ahh," he said. He lifted the mug and drank. He wiped his mouth with the back of his hand. He nodded. "Yup," he said, "the first one was with my wife. And like I say, I don't want, talk about that one." He raised the mug again and drank.

"Well, Roger," Norris said, "now, I see Candida today, I was telling Arthur. I seen her goin' right through town this afternoon in a car. She was riding in the car with Maggie Morgan. Now, didn't I tell you that, Arthur?"

"Goddamnit, Norris," Arthur said, "you never told me no such thing."

"Well, I did," Norris said. "I was sittin' right here and I said when I went down the doctor's office there today after we finally got that fire knocked down Robinson's ravine, goddamnit, and I was right there in the parking lot there and I seen Candida go by with Maggie Morgan, with your sister there, Roger, in Maggie Morgan's car there. Without Roger. And they was goin' someplace. And I told you that and you did not believe me. Now don't you go tryin' tell me, Arthur, I did not tell you that. Because I goddamned right well did."

"Yeah," Roger said. He emptied his mug and shoved it back toward Arthur. He pointed to it.

"So there you are, Arthur, goddamnit," Norris said. "Tryin', tell me that."

"Now goddamnit, Norris," Roger said, watching Arthur fill the mug, "now didn't I already tell you there when I come here that was something I didn't wanna talk about?"

"Well, Roger," Norris said, "that thing, that thing you said you didn't want to talk about, this didn't have nothing to do with that. That I told Arthur that I seen."

Roger nodded, accepting the full mug from Arthur. "Yeah," he said, "well, never mind about it then." He drank and set the mug down. He peered down the bar at Rosen once again. "You got to tell me," he said. "I know I seen you someplace, but I can't place it in my mind. Where the hell was it where I seen you?"

"Your gas station," Rosen said. "I bought some gas from you one night a while back. Back in May, I think it was. I was up here. I was on my way to Chicopee."

Roger frowned and drank his beer.

"Who'd you have the other fight with, Roger?" Arthur said.

Roger put the mug down. He belched again. "Dad," he said. He shook his head. "Shit." He spread his feet apart and lowered his head until he was facing down at the counter. He farted. "Ahh," he said. He straightened up again and raised the beer mug. "He got to thinking," he said, "he got to thinking I was Bernie again, and you know how he always thinks he's got a lot to say to me when he gets it in his head I'm Bernie. Jesus." He drank. He put the mug down. He shook his head. "Shit," he said, "I take the day off from the station and go up there like I think I should, put the car out front where he can see it, bring that fuckin' old blind dog I practically got to carry up the steps he's so goddamned old and his back legs give out if he even tries, stand up. And then I get in there at suppertime like he always says he wants that I should come around if I am gonna come at all, and then goddamnit after I go to all that goddamned trouble he decides I'm Bernie and he's gonna give me hell all afternoon." He belched again. "I get sick of it," he said. He growled. "That ain't right."

"Well, Roger," Arthur said, "it ain't right, certainly if you ain't Bernie and you didn't do what Bernie did that made him mad."

Roger gazed at Arthur with reddened eye. "Not that," he said. He jerked his right thumb toward Rosen. "Him," he said. He craned his neck around and looked at Rosen. "Hey," he said, "the guy with the beard there."

"Yeah?" Rosen said.

"Well, goddamnit," Roger said, "that ain't what you told me, that night that you was in and bought some gas."

"What?" Rosen said.

"That you was goin' to Chicopee," Roger said. "You didn't tell me that."

"I didn't?" Rosen said.

"No, goddamnit," Roger said, "you said you was goin' to Springfield. You was, you came in just a few days or so after that guy that we was talkin' about that had the red car there, Ferrari, had the brazeer thing on it. And we was talkin' about that and the bugs there from drivin' fast, and you told me that you was on your way to Springfield."

"Geez," Rosen said, shrugging and grinning, "could've, I guess. I really don't remember."

"Yeah," Roger said, raising his glass, "well, I do. It was Springfield you said." He drank and set the mug down again. "Springfield," he said to Arthur. He blinked. "And it was Bernie did them things, made Dad mad. Not me that was gettin' blamed for them today. Shit. And I hadda look at that supper they give them. It was pork tonight. Good goddamned thing all those people in there're crazy. That stuff, it just gets worse and worse."

"Yeah," Arthur said.

"He eats it," Roger said, "and he sits there and he don't know what the fuck he's eatin', and he's callin' me Bernie and telling me the first thing I have got to do the minute that the legislature's over and they both, the two of them get back to Proctor, he's got to get ahold of me and get me so I start taking decent care old Rocky there.

"Well, shit," Roger said. "That old dog there, ain't gettin' decent care? That goddamned old dog's gettin' better treatment'n I do, and I don't know why the fuck I give it to him That goddamned sick and blind old dog ain't good for nothin', and he's so goddamned fat he can't get out his own way half the time. He stinks. Candida says he don't stink, but he does. I want to say to Dad and tell him, you know, that the goddamned sick and blind old dog, well, he can't hardly walk enough, get outside and take a goddamned *piss,* and what I really ought to do since I am being Bernie there is get ahold of me and say: 'Now Roger, you take that sick and blind old dog there down the back meadow there and your shotgun there where Candida can't see you none, and you just put him out his misery.' That's what I oughta do. But I tell that to Dad, even if he does think I'm Bernie, and I know what's gonna happen then, sure as you're born. He's gonna start that goddamned moanin' and throwin' his head back that he does when he gets all upset at something and goddamn, I can't stand much of that.

"So," Roger said, "I just leave him go along and tell me that, and then he starts tellin' me another thing I got to do when I get back from Boston being Bernie, and that is that I got to tell Roger there to see if he can't do something about Candida there and all them things that he's been hearing from Katie and them about her, which of course is, the thing of that is that Katie's been dead there for more'n ten years or so, and anyway, I said I didn't want to talk about that." He picked up the beer, drank again, craned his neck, belched, and peered around at Rosen again. "Hey," he said, "you with that beard there, the fella with the motorcycle there that went to Chicopee when he told me that he was goin' out to Springfield."

"Yeah?" Rosen said.

"Well, goddamnit," Roger said, "I'd just like to know what the goddamned hell you're doing up here all the time, ridin' around on that goddamned motorcycle and mindin' people's business for them that don't want no part of you."

"Well," Rosen said.

"Hey," Norris said, "goddamnit, Roger. Now you leave Leo here alone, is what you oughta do, goddamnit. We're gettin' along perfectly all right here, till you come in here and you got to start all this goddamned foolishness of yours, you know. So you just shut up there and you leave Leo here alone. He ain't botherin' nobody."

"Well," Roger said, "that's maybe all right if you want to say it's all right, Norris, but he never went around up here and started tellin' you no stories like he did me, and I want to know what it is this son-of-a-bitch here is doin' here, is what I want to know, and I guess I got a right to ask him if it suits me. So, I asked you something there, mister. What the hell're you doin' around here and you're comin' around and mindin' everybody's business for them like this?"

Norris started to speak. Rosen touched him on the arm. "Hey, Norris," he said, "it's all right. I don't mind tellin' him what I'm doing here."

"Yeah," Roger said, "well, that's all right, because I already know what you're doin' here, all right? I just want to see, see if you'll tell me 'nother lie, like you did that time here back this spring when you was buyin' gas from me and tellin' me that you was on your way to Springfield, that's all." He belched and smirked at Rosen. "That's all, buddy boy. I got you figured out. I know what you're doin' up here. I jus' wanna see, how big a liar you are anyway."

"Hey," Norris said, starting to get off the stool, "now goddamnit, Roger, you come in here and you start sayin' things like that, my friend Leo here, I got to warn you, Roger."

"Shit," Roger said, belching again. He picked up his mug, drained it, and pushed it toward Arthur. "Now Arthur, goddamnit," he said, "you just go ahead and fill that up again for me, you hear? Yeah." He nodded. "Now you just listen me, Norris, is what you do. I know, I happen, know what this guy's doin' here." He nodded and leered. Arthur pushed the refilled mug back to him. He lifted it and drank half of it. He set it down and nodded again. "Yup," he said, "this here lyin' son-bitch here, he's up here workin' for Bernie, 's what he's doin'." He nodded solemnly. "That's right," he said, "he's out here for Bernie and that's why he's talkin' stories, people, don't want them actually know what he is doin'. Bernie." He picked up the mug and drank again.

"Well, goddamnit, Roger," Norris said, "now that's just your ordinary run of bullshit there, Roger. You don't know what the hell you're talkin' about most of the time, and this is one of them. This guy, we already talked about Bernie there, 'fore you come in here, and he don't even know Bernie. Know who Bernie is. Ain't that right, Leo," he said, nudging Rosen.

"That's right," Rosen said.

"Hah," Roger said gloomily, "that's more shit. All of Bernie's guys that he's got workin' for him say that, every last one of them. They all say that." He emptied the mug. He pushed it back to Arthur. "I got time, one more," he said. He reached into his pocket and pulled out crumpled bills. He lurched a little as he counted them. "Then," he said, trying to focus on the money, "I'm gonna, I got to go back the station there and see if any business comes along. Get me six-pack there and go back out the station." He farted again. "Oops," he said.

"Well shit, Roger," Norris said, "that's just shit, I guess, and there ain't no point in talkin' to you any further on it. Ain't that right, Leo?"

Rosen shrugged. "Guess so," he said. He emptied his mug. "Drink up, Norris," he said, "see if there's any left when Roger gets finished there and maybe Arthur give us some of it."

"Yeah," Roger said, accepting his fresh mug and putting the whole crumpled wad on the bar. "Now Arthur," he said, "you just take out that what I owe you there." He raised the mug, drank deeply, set it down, and addressed Rosen again. "Hey," he said, "guy with the hair on his face there, all right? You better watch out around here, ridin' around on that motorcycle and spyin' for Bernie. Understand me?" He nodded, raised the mug, and drank again.

Arthur had walked down to where Rosen and Norris sat and picked up their empty mugs. He was on his way back to the taps. He gestured toward Roger with the mugs. "Now Roger, goddamnit," he said, "that'll be just about enough we had out of you today, Roger. Now you just finish your own business there, you understand that? No call for no more your foolishness in this place about motorcycles."

Roger put the mug down, still about a quarter full, and glared at Arthur. "Yeah," he said, "well, that's all right, Arthur." He addressed Rosen. "But you better watch yourself, is all I got to say, Mister Beard here out on his motorcycle and mindin' people's business that don't concern him none. Because I know somethin' about them motorcycles there, and them fuckin' things can be dangerous, man don't know what the fuck he's doin', patch of sand or something. You just better watch your ass, is all I got to say." He picked up the mug again. Arthur made change from the wad, putting Rosen's mug and Norris's mug aside, and put the change back on the bar. He waited watchfully while Roger finished his beer and set the mug down. Then he seized it. "Hey," Roger said.

"Hey nothin', Roger, goddamnit," Arthur said, putting the mug in the sink with soapy water, dipping it into the rinse sink and standing it upside down to dry on the rack behind the bar, "you ain't having no more goddamned beer in this place tonight, Roger. Goddamnit, you come in here, it was just a few minutes ago, tellin' everybody in here how you done nothin' but start fights today and you lost both of them, and I'll be goddamned if you don't start right off and try to start another one in here. Now you just clear out of here and take your goddamned money there that you got left and get the hell out of here."

"Well, that's all right," Roger said, scooping up the money and stuffing it into his pocket. He nodded vigorously. "You can go ahead and throw me out if that's the way you feel, Arthur, and that's just fine with me. But you just remember that I told him there, he'd better watch his ass."

"Yeah," Arthur said, "well, if you was to ask me, Roger, man gets drunk as fast as you do like that, Bernie and them pass this new drunk drivin' thing I guess they did, you're the one'd better watch out, 'cause you're gonna find yourself down in the jail some night, you keep acting like you're acting now."

Roger pushed himself away from the bar, belching again. "That's all right, Arthur," he said, "that'll be all right. Just go down the package store there and get myself a six-pack and go home. Old Roger'll be all right. It's everybody else should worry." He belched again, then turned suddenly and pointed to Norris. "And you, goddamnit Norris, you just keep in mind what I told you here now, and don't say that I didn't tell you. That guy you're so friendly with there, he's one of Bernie's spies." He nodded. "Spies," he said. "Still didn't tell nobody what he's doin' here." He made his way unsteadily toward the door, opened it, and left.

Arthur picked up the two mugs. "Shit," he said, "now I can't remember which is which."

"Well, goddamnit, Arthur," Norris said, "you can give us two clean ones there. It ain't like it was something gonna kill you."

Arthur took two clean mugs from behind the bar. He started filling them. He shook his head. "Goddamnit," he said, "I don't know. That Roger there. He is a funny bastard, 's what he is. That ain't, you can't never know what to expect from that guy, you know? Ain't that right, Norris?"

"Well, goddamnit," Norris said, as Arthur brought the fresh mugs, "of course it's right and you know that." Norris turned to Rosen. "That guy Roger," he said, "he'll come in here nine times out of ten and he don't, you can't hardly get one word out of him. And then something like he did tonight, come in here with a hair across his ass before anybody had a chance to say a word to him, and no matter what you say there, he is gonna get mad at you for sayin' it. He would've gotten mad that everybody went the ball game, you wasn't here. Which, come to think of it, what are you doing here?"

"It's very simple," Rosen said.

"Of course you don't mind sayin'," Arthur said, "because you don't have to if that suits you. This here's a bar, and you can come in here and have some beer if you behave yourself without tellin' everybody what your business is."

"Well, goddamnit, Arthur," Rosen said, "no, I don't mind." He raised the mug. "Cheers," he said. He drank. "I'm with the state, just like he said," Rosen said, putting the mug down. "Not working for Bernie, though. Like I said, I don't even know the son of a bitch." He grinned. "Except you told me I shouldn't call him that. And what I'm doing, I'm with the Department of Mental Health and we're thinking of expanding the hospital there in Proctor that I guess's the one he was talking about, where his father is, and I've got to see somebody up there that's out of town all day and won't be back until tonight. So that's all. Nothing serious. But I wasn't gonna say that I was goin' to that hospital while he was still here. Not like he was talking."

"No," Arthur said, "well, that was smart. There he goes now." They turned on their stools and watched Roger walk unsteadily across the street, carrying a bag under his right arm. He stopped at the Kawasaki Spectre, stared at it, and then kicked the rear tire. "That guy, he sure don't like those motorcycles."

"Well," Rosen said, "I don't expect he'll hurt it any, kicking tires."

Roger got into the DeSoto and backed it away from the curb, the triple taillights in the upswept tailfins red in the gathering dark. "It's gonna be a long night at that gas station, I think, Arthur," Norris said. "That looked to be like two big six-packs was in that bag he had there with him."

Arthur began wiping the bar. "Yeah," he said. "And him with that load he made here in about five minutes. Pity Candida, she gets home 'fore it puts him to sleep and he's still sittin' up and nursing all that beer, drunker'n a goat and mad, too."

"I think I'll have another one," Rosen said, drinking his stein dry and placing it on the bar. "Let him get a few miles out the road toward home 'fore I start out on that motorcycle he doesn't like."

"Good idea," Norris said, emptying his mug and shoving it to Arthur, "good goddamned idea."

Roger went about four miles out of town on the Mercer Road until he came to a dirt road leading to an abandoned farmhouse set well off the highway. He backed the DeSoto into it and turned the engine and the headlights off. He opened the bag on the seat beside him and wrenched a can of Bud from its plastic collar. The dog slept, snuffling, in the backseat, occasionally whimpering in its dreams of hunting long ago. He popped the top and drank from it. "Goddamned Caldor store," he muttered, "goddamned lying bitch." He drank beer and he waited. In the middle of his third beer he heard the sound of an engine. He started the DeSoto and did not put the lights on. He sat crouched over the steering wheel, the can of beer between his legs, and watched as Rosen rode by on the Kawasaki Spectre, traveling at a moderate rate of speed. "Ahh, goddamnit," Roger said.

Roger put the DeSoto in gear after the motorcycle had gone by. Still with no lights he turned out of the dirt road and followed well behind the bike, his eyes fixed on the red taillight swinging through the curves beneath the overhanging maple limbs. As Rosen got closer to Robinson's ravine, where the smoke still rose from the fire, Roger began to close the gap. As Rosen crested the hill just before the ravine, Roger floored the DeSoto. He was less than five feet behind the bike on the downside of the hill when Rosen heard him and jerked his head around in the helmet to verify his ears. Roger brought the car up and turned the wheel slightly to the left as the bumper kissed Rosen's rear tire. The motorcycle slewed to the left, tilting toward the right, and Roger straightened out the steering wheel, catapulting the motorcycle into the ravine, Rosen flying forward over the handlebars and into the smoke as he dropped head first toward the rocks. Roger straightened out the wheel, turned on his headlights, and allowed the DeSoto to coast down to normal speed.

Roger parked the DeSoto in the service bay with the grease pit in the gas station. The dog got out of the backseat with difficulty and slowly ambled down to the trailer. Roger closed the door behind the car. He went into the office with his beer and sat down behind the desk. He reached behind him and shut off the two bulbs that illuminated the sign outside. He did not turn on the television set. The tire iron lay on the desk where it always was, glinting in the moonlight. He put his feet up on the desk and opened his fourth can of beer. He waited, grinning from time to time and saying, "Caldor store, huh. Don't believe that. Wait for her." He dozed.

Shortly after midnight, Roger woke up and heard the tires of Maggie's Grand Prix crunching on the gravel. He looked out the window and saw the white car shining in the moonlight. He could hear Maggie and Candida talking.

"Well, see, Maggie," Candida said, giggling a little, "he did just what I said and went to bed, the little lamb."

"I dunno," Maggie said, "the car, I don't see the car there. He could still be out, getting drunk down Knacky's or something like that."

"Nope," Candida said, slurring her words slightly, "he's asleep. Roger never lasted this late down at Knacky's. He goes down to Knacky's, he is always home by ten. Ten fifteen, the very latest. It costs him, he don't like having to spend all that money that it costs to drink at Knacky's, he can get himself drunk so much cheaper here." She giggled again.

"Well," Maggie said, also giggling, "he didn't get drunk half as cheap as we did."

"Nope," Candida said, also giggling. "Course, he didn't have to do nothing for it, neither."

Maggie thought that was very funny, and sputtered with laughter. "Well, Candida," she said, "you didn't *mind* doing what you had to do for all them drinks and that lovely dinner that you had."

"Nope," Candida said.

"Matter of fact," Maggie said, sputtering some more, "while you was where I could see what you was doing, you didn't seem, mind it at all. Ain't my friend's friend Theodore there, ain't he nice?"

"Teddy's very nice," Candida said firmly. "He's very considerate and polite, and . . ." She giggled. "And . . . he's a gentleman, and he's very nice."

"And," Maggie said, "he's got a nice, big cock, ain't he, Candida, huh?"

"Well, Maggie," Candida said, "now how on earth would I know that?" She also sputtered with laughter, which set Maggie off again and they both laughed loudly. "Bernie," Roger whispered to himself. He put his head down on his arms on the desk and began to weep into the cloth of his shirt sleeves. He did not sob or make any other noise. He heard Candida get out of the car, shut the door carefully and quietly, and walk across the gravel into the grass. He heard Maggie drive away. He heard Candida open and shut the screen door to the trailer, and heard her calling him. After a while she stopped calling, and Roger went to sleep at the desk.

25 "Yeah," Mahoney said, stuffing his khaki shirt into his khaki pants and shifting his shoulders back and forth in the sunlight of the parking lot outside the big white building of the Steamship Authority at Woods Hole. Behind him in the traffic line the cars and trucks moved erratically forward toward the loading-bay doors of the *Uncatena*. Toward the end of the line was a Mahoney Construction Co. two-and-one-half-ton truck loaded with twelve Johnny-on-the-Spot field toilets. He did not offer to shake hands with Hanrihan; he only stood and looked at him for a moment, then returned his gaze to Costello. Hanrihan in a white business shirt, open at the collar and with the sleeves rolled up, allowed his hand to drop back to his side. He did not add anything to his "pleased to meet you."

"Vinnie, Vinnie," Costello said, some irritation noticeable in his voice, "don't be like this. We talked about this, you and I, did we not?" The tourists in shorts, nagging at children and struggling with baggage, eddied impatiently around them toward the ferry.

"Yeah," Mahoney said, glancing once more at Hanrihan and then back to Costello, "yeah, we talked about it."

"And didn't I tell you then," Costello said, "that this is the guy, that Brian here has got a way that can maybe get us all out of this little problem that we have?"

"Yeah," Mahoney said, keeping his gaze on Costello, "yeah. You said that. And this guy here"—he looked back at Hanrihan—"all right, Mister Hanrihan?"

"Brian," Hanrihan said.

"Brian," Mahoney said, "look, all right? You understand, I haven't got nothing against you, all right? This, what I'm saying here, it's nothin' that I got against you. Hell, I never even met you, right? You and I, we never saw each other before in my life."

"Far as I know," Hanrihan said.

"Vinnie," Costello said, "I checked the guy out, all right? His father was all right, for Christ sake. He's all right, I'm telling you. The guy's a straight shooter, which is always nice. Especially when you're in the kind of box that you're in. And he's a smart lawyer, according to Dennis Patrick, who's the DA. Your DA, in fact, Dennis, told me personally, he was very, very sorry to lose Brian here, when he came in and offered his resignation from his staff. But he said no, he couldn't think of anything, anything in the world, that anybody could possibly say against him. Spoke very highly of him. So, this guy, Brian, isn't coming in here cold to this thing. He prosecuted Dussault. He knows the kind of guy that Dussault is. And he's a courtroom lawyer, a trial lawyer, which is the kind you need in a situation such as this. Not somebody like me, that's an office lawyer, or maybe Shipstead, who never gets off the island there. Somebody like Brian here that's used to the pit and he's lived in it, and it's just second nature to a guy like him."

"Yeah," Mahoney said.

"*Yeah*," Costello said.

"Mister Hanrihan," Mahoney said, "lemme ask you something, all right?" He squinted in the sunlight.

"Brian," Hanrihan said. "Sure, ask away."

"Brian," Mahoney said, nodding. "Okay, why you doing this, huh? Can you tell me that? Things're happening pretty fast around me all of a sudden, you know? I need some time here, get things straight in my own mind, make sure I understand what's going on. Which maybe I should've done a little while ago, before all this shit started happening and all of a sudden I was in it up to my eyeballs and I'm meeting guys like you never heard of that're supposed to be able, say magic words and get me out of it."

"Mister Mahoney," Hanrihan said, "I'm not claiming to know any magic words. Not that at all. Nothing like it. There aren't any, that I know of."

"Right," Mahoney said. He sighed.

"Vinnie," Costello said, "will you listen to me, please? I am telling you, all right? I checked the guy out. He is okay."

Mahoney shifted his gaze back to Costello. "Mister Costello," he said, "I don't mean nothing by this, okay? Just telling you something you already know. So don't get mad. You told me lots of things, already. Quite a few things. And I listened to you. And I did what you told me, even though I didn't want to do it. As you know. And you told me then that everything was okay and I would be all right if I would just do what you told me even though I didn't want to do it and it cost me a lot of money. And I did it.

"And now, Mister Costello," Mahoney said, "everything, I find out, isn't all right. Everything is pretty bad, as a matter of fact. I am in a lot of trouble. I am in more trouble than I have ever been in my whole life. Which would not be hard even if it was just a little trouble I was in, because I have never been in any trouble in my life until just now. But it is not a little trouble I am in for the first time in my life. It is one goddamned fucking shitload full of trouble I am in, and all of a sudden I find out that I don't see no way I'm going to get myself out of it."

Costello sighed. "Vinnie, Vinnie," he said, "I know. I know. If I'd've ever expected anything like this to happen, I would've . . . Look, can we go someplace and get a cup of coffee, something?"

"Uh uh," Mahoney said. He gestured with his left thumb back over his shoulder. "That boat there," he said, "that boat is loadin' up to go right back to where I'm supposed to be, mindin' the store. Especially since I kind of think there're probably people that're interested now in how I spend my time. I'm gonna be on that boat when it goes back, they get all the cars and trucks all loaded up including the truck that has got my stuff on it, my clean shithouses, that I told everybody I was coming over here to check out for myself this morning and make sure this time they sent me down the kind that I wanted in the first place." He laughed shortly. "And if anybody finds out I really made this trip mostly so I could see you guys, at least they can't say I was lying when I said I was coming over here to make sure everything was all right with the shithouse problem. Because that's exactly why I'm talking to you, and I can tell you right now, Mister Costello, it ain't."

"Anyway," he said, "I ain't gettin' no coffee. I ain't missing no boat. I had coffee coming over and I can have coffee going back. You guys want coffee, Mister Hanrihan, you'll have to wait 'till we get through."

"Fine by me," Hanrihan said.

"Okay, Vinnie," Costello said, "that's the way you want it, you've got so much experience in these things, you . . ."

"Mister Costello," Mahoney said, "I haven't got no experience in these things whatsoever. At least I didn't until now. And I didn't want none, neither. But I don't seem to be doing so good using yours, okay? Lemme try it on my own a minute.

"Mister Hanrihan," he said, "I asked you something: why you doing this? You doing this, this stuff you do in courtrooms all the time, you're doing it for money, right?"

"Right," Hanrihan said. "I get love at home."

"How much money, Mister Hanrihan?" Mahoney said.

"Vinnie, Vinnie," Costello said, "don't worry about the money. Mister Hanrihan's fee will be all taken care of."

"Mister Costello," Mahoney said, "I'm sure of that. I haven't got no doubt about that whatsoever. What bothers me is who's gonna be taking care of that fee, right? Is it me?"

"No," Costello said, "it is not you. Mister Hanrihan is being paid by somebody else. It doesn't need to concern you in the slightest."

Mahoney nodded once, firmly. "Mister Hanrihan," he said, "how much?"

"Vinnie," Costello said with anguish, "what the hell difference does it make to you? You're not paying it. I told you that."

"You told me that I wasn't paying him, Mister Costello," Mahoney said. "I just want to know how much somebody else is paying him. In case somebody else should happen to come up to me some fine day, when this is all over and Mister Hanrihan here done something with his magic wand that all of a sudden makes everyone happy once again, and says I owe him so much an amount of money on account of that's what it cost him to get somebody to come by and make everything all right again. Clear?"

"Yeah, Vinnie," Costello said resignedly. "Clear."

"How much, Mister Hanrihan?" Mahoney said.

"That's kind of hard to answer, Vinnie," Hanrihan said.

"Uh huh," Mahoney said, "I was afraid of that."

Hanrihan forced a laugh. "No, no," he said, "not for the reason you're thinking. The reason is that I've accepted new responsibilities as general counsel to the Speaker of the House of Representatives, and this matter is one of the things that's included in the retainer for that position. Even though it's not something that's part of my official responsibilities."

Mahoney frowned. "I ain't getting all of this," he said, "and I got the place now where I am by not following things like I maybe should've. You wanna start that up and run it by me again?"

Hanrihan sighed. "Sure," he said. "I quit my job, Vinnie. I did it to go to work as a lawyer for the Speaker. The job's full-time and it pays like the dickens, more'n I was getting where I was and it's something different too. Which is nice because I was getting tired of putting guys in jail. Mister Costello was the guy that got me the job. It doesn't start up for about a month, though. In the meantime, he told me, you've got this problem. He asked me whether, just as a matter of casual conversation, I could see any way to solve it for you. I said that I could. He asked me if I'd be willing to spend that month I've got until I start my new job, clearing up your problem. I said I would, but I couldn't do it for nothing. I've got this family, you see; that eats. Either I find something that pays me money to buy food so they can eat, or I somehow manage to convince them to stop eating for a month. Getting money's always seemed easier. Not easy, but easier. Mister Costello said he'd see to it that I got one-twelfth of my new salary for spending a month working on your problem. I said that was fair. Mister Costello paid me that money this morning. Here I am."

"You already got it," Mahoney said.

"Paid in full," Hanrihan said.

"How much?" Mahoney said.

Hanrihan glanced at Costello. Costello shrugged. "I didn't ask you nothing, Mister Costello," Mahoney said.

"Sixty-five hundred dollars," Hanrihan said.

"Sixty-five hundred dollars," Mahoney said. "Wow, I guess I wasn't wrong when I thought this was a serious amount of shit that I was in."

"Nope," Hanrihan said, "you weren't."

Mahoney grinned. "Although actually," he said, "you should've gotten another grand. That's what it cost me to get into this crap. You oughta get at least as much to get me out."

"Frank," Hanrihan said, "I want another grand."

"Eat shit," Costello said. He tried a smile. "Okay, Vinnie," he said, "now can we have some coffee?"

"No," Mahoney said. "Brian," he said, "talk to me. Keep it simple, like I say, 'cause I ain't used to this. And, I got a boat to catch."

"Got it," Hanrihan said. "First, you pay me one dollar. Got one on you?"

Mahoney smirked. "I thought you said you been paid."

"I've received a fee," Hanrihan said, "but not from you. When I show up in court to represent you, someone's sure to ask me if you paid me a fee. The answer will be yes. How much is nobody's business. If, that is, you do."

"One buck," Mahoney said, reaching into his pants pocket.

"One buck," Hanrihan said, holding out his hand.

Mahoney peeled a dollar off a roll of small bills. He held it out. "This is it?" he said. "No more?"

"This is it," Hanrihan said. He took it. He put it in his pocket. "Second thing you do," he said, "you ask me to represent you as your legal counsel."

"Mister Hanrihan," Mahoney said, "since you took my money, how about you being my lawyer?"

"Done," Hanrihan said. "Now, third thing: you tell anybody who asks that you will make no statements, written or oral, public or private, unless you are subpoenaed."

"I *ask* them," Mahoney said, "for a subpoena? I thought what people usually did with them things was try not to get them."

"You're different," Hanrihan said. "Without a subpoena, served to you in your paws, you got lockjaw and no memory as well."

"I try to duck it?" Mahoney said.

"Nope," Hanrihan said. "Anybody asks, and they will, you tell them it's just that you don't want it to look like you're a happy volunteer. You'll only talk if they make you. Or so it looks like they made you, at least."

"Got it," Mahoney said.

"Last thing," Hanrihan said, "tell me this, all right? Is there any way that they could make you testify, if there was a perfectly legal way for you to get out of it and you didn't want to talk?"

"Probably," Mahoney said. "There probably is."

"Oh oh," Hanrihan said. "Okay, tell me what it is."

"My foreman," Mahoney said. "He's got a rape charge on him. They already just as much as said to me, they'd hammer him on that if I didn't tell them what they knew I know."

"Would that make you talk?" Hanrihan said.

"Well," Mahoney said, "tell you the truth, it probably would. Besides, if he talked, I'd be in the shit personally. Mister Costello here and Mister Morgan, they wouldn't have nothing to worry about, but I would. They'd settle for just nailing me, I think. So what's the point? Ditch an old friend like Billy, and I'm still in it up to my eyeballs?"

"Isn't any," Hanrihan said. "Look, will Billy, whatever his last name is, will he listen to you, do what you say?"

"Yup," Mahoney said. "Except when he gets himself in scrapes like this one, he always does."

"Good," Hanrihan said, "tell him if they come after him, same thing."

"Subpoena," Mahoney said.

"Right," Hanrihan said. "Who's his lawyer?"

"Ours," Mahoney said. "Mister Shipstead, on the island."

Hanrihan looked inquiringly at Costello. Costello nodded. "Fine," Hanrihan said. "I'll talk to Shipstead. Any questions?"

"Yeah," Mahoney said, "although I'm actually sort of afraid, ask. How you gonna pull off this miracle?"

"My heart is pure," Hanrihan said. He clapped Mahoney on the shoulder. "Because of that, I have the strength of ten."

Mahoney grinned. "Bullshit," he said.

"Confidentially?" Hanrihan said.

"Confidentially," Mahoney said.

"Okay then," Hanrihan said. "Confidentially, I'm getting even. I have got a big grudge that I'm out to settle."

Mahoney's grin widened. He slapped Hanrihan on the shoulder. "Now," he said, "now I believe you."

26 Shortly before noon, Joe Gillis in his brown suit fresh from the cleaners met Paul Linder at Forgan Cahill's elevator in the basement of the southwest corner of the State House. Linder was wearing his maroon blazer and his maroon and white checked pants, with a white-on-white shirt and a maroon string tie. He looked very uneasy.

"Paul, my friend," Gillis said, "fancy meeting you here. The hell's a representative to the Great and General Court doing in the State House on a fine summer's day like today? How come you're not down the Cape, basking in the warm sun and making great plans for the fall elections?"

Linder frowned. He gestured toward the closed door of the elevator, including in his movement Forgan Cahill's stool next to it, and the folded *Armstrong* resting on it. "Forgan ain't here," he said.

"Well now," Gillis said, reaching his hand toward the spiral notebook in his jacket pocket, "I knew my faith would be rewarded. Nothing much doing around town, is there? Well, just mosey on over to the State House there and get ahold of Paul Linder. Guaranteed to give you the scoop of the day, every day, the straight poop sure to amaze and delight every reader. And here you've gone and done it again, a regular flash for the wires and hold the front page, damnit: Forgan's not here. What is he, Paul, risen? He goes before us into Galilee, as he promised?"

Linder shuffled his feet and jammed his hands in his jacket pockets. "Well," he said, "I been standing here, is all, waiting, and I didn't know if you maybe had some place you hadda be, so you didn't want to wait or something."

"Nah," Gillis said, staring up at the board that indicated which floor the elevator was on. "There isn't much of anything doing around today. I'd just as soon stand around and shoot the shit with you a while, wait for old reliable Forgan come back, take me where I want to go." He frowned. "Where the hell is he, though, huh? None the lights're on."

"Well, that's what I mean," Linder said desperately, "he evidently ain't here at all. I mean, he's not in the elevator, you know, like he was in it only he just happened to be somewhere else? Different floor? He ain't here at all. The thing ain't working." He shuffled his feet.

"Well, that's all right, Paul," Gillis said. "I guess he'll be back sooner or later." He glanced at Linder, who had taken his right hand out of his jacket pocket, put it in his pants pocket, and was jiggling change while he shifted his feet and looked anxiously at the board. "The hell's the matter with you, Paul?" he said. "You got to go the bathroom or something?"

Linder looked at him irritatedly. "No," he said, "I haven't got to go the bathroom, Joe, for Christ sake. I got to go to the Speaker's office, 's where I got to go, and I said I would be there and I come right over like I said and now Forgan ain't here."

"Paul," Gillis said, "is the Speaker here yet?"

"I don't know that," Linder said impatiently.

"Because if he isn't then it doesn't matter," Gillis said, "Forgan isn't here. The hell's the point, standing here and hoppin' around like you're gonna wet your pants or something because Forgan isn't here, it turns out when he gets here and he takes you up, the Speaker isn't even in yet. He does not exactly make a habit, early hours, Mister Morgan doesn't in the summer, I recall."

"Maybe I'm not seeing the Speaker," Linder said. "Jesus Christ, where the fuck is Forgan? Only goddamned elevator in the whole fucking building that's working, and now it isn't working. Must be off takin' a shit for himself or something. Shit."

"Well," Gillis said, "he can do that, I think. They allow that. It's okay when Forgan's on the job, he wants to go and take a shit for a minute. No complaint there."

"Yeah," Linder said, "but does he have to decide and go and do it just when I get here and want a ride up the third floor?"

"What's your hurry, Paul?" Gillis said. "Ray Archambault sneaking into Bernie's office 'fore he gets here this morning, cleaning out the tyrant's desk and heaving all his memorabilia out into the hall, maybe? Symbolize the end of an era? Maybe I should get a camera over here. Could also pick up a little change, maybe, drop a dime or two on the television people. Always appreciate a good tip like that, photo opportunity. Good visuals."

Linder glanced quickly at Gillis. "What're you talking about, Archambault?" he said.

"You know Ray Archambault, Paul," Gillis said. "Chairman of Ways and Means. Well-dressed guy? Comes from Avon. He's gonna be the next Speaker, people I've been listening to're saying. And pretty soon, too."

Linder looked back at the unlighted location board. "Bullshit," he said.

"No, Paul," Gillis said, "it's not bullshit. You must not be spending enough time in this building. Else you're spending it all here, standing in front of elevators that aren't working and waiting for guys that're in the bathroom. You're not gonna learn anything useful that way, Paul, my friend. You've got to exercise the old leg muscles, sacrifice the old shoe leather, get yourself some exercise so you won't be so edgy you can't even stand still while you're waiting for an elevator man to show up."

Linder gave him another glance. "Leave me alone, Joe," he said. He licked his lips. "You ain't in no position these days, go around bustin' guys' balls for them."

"Bustin' balls?" Gillis said, flaring his eyebrows in feigned shock. "How the hell can you say such a thing, Paul baby, that I am bustin' balls. Me? Joe Gillis? Jesus, she really has got your bowels in an uproar, hasn't she?"

"Who has?" Linder said desperately.

"Who?" Gillis said. "You mean to tell me, there's more'n one of them that's got your bowels in an uproar? Good God, Paul, you must've been one busy little beaver. So to speak. Who's the other one?"

"Who's the other one what," Linder said, swallowing several times and jingling the coins furiously in his pocket.

"Paul, Paul," Gillis said, returning his gaze to the elevator panel, "spare me this hollow charade, my friend. This is old Joe Gillis here, you're talking to. Have a heart, man."

Forgan Cahill came down the corridor to their right and turned the corner to the elevator. He was carrying a parcel wrapped in waxed paper and a small paper bag. He was whistling "Un bel' di." His face broke into a smile. "Paul, baby," he said, "and my old pal Joe. The fuck *are* you guys, anyway? Lost any more columns, the Jew boy lately, Joe?" He reached the elevator, picked the *Armstrong* off the stool, sat down and began to open the parcel.

"The hell're you talking about?" Gillis said.

"Yeah, Joe," Linder said, relaxing, "what about that, huh? Rosen get any more of your job out from under you, the last time I saw you?"

"Hey," Gillis said, "you guys talking about Leo Rosen, that works for my paper?"

Cahill looked at Linder inquiringly. Linder shrugged. Cahill looked back at Gillis. "Well, yeah, Joe, matter of fact," he said. "Leo Rosen. Yeah. The Jew that works for your paper and is now the guy that writes one of the columns you used to write. Him. You know him?"

"Of course I know him," Gillis said. "Perfectly nice guy."

"Well," Linder said to Cahill, "that explains it then. See, Paul? Joe here, he likes this Rosen kid so much, he prolly went in there, see Pucci, and said to him: 'Hey, Pucci there, my friend, this Rosen kid's a prince of a guy, you know, Dave? And I been thinking, right? I think a nice young man like that should take over one of my columns.' "

"Right," Cahill said. "And probably said to him: 'Hey, all right? We see how the kid works out, huh, maybe we give him the rest of my columns. Because, see, I been gettin' old lately, and I could use some up-and-coming young Jew boy, take over my job for me. You got anything opening up, covering one the little city halls down in Roxbury with the coons, maybe? Or how about Middleboro, maybe. I could get my cookies down in Middleboro, bet your ass, out with all the hayshakers all day.' "

Linder seemed to think this was hilarious. He laughed very loudly. Cahill contented himself with snickering and unwrapping the waxed paper.

"What the hell're you doing?" Gillis said, his face red.

"Me?" Cahill said, looking up.

"Yeah," Gillis said, "you."

"I'm having my sandwich," Cahill said, spreading the waxed paper over his lap and looking down at its contents. It was a small loaf of French bread with dribbles of catsup oozing out of the sides. There were two small gherkins nestled next to it. He looked up, smiling. "See? Mother Cahill's Special Meatloaf Sandwich, personally prepared with her own hands in her own kitchen on Albemarle Street in Jamaica Plain for the dining pleasure of her favorite son, Forgan." He picked it up and bit into it, tearing into the bread and ripping off a large chunk of it.

"You're having your sandwich," Gillis said.

Cahill nodded with gusto. He picked up the paper bag and lifted out a can of Budweiser, which he promptly slid back into the bag. He talked with his mouth full. "And in a minute or so," he said, "I am gonna wash Mother Cahill's Special Meatloaf down with a can of cold golden Budweiser. How about that, sports fans?" He grinned as he swallowed. "This Bud's for *me.*"

"The hell'd you get that?" Linder said.

"From my locker," Cahill said, swallowing the last of his first bite and preparing to take a second. "Hadda go out inna parking lot, see if the Speaker's car was in yet, and it wasn't, so on the way back I stop in Lonergan's office and ask him, call Connie inna Speaker's office and tell her: 'Nope, he ain't here yet,' and then I decide since I am there I might as well have lunch a little early and save myself a trip. Besides, I always eat Mother Cahill's Special Meatloaf early. Love the stuff."

"Looks like shit, you ask me," Gillis said. "All that ketchup in there gumming up the bread like it was bleeding piles, all that greasy old cold meatloaf squeezin' out of there the way dogshit does from under your shoes, you don't happen to watch where you're puttin' your feet when you're walkin' on the sidewalks around here. Looks like dogshit, too. Same color's dogshit from a dog that's been living all the time on them kibbles, there. Grey and greasy."

"I know it," Linder said. "Hot meatloaf I can hack, when it's right out the oven, you know? Nice and warm. Maybe slice of bacon on top, huh?"

"Right," Gillis said, "some onions in it, maybe some green peppers cut up in it, huh?"

"Uh uh," Linder said, making a face, "no green peppers in mine. Heartburn from them things. But cold? Shit, I wouldn't eat cold meatloaf if it was the last thing on earth."

Cahill swallowed his second bite and examined the sandwich to choose his site for the third attack. " 'S all right," he said, "you guys aren't bothering me none." He picked up the bag with the beer and took a drink, setting it down again. "I should have some potato chips with this," he said reflectively. "Should've gotten a bag of potato chips, I came in this morning. I got Mother Cahill's meatloaf, though. You guys haven't. And besides," he said, looking up with the happy thought, "what I been hearing about you lately, Linder, you're not the kind of guy'd know much about meatloaf anyway. *Letting* your meat loaf, at least."

Linder blushed at once. "The fuck're you talking about?" he said.

"Talking about?" Cahill said. "You know what I'm talking about, all right. Connie Mulready thinks you know what she's talkin' about anyway, and that's what I'm talkin' about. Connie kinda worried about something she missed all of a sudden? Like this month, maybe?"

Gillis thought that was very funny and started laughing loudly. "Yeah," Cahill said, glancing at him, "see, Paul? Joe heard that, too, Mulready missed her period. And she thinks you're to blame, is what I hear. Wants to talk to you about it." He laughed. "Shit," he said, "that's a good one too, now I think about it, Connie wantin', talk to guys could maybe know a little something—have them coming in, like they do down the Governor's Council when they're deciding who's getting the judgeships. Have all you guys lined up on chairs outside the Speaker's office there, waitin' for your interview with Connie." Gillis laughed even louder. Cahill stared at him. "There's a column there, Joe, I think," he said. "You oughta see if maybe Rosen'd like to write it." Gillis stopped laughing.

"Look, Forgie," Gillis said, "okay, fun's fun. But just by way of information, all right? Seeing's you apparently got time enough to run around all over the goddamned place seeing if Morgan's parked his car yet and keeping tabs on other pressing matters, is there any kind of possibility you might decide to run this goddamned elevator today?"

Cahill chewed and stared at Gillis. When he had room enough in his mouth to speak, he said: "Look, all right? Gallopin' around this building's not in my job specs, you got it? That thing, Connie asked me. Got a call the Speaker's wife and she says the Speaker's brother-in-law's disappeared up in the woods here and they're kind of worried about him. He ain't right inna head, Paul," Cahill said to Linder, "and they're lookin' for him."

"For this of course they got to have the Speaker right off," Gillis said. "The fuck is Bernie gonna do, his brother-in-law's out whacko in the woods, you wanna tell me that? Gonna put his goddamned boots on and go running through the bushes looking for him?"

"They don't know if he's in the woods, for Christ sake, Joe," Cahill said. "He could be in the woods, he could be someplace else. How the fuck'm I supposed to know where he is? All I'm supposed to do is find the Speaker, find out if the Speaker got here yet. I did that. He ain't. That's all. But I didn't just decide I was gonna do that myself. Connie asked me. And then since I hadda do it, I decided, I did decide, I was gonna take my lunch, all right? Which I happen to be doing now, as you can see." He put the rest of the sandwich in his mouth and chewed.

"Which means, I guess, Joe," Linder said, "he isn't going to run the elevator."

"Look," Cahill said, his voice muffled through the food, "in the first place there is always the stairs, which've been standing there without nobody using them ever since you two lazy bastards got in here and started giving me a lot of shit. Which if you was in a hurry to get up-stairs, you could've used the minute that you got here. And you didn't, Paul, because you're about as anxious, get onto that third floor, as the last guy was that they electrocuted over Charlestown and he hadda walk the last mile. Connie's waitin' for you up there, and you're standin' here and prayin' that if you wait long enough, she will get sick of waitin' for you and she'll leave and she'll be gone by the time you get there. So, no more of your shit.

"As for you," he said, turning to Gillis, "the only reason you don't see no reason to get off your ass and walk is . . ."

Roger Knox in his green uniform and Red Sox hat, walking with his left leg stiff and his shirttails out over his pants, came around the corner and stopped about twelve feet away from them. He stared at them and swallowed. He said: "Morning."

Cahill gazed at Roger Knox with interest, stopping in mid-chew. He swallowed some of what was in his mouth. "Morning," he said.

Roger resumed walking, very stiffly, and joined them. There was a protuberance just above the outside of his left kneecap. "This, ah," he said, "this where you take the elevator?"

"Yup," Cahill said. He picked up the paper bag and tilted the can up, finishing the beer. He put it back on the floor. "You, ah," he said, "you wanna go someplace?"

Knox looked at Gillis and moistened his lips. He looked at Linder and frowned, as though trying to place him. He looked back at Gillis. He shook his head. He refocused on Cahill. "Uh, yeah," he said. "Yeah. Is this, this where I take it?"

"Uh huh," Cahill said, wadding up his waxed paper and crumpling the bag shut around his beer can. "Soon's I finish picking up around here, take you right up." He balled all the trash up together and placed it carefully under his stool. He stood up and placed the *Armstrong* back on the stool. He dusted his hands. "Okay," he said, "all set." He looked inquiringly at Roger. "Which floor you want, mister?"

"The, ah, the third," Knox said. He nodded firmly. "Third floor."

"Geez, uh," Cahill said, "there's ah, there's not much of anything on the third floor, I know of. You know of anything, the third floor, Joe?"

"Uh uh," Gillis said, staring at the bulge above Knox's left knee. "Hardly anything, 'cept the House chambers."

"Yeah," Linder said enthusiastically, "that's really all there is up there. House chambers. No citizen complaints offices or like that where you could go."

Knox looked confused. "Well, ah," he said, "yeah. That's what I recalled. That's what I want. House."

"Yeah," Cahill said, "but the House ain't in session today. Am I right about that, Joe?"

"Well, it was," Gillis said. "Went into recess about ten thirty or so, I think it was. Nobody probably up there now."

"See?" Cahill said. "No point, going up there. You got, there may be something somebody else could help you with, that you could talk to?"

Knox's face furrowed deeply. "Look, goddamnit," he said, shaking his head slightly, "this shit. I don't need this shit. I know the fuck where I am going, where I want to go. I know what's on the third floor. I been there lots. My name is Knox, all right? You maybe don't remember me, but my father, my father was the Speaker of that House there, and I guess I know where it is and what's up there and I want to go there. Now don't you just go and start giving me a whole lot more of your shit here, Mister Whatever-your-name-is that's got ketchup on his face, goddamnit, or the two of you guys neither, because I know what I'm doing. And you just get in that goddamned elevator there and take me up there. I'm gonna see Bernie Morgan and it don't matter none to me what you think or what you say because I know he's up here in that goddamned office he took from my father."

"Well, as a matter of fact," Gillis said, "he isn't up there. I was just out the parking lot a few minutes ago, isn't this right, Forgie? And I happened to notice, his car wasn't there. So he ain't upstairs there."

"Bullshit," Knox said firmly, "what you did and what you seen and all that shit you say. I was just, I just come from that parking lot and I walked right past that goddamned car and it was sittin' right there with the goddamned hood of it all warm. I put my fuckin' hand on it, Mister, is how I know it was warm. And it was. So don't give me none that shit of yours."

"Huh," Cahill said to Gillis, "must've gone up the back way."

"Get in the goddamned elevator," Knox said.

"Hey," Linder said, "not me. I was just leaving." He started to back away from the group.

"Yeah, Paul, right," Gillis said, "you did say something, you hadda make a call to Connie right off, didn't you?"

Linder glanced at him nervously. "I uh, well," he said, "yeah. As a matter of fact, I did. I better call her right off." He did not quite accelerate into a trot as he got away from the group, but he walked very fast.

Knox gestured toward him. "Guy," he said thoughtfully, "guy's pussy-whipped." He nodded. "Pussy-whipped." He returned his attention to Gillis and Cahill. "You goin' up?" he said to Gillis.

"Yeah," Gillis said, "yeah, matter of fact. I was gonna ride up here with Forgie, yeah. Soon's he finished his lunch."

Knox looked at Cahill. He looked back at Gillis. "Well, goddamned," he said, "looks to me like he's finished it. Get in the goddamned car, you're going up." Gillis glanced at Cahill and passed in front of Knox. He stood facing the closed door of the elevator. Cahill stared at Knox. "Well, goddamnit," Knox said, "the fuck you waitin' for? Goddamned door isn't just gonna *open* for him, is it?"

"No," Cahill said.

"Well, goddamnit," Knox said, gesturing with his right hand, "open it for him. Jesus Christ. No wonder Bernie turned into such an asshole. All these years down here in this place, spendin' all his goddamned time a buncha assholes like you are. Waitin' for elevators, open their own doors. Go on, goddamnit, open it."

Cahill twisted the lock that started the elevator and opened the doors to the car. Gillis stepped in. Cahill stood next to the doors. "Well, goddamnit," Knox said, lamely stepping in behind Gillis, "now get in the goddamned elevator here and run the goddamned thing."

"Well, goddamnit, that's what I'm doing," Cahill said, getting into the elevator and shutting the doors. He pushed the button for the third floor and the elevator started up slowly.

Knox glanced at Gillis and grinned. "Goddamned things," he said. "This goddamned thing was slower'n a popcorn fart back years ago when my dad was runnin' this place. He was always gonna get it fixed. And he never did of course. They got him moving outta here faster'n they ever got the goddamned elevators running." He laughed, a short bark. "Course the goddamned difference was, they wanted him run out—they didn't give a shit about the elevators. Like this fat bastard here," he said, jabbing Forgan in the love handle with his thumb. "This guy here don't give a shit about nothing moving in the State House. Sit around and fill his big fat guts, drink his beer out of a bag so he thinks nobody can come in and smell it on his breath, don't know where he got that big fat belly, young guy like he is. Huh." He leaned close to Gillis and nudged him. Gillis drew away from his breath. "Fuckin' people work the State House," Roger said, "bastards're all out to screw us. Every single one of them. Do it, too. And that includes my goddamned brother-law, the Speaker of the goddamned House of fucking Representatives. Uh huh, certainly does." He nodded.

Gillis cleared his throat. "What the hell've you got in your pants there?" he said mildly.

"Hey," Knox said instantly, "fuckin' queer." His voice was loud at once and very threatening. He nudged Gillis again. "Old bastard there, huh? That what you are, fuckin' queer? Askin' man, what he's carryin' his pants? Huh. Just like the rest of them. Fuckin' bastards. Come in here, the State House, there's something wrong with all of them." He snorted. He stood up straight again. The elevator approached the second floor.

"Killed my old dog this morning," Knox said conversationally.

"That so?" Cahill said politely, as though responding to an announcement that he had mowed his lawn. Gillis shifted uncomfortably and said nothing.

"Yup," Knox said with satisfaction. "Now that's something I've been meaning to do a long time." He nodded several times. "Goddamned old good-for-nothing dog. Couldn't see. Couldn't hardly walk. Stunk. Every time he had a drink of water, five minutes later he'd be pissin' onna goddamned floor. Hadda feed him stuff practically was baby food, all slop. Didn't have no teeth. I been thinking for a year, I should put that old dog down. So I wake up this mornin' on the desk, see. I slept there last night. On the desk in the station. Wife's out whorin' on me again. That's Bernie's fault. Her and that sister mine. Both whores. Nothin' but good-for-nothin' whores. Out whorin' last night. Heard them come home. Slept in the station. Sleep no bed, no whore. Woke up and there was that old tire iron, mine. Saw it. Goddamned old dog over cryin' on the patio I built behind the house. Cryin' for his goddamned slops. Breakfast. Decided me. Picked up that tire iron there an' went right over there. Bashed him one, right the head. Didn't expect it. Seen me comin', much's he could, thought I was bringin' slops to him. Fuck him. Smashed him one right on the head there. Dropped him like a god-damned stone. Ton of bricks hit him. Cracked his old skull open like a fuckin' egg, yup. I hit him a couple of more times, but I didn't have to. I was just making sure." He patted his left pant leg. "This's here's one damned good thing to use," he said, "this here tire iron."

"You've, ah," Gillis said, speaking with difficulty, "you've got it with you then, huh?"

Knox glanced at him. "Oh sure," he said. "Brought her right along. I decided, I left that old dog there. Let her find the old bastard, she gets up and finds out I ain't there but Rocky is, dead on the patio and how's she gonna get him off of there without me around to help her, huh?" He snorted. "He was old and he couldn't hardly walk much, but he's a pretty heavy dog. Fat. Lot easier for her, movin' him around, he was alive and all she hadda do was call him and sooner, later, he'd get him-self over to where she was." Roger chuckled. "He ain't gonna do that no more, by Jesus. No sir. She can sit there in that goddamned lawn chair makin' those goddamned noises at him just's long's she goddamned right well likes, old whore, and he ain't gonna move one goddamned muscle. Just lie there and all the flies come over him, is what he's gonna do. Oh, she's gonna have a fine mess with that old dog lyin' down there dead's he can be right on that patio I built. Teach her a goddamned lesson." He laughed again.

The elevator halted jerkily at the third floor and the doors began to move slowly open. "Say," Gillis said casually, "you brought that thing with you, how about lettin' us see it?" Cahill gave him a stern warning glance which Knox, making his way out of the elevator, could not see, and Gillis ignored.

Knox paused on the threshold of the elevator. "Oh no, goddamnit," he said, "smart fuckin' bastard think you are, trick me that easy." He leaned back into the elevator and jabbed Gillis on the chest with his left forefinger. His teeth clicked as he talked. "How dumb you think I am, you bastard?" he said. He grinned craftily. "Already told you, god-damnit, my father was the Speaker. I know, know about the cop sits there at the desk outside the governor's office, probably couldn't see me anyway, even if he is there and not off someplace gettin' fat like him," he said, gesturing toward Cahill. "But he might be. And I ain't takin' no chances." He grinned triumphantly. He stepped off the elevator into the corridor, turned to his left, and lamely made his way toward the corner, heading for the Speaker's rooms. Cahill shut the elevator off. He exhaled noisily. "Well," he said, looking at Gillis, "the fuck we do now?"

"Not a hell of a lot we can do," Gillis said, " 'cept hope to Jesus Paul called Connie like he didn't want to."

"Yeah," Cahill said. "And that if he did, she shut her trap long enough about missing her period to hear what he was tryin', tell her. And that she had sense enough, lock the goddamned doors. *And . . .* that Lonergan could locate a few of his stout lads in uniform to get their asses up to Bernie's office and be standing by to grab the bastard. Jesus," Cahill said, "this joint is not exactly what you'd call set up to handle little happenings like this, is it?"

"Not hardly," Gillis said. He sighed. He patted his coat pocket. "Well," he said, "got my notebook. Guess I may as well mosey down the hall now to the battle scene and see what's going on." He started toward the front of the elevator.

Cahill stopped him by placing his hand on Gillis's forearm. "Jesus Christ, Joe," he said, "you're not going down there, are you?"

Gillis looked at him with some amusement. "Well, for Christ sake, Forgie," he said, "the hell else'd I be going? I'm still a reporter, goddamnit. Almost anybody can see something's going to happen down there in a few minutes, and since it's going to happen at the Speaker's offices, there's a reasonably good chance of its being news."

"Joe," Cahill said, "that fuckin' lunatic has got a tire iron, okay? He told you he killed a dog with it this morning, for Christ sake. You want him to decide, see how good it works cracking your skull open? Jesus H. Christ, man, you really must think quite of lot of Rosen. You go down there with that maniac, Rosen's liable end up writing the column all the time."

Gillis laughed. "Forgie, Forgie," he said, "Mister Knox doesn't know me from a hole in the ground. He's got no beef with me. And killing a dog's not the same thing as killing a man. Let go of me." He shook his arm free.

"Maybe not," Cahill said, "but it's good practice. You oughta stay away from that, I'm telling you."

"Ahh," Gillis said. He started down the hall, turned left, and walked toward the Speaker's rooms on his left. There were no sounds except murmured conversations unintelligible from the Hall of Flags below.

Roger Knox had reached the double paneled doors. He stood before them, both hands on the knob, shaking it and grumbling. Gillis could hear some of what he said as he wrenched back and forth at the doors. "Goddamned shit-eating bastards," Knox said as sort of a commentary, as though he'd been expecting something like this. He stepped back from the doors. He reached under his shirttail and into his waistband. He drew the tire iron out of his pants, using his right hand. First he held it up as though inspecting it. The silvered tip glinted. He drew it back in a cross-body blow and whacked it against the paneling. Small slivers of wood flew through the dim light in the hall and landed on the marble floor. The door vibrated audibly. He raised his voice. "Son of a bitch, Bernie, you bastard, you open up and you come out of there, you fuckin' bastard." He swung the tire iron again. The door vibrated again but did not give, and more small pieces of wood dropped to the floor. "Bastard," Knox said, his chest heaving from the effort and the shouting. "I'm warning you, goddamnit, Bernie," he shouted, "I'm coming in there after you, you fuckin' bastard turned my sister in a whore and now my wife goes with her, fuckin' bastard."

Gillis stopped about thirty feet away from the doors. Knox, catching his breath, noticed Gillis. He brandished the tire iron at him. "You watch, goddamnit, State House fuckin' bastard," he said. "You watch and see me if I don't get in there, fuckin' bastard." He swung the iron once more. Then he moved in close to the doors. He took the butt of the iron where it curved and gripped it in his left hand. He gripped the shaft of it with his right hand, about eight inches up from the point. He jammed the point deeply under the flange of the paired doors which covered the seam between them. The wood shattered and two large pieces of it cracked on the flange, hanging away from the door when he wrenched the iron out. He batted away at those pieces until they fell free and he had an unobstructed access to the bolt and its receptacle, which locked the doors together. He fitted the tire iron between the two doors, just over the bolt, and shifted his position so that he could press it horizontally against the door on the left, flexing the door on the right.

As Knox began to exert the pressure and the doors groaned, the left door opened suddenly. Knox toppled forward and was grabbed by the shirt by a man standing inside the Speaker's rooms. The fist closed around Knox's shirt and lifted him off his feet, jerking him forward against the opening door and into the Speaker's rooms. The door shut immediately, slamming behind him. Gillis heard the lock snap back in place.

Gillis walked quickly down the corridor. Behind him he could hear footsteps. He turned and saw Cahill, following slowly. Gillis reached the doors and poised his right hand to knock. Then he heard noise coming from the office. He lowered his hand without knocking. He stood and listened.

Cahill came up next to Gillis. He whispered. "The hell's going on in there, Joe?" Gillis shook his head for silence. There were sounds of furniture being smashed around and there was a repeated sound of a body falling. There were no cries, nor any shouts. After a short while there was silence behind the doors. Gillis grinned. "The hell is it, Joe?" Cahill whispered. Gillis shook his head again. He held up one finger, and winked. He waited for about forty-five seconds. Then he stepped forward again, his feet crunching on the slivers of wood on the floor, and knocked authoritatively.

From behind the door there was a brief pause. They could hear murmurs. Then a female voice, quavering at first, said: "Come in."

"Can't," Gillis called through the door. He shook the knob. "Locked."

"Oh," the voice said. "Sorry. Just a minute." There was more murmuring, and the sound of an interior door opening and closing. Gillis and Cahill heard the doors being unlocked. Connie Mulready, her face flushed and her hair somewhat out of place, opened the door. "Sorry," she said, "oh, Joe." She turned toward the interior. "It's Joe Gillis," she said warningly, "Joe Gillis from the *Commoner*, Andy." Gillis heard Andy Boyce tell her to let him in. "And Forgie," she said, opening the door. "Him too," Boyce said.

"Sorry, Joe, Forgie," she said, as she let them in. "I didn't realize. Somebody must've locked it."

Gillis and Cahill went in on the deep blue carpet. Andy Boyce, looking a little winded, was standing in the door to the Speaker's private office, rolling down his sleeves. "Joe," he said heartily. "For Christ sake, Joe Gillis. I haven't, we haven't seen you in this place since Christ knows when. How the fuck've you been, huh kid?" He gestured grandly toward Morgan's office. "Me an' the Speaker was just gettin' ready, salute to fallen comrades," he said. "Little preprandial before-lunch drink, huh?" He winked. "Wanna join us, strike a blow for liberty?" He peered over Gillis's shoulder. "Hey, Forgie," he said. "You too, my man."

"Uh," Cahill said, backing toward the door, "uh, no thanks. I left a hot elevator all by itself. Some other time." He backed out, closing the outside door behind him.

Gillis, with Boyce's hand on his shoulder, went in to the Speaker's office. Morgan, his face red, his sleeves rolled up, was preparing drinks. The knuckles of his right hand were bloody. There was a cut on his left arm, at the feet of the nude tattoo. As Gillis came in and sat without being asked to at the chair near the right corner of the Speaker's desk, Morgan placed a bourbon and water before him. He put a bourbon on the rocks in front of the seat in the middle, for Boyce, and lifted a double bourbon on the rocks for himself. "The top of the morning to ye, gentlemen," he said, "and the balance of the day to meself." He drank half of it, shook his wattles, blew like a racehorse, and sat down. "Whew," he said. "That okay, Joe? You still take it with water?"

Gillis sipped at his drink. "Perfect," he said. He set it down.

"Been a while since we've seen you," the Speaker said. "Been down the hall studying political science under Jack Tierney?" He laughed.

"Not exactly," Gillis said. "What I've been doing, actually, is studying in the sports department. Martial arts. Breaking doors down, that sort of thing."

"Oh," Morgan said, "sounds interesting. That what you're gonna be covering now, with this Rosen kid taking over the State House like he seems to be? He's a bright kid, Joe. I'll have to remember to say something to Dave Pucci, next time I run into him again for about the three hundredth time and he still doesn't remember who I am, compliment him on the fresh new blood he's bringing in here to the State House coverage."

"Yeah," Gillis said, sipping at his drink again. "Actually, I hear that's the trend around here in just about everything. House leadership, everything."

"No shit," Morgan said. "Hey, you hear that, Andy?"

Boyce shook his head, grinning. "Not lately, boss," he said. "Course, you can generally hear one thing, another, 'round this place, you want to."

"Right," Gillis said. "Like the sound of doors breaking on the Speaker's rooms. And sometimes you can even see something, like a guy with a tire iron. Breaking them."

"No," Morgan said. "You got to be shittin' me, Joe. Really?"

Gillis nodded. "Absolutely, Bernie," he said. "Saw it with my own baby blues, as a matter of fact. Not ten minutes ago."

"Well," Morgan said. "I'll be a son of a bitch. I didn't see anything like that. You see anything like that, Andy?"

Boyce shook his head solemnly. "Not me, boss."

"Well, goddamnit all," Morgan said, "obviously something's been happening here, we're not aware of. Don't look good for us, Andy. Tell you what, all right? You go check into what Joe says here, and him and me'll have our drink and then when you get back we'll just see about some lunch, okay? Oh, and while I think of it, tell Connie she don't hear from Paul again today, he hears from me. And he won't like what he hears from me, either. I'll ruin that little shit, he don't come around for her, at least."

"Gotcha," Boyce said. He put his drink down on the desk and left the room.

Morgan waited until he left the room and shut the door. Then he leaned across the desk, his face low to the wood. "Joe," he said, "the guy is my brother-in-law. He is on his way back to Proctor, where he will join his daddy, and he will not get out again. It was a mistake obviously, when we let him out the last time. Now, we been doing business a long time, you and me. We had our differences and that's all right. You do your job, I do mine. Give the other guy a little tickle every now and then? Okay, so long's it don't interfere with everybody else doing their job, am I right?"

"Let's say," Gillis said, savoring the aroma of the bourbon, "I've been here a long time, just like you."

"Okay then," Morgan said. He leaned back. "That being the case, I'm gonna trust you, because I always could in the past."

"Bernie," Gillis said, "I got to warn you. This is a pretty good story I'm sittin' on here, and I'm the only one who's sittin' on it. You don't want to ask too much of me here, all right?"

Morgan held up his hand. He shook his head. "Hey," he said, "I understand. Like I say, you got a job to do, and I know it. And like I say, this Rosen kid buzzin' around, it's probably pretty important for you to get that job done. Little something special wouldn't do you no harm at all, the papers, am I right?"

Gillis shrugged. "Seldom does," he said. "Never has, my experience."

Morgan nodded vigorously. "Okay," he said. "So I'm gonna give you the full story, of two stories, and you decide which one it is you really oughta print."

"But only one of them, is that it?" Gillis said.

"Right," Morgan said.

"Well, shit, Bernie," Gillis said, "that's no fuckin' deal. A scoop I got without you that I eat to get something from you that's maybe dogshit?"

"Oh no," Morgan said, "what I got isn't dogshit, Joe, no sir."

"That's what you say," Gillis said. "I'm the reporter. I'm the one has to decide."

"You're not the only reporter," Morgan said. "If you spill Wilf's non compos mentis kid all over the Boston *Commoner*, Joe, I'll give the one I got to Rosen, and that'll paint your fuckin' fence for you once and for fuckin' *all*. Because I want that little matter left where the Lord put it, and that is where it's gonna be left, too." Gillis licked his lips. Morgan nodded. "You'd better wonder, Joe, and you better think about how many times I ever lied to you or bluffed you in the whole of thirty years or so that we been doing business. I may've yelled at you and I may've told my people to forget your name before they ever told me who it was that called me, but I never once blew smoke up your ass, did I, Joe?" Gillis shook his head. "Right," Morgan said, "and I'm not gonna do it now. So: choose. What you got, or what I got that I can give you."

Gillis took another sip of his drink and considered the color of it in the glass, squinting in the light. "I've always been a gambling man," he said. "I'll go with what you got."

"This is embargoed until a week from Sunday," Morgan said. "Or that Monday column, if you want."

"Now wait a minute, Bernie," Gillis said, "what I got is fresh and hard, and I can use it right now. I got to wait till a week from Sunday to use what you're giving me?"

"That Sunday," Morgan said. "Nobody else in town will have it. Not even my own wife. Not Andy Boyce and not Connie Mulready. Nobody."

"Nobody," Gillis said.

"Nobody," Morgan said.

"Not even Frankie *Coss*-tello?" Gillis said.

Morgan grinned. "In his case, Joseph, an exception might be made. But would it matter, if I told the Sphinx? Not that I probably will. Right now I think I won't. But would it?"

"Nope," Gillis said. "Okay. Gimme."

"That Monday morning," Morgan said, "there's gonna be a special meeting of the House leadership committee. Plan for the new session in January. At that meeting, I am going to announce my retirement from the Speakership, and nominate Archambault to succeed me."

"Holy Jesus," Gillis said, taking out his pad. "I think maybe I better take some notes."

The Speaker stood and hoisted up his pants. "I think you should," he said, "the short-term memory goes first, Joe, and you're almost as old as I am."

Gillis popped his ballpoint open and wrote the date at the top of his page. "I won't need to put that down," he said. "Okay, how come?"

"I'm getting old," the Speaker said, walking to the windows and looking out over Beacon Hill in the flat noontime sunlight. "I must be—everybody's telling me I am. I've been at this long enough. My friends, like Billy Dealey, they're all dying or they've gone on to other things. My woman—don't print this; it'd piss her off for sure—has got cancer and she came back from the doctor's with a checkup the first part the week. It's spreading."

"Christ, Bernie," Gillis said, "I'm sorry to hear that. Anything they can do?"

The Speaker shrugged. "Could," he said, "but she won't let them. I guess I don't blame her. What's the point? She lets them and Maggie Gault dies in pieces, one chunk at a time. She doesn't let them and Maggie Gault all dies together. The pain's about the same, and the last choice's quicker and more dignified." He paused. He cleared his throat. "I dunno," he said. "The past few years, we haven't had a lot of time together. I'm gonna take July, then all of August, and then come back but mostly as a rep, and spend my time with her. Let Archambault learn the ropes with me still here. I will have the title, but he will do the job. I'll just be a figurehead." He paused again. He wheeled around.

"The real reason, Joe," he said, "is that I'm tired. They carted Wilfred out of here, when he was too far gone to know or care. I'm leaving on my feet."

"And there's the Ames Commission too, of course," Gillis said.

"Oh yeah," Morgan said, "the Ames Commission. A crazy old man and a nice enough black kid, I guess, still out chasing the old elephant after he's gotten too old and too damned tired to care much about them or about anybody else, chasing him much more. Fuck 'em. As long as I'm still here there'll be an Ames Commission, one kind or another. I leave and the fun's gone. Who wants to put an elder statesman in the can, huh? No excitement there."

He returned to the desk and toyed with the pen that lay on it. He looked up slowly. He folded his arms. "But the bottom line, Joe, is, and this is what I kind of hope you'll emphasize, all right? I'm tired. I've done my job. I'm through." He sighed and smiled. "It's time for Bernie Morgan to go home now."

27 In the early afternoon a soft southwesterly blew through the perforated green curtains that protected the tennis players on the red clay courts of the Nantucket Yacht Club from the wind and the view of daytrippers crowding up from the Steamship Authority ferry wharf. The *thwock* of new balls against tightly strung gut and an occasional well-mannered call were the only noises. Judge Warren Matte, his face in repose, sat by himself at a table set for four in the dining room and told the waiter he could clear away the remnants of his club sandwich. He said that he would have his coffee and Indian pudding.

Dory Feldman, wearing a dark blue polo shirt and khakis, arrived at the door to the dining room twirling his sunglasses by the bows in his left hand, and surveyed its occupants in the manner of a man who does not believe in wasting any time, especially that of his vacation. He located Warren Matte, smiled a declination of assistance by the maitre d', and headed straight for Matte's table. He came up behind the judge from his blind spot and tapped him on the right shoulder, bending toward him as he did so. "Pardon me, Your Honor," he whispered, as Matte started to turn, "the White House is on the line. Most important." He was grinning when Matte faced him. "Hullo, Judge," Feldman said, offering his right hand, "nice breeze up on the sound today, for those whose friends have sailboats." He was already moving toward the chair opposite the judge as he finished speaking.

Matte's face creased into a grin. "Dory," he said happily, "how the hell are you?"

Feldman nodded twice. "Very fine, fact, Your Honor," he said. "As a matter of fact, if all my friends who love good government are right, I have never been better."

Matte's grin retracted slightly, and the beginnings of a frown appeared above his eyes. "The Dussault thing, you mean?" he said.

Feldman nodded once again. "Uh huh," he said, "the Dussault thing. Apparently by losing that case—mind you, nobody's actually come out and said they think I took a dive on Jean to set him up for Otis Ames, but they do have a tendency to wink when they say anything about it—I've done more for civil liberties in Massachusetts than I managed in the entire thirty years that I spent trying cases before Jean's. Isn't that something?"

Matte shook his head. "I still cannot get over that damned jury," he said. "If I ever saw a case with the absolute minimum of evidence that a prosecutor could put in to get past a directed verdict, that was it."

"If it was the minimum," Feldman said with mild reproach. "You and I still differ on that. You should've directed for me, Warren, precisely so that none of this shit would've happened."

Matte raised his eyebrows. "You could be right," he said. "But still and all, with Hanrihan stomping around the courtroom there, showing off and striking poses like some third-rate actor in a fourth-rate melodrama, all his witnesses behaving as though he'd written their lines for them, who the hell in his right mind would have expected that the goddamned jury would go out and find your client guilty? I certainly didn't. And why should I direct and then get blasted by Joe Gillis or that Rosen kid, in the papers the next morning, when I know very well the jury will acquit and that'll be the end of it? Didn't make sense, Dory, with all the innuendo about my bias and prejudice that Hanrihan's spread all over the record. If I had directed, they would've been screaming for my impeachment in the *Commoner* and offering rewards for any citizens who'd form a mob to get you lynched." Matte shook his head. "I don't think so, Dory. Somehow, I don't think so."

Feldman sat silent for a moment to let Matte see he was debating whether to make further criticism. Then he shrugged and said: "Well, maybe, Warren. I've got to say, that kid was more resourceful than I thought he was when I went in against him." He chuckled. "First sign of advancing age," he said, "when you start thinking you can beat the newest whippersnapper just because you've beaten all the other whippersnappers."

"And forget the guy you beat that thought he had you stuffed back when *you* were the new whippersnapper," Matte said. He laughed lightly to show that he had not taken offense. "Happens to all of us, I guess," he said.

"Which does not," Feldman said, "make it more enjoyable though, Judge."

Matte regarded him narrowly. "Well, Dory," he said slowly, "nevertheless, I notice when the blow did fall on you, you managed to retain enough of your presence of mind to make sure that Hanrihan didn't get too much enjoyment from his victory."

The waiter brought the judge's coffee and dessert, and Feldman asked for Perrier and lime. "Should I have?" he said. "Dussault was on the edge of suing me for malpractice, because of course no convicted client ever stops to think it might be at least partly because he did it, and he looks like he did it, and the prosecutor had at least a smidgeon of evidence to prove that he did it."

"No, of course not," Matte said, dipping his spoon thoughtfully into Indian pudding, "a conviction is always the defense attorney's fault."

"So," Feldman said as the waiter returned with his Perrier, "I made my usual lightning estimate of the situation that confronted me, and I decided that there wasn't much point in me bargaining with Hanrihan for Jean's hide and liberty. Hanrihan couldn't guarantee Jean that he'd get his shirts back from the laundry Friday if he left them off for washing Monday. The only fellow who was worth negotiating with was the guy who was going to bounce old Brian off the case the minute that you brought Jean in for sentencing, and send his boy in front of you to ask for a postponement until Jean had had a chance to spill his guts. Choice for me was simple: eliminate the middleman; go cut a deal with Otis Ames. And that was what I did. Getting that wise little fucker Hanrihan stuffed at the same time was incidental, just a little bonus. Fun, though, I must admit. I did take some small pleasure in smashing all the spokes on his new bicycle, after those dirty little cracks he made about me. And about you, I might add, after the jury came in."

Matte grinned into his coffee. "Dory, Dory," he said. "Tempers always run high in a hotly contested trial. You must know that by now."

"I do, I do," Feldman said, "but still and all, as you say, when the opposition tells the evening news that he is up against the favorite mouthpiece of the political establishment, and it's perfectly obvious that Feldman's real client's not the man who's on trial before the jury, well, it does kind of eat at you, you know? It did not occur to me, Warren, at the beginning of that trial, to ask you to sequester that panel. I'm beginning to wonder if that wasn't a mistake on my part. Didn't occur to me that they'd be going home at night to hear the prosecutor telling them on television that they'd better hang Dussault or they'd be letting Bernie Morgan off the hook." He shook his head. "Maybe Jean's got something when he says I've lost my touch."

Matte finished his dessert and pushed the dish away from him. "Put your mind at ease, Dory," he said. "Wouldn't've made a particle of difference if you had moved to sequester. I would've denied your motion."

"And you would've been just as wrong to deny it," Feldman said, "as I was not to make it. You hear what Hanrihan was saying about you? 'The judge on this case is a well-connected politician in his own right'?"

Matte uttered one short explosive laugh. "Yeah," he said, dabbing at his eyes with his napkin, "I did have the pleasure of hearing that one. 'Well-connected politician,' right. I'm so well connected I got appointed out to pasture over twenty years ago, and there I am today, right where Wilfred Knox gave me the choice of going if I didn't relish the idea of being hounded out of office and left to spend the rest of my life trying to make a living trying uncontested divorces and bum check cases in the Quincy District Court. I was well connected, all right—they had me wired to somewhere in the neighborhood of fifty thousand volts, and just one taste of that power was enough to convince me, my friend."

Feldman snorted. "Okay," he said, "but I don't think it's funny." He glowered for a moment. "I'll tell you something, Warren," he said. "Much as I hate the guy today, and have since I remember, there are times when I almost kind of hope that Bernie beats the bastards."

"Really," Matte said conversationally. He reclined a little in his chair. "That's quite some admission, coming from you, Dory."

Feldman chuckled and tapped his fingertips on the table. "I know it," he said ruefully. "It kind of startles me that I'm making it. But Jesus Christ, you know? Morgan's an old crook, and everybody knows it, but at least he isn't in it for some sort of public adoration. Bernie never said we had to love him. Just leave him alone with the money box for a few minutes, that was all he asked. These guys like Ames and Putter that're lining up against him now, for God's sake, it's not enough for them if they just *win*. No, they've got to have hosannas and applause besides. They want us to be grateful and lead cheers for them. I don't mind saying Ames and Hanrihan and Putter, well, they make me a little queasy. Pompous sanctimonious windbags."

"Perhaps, Dory," Matte said, idly stirring coffee slowly, "you've been out at sea too long."

"Huh?" Feldman said.

"The queasiness," Matte said, clearing his throat and frowning as though suppressing some amusement. "How long've you been sailing?"

"Since I wrapped the deal with Putter," he said. "I was so damned disgusted I went up to Marblehead that night and told my crew they could load up the provisions and we'd leave on the morning tide. Went down to Camden, over to Newport, now we're on a mooring here. Why?"

Matte raised his eyebrows again. "Nothing," he said, "nothing. Just sort of wondering."

"You want to go out today?" Feldman said. "That was why I came looking for you here, actually. It really is a gorgeous breeze."

Matte frowned and sat up straight. He put his elbows on the table. "Love to," he said. "Thought you'd never ask. But I can't do it."

"You're tied up today?" Feldman said, looking genuinely disappointed.

"Yup," Matte said, nodding. "Just like these things always work, I finished what I had before me on the calendar this morning, but something else crops up for me to go back and listen to this afternoon. Never fails." He laughed. "Probably not surprising though," he said. "Best I can figure out, I'm the only Superior Court judge in captivity between here and Taunton today, and the plaintiffs're on the Vineyard. You had a choice for an emergency hearing, and your client was paying for it, where would you go? Nantucket or Taunton?"

Feldman nodded. "Injunction?"

"No," Matte said, "motion to quash. Also an application for a temporary order. *Mahoney* and *Another* versus *Ames*."

"Ames," Feldman said. "Not the, ah, Ames that springs immediately to mind when civic virtue is the topic, by any chance?"

"The very same," Matte said, grinning. "From the pleadings it appears that the defendant Otis Ames has issued and caused to be issued two subpoenas, which by their terms direct one Vincent Mahoney and one William Fucillo, plaintiffs, to appear before said Ames at ten o'clock in the forenoon, next Monday, at the Gardner Auditorium at Boston in the County of Suffolk, and to bring with them all documents relating or in any way pertaining to certain financial transactions, and to testify under oath as to such matters as the said Otis Ames may then and there inquire of them."

Feldman cocked his head. "Do I detect in the distance," he said, "the faint blare of trumpets and the sound of the hooves of the cavalry?"

"Well," Matte said, "somebody has, and somebody doesn't like it. So an effort is being made to head off the posse at the pass."

Feldman grinned. "Uh huh," he said. "Well, Francis Costello has been silent for quite some time now. I hope old Otis didn't let himself decide that meant Costello was sleeping. Who's arguing?"

"The Putter kid from Ames's office," Matte said. He smiled.

"Come on, Warren," Feldman said. "I'm on vacation now. There's no need to stall me around here. Who's arguing Costello's little monkey wrench into Otis Ames's gearbox? Is the old fox doing it himself, actually sticking his own head up in public for a change?"

"Dory," Matte said, "I'm surprised at you. Frank is not the sort of guy who surfaces during the preliminary skirmishing. You ought to know that, after all these years. No, it's an old pal of yours. Brian Hanrihan."

"Mercy," Feldman said. "The same Brian Hanrihan who so eloquently argued the sanctity of union contracts, not so long ago? The same guy who pilloried a poor miserable leg-breaker into a reproach to the brotherhood of man? The same guy who all but told the jury Jean Dussault was a running sore of corruption on the snowy garments of the Lord, and the prejudiced trial judge let him do it?"

"And convicted Jean Dussault," Matte said, grinning, "fully against the expectations of his counsel and quite to the surprise of that same presiding judge. No wonder I got banished to the islands. Put me down here like they were sending me back to Pawtucket for a little more seasoning in Triple-A ball, see if I can try a few bad-check cases without getting into any further trouble."

"Son of a bitch," Feldman said, nodding. "Now I have got to admit this is one of Frankie's neater little exercises. For the price of one ticket of admission, he gets a spotless young prosecutor who sometimes mispronounces words but has proved he has an actual, working brain, *and* a guy who next to Jean and me knows as much about what Jean can tell old Otis as anybody currently on earth. Very neat."

"And probably a good deal cheaper'n you would've been too, Dory," Matte said.

"Oh, unquestionably," Feldman said. "For a guess, figuring Brian's crediting half his take to publicity, which is kind of stupid but he'll learn after a while when it doesn't bring him any really juicy cases, and that his asking price is probably about a third of what mine is anyway, Francis is knocking this adventure down for about fifteen percent of actual cash value." He slapped the table. "Damn," he said, "Warren, you have got to hand it to him. That son of a bitch is smarter than a weasel with a doctorate in wizardry. The man is absolutely beautiful. When you think of all the years that guy's been orchestrating things, without anybody ever seeing him when the curtain's open, you have got to hand it to him. Boy, when it comes to crafty, I take my hat off to the guy. And of course you're going to grant Hanrihan's motion."

Matte shrugged. "Have I got much choice?" he said. "His pleadings say that Ames is proceeding under a statutory grant of powers equivalent to those of the attorney general."

"Which, I assume, he is," Feldman said.

"Correct," Matte said. "The brief alleges that said statutory powers are invalid because the constitution and the Declaration of Rights of the Commonwealth expressly reserve said powers of the attorney general to the attorney general."

"Right again," Feldman said. "Doesn't say one damned word about 'and also to Otis Ames.' Not as I recall."

"Nor I," Matte said. "From those authorities, Hanrihan reasons that the powers of the attorney general cannot be delegated, transferred, or maybe sort of divvied up among folks who aren't attorneys general, without a constitutional amendment. Which, Hanrihan says, Ames hasn't got."

"And he hasn't," Feldman said.

"So," Matte said, grinning, "doesn't leave much room for me to maneuver, does it? Near as I can see, Vincent Mahoney and William Fucillo've been ordered to do something by a man who hasn't got any power to order them to do anything. Which means that their subpoenas should be quashed. Now," he said, smirking, "maybe Lyle Putter has some ingenious argument on parchment in his portmanteau which he's going to pull out with a flourish in that airy courtroom over there this afternoon, and when he gets through showing it around the scales will have fallen from our eyes and I will understand how come it's okay to amend the constitution with an ordinary statute if your purpose is to give some power to Otis Ames. But if I were a betting man, Counselor, I would be inclined to put my cash on the nose of Brian Hanrihan. I don't like the little bastard, but then maybe Brian's grown up too as well. I think it's fun."

Feldman nodded. "Me too," he said. "Boy," he said, "just like that, huh? I figured Bernie'd blow the guy out of the water when Ames got around to charging him and dragging his big fat ass into the courtroom for arraignment. That I expected, and what difference would it've made? But that Francis'd find a way to put Ames's feet to the fire before he ever got a chance to daub some mud on Bernie, that I didn't think he could bring off." He snorted. "And where does he do it? Nantucket. In the afternoon. In the summer. Where if there does happen to be a reporter around, he probably won't have even the foggiest idea of what all this quiet argument means. So Ames's boat's not only going to sink, it isn't even going to leave an oil slick. Nifty, Warren, nifty."

"Well, Dory," Matte said, "not quite that nifty. The effect's the same, of course, but it really shouldn't be. There does happen to be a newspaperman from Boston here, and he does know about this hearing."

"Well," Feldman said, "at least old Otis'll get that comfort."

"Hardly," Matte said. "The newspaperman is David Pucci."

"He knows about it?" Feldman said. "What's he doing, flying in the whole city room on one of these Air Force cargo planes?"

Matte smiled. "He is playing tennis."

"Tennis," Feldman said.

"Tennis," Matte said. He nodded toward the courts. "He stopped by here right after I sat down. Had his whites on, two laminated Prince racquets under his arm, sweatbands and everything, looked like he was late for his curtain call in a Noel Coward festival, and I said something about that Rosen kid. His reporter there, the one that's in and out of coma."

"Yeah," Feldman said. He shook his head. "That was kind of tough there, young kid like that. They find out for sure whether it was an accident? Smelled kind of funny to me."

"Dory, Dory," Matte said, "your cynicism appalls me. It's just a good thing for the happy citizens of Boston, whose attitudes are shaped by the *Commoner* they read so faithfully, that Pooch Pucci doesn't have your suspicious mind."

"He doesn't think somebody might've run that kid off the road?" Feldman said. "Good God, does he think the kid just decided to hang a hard right and drive his bike into a flaming ditch? Clear night? Dry road? No other cars around for miles, and here's this kid nobody ever thought might be insane, all of a sudden decides he's Evel Knievel and he's gonna jump his wheels through the valley of fire?"

"He said Rosen'd evidently been doing some drinking in Mercer before it happened," Matte said. "Told me confidentially."

"Hell's bloody bells," Feldman said, "was he drinking loco potions or something? LSD? What in God's name could the kid've been drinking that'd get him completely out of his skull at that hour?"

Matte shrugged. "Just telling you what Pooch said. From all he heard, it looked like the kid skidded and went off the road. The ditch and the fire, gully, whatever it was, just happened to be next to the spot in the road where he skidded. 'Motorcycles're dangerous, you know.' Dave told me that. 'Told Leo that, Leo Rosen. Told him many times. We're thinking, thinking, starting up a campaign against them. Talented young people like that? Can't afford to be losing them like this.' "

" 'Motorcycles are dangerous,' " Feldman said.

"That's what the Pooch told me," Matte said.

Feldman nodded. "Well," he said, "that's certainly true. I wonder if he'd say the same thing if somebody'd shot Rosen. 'Guns're dangerous. Told him many times, don't stand in front of guns.' Jesus, what a specimen he is. Talk about a vacant attic—you could store fifty steamer trunks in his and have space enough left over for a couple of dress dummies and a complete set of living room furniture. How'd he react to the hearing?"

"By looking at his watch," Matte said. "He can't make it. He's playing doubles at two with an associate justice of the Supreme Court of the United States, the Undersecretary of Labor, and his old school chum, Ambassador Kenneth Wheelwright of the U.K."

"Ah yes," Feldman said. "In other words, he had an earlier engagement to swat the old fuzzy ball around with his idea of the celestial choirs."

"Right," Matte said.

They sipped for a while in silence. Feldman fished the wedge of lime from his glass, bent the peel back so that the pulp stood up, and began to gnaw on it.

"Cripes," Matte said, puckering, "how the hell can you do that?"

"It's good for you," Feldman said, glancing up and then resuming his gnawing. "British tars used to do it. Old custom of us mariners. Prevents scurvy. That's why Englishmen're called *limeys*."

"Oh," Matte said. "Are you English now, Dory?"

Feldman finished his lime and dropped it back into the glass. He dabbed at his lips with a napkin, sat back in the chair, and produced a pack of Luckies from his shirt pocket. He tapped one firm on the table, lighted it with a Zippo, spat a few shreds of tobacco from his lower lip, and grinned. "Hell," he said, "I've got all I can do just staying an American. Lemme ask you something, all right?"

"Sure," Matte said, "fire away."

"When you started out," Feldman said, "when you were just starting college, or law school, or whenever, it happened to hit you that you'd be middle-aged someday, all right?"

"Yeah," Matte said.

"Did you think," Feldman said, "did you look around you at the men you knew then who were the age that we are now, and see what they were doing with their lives?"

"Sure," Matte said.

"And what did you think yours was going to be?"

"Think?" Matte said. He laughed. "I didn't think, Dory, I knew. Mine was going to be different. I was going to make a difference."

"Yup," Feldman said, nodding, "so was I. And did you?"

"Nope," Matte said. "I guess I was mistaken."

"Me too," Feldman said. "So was I." He shook his head and laughed. "The only man who wasn't was the Speaker."

28 Walter Hackley's three years of experience as a security guard at the Prudential Towers had not prepared him to respond to frantic questioning conducted by reporters from four television stations, four newspapers, two wire services, and by Representative Paul Linder of the Massachusetts General Court, who did his best to outshout the reporters while at the same time interposing his body between Walter Hackley and the cameras. The cameramen moved agilely to exclude Paul Linder from the pictures they transmitted from the dishes on their vans outside the lobby of the Pru, and when Linder shifted his position to regain the limelight they nudged him out of it again. He became angry at this treatment and shoved one of them who lost his balance momentarily and lowered his minicam to glance at Linder with astonishment. Linder blustered at him and put up his fists as he vaguely recalled being taught to do when he had been a member of the CYO at the age of ten or eleven. The camerman looked at him and laughed, called him an asshole, and went back to shooting pictures of Walter Hackley. That effort required him to move repeatedly toward Hackley, who was recoiling and retreating from the microphones and lights that were being pushed into his face. At last he had his back against the wall; with his left hand serving as a visor to shade him from the lights, he requested mercy.

"Hey," Walter Hackley said, "I'm telling you that's all I saw, all right? I was just doing my job, like I do every day. I come on duty every night at ten thirty, and I stay mostly up here in the lobby unless I hear something. Every couple hours I take a look down in the garage and maybe I walk up and down a few aisles, make sure that I don't see nothing that I think should be reported.

"I did that last night," Hackley said. "I come on duty at ten thirty and it was a quiet night. I didn't see nothing. I saw some tenants that I know come in, and I said hello to them, and I seen them take the elevators and I walked around a little. I went down in the garage around one thirty and looked around, and I didn't see that anything was wrong.

After all, we got guys that just patrol the garage there and see who's coming in and going out and that's their job that they do. All I do is look around the part of the garage where the people that live in the building have their parking spaces, and also because I go down there to the room where we have our lunch and Cokes and things like that. And that is what I done."

A reporter from one of the television stations asked Hackley if he had noticed anything unusual when he went down into the garage at one thirty. "No," he said, and looked irritated, "I already told you that I didn't. That's what I already told you about eighteen times already. That I didn't see a thing that looked like it was unusual at one thirty, or when I come back up here about, it was around two or two fifteen, or when I went back down there around three thirty, or when I went down again around five thirty, I didn't see a damned thing that looked like I should report it. If the Speaker's car, if Mister Morgan's car was in there at one thirty, or if it wasn't there at one thirty but it was there at three thirty, I honestly don't know. I couldn't tell you. The only thing that I could tell you is that the car was there at five thirty, that much I am sure of. The Cadillac Seville that was the Speaker's, was in the garage when I went down into it at five thirty."

"Was the light on in it when you noticed it at five thirty?" Linder yelled at him from the fringe of the crowd of reporters.

"I don't know, sir," Hackley said. "I imagine that it must've been, because it was on when I came back out of the guardroom around ten of six there and I noticed it. I had my coffee and I come out and I went past the car again, and that was when I noticed that the inside dome light of the car was on. So I went over to it, 'cause I figured Mister Morgan must've come home some time in the night when I just happened not to see him come up to the lobby and take the elevator up to his apartment, like I was in the guardroom having lunch or something, and I just didn't see the light was on before or notice that the car was in. And I thought to myself, well, I should go over to the car and it was probably that he'd left the door to it open, and I should shut the door because if the light stayed on the battery'd run down and the Speaker couldn't start his car when he got up this morning. And I did that and I found the body."

"Did he appear to be alive at that time when you first saw him?" one of the female reporters shouted.

Hackley looked puzzled. "I don't know, ma'am," he said. "He didn't say nothing, if that's what you mean."

"Was he breathing?" she said, poking her microphone into his face. He drew back again, his eyes fixed on the mike as though it was a weapon. "I don't know, ma'am," he said, feebly pushing the mike away. "All I know is that when I got there, I tripped over something when I went in the stall where the car was, and I looked down and I couldn't see very well because it was dark and I wanted to see what it was that I stepped on. And I reached down and felt around, sort of, and I realized it was a body. And then I looked closer, bent over and sort of felt around it some more, and the door that was open, there was part of his coat that was stuck in the door and the rest of him was down there, sort of jammed in between the wall of the stall and the side of the car. There wasn't much room in there anyway, and he was a pretty big man, and I couldn't really get in there. So I backed out of there and I went and I called the police and I said what I found and I called up the number you call for the ambulance there, and they came. And that's what I know, just about. I don't know whether he was alive when I got to him, but he didn't say nothing when I stepped on him, and I didn't hear him make a noise or do any breathing. So I guess probably he wasn't. But I don't know."

"Do you realize," Linder bellowed, rising up on his toes at the fringe of the crowd and craning his neck at the same time, "this man was the Speaker and he was the target of a vendetta? That people wanted him dead?" He looked around eagerly after he said that. A few reporters looked at him with contempt. The cameras stayed focused on Hackley.

"No, sir," Hackley said, "I did not. The Speaker, I knew about that, that he was. But the other stuff, no, I did not. He was always a good guy to me. Very nice. Him and his wife also, too. Very nice."

The reporters and cameramen then by what seemed to be silent consensus shut off the lights and began to turn and disperse from the guard. He relaxed and permitted his shoulders to slump. Joe Gillis, his spiral pad out and his pen in his hand, threaded his way through the crowd and came up to Hackley. He identified himself. "Were you still there when they took out the body and looked at it?" he said.

"Yeah," Hackley said, heaving a deep breath and rotating his head on his neck, massaging the back of his neck with his hand, "I was standing right there."

"What did you see?" Gillis said.

Hackley frowned. He spread his feet apart, locked his hands together palms downward, and expanded his muscles. He closed his eyes while he thought and then spoke. "They dragged him out by the feet," he said, "and it was no little job of it, either. He was a big motherfucker, and he was really wedged in there."

"Could you see any blood?" Gillis said.

Hackley opened his eyes very wide, then closed them and rubbed them with the knuckles of his index fingers. "Uh huh," he said. "There was blood on his suitcoat on his right side, right about here." He placed his right hand on his right kidney. "There wasn't much blood, or anything like that, anything that you would say was a lot of blood there, but there was blood there, maybe a spot about six inches across."

"Anything else?" Gillis said.

"Yeah," Hackley said, breathing deeply. "When they got him out where they could look at him, they rolled him onto his back and they listened for whether his heart was beating and whether he had any pulse, and he didn't. Then they undid his coat and there was more blood on his shirt, all over his belly and the inside of his coat. It was dried. The blood had dried. And I heard the paramedic there, after he took a look at him, he said it looked like he'd been stabbed in the back as he came out of the stall. And then the cops, when the medics said he was dead, they took his watch and his wallet and his stuff like that, and they said it sure wasn't robbery unless whoever did it got scared off by something. And then they started asking me, did we have any problem with people getting attacked and mugged here, and I said we didn't. Which we do not. And they took him away." He frowned. "Oh," he said, "yeah. And there was *Kike* on the trunk of his car. Somebody scratched it." He shrugged.

"You got any theories?" Gillis said, ready to write on his pad.

"Sure," Hackley said, "sure I have. The guy parked his car and he was getting out of it, squeezing between it and the wall until he could get far enough from the door so that he could reach in and shut it. And somebody come up behind him and stabbed him in the kidney, and it hurt him enough so that he fell forward, and he was heavy enough so he slid down between the wall and the car. And the guy that'd stabbed him took off. But, why the guy stabbed him?" Hackley shrugged. "That I don't know," he said. "Or who scratched his car," he said as an afterthought.

"He was always nice to you," Gillis said.

Hackley nodded. "Absolutely," Hackley said. "Him and his wife, both very nice." He looked at Gillis suspiciously. "Otherwise," he said, "I wouldn't know. If it was politics, like that fellow there said, I wouldn't know about that."

"You wouldn't, huh?" Gillis said.

Hackley was very firm about that. "No sir, I wouldn't," he said. "I got nothing to do with no politics."

29 Saturday was hot and muggy, a grey day that made Hanrihan's skin and his spirit feel greasy and itchy and worn. Late in the morning he went to the deserted courthouse in Cambridge to clean out his office; it was a task he'd postponed as depressing and dull, and it seemed appropriate for the way he felt. He was sitting behind his desk with all the drawers open around him, a large cardboard carton on top of it filled with old files and red Lawyer's Diaries, Kiwanis plaques and framed award letters, empty cheap penholders and mostly used scratch pads, watching the bowling match on the little TV set, when Jim Cremmens came in on a similar errand and caught him disconsolate, chin in his hand.

Cremmens came to the First Assistant's cubicle and leaned against the doorjamb, his arms folded. "Brian," he said agreeably, "something going on?"

Hanrihan glanced up at him without lifting his chin, arched his eyebrows in a silent greeting, and said: "Yeah. Stasia Czernicki leads by eleven pins in the eighth frame, but the other lady's got a spare working."

Cremmens grinned. "You, ah," he said, "you got big money riding on this one, have you?"

Hanrihan snickered at that, raised his head off the support of his hand, and folded his arms across his stomach. "Actually, no," he said, conceding a lopsided grin. "Somehow my general outlook on this bright New England day did not inspire me to go out and get a few bets down. Not on anything, in fact. Not the way my luck's been going."

Cremmens registered mild surprise. "Christ, Brian," he said, "the hell do you mean, the way your luck's been going? You've been on a roll like nobody that I ever saw in my whole life before, lately. First you hook Dussault, when nobody thinks you're gonna . . ."

"Right," Hanrihan said bitterly, "and the old Yankee Clipper sends his little Brown Bomber right in to scoop the prisoner out from under me."

"Hey," Cremmens said, "you still complaining about that? You should be lighting candles in thanksgiving over the Cathedral. The big fat candles, too, for what losing Jean saved you from. You come out of that swap looking like Steinbrenner did when he lost that loser Torrez to the Red Sox. And anyway, that was Feldman pulled that little number on you, just in case you didn't know, hustling Jean over to see us. That wasn't anything that Ames did, or Lyle either, for that matter."

"Doesn't really matter who was sticking it to me," Hanrihan said, stretching in his chair and yawning luxuriously. "Point is that I had it stuck to me, no matter who was doing it, and I didn't like the feeling very much."

Cremmens shook his head. "Well," he said, "okay, I guess, if that's really how you want to feel. But it doesn't make good sense to me." He stood away from the door and turned as though to leave. "I got to go clean out my desk and stuff."

"The hell you mean," Hanrihan said, collapsing from the stretch, "saying that it doesn't mean anything? For Christ sake, Jimmy, when in hell did you get so damned charitable, it didn't mean a thing if some bastard stuck it to you? Don't give me that shit."

Cremmens wheeled back and stood in the doorway again. He hooked his thumbs in the belt loops of his jeans and shook his head at Hanrihan. "Brian," he said, "all right? This is me you're talking to, your old pal, Jimmy Cremmens. I know about things other people haven't even guessed at, right? I know about the big extortionist and labor racketeer that had his thumb on every contractor in Massachusetts and was fucking every union member out of everything he earned, the one that had his name in all the papers? Jean Dussault? And I happen to know that if we could've gone in there and proven every single goddamned case we even had a possibility of getting evidence about, and not just that two-bit little case with Ricky Mortimer that I still think was lying about half the time, the most we ever could've proven that Jean got from all his victims in a whole fucking year was less than twenty-seven thousand dollars."

"It was more than that," Hanrihan said uncomfortably, not looking at Cremmens but discovering some loose articles to play with in the top right-hand drawer of his desk.

"It wasn't much more, if it was," Cremmens said. "What we proved was that he got about six hundred bucks a month from Ricky Mortimer, which is seventy-two hundred bucks a year from that outfit, Brian, and that was probably the biggest tit he had. And that's assuming that Jean was lying when he claimed that Ricky bet him every game the NFL ever put on, and the only one that Ricky ever won from him was one day when the Pats forgot they are supposed to lose and beat the Raiders in a fuckin' flood." He jabbed his forefinger at Hanrihan, who was still hiding in the drawer and could pretend he did not see. "You know what your newest client there, Mahoney on the Vineyard, you know what he was paying Jean each week his guys could actually do work? Which is only when the weather's good, I should remind you, about half of the year around here or a little more. He was kicking back to Jean about two hundred fifty bucks a week, a thousand bucks a month for six months of the year, max. Between Mahoney and that ass-hole Mortimer, Jean was cleaning up a little over thirteen grand a year, and risking his ass out on the street to do it. Christ sake, man, you make over twice that, two and a half times that, just stomping in here every day and throwing your weight around all over the goddamned place, and you didn't even have to steal to do it. And it stands to reason if you quit this job to take this other one, the new one naturally pays even more, and it's all legal, too. I assume it is, at least," Cremmens finished slyly.

Hanrihan came out of the drawer and smiled at Cremmens. "Oh yeah, Jim," he said, "it's all legal. I looked into that before I took it."

"Okay," Cremmens said, looking very skeptical, "okay if you say so, Brian. But just the same, a man with my experience has got to wonder, right? A job that pays a lot more than this tit you had that paid you thirty thou a year for grandstanding in court like you admit you like to do, plus which you get your name in the paper all the time for being the next guy that's in line to succeed Jesus, and it's on Beacon Hill? With all them crooks and robbers you've been telling me for years're on the loose up in that State House there? A man in my position's got to won-der whether any job that good can actually be legal." He laughed with as much wickedness as he could muster.

Hanrihan's expression of amusement slowly disappeared. He nodded. He slammed the top right-hand drawer shut, hard. He let out a deep breath. "Well," he said slowly, "you can put your fears to rest, Jim. It does pay lots more money, like you say, and it is on Beacon Hill, but just the same it's perfectly within the law." He paused and looked at the carton on his desk. Absently he said it again: "Perfectly within the law." He rested his forearms on his thighs and seemed to stare at the box without seeing it.

Cremmens frowned. He shifted his position and leaned back further on the doorjamb. "Jesus, Brian," he said, "you act like, it almost seems like you're sorry you took it."

Hanrihan glanced up at him quickly. He thought about it and he nodded. "I am," he said, making a confession. "I am sorry, now that you mention it."

"Well, Jesus Christ, Brian," Cremmens said, "that doesn't make sense either. You're the one that took it, for Christ sake. You didn't have to leave here. Dennis, never mind all that regular bullshit that everybody always puts out for the papers when one of their important people's leaving. Dennis Patrick isn't any different from any other politician that I ever saw, when it comes to that shit. But Dennis around here was even saying that he hated like hell to see you going, to lose you, and he wished to God there was some way that he could offer you more money or something so you'd stay. He even said, Maria heard him talking to some friend of his, he said if he was just a little older, only about five or six years older so he could see his way clear to step down and let you have the job, he would do that. But he said that he thought about it and until his kids get out of college, he just can't do it, or he would. Dennis said you were the best assistant that he's ever had."

"Goddamnit, Jimmy," Hanrihan said, "I've been telling you that ever since the first day you came in here, for Christ sake. You have to hear it from Dennis before you can believe it?" He grinned.

"Well," Cremmens said, "I know that you believed it, of course, but I got to say it is a little unusual, hear a DA say it too. You were good at this."

"I was good at this," Hanrihan said, nodding. He looked vacantly around his official shambles and contemplated it. "And I also loved it, doing this." He looked back at Cremmens. "The thing of it is, Jim," he said, "I've been doing it for long enough. Nine years this July I will have been here, and that's long enough in any job. Came in the day after I finished taking bar exams. Didn't know a goddamned thing about the way you try a case, or how you keep a judge off balance, or what you do when some prick named Feldman gets bored in a trial and decides maybe he'll pass the time jerking your chain now and then. But I learned. I learned fast." He paused and considered. "I can honestly say," he said, "that I don't think any man on earth has ever had more fun with his first job than I have had with this one."

Hanrihan cleared his throat and frowned. He looked earnestly at Cremmens. "Unfortunately, Jim," he said, "the fact that you like something doesn't mean that you can say, or that you should say, that you're going to spend the rest of your whole life just doing it. Arrested development, you know? Bad for the outlook generally, and sometimes dangerous to your health and longevity. Men like me who stay in one place for too long have been known to start drinking too much, losing track of what they meant when they declared their wedding vows, and generally—"

Cremmens interrupted in a warning voice. "Watch it, Brian," he said, smiling, "with that casual shit there about wedding vows."

"Oh," Hanrihan said smiling. "Sorry, I forgot. No offense to you and the lovely Maria, James. I hope you two will be very happy."

"Most likely we will be," Cremmens said. "Most likely also, not with each other. But never mind that."

Hanrihan deliberated whether Cremmens really wanted him to leave that subject alone, and decided that he did. "Yeah," he said. "Well, anyway, it's just not a good idea for me to stay in this job here much longer. The opportunity came along and whomped me on the head to make the change. I thought about it and decided I would do it." He arched his eyebrows again. "I must confess," he said, "that the job of me being counsel to the chairman of Ways and Means, being the lawyer to Raymond Archambault, I don't think anybody talking about it conceived of the possibility I'd be acting as Archambault's attorney in his office as the Speaker of the House. At least not until a year from January. But that's a minor point, I guess."

"You were going to be Archambault's lawyer?" Cremmens said. His brows were furrowed. "Even before the Speaker got himself scragged there, you were going to work for Archambault?"

Hanrihan looked genuinely puzzled. "Sure," he said. "That was the agreement. Morgan had his own man, Sam Kilgore. Two of them'd worked together for about five, six years. Kilgore . . . sure. I was going to work for Ray. New job, created specially for me."

"Huh," Cremmens said.

"Why?" Hanrihan said.

"Well," Cremmens said, "nothing special or anything like that. It was just that, over the commission there, see, we knew the job was a new one that somebody'd set up for you."

"It was," Hanrihan said. "I just told you that."

"Yeah," Cremmens said. "Well, Lyle and Mister Ames there, and I guess as far as that goes, the rest of us along with them, they thought the new job was just camouflage, you know? Something they set up for you to cover up what they were paying you for throwing the monkey wrench into what we were trying to do, see?"

"Paying *off* to me, you mean," Hanrihan said reproachfully.

"Well," Cremmens said uncomfortably, "yeah, if you want to put it that way. Paying off to you. Seventy-eight grand a year is quite a lot, Brian, I think you got to admit, even for a guy as good as you are, for reading statutes and stuff like that for the chairman of the Ways and Means Committee."

"Yeah," Hanrihan said, "I suppose it is. But you have to keep in mind, Jim, that the whole idea of my job until they found the Speaker's body yesterday, was that Archambault would be doing both the chairman's and the Speaker's job for the rest of this year. And then all of next year, too."

"Morgan was resigning?" Cremmens said. "Holy shit. That we didn't know."

"Well," Hanrihan said, "not resigning, actually. He was announcing he was going to resign as of the end of the next session. And that Ray was going to have the power and authority until then, only not the title." He looked at Cremmens appraisingly. "You guys, Jim," he said, "you guys have no idea what you actually accomplished."

"Oh," Cremmens said, "I don't know about that. I think I've got a pretty good idea. Nothing, is what we accomplished. Absolutely nothing. We gave an old man another turn at bat, and he didn't hit a damned thing anybody threw at him. Too old and too daffy. We gave Lyle Putter a new job that opened with a fanfare and collapsed like a lead balloon. Me?" He shrugged. "I didn't have that much to gain when I got the assignment, so I didn't lose much when it got a puncture wound just as fatal as the Speaker's. Except what it did to me, of course, which doesn't matter. But what we accomplished, actually? Not a fucking thing."

"Well," Hanrihan said slowly, "I guess I've got to disagree with you then, James." He smiled. "Because," he said, "I know better."

"Yeah," Cremmens said defiantly, "you know better. If there was anything else to know, maybe, yeah, then I would say you might. Because after all, you've been up there on the Hill with all the people that know everything, over a week now, and I suppose that should be time enough to get just about everything.

"The trouble is though, Counselor Hanrihan sir," he said, "there isn't a damned thing else to know. Thanks to you and your little contribution there to the celebration we had going with Mahoney, the only chance we had of nailing Morgan went right up in smoke." He paused and glared at Hanrihan. He spoke very softly, but his eyes were menacing. "And we both, buddy boy," he said, "know where you got that idea, don't we? You double-dealing prick."

Hanrihan raised a hand to placate him. "Jim," he said mollifyingly, "hey, if what you're thinking is that—"

Cremmens held up his own hand and shook his head emphatically as he interrupted. "Uh uh, Brian," he said, "don't try to give me no nice song and dance now about how you didn't mean no harm and any of that shit, when you took what I told you like an asshole in that cafeteria there that night and went running right over to Costello as fast's your fat little legs would carry you. Uh uh, none of that shit, buddy. I kind of suspect maybe the old bar association overseers might be sort of interested in you getting information from me like that, and then using it to go right out and torpedo what it was that I was doing, supposedly in my official duties as a police officer, this Commonwealth, but so far you and I appear to be the only ones that realize what made you so smart so fast about Ames's case he was developing against Mahoney. And if it's all right with you, pal, I can assure you that it's perfectly all right with me if nobody else finds out. There's enough people around this state as it is, that are convinced that I am probably an asshole. I really don't see any need to prove it for them."

"Jim," Hanrihan began again.

"Nope," Cremmens said, "I mean it, Brian. I really, honestly do mean it. By the time the two of us left here that night, both of us knew just how important it was that me and Lyle Putter tipped that mealy-mouthed Mahoney over, the guy that wants everybody to feel sorry for him but he'll give out bribes if that's the only way he can screw somebody else out of the contract. The difference between us was that I'm a cop and I'm on salary and I can't sell the information that I get from being one. But you're a lawyer and the way that things're set up, lawyers can. So both of us knew the exact same thing, but you could go and sell it for seventy-eight big ones this year and God only knows how much next year, and then after that, the sky's the limit, right? Soon's you make your big fat bundle, what you take out of the State House plus what you can pick up on the side, right, Brian? Pretty nice. You and Barbara there'll be down with the summer place in Osterville before I even make sergeant, the way I'm going."

"Jim," Hanrihan said, believing he was finished, "I'm going to tell you this if—"

"Who you going into private practice with, Brian?" Cremmens said, a mocking smile on his face. "Ames when he found out about what happened and the name of the guy that did it to us, he said right off you'd be joining Frank Costello's firm. That right, Brian baby? Gonna take some lessons from the master on how to fix things so nobody gets caught with their fingers in the cookie jar?"

"Ray Archambault," Hanrihan said wearily. "I'm going into Ray Archambault's office and I'm going to see if maybe I can use all the worthless experience I've gotten trying criminal cases to make myself into a reasonably competent defendant's lawyer in civil cases. I'll be representing mostly the insurance companies, and I won't be getting any giggles out of it. No damned fun at all. Does that make you feel better?"

"Well," Cremmens said sarcastically, "a little bit, it does, yeah, now that you mention it. The way you made your debut there, I figured the next time I picked up the paper I'd see where you were representing the Godfather of the Mafia or something. But yeah, it does help some that you're not going whore completely."

"Oh for Christ sake, Jimmy," Hanrihan said wearily, "go and fuck yourself then, willya?"

"Hey," Cremmens said in feigned surprise, "did I get something wrong or something? Tell me where I'm wrong, that you're not turning whore. Sounds to me like you are. Nice salary plus all you're gonna get from the insurance boys. That's good money, Brian. Or is it just, I hurt your feelings there, calling it by its right name? Is that it, maybe?"

"Have it your way, Jim," Hanrihan said, dipping into the second drawer down on the right-hand side. "Think what you like. Just get the hell out of here and sort of leave me alone, huh?"

Cremmens gathered himself together. Then he paused and looked at Hanrihan again. "You, ah," he said tentatively, "you did say Morgan was resigning."

"Yeah," Hanrihan said from the depths of the desk, "Morgan was resigning. That's what I was going to tell you when you decided it'd be more fun to go flying off the goddamned handle. He was resigning and the boys were going to expand Knox State Hospital for him to play with. Morgan was resigning, but it was not Morgan's idea, not by a long shot.

"It was Frank Costello's idea, principally," Hanrihan said, emerging from the drawer, "his and Ray Archambault's, and they didn't want to have it either. They had it forced upon them, and they in turn forced it ipon Bernie. And the people that compelled them, all of them, into taking this action that none of them liked one bit better than he would've welcomed the idea of amputating his own dick, himself, were you, Bojangles there that aced me out of what really should've been my ob, and Cotton Mather, Esquire—you know, the guy that hates a Harp so much he'd rather put his last shot in the hands of a black rookie who will most likely screw it up, than give it to a mick who would know what to do with it. Shit," Hanrihan said bitterly, "you want to piss and moan a little, James? You want me to sit here and weep tears for you and Ames because I managed to have something to do with raining on the old bastard's parade? Forget it. Poetic justice if I did it, that's what that was."

Cremmens showed signs of suppressed excitement. He rubbed the palms of his hands on his jeans. "But you said, Brian," he said, "the commission had something to do with Morgan stepping down?"

"Yup," Hanrihan said placidly. "You guys were the last straw for Ray and Frank Costello. Also for Andy Boyce, as far as that goes. What they wanted was for Morgan to get the hell out of there before Ames took him out. And also, it was not what you would call a secret that the old dinosaur was drinking just a tad too much from time to time, either."

"It certainly wasn't," Cremmens said. "Waitresses in truck stops in New Bedford even knew that."

"Right," Hanrihan said. "So, they went to Morgan, and before that he just would not believe them when they told him Ames was gonna nail him. And they had me go through this routine they had all scripted out for me. That I was the one guy that could save him from Ames, because I knew about Mahoney, and furthermore I knew a way to muzzle what Mahoney would go in and say about him. But, and the way you evidently view me now, you may find this just a little hard to swallow, the story was that I'm fucking Galahad and Lancelot and King Arthur himself, all rolled up into one, when it comes to honesty and no stealing whatsoever from the government. And the only way that I would say that I would silence Mahoney and his foreman there, who otherwise were about to hand the Speaker's balls to you and the commission, was if Morgan'd agree to get his ass out of office. Which would make Ames go away because it would give him all that he was going to get, and all that interested him anyway. And at the same time it would keep Bernie's big fat ass out of Walpole.

"That idea," Hanrihan said, "appealed to Bernie. It was mostly bullshit, of course, as we both of us know, because Mahoney would've been chewed up in sixteen minutes by any defense lawyer who knew what he was doing, even if there didn't turn out to be anybody smart enough around to blow the whole goddamned commission right out of the water long before his case could ever come to trial. But Morgan was too tired to think about that, I guess, so he threw in the sponge." Hanrihan stared speculatively at Cremmens. "And that, James, is the honest truth. The fact of the matter is that you, by telling me what you had and didn't have in Vinnie Mahoney, actually accomplished the whole purpose that your boss set out to do. Or at least most of it."

Cremmens gazed back at Hanrihan with almost the same expression. "Uh huh," he said cynically, "if you believe it all, I guess, then that is what I did."

"Sort of funny, in a way, wouldn't you say?" Hanrihan said.

Cremmens shook his head. "No," he said, "no. Actually, I wouldn't, when you come right down to it. The old man? My guess is that he won't last too long. If he did do what he wanted, he won't ever believe it. He will think he failed. That Morgan beat him. Even if he is dead. That don't matter. Otis Ames is not the guy that killed him. That was just some damned mugger did that. Some damned accident. Nothing amusing there, that I can see.

"Lyle?" Cremmens said, continuing as though taking inventory in his mind. He shook his head again. He looked at Hanrihan. "You don't like Lyle," he said. "I guess in your position, I most likely wouldn't either. But Lyle is not a bad guy, Brian. He's smart too, just like you are. He wants what you want, to be rich and famous and well respected, and he took what looked to him like his best shot to get there. You can say that Morgan had to pay a high price, resigning and then getting killed, to cheat Lyle of the big success that he thought he had waiting for him, and that you therefore got the slightest bit of trouble feeling sorry for old Lyle. But your career is flying now, and his is wrecked. His old job's gone, because he was the only thing that kept the organization running and it fell apart when he left. Besides, he couldn't go back even if it was still there. He already did that. Just like you did this. And now he's pissed off at the world.

"That night," Cremmens said, "after you plastered our ass down there on the island?"

"Uh huh," Hanrihan said.

"Uh huh," Cremmens said wryly, "funny how much friendlier Judge Matte got to what you had to say when you were on the same side as his old pal Bernie Morgan, huh? I noticed that. When you were out there like a one-man gang hot after Jean Dussault, and old Judge Matte thought that you were going to use Jean to stir up a little trouble for his pals, he thought you were just about the nearest thing to catshit that he ever saw wearing a suit. But when you made your entrance down there on Nantucket like the guy that starts the circus going and says 'Ladies and Gentlemen, and Children of all ages,' I tell you it was just remarkable how Warren Matte's idea of you changed. If you'd've told him Bernie Morgan was the Son of God, for Christ sake, Warren Matte would've cried real tears of joy."

Hanrihan shook his head and chuckled. "Jimmy," he said, "I'll never convince you of this, but that's not the way it is. It just isn't, that's all. Lyle had the law solidly against him. The law was flat against him that day, that's all, and there was not a thing that he or Judge Matte could do about it. If I'd come in there representing Hitler on that case, Jim, Warren Matte would've had to rule in my favor."

"You're right once more, Counselor," Cremmens said, shaking his head and grinning like a simpleton. "By God, there ain't no fooling you, boss. You will never, no matter how hard and how long you may try, convince me of that fairy story that you just got through telling me. No sir."

Hanrihan nodded. "Okay," he said.

"That night," Cremmens said, "when we got back to Boston, Ames'd gone home and his daughter'd left word at the office would we please come out there. They've got this fucking estate out there that must take up most of Dover. So Lyle and I went out. And the old man was raving around like he was some kind of maniac, which I guess he is, when he gets like that anyway. And pretty soon his son-in-law, the doctor, he decided there wasn't going to be much of anything that he could do to calm the old boy down while he was still awake so he stuck him with a needle full of something and we all put him to bed. And you know something, Brian? I felt sorry for those people, too, his daughter and her husband there. They were really kind to him, moved in with him and put up with him, had Lyle and me in there when they most likely would much rather've been home by themselves every night, no old crazy man, a cop and a pissed-off black guy in the same house with them every time they turned around. And she just turned to him and said: 'Well, Ted, huh? In the long run, there isn't any harm done. I still have you, and Dad still has his fierce dreams all unharmed.' See, this was before Morgan got it, or anybody knew he did, at least. 'And we can probably convince Dad in the morning he can try for Morgan again next year.'

"Which, of course," Cremmens said, "they both knew damned right well he couldn't. Ames's finished this year. But it was nice, just the same, and I was sort of envying them there, kind of a reminder that there, there can be such a thing as marrying somebody that you love and that you'd rather be with than with anybody else. Not like that goddamned bandsaw that I picked. And Lyle jumps in and ruined it."

"How?" Hanrihan said. "What the hell could he do?"

"Ah, shit," Cremmens said, making a dismissing gesture with his hand, "he didn't mean to do it. It was just that he was all upset, like everybody else, after what you did to us, and he lit into them for doping Otis up and turning him loose on the world to play with people's lives and shit like that. He was feeling sorry for himself. But it bothered Doctor Scalley, really bothered him. I just didn't like to see it, Lyle yelling at them that they're just careless rich people who don't ever stop to think about what getting their own way and medicating Otis like that might end up doing to anybody else. Like him, of course, and he also said: me."

"Christ," Hanrihan said, "what the hell happened to you? They eject State Police when they don't get their man like Mounties now, for Christ sake?"

Cremmens snickered. "Might be better if they did," he said. "I bet it wasn't, oh, fifteen minutes on the wire that Morgan'd put all four feet up in the air than Major Boynton out there at ten-ten had my name on the teletype. Immediate transfer to emergency temporary duty out of North Adams. He transferred me any further, I'd be the only Mass. State Trooper you'd be likely to see making regular patrols on the New York Thruway. I reported in, he tells me: 'Morgan's dead, Corporal Cremmens. Commission isn't going to need you any more, for sure. Off you go.' Had this grin on his face that he gets when he does something mean like that to somebody and he really hates his ass."

"But why?" Hanrihan said. "I know Boynton, for Christ sake. He never seemed like a vindictive guy to me. Always very helpful, any time I had to ask him for something."

"Of course he was," Cremmens said. "You're a lawyer, and you might be powerful some day. Major Boynton has his eye on Secretary, Public Safety, when he finally retires. Major Boynton don't offend no hotshot young DAs, no sir. And if you think he loved you back when you were here, wait until he finds out how much weight you swing up at the State House now. He'll be polishing your shoes for you and asking if you want your car waxed or your lawn mowed Saturdays, for Christ sake." Cremmens laughed shortly.

"What he doesn't like," he said, "is lowly troopers such as yours truly, who get their names mentioned in the 'State House Viewpoint' column. Because they might attract the kind of attention that Major Boynton's got in mind for himself. That fucking Rosen. I told him not to use my name. I knew something like this was going to happen. But oh no, Rosen used it, and then of course it happened. Shit." He shook his head again. He looked ruefully at Hanrihan again. "So," he said, "if you're still worried about me and my marriage vows there, cheer up, old pal and buddy. North Adams should be far enough to put a real nice crease in anything that I had going with Maria. And besides, huh? It's not so bad, I guess. It at least gets me a long ride away from Sylvia. I suppose I should be gateful."

"Well," Hanrihan said, "you're better off than Rosen."

Cremmens nodded. "Yeah," he said. He laughed again. "You want to know how paranoid you get, working one of those commissions for a guy like Ames?" He shook his head again. "The minute that he heard about that, the Rosen accident, Otis said that Bernie'd had one of his boys catapult that damned reporter into the ravine. Because he was being too friendly about Otis, Lyle, and me. Can you beat that? The bartender at the place where he was drinking before he hit the ditch said that Rosen'd been matching beers and telling lies with one of Mercer's biggest drunks in Knacky's Place for just about two hours before he took off on that motorcycle. I even got the guy's statement, so Otis could just maybe see for once there was some bad thing that he couldn't blame on Morgan. 'See, Mister Ames?' I said. 'This guy Arthur here himself says that he personally begged the Rosen kid to stop drinking, and the guy just wouldn't listen.' Of course all bartenders say that, after there's an accident, but never mind. Otis still would not believe me."

Hanrihan stood up and stretched again. He hitched his pants up and then he arched his back. "Shit," he said, "where somebody like Morgan is concerned, lies are what people prefer to think."

"I suppose so," Cremmens said.

"They're used to them," Hanrihan said. "They look at somebody like

Morgan and they see the biggest crook since Francis Drake was out looting the Spanish Main. You know what they told me in his office yesterday?"

"You were in there yesterday?" Cremmens said.

"Yeah," Hanrihan said. "I was sort of at loose ends, you know? When I found out he was dead, I was supposed to be in meetings with Ray and Frank Costello all day long. But then there didn't seem to be much point in it. The big bad wolf'd gotten wiped out by some sneaky little hood out looking for a wallet. Picked a drunk too fat to roll, and when he stabbed the guy he fell on it so that the kid couldn't get it, and what the hell are we supposed to do? Nothing. So we had a sort of private wake in his office, a few drinks with those women he had working for him—Christ, Jim, you want something'll cure you from chasing the broads, my friend, you come around to that place some day and I'll make sure that you meet Connie. Jee-zuss."

"Rough, huh?" Cremmens said.

"Oh," Hanrihan said expansively, "no worse'n crushed stone, I suppose. But there's an example of something about the Speaker that you never heard about—this rep evidently knocked her up, and he won't do the right thing by her? So, they were talking about this yesterday when they were telling stories about him, Ray and Frank Costello and this guy, Andy Boyce. That one thing that they should not forget to do is take this guy's assignments all away from him and put the word out on the street in Needham, which is evidently where he lives, that the state leadership is looking for a clean young candidate to take him on with full support. That guy is finished, Jim, and the reason that they're gonna finish him is just because of that."

"Huh," Cremmens said without much interest.

"And another thing surprised me," Hanrihan said musingly. "You ever stop to think where most the money went that Morgan was supposed to be—that he was stealing all the time?"

"No," Cremmens said, "no, I can't say that I did."

"Well," Hanrihan said with the air of someone who has made a fairly interesting discovery, "evidently most of it these past few months or year or so, most of it was going to build up a nest egg for this Billy Dealey that is dying."

Cremmens yawned abruptly. "Yeah," he said, "him I did hear something about. He's the shitbird that protected all of those guys and did time when Ames thought he had a clean shot at them back in the fifties or the sixties, right? I forget which it was." He stretched and yawned again. "Jesus," he said, "I hope at least that I can get more sleep in North Adams." He collected himself and returned his attention to what Hanrihan was saying. "Got cancer, hasn't he?" he said. "This Dealey guy got cancer or something?"

"They're saying that," Hanrihan said. "What it is actually is cirrhosis. His liver's shot from drinking. Skin's all turning pus-colored. Yellow. Like a chicken in the market. Chicken skin. He was who Morgan was giving all the money to."

Cremmens jammed both hands in his front pockets and stood there grinning at Hanrihan. "A saint among men, Brian, right?" he said. "A prince of a guy?"

Hanrihan got somewhat flustered. He tried to think of something purposeful to do with his hands. He stuck them in front pockets and rocked back on his heels. "Well," he said, feeling a deep blush on his face, "he might not've been quite as bad as I admit I thought he was."

"Right," Cremmens said, still grinning. "And after a few years in hefty private practice there with Frank Costello, you'll—"

"Archambault," Hanrihan interrupted quickly, "I'll be in practice with Ray Archambault. Naturally, of course, I'll be paying close attention to anything that I can pick up from Costello, but I'll be practicing with Archambault."

"My mistake," Cremmens said, bowing elaborately, "Raymond Archambault. And then, after a few years of heaping the green high, a word in the friendly ear of Joe Gillis, and I'd imagine that we'll see a column or a dozen, maybe, saying how the next attorney general is going to be that champion of good government, well-respected Beacon Hill attorney Brian Hanrihan. Let's have a big hand, everybody, for the next attorney general of the Commonwealth of Massachusetts."

Hanrihan suddenly looked sad. He traced the tip of his right forefinger back and forth across the edge of his old desk as though he had expected to uncover magical incantations written in the dust. "No," he said softly, "somehow I do not think so, James."

Cremmens was astonished, or pretended that he was. "Brian," he said, "say it isn't so. This Commonwealth needs you. You've told me that yourself. You're clearly the best man it has, for any goddamned job it's got. You told me that, as well. You're saying you won't run after all?" He pretended to employ the back of his right hand to wipe sweat from his brow. He genuflected to one knee and stretched out his hands imploringly. He imitated sniffling. "Brian," he said, sobbing, "say, say it isn't so. That you will *reconsider,* man. That you'll accept a *draft.*"

Hanrihan snickered at him. "You're good, Jim," he said. "When you get going, you are good. But fuck off now, all right?"

Cremmens went back to normal. "You shittin' me, Brian?" he said. "The fancy cars, the summer place, the trips to Europe and the Ivy League schools for the kiddies, is that going to be enough for you? You sure that you can settle for just that?"

"Let me ask you something," Hanrihan said. "Remembering what you've said to me since you came in here, all the cracks that you've been making about how you just assume I must be crooked now, that I became a thief a little over a week, even though you know damned well it isn't so, all right?" Cremmens looked somewhat abashed and nodded. "Remembering what you've said, you that know me," Hanrihan said, "do you really think that after I've been branded in the public mind as the crusading DA that quit all of a sudden and went to work for Bernie Morgan, the guy that he was trying to convict, you think I could get elected?"

"Actually," Cremmens said, "since you put it that way? No."

"No," Hanrihan said, "and neither do I, either. And neither did the late Speaker of the House, or Frank Costello, either. You know what the Speaker said to me? Very shrewd remark, I thought. 'The people out there think the government in here ought to be run the way that Plato said in his *Republic,'* Morgan said. 'I can tell you that they're wrong. You can go out there after you've been in here for a while, and you can tell them that they're wrong. But they won't listen to me now, and they won't listen to you, then. Instead they'll say today that I'm a crook because I tell them that Plato's approach won't work. And tomorrow they will say that same damned thing to you.'

"So," Hanrihan said, "like I say, I thought that was shrewd, but I didn't really see the point. And Frank Costello said: 'What Bernie means, Brian, is that if you've got any elective office aspirations in your head, understand you'd better get them out before you come in here. And if you don't understand why you must resign yourself to that, then you can tell me the names of the last three real veterans of service in the legislature that went on to major statewide office.'

"I could think of one," Hanrihan said.

"Well, maybe two," Cremmens said. "Since I grew up, at least."

" 'And then,' Costello said, 'when you discover that you've got to go back some twenty years to find a couple, tell me why that is. And then what it is, convinces you you'll be the one to change the way things are.' And of course," Hanrihan said, "I couldn't do that, either. And Costello said to me: 'So, my friend, if you are staying, I recommend you understand that you are putting on your tar the instant you decide to do so. Don't plan to offer yourself in public after you do this. They have lots of feathers out there ready for you, and those feathers will stick to that tar.' "

Cremmens didn't speak for a few moments. Then he cleared his throat and offered his right hand. "Brian," he said, "I'll be thinking of you out there in the Berkshires, pal."

Hanrihan took it. They shook heartily. "Jim," he said, "we did have some fun, didn't we."

Cremmens paused in mid-shake, and he frowned. "Fun," he said, turning the idea over in his mind. "Fun. That may not be just the word I'd choose, Brian," he said.

"Interesting, then?" Hanrihan said with some brightness.

Cremmens nodded, closing his eyes once to show assent. "Interesting," he said with a final shake. "When I could still tell all the bad guys from the good guys, the minute that I spotted them, it was at least interesting."

30 On Sunday the *Commoner* featured Joe Gillis's long analytical piece on the Morgan years of the General Court. Gillis predicted that his style and his power would not be soon duplicated, and forecast a quiet, more collegial rule by Ray Archambault, his apparent successor. "Archambault," Joe Gillis wrote, "is the first of the new breed to achieve power in the legislature, and his tenure signals the dawn of a new era there. His choice of top-notch young attorney Brian Hanrihan to be his lawyer is taken as a clue to it. In many respects, observers are saying, it may well prove to be a quieter regime, less boisterous, less subject to one man's arbitrary moods.

"For," Gillis wrote, "there is no mistaking the fact that the late Speaker during his life was larger than life. He could be a tyrant, some said, and many agreed that he seldom would listen. Less of an innovator than his predecessor, his father-in-law, Wilfred Knox, Morgan rode roughshod over those who opposed him, brushed aside those who might disagree, made and unmade the careers of his supposed equals, and dared anyone who challenged him. Dared, and then demolished without mercy. When he died, his killer's motive as well as identity still an unfathomable secret, he died knowing he had once again, it appeared, fought off still another concerted attempt to destroy him. He was unarguably ruthless, and he was widely believed to be corrupt, but he was also, without any doubt, one of the most colorful figures that this generation is likely to see. As Ray Archambault put it, Bernie Morgan's a hard act to follow.

"For those of us like Archambault or this reporter," Gillis wrote, "and for everyone whose work made it necessary for him to spend much time on Beacon Hill and thus to come to grips with the Speaker who so completely ruled it, the suspicion is that it may be impossible. For those who knew him, it's indeed ironic that he died a victim of mindless, random violence, because this blustering, domineering politician who had in his younger days deserved a reputation as a brawler, in his later years was virtually all bluff. He tried without success to make people believe that he was still a bully, but anyone who knew him well, knew him to be a pussycat. 'Bernie Morgan,' as his close colleague Andy Boyce said of the man that he knew so well, 'was good at making lots of noise and scaring people half to death, but that was as far as he'd go. And if he liked you, well, it was not his great fists that you noticed—it was the size of his great heart. No friend of Bernie Morgan's who had hit a stretch of bad luck ever wondered if there was one man left on the earth who'd hold out a hand to help him. Nobody.'

"Tomorrow," Gillis concluded, "as Morgan had confided exclusively to this reporter, the Speaker had intended to inform a regular leadership caucus of the legislature that he would step down after this session was over. He was, he told me, tired, anxious to spend more time with his loved ones, satisfied after his long term in office that he had accomplished most of his important goals. He was convinced the time had ripened for him to depart gracefully. 'Most of all, Joe,' he said with a combination of real pride and equally real sadness, 'most of all what I want now in this world is to go home.' He outlined plans which would have kept him the speakership in name only, ceding the effective control of the House to his personally groomed successor, Ray Archambault. Then when the session ended, he would leave with his dignity intact and his powers undiminished, without anybody's forcing or affecting his decision, fully in control until his last hour in office. It would be, he told me, his last laugh on all his enemies.

"And that, perhaps, may be the final irony of Bernard Morgan's long and historical lifetime in office: that death, the only foe he could not vanquish or schedule for his own convenience, stepped in so abruptly to deprive him of his final triumph. Facing the Dark Angel, even Bernie Morgan was defenseless.

"May he rest in peace at last."

FINE WORKS OF FICTION
AVAILABLE IN QUALITY
PAPERBACK EDITIONS FROM
CARROLL & GRAF

- [ ] Asch, Sholem/THE APOSTLE $10.95
- [ ] Asch, Sholem/MARY $10.95
- [ ] Asch, Sholem/THE NAZARENE $10.95
- [ ] Asch, Sholem/THREE CITIES $10.50
- [ ] Ashley, Mike (ed.)/THE MAMMOTH BOOK OF SHORT HORROR NOVELS $8.95
- [ ] Asimov, Isaac/THE MAMMOTH BOOK OF CLASSIC SCIENCE FICTION (1930s) $8.95
- [ ] Asimov, Isaac et al/THE MAMMOTH BOOK OF GOLDEN AGE SCIENCE FICTION (1940) $8.95
- [ ] Babel, Isaac/YOU MUST KNOW EVERYTHING $8.95
- [ ] Balzac, Honore de/BEATRIX $8.95
- [ ] Balzac, Honoré de/CESAR BIROTTEAU $8.95
- [ ] Balzac, Honoré de/THE LILY OF THE VALLEY $9.95
- [ ] Bellaman, Henry/KINGS ROW $8.95
- [ ] Bernanos, George/DIARY OF A COUNTRY PRIEST $7.95
- [ ] Brand, Christianna/GREEN FOR DANGER $8.95
- [ ] Céline, Louis-Ferdinand/CASTLE TO CASTLE $8.95
- [ ] Chekov, Anton/LATE BLOOMING FLOWERS $8.95
- [ ] Conrad, Joseph/SEA STORIES $8.95
- [ ] Conrad, Joseph & Ford Madox Ford/ THE INHERITORS $7.95
- [ ] Conrad, Joseph & Ford Madox Ford/ROMANCE $8.95
- [ ] Coward, Noel/A WITHERED NOSEGAY $8.95
- [ ] de Montherlant, Henry/THE GIRLS $11.95
- [ ] Dos Passos, John/THREE SOLDIERS $9.95
- [ ] Feuchtwanger, Lion/JEW SUSS $8.95
- [ ] Feuchtwanger, Lion/THE OPPERMANNS $8.95
- [ ] Fisher, R.L./THE PRINCE OF WHALES $5.95
- [ ] Fitzgerald, Penelope/OFFSHORE $7.95
- [ ] Fitzgerald, Penelope/INNOCENCE $7.95
- [ ] Flaubert, Gustave/NOVEMBER $7.95
- [ ] Fonseca, Rubem/HIGH ART $7.95
- [ ] Fuchs, Daniel/SUMMER IN WILLIAMSBURG $8.95

☐ Neider, Charles (ed.)/GREAT SHORT
STORIES $11.95
☐ Neider, Charles (ed.)/SHORT NOVELS OF THE
MASTERS $12.95
☐ O'Faolain, Julia/THE OBEDIENT WIFE $7.95
☐ O'Faolain, Julia/NO COUNTRY FOR YOUNG
MEN $8.95
☐ O'Faolain, Julia/WOMEN IN THE WALL $8.95
☐ Olinto, Antonio/THE WATER HOUSE $9.95
☐ Plievier, Theodore/STALINGRAD $8.95
☐ Pronzini & Greenberg (eds.)/THE MAMMOTH
BOOK OF PRIVATE EYE NOVELS $8.95
☐ Rechy, John/BODIES AND SOULS $8.95
☐ Rechy, John/MARILYN'S DAUGHTER $8.95
☐ Rhys, Jean/QUARTET $6.95
☐ Sand, George/MARIANNE $7.95
☐ Scott, Evelyn/THE WAVE $9.95
☐ Sigal, Clancy/GOING AWAY $9.95
☐ Singer, I.J./THE BROTHERS ASHKENAZI $9.95
☐ Taylor, Peter/IN THE MIRO DISTRICT $7.95
☐ Tolstoy, Leo/TALES OF COURAGE AND
CONFLICT $11.95
☐ van Thal, Herbert/THE MAMMOTH BOOK OF
GREAT DETECTIVE STORIES $8.95
☐ Wassermann, Jacob/CASPAR HAUSER $9.95
☐ Wassermann, Jabob/THE MAURIZIUS CASE $9.95
☐ Werfel, Franz/THE FORTY DAYS OF MUSA
DAGH $9.95
☐ Winwood, John/THE MAMMOTH BOOK OF
SPY THRILLERS $8.95

Available from fine bookstores everywhere or use this coupon for ordering.

Carroll & Graf Publishers, Inc., 260 Fifth Avenue, N.Y., N.Y. 10001

Please send me the books I have checked above. I am enclosing
$_____ (please add $1.00 per title to cover postage and
handling.) Send check or money order—no cash or C.O.D.'s
please. N.Y. residents please add 8¼% sales tax.

Mr/Mrs/Ms _____

Address _____

City _____ State/Zip _____
Please allow four to six weeks for delivery.

FINE WORKS OF NON-FICTION AVAILABLE IN QUALITY PAPERBACK EDITIONS FROM CARROLL & GRAF

- ☐ Anderson, Nancy/WORK WITH PASSION $8.95
- ☐ Arlett, Robert/THE PIZZA GOURMET $10.95
- ☐ Asprey, Robert/THE PANTHER'S FEAST $9.95
- ☐ Athill, Diana/INSTEAD OF A LETTER $7.95
- ☐ Bedford, Sybille/ALDOUS HUXLEY $14.95
- ☐ Berton, Pierre/KLONDIKE FEVER $10.95
- ☐ Blake, Robert/DISRAELI $14.50
- ☐ Blanch, Lesley/PIERRE LOTI $10.95
- ☐ Blanch, Lesley/THE SABRES OF PARADISE $9.95
- ☐ Blanch, Lesley/THE WILDER SHORES OF LOVE $8.95
- ☐ Bowers, John/IN THE LAND OF NYX $7.95
- ☐ Buchan, John/PILGRIM'S WAY $10.95
- ☐ Carr, John Dickson/THE LIFE OF SIR ARTHUR CONAN DOYLE $8.95
- ☐ Carr, Virginia Spencer/THE LONELY HUNTER: A BIOGRAPHY OF CARSON McCULLERS $12.95
- ☐ Cherry-Garrard/THE WORST JOURNEY IN THE WORLD $13.95
- ☐ Conot, Robert/JUSTICE AT NUREMBURG $11.95
- ☐ Cooper, Duff/OLD MEN FORGET $10.95
- ☐ Cooper, Lady Diana/AUTOBIOGRAPHY $13.95
- ☐ De Jonge, Alex/THE LIFE AND TIMES OF GRIGORII RASPUTIN $10.95
- ☐ Edwards, Anne/SONYA: THE LIFE OF COUNTESS TOLSTOY $8.95
- ☐ Elkington, John/THE GENE FACTORY $8.95
- ☐ Farson, Negley/THE WAY OF A TRANSGRESSOR $9.95
- ☐ Garbus, Martin/TRAITORS AND HEROES $10.95
- ☐ Gill, Brendan/HERE AT THE NEW YORKER $12.95
- ☐ Goldin, Stephen & Sky, Kathleen/THE BUSINESS OF BEING A WRITER $8.95
- ☐ Golenbock, Peter/HOW TO WIN AT ROTISSERIE BASEBALL $8.95
- ☐ Green, Julian/DIARIES 1928–1957 $9.95

☐ Richelson, Hildy & Stan/INCOME WITHOUT
   TAXES $9.95
☐ Roy, Jules/THE BATTLE OF DIENBIENPHU $8.95
☐ Russell, Franklin/THE HUNTING ANIMAL $7.95
☐ Salisbury, Harrison/A JOURNEY FOR OUR
   TIMES $10.95
☐ Scott, Evelyn/ESCAPADE $9.95
☐ Sloan, Allan/THREE PLUS ONE EQUALS
   BILLIONS $8.95
☐ Stanway, Andrew/THE ART OF SENSUAL
   LOVING $15.95
☐ Stein, Leon/THE TRIANGLE FIRE $7.95
☐ Trench, Charles/THE ROAD TO
   KHARTOUM $10.95
☐ Werth, Alexander/RUSSIA AT WAR:
   1941–1945 $15.95
☐ White, Jon Manchip/CORTES $10.95
☐ Wilmot, Chester/STRUGGLE FOR EUROPE $14.95
☐ Wilson, Colin/THE MAMMOTH BOOK OF
   TRUE CRIME $8.95
☐ Zuckmayer, Carl/A PART OF MYSELF $9.95